JESSA HASTINGS

MAGNOLIA PARKS
INTO THE DARK

DUTTON

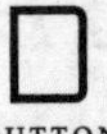

DUTTON
An imprint of Penguin Random House LLC
penguinrandomhouse.com

LIBRARY OF CONGRESS CATALOGING-IN-PUBLICATION DATA

Names: Hastings, Jessa, author.
Title: Magnolia Parks: into the dark / Jessa Hastings.
Other titles: Into the dark
Description: New York: Dutton, 2024.
Identifiers: LCCN 2023050389 (print) | LCCN 2023050390 (ebook) | ISBN 9780593474945 (paperback) | ISBN 9780593474952 (ebook)
Subjects: LCGFT: Romance fiction. | Novels.
Classification: LCC PS3608.A86144 M34 2024 (print) | LCC PS3608.A86144 (ebook) | DDC 813/.6—dc23/eng/20231107
LC record available at https://lccn.loc.gov/2023050389
LC ebook record available at https://lccn.loc.gov/2023050390

Printed in the United States of America

1st Printing

To anyone whom the more sting-y parts
of this book resonate with, anyone who's grieved
or is grieving or has lost or is losing,
anyone who worries about the black,
empty nothingness . . .
everything is going to be okay.

Okay? ♡

MAGNOLIA PARKS
INTO THE DARK

ONE
Magnolia

I look over at Henry leaning back on the bedhead on his brother's side of the bed. He's frowning at a sudoku puzzle. I don't know why he likes them but he always has, even when he was small. Back then it was find-a-words, but by the time we were at Varley, it was sudoku. He bites down on the pencil, and his eyes pinch more.

I peer over at it and point to one of the empty squares.

"Seven," I tell him before he brushes my hand away with a glare.

"I don't want your help."

I frown at him. "Rude."

"It is rude," he nods. "Your professed and fucking flagrant disinterest in the art of sudoku—"

"It's hardly an art," I tell him, and he ignores me.

"—is rude," he keeps going. "Because you're annoyingly good at it."

I roll my eyes at him and flip the page of this month's Italian *Vogue*.

He grumbles a little bit, says something about being a savant and that I really should have applied myself more in maths at school and I ignore him.

I flash him a picture of a dress I don't fancy. "They made that out of twill! How weird."

Henry's face pulls sarcastically. "So weird."

"It's summertime—" I let it hang there, though it doesn't

elicit from him the horror I anticipated. "That's a winter fabric," I remind him, and he gives his puzzle a look instead of me.

Then the front door slams and Henry and I catch eyes.

"Parksy?" BJ calls for me.

I like it when he calls me that—it makes me feel fifteen again. That's what he'd call me when we were in school, when we were together before. It sort of just showed back up once we got engaged.

"In here!" I call back to him as I dive out of the bed. "—quick!" I yell, straightening the duvet out, waving my hands like mad at Henry. "Quick! Get out—!"

Henry tugs his corner straight and flings his sudoku book to the other side of the room—unfortunately, it hits his brother square in the face as he walks into our bedroom.

I laugh breezily and lean awkwardly against our custom Savoir Winston & N°4v bed that I had them make in cream boucle.

"Hi!" I give him my brightest smile.

BJ's eyes pinch. "Hey."

Christian pokes his head in through the door and looks from me to Henry, then starts laughing as he sidles up next to BJ.

Beej nods his head at us. "You two in bed?"

"No." I shake my head emphatically.

Henry shakes his head with a dismissive shrug.

"No." My head keeps shaking. "You told us to stop doing that and we definitely did truly listen."

Henry nods along.

"And though it goes without saying, Henry definitely didn't eat a sandwich on your side of the bed because"—I toss Henry a look and say through clenched teeth—"that would be crazy and would have given it away if there was anything to give away—which there isn't—but if you were to say, hypothetically feel something crumb-adjacent, I think it would just be from a mouse or—um, a hungry ghoul or something."

BJ shoves his hands through his hair and groans.

"Why won't you sit in the fucking living room?" He looks between us, annoyed. "It looks sick."

Beej designed it and he's very proud.

"It does." Henry nods again.

And actually, it does, he's right—it looks incredible.

Christian leans against the door frame, peering between all of us, amused.

"*AD* did a piece on it—" BJ reminds us.

Which is also true. *Architectural Digest* did do a YouTube walkthrough of it—though the timing of which is considered controversial amongst the Box Set, and at the mention of it, Christian lets out an angry, defensive little grunt.

I flick him a look because BJ's not just very proud of the living room, he's admittedly rather oddly proud of the living room. The sort of pride one might imagine you'd possess for—I don't know—birthing a child?

So yes, it's a tad overzealous, but I don't much care for anyone being disparaging towards any of BJ's endeavours, even the ones I'm not sure that I myself entirely grasp.

"All things considered," I give Beej a reassuring look and float over to him, wrapping his arms around me. "I love it. You did an amazing job."

My fiancé lifts an eyebrow. "But . . . ?"

And I say nothing! I press my lips together demurely, not wanting to crush the boy I love most in all the world because he did do an excellent job. It really (truly) does look incredible. Mid-century modern, light and warm, it's just—

Henry grimaces.

"It's a bit angular out there, man." He gives his brother a shrug, and Beej rolls his eyes, muttering under his breath. "And like, it's hard to get a grip on that love seat—"

"That is true—" I nod.

"It's a Hans J. Wegner!" BJ looks between us, incredulous. "It's a £37,000 bench."

"Yeah—" Christian shrugs unhelpfully. "Can't really put a price on comfort though, can you?"

"But clearly you can put one on discomfort, ey Beej?" Henry tosses his brother a wink, and BJ flicks me an unimpressed look.

I stare up at BJ with big, sorry eyes.

"You do sort of just . . . slip off. You know that—" I tell him, eyebrows up. "We tried to have sex on there and I slid right off it! Like a penguin on ice."

His eyebrows go up.

"We found a way to make it work."

I shake my head a little. "No, we didn't, we just had sex on the floor."

BJ thinks back to the moment and then a little smile rolls over his face as more of the details come back to him. We're the best at sex, he and I.

"Oh, yeah." He locks eyes with me and from behind us Henry grimaces.

Christian nods and smacks me in the arm as he walks further into our room. "Nice . . . Floor sex—didn't think you had it in you, Parks."

BJ gives me a little wink.

Henry stretches his arms up over his head and sits back down on our bed. Beej picks up Henry's sudoku and pelts it over at him.

"Stop hanging out in our bed!"

Henry shakes his head.

"Oh, we can't," he says, sounding sorry.

BJ's eyebrows go up. "Why's that?"

"Too comfy." Henry rolls around just to annoy him. "Actually, can I get one of these in my room?"

"How many fucking times, man—" BJ gives his brother a look. "You don't have a room here."

"Well—" I jostle my head around, undecided.

"Kind of do," Henry says.

Christian's not around their place so much anymore—I'm not sure why—? I don't even know if I could in good conscience any longer call it 'their place.' And once upon a time, I think that would have been fine—welcome, even, but now, Henry, who generally loves to be alone, loves it much, much less these days.

So even if Henry 'doesn't have a room here' because his

brother doesn't want to live with his brother, he actually does have a room here.

Christian lays down next to him for a few seconds then props himself up, looking over at us. "Woah, bro, this is cozy as fuck!"

I scramble back onto the bed, sitting in the middle of it.

"Isn't it?" I beam at them.

Christian nods slowly, basking in the comfort.

"Way comfier in here than out there—"

BJ breathes loudly out his nose and then lays down on the bed too, picking up a shitty magazine and starts flipping through it.

I know I shouldn't even bother having them, but we're always in them and I like to know what people are saying about us.

I look around our bedroom—white walls, giant white bed like a cloud, big, billowy white curtains . . . I love having an "our bedroom" with him. We've never had one, not in all the years we were together.

In school we, of course, had our respective dorms and we'd sneak into one another's as much as physically possible. On weekends we'd stay at one of our parents' houses together in either of our respective rooms. We've shared each other's rooms and beds infinity times over the course of our lives but we've never had one that's just ours, in a bed we've never shared with other people, in a room that every night we both fall asleep in next to each other, and every morning I wake up and he's beside me. Our room could be a cardboard box and I'd love it if he was in it.

No, I wouldn't, that was a lie and I was absolutely being hyperbolic, but you do see my point, yes?

BJ did our whole entire house, picked every single piece of art and furniture—I didn't have the—I couldn't at the time, you know? It wasn't too long after what happened, and I just couldn't. The only thing I picked in the whole flat was our bed and our mattress, and it's not a competition and even if it was, I'd want him to win it, but our bed definitely is the most comfortable place in our entire home.

I wriggle down the giant cloud we're all nestled upon and

over towards my fiancé, rolling in towards him, batting my eyes so he likes me again.

His face pinches suspiciously. "Don't you point those things at me."

I shrug innocently. "Well, I'd point them at our sofa but they'd slip right off."

BJ suppresses a laugh, shaking his head as he flips the page.

And then I see it.

"London Lovers" is the title of the "article" (and I do mean that in the loosest possible way), and it's a few photos of us and other people like us, being romantic and cutesy around London. Suki Waterhouse and Robert Pattinson. Rachel McAdams and her husband. Jamie Dornan and Amelia.

"Oh no," I gasp as I smack my finger down on the photo of he and I in the magazine.

It's a paparazzi shot. Me on his lap, his chin on my shoulder, both of us reading what's really a menu but rather unfortunately looks like a leather-bound book.

"What?" Beej glances over, pressing his mouth into my arm. "We look fine."

"No—" I sigh, forlorn. "No, we look like the kind of couple who would tag one another in their Instagram biographies."

"Oh, fuck—" BJ starts to laugh. "We do a bit."

"What's wrong with that?" Henry asks, peering over curiously, and I can't help but smile at the sweetness of him. He's so pure and evergreen and ready to love someone properly (and please rest assured when that happens I will be confiscating his phone, locking him out of his Instagram and making sure all biographies remain undisgusting).

Christian throws him an off look.

"Everything. The only thing worse than mentioning your partner in your bio is a joint account." He huffs, much less pure and much less evergreen than Henry because, I suppose, to be fair, Christian has loved someone really, truly properly, and where has it gotten him?

Daisy's still gone—not a word for three months now. It's

hard to tell how he's coping with that. He's not how he used to be—he's not outworking how much he misses her with alcohol and other girls, but then, he wouldn't. Because he also doesn't even know if they're not together. Because they just left. Both of them. They left and then nothing. Not a word from either of them since. Not even when—

I shake my head at myself.

I don't want to think about that.

Henry's phone chimes. He pulls it from his pocket and looks down at it. A familiar look rolls over his face—sort of pained, sort of frustrated—he breathes out his nose before he puts his phone away.

Taura. That's his Taura face now.

That's taken a nosedive too.

Taurs finally picked Henry, did you know? I suppose probably not—she didn't tell anyone but me. She told me she picked Henry, that it was Henry she wanted, Henry she really, properly loved and wanted to be with . . . right before Jonah's mum went into a coma.

So she didn't tell Henry then, because she didn't feel as though she could do it to Jo, so on and on it went, how it had been before except worse because she had picked and I knew and she knew, but the boys didn't know and she didn't know how to tell them, not without hurting Jonah, who is so overtly hurting these days that she couldn't bear it. So she said nothing to spare him and then lost them both in the end.

I glance back at the photo of Beej and I, and sigh.

"I suppose we just must endeavour to be less adorable in public," I tell him rather firmly.

"Or—" Henry snaps his fingers at me, his pensive moment gone, all the sadness I saw on him a second ago packed away somewhere distant. "You could just give your democratisation of luxury speech loudly in public and I promise they'll stop adoring you."

I put my nose in the air. "I wouldn't bet on that."
BJ tosses his brother a glance. "I would."
"It's a vastly unexplored phenomenon in modern consumerism, and I for one"—I lay my hand on my chest—"am gravely concerned."
Christian rolls his eyes and BJ shakes his head, keeps flipping through the magazine. A few pages and then suddenly, Beej jerks it away from me as he closes it.
I frown over at him.
"What's that?"
"Nothing—"
"What is it?"
"Just a stupid article." BJ shrugs, moving the magazine away from me.
"About what?"
A pause from him.
". . . Me."
"Oh." I purse my lips. "Well, let me see it—"
BJ scrunches his face up then shakes his head.
"Nah."
BJ passes it over my head to Christian.
"What does it say?" I ask as I reach for it, but Christian holds it out of my reach.
"Nothing." Christian shrugs. "It's dumb."
Then he tosses it to Henry, which was stupid because I have absolutely zero qualms about tackling Henry, so I lunge towards him and he flings it back to BJ as I do, who jumps off the bed and hides it behind his back.
I scramble up after him—
"BJ, this isn't funny—let me see."
He lifts a gentle eyebrow.
"Do you trust me?"
"Yes," I say, automatically.
He offers me a hopeful shrug. "Then trust that you don't want to see it."

I look from him to his brother and his best friend.

"Have you done something?"

He blinks twice.

"No," he says, and maybe if I wasn't being such a bulldog about all this I'd have seen how that hurt him a little, but I don't.

I hold my hand out in front of me waiting for him to hand it over.

He licks his bottom lip and sighs big as he drops it into my hands.

"THE SECRET LIFE OF BRIDGET PARKS" is what the page reads in big block letters.

My mouth falls open a little and my stomach drops to its knees.

They didn't care about Bridget when she was alive, that's the awful truth of it. Because she didn't want them to. She lived a life that was so spectacularly unassuming and so regular, the only times you'd see her in the papers was when she was with me or our parents. She despises celebrity. Despised, I mean. She could have been like me if she liked—she could have been whatever she wanted. She just found none of it fulfilling. And none of it is, it's all meaningless. Her whole life she was above it and avoided it and then in her death, they came for her anyway.

I glare down at it and my blood goes hot. It's a series of photos of my sister from various times in her life, ranging from when she was at Varley up until recently. They're all strange and out of context.

There's one where she's lying down pretending to be passed out in the middle of a pile of bottles. It's from her Instagram. She was fully sober, the caption read: "Who am I?? @jonahhemmes?" There's another photo, also from her Instagram, where she's leaning down, chin in hand, on our kitchen bench at Holland Park, BJ grinning away next to her with lines of what looks like cocaine in front of her, but the photo is cropped. In real life, unseen in picture displayed also is Marsaili, eyes mid-roll. Also unseen are the ingredients scattered around from all the baking Bridget was actually doing. BJ and I had walked into the kitchen and somehow, cocaine had come up, and Bridge asked him if it hurt your nose to do it, and he arranged little bumps of icing sugar for her and they did them together.

There's a photo of her and a boy kissing in a corner, I don't know his name but I remember the night. It wasn't secretive. She wasn't hiding this from anyone. A few more like those, all moments that were completely normal life moments which someone's trying now to pervert for a story and I hate them for it.

Bridget's Instagram, by the way, is and always has been private. She only has about three hundred followers. So someone she loves and trusts is betraying that trust she gave them for a quick buck.

I swallow down the lump I feel rising in my throat and ignore the heavy looks resting upon me from all the boys I love.

"I'm fine," I tell them, flashing them a quick smile even though none of them asked.

Henry nods big like he doesn't believe me, and BJ touches my face.

"Want to go for dinner?"

"I'm starved," Christian says, trying to move the moment along.

I nod quickly then stand.

"Just—I'll be a minute." Another quick smile from me before I push up from our bed and walk through our giant walk-in wardrobe and through to our en suite.

I stand at the vanity, grip it tight as I feel my heart clench. I breathe out my nose as measured as I can and stare at my reflection, waiting for her to arrive.

It takes about a minute but then I see her. She's always wearing what she was the night I last saw her. Rainbow crystal–embellished striped cardigan from Miu Miu and the Rag & Bone knit ribbed bike shorts with the black Oh Yeah slides from UGG.

"Dinner?" my sister would say. "Really?" And I'd ignore her, push my hair behind my ears, lift my chin a little bit. I'd stare at her brown eyes defiantly like I have most days of our lives til she left it.

"Is this a thing again?" she'd ask, and I'd roll my eyes because she can't roll hers and I miss them.

"I'm fine," I'd say, even though that wasn't what she would have asked and she'd give me a look.

"You're in a bathroom talking to your dead sister," she'd tell me, and I'd stare at her with hurt in my eyes because Bridget is notorious for not pulling punches and occasionally getting carried away, and I think we can all agree that dying on me was a skosh too far.

She wouldn't care though.

"What—?" She'd shrug anyway, push her hair back behind her shoulders and cross her arms over her chest. "You are."

"You good?" Beej asks, standing in the frame of the bathroom door watching me with cautious eyes.

"Yes," I nod quickly. "Grand."

"Ready to go?"

I look down at myself. The patchwork leather & crocheted cotton minidress from Chloé with Allude's white cable-knit cashmere cardigan.

"Do I look okay?"

He walks towards me and puts his hand on my waist.

"Always."

I look back at myself, touch my acromion bone and press my tongue into my top lip. "Are we dri—" I bunch up a bit. Swallow. "Taking a car or—?"

"Walking, Parks," he tells me gently as he comes behind me, slipping his arms around my waist and looking at me through the mirror.

I nod quickly. Can't say I'm much for cars these days. Unavoidable of course, on certain occasions. And on such occasions, I have a driver. These days I actually sort of have two. A regular driver and Daniela. Who's not technically a driver, but she does drive a lot. She's a personal assistant. Jonah said I was dropping too many balls, so he's paid her salary for a year as an 'early birthday present,' is what we tell people publically, but actually, he told me it was a 'your sister died present.' Admittedly, both Ballentines thought it was a strange milestone to christen with a gift, but I thought it was okay because I understand. Jonah and Christian have, for a long while now, been members of a terrible, exclusive club; one which—against my will—I've recently joined now also.

That was thoughtful of him, don't you think? She's from Brazil. She's fairly quiet and I wouldn't say she's overly organised, but she drives me everywhere and she sort of always seems to be around to help if I need it, which is nice.

"Are there many downstairs?" I ask BJ quietly.

"No more than normal." He shrugs. "Dani said there's five or six down there at the minute."

I nod before looking at myself in the mirror again.

Fascination for BJ and I has been at an all-time high since the engagement and then Bridget. It can feel rather invasive at times.

BJ nudges me with his elbow. "Just a dinner with me and the boys."

My eyes pinch at my reflection.

"I don't want them to call me mismatched again."

His head tilts. "That was a week after your sister had died, Parks. A monster wrote that one—" A dark look rolls over his face. "No human could have done it."

He slips his hand in mine and pulls me out of the bathroom and into the wardrobe, he pushes me down onto the nineteenth-century French carved and giltwood upholstered bench that he picked—it divides my side of the wardrobe from his—then he goes to my shoe shelf.

Chloé's Mallo high boot in brunet brown is what he brings me. Well picked.

I give him a tired smile and he gives me one back.

He drops to his knees and slips one on each foot, then stays down there so we're eye level.

He puts his nose against mine.

"We can stay in," he tells me.

I shrug. "Whatever you like."

He nods.

"Let's get a bite then."

He brushes his lips over mine and climbs to his feet, pulling me up with him.

Henry and Christian are waiting by the front door when we walk out.

My best friend gives me a smile that I think is meant to make me feel brave but sort of just makes me feel sad. Everyone moves around me these days like I'm made of glass. Like one wrong look and I'll shatter. Little do they know that it's too late . . . All of me already is all shattered.

A mosaic of cracks and agony.

Henry hands me my enamel sunglasses from Christian Dior's 1969 collection.

We step into the elevator.

"Shades on," BJ says, and we all suit up.

He looks down at me. "Ready?"

I nod, sort of. He slips his hand into mine and—ding!—the doors open.

As soon as we step into the foyer the cameras start flashing from outside.

The boys form a little triangle around me: BJ at the front, Henry to my right, Christian to my left.

They yell our names, mine in particular.

"When's the wedding!" "Who will you wear?" "Have you spoken to Paili Blythe?" "Will you honour your sister at the wedding—" one starts to ask, but Christian breaks away from the triangle to grab him by the neck of his shirt and shove him back into the wall behind him.

"Fuck off," my old friend spits at the reporter before he jogs after us and falls back in line.

I give him a tiny, grateful smile and he gives me a little chin nod.

They follow us the whole way to Zuaya on Kensington High Street, and it's a fairly accurate example of how it feels to be alive right now.

Yelled at and watched, invaded upon and never left alone, but somehow completely, entirely, wholly alone all at once.

Which isn't a commentary on BJ or Henry or Taura, or anyone even—it's just a strange, new frontier that I've found myself on. It's where I live now.

All alone in my mind, just wandering further and further into the dark that is the absence of her.

11:23

Bushka 🍸 ♥

Will yoi brinf me tea

What?

Tea

Where are you?

Himw

What?

I am home

I'm not at your house

Wherw are you

Notting Hill.

So close. Brinh tea

I do regret buying you an iPhone

I don't. Independoent lady

Do you know what 'independent' means?

Hurry up

Do you want any food?

Ok

What?

Ok yes

BJ with?

Yes

👍👍

TWO

BJ

I've got a few memories of Parks that live on a pedestal in my mind. Her face—beautiful, right? But that's not what it's about. I see her face and it sets off some old ache in me . . . Transports me somewhere else—her in my garden when I was six, all that light behind her that I can't tell anymore whether the light was real or if it was just her. That day I got to St Barts, her in that yellow bikini. Her in the lilac bikini on that boat too, actually. When I gave her my family crest ring when we were at school. When I gave her it again when we were adults.

Other times too that I remember—this look in her eyes—this visceral, almost-punching that I feel sometimes like a phantom.

Like when I told her I cheated on her. Or when we lost Billie. When she found out it was Paili, the night she slept with Tom, Bridget . . .

I don't think I'll be able to get it out of my head, that girl I love on her knees at the side of her sister's bed, holding her dead sister's hand, weeping in this quiet way.

It was worse that it was quiet for some reason.

She's easier to console when she goes big.

I remember standing there with Hen, waiting for the ambulance to get there, and we both just stared at Parks, bunched up by her dead sister's body.

The ambulance arrived and Henry let them in.

She didn't move away from Bridge by herself, I had to pull her away. Wrapped my arms around her, pulled her back into me.

I remember being glad I got to hold Parks then, because there's something about losing someone how we were losing Bridge in that moment that makes you feel like you need to. Like if I hadn't, I might have lost her too.

They tried to resuscitate Bridge on the spot but nothing.

"She needs to get to a hospital," an A&E girl told us.

Magnolia stood. "I'll ride with her."

The emergency worker looked at me, eyes communicating something.

"Maybe you stick with me, Parks." I nodded at her.

She shook her head.

"I need to be with Bridge."

"You will be." I gave her a gentle smile. "We'll be right behind her."

Magnolia shook her head. "She really shouldn't be alone—"

"She won't be." I told her with a nod towards the medic standing there.

"I'll be with her—" The A&E worker flashed Magnolia a weary smile. "My name's Amy, and I'll be with her the whole time."

Henry's unbelievable in situations like this. Packed us a bag. Hoodies, wallets, water. Things you'd never think about like phone chargers.

We got in the car. I can't really remember how.

Henry drove. I sat in the back with Parks.

She sat in the middle. Put her head down in my lap, closed her eyes.

Feels like about then that her PTSD with cars really started to show its face around these parts.

A couple of years ago I tried to get her to walk from Selfridges on Oxford just to Saint Laurent on Old Bond and she bit my fucking head off. If you aren't from London, that's maybe a fifteen-minute walk. Less, with legs as long as hers. Take you more time to catch a fucking taxi, and it did.

But she'll walk anywhere to avoid getting into a car now. She wasn't like that before.

I don't remember much of that drive, just my fingers in her

hair and how Henry didn't put anything on the radio as we followed the ambulance over to Chelsea and Westminster. The silence was loud enough. The rushing sounds of London around us as we raced through her, and this strange sense of knowing—

I didn't have a lot of hope that Bridget was going to be okay—I don't know why. I feel bad about that. Like maybe if I had more, she might still be here, but I just had a feeling, you know? As we pulled up to the hospital, the feeling got worse. Never wanted to be wrong so badly in my life.

It all happened pretty quickly once we got there—pulled into this room where they started trying to resuscitate her, and then we got sent out into a hallway after about a minute. Felt like a bad sign.

Henry knew it too, I could see it on him. I think Parks might have as well, because as soon as we were in the hall she was trembling. Her whole little body shaking and jittery, teeth chattering away.

I called her parents—don't remember at what time that was. It needed to come from either me or her, and she couldn't string words together so, me.

"What?" is how Harley answered the phone.

It was late by then. Not like I ever call him just for a chat, so I don't know why he'd think I'd be calling him for any reason besides an emergency.

"We're at the hospital, something's wrong," I said as no-frills as possible—not to be an arsehole, but because I needed him to hear the facts. "Bridget's unconscious. We don't know what happened."

Pause.

"Is she okay?" their dad asked.

Pause.

"I don't know, man."

He said nothing.

"Should I call Arrie?" I asked. My voice was weird. Strangely calm. Sounded less scared than I was.

"No," he said. Also calm. "I'll do it."

"Okay."

"Which hospital?" he asked.

I told him. Shared my location so he could find us easier.

Then I called Jo; Jo then Christian then Taurs.

Didn't take them long to get there, all six of us in that hallway.

They got there before her parents did.

Magnolia looked up at them all blankly. Christian kissed her on her head, grabbed my shoulder before sitting down on the floor opposite us.

Taurs gets real twitchy in emergencies. Flits around all busy and nervous. Got snacks and water for everyone, tried to make Parks sip some but she wouldn't.

I think Jo knew. He has a sense for these things. Stared at me for a second, face heavy, said nothing but something about how he looked—I know he knew.

The chain of events feel weird in my memory—fractured—like parts of a dream.

I remember Henry pacing around the waiting area, Parks on my lap just staring at me. Eyes big and round like they were on our other worst day.

I wanted to be able to tell her it was going to be okay, but I couldn't bring myself to say the words. I think I knew it wasn't going to be—? Didn't want to lie to her. That felt worse somehow too.

There was so much going on around us, even in that hallway late at night—and Parksy, right?—loves a distraction. Loves avoiding uncomfortable things, tries her hardest on a fucking daily basis to ignore them, but she didn't look around, just kept her eyes on me.

Could have felt it, I reckon—if I knew to look for it—that mantle Bridget had being passed on down to me.

Because Magnolia looks at her sister when shit's going down, always has. Maybe she'd look at me if I hadn't been the shit that was usually going down. She's never looked to her dad—why would she? Sometimes Hen would get a glance, but because of me, I think she felt like she was putting Hen in a shit position.

You know how ballerinas pick a spot to look at when they're doing a pirouette so they don't get dizzy?

Bridget was Magnolia's spot on the wall.

When their parents arrived, it was Harley and Mars first.

They burst through the doors, stared over at us—he pressed his hand into his mouth when he saw Magnolia and then he looked away.

Turned to a nurse. Asked her a question I couldn't hear.

Mars rushed over, pulled Magnolia up off my lap and hugged her.

Parks didn't hug her back, but I don't think that was for any particular reason, she was just sort of not there.

I remember I watched over at her dad, watched him not come to her.

"She's going to be okay, Magnolia," Mars told her, pulling away as she nodded vigorously.

Don't like it when people say things they don't really mean.

Parks barely nodded back but managed a few before she retreated back to me.

A little ball on my lap.

Arrie blew in not long after that.

Cyclone Arrie. Massive trench coat, some kind of negligee, heels and oversized sunglasses.

That Nathan guy with her, standing nervous by the door. Afraid of Harley or just fucking way in over his head, it was hard to tell.

"Where is she?" Arrie asked loudly.

Harley spoke to her in low words we couldn't hear.

Mars made her way over, put her hand on Arrie's arm.

Henry and me, we caught eyes.

Both thought it was weird that neither one of their parents came over to check on their other daughter.

Thought about calling my mum but decided—nah, it's too many cooks—that tiny room was already too full.

Time goes funny in places like hospitals, don't you think?

From when her parents arrived til a doctor came out to speak to us, I don't know how much time passed. Hours? Minutes?

All I really remember is holding Parks' hand and pressing my family ring into her.

Hadn't taken to wearing the diamonds yet.

Now she wears the crest on a pendant how she used to and the diamonds on her finger. The crest ring never fit her anyway. She had to wear a little ring on top of it to stop it from coming off.

I was spinning the ring around her finger, trying to think of anything but what life might look like if what I was worried was happening actually happened and Magnolia's head was resting heavy on my chest when the door opened and a doctor came out—

Magnolia scrambled onto her feet, eyes desperate. I stood up after her, eyed the doctor, nervous.

Wouldn't fancy his chance at poker. Didn't need to say the words—he still said them anyway.

"I'm sorry," he told us solemnly. "We did everything we could."

Arrie let out this wail that surprised all of us, I think. Guttural.

Next surprise on the agenda was Harley turning from Marsaili and holding his ex-wife.

Least surprising of all, neither of them clock Magnolia.

But fuck them because she doesn't need her parents anyway; she never has, even if she thinks she does. She doesn't. She has us.

She turned around to face me, eyes all glassy. She said nothing, I said nothing—just grabbed her and held her.

She didn't cry. Not then, anyway.

She saved it all up for later that night when it was just me and her in my old bedroom at my mum's house.

In the hospital, the little family she built for herself gathered around her, locked arms and didn't let go. Didn't budge til Harley finally came over, told us it was time to leave.

Parks stared over at him, eyes probably more defiant than I've ever seen them and fuck, I've seen them defiant—

"I'm not leaving her," she told her dad.

He swallowed heavy, looked over at me for help.

Didn't offer him any more than a nod of my chin.

"We're good here," I told him.

He nodded his head subtly towards Magnolia. She didn't see. Asked me without asking me to look after her. Like I haven't been doing it all my life anyway—like I needed the prompting.

He's always been a bit like that. Nods his chin at her when she's not looking. He cares more than she realises, I've told her that. She says if he cared at all he'd nod his chin at her less and just look after her himself.

Hard to argue with that.

Henry sat down against a hospital wall and patted the ground next to him once.

Magnolia went and sat next to him wordlessly. Christian sat on her other side, didn't say anything, didn't look at her, just stared straight ahead with a look that's hard to place. He lost a sister too. Wasn't a grimace, not a smile. He was sorry for her. Knew there was nothing he could say.

Before her parents left, Marsaili tried to get Parks to go home with them, but she wouldn't budge.

"I'll make you a tea at home, darling. Come," Mars told her with a gentle smile.

Magnolia's eyes drifted over to her stepmother's, stared at her, blinked twice, then looked over at me.

Mars followed her gaze, breathed out tired when our eyes caught.

I did my best to give her a reassuring nod. "I've got her."

Marsaili walked over, held my face in her hand.

"Yes, you do."

Might be the heaviest thing anyone's ever said to me, actually.

After that, I don't know how long we stayed for. Time slips and drags in moments like those. Well into the night though. Parks didn't move, sandwiched between my brother and Christian, just shifted her head between their shoulders, eyes on me.

I sat down across from her. Leant against the opposite wall, took a minute to take stock of myself.

Pushed down all the feelings I felt. Tried to pack away that I lost someone too. Someone who might as well have been my own sister, someone who's shaped my life and how I now live it as much if not maybe more than anyone, besides Parks—maybe even more than Parks?

Tausie and Jo went for a McDonald's run somewhere around two a.m. Magnolia didn't have a bite. Didn't cross my mind at that time what that might've signalled. Henry put a straw in a bottle of water, raised it to her lips. She sipped on it, rubbed on those eyes of hers all tired. Still didn't look away from me.

"You okay?" Jo asked as he sat down next to me.

I shook my head slightly, didn't want her to see.

"I can't have this conversation right now—" I barely looked him in the eyes. "I need to be—"

Jo nodded, gave me a solemn look. "I know."

He threw his arm around me and didn't say anything else after that.

A few hours later, when Magnolia's blinks started to turn to drags, a very brave Taura asked her if maybe it was time we headed home.

Magnolia glared over at her, shook her head.

Christian elbowed her. "What do you need, Parks?"

She stared at him a few seconds. "To see her."

Christian looked over at me and nodded once.

He stood, I followed after him over to the girl at a desk. He gave her a tight smile as he pointed over at Parks.

"She needs to see her sister."

The girl shook her head. "That's not really how—"

He cut her off. "I'll transfer you £10,000 right now, on the spot, if you let her in to see her."

The nurse's face faltered.

Christian shrugged. "It's four in the morning. No one's here. We won't tell anyone. No one's going to go in with her besides him—" He gestured to me. "She won't go home til she sees her—" He leant in closer to the woman and said in a low, tired voice. "And I really fucking want to go home."

The woman nodded once.

I walked back over to Parks, offered her my hand. She took it without thinking and I pulled her to her feet.

"Let's go see her."

Her eyes went wide and her face got nervous.

I squeezed her hand to make her feel a bit safer in a world that had just become undeniably less safe for all of us a couple of hours ago.

The nurse led us into the room.

Parks stood in front of me, not letting go of my hand.

Worse than you think it's going to be . . . And it wasn't like it was gory or bloody or scary, even—

It's just this girl we love, all fucking still on a table.

Magnolia did this quiet little gasp I think I'll hear on repeat in my brain forever. Hated it. Made me want to die. Never want to hear her make that sound again.

She squeezed my hand after that. Dug her nails in so deep I'd find cuts later.

Bridge looked normal, really. Lips were maybe a tiny bit paler.

Like she was sleeping.

Magnolia's trembling hand reached out and touched her sister's face.

She barely brushed it before she snatched her hand back, like death is a thing you can catch.

I slipped my arms around her waist, pressed my mouth into the back of her head, tried to steady her without having to lie.

"It's okay" was a lie, so I didn't say it to her.

It wasn't okay. Couldn't see how it would be okay anytime soon or ever even, if I'm honest.

"Will I see her again?" Parks' smallest voice asked.

"I'm not sure," I told her, but it was muffled by her hair.

"Then I don't want to go," she said.

I breathed out, kissed the back of her head.

"We can stay as long as you like, Parksy—" She nodded quickly and I kept going, as I nodded at the body on the table. "But she doesn't live in this anymore."

She turned around in my arms and looked up at me, tired.

She blinked a few times, lids dragging over her eyes like they were made of sandpaper.

"I'm scared, Beej," she told me, eyes made of glass.

She didn't say of what. Didn't need to.

When we walked out of that room, it would be real. Everything would change forever. We knew, once we walked out of that room, we would live in a world where Bridget Parks is dead. Not 'could be dead,' not 'maybe dying somewhere in a hospital room' with the chance of being revived—but properly dead, life gone, body cold with a strange stillness we won't ever all the way unsee.

"I'm scared too," I told Magnolia as I kissed the top of her head.

She turned back to her sister's body, crouched down close to her ear.

"Please come back," she whispered, her voice cracking. "Please?"

She waited a few seconds that felt like decades and nothing happened—of course nothing happened. Bridge was very gone at that point. I think she'd been gone since the flat, really.

Magnolia's hands flew to her face, covering it. In public, trying to stay composed.

It's habit, wasn't conscious.

She rushed past me to leave the room and I knew I needed to go after her, knew that then was not the time or the place for me to feel anything, but you know what, I loved her too.

I swiped my face, brushed away the tears, and then I bent down, my chin shaking. I reckon me and Parks probably only found our way back to each other because of her sister. Reckon I'm clean probably because of her too.

I kissed the head of the straightest shooter I'll ever know.

I couldn't tell whether it felt strange and waxy in my mind because she was dead or because bodies actually just do feel different once life leaves them.

Put away how sick I felt and ran after Parks. Found her in my brother's arms.

Hen nodded his head towards the door.

We pulled up outside the girls' Grosvenor Street flat. Magnolia's head in my lap, took me and Henry a solid five seconds to realise no fucking way in hell should we have brought Parks back to the place she found her sister dead in her bed.

Hen peeled out, headed to the safest place we know.

My parents have lived in the same house my whole life. Cadogan Place in Belgravia. Whenever anyone would get too fucked up, too drunk, too sad—whatever—they'd come here.

Mum's good for it. Doesn't judge you. Just wants to help you.

Henry must have called her at some point, I guess because when I helped Magnolia walk up the front steps, the door swung open before we were at the top of them and my mum swooped. Threw her arms around the love of my life, started crying on her behalf.

Magnolia let Mum hold her. Didn't cry though.

That made me nervous.

Mum looked over at me, eyes heavy and sad for us. For Parks. For my sister.

"Allie doesn't know," Mum mouthed to me over Parks' shoulder.

I nodded.

She pulled back to look at Magnolia.

"You should sleep, darling," Mum told her.

Magnolia shook her head.

"I can't," she told Mum, looking past her in a distant way.

Mum's brows furrowed in concern. "Oh?"

"She needs a shower," I told Mum quietly.

Mum reached for her wrist. "It's so late, sweetheart. Perhaps just shower in the m—"

"She can't, Mum," I said, firmer now. Magnolia looked over her shoulder at me and our eyes caught like she's grateful for something.

Mum's face faltered. "Why?"

"Dead people," Parks and I said at the same time.

"Germs," I added, with a subtle tap on my head.

Mum swallowed and nodded once, looked embarrassed like she should have known that herself. It's not necessarily the kind of thing that lives on the forefront of someone else's mind if you don't live with a maniac who feels germs in her mind, not just on her body.

"Room's ready. Towels are on the bed. Can I make you something to eat?"

Magnolia shook her head.

"A tea?"

She shook her head again.

"Some water, Mum," Henry told her with a nod towards the kitchen.

"Come on." I slipped my hand back in hers and led her up the stairs.

I moved her through this house we both grew up in, through into my old bedroom that I'd sneak her into every fucking chance I got, and then into the bathroom.

I turned on the shower and the room fogged up quickly because I suppose the world got colder the moment Bridget left it.

Parks stared over at me, eyes so heavy I didn't know how to hold them.

She was still in the white dress she was in from dinner. In the few weeks between when we got engaged til that moment in time when everything changed, Magnolia took every chance she got to look like a bride.

I stood behind her, unzipped the dress. Monique something. Very bride-y. It fell to the ground.

I crouched down to the floor, lifted her ankle and pulled her heel off her foot. Lifted her other ankle, took the other one off.

Couldn't believe she spent the night in heels. Hadn't even noticed.

She was standing there, not moving, staring at herself in the mirror.

Strapless bra from Fleur du Mal. Know that one. Picked it myself. Matching knickers.

I slipped my T-shirt off over my head. Tugged off my jeans, kicked off my shoes.

I reached behind her back for the clasp of her bra, didn't look down, didn't look sideways. My eyes held hers and I could see for the first time since we left her house that there was a tear sitting on the edge of her eyelashes.

I brought her into the shower.

Washed her down. Didn't miss an inch of her because it's a mind thing. It's hard to articulate but I think she worries that outside things can seep in. Once we were on the street and a crazy man yelled at her, kind of got in her face a bit, towered over her for a few seconds before I got over to her. We had about five showers that night. We weren't together at the time—I mean, we were. Who are we kidding?—but she let me in the shower that night.

Scrubbed her down. Tried to wash that feeling off her.

Didn't know how I was going to wash this one off her though.

Any other night, it would've been fucking hot—her eyes locked on me, all naked, the most beautiful girl in the world—maybe the most broken now too.

Washed myself quickly. There was death on me too.

Turned off the water, wrapped a towel around her shoulders and one around my waist before I dried her like you might a little kid.

Found her a T-shirt of mine and tugged it on over her head. Pulled on some sweatpants myself and then I moved her over towards the bed.

Made me feel nervous because I knew what's coming.

The bed was where she'd feel like we were alone and I knew that's where it'd happen.

I laid down first, pulled her with me. She folded like an envelope into my chest and I counted to three in my mind but she only made it to two before she broke like a dam and cried like she hadn't let herself all night.

I kissed the top of her head a thousand times, held her as tight as I could.

"I'm so sorry, Parks," I told her like it counted for anything. "I'm so sorry."

23:42

Bridge 💩✨

I ordered you a book on the etymology of 30,000 common British words because you're a loser and I thought you'd like it.

It'll be here tomorrow.

You're welcome.

•••

THREE
Magnolia

I run into our master bathroom to find a specific lip colour I'm after only to find BJ and the contractor both staring, hands on hips, at the giant marble mantelpiece that should hang over the bath all cracked and broken in the now also-broken bath.

"We've had an incident." Beej grimaces.

"I see." I nod as I peer in.

The contractor flashes me an apologetic smile. "Sorry."

"No—" I shake my head. "That's quite alright. We're actually not really a bath household—"

BJ suppresses a smile but the contractor's gawping at me.

"You don't like baths?"

My face falters and I flash him a quick smile.

I clear my throat. "You don't read the papers?"

BJ leans in towards me and whispers, "I don't think the papers have all the details."

I flick him a look. "Lucky them."

Beej breathes out—it's weary, almost. Like he's tired, or that it hurt him. Maybe I did? I shake my head quickly.

"I'm kidding!" I kiss him on the cheek. I kiss him again for good measure.

I'm not kidding.

I think in general I'm feeling better about all that—I don't have this morbid fascination about them. I don't scroll through Paili's Instagram at nighttime and I don't stare at old photos of us all, looking for clues. And I did, admittedly, do that for a while.

I don't know that I'm an innately distrustful person, perhaps it's because I'm not that what happened then happened. Maybe if I had been more suspicious or astute or I'd studied the way Paili stared at BJ with eyes that weren't so wrapped up in loving him and believing in him at all costs, I'd have seen the potential for all the terrible before us, at least in her. He's said so many times that it wasn't planned, it wasn't about her, it could have been anyone, she was just who followed him downstairs. And I think I believe him—but then when your sister's dead and your friends are all in varying crises of their own and there's no one really to unpack something that happened five years ago with because everyone's tired of talking about it but it's still the biggest deal in the world to you even though it isn't and everything's fine—sometimes the mind does wonder, you know?

Because of our history, BJ and I have an open-phone policy. I know his passcode, he knows mine, if I want to read his messages I can and I would. His DMs too. Honestly, his texts are fine, if not a bit beige, actually.

His DMs though—they're wild. The incoming ones (to clarify). Girls are thirsty, insane, little cretins with a horrible disregard for the sacrality of a relationship.

"This is a funny kind of trusting him," my sister would say every time I did it if she was still on the planet.

She'd be peering over my shoulder and down at my fiancé's phone as I read as quickly as I could a thousand things people say to him that make me want to die a little bit.

They range from fairly mild like "👄👅💦," to a touch more aggressive, like "Any time, any place, say the word and I'm down," to girls he's been with in the past messaging him "remember when"s, to downright insane things like "We belong together, I know we are meant to be."

And to BJ's credit, he never responds. They just sit in his requested.

"I do trust him," I'd say, and she'd give me a look.

"I can tell." She'd eyeball me, and there's nothing I love more than proving my sister wrong so then eventually I stopped reading his phone and now I sort of just smack away my curiosity and paranoia with the baseball bat that lives in my mind that I use to keep safe what we have.

"It'll be a couple of months' wait on the marble." The contractor grimaces in our bathroom.

"Months?" BJ sighs.

"Statuario marble—" The contractor shrugs. "In white? This size—" He gestures to the now-cracked piece of it laying in our unused, now-broken bath. "Months, easy."

"That's fine—" I swat my hand at him and give BJ a look, telling him to leave it. "What's it matter? When are we going to use it anyway?"

Beej puts his hand on my waist and leads me out of the bathroom.

"How are you getting to dinner?" He gives me a patient smile.

I shrug. "Walking."

His face pulls. "That's about an hour's walk."

"So?" I shrug again.

"I'll drive you."

I shake my head.

He tries again. "Dani will drive you."

"Happily—!" Daniela calls from the other room. I actually hadn't really noticed she was there. Quiet and sneaky as a mouse.

"I'll catch the tube with you?" Beej offers, and I give him a sharp look.

"I beg your pardon?"

"Harry Styles catches the tube," he offers.

I shake my head as I grip my throat. "He also chokes people with a sea view."

Beej shrugs and blows some air out of his mouth.

"Probably better than choking someone with a garden view—?"

I shoot him a look.

"Meu Deus!" Daniela sighs under her breath, appearing in the doorway. "I will drive."

"Want me to come for the drive?" he offers again because he's a bit perfect like that.

I think about saying yes because I hate cars and driving now and he makes bad things a little bit better, but I want him to think I'm more functional than I think I really am.

"I'll be fine!" I tell him and flash him my most brilliant smile.

I'm silent with white knuckles the whole twelve-minute drive over to St James and Taura is waiting for me out front of the Sofitel. Dinner at Wild Honey, just me and her. I still see her a few times a week but it's been harder lately.

Well, not harder—harder implies the wrong sentiment—it just takes a more conscious effort now to see her after everything that's happened over the last few months with her and the boys. Before we were all always together—now, not so much.

Taura gives me a big smile as she tosses her arms around my neck.

"Love this." She nods down at my outfit: pink and red houndstooth pattern miniskirt from Versace; white cropped embroidered ribbed stretch-cotton jersey tank from Loewe; the hooded belted shearling coat in Bottega green from them (obviously) and the 'Brick Phone Text Me' crystal-embellished silver-tone clutch from Judith Leiber Couture. "God, you look beautiful—Daniela!" She beams over at her. "Hi! Are you going to sit with u—"

"No," Daniela says before leading us into the restaurant.

She does stick close, that Daniela, I will say that.

I thought it was odd at first, how she was just a bit of a shadow but then, she is handy I suppose—? Driving and smacking away photographers—and you know me, not one to bring someone new into the fold, but when she first started to work for me, out of sheer politeness and a fear of feeling paralysingly awkward otherwise, I'd invite her to sit with us and she just never would. Ever. Which then initially felt rude and confusing because—who wouldn't want to sit with us?—but Christian told me not to think too much into it, and also that I can be annoying sometimes and if I gave him the choice not to sit with me sometimes, he'd probably take it too.

Daniela checks us in with the maître d' and then sits at the bar where she looks around, eagle-eyed and observant.

She's admittedly rather strange. I do like her though. Naturally blonde hair, petite features, quite tall, bright eyes.

Taura nods her head towards her.

"Loves a people watch, that one."

"Yes—" My brow folds in the middle. "She does, doesn't she?"

"Bit weird."

"People bird watch . . . ?" I offer her with a shrug.

Taura shakes her head.

"I don't think the two are necessarily connected," she tells me, then orders a bottle of orange wine before she settles into her seat. "How's Beej?"

"Good," I give her a warm smile. "He's got a rather big shoot tomorrow with Versace so he's just having an early night."

"And Christian?"

"Grumpy and a bit sullen and kind of annoying, so normal?" I shrug. "Fine—" I add as an afterthought. "Missing Daisy," I say finally, which I suppose is the real answer and the only one that matters.

Taura nods along, eager to get to the question she really wants to ask. "And the boys?"

I stare over at my friend. Try my best not to sigh aloud. "They're fine, Taurs."

She breathes out, face tugging in anguish.

I hate this, it's the worst. I smile uncomfortably.

"How is he?" she asks quickly, all laced with hope.

I do sigh now. "Taura—"

"Sorry—" She shakes her head quickly. "Sorry! I know, I know but he's not talking to—"

"He's not . . . not talking to you," I interrupt her. "He's just taking some—"

"Space," she tells me, nodding quickly, and I think she's trying not to cry.

I hate her being sad. And not just sad but stressed. You know the feeling? When you like someone and they liked you back and then something shifts for them but not for you and you're left standing there wondering what happened and what changed?

That's actually never happened to me. Sort of briefly that time that Julian dropped me off outside of my old flat because he didn't like it when I asked him if he had PTSD, and if that's what this is then I can confirm, it's not the best feeling.

"It's just so much space." Taura covers her face with her hands. "God. Did I fuck it?"

"No . . ." I say weakly, tugging on my pink mushroom 14-karat gold, silk, enamel and diamond necklace by Marie Lichtenberg.

Her eyes tighten.

"You're lying," she tells me, and my mouth purses.

I am lying, I'm afraid. I don't know whether that's the official consensus but I'm quite sure it'll be the ultimate outcome. Especially after that night—fuck—I shake my head at the memory of it. Such an unbelievable mess.

I pinch my bottom lip absentmindedly.

"Well, I just wonder if perhaps you all left it too long?"

She sort of scoffs and waves her hand at me. "You and Beej strung each other along for years—"

"Yes, but—" I shake my head. "Henry isn't BJ. He's far more pragmatic and, god, Taura—!" I roll my eyes at her. "Please, don't ever look at us as a reference, it's not the same—"

She shakes her head. "Why?"

"Because it's literally not the same." I reach over and squeeze her hand. "For far, far better and for worse, between you and Henry, you don't have all the drama and the shit that bogged Beej and I down and tied us together—"

"Yeah, but—"

"And thank god you don't, Tausie!" I add quickly. "Because those years were hell."

"But you're—"

"Taura." I give her a long look. "BJ and I are not a relationship map. I'm grateful we are where we are and I love him and I wouldn't change a thing—"

I stop myself short and we exchange looks, both knowing that there are, in fact, many, many things I would change.

I shake my head and regroup. "There's no one on the planet I'd rather be with. And yes, for us, it worked out in the end, but you can't use us as a guide—no one should—we barely made it out alive."

She picks at her finger nervously.

"So, you're saying you think it's over?"

I sigh and I wish I could give her more than the shrug that I do.

"I don't know," I say, but I think I do know. I think so does she because they came to blows.

I'd never seen Henry and Jonah fight before—not each other. It was kind of scary. BJ and Christian, they fought often (whoops, sorry)—and I'd seen Hen and Jo get into fights with other people handfuls of times over the course of growing up, but never the two of them just against one another.

Henry's usually so calm and Jonah's so silly—most of the time—but he's proud. Pride is quite dangerous, did you know? And this had been brewing for a while. Their collective relationship had become the wobbliest Jenga tower in the world, just all of us crouched around a table with bated breath, waiting for the wrong brick to be pulled before the imminent collapse.

We were at dinner at few weeks ago at Blacklock, the Soho one. BJ's favourite Sunday roast is there besides the one Lily cooks, and it was he and I, Christian and Henry. And maybe it was my fault, because the last few months before Bridget, I'd been running defence. I always tried to find out where Taura was going to be so that the other one didn't see it, but after Bridge, I suppose I got sloppy. Forgetful, or something—?

I should have asked. I knew it was 'Jonah's night'—I even thought to ask, but when we left the flat there were so many people downstairs waiting for us, yelling at me these terrible questions about my sister's private life. It was around then that the boy she lost her virginity to at school sold the story to the red tops, so all the questions people were yelling at me, I don't know—I just forgot.

Anyway, it was 'Jonah's night'—because even though she knew she picked Henry, and I knew she picked Henry, she didn't know how to end it with Jonah when his mum was still in the hospital, so things between them kept sort of pottering along how they had been before she made a choice—anyway, we were at dinner just the four of us and then who should waltz down the stairs but the rest of our little Box Set. Both of them drunk, but Jonah worse than Taura.

I saw them first and kicked Christian under the table because honestly, I feel less weird about putting him between Jonah and Henry than I do BJ, but Beej caught it anyway.

He tilted his head, gave me a confused look, and I gestured with my eyebrows, keeping my head as still as I could—he clocked them, face pulling.

I turned to Henry quickly. "Come to the bathroom with me?"

"What?" His face scrunched up. "No."

"But"—I swallowed—"I'm going to vomit."

Christian was holding his breath.

"Right." Henry nodded. "I'm going to stick with no—"

Henry flashed me a quick smile and I gave him pleading eyes. His head rolled back and he gestured to Beej.

"Your betrothed will take you."

BJ scratched the back of his neck and shrugged.

"Nah—" he said, but it came out a bit high. "I'd rather not get sick."

Henry stared over at his brother, annoyed. "I'd rather not get sick!"

I made a noise in the back of my throat. "Well, not absolutely everything is about you, Henr—" I started, but I was cut off by Tausie, who spotted us with her bleary eyes in the arms of the elder Hemmes.

"Oh, hi—" She froze up.

When I think back to that moment, the thing I remember,

the part that sticks out the most in my mind, is the way Henry's breath sucked in.

I heard it. This quick intake, two sharp, short breaths—then silence.

Jonah's hands were really low on Taura's body. Like, arse low and Henry's eyes fell to their placement immediately.

His jaw went tight. He said nothing.

"Hey, Hen," Jonah said blearily, kind of staring him down because he can be a bit belligerent when he's legless.

"Hey." Beej jumped to his feet, giving his best friend a disarming smile. He placed himself between Jonah and Henry's line of sight and held Jonah's eyes. "Why don't you nick over to Bill's? Bit of a weird vibe here—"

"Why's it weird for?" Jonah asked him with his chin, and that was sort of when I had a feeling that the night was going to go sideways.

Jonah and BJ are each other's horse whisperers. If anyone can de-escalate a situation, it's one of them for the other. Except that Jonah didn't want to be de-escalated, he wanted a place to point how hurt he was Taura still hadn't made a call and how scared he was about his mum, and the place he chose was Henry.

"Erm—" Christian tossed a thumb in my direction. "Magnolia's vomiting."

Jonah rolled his eyes. "So what else is new?"

I tensed up a little bit and told my hurt feelings he was just drunk and sad, which he was, I suppose. BJ tapped two fingers on his best friend's chest.

"Nope." He gave Jonah a stern look, but by then Henry was already on his feet.

"Oi, take that back and then piss off." Henry nodded his head back towards the exit.

Jonah pointed to himself. "Are you talking to me?"

Taura went stiff.

"Who the fuck else would I be talking to?" Henry asked, an eyebrow up.

"It's fine, Hen!" I stood up, smiling as sincerely as I could muster. "He's just in a mood—"

"Yeah, Hen—" Jonah smiled, barely. "I'm just in a mood."

And then he laughed and it was all drunk and hollow, and from behind, he buried himself in the curve of Taura's neck, kissing her. She squirmed uncomfortably.

"Stop—" she said quietly.

"Stop?" Jonah said, pulling back. He looked angry but it was a very thin mask for hurt.

"Yeah, Jo—" Henry said, coolly. Not the good kind of cool, but the bad. "She wants you to stop."

Jonah looked over at Henry and gave him a tight smile, a little sniff of a laugh—and then he lunged for him.

Tackled him to the floor and punched him.

They knocked over a poor server in the process and Taura rushed to their aid at the same time Henry took a swing. A big one in the eye right before he elbowed Jo in the lip.

BJ and Christian dove towards them, Christian dragged Henry away, Beej grabbed Jonah, who was thrashing in his arms, doing his best to kick Henry on the way out.

I was useless—sort of normal for me these days—I just stood there, looking between my two old friends and the girl they were fighting over.

Taura was still helping the server up, apologising profusely. She was teary—the whole restaurant was silent, a few phones out because it was us.

"What are you all fucking staring at?" Jonah yelled, eyeing them all down.

So naturally, more phones came out.

"Come on—" Beej said, shoving him towards the stairs. He caught my eye, gaze heavy. "I'm gonna take him back to his place."

I nodded.

Beej nodded his head towards me.

"Take her home," he told Christian.

Christian sighed, looking around, then gave BJ a quick yes with his eyes before he smacked someone's phone out of their hand.

"Piss off," he growled at the young guy, early twenties, grinning at the drama.

The guy looked both scolded and offended.

I grabbed some ice from the wine bucket and wrapped it in a napkin, and then dabbed it gently on the cut above Henry's eye.

He shooed me off—he doesn't like to be looked after. Never has. He took the napkin from my hand and held it himself.

"Are you okay?" Taura asked gingerly as she walked over.

Christian and I stood there uncomfortably, sort of stuck, not sure whether to leave or to stay, kind of just frozen like idiots. We looked like idiots too, when *The Sun* ran the story the next day, the photos of Christian and I standing there make us look like the twins from *The Shining*, so stiff and weird.

Henry stared over at Taura, eyes as heavy as I could tell his heart was.

"I can't do this anymore, Taurs," he told her.

She shook her head quickly.

There are a few flashes of cameras around us.

"Henry—" She reached for him but he recoiled from her touch.

"Maybe we shouldn't do this here—" I said gently, peering around at the entire silent room.

Henry shook his head. "I don't care who sees, Parks. I'm done."

Taura breathed out, barely holding it together. "Hen—"

"I said I'm done." He raised his hands in surrender and his face looked like he meant it.

He did mean it.

Sort of.

The next day he was lying face down in our bed yelling that he made a huge mistake and that he'd cocked up. That lasted for about a day and a half and then we dragged him out to dinner, which proved to be a bit of a faux pas on our behalf, because then Henry got kind of sloshed and then made us go to a bar, where he proceeded to hook up with some girl.

It was really quite stressful. Not just because it made me feel like I was somehow cheating on Taura but because it was also just sort of out of character for Henry—

Even before Taura, Henry hooked up the least out of all the boys—which is not to say that he never did, nor that he couldn't—he's just not really like that.

But there he was—tongue down the throat of this honestly (fair play to her) really beautiful blonde girl, hands all over the place, up in her hair—and honestly, to be frank, he's a good kisser. We've kissed twice because of stupid games, and firstly, yuck. But secondly, not yuck because he's actually very good at it. Girls go puddly for him the same way they do for BJ, except Henry is less approachable somehow.

It might surprise you to know, but BJ is really rather approachable. He's friendly to everyone, smiley. Warm, like picnic in the middle of the park on a sunny day. The sandwiches are out, the tea's poured, everyone's invited. He's happy to chat, happy to see you.

Henry is a man reading on a park bench . . . you don't really talk to him unless he's talking to you.

BJ and I stood there, blinking at what was unfolding in front of us—Henry and that girl, and whatever was going to happen next.

"Oh." I reached for his hand. "I feel like this might be a bit of a headache."

"Yep." Beej nodded, his brows all low with worry for his brother, then he nodded his head to the door. "Let's leave him to it."

And we did leave him to it. That night Henry did proceed to do it with that girl. Do you know how I know? Because he did it with her in our home! In our guest room—which, for one—disgusting!—and two—absolutely not and never again, thank you very much, Henry Austin. My eyes nearly fell out of my fucking head when she crept past us in the living room towards the front door the following morning.

Henry wandered out a few minutes later in only sweatpants, rubbing the back of his neck as though he pulled a muscle. He gave us a bleary smile and I stared at him in googly-eyed horror.

"Oi—" Beej nodded his chin towards the guest room. "Like, man to man . . . Never again."

"Come off it." Henry rolled his eyes. "How many people have you shagged at my place?"

I turn to BJ sharply, a finger up to silence him. "Do not answer that—" And then I turn back to his brother, pointing. "And you, that was very rude—" I glared at him. "In no world, Henry—" I shook my head. "You have a Coutts card and a giant inheritance. Get a fucking hotel room."

Henry rolled his eyes at me.

"The nerve." I eyeballed him before pointing towards the front door. "Go and buy me some new sheets immediately—"

He rolled his eyes again. "Magnoli—"

"IMMEDIATELY!" I yelled. "King size, Egyptian cotton, twelve hundred thread count, minimum. Somewhere in the colour-wheel between linen white and mother of pearl."

Henry growled under his breath.

"And I will be telling your mother!" I call after him as he retreated back towards the guest room.

"No!" He spun around, looking at me with desperate eyes.

"Yes," I told him, nose in the air all defiant.

In the restaurant, Taura blinks at me sadly before she throws back her wine.

"I'm sorry," I tell her.

She nods quickly, eyes busy and unable to settle on a place in the room.

"Is he fucking around a lot?" She asks that without looking at me, afraid of the answer, I think. I stare over at her—or maybe I glare, if I'm being entirely truthful. I don't like the position I've found myself in.

"Please?" she asks quietly.

I breathe out my nose and lick my bottom lip.

"He hasn't gone full Beej."

"Yeah but—" She shrugs. "No one goes full Beej like Beej."

I give her a look.

"Sorry." She stares down at her half-eaten plate.

"He's dating," I offer her.

"Oh." Her face falls a bit.

"No one in particular—" I shake my head quickly, wanting to make her feel better. "He's just going on dates."

"Right." She nods, thinking it through. "Does he ask about me?"

"Well, I mean—he's very principled." My face pulls as I see the answer hurting her again. "He's trying his best not to."

"Right," she says again before she shakes it off and nods over at my full plate of food. "You don't like it?"

"Hmm?" I blink, glancing down at it. "No, I love it. I just had a late lunch." I flash her a quick smile.

I get home close to eleven p.m., and Daniela walks me inside and says she's going to clean up a bit before she goes home. I thank her for driving me before I head to the comfiest, least angular room in the house.

And there he is, sitting in bed, shirtless, just how I like him, *The Little Prince* in hand. He lowers it when he sees me, smiling all tired and beautiful.

"Hey."

"Hi." I crawl over to him.

He touches my face. "How was dinner?"

"Good."

"You have fun?"

I nod.

"What'd you have?"

"For dinner?" I blink and shrug. "The halibut."

He pulls me in towards him and up onto his lap, kissing my shoulder.

I turn back to look at him.

"What are you up for? It's supposed to be an early night."

He shakes his head. "I never sleep til you're home."

"Ever?"

"Nope."

"What about in our lost years?" I ask, turning around to face him.

"In our lost years"—he slips his arms around my waist—"we still shared locations—I'd just watch and wait til you got home."

"Oh my god!" I laugh, straddling him now. "How exhausting—that's practically a full-time job!"

"I fucking know, right!" He rolls his eyes. "Will you tell my dad that?"

I tilt my head as I touch his cheek. He meant it as a joke but there's a heaviness to it.

"Is he giving you a hard time still?"

His head falls back a bit and he breathes out, shrugging like he doesn't care except that he does.

"Just the usual 'what are you doing with your life?' shit."

He stares up at me with this strange heaviness, pushes his hands through my hair, and I can feel a struggle in him that I don't know how to pull to the surface. I don't know what he's doing with his life, if I'm completely honest. I think, before, *I* was the thing he was doing with his life. Getting me back was his raison d'être and now he has me and then what? I don't think he knows.

He shakes his head.

"I'll figure it out." He gives me a quick but perfect smile. It does look a bit sad though.

I brush my lips over his. "I'm going to shower."

"Want me to come?" he offers for old times' sake.

I shake my head.

"You have an early morning." I tell him before I kiss him again.

I take my time in the shower, and then ages to do my skin routine because I need him to be asleep before I get into bed.

I've had to add in like four extra steps to my bedtime routine so that he gets bored of waiting for me and gives up and goes to sleep—not because I'm avoiding sex with him—my god, don't be insane! Look at him, he's ever the vision. Always has been, always will be.

No, I need him to be asleep so my second nightly routine can begin.

I tiptoe back into our room and climb into our bed next to him.

At the motion of me, he shifts a little in his sleep, makes a tiny sound that's so cute I want to die and through me surges this great wave of loving him. Loving him so much, it feels almost like I'm choking on it.

He moves again, rolling in towards me, and I stare at him, the great love of my life.

It was always him. I knew that, even at the time, even when I tried to fill the gap he left in me with other people, it was and always will be him.

I put my hand on his chest and swallow heavy.

I love this body.

I think I know it better than I know my own.

The two freckles he has just left to the centre of his chest.

The way his abdomen ripples down down down, like he's been moulded—like he's not really real. The curves of his chest carved into my memory the same way you won't ever forget your best day. He is my best day.

I so vividly remember undressing him for the first time.

It was strange because I'd seen him fairly naked before—hard not to when you've grown up around each other—but not all the way naked.

It was at school, in my dorm room.

We'd only been together a month or two, depending on the undecided date of our togetherness. He says we were together since the holiday, but there was a week where he didn't talk to me much (Christian told him to play it cool) and that week was an absolute torture. I don't personally count us as together until he kissed me in front of my entire dorm.

We were quick-sticks after that, in a free-for-all for loving each other.

A month later, he was in my dorm room, me pressed up against a post of my bed, his hand up my uniform skirt for a second before I was unbuttoning his shirt.

I felt so grown-up. We were so small.

Back in our bed tonight, I trace the wave his biceps make and down his arm, tracing the veins to his wrist, where I let my fingers rest, feeling for a pulse.

I think death brushes up against nearly everyone at some point or another, but it's properly danced with me. Grabbed me by the hand, spun me, dipped me . . . taught me to waltz. I knew life through the prism of loss, secretly at first, but now it's coloured my world. It's the summertime here at the minute, but I'm terrified of the autumn because then death is everywhere. And it masks itself in colours all bright, but it's still a season of dying. And I'll have to walk the streets under the sweet gum trees that line our street and death will rain on me all gold and orange, and it'll be inescapable and unavoidable . . . All the ways I could die—or worse—all the ways he could and I'd lose him too.

65,000,000 people die every year, did you know?

Bridget is one of those statistics now. One of the 65 million that died this year.

And I guess, sure, statistically, 32,500,000 of those deaths are probably old age. But what about the other half of them?

If 65,000,000 people are dying every year, that means there's 178,000 each day. Which is 7,425 each hour, and get this—that's 120 people dying each minute. Two per second.

24,000 people annually die from lightning strikes. How do you think that'd be? I wonder, does it cook you a bit? From the inside out? Do you see light as it hits you?

At least 270 will die from a fire each day, which I think maybe is a bad way to go, don't you? I think you know with a fire—that if you're trapped with it, it's going to get you. But then the way flames lick your skin and it's not quite quick enough. I think you'd probably feel it all.

I caught on fire once, at a club. I was wearing a loose-fitting top, and it was too close to a candle. My back had a third-degree burn the size of my hand; BJ and I had to spend the night in hospital. I hated the smell. I wonder, could you smell your skin burning when you're on fire?

It's a similar number for drowning as well. About 100,000 a year. I've read that's a nice way to die. After the initial shock passes, after your lungs stop trying to breathe, apparently this euphoria hits you, and it's this dreamy, tired feeling, quite like falling to sleep.

More than 21,917 people will die every day from smoking and smoking-adjacent things, and part of me feels like "you know what, you invited death to the table by smoking, you idiots" but then actually, did you know that more than 10 percent of those 21,917 people (which is more than 2,190) who die every day because of cigarettes die because someone else smoked them? That's not fair.

But I suppose not much about death is.

500,000 people are murdered every year—also not fair. Also horrible, and terrifying, and speaks to a darkness in our world that is so catastrophically unbearable and uncontainable and if there are 500,000 people being murdered, then it would be fair to infer that there are then too approximately 500,000 murderers, so then what's to stop the random man on the street turning around and knifing you in the head because he felt like it? Heads are important.

More than 1,000 people every week will die from some sort of head injury, like falling. Pavements are uneven. There are curbs and walls and low ceilings—BJ's tall, and he's always talking or on his phone—there might be a low hanging pipe somewhere, and then what?

And then of course—the big C.

That kills a lot of people, doesn't it? 4,342 every day. Does it ever surprise them, I wonder? Or do you think you always know you're dying from cancer before it happens? I think surprise deaths are the worst.

Do you ever think about it? How you love a person who's made of mostly bone? Because it's all I think about now. That the thing protecting the heart I would do anything for—that I'd die for—all that's protecting it is a ribby cage made from collagen, calcium phosphate and calcium carbonate. That's it.

And some muscle.

These are the things holding Baxter James Ballentine together. Bones and sinew.

And I've seen him break bones before. A million times over the course of our lives up til now. Fingers and toes and wrists. I've seen him snap his arm in a way where a tiny bit of the bone pierced through the skin. Bodies tear apart so easily.

And that mind of his. I love his brain. I love how he sees the world, like everyone is good and everything is fun and exciting and sweet; he has the most lovely, sunny disposition because his mind is good and pure, but do you know how easy it is to sustain a brain injury?

One bad whack in the temple and your brain can swell and then—poof!—you're a goner.

BJ doesn't chew his food very well either. He sort of swallows it whole. Always has . . . Did you know 3,000 grown-ups will die from choking on food every year? And I don't know the Heimlich. What would I do if he were to start choking?

He just never chews properly. He's always hungry so he always eats too fast, you're meant to chew each bite thirty-five times or something, which like—come off it, as if! That's absolute pure madness—but I don't think he'd be doing three before a swallow, which means he's doing like, an eleventh of the chews he's meant to, and I don't like those odds.

Plus, he's so bad at seat belts. I don't know whether he thinks he's James fucking Dean but he never wears one, even though 3,287 people die every day from car accidents, which is more than you want because cars are so normal and people are in them all the time. Us less so now because I don't like cars much these days after—well, you know what after—but because of that, I can say that I'm quite sure that a car accident is a bad way to die. Now that I've been in one and all. Because your skin is so thin, and underneath it there isn't anything that can help you against a tonne of twisty, sharp metal that's just trying to scrape the meat of you clean off your bones. The metal wraps around you and tries to make you one with it, like it's an intimate moment between you, and maybe that's because all death is.

An intimate moment that's coming for you, and it'll take you whether you're ready or not. It asks no questions and it leaves no answers—

I need some answers.

I reach for my bedside table drawer and quietly remove a few items from it.

"This is peak dysfunction," I think I hear Bridget whispering to me.

"Quiet," I tell her, though I never want her to be.

The touchless forehead thermometer—"At least it's touchless," my sister would say—the little oximeter I clip onto his finger—"Oximetry, Magnolia? Really?"—and the little notebook I write his vitals down in to keep track.

"You know about vitals, then?" she'd say to me, and I stick my nose in the air to spite her like she's still on the planet to watch me do so.

37.2 degrees Celsius today. 97—SpO_2%; 63 bpm.

Hm. I purse my lips.

"He's fine," she'd tell me, but what would I even believe her for, the traitor?

Yesterday he was 98—SpO_2%; 61 bpm. Those are numbers I like better.

Nevertheless, I write them down and then tuck all my secret doctor tools away and back in my drawer.

"Well, now he'll never die, ever!" she'd tell me with an annoying look, and I feel cross at her for it even though she's not here to say it in real life, and my heart lurches for her and it lands on an empty plot in Highgate because her ashes are here at the foot of our bed.

I wriggle in towards Beej, wrap his arms around me myself and then I lay my head down on his chest.

This is how I sleep now.

To the beat of his aliveness.

FOUR

BJ

I have three regrets from my lifetime. More, probably. But if a genie's handing out wishes, these three are what I'm changing.

The first one you know: Paili and the bath. What I would give to go back in time and walk out my door instead of down those stairs. Go straight to Parks, tell her everything, skip all the breaking we did to each other between then and now.

The second, I don't want to talk about, but the third one—probably not hard to guess.

When I think back to that day in the hospital, Magnolia all banged up and bruised in the bed, still unconscious—that's the screaming image in my mind. How much it fucked me up seeing her all hurt like that, it was nearly impossible for me, in that moment, to see past her—but if I do, pull a curtain closed on her—tell my mind she's fine, she's completely fine, she'll make it, she's good, we're good—if I tell my past-self that, peer back in my memory, let me remember some other things . . .

Bridget in that chair still in the clothes from the crash.

A little cut on her lip. Her arm bleeding. A light graze on her forehead.

She looked fine. Tired, but fine.

And I fucking told her to go.

Me and Claire have talked about this. How the doctors already cleared her and I'm not a doctor, so how was I supposed to know? Fair question, I s'pose, but I feel like I should have anyway.

Because I know her. All her life I have, so I should have seen it. It feels like the sort of thing I should have seen in her.

★

I was her first kiss, did you know? Bridget's, I mean.

Funny.

Magnolia and I had been together just a few months by then, it was a Sunday night before we would go back to Varley the next day.

Me and Parks were lying on her bed watching TV when her sister walked past the bedroom door.

"Bridget," she called to her, and Bridge poked her head in the door.

"What?" Bridge asked, already rolling her eyes because they've always been how they've always been. Even at thirteen and fifteen. Even at three and five.

Magnolia sat up, back tall, eyes pinched.

"At a party last night, did you play seven minutes in heaven with Dean Vinograd—arguably the hottest person in your year—" Magnolia looked from Bridge to me to further her point. "Only to not kiss him at all, the entire time?"

I sniffed a laugh and then Bridge crossed her arms uncomfortably.

"So what if I did?"

Magnolia eyed her suspiciously. "Well, why wouldn't you? It's just a kiss."

Bridget shifted her weight between her feet.

"Right?" Magnolia blinked over at her.

Bridge glared over at her, chest getting a bit huffy as her face pinched.

"I've never kissed anyone before," Bridget said, nose in the air like her sister's goes.

"What!?" Magnolia yelled dramatically before falling backwards on her bed. Like she was so fucking experienced. We hadn't done much yet. A little bit because she's handsy, but not much.

Bridget's face went embarrassed and she rushed further into the room to defend herself. "I just—I haven't—" She takes a breath. "And now I'm—" She doesn't say it, but I could see it on her face.

Scared.

"That's fine," I told her, shaking my head.

She blinked. "Is it?"

I nodded. "Yeah."

"No, it's not." Magnolia pouted. "It's weird."

Bridget huffed again, breathed out her nose, now pouting too. "It's just I don't know how—I don't want to look stupid."

"You couldn't," I told her.

"You definitely could," Magnolia said matter-of-factly, and I gave her a look.

"I couldn't kiss Dean last night!" Bridget yelled suddenly. "What if it was bad and he hated it and then he told everyone and then I was a big loser?"

Magnolia scrunched her face up. "What if you had the opportunity to kiss the hottest boy in your year, you didn't, and then he tells everyone and you're a big loser? Oh, wait—" She tossed her sister a look.

"I didn't know what to do!" Bridget yelled.

"I'll kiss you," I told her.

Bridget blinks twice. "What?"

"Yeah." Magnolia stared at me. "What?"

"I'll just kiss her." I glanced at Parks and gave her a shrug before looking back at Bridge. "Then it's done and you've done it, and you won't feel scared the next time it comes up."

Bridget eyed me indignantly. "I didn't say I was scared."

"You didn't," I conceded. "But were you?"

She pinched the tip of her finger. "Maybe."

"Hold on a minute!" Magnolia said, sitting back up, eyebrows arched. "You're going to kiss her?"

I nodded. "Yeah, if she wants."

"My sister?" Magnolia clarified, all horrified.

I leant in towards her and caught her eyes. Gave her the look I'll give her infinity times over our lifetime together that turns her to puddles.

"It's just a kiss," I whispered to her with a shrug.

Her face softened and I stood, turning towards her sister.

"Ready?"

Bridge nodded, swallowed heavy.

"It's nothing." I gave her another shrug. "Just a kiss."

She nodded again and then I slipped my hand behind her head and gave her a proper good snog.

Don't have anything poetic to say about it, no nautical metaphors or exploding skies, no fireworks—can you imagine? What a fucking mess—solid little kisser though.

It was about two seconds into our practice kiss that Harley walked past the open door and bellowed, "What the fuck?"

Magnolia proper screamed, Bridget yelped, jumping backwards and away from me, and Harley charged towards me, shoving me away from his fourteen-year-old. Which, honestly, fair play . . .

"No, no!" Magnolia dove between us.

"What in the absolute fuck is going on in here?" He looked from Magnolia to me, blood visibly boiling on his face.

Pretty scary at sixteen, I won't lie.

"Nothing!" Magnolia started shaking her head wildly. "Bridget's just a big loser, that's all—!"

Some heavy breathing from Harley and a glare at his eldest.

"What?"

"Because of Dean Vinograd!" Bridget scurried over to us, nodding.

Harley's face pulled. "Who?"

"In the closet?" Magnolia nods, eyes wide.

Harley's face scrunches. "What?"

"So embarrassing—" Magnolia takes the chance to toss her little sister a filthy look. "She just talked—"

"Who talked?"

I pointed to Bridge. "She did."

Magnolia went back to head shaking. "Sullying my good name!" Tossed her father a courtesy head nod. "And yours too, I suppose, Harley."

He gestured to himself. "My good name?"

Both his daughters nodded quickly with big eyes.

"So sullied," Magnolia told him earnestly.

"Mmm-hmm," Bridge said, and when I think back to it now, it's so cute, the two of them creating a little barrier between me and their dad. Like I would have stood a fucking chance if he wanted to hurt me.

You know how there are men who thrive when they have daughters? Obama, Kobe Bryant, the Rock—the whole girl-dad thing? My dad's one of them—loves having girls.

Harley's not a girl-dad. Never has been. Don't think he ever will be.

His face by then was in the depths of misunderstanding, not tracking a single thing they were panic screaming, except for maybe the one thing they wouldn't have wanted him to catch.

Harley nodded his head at Parks.

"You have a good name for kissing people in closets?"

Bridget's lips formed a little "o" shape, and Magnolia's mouth fell open.

"Erm." She cleared her throat then shook her head quickly. "No?"

Except that the "no" came out real high.

Harley's face got a bit dark.

"Yeah, no . . ." I said, pushing between them, feeling like I should take over. "No. Like, we—actually . . . don't even really, like, hook up—"

Their dad's eyebrow went up. "Uh-huh."

I shrugged. "She's a massive prude, like we've done nothing—"

"I am not!" Magnolia cut me off, so I spoke over her, louder.

"No, like, man to man—" I shook my head. "We've done nothing—"

Magnolia's face went so cross, little fists into balls.

She got out a "We do so—" before Bridget clamped her hand over her big sister's mouth, who has been (to this day) always weirdly into confessing things she doesn't need to.

Harley looked between us all, eyes pinched.

"I hate this." He breathed out loudly.

I gave him a big hopeless smile and a half-hearted shrug.

"Yeah, same."

After that, he left and then the three of us fell on Parks' bed, laughing.

But it wasn't a "yeah, same." I didn't hate it. Never have. Never will.

I love that memory.

By the time me and Parks were engaged, even Harley was laughing at it.

Fuck, I miss her.

So, yeah . . . The third one of my three great regrets is that Bridget's dead and I'll wonder forever if we caught it, if maybe she wouldn't be.

14:19

Parksy

Hi

what are you wearing

Bit sexy!

Fun though.

I'm in.

What do you want me to be wearing?

. . . to our wedding.

Ah.

Less sexy

I mean—

God.

Hopefully not?

Hah

. . .

I’m not telling you

Please?

Nope

🌩️

❄️

Don’t be rude

🙂

That seems racially charged

🌬️

FIVE
Magnolia

They closed Saint Laurent on Old Bond early for me in the late afternoon so that I could take Henry and Christian suit shopping without having to deal with crazy people and cruel questions.

As far as the wedding goes—style-wise—as I'm sure you can imagine, I'm running a fairly tight ship.

It might come as a bit of a surprise to you (because we all know I love colours and have an aversion to the boring) but the dress palette for our wedding is black, white and neutrals.

That, of course, is not the overarching colour palette of the entire day—I'm not depressed—but unless BJ and I were to forsake tradition and wear colourful dresses and suits ourselves, the others in colours just looks a bit like a circus.

"You know," Henry peers at me through a rack of clothes. "We are capable of dressing ourselves."

I pivot in my pink and red rose appliquéd satin sandals from Magda Butrym, eyebrows up.

"When have you ever?"

"This morning," Henry tells me defiantly.

I eyeball him. "And what are you wearing?"

"An outfit of my own choosing—" Henry says smugly, "—from the capsule wardrobe you gave to me at the start of the season," he adds at the end, a fraction more sheepish.

"I like not dressing myself," Christian announces.

I give him a merry shrug. "And I like having cute boy dolls to dress—"

He scrunches that cute nose of his. "I like it a bit less after that."

"Oh no." I yawn as I flip through a rack of dress shirts.

Christian grunts under his breath before he asks, "Are you dressing Beej for the wedding?"

"I'm not," I huff, looking at him with my arms crossed. "But I do know he's wearing Saint Laurent Oxfords and custom Gucci."

"You mean Tom Ford," Henry corrects me.

I give him a sneaky smile.

"Magnolia!" Henry groans. "He's going to fucking kill me—"

I smile at him, smug. "You're too easy—"

"Parks—" Henry viciously pulls a shirt he likes off the rack.

"You walked into that, man—" Christian shakes his head at his best friend. "That was vintage Parks, she's a fucking sneak."

I aggressively elbow my way past him, mostly just to elbow him but I disguise it to look as though I'm trying to get to the rack behind him. "Excuse you! I'm not sneaky—"

"Oh no," Christian rolls his eyes. "You're right, everything's always face value with you."

I give him a glare and hand him a jacket, trouser and shirt combination. He stares at the clothes for a few seconds then snatches them out of my hand with another roll of his eyes.

Henry bustles past me, still cross.

"Brat," he calls me, and I scurry after him, wrapping my arms around his waist, and cuddle him, batting my eyes.

He throws a reluctant arm around me and kisses the top of my head. "Don't tell him you know."

I zip my mouth shut.

Christian reappears then proceeds to stare at himself in the mirror.

Single-breasted tuxedo jacket in Grain de Poudre over white slim-fit cotton poplin with Yves collar, tucked into the tailored trousers in Saint Laurent Gabardine.

He squints, pretending he's trying to decide whether or not he likes it, but I can tell he does.

I hand him the black silk satin Yves bow tie, and he begins to fasten it to himself as I stand in front of him, tugging at the jacket.

Handsome, like always. Never doesn't look handsome though, I suppose that's the thing with him. Especially in a tux.

I take his arms and adjust the sleeves, I can feel him staring down at me, watching me.

I flick my eyes up at him. "What?"

His face pulls in some discomfort.

"Sorry if this is a shit question to ask—but like, who are your bridesmaids now?"

I breathe out the question and don't let the way it stabs me in my heart show on my face. I take a breath, rubbing the fabric of my bead-embellished sequined tulle minidress from Valentino Garavani between my fingers.

Bridget's absence (if that's what we're calling it) has highlighted a great many things, but one in particular is how few female friends I actually have.

Who would I have stand next to me in lieu of her?

There is no in lieu of her.

No one comes close. Not really. Except maybe . . .

"Me," Henry says, sidling up next to me with broad smile. He tosses his arm around me again. "I'm her mate-of-honour."

I give Christian a long-suffering look. "He came up with that himself."

Christian smirks. "You don't say."

"I am your mate-of-honour," Henry tells me, proud.

"You are my m—" I mash my mouth together and shake my head. "An honoured position in my life."

Henry points his thumb in my direction. "She doesn't like the M-word."

"The M-word?" Christian blinks. "Mate?"

"God, you're ridiculous," my sister would say, and I'd ignore her.

I shake my head despondently. "Hateful."

"What?" His face scrunches up. "It's not even a swear word. Like, I get why you don't necessarily like the word cun—"

And then I let out a scream to silence him, clamping my hand over his mouth.

"Never!" I shake my head at him. Henry rolls his eyes at me but

I ignore him because we don't say the C-word. "My god! Did you slip and fall into a lower socioeconomic bracket where that word would perhaps, at a push, on a terrible day, be acceptable to say?"

Christian rolls his eyes too.

"Absolutely never—" I keep shaking my head, my nose in the air. "So vulgar."

"Such an idiot." My sister would shake her head.

"Right." Christian's whole face pinches. "But 'mate'?"

"It just sits funny in my mouth, that's all." I shrug. "I can't say it properly."

"You can't say lots of words properly though, that's hardly the word's fault now, is it?" Bridget would pipe in and I'd be cross at her for that one.

"Why?" Christian asks, exasperated.

"Because I'm not poor." I give him a curt smile. "And nor are you, it's worth noting."

Christian ignores me and looks over at Henry.

"So, you're going to be standing at the top of an aisle with your ex. How are we feeling about that?"

Henry's jaw juts a little and he swallows.

"Fine."

"Yeah?" Christian tilts his head, not buying it. "See yourself standing at the top of any aisles with her anytime soon?"

"Nope." Henry says, pretending to look at the jewellery. And then he looks up and gives Christian a dark look. "Heard from Daisy?"

Christian says nothing, just walks back into the changing room.

I toss Henry a look, because yes, Christian was being annoying and borderline unkind, but that was meaner.

I walk towards the changing room and call through the mirror-door. "No word?"

"Nope," he says gruffly.

"Nothing at all?"

"No, Magnolia."

"Have you spoken to J—"

The door swings open, and Christian plonks the clothes into my hands.

"I have spoken to no Haites since the day they left."

I nod once, my heart feeling as heavy as his eyes look.

It did surprise me, if not perhaps hurt my feelings just a little, that I didn't hear from Julian at all. Not when I had my accident, not even when Bridget d—

Well, you know what Bridget went and did.

"Right." I tug my ear mindlessly then shake my head. "Okay. Now shoes."

22:37

Gus W ♡

Miss you

Same

Lunch soon?

Yeah. Friday?

Yes!

I can't wait!

Alright though?

Are you ok?

I'm brilliant.

I just bought the Cherry Lunch Box Clutch from Gucci and Judith Leiber, it's honestly perfect.

Wear it friday, dying to see it x

SIX

BJ

I wanted a burger. Been thinking about one for weeks.

Don't get a lot of burgers in at the minute. Magnolia's a bit weird about them. Bit weird about a lot of things, honestly.

She had to work late tonight and I was sort of happy to have the night with the boys. One more meal from Farmacy and my head's going to fucking explode. It's not bad food—nice enough, actually. Just all she'll eat right now. Suppose I should be happy she's eating at all at the minute—

I just wanted something greasy, so here I am. Patty&Bun on James Street because they're arguably the best. Wasn't a big, planned thing.

I called Hen, he was with Christian, who called Jo, who was with Banksy and now we're here.

How's it between Hen and Jo, you're wondering?

Fine.

Weird, I know, but then Christian and me were like this for years. Buried shit, ignored it.

Only that—I don't know—Henry's weird with things like this. He can switch off his mind like a valve.

He said he was done with Taus, he's been done with her since.

Which, then I know you're wondering—did he even properly love her?

And yep.

He and I aren't the same like that. He's too pragmatic. How it all went down with me and Parks—would have driven him mental.

I kind of can't believe he lasted as long as he did with Taura. That's how I know he loved her, he wouldn't have tried to figure it out as long as he did otherwise.

I think that's a thing. Like how the family of cancer patients grieve the death of their loved one before they actually pass, and then once they finally do pass, they're often able to move on a bit faster than say, when your sister suddenly dies from a brain aneurysm no one knew she had.

I think Henry felt like he was losing Taura all along.

He turned off the valve.

And Jo? He's spending a lot of time with Bianca Harrington these days. More than usual . . . Interesting, I know. He keeps banging on that he's not into her but it's shit, I can tell it's shit. Because Banksy's got a new boyfriend (who might actually be an old boyfriend? I can't follow) and Jo's real worked up about it.

It's funny watching them together.

They kind of remind me of me and Parks way back when.

Friends, but more than that. His arm around her chair. Her eating his chips. Sort of leaning into him without properly leaning into him. I don't even know if they know they're doing it. But I know they're doing it, and I'm watching them with pinched eyes and an amused smile.

"What?" Jo mouths, frowning.

I smirk, shaking my head when my phone rings.

Parks.

I answer it. "Hey."

"Hi," says the best voice in the world. "Where are you?"

"Just out for dinner with the boys and Banks."

"Oh, nice!" she says. Means it. "Where at?"

"Um." I pause. It's not going to be worth the drama of telling her I'm eating a burger. She'll freak out, make me go on a reset juice cleanse for the havoc the fried food is causing my gut.

"Malibu Kitchen," I lie, and everyone else at the table frowns at me, confused.

"Oh, good!" Magnolia says on the phone, appeased. "I love that place."

Henry mouths, "What?" and I shake my head at him, standing up from the table and taking a step away.

"Yeah, me too—" I tell her. "Was your day good?"

"Mm-hm—" she says mindlessly. "Yeah, I had that meeting with—"

"Oh yeah," I rub the back of my neck. "How's Rich?"

"Good," she answers.

"Happy with it all?"

"Yeah."

I nod, chuffed for her. "Knew he would be."

"Will you be home late?" she asks.

"No, not too late—" I tell her, glancing back at the table, who are all watching me. "We'll finish up here soon. I'll come home straight after."

"You don't have to," she tells me quickly because she doesn't like to be needy when she's actually needy.

Spent the last five years being needy and demanding as fuck for no reason at all, and now she has every right to and she won't be.

"I want to," I tell her.

A pause.

"Okay," she says, but I can hear the relief in her voice.

Tell her I love her and hang up.

Christian nods his chin at me as I sit back down. "Did you just lie to her?"

"What?" I blink mindlessly. "No—not really."

"Why'd you say we were somewhere else?" Jo frowns.

I roll my eyes at them.

"She's been a bit weird about food, hasn't she, Hen?"

My brother gives me a long look, brows dip in the middle, before he nods reluctantly. "A bit, yeah."

And then the conversation moves on to what we're going to do for her birthday, because it's soon. Feels weird for a few reasons.

One, we're together.

All recent birthdays til now I've had to celebrate at half-mast or not at all. Last year she was in New York without me. I sent her a present, said she kept it but never opened it. She opened it after we were together.

First edition of *The Little Prince*, with all the parts that remind me of her highlighted. Bit of a joke because it all reminds me of her. She's the rose, the thing that tamed me.

"Of course I love you. It is my fault that you have not known it all the while" is what I wrote in the front of it.

She loved it how I knew she would. Cried actually.

She expects a lot for her birthday. Loves an event.

We've had a lot of good ones . . . Couple of bad ones too.

Her eighteenth birthday was a doozy. I took her camping.

No, I know—stop, you don't need to say—I don't know what the fuck I was thinking. She took it about as well as you'd imagine.

"Do you have an idea for my birthday this year?" she asked brightly. We were sitting on my bed late in the summer.

It was well after Billie and a good deal before all the shit with Paili. Pretty sewn together by then. Makes me laugh now, thinking that she'd ever fucking go for it.

"Yep." I nodded, proud of myself for some reason.

She lifted her eyebrows in hopeful expectation.

Other things I could have done for her birthday: Taken her to Paris. Taken her sailing around French Polynesia. Thrown her a regular birthday party. Taken her to a fucking Nando's.

Any and all of these would have been preferable to her over what I did plan.

"Camping," I told her with a big smile.

She blinked about twenty-five times.

"Sorry, what?"

"Camping!" I told her again. "You and me. And the boys." I added as a caveat.

Her whole face scrunched.

"It'll be fun!" I said with a laugh, nudging her head with mine.

She pulled back, looked at me really carefully, then swallowed and touched my hand gently.

"BJ," she cleared her throat before she delicately said, "Is everything okay with your family business?"

"What?" I snorted. "Yeah—why?"

She looked at me dubiously.

"This just sounds like something a poor person might suggest . . ."

I rolled my eyes. "I thought it would be fun."

She stared at me a few seconds then shook her head.

"If you've fallen on hard times, Beej, I promise nothing will change between us, but—if that's the case, I love you and please just let me plan my own birthday—"

"I'm not poor." I frowned at her. "I think you'll like it."

Her eyes pinched. "Have you hit your head?"

"Parksy—" I started laughing. "Just think . . . you and me . . ." I lifted my eyebrows, trying to convince her. "In a tent . . ."

"No." She shook her head.

"Under the brightest stars you've ever seen . . ." I elbowed her playfully and the stars got her a bit because we're in them. Her face started to soften. "In a sleeping bag—"

"—In an excuse me what?" she interrupted.

I grimaced. "A sleeping bag."

She looked at me all suspicious. "What's that?"

"It's a bag you sleep in while you're camping."

That got her attention. Loves a bag. Honestly, same. But not anymore, and it was a different kind of bag to her anyway.

"Made of what?" she asked, interest piqued.

"Like, a zipped-in duvet or something?"

"Hm." She frowned, considering it all. "Interesting."

I leaned in towards her, started kissing her neck. "You know camping gear can be quite expensive . . ."

She eyeballed me how she has a million times over the course of our lives. "So too can a trip to the Amalfi Coast, and I should imagine I'd enjoy that a good bit more, and yet here we are."

That made me laugh.

Wish I didn't think it was funny when she's a brat but I still do. I've made her into a monster. Wouldn't change a thing though.

We did go camping. Switzerland. It wasn't a hit.

We lasted thirty-two hours before her and Paili cried so much we had to find a nearby motel.

Motel didn't go down so well either, she cried there too.

She went to the loo once in those thirty-two hours. Came home with a UTI, so we all paid a price that weekend.

Second reason this year's birthday is different is the obvious one.

No Bridge. And something about Bridget not being here's dulled it for her. Like she can't celebrate now, like maybe it wouldn't be right.

And it's popping out in weird ways.

I asked her what she wanted, she said nothing.

I said, "Who are you and what have you done with Magnolia Parks?" and she gave me a weak smile before she just started crying. Fucking kill me. Crushed me because I can't fix this shit.

First birthday we've been proper together for in what—five?—six years? That should be reason enough for a parade but it's all shit anyway because it's the first birthday without Bridge and we feel it in everything.

I want so bad to be able to fix this for Parks, but I can't. It's a steep dip down on a roller coaster we're already strapped in on. The ride's already started.

After dinner, Henry and I walk home.

Habit now. She's off cars so I am too.

He's quiet for the first fifteen minutes.

Conversationally like getting a stone to bleed.

"You good?" I eventually ask him with a nudge.

Hen shakes his head a bit.

"Don't do that again."

My face pulls. "Do what?"

"Pit me against her." His jaw goes tight. "Make me lie for you."

I shake my head at him. "Bro, she has been crazy about food again, you said it yourself—"

"Okay." He nods, impatient. "So what are we going to do about it?"

"I—" My mouth falls open and for some reason how he's talking about it feels like a punch. Fuck. I shake my head again. Hope I look less threadbare than I feel. "I'm not ready—"

Henry's face falters. "What?"

"Nothing." I walk a few paces ahead. Can't get into this at the minute. "It's—fine." I look back at him to make sure he believes it. "I'm fine. I won't lie to her again, yeah?"

Except even that was a lie.

I am lying to her, actively.

Every day at the minute.

Everything's fucked.

You have no idea.

SEVEN

BJ

I don't really know when it started.

Can't have been long after Bridge.

I don't know what it was . . . Heightened emotions or something? Everyone distracted? Maybe the sneaking around was hot, I don't know—? I don't think it was planned. Just happened, I s'pose.

We're at her parents for her birthday, which is tomorrow.

Family dinner. Hers and mine.

When we walk into the living room, Arrie's sitting down across from Mars and Harley, and our eyes catch. Hers go guilty. Makes me think she knows it's wrong.

I mean—fuck—we all know it's wrong.

It's not a grey area, it's proper fucked.

I look away because I don't want Parks to know, don't want her to see anything, think into anything. I know I'm going to have to tell her eventually, I just don't think she could stomach it right now. It'd do her head in. I don't even know how she'd start to process it without Bridge, you know?

Don't think she's processing much at all without Bridget around, if I'm honest.

Harley's about as clueless as ever.

What do you reckon her dad got her for her birthday?

A car.

A white 2023 Mercedes-Benz S 580. Brown interior. Four-liter, eight-cylinder engine. Nice car, honestly . . .

But way to read the fucking room, you twat. Haven't ridden in a car with her for four months where she hasn't dug her nails so hard into my hand that she's made me bleed.

She doesn't know that. She doesn't know she's as scared as she is.

Everyone else does though, at least they do if they're paying a fucking lick of attention, and maybe that's the problem. I don't think any of them are.

Mars had tonight catered. Doesn't cook much these days. Kind of shit because she's a fucking excellent cook, but I guess you wouldn't if you didn't have to, maybe? After years of serving people you'd probably be pretty off cooking for them if you didn't have to.

Bit funny though I think. Because Mars was the mum. Even though she wasn't the mum, she was the mum. The anchor in their home, the thing that made everything make sense for the girls. That's why when she was fucking Harley, Parks lost the plot. I don't like how she doesn't cook for the girls anymore—for Parks anymore, I guess—makes it seem like it was all an act.

Not that you have to cook to be a mum. 2023 and all that fucking jazz, I get it. Motherhood looks a thousand different ways. I don't think for a second that when Parks is a mum that she's suddenly going to be huddled over a stove with a ladle—don't even know if she'd know what a ladle is. I don't know—my mum cooks because she loves it—loves the praise of cooking, probably, if I'm honest. She barely ever orders in. And Mars cooked every day she worked for the Parkses, and it seems like not a day goes by anymore where shit's not being cooked by a private chef or brought in. Can't quite put my finger on why that reads weird to me but it does.

Hen arrives not long after us, then my parents arrive with Allie and Maddie.

They give her a Panthère de Cartier watch. Mini, yellow gold, diamonds. She likes it, I can tell she does. Her face lights up a bit. Not all the way up but a bit of the way.

Al's taken Bridge hard too, about how you would if your best friend died. It makes Magnolia happy to see her, makes her feel closer to her sister. Distracts her from herself—I get it. I was able to avoid the shit that happened that night to me for years by throwing myself into making sure Parks never felt pain. Doesn't get rid of your own shit, just displaces it.

Pain doesn't like that though, doesn't like to be relocated, doesn't like to be ignored. It demands to be felt, and Magnolia's only feeling it in bursts that feel like pain is in the air and she's holding her breath. Every now and then she gasps, breathes it in, feels the weight, crumbles under it. Most of the time though she just ignores it.

Dinner's served and we start eating. Most of us anyway.

Parks and Henry are regaling a story about their baby days at school, when Magnolia made up an elaborate lie about why Henry was absent (a girl) that escalated so beyond belief when she told Henry's housemaster that he had come down with this fucking hectic cold and then went on to accidentally describe the symptoms of the bubonic plague. His dorm had to be quarantined.

A bit into the story, Harley looks at his phone.

"Fuck," he sighs, then apologises to my parents like it's not my every second word. "I've just got to take this."

He kisses Mars' cheek.

Magnolia is well distracted by now. Maddie has seventy-five thousand questions about our wedding—what she should wear, who's coming, what kind of cake, what song are we dancing to, who are her bridesmaids, etc., etc., and Parks answers them all like every answer she gives doesn't crush her in context of it all happening without her sister.

And don't think for a second that it's lost on me, Arrie excusing herself from the table.

My jaw goes tight as she stands and our eyes catch as she does. She swallows, sheepish.

Something in me sinks and under my skin goes hot.

Not again.

I toss my drink back, wait a couple of minutes and then say I'm going to the bathroom.

I wish I was going to the bathroom but I don't. I go straight to Harley's office, reach for the handle—brace myself—swing the door open. It's not even fucking locked.

And there it is. What I knew I was about to see.

Arina Parks, dress hiked up and legs wrapped around the waist of her ex-husband.

Takes a fraction of a second for them to see me and then Harley swears under his breath and Arrie dismounts.

"What the fuck?" I shake my head at them.

"Don't," Harley growls as he zips his pants back up.

"No—" I glare at him, stepping into the office and closing the door behind me. "You fucking don't."

"We didn't plan it!" Arrie insists as she straightens her dress back down.

"Really?" I toss her a look. "Cause it kind of looks like you did."

She tucks her hair behind her ears. "I meant the affair."

I breathe out my nose, glare over at them.

"So this is an affair?"

Harley tosses me a disparaging look. "'Course it's a goddamn affair."

I nod once, face all grimaced.

Harley eyes me. "Can't see how it's any of your business—"

I blink a couple of times, look between the two of them. "Can't see how it's not."

"Because neither one of us is fucking you," he tells me.

"Just purely because of Magnolia, darling. Don't read into it otherwise—" Arrie tells me. "Believe me, if you weren't with my daughter—"

Harley shakes his head firmly. "Nope. No, hate that."

Arrie shrugs fairly merrily.

"You have to stop." I shake my head at both of them. "She can't deal with this right now—"

Harley rolls his eyes. "How's it got anything to do with her?"

I stare over at him, eyes wide. "If you're not joking, man, then you're a shittier dad than I thought—"

Harley scoffs. "What'd you say, big man?"

I square my shoulders. I'm ready to fight. Honestly, I wouldn't mind hitting something. Of all the things I could hit right now, Harley Parks is pretty top-tier.

I move in towards his direction and Arrie tenses up next to him the same way Magnolia does when she's nervous.

And then the door swings open behind me and the only voice in the world I actually care about says, "Oh, there you are."

I turn around to face her. Dissolve from my face as quick as I can all the ways a second ago I planned on fucking her dad up, give her a big smile instead.

"Here I am." I slip my hands around her waist and pull her in towards me—still not old—kiss the top of her head.

She looks confused, eyes flicking from me to her parents. "What are you all doing in here?"

"Oh." I shrug, and look back at her dad. "Just tell her, Harley."

He freezes, the Big Man himself. Doesn't say a fucking thing.

"Can't keep a secret from her to save my life—" Swipe my hand through the air and scoff like I'm the idiot. "Your dad realised that a car was a bit of a shit present—" I catch his eye. "He got you an island too."

Harley shifts on his heel and Arrie might stifle a smile.

Magnolia's eyes go wide. "An island! Really?"

I nod once. "In the Caribbean."

She smiles, curious, looking at me, not her dad. "Bigger than yours?"

I bite back a smile. "Much."

Her dad's jaw goes tight and then Parks spins on her heel around to him.

"Thank you!" She beams at him. "That's a lovely gift."

"Yeah—" he chokes out, nods. "Of course. Yeah."

She moves towards him for a second, like she has the impulse to hug him but stops herself in her tracks—reaches out and pats his arm twice instead.

He nods at her, about as uncomfortable (if not more) than she is.

She bounces out of the room, and I toss her dad a shit-eating grin before I follow after her.

The night bumbles on after that. Parents planning out the wedding. Parksy's annual Lily Vanilli birthday cake—the only cake I've ever seen her eat, really. More wedding questions from my sisters. Me and her dad tossing daggers at each other across the table; he doesn't like being told what to do, I don't like anyone doing anything that might hurt her. How fucking grand would life be if it was the other way around? Me not liking being told what to do, her dad not liking anyone doing anything to hurt her—and yet here we are.

Took her home after that. Left the car they bought her on the street and walked. In silence, for the most part, but I loved every second of it. She held my one hand with both of hers, leant into me and against me the whole time.

I love how it feels to be needed by her.

I haven't found a better high, and I've looked everywhere. Only thing that comes close is being wanted by her, but even then it's not the same.

Want is a luxury, but need is necessary. Can't do without. It's an inherent purpose.

When we get home we have sex in the shower. One of my favourite things about us, and I probably forgot about it for a while—because it would have been fucking shit to remember it the whole time we were apart—but I forgot how good we are together.

How we don't need words, how we have a whole language in our looks.

She didn't say a thing, just walked into the bathroom and turned around to face me. Rushed her, clothes off, shower on.

She clung to me tight tonight, but she does most times these days. Like she's worried she's losing me too.

We went to sleep after that. Wish I could say I woke up early her birthday morning and snuck out of bed to do all the shit; flowers, coffees, balloons—you know? Can't.

She wakes too easy. Always been a light sleeper. These days I'm not even sure she really sleeps at all, and if she does it's on my chest.

Her birthday morning she blinks awake, I smile down at her, touch her face how I usually do and then she just crumbles.

Remember those gasps of air I talked about? Where she gulps in pain like breath? One of those times.

It's the worst feeling in the world, having her whole body tremble in my arms and there not be a thing I can do to fix it.

Just hold her. What the fuck else could I do?

Cry with her a bit.

Tell her it's going to be okay and sometimes I believe it but right now it feels like a lie.

After about twenty minutes, she takes a big breath and wipes her face—tucks the mess she let out for a second all back in again and gives me a smile that's completely, overtly, entirely fucking perfect in every way and yet still, it doesn't make me feel like for even a minute that she's okay.

"Fancy Bridget Dorothy Parks ruining my birthday from beyond the grave," she says as she sits up, eyeing her sister's ashes that are on the windowsill now. She moves them around a lot. Like she thinks Bridge might get bored from being in one place.

I sniff a laugh. "Seems on brand."

"I suppose it does." She gives me a tender smile. She sniffs again and presses her lips together. Swallows. Big smile again. "So, what did you get me?"

I lean in, brush my lips over hers. "Not enough."

Bought her everything I could think of that would maybe make her happy, even though I don't think any of it did.

Another edition of *The Little Prince* book because I think I'm collecting them for her now, couple of bags, shoes, a Harry Winston diamond bracelet I knew she wanted, a holiday we'll go on soon, a vintage Paddington bear from the year she was born . . .

She liked the bear actually, and the book. She's gone sentimental.

But that's it—things for her, a dime a dozen, isn't it? She's seen it all, can buy it all herself.

Only one thing she wants anyway, and it's the only thing I can't give to her.

23:02

Bridge 💩✨

Today BJ and I took Bushka to lunch and Jason Statham was at the restaurant, and she had a crack.

I mean, a genuine, red hot go.

That poor man.

I mean, I didn't try to stop her or anything, but still poor, poor man.

•••

EIGHT
Magnolia

Beej took Tausie and I to Clos Maggiore for lunch. It's one of my favourites, that's why he chose it.

I pretend I don't see his face fall a little when I order just the parsnip soup, which seemed like the lightest thing on the menu, and plus it really is very delicious—I've had it before—except that after I order it, I remember that parsnips can be dangerous.

BJ nods his chin towards my mostly full bowl. "You don't like it?"

I shake my head quickly, "No, I love it—"

His eyes flicker down to my plate that's barely touched.

I shake my head at him like he's silly.

"It's just that parsnips are really high in potassium, which is great except if there's too much of it and then your blood can go hyperkalemic and you get nauseous, fatigued and all crampy."

Taura frowns over at me. "Had a lot of potassium lately then, have you?"

I put my nose in the air. "I had a banana smoothie for breakfast."

No, I didn't.

Taura's face scrunches up. "Why'd you order it then?"

I say nothing and pick up my soup spoon to placate them.

BJ's watching me closer than I want him to.

"Do you want to go somewhere else?" he asks.

I shake my head.

"Order something else then," he says with a hopeful smile.

So I do, the French beans and the mixed leaves in a French dressing, but I don't think that placates him.

"Much better," my sister would say with a roll of her eyes if she was here. Except she isn't here, so.

Afterwards, we go to grab a coffee from % Arabica across the road and BJ holds my hand with both of his and something about it makes me feel nervous.

I think it's because something about him feels nervous. And BJ's never nervous? He's always brave, always cocky, always sure of himself, but this afternoon there's a bend in his brow and my hand's being squeezed half to death, and so I look up at him, my eyes wide with worry, and I wish he'd just laugh how he did before and feel light and sunny and carefree, but he just smiles and it's cloudy and care-filled.

I know you wouldn't think it because of all the insanity of the years of us you've borne witness to, but really, in real life, BJ and I are honestly rather uneventful. Usually, anyway. Or we were five or so years ago.

He would have smiled before, blown all my worries away, but he doesn't—something about his face ushers more in and I wonder, very, very quietly, whether perhaps, maybe, could he be cheating on me—?

The thought has barely found its legs before I curse at it under my mind's breath—of course, he isn't—he wouldn't—

Except that he has—?

And in a quick, unconscious second, I think about how I need to call my sister to talk my mind down from this ledge and I reach for my phone to text her—and then I remember. I'm hit by one of those trains.

I do text her sometimes.

It's pretty one-sided though these days. Though actually, if I'm honest, it was pretty one-sided before as well.

I keep her phone on charge in the guest room so that the iMessage always sends through in blue because I can't bear the thought of messaging her and it sending through in green. There's something bizarrely final to a green text, don't you think?

Twice it's happened since Bridget died that BJ's been out, once with the boys and once on a shoot where his phone died.

I didn't worry before when it didn't say "Delivered" under my blue bubble, it just used to annoy me. But now if it doesn't say "Delivered"—or worse—it goes green, immediately I feel like maybe he's died.

To be fair, neither time it's happened has been death-related; they've been both because despite Apple driving up the prices of their devices, they've simultaneously been lowering the quality of them.

What was I saying—?

I can't talk to my sister, even though I need to. That's my point.

And I can't say it out loud to anyone else because who could I say it to?

If I say it to Henry, he might tell him. If I say it to Taura, I mean historically, chances are, that's who he's cheating on me with. Best friend, I mean, not Taura specifically.

Not that I think that he is, because I don't think that he is—he wouldn't—except again, he has. But even still, she wouldn't—except that, I guess they already have?

Things happen, accidents and whatever. People spend long stretches of time with one another, you get too comfortable. Late nights where they're both looking after me, their common thread, who's a sloppy, little, devastated mess—it could happen, you know? It wouldn't be the wildest thing in the world—

I'm knee-deep wondering when it happened and how many times it's happened when Taura's face appears in front of me with her eyebrows up, waiting impatiently.

"What?" I blink a lot.

She nods her head behind her. We're at the coffee shop now. I didn't realise.

"What do you want?"

"Oh." I frown. "A cortado, please."

BJ tilts his head, frowning more, worried more. "You okay?"

"Hmm?" I smile at him as bright as I can. "I'm wonderful."

That does nothing to convince him.

"Your face looks weird."

I frown. "That's rather rude."

"Alright." He sniffs a smile then brushes his mouth over mine. "Your face looks great. Your expression is weird."

I shake my head quickly. "No expression."

He touches my face and I know him too well to even let myself think for a moment that he believes me, but he says "Okay" anyway and I feel lonely and alone, which are similar things but they aren't the same and it's awful to feel them both at once and it frightens me, so I reach for his hand that's still on my face and hold it against me.

"Do you love me?" I ask him so quiet it's at a whisper.

"What?" His face falls to confusion. "Are you— Do we need to go—?"

I say nothing, just stare up at him with big eyes, waiting for him to answer me even though I know the answer.

"Parks—" he says again.

"Please?" I blink.

He ducks a little so our eyes are level. "Not a day has gone by since I met you where I've not loved you."

I drink in those words like they're water, let them douse the burning fear that lives inside of me that he'll hurt me again.

"Promise?"

He nods back as he gives me a quarter of a confused smile. "Promise."

"Oh my god—" Taura says, elbowing me. "That's Daisy's ex."

"The sexy policeman?" I perk up, looking around.

Taura nods, nodding her nose in the direction behind me.

He's standing there by himself, waiting for his coffee.

Faded light blue distressed straight-leg jeans from Palm Angels; the black embroidered cotton hoodie from AMI Paris and steel grey Converse x Comme Des Garçons Play Chucks.

"How sexy are we talking?" BJ glances over his shoulder, very unsubtly.

"Like, very—" Taura gives Beej a look.

BJ spots Killian Tiller and just his mouth pulls concedingly before he looks back at us, nodding.

"Total fucking smoke show, yeah—wow."

Taura's gone oddly quiet.

"He is a smoke show, isn't he—" I eye her suspiciously. "Do you think he's a smoke show, Taura?"

"What?" She blinks, cheeks going a little pink. "No—yeah. Like, he's handsome. Obviously—but, no, because—"

Oh my god.

"Let's bring him over," I announce.

"No!" Taura says quickly, shaking her head.

"Yes!" I nod, excited.

Tausie shakes her head at me, jaw clenched. "Don't you—"

"Tiller!" I wave at him.

Taura careens away from us back into the line to order something she doesn't need.

He walks towards us and sounds surprised to see me. "Magnolia."

He gives me a hug. He's a good hugger, I'll say that. Better than all those boys would want him to be. You shouldn't be dead sexy and incredibly sweet, it feels illegal.

Tiller pulls back and gives me a warm smile, then looks from me to BJ then back to me.

He shakes his head, nodding his head between Beej and I.

"I didn't realise you were back together."

"A few months now." BJ nods. "I don't know if we've ever properly met. BJ."

He offers Tiller his hand, who shakes it.

I look up at Tiller. "Did you really not know that we're back together?"

Tiller presses his lips together, smiling tightly.

"I really didn't."

My face falters. "Do you not read the society pages?"

Tiller's eyebrows go up and he flicks BJ a look. "I can't say that I do, no—"

"Oh." I frown. "Why not?"

He shrugs. "I don't know anyone in them . . ."

"Oh," I sigh. "I'm sorry."

"That's—" He and BJ catch eyes again, and maybe they're smirking over top of my head. "—fine."

I put my hands on my hips, thinking it through. "So, how do you keep up with your friends, then?"

Tiller glances to BJ and then back to me. "I . . . talk to them."

My eyes bulge. "All of them?"

He shrugs. "Well, I don't have a football team of them, so—"

I grimace for him.

"What are you on about?" BJ pulls a face. "You have four friends." He shrugs to himself. "Five, if you include me—"

"Which I don't when you've got an attitude like the one you're currently sporting." I give him a look and he rolls his eyes. I look back at Tiller. "Well, so, you look great. How long's it been? Probably not since—"

"We both know since when." He nods quickly. "You don't need to say it."

"Oh." I nod. "Is this a sensitive issue still?"

"Uh—" Tiller's face pulls.

"Because of unresolved feelings that you're harbouring for her?"

"Um—" Tiller glances over at BJ, maybe for help.

"Because you're still in love with her?" I press.

"What—?" His head pulls back. "I—no. I didn't—"

"So you aren't still in love with her?" I ask, eyebrows up, curious. "You're over it? Over her? Sayonara, Daisy—"

"Well—" His brows bend in the middle.

BJ gives me a gentle but firm smile. "Magnolia."

"Oh—" I look at my fiancé. "Too much?"

He gives me a tight smile. "You could try not talking for twenty seconds. See what happens."

I don't do that. Instead I give Tiller an apologetic smile.

"See, I was recently diagnosed with ADHD—"

"Oh." Tiller nods, not knowing what to say.

"It impairs my prefrontal cortex—something about a neurotransmitter in the brain and then also lower levels of dopamine—which is so rude—don't you think that's so rude? Dopamine's pretty nice—my doctor said it's probably why I love shopping so much. And sex—"

"She's not—doesn't have a great filter," BJ cuts me off, nodding his head.

Tiller's nodding along, a bit wide-eyed and saying nothing.

"My doctor said if my parents had paid more attention to me and if my nanny wasn't having an affair with my father that probably they might have noticed it, but in their defence—of which I can't say much—it is much harder to diagnose in girls than it is in boys—"

"I mean—" BJ tilts his head. "I feel like I knew you had ADHD."

"How?" I frown at him.

"Uh—" Baxter James Ballentine flashes me a quick smile. "Mostly because I've met you."

I fold my arms over my chest and my eyes pinch at him—so rude, I'm going to tell his mother on him for that later—I turn to Tiller.

"Well, I definitely only have four friends today. Have you met this one—?" I reach for Taura and yank her out of the line. "Do you know Taura?"

"I—" He nods once and maybe, possibly—oh my god!—maybe his eyes fall down her sexy little body. "—I know who you are, yeah. Hey."

"Hi," she says, possibly quieter than I've ever heard her talk.

She's never quiet. Like, ever.

Not even in school before we were friends. She was always so loud—I thought it was annoying back then, some sort of overbearing bravado, but actually, now that I know her, I think she just knew back then that she was the best because she is.

Tiller points at her and gives her a grim smile.

"Nazi painting in the basement."

She rolls her eyes. "We're very proud."

To clarify, they weren't.

"You gave it back," Tiller says, as though that's much of a consolation for all the pillaging her ancestor was a part of.

"We did." She smiles uncomfortably.

"And she made a sizeable donation to the Jewish National

Fund!" I tell him quickly so he doesn't think she's some terrible racist. "Taura loves Jews!"

Tiller lets out a confused laugh. "Okay."

"We all do!" I tell him enthusiastically, and BJ covers his mouth with his hand. "Are you Jewish?" I ask Tiller.

"Yeah." He nods, smiling, maybe a touch baffled. "On Mum's side."

"Well—" I laugh, incredulous, barely able to contain my glee. I lean in towards BJ and whisper, "What a story for the grandkids—!" And then he tells me to "Cool it," so I clear my throat again and try a different route.

I smile over at Taura fondly. "Isn't she just gorgeous?"

"Um—" Tiller's face falters. "Yes."

My eyes go to slits. "Interesting."

BJ growls under his breath, giving me warning eyes. "Magnolia—"

"What?" I shrug innocently because I am, regardless of what that boy I love might say, an innocent.

BJ rolls his eyes as he gestures to the increasingly awkward Tiller.

"He can hardly say no, can he? She's right fucking there—"

"On what planet is he saying no?" I stomp my foot and wave towards her. "Look at her face!"

"I'm leaving." Taura nods then glances at Tiller. "Sorry—she's like—the human personification of verbal diarrhea—"

"Revolting." I glare at her before I look back at Tiller, nodding my head at her. "Great grasp of the English language though, don't you think?"

"I'm going to grasp your throat in a second," Taura says through a tense smile, teeth all clenched and the big vein in her head becoming (regrettably) obvious and visible for all the world (and Tiller) to see.

"She's joking," I tell Tiller. "She's actually very loving."

Taura's eyes pinch and she points a finger in my face. "Stop not taking your medicine."

I tuck my chin and glare at her. "Mind your own business!"

She looks from me to Tiller and back to me as if to communicate some point that I'm happy to let float right on over my head and then she stalks out.

I apologise profusely to Tiller, make a joke about German manners (which BJ would later scold me for), and then I scurry after her.

Taura thunders down King Street, darting across the road.

"Did you feel a spark?" I call after her.

"You're so annoying," she calls back to me without turning around.

I turn to BJ.

"I felt a spark between them— Did you—?"

"Was it the spark of fury?" he asks, and I roll my eyes at him.

"Did you?" I ask again.

"Maybe?" He grimaces, not wanting to be on Taura's bad side. "I don't—"

"There was no spark," Taura says, all annoyed as she walks into Sandro and doesn't hold the door for us. Closes it—bang!—right in my face.

The gall.

"I mean, truthfully, that man is so sexy he could have a spark with a wet fish—" I whisper to BJ under my breath.

He rolls his eyes as he opens the door for me. "Calm down."

I wander over to a rack, flick through it. Act like I'm seeing the pointelle knit coatigan for the first time, like I don't already own it myself.

There's a sleeveless cardigan. Tricot knit—cream and black—contrasting stripes and pockets. *Bridget would have looked perfect in it*, I think to myself as I frown at it.

BJ sees. I can feel his eyes on me. He hugs me from behind.

"Her vibe for sure," he tells me before he kisses my cheek.

Taura flicks through a rack nearby.

"Could you fancy him, Taurs?" BJ asks a bit more gently than I had been.

"Tiller?" She stares at him. "No! He was with Daisy—"

"So?" I blurt, and Beej pokes me quiet in the ribs.

"So it's weird!" She frowns.

BJ shrugs. "You dated two best friends at the same time—"

Taura gives him a look. "Yeah, and I think we can all agree that it got pretty fucking weird."

BJ nods, looking at our friend closely. "You not over him?"

She looks at him like she's losing something.

"Are you saying I need to be?"

His face falls a little for our friend and then she nods once even though none of us say a word.

22:04

Tausie ❤

But would you though?

You're like a fucking dog with a bone

My sister died

!!!!!

Not fair

. . .

I don't know.

Of everyone not to cross, Magnolia . . .

She's in love with Christian!

Isn't she?

????

I don't know.

I heard wherever she is, she's with Romeo.

oh.

Yeah. So—

I don't know.

Have you spoken to them?

Her, I mean.

No one has

But she's definitely in love with Christian.

She was so in love before, that doesn't just stop.

Well then. She can't be greedy . . .

You wouldn't like it if someone dated your ex-boyfriend

Someone is dating my ex-boyfriend

Her name is Daisy Haites.

Are we calling Christian your ex now?

For conversational supremacy, yes

How does BJ feel about this?

Brilliant probably.

He loves for me to win arguments

Vrkfjghkjbn

Fkgj

You added **Beej** 🌞 🐺 to the conversation

Gtgh

Tausie

?

Beej

Don't love it.

Go away

He added himself.

Tausie

Oh good.

Hey beej

Beej

Hey taus

@parks but so were you boyfriend girlfriend though

Tausie 💖 has left the conversation

Wow

hah

NINE
BJ

When we were little, I used to think Parks was just like, the coolest, ballsiest girl because she always tried to get exactly what she wanted no matter what.

The ADHD thing, Mum was the one that spotted it first, really. You look back over her life, who she is, how she is, it's been there all along. Woven into her, part of the reason she's as fucking nuts and brilliant as she is. But it was my mum who spotted it, really. In adulthood, anyway.

After we told them about the baby, we had a conversation about how we got pregnant because though outwardly ignorant to the fact that we were having sex, Mum said she knew Dad had spoken to me about safe sex and through that she also knew that Arrie put Parks on birth control, so what had happened?

Magnolia had happened, really. Forgot to take her pill, and when we could have stopped, didn't want to because why would we? *Future myopia*, that's a term they've coined.

For the record, I don't have ADHD, and I didn't stop, didn't want to—of course I didn't want to.

I can look back now over our life and see it in traces of everything. Good and bad. Great and terrible. Bit of a short straw to call it a disorder, I think. It's a shit hat to make her wear all the time because she's got the best brain in the world, I love how she looks at everything, how she sees it all—I don't even mind the part where she just says whatever the fuck floats into her head at any given moment—the only part of it that I struggle with these day—all days, I s'pose—is the future myopia.

*

"How's she doing?" Claire asks, watching me carefully.

"I'm not sure—" My face pulls. "Weird, I think."

"Weird?" she asks gently.

"Her eating disorder's back," I say suddenly. First time I've said it out loud.

There's this pit in my stomach that feels a bit bottomless.

Being in love is so fucked up . . . How their pain is your pain? Can't believe we're back here again—like, after fucking everything, I can't believe it.

Claire's face pulls into a frown-y smile. "Is it?"

I nod.

"How do you feel?" she asks.

"Shit," I say with a nod. Swallow once. "Scared."

She nods.

"That's fair, considering—" She gives me a tight smile and I don't take the bait. I don't want to talk about that.

She looks down at her notes. "Do you remember where we left off last week?"

I nod. "Billie."

"Right." She nods. "And how you never told anyone."

"We decided not to." I shrug.

"Did you want to?"

I purse my mouth, thinking about it. "Maybe. Sometimes."

"But you didn't."

I shake my head. "It wasn't about me."

Was a bit, I guess, but not in the same way.

My body didn't change, she wasn't in me, wasn't my body bleeding and cramping. The loss deflated me, yeah—kind of flattened her though.

The ED got worse before it got better after that. Another stint at Bloxham.

If she was doing better, maybe I'd have done worse, but we were the only two who knew, and one of us needed to be okay.

She started looking at me differently after Billie—but same, I guess.

We were pretty tied up by then anyway, but once me and Parks are dead, they'll probably look back at our lives and call the time around Billie our 'inoculation period.'

Stopped looking at me like I was her boyfriend that she loved, starting looking at me like I was all she had.

Felt the pressure of that too, but I liked it. Felt like purpose.

I can see now, looking back, how much of a fucking mess it was.

Her and her shitty parents, all her dysfunctions that stemmed from that, how her brain works; then me never feeling like, good enough for my dad. And kind of undeserving of everything I've got . . . Got worse after I got hurt and couldn't play rugby anymore.

I can see on Claire's face she doesn't agree that it's not about me, but she doesn't push it.

I appreciate that. She's never been pushy. Always sort of let me arrive wherever I'm headed myself.

"And you said after Billie died that you began to feel—" She pauses to choose her words. "—Listless."

Her words, not mine. I wouldn't say 'listless,' I'm not fucking Shakespeare.

I flash her a smile, amused. "Sure. Yeah."

Even though I think my actual words were, 'After she died everything got fucked.'

"Why is that?" she asks, warm smile, brows up.

I shrug. "Just did."

She gives me a look. "Come on."

I sigh. "Rugby was always the plan. Only thing I was ever really good at—"

"And you were injured?"

I nod. "Tore my hamstring pretty much clean off the bone in the middle of preseason training."

I'd been scouted by both Ulster and the Harlequins.

Would have rather played for Ulster for Dad, but I thought my mum and Parks would fucking flip it if I left London.

The whole thing was so shit, when the tear happened—it was

just a fuck about. Me and the boys used to do football or rugby on Saturday mornings at Paddington Recreational Ground with some old boys from Varley.

The games drew a bit of a crowd. Partly because we were good, partly just to watch us, I think.

It was towards the end of July. I'd just finished school that May.

I'd had some hamstring injuries before. Couple of stage one tears, one stage two, but I'd been good for about a year, I reckon; all it took was one fucked-up lunge for the ball, and pop.

Jo swears he heard the pop too.

Now listen, I've got a good pain tolerance. I've dislocated shoulders, like, fucking infinity times—mid-game—just popped them right back in and kept playing. I've broken fingers punching people and kept punching them anyway.

I've had a doctor realign a snapped bone with no pain medication (but that one was fucking rough)—but this took me down.

I can't really tell, when I think back to the moment—whether it hurt how it hurt because it literally hurt how I remember it hurting, or if it felt like that because I knew even then that shit was fucked and I was done.

I remember falling to the ground, and I looked over to Mum and Parks on the sidelines—their faces kind of did the same thing—the slow-motion breathe-out where they're watching me to see if I'll get back up again, the hope hanging on their faces for a second or two and then the fear comes.

They both ran to me but Parks got there first because she's faster than everyone. Dove on the ground, and I had this weird moment where like, my whole world changed in a second.

I went from knowing exactly what I was going to do with my life to not knowing a fucking thing. Rugby at school, it was a bit of an identity.

And Mum and Dad, they were proper proud of how good I was.

Didn't really feel like my dad was proud of me much outside of that, you know? Like, the girls are the girls, and my dad's a fucking softie, and Henry was the golden child. Good grades, good enough at rugby but better at football.

But me—I don't know—higher expectations being the eldest boy, maybe? Parks says it's in my head, that he loves me plain as day, and he does.

I haven't ever thought he doesn't love me. Don't know that he's proud of me, though.

"And you couldn't play anymore?" Claire asks.

"Yep," I nod coolly. "That was me done."

"With rugby," she clarifies with a look.

"Yeah." I shrug.

She sits back in her chair. "So when rugby was suddenly off the table, what did that mean for you?"

I give her a shrug.

"Were you scared?" she asks.

"I guess."

She leans forward a bit. "Still?"

That throws me and I think it shows on my face.

I swallow.

"Sometimes."

She nods, sitting back in her chair. "Control is a really interesting thing, BJ. It's important to feel like you have some, and from what you're saying, in your life, up until now—you probably haven't felt all that in control of much."

"Right." I cross my arms over my chest. Can't say I'm loving hearing this.

"Billie; your injury; what happened with Zadie; Magnolia breaking up with you; Magnolia running away; Magnolia dating Christian; Bridget dying—it's all—"

"—Fucked," I interrupt her, nodding my head.

She puts her pen down.

"I suppose it is." She gives me a curt smile. "Now what are you going to do about it?"

TEN

Magnolia

Beej, Hen and I go for dinner at Chiltern Firehouse, which isn't really in line with my organic kick, but I thought I'd throw them a bone. Besides, they have a celeriac dauphinoise there that I quite like.

When I order just that, Henry does a little shift in his seat and he catches eyes with his brother and it makes me feel worried that they've been talking about me and I don't want to get into trouble, so I order the radish and grapefruit salad as well, which I definitely won't eat because I don't think that a radish has any business touching a grapefruit, and I suspect BJ knows as much because his eyes pinch as I order it.

I ignore his gaze and focus on his brother across from me, who's making eyes with a random girl at the bar who's sitting by Daniela, and I must say, this isn't my favourite colour on Henry.

"She's pretty," Beej tells Henry as he tosses his arm around me. "Ask for her number."

I give BJ a look. "Don't encourage him."

Henry rolls his eyes. "I've hardly gone full Beej—"

"Right," BJ grunts. "When's that one heading into retirement?"

"Never," Henry and I say at the same time and then BJ orders another negroni.

I kiss his cheek and tell him I love him more than everything else in the world without telling him out loud, and he traces a heart on my upper thigh with his finger.

Henry gives BJ a look across the table.

"Skipped out on the board meeting again."

Beej rolls his eyes. "It's a courtesy invite."

Hen tosses him a look. "It's not—"

"It is."

"It's not." Henry glances from me to his brother. "You're on the board."

"Yeah, but I'm not fit to be on the board, man—it's nepotism."

"Yeah, so?" Henry shrugs. "It's going to be ours one day. Might as well pay attention to it."

I look over at BJ. "Was your dad cross that you missed it?"

He takes a sip of his drink. "Yeah."

"You should have gone." I poke him in the arm.

He shrugs, helpless. "I just don't care what's happening in a supermarket."

Henry sniffs, annoyed.

"Not *a* supermarket—" I give BJ a look. "The *largest* supermarket chain in Britain."

Beej tucks his chin to his chest. "What the fuck are you on about? You've never stepped foot in a supermarket."

"Correct." I nod, giving him a tight smile. "And I'd love for that to keep being my lot in life, so do be a dear and go to those meetings with the only father either of us have on the horizon."

He says nothing, just scratches the back of his neck and has another drink.

"Oh my god." Henry suddenly says, freezing up.

"What?" I sit up straighter, feeling a bit on edge. I'm always on edge these days though.

"Shit." Henry looks down at the butterflied prawns in front of him.

BJ looks around, frowning. "What?"

"Shit, shit, fuck—" Henry's hands ball into knuckles before his eyes peer up at me wide and maybe nervous. "Romilly's here."

"What?" My neck snaps as I peer around the room.

Romilly Followill. You've heard me talk about her before, surely? Henry's first proper love, do you remember? I don't know if they were ever really properly, officially together—I don't know if she was ever quite his girlfriend, but I don't know whether that ever really mattered to Henry. He was besotted either way. Adored her completely. They were sort of best friends as well, they just couldn't seem to get their timings right. And then when they were seventeen, finally, they had sex. She lost her virginity to him and somehow her crazy American pastor dad found out and moved their whole family back to America—kind of out of the blue and in the middle of the night. It was terrible.

Hen drove her home afterwards, told her he loved her, she went inside, and somehow her dad figured it out. They moved to America the next week.

Henry was devastated. I never really saw him like anyone else again til Taura.

"Go talk to her." Henry nods his head towards her and gives me a little kick under the table.

"What?" My head pulls back. "Me?"

"You." He gives me another small kick. "Go. Now."

"Ow—! No!" I stomp my foot. "You go! Don't be a baby—"

"She was your friend!" He gestures towards me, annoyed.

I gesture back, imitating him. "She was your friend too!"

Henry pulls an annoyed face. "More than my friend."

"Yes—" I give him a look. "Much to my point . . ."

Henry looks at me with slightly wild, definitely desperate eyes.

"After all the fucking grief you two idiots put me through for years—years, Magnolia!—Years!"

"Oh, go on." BJ nudges me with his elbow and I look over at him, eyes wide that he's not taking my side, but he stares at me, unmoved, then gives me a bit of an impatient frown as he nods his head towards our old friend. "Pip pip."

I scoff at his audacity but do what I'm told anyway because—I don't know, actually? It feels father-issues adjacent.

I walk towards the very beautiful girl in front of me, beautiful in the way mixed girls usually are, not to ring my own bell, but whatever, you get it—

Big brown eyes, brown skin, pink lips, caramel hair.

"Erm—" I clear my throat and toss the boys a quick, angry look. "Romilly?"

She looks over at me and gawps for a few seconds.

"Oh my god," she says eventually, blinking a lot. "Magnolia."

"Hi—" I give her an unsure smile because "Oh my god, Magnolia" isn't usually the response I get when I cold-contact someone.

"Hi!" She then suddenly flings both her arms around me and I hate Henry for this. I hate hugs from people I don't know and even from some I do know. But then I feel my body un-tense a little, and I don't understand it.

"How incredible to see you—" She beams at me, stepping back, looking down at the cream cropped embellished bouclé-knit cardigan from Self Portrait buttoned down and meticulously (and strategically) fastened with Hollywood tape to reveal Cult Gaia's Asha bralette chain, paired with the black and gold tweed pleated miniskirt from Balmain and Saint Laurent's Diane buckled glossed-leather knee boots. "My god, you look amazing."

"Thank you!" I smile at her fondly. "So do you. Your hair, it's lighter—I love it—"

"Magnolia—" She sighs my name as she tilts her head. Grief makes people's heads go sideways. "I heard about Bridget, I'm so sorry, I—"

"Thank you, it's fine," I say quickly because it's not and it won't ever be but I can't start crying in front of this girl who I haven't seen in like seven years and I will because there's something about an old friend who's safe and familiar and they have the ability to undo you and I don't want to be undone in the middle of Chiltern Firehouse on a Thursday night, I want to be incredibly, very tightly done up, and so I stare down at her shoes. I blink down at the caramel brown patent-leather sling-backs she's wearing and take a tiny breath and then look back up at her with my best smile.

"Saint Laurent?" I nod at them.

She nods and laughs once. "You haven't changed."

"You're in London." I give her a big smile.

"I am." She nods. "I'm back."

Oh god—my face freezes—Henry's going to lose his marbles.

I look past her to the man behind her, now aware—for all our sakes—that I need to glean as much information as humanly possible.

"Is this your boyfriend?" I gesture to the rather striking gentleman next to her.

"No!" She pulls a face and laughs. "This is my brother—"

He turns around on cue.

"Cassius!" I stare up at him. He was the year below us. "Oh my god, you're huge!"

Six feet five inches, easy—and a real fuckboi energy about him . . . He's devilishly handsome and without a doubt knows a TikTok dance or three.

He laughs, breezy, then speaks with a bit of an accent. Not all the way American, but not as British as me. "And you're like, woah—" He pulls back and overtly looks me up and down. "I always thought you were—you know—but . . . fuck."

Romilly looks up at her brother, face scrunched, and I open my mouth to say I don't know what, because what do you say to that?—when an arm goes around my shoulder from behind and we're all conversationally spared.

"Hey, man—" BJ says a tiny bit loudly, and I wonder whether he's making a point as he extends his other hand out to Cassius.

"Ballentine!" Cassius grins, shaking it. "Been a long time, bro—"

Beej turns to look at Romilly and his face lights up all bright with a sweet happiness that's not on his face for him.

"Rom." He gives her this warm smile, bending down to kiss her cheek.

She looks flustered—instantly—at the sight of a Ballentine, because now I know she's wondering . . .

Jonah and BJ, they weren't all that close to her because they were older than us, but you have to understand, Henry and Christian, Paili and I, we were all very close with her. I mean, at Varley—Romilly would have been like, second-tier social circle friend. Truthfully, she'd probably have been first circle were circumstances different. It was just that her parents never let her go anywhere with us, they called my parents a lot of names (most were true, but it was a strange thing to hear a Christian say when they don't know you can hear them). They were weird in general though. She was born in America, and they were pastors of like—you know, those money churches? The ones with the jets and the gold chains and the fuckery that's a bit confusing to comprehend from the outside looking in.

The dad had an affair and just sort of dipped, fleeing the country with his family, moving to England—where Romilly's mum is originally from. Eventually he became the pastor of a little church out in Kent, but he still had all that money from before, and so she wound up at our school. And Henry—my god, he just completely adored her—

So what happens here next feels like this sort of weighted, holy moment.

From behind me, Henry appears—his sweet chest going up and down with those old nerves.

The metaphorical sky lights up and the sea parts and their eyes lock and Henry just stands there like a dummy, his arms heavy at his sides, like he's scared of her. I think he is. I think he's always been.

He swallows.

"Hey." His eyes go soft like he's looking at an old photo. He kind of is. She looks the same, for the most part. Her hair's lighter now than it was when we were at school.

"Hey," she says softly.

And then neither of them do anything. They just stand there like weirdos for way too many seconds just staring until BJ elbows Henry.

"You're back?" Henry sort of chokes.

Romilly nods, cheeks pink. "Yeah, I'm back."

"For good?" he asks, staring over at her.

She nods, but barely. "Yes."

And then they don't say anything again.

I look over at BJ, equal parts flummoxed and perturbed—I

nod my head towards them as subtly as possible. Ask him with my eyes *'Now what?'* Beej shrugs, a bit confused and grossed out.

"Um." I look between Romilly and Cassius. "Do you want to sit down with us?"

"Actually," Cassius scrunches his nose and rubs the back of his neck. "There's a girl I'm on the tune with over there, so I'll catch ya—"

He walks away and Henry and Romilly, once again, don't move, so I point towards the table and BJ shoves his brother so he starts walking.

"I can't believe it," Romilly says as she sits down to all of us but really she's just looking at Henry.

Hen shakes his head, eyes all sparkly. "How long's it been?"

"Um—" Rom's eyelids flutter. "Sev—eight? Eight . . . years."

Henry's face pulls like the time that's passed has hurt him. Time can be a bit like that, don't you think? It doesn't hurt when you're losing it as much as it does when you see in retrospect how much you lost. I feel that way about Beej and I sometimes. Sometimes, if I'm not careful, all the time we wasted will creep up on me and knock the air out of my heart. Years I wasted without him, days I wasted with my sister, and I know days don't sound like much but they do when you don't have them anymore—and then for the second time in two minutes, Bridget's death creeps up behind me and puts a plastic bag over my head. I'm suffocating. Choking inside myself for a lick of relief, for some kind of breath that actually feels like air as opposed to the fire that is the grief that lives inside of me now.

And I think I could be starting to have a panic attack—I need to go to the bathroom—I'm looking around for a quick escape—and then BJ reaches for my wrist and flips it over.

I look over at him and he gives me a quarter smile, gentle, laced with this specific brand of sadness he keeps on the highest-up shelf just for me, then he fishes an ice cube out of his water glass and holds it against my wrist, drawing circles. It distracts me enough, pulls me out of the moment, grounds me.

My breathing changes quickly, and I look over all grateful

with my eyes in a way my mouth couldn't speak anyway. BJ gives me a subtle wink then slips his hand into mine, and I know—even though I knew it already—that I'm marrying the right person.

"Eight." Henry breathes out in disbelief then swallows heavy.

Then they just stare at each other—as though BJ and I aren't there!—which I know, sounds incredibly unlikely, we're like, impossible to ignore, and honestly, it's actually not something I've hitherto ever experienced. But I have now, and I can't say that I was overly fond of it.

It's like we're invisible. Truly. I mean that. Henry and Romilly are locked on each other the way BJ and I do across rooms, and I suddenly understand in a single moment how completely unbearably excruciating we must be almost all of the time.

"Say something," BJ whispers urgently to me under his breath. "Make it stop, make it stop."

"So." I cough as I pick up the bread basket in front of them and rattle it between them to snap them out of it. Henry gives me angry eyes but BJ starts laugh.

"Um." I give Romilly a big smile, not having thought about what to say next. "America."

"Yeah," she nods, tucking her hair behind her ears as she glances at Henry quickly. "You had a stint there, didn't you?"

"I did." I nod. "Yes."

"I heard you two broke up for a spell—" She looks between Beej and I.

"Well, as I'm sure you know, BJ had an affair with Paili, so—"

"I—wow—didn't, actually. Fuck."

BJ nods once. "Thanks for that, Parksy."

I can see her mind trying to process it. "Paili? Shit. Are you—"

"I mean," I scoff. "She and I aren't—"

"Dead to us," Henry says, nodding.

"But we—" I gestured between BJ and I as I give her a bright smile. "We're fine."

Henry tosses us a glare. "Only took them nine hundred years . . ."

"Worth it though," BJ tells his brother before looking at me with heavy eyes.

"What part of America were you in?" I ask her because I'm acutely aware now of romantic, annoying gazes.

"California." She reaches over and takes a sip of Henry's drink. He's been on a bit of a Gibson kick lately. She drinks it to flirt with him, not because it's a nice drink, because it's yuck and she and I both know it. I see a flicker of a grimace dance over her face and I fight off a smile.

"Laguna, mostly." She takes another sip of the Gibson before she hands it back to Henry and the tips of their fingers brush. "You were in New York, right?"

"Right." I nod.

"You were dating that sexy, blonde one, weren't you? In the movies?" She looks from BJ to me for confirmation.

Henry makes an awkward noise and tosses back the rest of his drink.

I roll my eyes at him. "We weren't dating-dating."

"Definitely dating!" Henry roars at the same time BJ loudly says, "So fucking dating!" and I glare at them both.

"Right—" I say to silence them, and then lock eyes with Romilly. "So what was your least favourite part about America?"

"The tampons," she says without missing a beat.

"Oh my god!" My head rolls back in mental despair. "The tampons!"

"Awful." She shakes her head, sincerely.

BJ pulls a face. "Why?"

"Well." I fold my hands on the table in front of me. "I can't be entirely certain, but the tampons over there feel distinctly as though they were made by a virgin male."

Henry's eyes pinch. "How's that now?"

Romilly tilts her head. "It's almost as though upon contact with a liquid agent, they less so seem to expand as much as they do unfold. Like Japanese room dividers."

Henry looks upset by this. "Why?"

"Why, indeed! Yes." I nod. "One can only presume that they

either want you to leak all over your ribbed knit minidress from Balmain or that the designers of these so-called feminine hygiene products have never seen the shape of a uterus, nor are they either overly concerned with hygiene." I give them all a collective, conceding shrug. "Either way, no matter how you slice it, the American tampon wasn't designed for the Commonwealian menses," I announce, and Henry chokes a little on his water, which makes Romilly laugh.

"Oi—" BJ flicks his brother from across the table. "Between us, I reckon we could probably design like, a pretty decent tampon—"

I give him a polite smile. "Let's not brag about that, shall we?"

Romilly looks over at Beej, eyebrows up and playful.

"Have you peered into many uteri then?"

"No," I shake my head. "Just poked around in several hundred."

BJ rolls his eyes and Henry starts smirking.

"Oh." Romilly looks over at him, confused. "Are you a gynaecologist?"

"No," he tells her with a firm smile at the same time that I shrug and say, "Practically."

"Oh fuck." He rubs his face, tired, before he peers over at me. "Parks, you don't actually think that when we're having sex, that I'm touching your . . . uterus . . ." He stares at me for a few seconds. "Do you?"

I shrug, happy enough. "I feel like you are."

Romilly's face pulls, slightly impressed. "Mazel tov."

"Thank you," I tell her, my nose in the air.

"I'm not—" BJ says, looking from me to Romilly, eyebrows all tall. "I'm definitely not—" He shakes his head. "God, who taught you about sex?"

I gesture towards him emphatically. "You."

"Nope—" He shakes his head. "We just did it a bunch. Never talked about it—"

I lean in towards him and whisper, "No wonder we got pregnant."

He lets out my favourite laugh that feels like a cup of tea on a rainy day, and his face looks the kind of happy I always want it to with a smile that touches his eyes.

He kisses the corner of my mouth.

"God." She stares over at us. "It's like nothing's changed."

"Actually," I take a sip of my drink. "Very much has changed."

"Yeah, well—" She grimaces. "I guess that figures. Do you know what?"

"What?" Henry asks even though I don't think she was really actually talking to him.

She shakes her head. "Never mind."

"No," I flash her a confused smile. "What?"

Her face pulls, and she shrugs her shoulders before she looks over at Beej. "I always thought Paili might have fancied you."

He nods. "Yeah." Then he gives her an uncomfortable smile, and we both stiffen up even though we don't mean to. I try not to care about it. We've moved on, we're totally moved on from it—except sometimes it's still a thing I have bad dreams about, and sometimes I wonder if, when I'm not looking, if he's maybe flirting with other people, and then I think—no, he'd never, and then I think, except that he did for years.

And if Bridget were alive she'd say to me, "And so did you, you manky twat." And then I'd be upset that she called me manky, but not so much a twat because I can be a bit of one sometimes, I suppose.

Am I one for worrying that he might cheat on me again? Maybe. Who's to say?

"She said something once," Romilly says, mind somewhere else for a moment before she looks back at me. "That night—the party at your house in Dartmouth—"

BJ reaches over, takes my hand and squeezes it, not saying anything.

I swallow. "What did she say?"

"You kicked us out of the room, remember? Me and her"—she says to BJ. He nods—"Well, on the way down the stairs she said something like, 'What do you think it is about her?' And I was like, 'What?' And she said, 'What do you think it is about her that he loves?' And I sort of shrugged it off. I don't even remember what I said—something like 'Whatever, they're perfect together.' And she said, 'Do you think?' And it was weird—I thought it was weird—and I wondered if—you know"—she looks at BJ uncomfortably—"I mean, you obviously know."

He takes a big breath then breathes it out, and his eyes look a bit dimmer for a moment, which is possibly my fault and any kind of dimming of him is a crime against humanity, and I will pay for it later.

"Anyway, you'd be glad you left, Rom." Henry nods his head over to us. "They were a fucking disaster—"

"Easy there, champ—" Beej scoffs. "Wanna catch her up on your love life lately then?"

Henry tosses him a dirty look. "No, not really."

"Ooh," she coos, leaning in. "Catch me up."

"Yeah, Hen." I give him a playful glare. "Catch her up."

Henry runs his tongue over his bottom lip. "Nothing really, just like—it's not a big deal—"

Beej pulls a face. "That why you've been a fucking deadweight in our guest room these last three months?"

"No," Hen sniffs, annoyed. "I just like the bed."

BJ gives him a steep look. "Bro, I will fucking give you that bed if you leave—"

"No, we won't," I interrupt quickly. "It was custom designed for the room—"

"Tell me about your love life," Romilly says, re-harnessing the conversation.

Henry sighs.

"Do you remember Taura Sax?"

"Yeah." She nods, eyes going a bit round. "Really striking, funny. Daddy issues . . ."

"Yeah, but—" I shrug. "Who doesn't have those?"

"I just kind of fell in love with her." Henry shrugs.

Romilly stares over at him for a few seconds.

"Just kind of."

"Mm-hm." Henry nods lowly.

"I mean—I get it," she says, and I can see it on her face that it's an uncomfortable thing for her to hear, and I think it's amazing how time and space mean naught in matters of the heart. "What's so bad about that?"

"He fell in love with her the same time that Jonah did," BJ announces unceremoniously.

"Oh, yeah—" She nods. "That's much worse."

"Yeah." Henry sniffs a laugh.

Romilly grimaces. "That's so awful."

Hen shrugs. "It's fine?"

"Is it?" she asks, eyebrows up.

"I mean—" He lifts his shoulders again, tilting his head. "We're not fine, we're—done."

"I'm sorry." She gives him a tender smile, but Henry shakes his head.

"No—don't be." He stares over at her. "I'm happy for it now."

BJ elbows me, eyes wide, and I stare over at the two of them, a little in disbelief.

And I am so excited for my best friend. So excited that I can see in his eyes that he's hopeful, that he sees an old promise he forgot about maybe being kept. To have been allowed to be here to see this, it's as though the universe peeled back a secret curtain to watch this unfold, and I want you to hear me that I am genuinely, truly delighted.

And then I think of Taura.

ELEVEN
BJ

Around the one-week mark after Bridge passed, we planned to meet their parents at The Savoy. Really it was to plan what to do with her body, which is fucked. Taura asked her why she wanted to decide that in public and Magnolia said it was because it was dignified, but I know it was really because she's got a better handle on herself when eyes are on her and she didn't want to be crushed by the weight of the decision.

Only thing is, her parents didn't show.

I told Parks to forget it, that we didn't need them—she was pretty riled up about it. Which, fair play.

She speed-walked all the way from Covent Garden to Holland Park, which honestly like, her regular walking pace is a bit like speed-walking, so when she's actually angry-speed-walking, you don't stand a fucking chance.

It's a decent walk too. Thought she might have lost steam somewhere in the sixty-eight minutes it took us to get there. Didn't. Probably would have gotten there sooner if she hadn't worn such impractical shoes.

"Did you not know you were going for a jog today?" Taura called after her wryly, just trying to keep pace.

Mars was at the girls' house, packing up, sorting things out—Magnolia didn't step back into their Grosvenor Square flat once Bridge died. Hasn't been back still and it's been four months.

Only reason Harley missed The Savoy that morning would have been because he can't organise shit himself, and Mars wasn't there to organise him.

Magnolia clomped up my favourite front steps in the world and threw open the door for us before she slammed it behind her loudly.

And then—nothing.

Her face faltered like there was a glitch in her brain.

She moved back over to the door and reopened it, then slammed it again.

I tried not to smile because—all things considered—none of it was funny.

Only that it was just like, fucking vintage Parks. And she's always funny.

"Hello?" Magnolia yelled, loud as she possibly could, stomping her foot at the same time.

"Magnolia, darling!" Arrie called from the sitting room.

Couldn't figure for the life of me at the time why she was there, but honestly didn't think too much of it in the moment.

"Oh god," Taura said under her breath.

Parks marched over to her, arms all crossed—kind of novel whenever she's pissed off at someone who isn't me—stood in the doorway, eyebrow arched.

"What are you doing here?" Parks asked her mother before she eyed the stranger sitting across from her. A woman with a Dictaphone. She looked at Parks and gave her a smile that struck me as circumstantially strange, so I threw an arm around my girl and pulled her back into me.

"Arrie," I looked over at her, brows low. "Who's this?"

She stared over at me kind of blankly, not answering. She might have been high, now that I'm thinking of it.

The woman stood and extended her hand to me and I—cautiously—took it with the one that wasn't around Parks.

"Sally Belasco. *Mind, Body, Soul, Woman.*"

A reporter? Parks tensed up and I kissed the back of her head so she remembered I was there still.

Taura folded her arms. "And what are you doing here, Sally Belasco?"

"We're doing a piece on grief," her mother announced with a vacant smile.

"Sure." Parks stared at her mum. "Okay. An expert in that now, are you?"

"It's just very topical in our lives now, darling. Incredibly relevant, wouldn't you say, sweetheart—"

"Right." Parks nodded once. "You and Harley were meant to meet me an hour ago at The Savoy."

Arrie blinked over at her, confused. "Was I?"

"To discuss the body," Parks said, eyebrows up.

"Oh—" Arrie swallowed and swatted her hand. "No. No, you decide that."

"What?" Magnolia said, but really, it came out sort of like a whisper.

I could feel her breathing getting faster, so I held her tighter.

"You decide, darling." She shook her head, smiling in this sort of distracted, absent way. "Completely up to you—"

Kind of sing-songed that last part, like she asked Parks to pick what's for dinner.

"Sally," Taura extended her hand to the reporter who took it and was then pulled to her feet by Taura. "You know what, this isn't—believe it or not—actually all that great a time for an interview."

Arrie stood, shaking her head. "Don't be so silly, Taura sweetheart, it's fine—it's a fine time."

Magnolia said nothing, just shook her head a little.

"Darling," Arrie sighed. "As a family, now more than ever, we need to present a unified front."

Parks stared at her. "A what?"

"A unified front, darling."

"We're not unified, Mum." Magnolia shook her head more. "I don't know that we've ever been—"

"Magnolia, sweetheart—" Arrie's cheeks went flushed—Parks' go the same when she's embarrassed—Arrie glanced at the reporter before she looked back at Magnolia, straightening her skirt, trying to regain her composure. "Don't be so silly."

Parksy gestured between them.

"You're divorced, Harley's remarried, you're dating some

fucking Bratwurst from fucking Germany, you don't live with Bushka, I don't live here, and Bridget's dead." Topped all that with her best brat smile. "We're literally as un-unified as a family unit can possibly be."

Sally's eyes went wide with the scoop of a fucking lifetime that she was getting, but then Taura snatched the Dictaphone out of her hands and cleared it, and fuck, I love her. You ever get grateful for other people who love your person proper good? I get a surge of that.

"Hey!" The woman growled. "That's my work!"

Taura straightened up and looked her square in the eye. "Get out. Find some class."

Arrie didn't say anything else, just watched Sally scoop up her belongings and leave with her tail between her legs.

"That was a little bit rude, sweetheart." Her mother gave Taura an awkward smile once Sally was gone.

Parks tilted her head back and forth. "Rude or fucked?"

I tightened my grip on her a little, tried to remind her I'm with her without having to say it out loud.

"Nevertheless," Arrie clapped twice. "Follow me,"

Then she led us to the dining room and sort of like, silently 'ta-da'ed us on entry.

Bushka was sitting at the table, eyes red, head in her hands—that was my heart done for the day—she gave me a weary smile. I gave Parks a peck on the cheek and jogged over to her grandma, wrapping my arms around her.

"How are you doing?"

She looked up at me with glassy eyes and tried to smile. "No good."

"Yeah?" I frowned. "Anything I can do?"

She nodded her head towards Parks, lowered that croaky Russian voice. "Look after."

I gave her my most reassuring smile. "I am."

She grabbed me by the arm and pulled me down to whisper something.

"Will be bent til she crack." She pointed not all that subtly at Magnolia.

I nodded, forced myself to smile like that wasn't the fucking scariest sentence anyone could ever say to me, ever.

And then I looked down at the dining room table, tuning back in to what was happening around us. It was covered in like a billion handkerchiefs.

"Party favours," Arrie told me, hands on her hips as she looked down intently.

"What?" Magnolia blinked.

"Party favours," Arrie gave her a brilliant, kind of manic smile.

I scratched the back of my neck, cleared my throat before I asked as gentle as I could, "For which party, Arrie?"

She stared over at me, her eyes this familiar sort of numb. I knew it. Done it myself.

No judgment. Pretty fucking hard to watch though.

"The funeral, darling, of course." She laughed like it was a dumb thing to wonder. "We'll leave handkerchiefs with Bridget's initials embroidered on the chairs of the memorial service. It will be spectacular."

Magnolia shook her head.

"No."

"You don't like the materials?" her mother asked, glancing up. "These are only prototypes, of course. This one"—she threw Parks a pale cream square with the monogram of "BDP" embroidered in gold in the corner—"that's vicuña wool."

"Is that—?" Taura started, but Arrie cut her off.

"Gold thread? Of course," she said airily.

Taura tossed me a "What the fuck?" look, and I frowned.

"No," Parks said, and I could hear it in her voice, how close she was to cracking.

"You're right. Wool's silly for a handkerchief." Arrie drummed her fingers on her waist, shaking her head at herself. "I don't know if linen's soft enough though. What do you think?" She looked up at me, deeply concerned.

"You're insane," Magnolia told her, eyes wide.

Arrie stared over at Parks, blinking. A few seconds hung there—tense and thick, like all the breath was gone from the room—and then Arrie suddenly said, "A linen-silk blend, perhaps?"

"No!" Parks growled, stomping her foot, and I slipped my hand into hers, trying to keep her steady.

"Darling," Arrie smiled at her with a weird, sort of glued-on patience. "That's fine, don't worry about helping me choose the fabric, I'll work it out myself." Then looked past her to me. "What about plain silk?"

"Mum!" she yelled.

Arrie shook her head. "Linen silk, you're right. Embroidering on plain silk is like trying to stitch water."

"What the fuck is the matter with you!" Magnolia cried, and all noise gets sucked out. Taura's buttoned up. I didn't say anything, not yet—just watching to see how it might pace out.

Arrie stared over at her eldest daughter, eyes a bit blank. Stared at her, but also past her.

Then Arrie snapped her fingers.

"I could print on it!" she told no one in particular. "You can print on silk. A monogram-style silk handkerchief with her initials in the pattern in gold."

"Bridget hates gold," Parks told her, voice started to crack a little. I shifted uncomfortably next to her.

"What?" Arrie frowned. "Since when?"

Magnolia swallowed, steeled herself. "Since always."

"Are you sure?" She put her hands on her hips.

"Yes."

"Oh well," Arrie sighed. "She'd have appreciated the effort—"

"You've lost the plot," Magnolia stared over at her, looking at her mother like she was a stranger. "She's dead. And you're prattling on about a handkerchief and an interview so you can show England that we're fine—we're not fine. You're not fine—your daughter is dead and you're giving TED Talks on fucking grief and you don't even know that she doesn't like gold—what kind of mother are you?"

"Parks—" I said quietly to her, the same time her mother shook her head and barely whispered, "Stop."

"You gave birth to her." Magnolia gestured to Arrie. "She lived inside your body. And now she's dead. And all you can talk about is handkerchiefs? What's wrong with you?"

A single tear slipped from her mother's eye, then she flicked her eyes up as she pressed it into her face before she quickly wiped it away.

She took this big, deep, sobering breath then blinked twice.

"Maybe the handkerchiefs should be embellished." She nodded to herself. "I can give Swarovski a call." Then she gathered some papers in front of her into a half-baked pile, scooped them up and left the room.

Parks turned around to face me and Taura—her eyes heavy and all rimmed with tears, so I took her wrist and pulled her in towards me.

"Try not to fight with her, Parksy," I said to her gently.

"She's certifiably insane!" She sniffed, face buried in my chest.

"Yeah," I pulled back and looked down at her, tilting my head. "Always has been though."

Parks' bottom lip started to wobble. "She's ruining Bridge."

"No one could ruin Bridge," Taura said, rushing towards her. "She's unruinable!"

I pushed some hair behind Parks' ears. "She's just—I think your mum's grieving the only way she knows how . . ." Gave her a little shrug. "Like, being as fine as your mum's being—that's a kind of grief, Parks—no one gives a fuck about handkerchiefs the way your mum is fucking about with those handkerchiefs." I gave Parks a look, poked her in the ribs, tried to make her smile because otherwise it's too fucked up and sad. "Not even at the funeral of the guy who invented the handkerchief did anyone give this many fucks about handkerchiefs—" Moved some hair behind her ear. "She's grieving, Parksy. And it might look different to yours. It might sound different. It mightn't even sound like anything at all to you, but it's there—I can see it in her."

"What's this about you not liking the handkerchiefs?" her dad said from the doorway Arrie had just walked through.

Parks stared over at him. "Of course I don't like the fucking handkerchiefs."

Harley folded his arms over his chest. "Do you think you're making this a bit about yourself?"

Taura's face pulled, confused. My eyebrows went up.

Magnolia eyed him carefully. "You actually want there to be handkerchiefs?"

He shrugged, baffled. "Why do you hate handkerchiefs so much?"

"It's not about the handkerchiefs!" Magnolia yelled, sounded a bit frantic.

"Then what the fuck's it about?" Harley said a little louder than I wanted him to.

Parks pointed to her mum, who'd just reemerged, standing behind her dad.

"She's always been insane, I expect this shit from her, but you—" Parks took this breath that sounded like she was cracking. "Harley, you're like—"

His face turned to a scowl as he cut her off. "Are you saying she doesn't—that we don't know our own daughter?"

Magnolia breathed in through her nose, sharp and quick, and I could tell where this was going—

"Yes," she told them both, unflinching. "If you're saying you think she'd want this, then yes."

Harley glowered over at her, pressed his tongue into the side of his cheek, stared over at Parks all dark and I could have killed him for it, maybe—

Harley's a hard one to pick. Would never hurt her—not on purpose—watched him try to work through his guilt about what happened before for the last decade, and it messed him up—that thing that happened when Parks was fucking about with Tom. The lamp, remember? He was fucked up about that for a while,

Bridge told me—but there's an edge to him that you don't play with. He's got a precision strike with his words, poison in the tongue—got some fire in those fists, I'm betting too.

Only person I've ever seen go toe-to-toe with him is the girl who lives in my arms, and I remember not liking how he was looking at her in the moment.

"I think you're a bit worked up, darling," he said to her. Except that "darling" sounded like a slur the way he said it. "Why don't you go for a walk, cool off a bit, come back later—"

Magnolia's eyes pinched. "Why don't you fuck off?"

Her dad's head pulled back. "Excuse me?"

Oh, fuck—I breathed out my nose, cracked my back—remember thinking, *I'm going to have to fight her dad, aren't I?*

"You're going to talk to me like that?" He pointed over at her, a bit menacing. "You're in my house."

"No, I'm not—" She started backing away. "I'm going for a walk, remember?"

Harley rolled his eyes at the same time she turned and walked away.

Me and Tausie jogged after her and she burst into tears on the front porch.

"Hey—" I wrapped my arms around her, put my head on top of hers. "You're good, it's okay—"

She had one of her burst-dam cries where all her grief poured out of her in this one, precise moment where she cyclops laser fires all her emotion out at once—then she pulled back, stopping suddenly.

"Oh—" She shook her head. "I left my bag inside—"

I nodded. "I'll grab it. You wait—"

Kissed the top of her head then darted inside and back into the dining room where I stopped in my fucking tracks.

Standing there was Harley holding Arrie's face with his hands. She was teary, looking down. And it was this weird tenderness between them that I don't think I'd ever seen before. I don't think in—what? Twenty-two years?—I'd ever seen them act like that towards one another.

It was strangely intimate. Would've been sweet if Harley wasn't newly remarried with a dead kid in a freezer somewhere and a live one he was ignoring just out on the front step.

I cleared my throat and they jerked apart.

They both stared over at me, different vibes though.

Harley was pissed. Arrie was embarrassed.

"What?" Harley barked.

I pointed to Parks' bag, unfazed.

Harley waved his hand dismissively, like I was waiting for his permission—

Walked over, grabbed the bag. I like this bag. Gucci; brown leather bag with a wavy flap—wearing a lot of brown lately, actually—suits him. Bought this one for her a few weeks back.

Then I paused, eyeing her parents.

"No." I pointed between them. "Whatever the fuck this is . . . no."

Harley's proud face resurfaced. "Do you think—"

"Nope." I cut him off and pointed to him directly. "Fucking shut it and tighten up."

TWELVE

BJ

Mum's birthday tonight. Fifty-two. Party's at Claridge's. We drove. Took a minute to convince Parks of that. Held my hand the whole time, which sounds nice but is sort of pretty sad when you think of it.

We walk into the Ballroom and everyone stares.

Everyone's always stared—the eyes aren't the problem, we're used to them by now—it's what they're saying.

The hushed whispers, the shallow worries about my fiancée who's maybe now thin enough for people to be asking questions—

And don't get me wrong—she's her—perfect—I love her and I'll take her as she is. Best girl in every room, but she used to squeeze my hand with this giddy excitement when we'd walk into places and everyone would watch us. Tonight she squeezed my hand the same way she does now when we're in a car. Like the whole world's a threat.

Magnolia spots Allie and beelines for her. They've always been close but since Bridget, they use each other like a bridge to be close to her still.

She grabs my sister's hand and pulls her down onto a chair next to her, then doesn't let go of that hand.

Parks is laughing in this genuine way at a story Al is telling her about Bridget. They had this trip planned before everything happened—backpacking around southeast Asia—Bridge booked the flights. Booked them in economy.

"On purpose?" Magnolia asks my sister loudly as a server

comes by. He offers them some food—Allie takes one—onion tart. Good. Tiny.

Parks says no. Tell myself it doesn't mean what I think it means. Still hurts me the same. Grab a negroni.

I look around for Hen but I can't find him. Do spot the rest of the Parkses though.

I walk over and give Bushka a hug.

She smiles up at me, patting my chest. "Sexy boy."

"Ahh." I smile down at my suit that her granddaughter picked out. "Like it?"

She nods. "I like better off."

I laugh, waving my drink at her. "Might need a couple more of these."

"Bartender!" she calls, and I laugh more.

Marsaili catches my eye.

"How's she doing?"

I shrug. "You know . . ."

And credit where it's due, she probably does know. If anyone else was going to know if she was actually—you know—it'd probably be Mars . . . She was there for it all the first time.

Mars sighs as she watches her. "Is she down a size?"

My mouth goes dry. She could be down two, but I shake my head because I don't want it to be true. "I don't know."

"Has she done extra shopping lately?" she asks, looking for the signs we used to see, but I give her a look.

"She always does extra shopping."

She sniffs a laugh but it's sad, all laced with worry. I know it well, do it myself a lot these days.

She touches my arm in this way she'd never have done a year ago—kind of nice—then she goes off to help Bushka get some food.

Arrie walks over to me gingerly, gives me a nervous smile and a hug.

"BJ—" Her face is strained. "Always a pleasure. So handsome."

Harley appears behind her, extending his hand to me. "BJ."

I stare him down for a second, then shake it. "Harley."

"Harley! Arrie!" my mother coos, fluttering over and hugging them both before she turns to me. "Darling, darling! Oh, you look so handsome! Look at this suit—! Did Magnolia dress you? Where is she—?" She looks around for her and I don't say anything, she's not actually asking me, she's just talking to talk.

She spots Parks with Al, then she looks back at me, eyes all tender. Teary, even.

"Isn't she just beautiful . . ." my mum says, staring at my fiancée, who's now surrounded by various members of London's social set, some nosy, some intrigued, some just want to be near her.

And I will say this—Magnolia is on today. It's her coping mechanism. She can't be vulnerable around these people, there are too many, too many ways for someone to see something and misinterpret it, accidentally or on purpose.

She looks insane—big, candy-pink ballgown from Oscar de la Renta, these heels that are pink or purple depending on the light she's in, the most ridiculous crystal bunny bag and a headband with crystal flowers—so beautiful it's hard to look at her in the eye, but she's done it on purpose.

It was a hard lesson to learn, and it's one she learnt a while ago: beauty is a tool and a currency. She's not exchanging it for anything tonight, but she's using it to destabilise everyone else around her, make sure she's in control of the situation. This fineness she's plastered all over her face—the fineness that the few of us who actually know her can see right through—everyone else is dazzled by it, by her bravery, by her will to carrying on—she's sitting there, shoulders square, ankles crossed, answering my fucking pill of a great-aunt's nosy-arse questions about our wedding and the seating arrangements and her dress and whatever the fuck else Aunt Sandra wants to know, and Parks is laughing and smiling and nodding and making everyone around her feel special. But I can see it in the gaps between her sentences, in every breath she takes, it hangs there—this fucking hideous grief that she can't outrun, that follows her everywhere she goes.

I hear Parks talking to her sometimes. To Bridge. I know it's her—only person she'd ever be that fucking rude to, besides me.

Talking to her dead sister when she thinks no one can hear her?

Fuck.

"And coping so well," Arrie says, head tilted, proud like she has a part in that wellness.

I stare over at her, surprised, actually. "You think?"

Harley nods. "We're very proud."

I clock him, eyebrows up. "Are you?"

My mum gives me aggressive eyebrows, tells me to be quiet without saying a thing, the way mothers just can. I can tell she wants me to say sorry, but I don't. Don't want to, they don't deserve it. So I just shake my head like I'm tired of their shit because I am, and I walk away.

Find the Hemmes boys over in a corner and spot Hen stuck with my mum's dullest friend from university—give her an apologetic smile, tell her I need to borrow him for just one second.

He gives me a grateful look as he sidles up next to Jo.

Christian gives me a half-baked smile.

Not taking Daisy's absence too well, but not in the ways you might think. He hasn't fucked about, he's sort of just like, stuck on her—lost to her, or something—doesn't even know where she is, Jo told me.

"Oi," Jo nods his chin at me.

Henry's eyes pinch. "You good?"

"Yep—" I nod quick, not wanting to get into it.

"Oi, man—" Jo thumps Henry in the chest. "Where've you been? I feel like I haven't seen you in ages?" A couple of weeks ago, that question would have felt dangerously loaded, but now it's just a question.

I peek over at my brother. "You didn't tell them?"

Christian frowns, looking interested. "Tell us what?"

Hen gives me a glare and I give him a big smile just to piss him off.

He rolls his eyes. "Romilly's back."

Jonah stares over at him. "Fuck off."

"You're joking?" Christian's eyebrows shoot up.

I nod along, happy for him. "Wild, right?"

Henry rolls his eyes, shakes his head. "It's not a big deal . . ."

"Really?" I pull a face. "First time you've come up for air in like a week and a half . . ."

Hen gives me another glare and I give him another smile.

Christian nods his head at Henry. "She still fit?"

Henry sniffs. "Yeah."

"Good for you, man," I hear Jo say as I watch Parks politely decline the fourth waiter I've seen offer her food.

Makes my stomach drop. They're crudités. So small, it's not even a mouthful. It's like eating a fucking gumdrop.

Then Jo elbows me and lowers his voice. "You okay?"

"What? Yeah." I shake my head quickly. "Fine."

Doesn't buy it. "Yeah?"

I nod. "Mm-hm."

Jonah tilts his head a little. "Your face is, like—you look a bit fucked off . . ."

My mouth pulls. "I'm not fucked off."

He follows my line of sight over to her—sipping on a martini, laughing at something a marchioness is saying to her.

"But you're worried about her."

I nod. "Yeah."

Jo pats me on the back, trying to make it better.

"She's always gone a bit like this when she's stressed." He tells me like I don't know, like it makes it easier to see the person you love wilting away.

"Yeah" is all I say, because he doesn't get it. He can't. He's never loved anything how I love her.

Just power, maybe.

Parks looks over at me from the other side of the room and our eyes catch like they have since the day they first found each other.

I give her a wink and she gives me a tiny smile. I nod my head towards the exit.

'Want to go?' I mouth.

She nods.

Takes about fifteen minutes with all the goodbyes, but we make it out eventually.

It's just more than a thirty-five-minute walk through the park from Claridge's back to our place, and sure—the walks are a touch dysfunctional, but I kind of like them. Like how mundane they are. We used to take those long drives together, now we take walks. Long ones, short ones, any ones that mean she doesn't have to get into a car.

And I don't plan on it—don't start the walk thinking I'm going to say anything—but then I take my jacket off to put around her shoulders and she doesn't look like she's swimming in it but drowning. She's worn this jacket before. Bunch of times . . . Today it's hanging off her like she's a bag of bones.

I sigh. "How long are we going to do this for?"

She looks up at me, maybe genuinely confused.

"What are you talking about?"

I rub my mouth. "Did you eat today?"

For a quarter of a second she stops walking—barely—it's more like a jerk than anything, I s'pose—then she keeps walking.

"Of course I ate today."

"When?" I look over at her. "Didn't see you eat at the party—"

She glares up at me. "You're watching me?"

"Always." I nod emphatically. "Tell me what you ate."

She laughs all light and breezy, but it's controlled.

"I don't remember," she says like it's nothing, and then shakes that head of hers and gives me the same smile she's used all night to trick everyone else, but it doesn't work on me.

Jut my jaw. "Bullshit."

"Not bullshit!" She stomps her foot and then recomposes herself, gives me a restrained smile. "I have very poor short-term memory retention—"

I roll my eyes. "No, I know—"

"Maybe I had a burger!" She shrugs dramatically, but I give her a look. "You don't know!"

"I do know," I tell her. "Haven't seen you soberly eat a burger in about nine years."

She gives me a dumb look. "Who says I'm sober?"

Shake my head, proper annoyed now. "This isn't fucking funny."

"Beej!" She lets out a single laugh but it doesn't sound like hers. "I'm fine!"

I give her a look. She's full of shit. Even she doesn't think she's fine.

She stops walking, breathes out her nose, rolls her eyes.

"Relatively speaking, I'm fine." Crosses her arms over her chest. "Like, I'm—of course, I'm sad and I'm—" She stops short. Shakes her head. Breathes out her nose again. "All things considered, I'm good. Everyone says I'm coping really well—" she tells me, that nose in the air.

I give her a look. "Everyone—"

"Yes." She doubles down.

Give her an eyebrow. "Who's everyone?"

"I don't know—" She rolls her eyes. "Everyone."

I can feel myself getting worked up, and I should know better—we're not good at fighting these days—it's always zero to a hundred, and I know I should leave it but I love her and she's hurting her and I'm angry because we've already fucking done this one.

"Cool—" I nod. "Just throw me a couple of names because we have like, four friends and not one of them thinks you're okay."

I stare her down, brows low, jaw set. She says nothing, just glares up at me.

I nod my head back towards Claridge's.

"You mean the people you trick at parties?" I shake my head at her. "Doesn't count—you're a fucking snake charmer."

"Stop." She sighs, walking ahead.

I shake my head at her. "You're not fine."

"Yes, I am."

"Yeah?" I call after.

"Yes." She's still walking.

"Okay." I nod and tell her with a distance between us, "Don't take my pulse tonight, then."

She stops in her tracks, turns around. "What?" she says quietly.

"Don't take my pulse." I nod, coolly. "Don't take my temperature, don't put that fucking little clip on my finger—if you're fine, act fine—"

She lets out this little puff of air and turns on her heel, hailing a taxi.

I roll my eyes.

"Where are you going?"

"I'm going to go stay at a hotel," she tells me without missing a beat.

Pretend it doesn't sting me, doesn't scare the living fuck out of me that maybe I'm the prick and she's leaving me again.

Can't say that though so I just nod.

"Yep." Give her a tight smile. "Sounds about right."

"Fuck you," she spits as she climbs in.

I flip her off from the street and then she drives away.

22:47

Beej 🌞 🐺

Are you ok

Yes

Safe?

Yes

I shouldn't have cracked it how I did.

I'm sorry

Me too 🖤 🖤 🖤

You can take my pulse again

I don't know what you're even talking about.

Okay. X

You can't be bothered to come down to the Mandarin and spend the night with me, can you?

I'm just already in bed.

I'll be up in a minute

?? What

You're very predictable.

And I'm in the lobby.

THIRTEEN
Magnolia

He did come up and we made good use of that hotel room, in case you were wondering.

In the lobby, texting me? So cute.

I can't say that I love that he knew about the pulse at night-time though, that made me feel silly.

I refused to take it that night and I slept incredibly badly because of it. And by "incredibly badly" I do mean barely at all.

I was up bright and early in the morning—early enough that I could have myself run home to get us some clothes, but I had Daniela ferry them over to us instead because BJ said to let the assistant assist.

I had to FaceTime her to walk her through what to pick out.

She's not completely stylistically inept, but I shouldn't be running to her for fashion advice anytime soon.

The real star of the show is the MacAndreas Tartan Faux Fur Trim Skirt from Vivienne Westwood's A/W 1993 collection, which I had her pair with the red picot-trim satin bustier top from Dolce & Gabbana, the Lispa black suede knee boots from Isabel Marant, the Thea double-breasted wool-blend coat from Rag & Bone, and lastly Chloé's red Marcie mini embellished leather-trimmed suede bucket bag.

Beej walks out of the shower, just a white towel round his waist, perfect hair flopped forward, all wet.

I peek over at him and the back of my neck feels hot.

It's unfair how good he looks in natural lighting.

He walks over to me, slips his arms around my waist and brushes his lips over mine.

I beam up at him.

"How nice is us having a fight and you not like, fucking a random girl at the bar."

"Right?" He nods. "And you not running awa—oh, wait—" He gives me a look and I glare up at him.

He laughs, smiling down at me.

"It's pretty grown-up shit, all this, Parks." He does a fake-sigh, as though it's a bad thing. "We're in deep."

"We're also going to be late—" I poke him in his bare ribs and he laughs, darting away.

We make our way downstairs and wander around the hotel like we haven't been here a thousand times before. We'd umm-ed and ahh-ed about whether we should have the wedding here—in so many ways, having it out of London might be easier—? Less press, less fuss, but then I don't think either of our families is interested in that. Mine certainly doesn't want less press and his definitely doesn't want less fuss.

Lily and (apparently) my mother have dreamed of this wedding since we were tiny.

"Before you were even together!" Lily told me a couple of months ago. "I just knew it."

I said that I didn't quite believe her and she said a mother always knows. I asked my mum a few weeks later if she knew and she looked at me sort of puzzled and said, "Of course."

It did, however, become fairly clear rather early on that our wedding was less about BJ and I and more about the long-awaited occasion of our two fine families coming together—at last.

It made me sad at first—it felt unfair that after everything we'd been through to get here, it was all being taken away to appease a great-aunt on BJ's father's side I've spoken to thrice in my life. Not her literally, but her figuratively.

I cried after our first meeting with our parents about the wedding. My dream wedding—I bet you couldn't pick it.

Me and BJ, our friends—just the true ones—his family, mine

too, I suppose—somewhere hidden in a far-off corner in England somewhere. No eyes or whispers, just us.

I realised that night that that kind of wedding was completely off the cards for us. For one, Bridget wouldn't be there and that was already something I still haven't really figured out how to be okay with. In some ways Bridget not being there made an unintimate wedding feel a tiny bit better, like it might drown her absence out a bit. That aside, my mother had already gone ahead and organised for me to be in *Vogue*, for BJ to be in *GQ* and the wedding to be exclusively featured in *Vanity Fair*.

Privacy was already out the window. Plus—as BJ keeps saying so rudely—we have like, four or five friends. The majority of the guest list was being filled out by the respective Parkses and Ballentines that aren't us.

So we started to look at venues in London. Mostly because I didn't want to be stuck somewhere far away with a bunch of people I'm not mad on, you know?

We looked at the Four Seasons. We looked at the Natural History Museum and I really liked it, actually—but I felt like Christian and Daisy should get married there if they can sort themselves out, so I didn't book it.

Old Billingsgate actually is very beautiful, but it's kind of just a venue, you know?

One Marylebone's a bit done, in my opinion. The Savoy is gorgeous, and so is Claridge's, but we're there already a bit, which makes it less shiny—

And then Beej made a suggestion and it felt like the most obvious thing in the world and so we're here now.

The Mandarin.

Like there's anywhere else in London we could possibly get married, anyway. I mean—yes, St Paul's Cathedral, sure—but actually, this is our church.

I'd been unsure initially about the lack of tradition, but when they showed us the space, when we stood in it across from each other, staring like we were at the top of a fake aisle, there was this gravity to it because of what this place means to us. A holiness, almost.

It was funny, standing there with him, like that. We've probably stood facing each other a million times, held hands double that—and yet here, now, in this place, with what it means to us—this is it.

Beej lifts his eyebrows up, asking the question without asking the question, gives me a hopeful smile.

"Yes."

"Yes!" He grins, clapping his hands a couple of times, and then he kisses me.

"And they said you'd be a ball-ache of a bride."

My face falters, mouth ajar. "Sorry—who said that?"

"Er—no one—" He shrugs. "None of our friends."

I give him an unimpressed look and he laughs, kissing me again. "Come on."

He leads me out and we go and pay the deposit.

June fifth, next year.

I know it's a ways away, but summer's past here now, and who wants a winter wedding in London? Maybe if we were doing it in the country, but in London when it's cold and the snow turns to brown slush, it's just yuck.

We get into the lift to go back upstairs to our room and he grins over at me as he tucks away the deposit receipt.

"We're locked in now, Parks."

I give him a little look. "You were locked in before, Ballentine."

He goes "Hah," and I toss my arms around his neck, kissing him in the corner.

And then the lift doors open and BJ goes, "Oh shit—" and stops kissing me, head pulled back.

I turn around to find Harley Parks standing there.

Level five of the Mandarin Hotel.

"Harley." I stare at him.

He lets out a dry laugh.

"Magnolia, hi." He moves in to hug me. He does. It's awful,

all awkward—I freeze up. He never hugs me. What the fuck is he hugging me for?

BJ and I shuffle out of the lift.

"What are you two doing here?"

BJ's saying nothing, his jaw's tight though. He looks weird. Angry, or something.

Maybe that he hugged me? I don't know.

I give him a quick smile. "We had a wedding thing."

"Yeah?"

I nod. "We booked it here."

"Here?" He tilts his head, a bit surprised.

I nod. "For the ceremony, not the reception."

He's surprised again. "Interesting. Why?"

"I lost my virgini—" I start to say, but BJ clamps his hand over my mouth.

"Sentimental—" BJ says instead as he drags me backwards.

Harley rolls his eyes and moves further into the lift.

"What are you doing here?" I ask him, frowning, a bit curious.

"Meeting." He nods.

My face falters. "On level five—?"

"Needed a room." He shrugs.

"For what?" I pull a face.

He pulls one back. "Is everything about sex with you?"

I cross my arms over my chest, irked. "Harley, don't say sex."

"Sex," he says as he pushes the closed button on the elevator and gives me a smug smile.

BJ breathes out his mouth and starts walking down the hallway towards our room.

"Weird," I say, walking after him. Beej nods, doesn't say much.

"He hugged me."

BJ looks over at me, pulling a face. "Pretty weird, yeah."

"Do you think he's having an affair?" I ask.

"What?" BJ laughs once. Sort of like a scoff. "No—why? Because he hugged you? Parks, he's your dad."

I shrug. "He's just not ever been a hugger, really."

BJ shrugs back. "Maybe he's trying to change."

FOURTEEN

BJ

Felt like fucking shit lying to her like that.

That fucked me up.

Making her sound like she's crazy for thinking it's weird her dad hugged her—for one, fuck him for being like that—that he shows his daughter affection and it immediately flags to her as something's off and secondly, she's completely right, it was fucking weird and he's a fucking prick.

Tried to palm it off quick as I could—and I know what you're thinking—I need to tell her, I know I do, but I can't yet. Especially not now. Since I made that comment about my pulse like a fucking idiot, she hasn't taken it again. You know what else she hasn't done since then? Sleep.

She hasn't slept in like, a week and a half. She's slow-motion falling into madness. She's a tin-foil hat away from being a fucking flat-earther.

Paranoid about everything. Safety, food, her dad cheating on Mars. She followed him, she told me. For a day. I nearly passed the fuck out when she said that. She could have seen them.

I had to laugh it off, tell her she was being stupid—nothing was going on—I'm like, gaslighting her and for what—? So her dad can shag her mum and she's none the wiser? It's fucked. I'm fucked.

I did think about it . . . Thought about sitting her down, telling her—but she won't see a psychologist.

I ask every few weeks if she wants to come with me to mine

and she gives me a big smile and says, "Oh no, I'm feeling fine today, thank you though!"

But I'm genuinely a bit worried about what happens next here if she finds out now.

Without Bridge or at least a therapist, she's fucking adrift.

And this week in particular, she's crazy unhinged.

Never done too well without sleep. Cries a lot in general when she's underslept.

That perfect face of hers hollows out, eyes go dark.

She starts accidentally spelling things hyperphonetically in her texts and it's fucking typos galore at the minute.

We have her birthday trip coming up, thank god. Get her out of London.

Henry asked if he could bring Romilly, and Parks asked if he'd talked to Taura yet, and he said no so she said no and then they had their singular fight of the year so I mean, honestly—fuck it, I'm exhausted.

I get into bed early that night because when she doesn't sleep, I don't sleep. I mean, I do, but way worse. She's a wriggler at the best of times. When she's restless, it's a nightmare.

I think about slipping her a melatonin tonight. She needs it.

Seems like it might be of questionable legality so I decide not to in the end.

Made her a sleepy-time tea though; she was so fucking offended by the taste she spat it back out into the teacup.

"Are you mad!" She stared at me eyes all wide before she thrust it back. "Absolutely not."

It's about eleven p.m., and I've been in bed since just after eight trying to sleep. Still haven't really slept because I share a bed with a fucking Theragun, so I start texting her dad because he seems like the most reasonable thing to point my frustrations at.

23:04

Harley Parks

Tell me you weren't with Arrie the other day.

Ok

Mate

Don't mate me

What the fuck are you doing?

None of your fucking business

And then I'm typing back, well pissed now, when Parks leans in towards me and tries to look at my phone.

"Who are you texting?" she asks sweetly.

"No one." I click my phone off.

She goes kind of still.

"What?"

I give her a look, toss her a quick smile. "No one."

She lifts her eyebrows. "Well, it was obviously someone . . ."

"No one," I tell her, pressing my lips against hers quickly, hoping she drops it.

She lays there, staring at the ceiling. Says nothing for a good two minutes.

I watch her, trying to figure out what's going on.

She's gone weird—I wonder if she saw it? Figured it out.

And then she says something that knocks me for fucking six.

"Are you cheating on me?"

I stare over at her. "What?"

She rolls in towards me, sort of rolling up into a ball.

"Are you?" she asks, voice tiny. "Cheating on me?"

I feel like the air's been kicked clean out of my lungs.

"Parks—"

"It's okay if you are—" she says quickly.

"—It's okay if I am?" I cut her off.

"Well, no—" She sighs. "But I just want to know."

I roll onto my back and stare up at the ceiling, feel like shit. "Fuck."

She keeps staring at me, eyes big. Scared now too.

"Just answer the question—"

I look at her with a scowl. "When the fuck do I have a minute to cheat on you?"

Her eyes go dark. "You've found time before."

"Once!" I yell and jump out of bed. "One time!"

I shake my head at her, she sighs and doesn't say anything.

I'm fucking pissed. Or hurt? Maybe I'm hurt.

"Alright, so who am I cheating on you with, then?"

She sits up and wriggles back into the head of the bed; swallows, nervous.

"Taura?" she says quietly, tucking her legs up under herself.

I stare at her, proper horrified. "Is your head fucking cut?"

Her breathing gets quicker. "You still haven't answered the question."

I stare at her with ragged eyes, wonder who this is harder for—me or her?

I don't know anymore.

"No, Parks—" I glare at her. "I'm not fucking cheating on you."

She nods quickly. "Okay."

"How—?" I stare over at her. "Why would you—?"

"I don't know!" She jumps to her feet. "I don't know! I had a weird feeling—"

I shake my head, kind of can't believe it. After everything?

"About me cheating on you?"

She breathes out her mouth and shakes her head, looking confused at herself.

"Like you were nervous or guilty or hiding something from me, I don't know—"

She shakes her head at herself and instantly I feel shit because her instincts are dead on, even if her conclusions are out of this fucking world.

I scratch my neck, drop my eyes from hers.

"And that was the first place your mind went?"

"Yes," she says, like she's ashamed to admit it.

I nod a few times.

"We need to go to therapy," I tell her, and she shakes her head immediately.

"It's perfectly normal that I would have trust issues with you!"

"Sure, yeah—" I nod. "But how about we have a crack at getting rid of them?"

"There's nothing wrong with how I feel!" She keeps going. "I just need to learn to trust you again—"

"And how's that going?" I jump in. "You think I'm fucking your best friend. My fucking brother's ex—?" I shake my head. "Jo's ex?"

That sits on me heavy, fucks me up a bit in my head actually, because if she thinks I'm that much of a cock-up—she who knows me better than anyone, loves me more than anyone, then fuck—maybe I am?

I walk away because I don't want her to see it on my face how my chest feels.

Go to our bathroom—*our* bathroom. Even thinking it now when I hate her it still sounds like a novelty—"our" anything.

I close the door and walk over to the sink. Run the tap, splash my face with some water and my eyes catch on something behind me.

The bath. Just lying there under a clear bit of tarpaulin. Still cracked, still a mess, still there. Bit of a metaphor for us, isn't it?

"Beej?" says a small voice from the door frame. I look over at her. "I'm sorry," she says, and I can tell from her eyes she means it. "I shouldn't have thought—I'm just ti—"

"I wouldn't do that to you," I tell her, turning the tap off. Swallow, shake my head, hate myself for a quarter of a second. "Again."

She nods quickly. "No, I know."

I walk towards her and slip my arms around her waist, ducking til I find her eyes.

"Do you really know?" I ask her. I sound desperate? I am, I guess.

She stares up at me. "I'm—" She swallows. "I'm—trying to know."

I nod. Hate it, but there's not much more I can ask of her than that.

"Hey," I tilt my head as I look down at her. "I know you do it as, like, a coping mechanism or something—but, do you think you could stop with the jokes about it?"

The blinks, confused. "What?"

I lick my bottom lip.

"Parks, what I did is never going to be funny to me—and I know I did it to you so I can't really ask you to stop because it's yours to process however you want—but I'm asking anyway because it makes me feel like shit."

"Oh," she says quietly, staring at the ground. Then she looks up at me, nodding. "Okay."

I give her a tired smile. "Thanks."

FIFTEEN
Magnolia

France is where we're going for my birthday trip and we take my plane because it's better than everyone else's. It has a bedroom on it, which isn't oft used for sleeping, but considering I've not been allowed to take BJ's pulse for nearly two weeks, my quality of sleep has gone downhill because I sort of just lie there awake, making sure he doesn't accidentally die in his sleep.

Every now and then I doze off but then after a few minutes I jerk back awake with the feeling inside of myself like I've left the straightener on and something's about to catch on fire.

Henry and I are still on a strange foot, which I guess tells you what you need to know about Romilly. That's how much he cares about her.

It's as though his affections for her, he just packed them away in a box. Didn't resolve them, didn't try to work them through, just—took them as they were when we were seventeen, put them away, and sat on them.

Now that the box is open, they've sprung back to life size instantly.

He's cross I said she couldn't come. I'd have liked her to because I do like her, it's just—Taura. And I didn't say she couldn't come, I said that he had to talk to Taura first before she *could* come, and then he didn't so she couldn't.

It was already so hard to get Taura to agree to come away with both boys.

I think BJ had to pull the dead sister card, which I know he tries to reserve only for very special circumstances.

Gus came with us too, of course. He's on Taura duty, and there does need to be a duty.

Henry's being such a twat about it all. He said he didn't think he owed her a conversation, but I'm not sure I entirely agree with that. Nevertheless, I told her about Romilly because at the rate Henry and Romilly are hurtling down memory lane, someone needed to. It was quite sad.

Tausie did go to our school though, so she knew about Romilly already. Remembered how they were.

She cried and wondered if she hadn't dated both boys what would have happened, if it would have been different. It would have, I'm very sure—when Henry's in, he's in. But it works both ways, because when Henry's out, he's out. Her knowing it could have been different if she'd only chosen faster isn't the sort of thing I should like her to know at the minute when everything about it is already causing her some sort of anguish.

It's better for her to think Henry and Rom are a cosmic force she never stood a chance against no matter what because that's not a thread she'd pull at.

Henry's sitting in a window seat, scowling at the clouds as though he's being dragged to his own hanging, not the French Riviera.

Christian was trying to talk to him before but got bored and gave up, and now he, Beej and Jo are playing *Halo*, that's when I feel it creeping up behind me like a shadow in a dark alley.

Ominous, ill-intended, my worst nightmare.

And then it grabs my shoulder and it feels like I'm choking so I stand up and excuse myself even though I'm not technically sitting with anyone or engaged in any kind of conversation.

I walk quickly as I can to the bathroom and lock the door behind me.

It's the worst realization I've ever come to: how many people you're surrounded by has absolutely no correlation at all to how alone you really are.

And I'm afraid that I am, in fact, incredibly alone.

Alone in my grief, alone in my thoughts, alone in my mind. Just . . . alone.

I take a big breath, breathe it out, close my eyes as tight as I can and wait for her to arrive.

"Bit squashy." She'd shoulder me out of the way.

"Are you calling me fat?" I'd frown at her.

And she wouldn't say anything, she'd just give me a look like the ones BJ keeps giving me lately but he doesn't know I see them.

She'd cross her arms over her chest.

"Isn't this a sad sight?"

"Isn't what?" I'd pout over at her.

She'd shrug, look at her nails as though they ever knew a manicurist a bloody day in their life.

"A plane full of people and you're talking to your dead sister in the loo—"

"You're my favourite person," I'd say in a small voice.

"Liar." Her eyes would roll. "Your favourite person's sitting out there, all warm-blooded and adoring—" An eyebrow of hers would lift. "Tall, bright-eyed, body like a marble statue—do you know who I mean?"

I'd roll my eyes back. "Besides him, you are."

She'd flick me a look. "You never said shit like that to me what I was alive . . ."

"Well—" I'd give her one back. "That's because you were a fucking pain in the arse when you were alive."

"Speaking of arses—" She'd give me a smug look. God, I'd give anything for her to give me a smug look again. "How's about when you made one of yourself the other day?"

"Excuse me?"

"BJ and Taura?" She'd stare at me, incredulous.

My head hangs. "Oh."

She'd shake her head. "You've lost the plot."

I'd cover my eyes and breathe out. "I don't know why I thought it—he was being weird on his phone."

"He would never do that to you . . ." she'd say, sincerely, and I'd give her a look and she'd reluctantly concede. "Again."

I'd give her a careful look. "We would have said he'd never do it to me the first time."

She'd nod. "I suppose that's true enough." Then a shrug. "Taura wouldn't either."

"I know."

"She really loves you," she'd tell me.

I nod. "I know."

I close the lid of the loo and sit down on top of it, looking up at where I imagine my sister to be.

"So, what are you doing today?"

"Oh, you know—" She'd shrug. "Just wandering over meadows of clouds, playing with puppies—"

"Really!"

"No, Magnolia!" she'd snap. "I'm dead. And this is a construct you've invented in your mind as a means of processing my absence."

She'd say that like it was nothing, I know she would, then she'd follow it up with the second jab.

"You think by talking to me you're circumnavigating the need for a psycholo—"

"—I don't need one of those." I'd cut her off and then she'd look at me like I was insane. I fix my hair in the mirror. "Stop looking at me like that."

She'd shrug. "Stop talking to the ghost of me in bathrooms."

I'd peer over at her. "No."

She'd lift an eyebrow again. "Then also no."

I'd growl under my breath. "You're so annoying."

"And you—" She'd give me a persnickety look because if you recall, my sister is unbearably persnickety. Was. "—have a very rudimentary understanding of the afterlife." Another persnickety look. "You might want to reconsider what happens after one dies, Magnolia."

I stare over at where her reflection should be, a bit hurt now. "Why would you say that to me?"

"Because you're scared of it," she'd say.

I tug on my opal and diamond Orbit necklace from Balint Samad. "No, I'm not."

"You don't know where I am—" she'd start. "Or where Billie is . . . If we're safe—"

"Stop." I shake my head.

"If we still exist in some way—"

"Stop it," I say again because it's hurting me now.

"Whether you'll see us again—"

"I said stop it!" I yell and then she's gone.

I stand there looking at myself in the mirror as I grip the sink and push down and away everything and all the ways it all might unravel me.

They are safe, they do exist somewhere, and I will see them again.

I run the water over my wrists for a few seconds, then I walk back into the cabin and everyone looks up at me with varying degrees of concern that makes me feel self-conscious and stupid.

I was loud just now, I suppose. I'd hoped that the sounds of the plane would drown me out but alas, it would appear it didn't.

BJ stands and walks over to me.

He's got his concerned head tilt on already.

"You okay?" he asks me softly.

I nod. "Mm-hm."

He nods back, watching me carefully. "You look tired."

"Oh," I shrug airily. "I'm fine."

Ish.

His brows go low. "You sleep okay last night?"

I nod, give him a tight smile. "Great."

Not great.

He pulls me away into the galley, frowns like he's worried about me because he is.

"How many hours?"

"Millions!"

He gives me a look. "Parks."

"I don't know—" I say softly, shaking my head. "One or two, maybe."

He presses his tongue into his top lip and sighs before he nods.

He takes my hand and then he places my index finger and my middle finger over his carotid artery, and I feel it drumming away under his skin, all steady and constant and life-affirming, and I don't mean to, but I breathe out a breath I didn't know I was holding and swallow down that strange new fear that grips me even though I pretend it doesn't.

BJ's eyes go soft.

"Should we go lie down and have a rest?"

I lift my shoulders all breezy. "Only if you need one, because I'm fine."

His mouth twitches a smile. "Yeah, I'm knackered."

Then he takes my hand and we go back to the suite.

Him letting me feeling his pulse felt like—for some bizarre reason—one of the most romantic things he's done for me in recent memory, and I wish I didn't fall asleep the second we lay down because it's a wasted opportunity, but I do—the moment my head touches his chest. I count his heartbeats instead of sheep and I don't think I even make it to fifteen.

When we walk out of the room everyone makes a dumb "Ooooh" noise because they're children—except for Henry because evidently we're still fighting enough for him to not partake in any sort of merriment that's in my general direction.

I'm not even sure why he came—? Now that he's here and not speaking to me.

He and Beej are passive-aggressive the entire drive to the hotel, and BJ and Henry being passive-aggressive towards one another is more distressing to me than Henry and I just fighting ourselves—which we rarely ever do by the way, but when we do, I'm of course very stressed. But BJ and Henry fighting is a bit like BJ and I fighting; they know each other too well. It's too easy to hurt one another, and they're too familiar not to.

"What's your problem?" BJ says to Henry, who's been death-staring my hand in his brother's for the entire drive so far.

Henry's eyes pinch over at me. "She is."

Taura's eyes go wide in surprise, and I just blink over at Henry with dark, unimpressed eyes, but BJ scoffs.

"What?" BJ asks—dares, even—with his eyebrows up and his jaw already set.

"She's my problem—" Henry says, glaring at me.

Beej gives him a look, angling his head. "Toss her a fucking look one more time—"

"This is fucking bullshit—" Henry tells BJ now, not me.

"Boys—" Jo warns, voice low. "Wind it in."

BJ scrunches his face up. "I'm not even saying fucking anything—"

"You are, actually"—I lay my hand on my fiancé gently—"literally, saying things. You are not, however, the instigator. Just—" I shake my head. "Leave him alone. Just stop engaging with him."

"What am I?" Henry scoffs. "A fucking madman on the street—?"

"Definitely a bit of a prick on the street—" Christian says as he eyeballs him. "For sure."

Henry flips off his best friend, who flips him off back.

"Just leave it," I tell Christian, a different kind of tired now. "It's fine."

"No, it's not fine—" Henry says to me, testy again now.

Beej leans forward, angry as he points at his brother. "Raise your voice at her again—"

"Beej—" I start with a sigh but Henry speaks over me.

"Come on, then." Henry nods as he motions towards BJ, and then I move between them.

"Shut up," I say, sitting up straighter, to block him. "You want to have a strop because I said no to Romilly coming here, fine. Strop away." I give him a curt smile. "But do remember, I did say she could come if you spoke to Taura yourself and you didn't, because you were uncharacteristically cowardly."

Jonah's mouth forms a little "o" shape.

"And now—" I continue, and Henry's eyes pinch so I pinch mine back, "—you're being uncharacteristically arseholey."

"Arseholey," sniggers Jo, but Hen shoots him a look so he wipes it away.

"BJ didn't say no to you, Henry, I said no to you." I cross my arms over my chest. "So if you want to be cross at anyone, be cross at me, except don't be cross at me because this is my trip." I look at my Panthère de Cartier watch the Ballentines gave me for my birthday. "Go home if you like, I don't care. Charter your own plane to get there."

Henry's head pulls back, all annoyed, brows low. "W—"

"No—" I interrupt him, hand in the air. "I don't want you to talk anymore—you're irredeemably annoying."

"I fucking love it when she's pissed at someone else," I hear BJ whisper to Jo.

I give him a look, and he gives me an apologetic, overly large grin.

Henry doesn't charter a plane home because that would have been embarrassing and he's not that petty, but he does go to his room and pout the whole day. One can't blame him entirely because the suites at Hôtel de Paris Monte-Carlo are very beautiful, but you know what—so is the Riviera, which is where the rest of us spent the day.

The Hemmes have a yacht they keep docked here, so we lounged about on that.

Jo and Taura are doing okay. Sort of weird. Because they're still maybe a little bit flirty—they've always been though, that's their only setting—and I asked Beej if he thought that meant it might happen between them still but he said he thinks Jonah likes Bianca Harrington, but that also Jonah doesn't know he likes Bianca Harrington.

After the third time Jonah threw Taura off the side of the yacht, I grabbed her and asked whether she wanted something to happen with Jonah now and she gave me this weird look and said, "No, Magnolia—" with a very firm head shake. "He obviously likes Banksy."

And then she looked sad, but less sad than she did about Henry, and I realise I'm possibly not the only one on this trip who feels alone.

We head back to the hotel to get ready to go to the casino.

I don't love gambling personally, but for some reason, BJ's really quite good at blackjack, which I find a little bit sexy.

Plus I love him in a suit, so any excuse—

He walks out of the bathroom—freshly showered—and drops his towel.

I press my lips together, try to pretend I don't know I'm blushing and instead go to help him get dressed into the suit I lay out for him.

Not that he needs my help getting dressed, but I've always liked doing up his buttons and tucking him in. There's something nearly as sexy about dressing someone as there is undressing them.

He's watching me, head to the side, tongue pressed into his bottom lip.

"Are you happy?" he asks sort of suddenly.

I pull back, surprised. "In what way?"

"In every way, Parks—" He shakes his head. "It's all I care about."

I stare up at him and lift an eyebrow. "You should probably care about other things."

He shakes his head. "Not until you're happy again."

"Ah," I breathe out. "I'm afraid you can't fix this one."

"Fuck off—" he growls, poking me in the ribs playfully. "Lil always told me I can do anything—"

I purse my lips, smiling a little.

"Oi—" He pokes me again.

"Mm?"

He gives me a little grin. "I'm really excited I get to marry you."

I slip my arms around his neck. "Me too."

He lifts an eyebrow. "Are you sure you don't want to do it sooner?"

"BJ—" I roll my head back. "I can't get married in the winter, think of my dress and the slush and—"

"Parksy, I honestly don't give a fuck if your dress gets ruined—"

I interrupt him with a look. "—Not the way to get me to marry you faster."

"I just want to marry you," he tells me. "I'll buy you another dress if the slush gets it."

"Beej, I don't honestly imagine our married life will be all that different to our current one."

"I don't know." He shrugs. "There's something about all that 'outward commitment' shit I've got a soft spot for . . ."

"*Outward commitment shit*?" I repeat with a laugh.

"Yeah." He nods.

I roll my eyes. "How romantic."

His eyes pinch. "I'll marry you right now, if you let me."

And I think about it for a second—because, that would be the dream. Just us and our favourites—but it would kill our families.

I do up the button on his shirt sleeve instead. "Behave."

"With you?" He smiles down at me. "Never."

SIXTEEN

BJ

It's a good couple of days here in Monaco, besides Henry turning into an absolute fucking fuckwit. It doesn't sound like him, I know—I just like, I can't explain it. He's always gone weird around Romilly.

Makes her sound bad, but it's not her fault.

Just doesn't see straight when it comes to her, do you get me? A bit like me with Parks, like it's not that—nothing ever will be—but like, let's liken it as a visual representation so you don't think my brother's just turning into a fucking prat out of the blue for no good reason.

We're down at the pool, all of us, even Henry who's back in the sudoku—Taura's trying to teach Gus and Christian a TikTok dance and Jo's filming because they all look stupid, and me and Parks? On a sun lounge, her head on my chest, both reading books, and I can't really believe my luck that this is my life now.

That we figured it out, that despite all the fucking drama, that we're together—like properly and shit. This is what I'm genuinely thinking—and maybe it was too picturesque, I should have taken the hint, but I didn't. Sometimes life feels good and you want to bask in it. About then is usually when it creeps up on you and cracks you over the head.

And that's when Henry loudly goes, "Oh, fuck."

Jo looks over. Always alert these days. Bit weird.

"What?" he asks.

Henry nods his head at something and I follow his line of

sight, where I see Paili Blythe and Perry Lorcan standing there in front of me and Parks, towels in hand.

"Shit," I say under my breath.

"What?" Magnolia looks back at me before she looks around and then her eyes spot them.

"Magnolia!" Paili says, taking her sunglasses off.

"Oh no." Magnolia shakes her head quickly.

"Hi!" Paili says, hopeful.

"No," Magnolia says quick, keeps shaking her head. And then—zip—Henry's at her side. Parks looks up at him. Shakes her head, swallows nervous.

I feel sick.

"Boys!" Perry grins.

Christian and Gus fold their arms over their chests.

"What are the chances?" Paili lets out a laugh that sounds breezy but we've all known each other too long. It's fucking forced.

Magnolia turns to me. "I want to leave."

I nod. "Yep."

"Parks—" Perry steps towards her.

"Now." She looks at Henry, eyes big.

"Magnolia, listen—" Perry tilts his head as though she's being unreasonable.

"No." She shakes her head.

"Magnolia," Paili says, peering around Perry. "I'm so sorry about Bridget."

Henry's head pulls back. "Is your motherfucking head cut?"

Paili breathes out. "Henry—"

"Hi," Taura says, stepping into frame. "Remember me?"

Paili's mouth tugs. She's uncomfortable.

I throw an arm around Parks, try to make her feel safe in this fucking dumpster fire.

Taura looks from Paili to Perry, giving them both a tight smile. "I'm still waiting on my apology."

Perry scoffs. "Apology for what?"

"So glad you asked!" Tausie claps her hands together. She starts listing things off her fingers. "For lying about me. For perpetuating a rumour. For keeping me apart from my fated best friend. For running my name through the mud—"

Perry rolls his eyes. "Your name was in the mud at school."

Jonah points at him. "The balls on you, man—"

"Are you going to say sorry to me or not?"

Perry shakes his head, unfazed. "Not."

Paili stands there, uncomfortable.

Henry's hands ball to fists and he locks eyes with Christian in case a fight breaks out.

"What happened to you?" Magnolia says, staring at her old friend.

"Me? You're talking to me?" Perry asks, eyebrows up, and I don't fucking like his tone. "What happened? Let's see . . . You found out something that was so fucking obvious, everyone else knew—"

Hen shakes his head and Christian sidles up next to him.

"Not everyone."

"Oh, now you speak?" He sniffs. "Classic. Everyone knew but you and these two apparently—"

"Which isn't everybody, by the way," Taura interjects. "That's four people. On the planet. Five if you include me because I knew. But still, five people is statistically an undeniable minority."

"You fucked up my life," Perry suddenly kind of yells at Parks, then he nods at Paili behind him. "Hers too."

Magnolia stands, offended. "I didn't even say a word to you for a year!"

"So neither did anyone else," Perry tells her.

She shakes her head. "I didn't ask anyone to not speak to you—"

Paili gives her a hurt look. "But you not doing it was enough."

Magnolia looks back at me, incredulous, and I stand up too.

"For what!?" Parks asks.

"For us to become fucking social pariahs!" Perry yells.

"Are you being serious?" Parks stares at him for a few seconds. Blinks a handful of times. "There are many at fault in what happened—many things done wrong, so many lines crossed—none of them—none!"—she thumps her little index finger against her own chest—"were crossed by me."

Perry grimaces and eyes down my fiancée—Henry can hit him now, I'd be happy for it—he purses his mouth.

"Well, that's not strictly true though, is it, darling?"

Paili tugs on his sleeve. "Stop."

Magnolia shakes her head, confused. "What are you talking about?"

"Perry, stop—" Paili tells him, and so Parks turns her eyes to her.

Girls have always done what she's said, with the exception of her sister. And Daisy, I guess. Magnolia tends to be the alpha in a room of girls. Don't think she knows it—think she thinks she's always right and just always has great ideas—she's not and she doesn't—she's just not the kind of person you can easily deny. Doesn't matter who you are.

Magnolia stares over at Paili, squares her shoulders and holds her gaze in a way that—honestly, would scare me if I was the recipient.

"What is he talking about?" She overenunciates.

Paili sighs, rolls her eyes. Swallows. Swallows again like she's trying not to say it out loud. Stares at her defiantly for about two solid seconds before the veneer crumbles.

"The bottle landed on me."

I blow air out my mouth, shake my head.

Jonah lets out a *'hah'* and stares over at her. "You're fucking cooked—"

"No, I'm not—" Paili says. "I could see it sometimes, with the way you'd look at me before, it—"

I breathe out loudly, jaw set, keep shaking my head. Don't even look at her fucking face, just grab Parks by the wrist and turn her towards me.

She doesn't say a word—doesn't have to, her eyes say it for her. *'What the fuck is she talking about?'*

I lift my eyebrows, give her this look, say without saying that she's fucked in the head.

"I saw it," Perry announces to no one.

And then Henry shoves him. "Bullshit you fucking did—"

Perry catches himself and straightens up.

"Do you want to go?"

"So bad, man—" Henry nods. "Let's do this."

"Stop." I put my hand on Hen's shoulder then look over at Paili. "You and me need to have a talk."

Magnolia's mouth falls open, stares at me like I've lost my mind.

I nod my head away from everyone, but she shakes hers, quickly, angry.

"Parks—" I pull her away from the others and put both my hands on her waist.

"Magnolia, I need to talk to her."

She stares up at me, eyes wide and saying nothing.

I gesture back towards Paili, exasperated. "She's out of her fucking mind, and she doesn't get what that night was really about—"

Parks frowns, breathes loudly through her nose—her reluctant sounds of coming-to-reason.

Crosses her arms over her chest, finds the next thing to be pissed off about. "What's she talking about—? How you looked at her—"

I cover my face with my hands for a second and sigh.

"Girls see what they want to see, Parks." I shake my head. "I have girls in my DMs telling me they thought they'd send me a message because they saw me looking at them at Sketch once four years ago. And I swear to god, ninety-eight percent of the time, I've never fucking seen them in my life—"

"But this is different!" She stomps a foot. "You slept with her."

"That's why I need to talk to her." I sigh. "Come—" I tell her, mean it too. "Sit there. Come with me. I don't care—"

"I don't want to sit there!" she says loudly—louder than she'd want it to be out here in front of all these other people, so she swallows, regroups. "I don't want to hear that."

"Parksy," I breathe out, touch her face. "If you don't want me to talk to her, I won't—but I think I should. I think I should wrap it—"

"What the fuck, BJ?" She thumps me in the chest, face pinched and distraught. "Why isn't it already fucking wrapped?"

I duck down to her eye level. "Because I never wanted to be alone with her again after it happened—"

"Even after I lef—"

"Especially after you left, Parks!" I interrupt her. "I didn't want you to see me photographed with her, I didn't want you to think that when you left, that's where I went—" I shake my head and breathe out. "She tried to talk to me once after it all went down and Jonah physically removed her from the building."

Would have been pretty funny if I wasn't completely fucking distraught.

Someone took a photo, she cornered me—me and the boys were out at dinner and she got me on the way back to the bathroom, and some prick took a photo—and Christian, fucking bless him, broke the phone (I love that temper of his when it works in my favour)—and I told her to sod off and she started crying and kept trying to talk to me, so Jonah picked her up and carried her away.

"I want to be done with this," I tell her. "I don't want to marry you with this shit over our heads. We might bump into her forever—"

She gawps at me. "I should hope not!"

"But we might." I nod. "And if we do, I want it to be nothing—"

Her face flickers, hurt. "It's never going to be nothing to me."

I breathe out, reach for her hand. "That's not what I mean. I mean like, it's just a blip. Like, it means nothing if we see her because it's been put to bed—"

She stares up at me.

I nod my head towards Paili. "I'm going to go talk to her. Do you want to come?"

She shakes her head.

"Do you trust me?" I ask.

She shrugs, sort of weakly. "I guess."

I brush my lips over hers and then she walks back over to our friends, holding her own hands because she's nervous.

I clock Paili and nod my head away from everyone else. "Let's you and me have a chat—"

Henry's head pulls back. "No—"

Christian's face scrunches. "Are you insane?"

"It's fine," Magnolia says quietly, eyes locked on me, nodding. Telling me it's fine but also a bit asking if it is because I'm the thing she looks at to regulate.

"I trust him," she tells everyone, even though I know it myself that it's a stretch.

Perry smiles at her, sneers almost. "Brave."

"Mmm." Henry breathes in and gives him a tight smile. "Yeah, I'm going to give you three seconds to shut the fuck up and walk away, or I feel like I'm going to hit you—"

Perry rolls his eyes. "Really, Hen?"

"Three." Henry starts nodding.

"When did you turn into such a child?" Perry asks, folding his arms over his chest.

"Two." Henry keeps going.

"Bro, I'd leave—" Christian tells him.

"One," Henry says, rolling up his sleeves, and Magnolia looks at me, eyes wide, worried and not wanting the spectacle.

"Paili," Perry says, annoyed but stepping away. "Let's go."

Pails adjusts the towel around her. "I'm going to talk to Beej."

"And you—" Jonah ducks into Perry's line of sight. "Are going to hit the road."

Perry rolls his eyes. "We're staying here."

"You mean you were." Gus gives him a curt smile. "Come on, I'll help you pack your bags."

"No—" Perry shakes his head, proper annoyed now. "I—"

"Or—" Jonah gives him a bored smile. "If you'd rather, you can help me feed the fish?"

Perry breathes out as he glares over at Jo, and then Gus leads him away.

I look over at Magnolia, eyes so big and scared they look like pools you could fall into.

"I love you," I tell her.

She says nothing back, just gives me a nervous smile. Henry tosses his arm around her and pulls her to the bar.

I walk a bit away, find some empty lounge chairs, sit down and gesture for Paili to sit across from me.

She does. Gives me this weird smile. Could be a bit hopeful maybe? Nervous too, I don't know—? Blows my mind that she can even muster a smile anywhere near this because I still can't think about that night without feeling like I'm on fire in a bad dream.

Everything's in slow motion, I can't stop it, can't put how much it's all hurting me out—it's one of those memories that sting my bones when I think about it. Not just because I did something that now if I were to properly try to think about, I'd probably be literally physically sick, but because of how it hurt Parks, how badly it threw us off track.

Claire and I talk about it sometimes, mostly because I think it's still an issue for Magnolia. Claire said it'll keep on being an issue for her until she confronts it, which is true, I know. Don't know how much wriggle room I have to push with her at the minute, just?

Anyway, this part of it, it isn't hers to confront.

Paili lifts her eyebrows, waiting, pinches her index finger as she does.

"Paili, listen—" I start. "I'm really sorry for what happened."

"I'm not," she says, and it takes me fucking aback how confident she is. "I know I should be, but I'm not. I'm sad it hurt her—" She shrugs. "But—"

"No." I shake my head. "There's no follow-up there, just—be sorry that it hurt her."

She sighs and offers me a smile. "I feel like . . . we could have maybe been great together."

I shake my head. "No."

"And I know that you're with her now—" She's talking with her hands a lot and it feels rehearsed. Like maybe she's had this conversation before in her mind?

"Paili—"

I shake my head, look away from her, and if you can believe

it—she fucking reaches for me. I snatch my hand away. Look over for Magnolia to see if she saw, but I can't spot her.

"I don't mean it in the way where I'm trying to stir anything up—" Paili tells me.

"Stop it."

"But I think there was something there that night," she tells me earnestly.

"Pails, no—" Shake my head. "I was a fucking mess that night."

"You weren't drunk, Beej!" she tells me. "I remember."

I sigh, tired. "I told you, Paili, I mean, I was truly fucked. Just—not in a way you know about—"

"So tell me!"

"No." I stare over at her. "I don't—we're not—"

"But we were."

"And now we aren't." I tell her firmly.

"BJ—" She gives me a look, tilts her head and shit. "That night meant more than you're allowed to say, I know that y—"

"Oh fuck—" I sigh, feeling a bit stressed now—cover my mouth with my hand—bit like I've opened Pandora's box. "You're cooked."

"I know it did!" she insists. "I felt it. I know you, and I know your faces and I always ha—"

"This is— Right." I shake my head. "Could have been anyone, Paili, literally anyone. Any female, in that moment, I would have done the exact same thing with them—" Her face starts to fall. "Wouldn't have thought twice about it—it was never about you. You were just there."

She frowns. "But—"

"No, let me finish." I hold up my hand to tell her to let me talk. "And that's fucked up of me because I reckon I knew. I knew you had a bit of a crush on me. I did know that, and that's fucked up and that's for me to wear. But I need you to understand, and like, properly understand, and then leave us alone—"

Her head rolls a bit, and she looks at me, nervous. "You don't mean that—"

"Listen—" I eye her. "I really do."

The frown deepens.

"I've never ever had even sort-of romantic feelings for you, Paili. Never looked at you and like, tenderly remembered what we did. I have no positive connotations towards you or to that night. I look at you and see . . ." I purse my mouth. Try to think of a metaphor. "The thing I used to drive my life off a cliff."

She pulls back. "Thing?"

Didn't like that one.

"Yeah."

"You just used me?"

"Yeah." I nod, because I've accepted that part of who I was. "And I'm really sor—"

And then she slaps me.

Clean across the face. Tears in her eyes, cheeks pink from embarrassment, she stands, glares at me and then has to push past Magnolia to get away.

Don't know when in the conversation she turned up—

Parks watches over at me, brows bent in the middle, probably looks a bit pleased that I just got smacked in the face.

She walks over to me and sits on my lap.

"You eavesdropping?" I ask, rubbing my cheek.

"Eavesdropping?" She blinks. "I was down-and-out spying."

I sniff, amused.

"Excuse me—" She stops a waiter. "Can we please get some ice?"

Parks looks back at me and touches my face gently. "She got you quite good."

I nod. "I deserved it."

She nods back. "I suppose you did."

I kiss her shoulder. "You feel okay?"

"No, not really." She shakes her head and I sigh, but fair enough, I s'pose.

She pushes her hand through my hair. "But I love you anyway."

SEVENTEEN

BJ

I lean back in my chair at The Guinea Grill, stretch my arms up over my head, when Henry asks out of the blue, "What birth control does Magnolia use?"

I stare at him, blinking a few times. "What?"

He shrugs. "Birth control. She used to be on the pill in school—"

"Weird," I tell him with a pinched look.

He rolls his eyes. "She's my best friend."

I toss him a look. "Then ask her yourself."

"Oh, no—" He shakes his head. "She'd bite my head clean off."

I sniff a laugh then roll my eyes before I answer.

"Condoms. Why?"

"Condoms!" he repeats, surprised.

"Yeah," I nod with a frown. "Condoms."

Condoms, if you were wondering, because she gets migraines now, so she can't be on the pill anymore. And then she tried the IUD for a while but went fucking mental, so yeah, condoms while we figure it out.

"Why?" I ask again.

"Just—" He shakes his head. "Not really like, Rom's natural comfort zone. Trying to figure shit out."

"Ah," I nod, before I eye my brother. "Fuck, you were annoying on that trip—"

"Sorry, yeah. I know—" Hen's face pulls. "Rom was pretty cut not to be invited."

Steaming along, those two are. Funny, but it's not like—overly sexually based, from what I can tell. I reckon it is, like—but—kind of on brand for them. Do you know their deal? Can't remember if we've talked about it before or not—they were best friends at school, like Parks and Henry but with chemistry, I guess. They met at Varley, Rom didn't go to the same prep as them. Henry was fucking besotted with her from the moment they met. Pretty will-they-won't-they for ages, I don't know why. Think he liked her so much, he was scared he was going to fuck it up.

One day but, he finally balled up and kissed her and they had this brief spell where they were on. Had sex. Her crazy pastor dad found out, moved her back to America the next week. Tore him up, actually. Never saw him properly like another girl until Tausie.

Give him a sympathetic smile. "Wasn't about her."

"I know but—"

"I should have filmed you and sent it to Romilly." I give him a look. "She'd have sorted you out."

Hen rolls his eyes. "I wasn't that bad."

"You were a proper sullen bitch actually, man, yeah . . ." I give him a smile. "Hated it."

He throws back some wine. "She just loves Parks."

"And Parks loves her, but bro—you've got to understand like, Taura for her is massive—first friend she's made in years—"

"I know," Henry sighs. "But her and Romilly are—"

"She loves Romilly, Henry." I give him a shrug. "Just don't expect her loyalty to shift overnight, you know."

My brother stares over at me, eyes go all heavy in thought, then his face pulls uncomfortably.

"Do you think I might love her?" he asks his wine glass, not me.

I sniff a laugh. "Yeah, man—"

He looks up, bit alarmed. "Do you think?"

I nod. "Yeah."

He frowns. "Is that mad?"

"Yeah." I nod again then shrug. "But like—who am I to talk?"

He says bugger all. Too pragmatic for love, in a lot of ways, Henry.

Not in the way where he's robotic, he's not—you know what he's like—loyal as a dog, but he likes plans, likes things to be measured, wants to take his time. Falling in love—like, proper falling. Falling, without his permission—that wasn't on the cards.

"You can't quantify it, man—can't make it make sense. It is what it is." I shrug. "One day, you're fine, everything's normal, and then, bang—" I bring my fist down onto the table and the woman next to us gives me a look. Flash her an apologetic smile and she perks up a bit as I do. "You're in love, nothing's fine, everything fucked and even still, somehow it's better."

This doesn't offer my brother the mental reprieve I thought it might—he doesn't work like that.

"You've like—" I scrunch my nose. "Done it though, right?"

Henry pulls a face. "What?"

"You and Romilly."

He looks annoyed. "You know we have—"

Roll my eyes and clarify. "Recently."

"Oh." He frowns. "Fuck off, that's none of your business."

"So you have."

"Fuck off," he grunts.

I sniff. "You love her."

He points over at me, looks annoyed. Doesn't like to be pushed, my brother. "Fuck off."

I nod my chin over at him.

"You spoken to Taurs since?"

He shakes his head. "No."

He did talk to her on the plane on the way home, thank God. Tried to clear the air, think it worked—she looked a bit tender after it. But grateful, maybe?

Told her he was going to date Romilly, that she's great, hopes it's not weird for her, understands if it is and he'll try to be mindful of it but he's not going to not bring her around just because Taura's going to be there.

Said he had to watch her also date his best friend the whole of last year so he reckons she'll be alright.

Don't know really how that'll ultimately go down but it's better than it was before.

Taura and Jo are fine, which I guess is a testament to what they actually were.

Don't know if Henry hadn't fallen for her how he did if Jo would have found her all that interesting. Sounds shit, not a slight against Taurs . . . He's just like that.

Hates to lose, can't lose. And once he has something, he finds it like, proper difficult to relinquish control of it—even if he doesn't really want it anymore. Don't think he knew he didn't really want Taura, I think he thought he did. Don't think he suspects of himself that his interest in being exclusive with her was possibly rooted in her wanting to be exclusive with someone else.

All sounds pretty dramatic, but it's all in the undercurrents.

Anyway, I can't prove it, like I'd—can't imagine that'd go too well with Hen . . . just my feeling, is all.

And then this beautiful girl rounds a corner and kisses my brother's cheek and takes a seat on his lap. Not overly roomy, The Guinea.

"Hi!" Romilly beams over at me.

"Hey." Flash her a smile. "Good day?"

"Yeah." She slips an arm around Henry's shoulder. "Just figuring out where to live—"

"Oh, yeah?" I lean over and nick a wine glass off the table next to ours, pour her a glass and hand it to her. "Any leads?"

"Yeah!" She nods. "There's this great place in Kensington Square—"

My brows lift at that. Would be kind of nice—

"Hear it's got a stupid comfy bed and some really pointy furniture."

Henry presses his lips together and sniffs a laugh into her shoulder.

I retain a laugh—don't want to give them the satisfaction—roll my eyes instead. "Not on your life."

She grins away, pleased, and then her face shifts.

"How's Parks been doing anyway?"

"Oh, you know—" I shrug, because I don't know what to say.

"Bad?"

Shrug again. "Depends on the day."

"Is she not eating again?"

I snap my head towards Henry, stare him down—the fucking traitor.

He shakes his head quickly. "I didn't—I swear, I didn't say—"

Romilly frowns at me, almost looks offended.

"*Panton nos postulo*," she says, looking me in the eye, and I sit back in my chair, feeling like I'm falling through time. Latin, they made us all take it at Varley. Old schools fucking love Latin, don't they?

"Fuck." Henry breathes out. "Haven't thought of that in years."

Something we used to say to each other at school whenever things felt particularly shit.

Romilly tilts her head at me and gives me a gentle smile. "I was there the first time, remember?"

I breathe in through my nose. Don't really want to remember, actually.

Probably could start crying if I let myself, so I jut my jaw and toss back some wine.

"She'll be okay," I tell them both.

Kind of worried it's a lie, though.

EIGHTEEN
Magnolia

I stared at myself in the mirror.

I liked the dress I chose, it was incredibly beautiful—is still, even though my heart pangs when I think of it, but I think my heart always pangs these days. There is something a bit heartbreaking about this dress though—black, of course. Corset bodice, divinely layered Chantilly lace—and it felt beautiful enough to honour my sister, and timeless enough that the magazines won't mock me for it a year from now.

"Who even cares what you wear?" you might ask, if you're a fool. The answer is everyone. Everyone cares what I wear, all the time, but more than ever then, at that specific event, they were watching me. BJ's tried to hide the articles from me, but I saw one a week or so before in the newsstand. The fucking *Daily Star* predicting it to be the most fashionable funeral of the century.

What does that even mean?

In some ways, the conversation around what I might have worn to my sister's funeral was nearly enough to make me want to wear just leggings or something awful—I don't have any of those anyway, so bit of a moot point there—but it mattered to me.

It didn't matter in the grand scheme of life, I know that—it didn't and it doesn't matter, actually, in a truly consequential way, whatever I wore wouldn't bring my sister back, but it did give me a sliver of control . . . Control of how they see me, control of how they judge me, and they do judge me—they always have. "Sad but Strong" was a title that came out a few days after news of Bridget's death broke. The brave thing I was doing? Beej and I nipped down the road for a coffee at Holland St. Kitchen. Intrepid, I know—truly groundbreaking stuff. Feeding myself, or something adjacent to it, and I'm brave?

They're nice about me at the minute, they have been since she died. They like me these days because I'm sad so I'm fascinating. But they're wrong, I'm not sad, I'm destroyed; I'm not fascinating, I'm just a shell.

So I wore a dress that was exquisite and beautiful and made my heart sink when I looked at it, knowing that they'd write about it, what shoes I paired it with, which bag, the jewellery—the black bow-detail Chantilly lace gown from Giambattista Valli, the black Cloud clutch bag from Jimmy Choo and handfuls of pearl bracelets from Mizuki, Sydney Evan and Sophie Bille Brahe—if the outfit was sensational enough, I thought maybe I might have gotten a minute to myself to grieve my sister without being under a microscope.

There was a knock on my bedroom door—I mumbled at it, I think—then it opened—BJ and Henry filled the frame.

"You look b—" BJ started and I looked over at him, I said nothing and he stopped talking anyway. Closed his mouth, gave me a sad smile instead.

The black wool mohair Shelton Tuxedo and the white cotton poplin slim fit shirt with the Onyx Round cufflinks, all from Tom Ford, and then the Chambeliss grosgrain-trimmed embellished leather derby shoes from Louboutin. Handsome like always. I dressed everyone that day, did you know? Everyone. All the boys let me pick everything, top to tail. Even Harley.

Henry put his hands on my shoulders. "You feeling okay?"

I turned around to face him, stared up at him and said quite calmly, "No."

He breathed out, that's all. Didn't say anything else. What could he say?

BJ gestured his head over at my black satin Hangisi 90 jewel buckle pumps from Manolo Blahnik. "You wearing these?"

I nodded and he went and retrieved them, dropped to his

knees and put them on me. He didn't look at me as he did it—he couldn't—he was barely holding it together himself.

The door tapped twice and Gus poked his head in. "Car's here, babe."

I stared over at him, nodded or something close to that. Stared at the navy Tom Ford Shelton Wool Suit Jacket, crystal-embellished pale blue cotton shirt from Gucci and ETRO's pressed-crease tailored trousers that he's wearing like I told him, but he went rogue on the cufflinks. The Gold-Plated Mother-of-Pearl Cufflinks from Lanvin. *Interesting*, I remember thinking. *They are nice though. Well picked.*

"Ready?" Mars asked tearily from behind him.

Beej stood up and slipped his hand in mine. "Never been less."

He squeezed it and led me out of my room and downstairs into the waiting black town car. Mulliner, Bentley. BJ and I drove separate to everyone else, I don't why but I was grateful for it. I didn't like cars by then already. I tried quite hard to arrange for me to be able to walk there, but the consensus was that I'd probably be late if I walked. Marsaili offered to walk with me, to keep me right with time, but the funeral planner said we'd probably be followed by the papers the whole way there, and then that was enough to put me off.

I climbed in first and then Beej after me. Pulled me over to him as soon as he was in. Slipped one arm around my shoulders and with his other hand picked up mine and kissed it the whole way to the cathedral.

We don't go to church much—if ever—Harley thinks he's an agnostic, but he's not, he's just too wealthy to need to know about any god that may exist, and until all this with my sister, there haven't been a great many undercuts to his life in other ways either.

"Fine people don't need a god," I heard him say once to a rapper.

I don't think that's what it is, though. I think if you believe in a god, you have to adhere to said god's moral code; fucking models and drugs and affairs and being an absent husband and father—they're not in the code, and the code is the thought that carried me into the church. I'm still thinking about it when I realise I'm on the front steps of the venue, and it was precisely, in that specific moment, that I realised the next time I'd envisioned myself in a church was me walking down an aisle to BJ.

Funny, isn't it, that on that day still I did walk down an aisle with BJ. However, circumstantially, it was quite different than what I'd originally anticipated.

The funeral was beautiful and hateful. Mum went ahead with the gold. There was gold everywhere. And a million white Vendetta roses. Quite possibly, literally a million. If there was a white rose left in England the day after the funeral, you could knock me over with a feather. Bridget's not mad on roses, actually. Geum prairie smokes are her favourite flower—because, of course they are. Weird and inaccessible, I'm rather sure she likes them because no one else knows about them, and in my mother's defence I wouldn't either have lined the aisles of Brompton Oratory with fucking Geum prairie smokes, but then nor would I have lined it with roses. Maybe a Senlitsu rose? Or ranunculus, even? Some green amaranth as well. Bridge would have liked that.

Instead, it was this explosion of Vendetta roses and some kind of vine creeping from the entrance down to the front—it looked like a wedding and not a funeral and something about that stung severely, particularly in the light of my sister henceforth being glaringly absent from mine.

There was a blown-up photo of her sitting up on an easel by her casket. I know with some certainty that it's a photo she hates. I know because I took it.

It was a beautiful photo. Not because I took it, but because she is—don't tell her I said that though—she doesn't like it because it looks like she's posing. Didn't like it, I mean. I didn't give it to them. I don't know how the planners got ahold of it.

It was unseasonably warm that day—unkind of the weather, don't you think? You do so want it to be raining on the day of a funeral, so wonderfully melancholy, and yet there we were, the church all lit up spectacular by the fucking ever-bright sun, casting all of London's high society in a glowy light that none of us deserve because light like this is reserved specifically and exclusively for my sister and BJ alone.

All those people there who know us and know our family but they don't really know us, they didn't really know her—wet eyes that I spotted from people who really, I think my sister would have truly probably referred to as a stranger—maybe an acquaintance at best—they weren't crying for her, I know that.

For one, the funeral hadn't started, as I saw their crying eyes while being led to the front of the church by BJ—but secondly, I know they weren't crying for her because they'd no right to.

They were crying because death is scary and uncomfortable and highlights certain things within ourselves that without the threat of mortality pressing in on our consciousness, we'd otherwise ignore, but those such things demand attention at a funeral. Mortality doesn't just press against you, it body slams you to the floor.

I sat on the front row with my family sandwiched between the Ballentine boys—the rest of the Ballentines, Taura, Gus and the Hemmes were behind us—and the minister stood up to start the worst thing that's ever happened in the history of time, ever. BJ hadn't let go of my hand since we left Holland Park, but he squeezed it again for good measure.

The service started and they played a song that I'm sure my sister never listened to and the minister talked about her like he knew her but he didn't.

And he talked about death in that airy-fairy way Christians do where death is laced with hope because it's not the end and Jesus died so that we could live but that didn't work for Billie and it didn't work for my sister, so I stopped listening. I don't want to know about those pearly gates or the arms of the saints they'll be found in. I didn't want to hear that she's gone home and that she's found peace, because her home is here with me and I'm not that noisy anyway. A bit noisy, I suppose, but not enough to die over.

My mum wore a black veil, which was so insanely dramatic it

made me want to yank it off her dumb head—also a bit because I was jealous that I didn't think to do that because when the fuck else is it okay to wear a black veil? Such a missed opportunity on my behalf, and it made me angry at Bridget because it's her fault, all of it is, somehow—if I'd missed her less, maybe I'd have thought of a black veil. Or, I suppose, if she'd just not gone ahead and died, none of us would have any need for a black veil, and I wouldn't have been sitting on the front row of the church glowering at my mother, wondering who she got to design it for her.

She didn't get up to say anything though. Neither did Marsaili, they held hands. Strange, I thought. I wished so badly that Bridget was there to dissect the strangeness of that with me but she wasn't. Isn't, I suppose.

Harley didn't say anything either, but he did get up and play the piano for Stevie Nicks when she sang "Landslide."

Allie got up and said something, talked about all the plans they had, the things they were going to do, trips they were going to take, an essay Bridget was going to write for a class which she'd never pass now and she wondered how she'd explain to her university professors the sudden dip in the quality of her work in that class, and I remember thinking Bridget must really love Allie to do her homework, because I asked her to do mine for years and she was always so rude about it. She talked about how she'd never find another best friend like Bridge, so sure she wouldn't even bother looking, she'll just miss her forever.

Bushka didn't say anything, but I didn't expect her to. She was actually really just very still. Oddly so? Still enough that I became convinced they'd given her something to calm her, because she wasn't just still, she was muted. All she did was stare at the coffin, frowning at it. Like it was a puzzle she couldn't understand.

The service moved on, the orchestra played again, and yes—before you ask, she went with the linen silk handkerchiefs—and then the minister eyed me.

"I believe Bridget's sister, Magnolia, is going to share a few words." He gave me an encouraging smile.

BJ gave my knee a reassuring squeeze as Henry passed me the package I'd asked him to carry in.

I lugged up the giant oil portrait of myself I'd had painted in advance for Bridget's next birthday and placed it on the floor next to her casket before I walked over to the pulpit. There was a murmur of confusion.

"Um." I glanced over at it and then back to the crowd, pursing my lips together. "That's not going to make sense to anyone, but I had this painted as part of her birthday gift and she would have hated it so much, and so I had to."

The room sniffed a laugh.

"That was kind of our thing, I suppose. Nothing quite says 'Good morning, I love you' in Bridget more than 'That's the stupidest skirt I've ever seen' and some terrible fact about the origin of toast." I breathed out my nose, and my eyes landed on BJ. He gave me an encouraging smile and I bit down on my bottom lip. "We didn't have great examples in that—how to love someone well—" I pressed my lips together, shifting uncomfortably. "My parents will think that's a slight against them, but I don't mean it to be." I shook my head and caught Tom England—that sweet man—sitting in the crowd with his parents, Clara and that boyfriend of hers. Tom gave me a weighted smile and my eyes filled up with tears that I blinked away quickly.

"They're divorced now though," I said quickly, as though every present man and his dog wasn't already completely aware of my parents' divorce, like it wasn't what kept the fucking *Daily Mail* afloat for the entirety of the last year and a half. "So I don't think either of them are under the illusion that they loved one another well—"

The room laughed again and I feel guilty for a second because I wasn't trying to embarrass them.

"They did love each other within pockets of dysfunction," I clarified, nodding, and Henry shifted in his seat, bowing his head, and Beej pressed his hand into his mouth, eyes lit up with an amusement that wasn't allowed to be there.

"My mother always did my father's buttons up, every morning, for every meeting, every dinner, even the times I think she probably knew the dinners or the trips were extramarital in nature—" Another murmur. Oh well. "She did his buttons. She did it this morning, still. And Harley would buy me everything, and my mother too—I don't know if that was a guilt thing?"

BJ pressed both hands into his mouth at that point and I wondered if I should have written all that down before I got up there. I don't really get nervous about public speaking, truthfully. The public is always speaking anyway, I quite like it when I have the floor and I have a minute to say what I like.

"Maybe it was an easy way to buy our love—" I pondered out loud and then there was another murmur, and I watched Lily reach over and flick Jonah in the arm because he's always been the naughtiest boy.

"But for what it's worth—" I told them loudly. "I love stuff, but Bridge didn't. Harley would try to buy her stuff too, she was just never that interested. Sometimes she'd even just ask him to donate money to charities instead, which I know—comes off as pious, and good eye, you're right—she was."

They laughed again.

"It was sincere though, I believe," I said, nodding. "And even if it wasn't, it's still a rather glorious rebellion, don't you think?"

I sniffed and breathed out before I squared my shoulders.

"Did you know that you can send your ashes to space now? Or turn them into fireworks or a coral reef rehabilitation program. And a diamond. You can have your ashes compressed into a diamond. Strange, to wear a dead girl on your finger, don't you think? The reef one isn't so bad—" BJ was back to smiling by then, eyes all heavy with how much he loves me, with a hint of how silly he thinks I am also—a look which I think he was sporting on that particular day on behalf of my sister.

"I mean, I don't hate it. Except that they mix your ashes

with cement—" My hands made a mixing gesture. "Which is yuck, no?"

Christian let out a laugh that was loud enough for me to hear him and his mother smacked him.

"There's um—" I sniffed. "There's actually not a body in that coffin." I pointed to it. "Not because something bad happened. Not because Bridget isn't still the most beautiful, sullen girl in the whole world . . . This would have been my one shot to dress her without her smarmy comments, but I couldn't because she's not in there. Because I can't decide what to do with her body. She would have told me what to do. But um, she's—" I cleared my throat. "Foreseeably unavailable—" I forced a smile because I was very close to being completely undone. "So I have to decide what to do with her body by myself, and I don't know, because I can't yet. So I haven't, so that's just a box." I point to it.

"How many loves do you get in a lifetime? That's a question I've wondered before . . . If you ask *The Sun*, I've had far too many, and in some ways that's true, I have. But actually, I've only had two great ones." I avoided the eyes of both Tom and Christian as I stared at the only great one I have left.

"One sits here today, holding my grandmother's hand, and the other is dead in a refrigerator on Weymouth Street because I don't know what the fuck to do, and I don't know how to choose it without her. I worry that people will look at my sister's life, and they'll lament over the brevity of it. That she was twenty-two. That's a Taylor Swift song she pretended to hate but loved, but it's also not a lot of years clocked, is it? And there are so many bad parts about my sister dying. One of the worst to her, I'd imagine, might be the pity of strangers, that her life was barely lived. That she didn't do anything big, she didn't have time to solve cancer yet, or poverty or—and she would have." I looked up to tell them sternly. "She would have, were she afforded the time to do so; she'd have done it all. She would have had a legacy that people would've remembered and honoured her for, for centuries to come. And it's crazy to me—it makes me feel almost a bit sick, actually—that years from now, you probably won't think of her at all, but I will."

A tear slipped out my eye and I smacked it away quickly, but if you can believe the fucking nerve of people, I saw a flash or two of a camera.

"She's shaped me, she grounded me, she steadied me, protected me, when every single other person in my life has failed me, she has never—" I was crying by then, so I glanced up at BJ to steady myself but he was crying too, which was worse, so I looked at Christian because he's professionally stoic. He nodded once and gave me a tiny wink.

I wiped my face, took a breath.

"She was a terrible pain in the arse but a very good sister," I laugh-cried, before I shook my head.

"I'm not going to say something inspiring . . . Nothing about how now that she's gone, I'm going to live my best life. I don't know how to live my best life without her, I don't know how to do anything without her." I gave them the bravest smile I could muster but it was impossibly weak at best. They—anyone, really—could see right through me, like I was a prism made of glass and loss. "You're all here to bury the smartest girl, the sharpest shooter in the whole wide world. But I'm burying my guiding light."

NINETEEN

BJ

The wake was a fucking head spin no matter how you slice it.

I know you don't walk into those kind of days like, anticipating the smoothest day of your life—but it was probably a bit more chaotic than I'd anticipated.

For one, the cracks between Hen, Jo and Taura were well surfacing by then.

It was also definitely when Parks started talking to Bridge. Heard her in the en suite. Didn't know I was there, peeked through the crack in the door.

"How could you do this to me?" she asked the no one in the bathroom. Covered her face, let out a little sob.

"I don't know what to do without you," she said, and I was about to walk in when she turned her head slightly to the right, as though she was properly looking at someone.

"Of course I don't," she said.

I craned my neck to see who she was talking to—definitely no one there, right? I doubled-checked. Thought I was going mad—then she spoke again.

"I don't, why would I say that I don't if I do—?"—that face I love fell to a pout. "I am not dramatic!"—a pause—"Sometimes, I guess, fine."—another pause—"No, I don't want to go downstairs. I like it better up here with you."

Thought about walking in, but it felt too personal. Like, she'd be embarrassed if she knew I'd seen them—or her, I guess. I hate embarrassing her in general, but definitely didn't want to make her feel weird on that day.

Waited for her in the hall outside the bedroom and her eyes went big when she saw me.

Gave her a tired smile, and she walked straight into my arms, bowed her head into my chest. Wrapped her up in me, and she let out another little cry before she shook her head, got a handle of herself and squared her shoulders.

"Do I look like I've been crying?"

"No" is the answer she wanted to hear, but her eyes looked like fucking gemstones so yes, was the truth. My face pulled.

"A bit."

She wiped her face, sniffing.

"You're allowed to cry—" I told her.

"No." She shook her head. "I don't want them to see me like this."

I frowned at her, confused. "Sad?"

Her brows bent low, resolute. "Vulnerable."

"Parks—" I sighed.

"They'll use it against me," she told me as she straightened out her dress.

"How?" I asked, watching her closely.

She shrugged as she started walking down the hall. "They always do."

She's right though, they do.

Jogged after her because she's a fast little walker and took her hand as she walked back down the stairs, and who was standing at the bottom of them other than head spin number three:

England.

The ex, not the nation. Although, probably an argument could be made in the case of the nation as well because a fuck tonne of people were there.

Parks was happy to see him . . . You'd think that would have made me feel shit but it didn't. She doesn't look at him how she looks at me, never has—that was the problem, I s'pose—for them, not for me. Great for me, bad for England.

He gave her this casual, fucking handsome smile as she moved towards him shyly.

Stayed a few steps up from the ground so they were eye level—he's tall, I'll give him that—she stared over at him.

"You came."

"Of course I came." He sniffed a laugh. "You think I'd miss the funeral of the second most terrifying person I know?"

She squared her shoulders. "Who's the first?"

His smile went bigger. "I'm looking at her."

Her face broke a little, relieved or something. Parks can't be on the wrong foot with someone, makes her go all uneasy. Must have wrecked her, Tom not talking to her all this time.

He reached past her to shake my hand, gave me a warm smile.

"I really can't believe you're here." She looked over at him a bit in awe.

He took her by the hand and pulled her in towards him.

"I really can't believe you thought I wouldn't be."

"Oh really?" She pulled back and looked up at him and then over at me. "Can you not believe that? Tell me then, how are your positively hateful matching tattoos?"

She gave him a curt grin.

He went "Hah" and clocked me. "Thriving."

I grimaced. "Three sessions deep and at a slight fade."

Tom tossed me a playful glare. "Traitor."

I shrugged like I couldn't help it and nodded my head at Parks. "I'm marrying her."

"Traitor again." He shook his head like he was disappointed but he was smiling a bit. "I'm kidding—I'm glad for you." Gave me a sincere look. "Both of you. Congratulations—I mean it."

Parksy smiled up at him. "Thank you."

He nodded. "About fucking time, really—"

"Oh, my god!" Gus clapped his hands together as he came up behind them. "Be still my heart! My world back in balance!"

I leant in towards Parks, whispered I'm going to run to the bathroom, asked if she was good for a minute—she gave me a quick smile and a nod then kept talking to the boys, so I jogged back up the stairs. Too many people milling about the downstairs one. Kind of wanted a minute to myself so I walked to the furthest-away one. Wanted to feel sad by myself for a second, you know? Me being sad is irrelevant at the minute, in general, but especially on that day. I knew that. Still felt it but, just wanted to feel it by myself, so I did.

Number one reason why that day was a fucking twist?

Went to a bathroom no one goes to, mindlessly opened the door.

About as mindlessly as they didn't lock it—and there they were.

Arrie up on the bathroom vanity, dress hitched up around her waist, Harley pumping away.

"Woah! Fuck!" I yelled, before I slammed the door back closed.

Stood there, frozen. Blinking, trying to piece together what I just saw.

Cupped my hand over my mouth as my brain went into overdrive trying to figure out what that might mean.

Is that an affair? Technically, yeah, I guess. But then—he cheated on Arrie with Mars, so—is it? Was it just balance being restored? And what are they doing? Was it like, a proper thing or a quick fuck at a weird time?

And what about how—

The bathroom door opened again, and this time Harley filled the frame, clearing his throat.

Arrie stood behind him, the bridge of her nose was flushed, cheeks too—same thing happens to Parks when we—

I pressed my hands into my mouth, shook my head.

"What the fuck?" I stared at him.

"Listen—" He shook his head. "It just happened."

Shook my head more. "What just happened? What is this—"

"It's nothing!" Arrie said quickly, moving towards us, straightening out her dress. "It was nothing. And you stopped it!" she added as an afterthought.

I gave her a look. "No, I didn't—you fucking—I saw you—"

"BJ—" Harley started.

"It's her funeral!" I cut him off. "Her funeral."

"I know!" he yelled loudly, and Arrie stiffened up, pressed her lips together.

She touched his arm to quieten him and stood between us—probably not a bad idea—don't much like being yelled at by anyone really, but especially by fuckwits who are casually hurling around something that might knock Parks clean off her feet.

"It's nothing." Arrie nodded, eyes begging me to drop it. "I was upset, I came up here, he followed me. We kissed, accidentally—"

"—You more than kissed," I cut in.

"Yes." She nodded, solemnly. "But it won't happen again."

I nodded once, eyeing them both. "You're fucking right it won't."

TWENTY
Magnolia

Gus, Taura and I go to see *Mamma Mia* at the Novello. We've all obviously seen it a billion times before—honestly I'll probably see it again next week—it's one of those things we just seem to do now. It was Gus's idea.

I've always enjoyed the West End as much as the next person. I've never been absolutely gagging for it, but enjoyed it enough—until recently, that is.

Now I quite love it.

There aren't a great many places I can go to in London at the minute that afford me much privacy. But there, it's a given. There, I'm not the show. No one's watching me, and even if they are, the lights go dim anyway.

We sort of go to whichever show, depending on my mood. If I need to cry, we'll see *Les Misérables* or *Miss Saigon*. If I'm feeling okay, we'll see *Wicked* or *Mamma Mia*, *The Lion King*, maybe . . . Taura always wants to see the Harry Potter one but I'm so-so about it. I know they call it canon, but let's all just hold on a minute about that, okay?

Anyway—it's something I can do with my friends that doesn't really require very much of me. Just, get dressed, show up, say hi. I scarcely have to hold a conversation except through the intermission, and honestly, Taura and Gus can tell on the night whether or not I have much in me to say.

I did tonight, I was chatty, actually.

Happy to hear about Gus and Jack and ever-unfolding drama of them. Gus says he's over it, I can tell he's far from it. He's knee-deep in it and wishes he wasn't, because Jack is still—allegedly—rather hung up on Taj Owen.

They're trying to be friends—Gus is actually really good at boundaries. Well—usually anyway. But Jack's hard for him. For one, he's impossibly beautiful—like, would rival BJ on the beauty front, which we all know is saying something, so you can scarcely blame poor Gus. As well, I think Jack might just be "that" person for Gus. Which I sort of hate for him, because I sometimes wonder if "that" person for Jack is Taj.

It's rather unfortunate when you have a person and that person's person isn't you. BJ's always been my person. Sometimes people shift persons. I was Christian's once, though I'm most certainly not anymore. People can change. Hearts can press forward. Maybe Jack's will—? I would be ever so glad for them.

"Oh, fuck," Taura says suddenly. We were mid-walk a moment ago, my sweet friends agreeing to the hour's walk home for my sake—she's standing frozen now, staring into a shop window.

"What?" Gus stops, following her gaze. "Shit."

I look from them into the shop and it takes me a minute to see but then I do. Right there on the cover of *The Sun*:

BALLENTINE'S SECRET SCHOOL LOVER
SPILLS ALL!

I shake my head, march into the store and pluck it from the shelf.

"Magnolia," Taura sighs. "Honestly, it's just going to be shit—"

"Yeah, babe—" Gus shakes his head. "It's not worth it, it's—"

I ignore them, flicking through until I find it. A double spread. A giant photo of Beej on the left and on the right, his alleged secret school lover.

Allegra Fiscella.

Taura's face falters when she recognises her. "Fuck."

Allegra was obsessed with BJ, for years. Everyone knew. She was worse than Alexis Blau, and everyone knew how bad Alexis had it for BJ.

But Allegra took every chance she got, every single chance—until recently, even—right before BJ proposed, I overheard Henry telling Christian that they were out and Allegra tried to take him home. She's completely mad, like a proper little nutter, but my god, she is beautiful.

And accurate, actually. Scarily so.

> *"He loves to be kissed on his neck," she confesses with a giggle. "His neck is really sensitive. And he likes it when you play with his hair."*

I feel myself frowning because that's true.

> *"I always felt a little bit bad when we were at school because he was with Magnolia most of the time—"*

"Most of the time?" growls Taura. "When the fuck were you not together at school?" (She looks at Gus and adds under her breath, "A bit annoying, really.")

I shrug weakly. "Before we went away, I guess?"

"It isn't true, Parksy—" Taura tells me, voice sounding stressed. "You know that, right?"

I look at Gus and he says nothing.

I look back down and keep reading.

> *"Magnolia and I were in most of the same classes. I liked her. That made me feel bad sometimes, but BJ and I had such a special connection, it was hard to ignore. I was in a different dorm house to Magnolia so it was fairly easy to sneak him into my room or me into his. I always loved his room—four-poster bed, these grey sheets that were so comfy, like a flannel material. He had a photo of Magnolia stuck*

to the wall by his bed. Sometimes he'd take it down when we were—" Her voice trails and she looks embarrassed, but perhaps worth noting, not ashamed.

"Is that true?" Gus looks over at me. "What she's saying about his room?"

I think I'm going to be sick. I nod.

When asked why she's finally breaking her silence about their years-long affair, she smiles as though she's sad.

"I just think Magnolia ought to know the kind of person she's marrying. That while she was taking tennis lessons, we were having sex under her dormitory stairs."

My blood goes cold when I read that last part. Like I've fallen into a lake, or all my air's been kicked out of me.

I roll up the magazine.

"I'm taking this," I yell to the shopman.

"That's £1.10!" he calls after me gruffly. "You have to pay for that!"

Taura turns and eyes him sharply. "She's paid for it enough already, don't you think?"

I flag down a taxi and climb in—I don't even think about how much being in a car scares me because this scares me more.

The whole drive there Taura's telling me it's probably not true, but Gus is quiet and I find that rather frightening.

I don't really remember how I get from the taxi into our flat, but I tumble through our front door and only vaguely clock that in the room isn't just BJ but also all the boys and Romilly.

I must look funny because BJ jumps to his feet quickly—says my name and reaches for me but I don't let him touch me.

I hold my hand out to keep him at bay. He frowns, confused, and then sees the magazine in my hand.

Beej grabs it from me as Henry stands up, walking over and standing next to me, arms folded as he stares at his brother, waiting to understand.

BJ looks at the cover and then his face falls.

"Parks—" he starts with a sigh, and Jo jumps to his feet, looking over his best friend's shoulder.

"Is it true?" I ask, glaring at him.

"What?" He blinks over at me.

"Is it true!" I ask louder, overenunciating.

The whole room gets sucked into a vacuum of silence.

Beej takes a big breath and looks confused about how to proceed.

The entire universe hangs on a wire over a volcano that's waiting to consume it whole.

"I mean—" He breathes out, glances around the room self-consciously. "Yeah, we've had sex—"

"Oh, fuck—" Christian groans as he covers his face with his hands.

BJ glances over his shoulder, angry, and then he gives me a look. "But I didn't cheat on you to do it."

"So then how does she know about the photo of me by your bed?"

He shrugs. "Guessed?"

Henry frowns a little.

"How does she know about your grey sheets?" I ask him, glaring.

BJ frowns now. "My grey what?"

"Your sheets—" I growl. "How did she know what colour they were?"

"I don't know?" He shrugs again, looking around the room for help but no one really offers him any.

I lift my eyebrow. "And that they were flannel."

BJ's brows pinch. "No, they weren't."

I snatch the magazine from him and flip it to the article, pointing to the quote.

He rolls his eyes at me, like I'm an idiot.

"Oh, well, fuck—! If *The Sun* says it, it must be true." He takes the magazine back, shaking his head and looking at it himself. "I hate flannel sheets—they're too hot to sleep in. The fucking boiler was so hot in the Carver dorm—"

"It was—" Jonah nods.

I look up at Henry and he nods too, so maybe I might believe an inch of them.

"Mine were jersey," BJ tells me, brows low.

I purse my lips, thinking back to his dormitory bed, all those evenings I spent in it, the sheets he used to wrap me up in and then my eyes go wide.

"Shit, they were jersey."

He gives me a "told you so" nod.

I fold my arms over my chest, not ready to stop being cross just yet.

"Well, so, how does she know about under the stairs then?"

"I don't know—?" He shrugs again, and if I'm being entirely truthful—knowing a face as well as I know his, I can tell he's genuinely confused. "Like I said—I've slept with her since. Maybe she asked—wouldn't have been secretive about it fucking ten years after the fact—"

Henry folds his arms over his chest.

"How'd she know your sheets were even grey, but?"

BJ looks over to his brother, hurt by the question he asked, but Henry is unflinching and just lifts an eyebrow, waiting.

"I mean—" Jonah steps forward. "I fucked around with her a bit in school. We shared a dorm."

My eyes fall to my old friend suspiciously.

"You've lied for him before."

BJ breathes out loudly, shaking his head—hurt more still—Jonah's face grows a little dark, and the whole room goes more tense.

"Well, I'm not fucking lying now."

I look from BJ to Jonah. "So, she's just lying then?"

"Yes." BJ nods, sure now.

The anger starts to lift from me and I feel a bit floaty, not in a nice way. A bit how it might feel when you're small and you find out Santa isn't real.

I try to take a breath but then I think I take about four on accident. "Why would she do that?"

He looks over at me, exasperated.

"Because people are shit—" His face softens back to sad, maybe even scared. I hate it when he's scared. "You have to believe me, Parks—I'm telling you—I might be a fuck-up, but I'm not a liar. I didn't—"

"Okay." I nod.

"I promise," he tells me.

I nod again. "Okay. Sorry." I look past him to everyone else in the room—my neck feels hot, cheeks feel burn-y. "Sorry," I tell them all before I turn on my heel and leave the room.

"Hi, Taura," I hear Romilly say nervously on my way out.

"Hi—" Taura says back, also nervous.

And I feel conflicted because I've wanted so badly to see how they'd go in the same room, but not as much as I want to hide from everyone because now they all know my awful, burning secret: that I sit here, waiting every day to find out that he's done it again.

"Hey—" BJ walks after me, grabs me by the wrist and pulls me into a spare room. He tilts his head. "You good?"

"Yeah—" I shake my head. "I'm sorry. That was stupid. I shouldn't have—"

"No, I'm sorry." He ducks his head so our eyes are level. "I know that would have been hard to read."

I nod.

He pushes his hand through my hair and I look up at him, feeling beaten.

"Can people really be so awful?"

He shakes his head. "She was always fucked, Parks—do you not remember that whole thing with my jersey?"

I stare at him, squinting, thinking back.

"Remember—" He nods. "I couldn't find my rugby jersey for like, a week, and Bardwell was so fucking mad about it and then she turned up to the game wearing it?"

"Oh shit—!" I blink a few times. "I forgot about that."

"Yeah." He nods. "She was weird."

I smack his arm immediately. "So why did you later then sleep with her?"

"Ah, well—come on." He shrugs. "She's pretty fit?"

I open my eyes wide and stare at him. "What's that now?"

"I mean—" He shakes his head, smirking. "Lost without you! Lost all sense, I was—went mad. Completely lost the plot—"

I glare up at him, trying not to smile. "Mm-hm."

He wraps his arms around me. "I love you."

I settle in against him. "I love you too."

He says nothing for a few seconds and then he breathes out. "Thanks for believing me."

TWENTY-ONE

BJ

Weekly dinners at my parents, we've always had them.

It's the kind of place you always want to come back to. Like, all of London is, but Belgravia in particular—for me, at least. Three-storey townhouse on Cadogan Place, pretty hard to say no to.

Same house I first saw Parks in—hope they never sell it, I'll have to buy it if they do.

She's in the kitchen helping Mum tidy up—a figure of speech—she's definitely not doing that. Never has tidied a thing a day in her life, she's just following Mum around the kitchen, holding things, opening drawers, you know—eventually, she'll make my mum a tea and sit on the bench while Mum does the actual cleaning, but she's happy and Mum's happy, so I'm happy. Mum loves her in our house, always has.

She's always felt a maternal responsibility for both Parks girls, I think. Once she saw how shit Arrie and Harley could be, she kind of made it her mission to just bring them in.

They're still close though, don't get me wrong. My parents would consider hers to be among their closest friends. But you can have close friends whose lives you don't completely agree with. Take me and Jo, for example—can't say I love his day job, but here we are. Been my best friend since we were—I don't know—eleven?

Came outside tonight to kick a ball around. Actually—honestly—I came outside because my dad had a look about him and I could tell I was about to cop an earful because I didn't go to the board meeting again.

Henry said Dad was pissed—*'What even is the point of having him on here if he never attends?'*—which, my question exactly—please, for fuck's sake, take me off it. I don't want it.

I shouldn't have come outside though—rookie move of mine. If I want to be left alone, only shield I need is Parks. If she was out here with me he'd never have come out—but it's a catch-22 because if it was me and Mum and Parks in the kitchen, he'd have come in and asked me for a walk.

So I guess it's inevitable, this—whatever's coming—as he walks out and over to me.

Stands on the other side of the garden and waits for me to kick the ball to him.

Take a breath. Steel myself.

Kick it.

"Had something on today, then?" he asks, trying to sound casual, not pissed.

I nod, coolly. "Yeah, Parks needed me."

Not entirely true—feel shit lying like that. I'm lying a bit these days, don't know why.

"Is she okay?"

I shrug. Don't really want to get into all that.

"She couldn't go an hour without you?" he presses.

I give him a look.

She worked most of the day, truthfully. Used my lap instead of a desk chair, though.

And me? I okay-ed some tiles for a house I'm flipping in Saint-Jean-Cap-Ferrat. Moved some money from Ethereum to XRC just to see what happens. Slow day, really.

I could have gone. I just—it's not for me.

"There's more to being a husband than being physically there, BJ."

Look at him suspiciously. "Arguably, though, the most important part . . ."

"One of." He nods, watching me. Then kicks the ball back

to me. "How are you going to look after her? Financially—?" He clarifies at the end there.

I stare at him for a second, look baffled. "She's fine."

There were five grandchildren in line to inherit Bushka's fortune. Four now, just. Alexey told Parks after Bridget died that Bushka was reallocating Bridget's inheritance to our children instead.

Not that I'm going to be dipping into it or anything, but money's just not a thought for us.

"And what about you?" Dad asks.

"I'm fine too."

He gives me a look. "With the money that I gave you."

I rub my eyes, tired—try to put my game face on and have a run at this ball we've kicked back and forth so many times already.

"That your father gave you, Dad—that I've diversified myself"—I give him a look—"I have high-revenue passive income from like, twenty properties. My portfolio is solid. I'm pretty interested in mineral acquisitions. My stocks are—"

"In crypto," he interrupts, kicking the literal ball back to me.

"Yes, in crypto." I roll my eyes.

He eyeballs me. "Dangerous."

"Risk pays," I tell him, kick it back. "High. In dividends. You taught me that."

"Did I forget to teach you how to have a work ethic?" he shoots back.

Put my hands on my head, drop my head back and breathe out my mouth.

"Fuck." I sigh under my breath. Blink a few times before I stare over at him.

"I have a good work ethic—at school I'd wake up every morning at four to work out for two hours, then go to swimming practice and then rugby practice after school—"

Dad nods. Can't deny that. I worked fucking hard at school.

"And now?" he asks, watching me.

"I'm one of the most in-demand models on my agency's books." I tell him, and I see it—watch my dad restrain himself from rolling his eyes—good for him. Probably pulled a muscle holding that back, kind of hope he did.

"It's hardly hard work, Beej—" he tells me, and I don't react even though it's shit.

Anyone who's modelled knows that's not true. It's fucking hard sometimes. Is it rocket science? No. But neither is sitting on a board for a supermarket chain.

"If you were half as committed to a job as you are to Magnolia, you'd be—"

Shake my head.

"Stop," I tell him.

He doesn't.

"What if you get to the end of your life and you have nothing to show for it?"

I glare over at him a bit. "Define 'show'—?"

He rolls his eyes because he fucking hates a technicality. "BJ—"

"No—" I nod my chin at him. "I mean it. Tell me what 'show' means. What am I showing? Because what if I get to the end of my life and I have a good marriage and kids who like me—"

"Are you saying you don't like me?"

"Well, not right now." I sniff, rolling my eyes.

His head pulls back a bit. That hurt him. Didn't mean for it to. Maybe I did—? I can't tell.

"I'm just trying to help you," he tells me.

"To be like you." I finish that sentence off for him. "I'm not like you, Dad. Henry is, I'm not—"

"I'm not trying to make you like me, BJ." He sighs. "I'm trying to make sure you're set up for the rest of your life. That you're going to be able to look after her—" He gestures to Magnolia through the glass doors that lead into the kitchen. I was right. She's sitting on the bench now, tea in hand. "For the rest of her life."

I stare over at him, kind of feel a bit like he's hit me. Like he's implying something.

"I've looked after her my whole life," I tell him, and his face pulls again, like he doesn't think that quite checks out, and I feel something snap in me.

"Shut up." I point over at him. Could count on one hand the number of times in my life I've told my old man to shut up. "I have."

He doesn't say anything, just stares at me, so I look away and walk back into the house and into the kitchen.

"Come on," I say to Parks, lifting her off the bench and planting her on the floor. "We're going."

"What, darling?" Mum blinks.

Magnolia looks up at me, confused. "Are you okay?"

Dad walks in behind me, says nothing.

"What happened?" Mum asks, immediately sensing something. She frowns from me to Dad.

I grab Parks' hand. "Let's go—"

"Hamish, what happened?" Mum asks. I say nothing, kiss her on the cheek and lead Parksy out of the kitchen towards the front door.

"Thank you for dinner!" she calls back to them.

"BJ, darling—" Mum calls after me, but I don't stop.

"No, let him go." I hear Dad say and then I close their front door.

Keep holding her hand as I lead her—*pull her*, is probably more accurate—down the street towards the embassy.

She doesn't say anything for about half a minute.

"What happened?" she asks eventually.

"Nothing," I tell her without looking at her. "Want to stop by Muse for a drink?"

"No—" She stops walking. "I want you to tell me what happened."

I breathe out and turn to face her.

Feel myself feeling sadder than I want to.

"I've looked after you, right?" I say it without even thinking about it, because I want her to tell me that I have. Need her to.

"What?" She blinks, confused. "Yes."

"And I know I've cocked up—" I shake my head. "But you're okay. Like, we're okay—"

"Yes." She nods, frowning.

"And we're going to keep being okay."

She nods again. "Yes."

I breathe out.

"I just don't have much to show for it."

She's back to confused. "For what?"

"For life."

"BJ." She coughs a laugh, puts both her hands on my waist. "What's going on?"

"I can't—" I shake my head, annoyed. Not at her—just annoyed. "It's hard to explain."

Hard to quantify, actually. What do I have to show for this life?

Her. It's her. Loving her. That's all I've got, and he's saying I've not even fucking done that well.

Everyone has markers for their life. Ways they remember certain things and times. Stakes in the ground.

She's mine. My whole life, all dotted with and by things I remember about her. She's how I frame the world.

I never thought that was bad before. Is it bad?

Tilt my head as I stare down at her.

"Tom and Julian, did you like them because they did stuff?"

Her brows fall. "What?"

"Rush—" I shrug. "He was an actor . . ."

She blinks. "What are you talking about?"

"I don't do anything!" I say louder than I mean to.

Actually, I didn't mean to say it at all.

She stares over at me, most beautiful face in the world—looks dumbstruck. Sad maybe, even?

"Is that what your dad said?"

I sigh, shake my head. "He asked how I'm going to look after you."

"Financially?"

"Yeah."

Her face pulls, amused. "I'm fairly set."

"I know."

She folds her arms over her chest. "Does he think I'm poor?"

I sniff a laugh. "No."

She glances down at herself, suddenly self-conscious. "Do I look poor?"

"No—" I roll my eyes. "Can we ju—?"

"Sorry. Right." She nods. "Do you feel like you don't do anything?" she asks, carefully.

"I don't know—I—" I shake my head. "You were the thing I did," I tell her, and her face softens. "For so long. Getting you back, us working out was like—the reason I got up in the morning."

"Beej—" she says and looks like she's about to kiss me.

"And I've got you now—" I shrug.

She shrugs back. "You always had me."

I give her a look. "You know what I mean."

She watches me, eyes searching my face. "Not really—?"

So I laugh. Not because it's funny but because I don't know how to keep talking about this anymore, how it pulls at the thread in my mind about how I'm not good enough for her. I'm not, really—don't want her to realise that though—so I slip my arms around her and pull her into me. Kiss the top of her head.

"Sorry," I tell her, give her a smile. Hope it distracts her.

It doesn't.

She sort of frowns and smiles at once. "Beej—"

"Parks, I'm fine—" Another shrug. "Dad just got into my head—I'm good."

"BJ—" She says my name again so I kiss her to make her stop.

"I said I'm good."

22:17

Mum

BJ darling, are you ok

Fine mum ❤

Don't mind your father, he's just old fashioned

I know modelling is hard my darling

You're very good at it

Thanks mum

He'll come around.

Please don't let this ruin the Yacht

I won't

Promise

Thank you

I love you!

Love you too.

I don't care that he doesn't think modeling's hard by the way . . .

If you say so, darling

TWENTY-TWO

Magnolia

I get a hotel room at the Mandarin and have Daniela pick up all the dresses I'm so far interested in.

It's been a bit of a kerfuffle, trying to find a dress without the world finding out which ones they may be.

I know they'll find out eventually, but I should like for it to be a secret for just at least a moment. I'd like at least for BJ to know what it is before the rest of all sodding London.

Every time I go into any store lately, there's always a bit of a frenzy—"Is this the designer?" "Who are you wearing?" "Give us a hint!"—and please imagine what a personal dilemma that presents for me. I love going into stores.

Which is how this idea came to be:

Someone else would go and collect all the dresses I'm interested in, and I'd try them on away from the prying eyes of *OK! Magazine*.

Daniela's waiting on the other side of the door. She said it's to make sure no one's out there, but I actually just don't think she's terribly invested in my dresses, which I sort of like but also find a bit strange and frankly confusing.

"What am I here for?" Henry asks grumpily as he leans back on the bed eyeing the number of garment bags Taura's hanging up around the room. "Can't I wait outside too?"

"You're my maid of honour," I tell him without glancing at him.

"*Mate*," he corrects me, and I give him a sharp look.

Taura sniffs a laugh at us and pours some champagne, offering it to him before me, which feels rude, but his face implies he may need it more.

He gestures to all the gowns.

"I'm a boy," he whines.

"Oh my god—!" I look up at him as though it's a genuine revelation. "Are you?"

"Yeah—!" Taura nods brightly, playing along. "I've seen it."

Henry glares between us, and then I shake my head apologetically.

"I'm so sorry, I forgot that it's 1956 when men weren't allowed to give a shit about clothes—"

"But I don't give a shit about clothes," he whines.

I stare down my nose at him before I pluck a garment bag at random and close the bathroom door. (But leave it a little ajar because I'm nosy and I want to hear them.)

"Henry," I hear Taura say quietly, unimpressed.

"Sorry—" He sighs. He sounds a wee bit disappointed in himself, which is cute of him. "In my defence—" he calls loudly to me, "neither did Bridge, so I'm filling her role here well—"

"She would have pretended to care," Taura tells him.

"No," Henry says, and he sounds sad now. "She would have cared for real."

That makes me feel like I could cry, so I close my eyes as tight as I can squeeze them and tell myself that I'll talk to her later.

"I care for real, Parks," Hen calls to me. "Show me what you've got."

("Good boy," I hear Taura say. "Convincing?" he asks, chuffed with himself, and that makes me laugh a bit.)

I take a big breath.

"Okay—" I clear my throat. "I'm going to come out now and I'm going to be wearing one that looks—I think it looks lovely, but it's probably more of like, maybe the reception dress as opposed to the walking-down-the-aisle dress—"

"Out of curiosity—" Henry calls. "How many dresses will there—" then I hear a strange thud sound and a yelp then Henry clears his throat. "Never mind—! Not enough, probably. Never enough dresses in my opinion! You could—wear twelve dresses and I'd still think, 'Fuck, I wish there were more dr—'"

"Do stop," I tell him from the bathroom.

"Yep, okay."

"Remember—" I take a big breath. "Not the aisle dress."

And then I step out into the room wearing the Hunter gown from Alon Livné. A corset bodice, off-shoulder sleeves with a long train—it's sort of sheer all over, tulle-draped. Completely gorgeous.

"Holy shit," Taura says, staring at me.

"Fuck," Henry says, and his face pulls funny. "You look—"

He stops short.

I stare over at him, self-conscious, waiting. But he still doesn't say anything.

"Bad?" I offer.

His head shakes and then I think I see—

"Are you crying?" I blink at him.

"No," he scoffs. "Piss off."

"Are you?" Taura asks, getting right up close to his face. "He is!"

Henry shoves her away and I feel a bit relieved that they seem this okay.

I go back to the bathroom, Taura coming with me to help get me out of it and put on the next one.

"He's going to fucking collapse when he sees you," Henry calls.

"I said this wasn't my aisle dress—"

Henry groans.

"*Vogue* is covering the wedding—" Taura tells him, poking her head out from the bathroom door. "She has to have multiple outfits."

"Well, come on then—" Henry stands up, looking a little bit invested now. "What are you wearing down the aisle?"

I breathe out my nose.

"I don't know yet."

I'm a bit stressed about it, to be entirely honest.

"It has to be big," Taura tells him.

"Big, like—poofy?" Henry asks.

Taura tosses him a look. "Big, like *worthy*."

I sigh again and step into the next dress.

This one I had to pull some strings to get. A powder pink sculpted corset-bodice ballgown from Zac's Spring 2014 RTW runway. The skirt is so big you'd think there's a hoop in it, but there's not, it's just kilometres of this crushed (I want to say . . .) silk-taffeta. It's dramatic and beautiful and it makes sense for the sort of wedding we're going to be having.

"It's a bit of a spectacle, the wedding you know?" she tells him.

"Well, that's bullshit," Henry grunts from the room.

"The wedding's not for us, Hen," I tell him, try my best not to sound too sad about it.

"So who the fuck's it for then?"

I poke my head out the bathroom door and give him a smile like he's silly for not knowing the answer.

"Everyone else."

His face falls a bit. "Magnolia—"

"It's fine, Henry." I give him a big smile. "Now, how about this Zac Posen?"

TWENTY-THREE
Magnolia

A few weeks after Bridget had died—after the funeral—I woke up one morning and walked out into the living room.

"Woke up" is a loose term, I suppose. Sleep is funny for me since she left. That stretch of time where my eyes are closed is neither long nor short. I'm never rested, I don't get peace. I close my eyes, I wrestle the darkness that took my sister and then it's morning.

On that particular morning when my eyes opened, BJ wasn't there with me.

Strange, I thought—he'd not left my side since it happened—and then I heard him. Other voices too. Two of my favourites.

Henry and Taura.

They weren't technically at odds at the time, but then—I guess, perhaps maybe they were? Death has a frightening tendency to jostle up feelings that have been long subdued. I wonder, in retrospect—if Taura was losing Henry before either of them knew that she was.

I walked out in my pyjamas. The little satin briefs from Miu Miu in cloudy grey with a sweater of BJ's that I was sleeping in because it makes the darkness in my sleep a little bit less dark.

They all looked over at me, eyes big like they were collectively nervous.

BJ patted down on the couch next to him.

I frowned for a second but sat with him all the same.

Henry caught my eye and the heaviness of it made me feel a funny kind of sick.

"Parksy," Beej took my hand and then breathed out. He cleared his throat. Breathed out again. "We need to talk."

"Okay." I felt that frown of mine deepen and Henry sat down on the coffee table across from me, Taura kneeling down on the floor in front of me, offering me a tea.

I glanced down at it suspiciously. "How many sugars?"

Her lips pursed. "Two."

Shit. I blinked, looking between them all.

"What's going on?" I frowned, suspiciously.

"Marsaili called again." Beej cleared his throat. "They, uh—they need a decision on what to do with the body."

My brows furrowed. "What body?"

Still didn't feel real.

The corners of his mouth turned down. "Bridget's, Parksy."

And then it hit me again, like a train, that she's dead—always with the death trains—every morning, it's like a reset in my brain—how long will that last, I wondered? Still wonder, actually, now. How long til it stops radiating through me, and just becomes this permanent hum of knowing, where I don't have to remember afresh every day that my sister is dead and I don't have to lose her anew every time I remember it? Months, I'd find out—it'd take me months for it to not daily feel like brand-new information. It would take months of me being hit by these trains every day and months of me daily having the loss of her hit me like I am a small boat and grief is the wave that capsizes me.

Taura put her hands on my right knee, eyes all big and teary.

As we all know, I'm not very touchy, so I suppose in a way that kind of affection is rather odd, but it made me feel less alone, and Bridget always said I was afraid of being alone so I allowed it.

We'd already had the funeral—twelve days after she'd died—they tried to have us decide what to do with the body before then, but I couldn't—how could I? I couldn't even get my head around the part where she was gone; deciding what to do with her body felt impossible when I hadn't yet accepted her absence.

I still haven't.

Beej nudged my chin so I faced him.

"Your parents thought you'd like to decide, remember—?" Beej continued.

I said nothing, I just stared at him, all dressed down. The grey logo-print cotton hoodie from Palm Angels, Gucci's black star print track pants and the black Tasmans from UGG. I love him in grey. I wonder if he wore it to soften the blow? He suits the colour, he always has.

Tausie wiped a tear that found its way to her cheek and Henry tilted his head, sorry for me, then suddenly I'm drowning and nothing that anyone was wearing was enough to keep me afloat.

I looked over at BJ because for like, most of my life, even when nothing at all makes sense, somehow he still does.

I shook my head. "I can't—Beej, I c—"

"You don't have to," he told me, shaking his head quickly. "If it's too hard, you don't have to."

He looked cross, actually. I could see it on him, jaw set, brows low, knuckles white.

Really, without thinking, I reached for him and his face softened.

Henry shifted across from me before he gently said, "But do you really want them choosing what to do with her?"

I stared over at him as I thought about what he was asking me.

I shook my head quickly. BJ leaned in towards me and kissed my cheek, then pulled me further back onto the couch.

"So," BJ sniffed as he tossed an arm around me and buried his nose into my hair. "The most common ways of laying bodies to rest are burying them or cremating them—"

I stared at my tea, not drinking it.

"Burying," Taura said. "You pick a coffin, you pick a cemetery and a gravestone. Highgate Cemetery is really beautiful—" She offered me a sad smile. "That's where I want to be buried."

I stared over at her. "You want to be buried?"

She nodded.

"Why?"

"I don't know." She shrugged rather demurely. "I just think there's something quite dignified about it."

I blinked twice.

"About rotting in a box?" I stared over at her and she said nothing.

BJ took the tea from my hands that I wasn't drinking anyway, put it on the table next to Henry and then took my hand in his.

"The other option," Beej squeezed my hand, "is cremating her."

I snapped my neck in his direction. "You want me to set my sister on fire?"

His eyes went sad and probably if I wasn't in a vacuum of my own grief, I'd have been able to see that this conversation was hurting him also. I wasn't very interested in other people's pain at the time though. It's hard to be when every morsel of your own self is completely ablaze with it.

"It's bacteria, did you know?" I looked between them all. "That lives in your body, that eats you. That's how you decompose."

Beej nodded a couple of times. "We watched that one together."

Henry frowned. "What the fuck are you two watching?"

"National Geographic," Beej and I said in sync, except he sounded tender and I sounded toneless.

Henry pursed his mouth. "You know there are these biodegradable coffins where the coffin and your body degrade at the same time and then soon you become like, grass or flowers—" He leant over and touched my knee. "That's kind of nice, right?"

I shrugged, unconvinced. I looked at BJ. "Do you think I should just leave her to rot in a box?"

He gave me a long look, breathed out, his shoulders slumped—his shoulders never slumped—then shook his head. "Parksy, I don't think there's ever going to be a right way for you to bury your sister." He gave me a doleful shrug. "So just do the one that's going to hurt you the least, or the one that's going to somehow feel like the most closure."

"What do you think I should do?" I looked at Henry, pursing my lips together. "What would she do?" I asked them collectively, and somehow it felt like a beg.

Taura gave me a faint smile as she pulled out a notepad and a pen. "She'd make a pros and cons list . . ."

So that's what we did. We took our time. Found ourselves googling the weirdest things in the universe—like those people I mentioned at the funeral, remember? 'Ashes into diamonds'—what a metaphor. But imagine that—wearing a dead person on your finger. Is it serial killer-y? Part of me would like the closeness of her always being there, but then—my god, can you imagine? Bridget would absolutely keel over and die were she not already—you know—well, what I mean to say is she'd have hated it.

TURNING BRIDGET INTO A DIAMOND

Pro: Bridget would hate it; she would always be close to me.

Con: She would very likely haunt me.

There's a thing these days called aquamation where they used chemicals to like, melt your body down or something and turn you into a sterile liquid you get to keep in a jar, which at first I thought sounded interesting and then I found Big Manny the Instagram scientist doing it to a chicken breast on Instagram, and Henry actually vomited, so—

AQUAMATION

Pro: Better for the environment. (Bridget would care about.)

Con: Super gross.

There's something called a mushroom burial suit, and it's where you get buried in this suit that has mushroom spores sewn on the inside of it that accelerate the rate of decomposition and somehow they neutralise a lot of the bad things that live in our body like lead and mercury that are bad for the environment when they're released.

"What if someone accidentally eats the mushrooms?" Henry asks uncomfortably.

Taura's face pulled and BJ swore and pinched the bridge of his nose.

MUSHROOM BURIAL SUIT

Pro: Bridget would probably like it.

Con: Bit weird; someone might eat her as a mushroom; sounds about as fashionable as Bridget's wardrobe.

"Wicker coffins are quite beautiful," Taura suggested—and they are actually—there's something rather whimsical about them, and maybe that's something Bridge would have liked, but it was hard for me to have any sense of whimsy about her death at the time. Or now.

WICKER COFFINS

Pro: Beautiful.

Con: Reminds me of a picnic basket.

There's a new type of burial that essentially turns your dead body into human compost, which seems just so unbearably undignified, I don't even know how to fully process that one, and I refused to write it down.

Then there's a water burial—like, as in, buried at sea. But I don't think I ever heard my sister mention the ocean once in her life. Except it does sound rather peaceful, don't you think? The ocean being her final resting place.

WATER BURIAL

Pro: Calm and a bit lovely.

Con: Can't visit; bit random?; also, sharks.

"We could bury her at the tree," Beej offered, eyebrows up.

"Our tree?" I looked over at him.

He nodded.

"But my parents don't know."

He shrugs. "We could tell them?"

I shook my head quickly.

He pulled a face. "What—do you think we're going to get in trouble? We're engaged—what would they even—"

But I shook my head more and he stopped.

I can't really explain why it felt like in that moment, my parents knowing it would ruin it or harken us into a different time that I wasn't yet willing to visit, it just didn't feel like a good idea.

For a while longer, we kept googling things that probably now have us on MI6's watch list until all we were left with was this horrible, odd list of ways I might dispose of my sister's body, and it felt strange and abstract and not real at all.

"Does this mean we have the autopsy results?" I ask the piece of paper in front of me.

Beej shook his head, brows low, he licked his top lip.

"They need to know what they're doing with the body before they—"

"Oh." I looked down at my hands and felt more ill than I did a moment ago.

Taura nudged me gently. "Any thoughts, babe?"

Beej lifted my hand to his mouth and kissed it absentmindedly. "Let's just sleep on it?"

"No," I said quickly. "I want this to be over. I just don't know what the right thing to do is—"

"There's no right thing to do—" Beej told me gently. "Whatever you want to do, we do."

I looked at Henry and nodded my head at him. "What's your vote?"

He shook his head sheepishly. "My vote doesn't matter."

"It matters to me."

My best friend nodded once. "Cremation."

I looked over at Taura, eyebrows up.

"Highgate," she told me. "Or one of the other Magnificent Seven."

"So you think a coffin?" I looked between them, biting down on my bottom lip. "Do you know I read somewhere that a solid oak coffin slows down decomposition for . . . ages. Almost fifty years for a body to decompose—" They all frowned as I said that. "Is that a good thing or a bad thing, do you think?"

"Parksy, there's no such thing as 'good' here." Beej shook his head, then he pulled me up into his lap, angled my body away from the others so it was just us in the room even though it wasn't. He stared at me with the eyes I love most and everything went to black in the good way, even though the circumstance at large was overtly and undeniably un-good.

He pressed his lips together and swallowed. "It's all fucked, yeah—?" He gave me another gentle look. "She shouldn't be dead and you shouldn't have to choose, but she is and you do and it's all fucked." He tucked some hair behind my ears. "But here's the thing—knowing you, knowing how your brain works, you're going to think about her body in a box all the time. It'll hang you up. You won't ever get peace. You'll just wonder how far along in the decomposing process she is and that's what you'll see when you close your eyes."

I gave him a small nod. He was right.

I was already wondering that. Stage three would be my guess if they haven't embalmed her. They must have. My god, the panic in my chest at the time as I hoped they had.

I pressed my fingers into my eyes and breathed out my mouth, trying not to see my sister's body getting greener in a body-long refrigerator.

I breathed out a shaky breath.

"So, you think I should cremate her?" I said to BJ.

He glanced at Hen then back at me with a gentle shrug. "I think there's less threads for your brain to pull at."

"Okay." I nodded.

He nodded back. "Okay."

TWENTY-FOUR

Magnolia

You're not going to believe it, but guess who's back.

Daisy.

Just Daisy—in case you were wondering—not Julian. Which is fine, doesn't matter—I don't need to see him, don't even want to. I haven't heard from—whatever.

I'm just glad for Christian.

Glad for us too because they've seemingly picked up right where they left off, and it appears none of us are going to have to go through the rigmarole of their whole will-they-won't-they, so it's a Box Set dinner at Scott's Richmond.

Which is in Richmond, did you know? That's so far away, but BJ has been wanting to go there and I don't really care for leaving London unless I'm actually leaving London.

Definitely couldn't walk there, I'll tell you that much for free.

When Beej and I arrive, everyone else is already there—regular Box Set + Daisy + Romilly.

Taura's sitting next to Daisy, a seat free on her other side, waiting for me to come and sew her in so she's shielded from Rom.

Jonah whistles, staring at me across the table.

I look down at myself. Dolce & Gabbana's rhinestone-embellished cherry-print minidress with the sequin embellished cashmere cardigan from Saint Laurent on top. Black Ava crystal-embellished sandals by Balmain on my feet with some black mostly-sheer back-seam tights from Wolford. I'm holding the 1995 Chanel's CC diamond-quilted round top-handle bag, the red Tori padded velvet headband from Jennifer Behr atop my little head.

"What?"

"If you'd just put that dress on for him two and a half years ago, you would have saved us all a lot of grief."

BJ sniffs a laugh and kisses his best friend on top of his head.

"Oh—" Daisy stands, smiling at me. "I don't know about that."

She throws her arms around me.

"So good to see you." I smile at her.

She grips my shoulder. "Magnolia, I'm so sorry about Br—"

"Oh, pff!" I swat my hand through the air as though I've not got a care in the world. As though I don't have to stop people from saying her name out loud in case the shell of me cracks right there in front of them from all the weight of my grief.

"In case you didn't catch that"—Henry eyes me as he stands up to hug me—"that was 'oh, pff' . . ."

I give him a look, partly because he's the only one brave enough and stupid enough to make something even close to a joke within the realm of my sister.

Daisy stares, zeroing in on me in that strange way she can.

"Are you okay?"

I blink over at her and I can feel it bubbling up inside of me. My great, big no.

I take a breath and go to say something right as I realise that I don't know how to answer it so I tug on the hem of her black, sleeveless denim minidress from Saint Laurent.

"This is so cute, I love it. Did you pick it yourself?"

"Picked it myself—?" she growls, offended. "You're not Anna fucking Wintour."

"And for that you should be grateful," I tell her as I eye her black oil leather T-bar pumps from Chloé. "Pairing this with those when it's absolutely gasping for a knee high boot? She'd eat you for breakfast and then probably spit you back out because of your Mary Janes."

Daisy stares over at me for a few seconds then snorts a laugh, smiling like maybe she missed me. She nods her head at Taura.

"Swap with me," she tells Tausie because she's bossier than I am, and that's hard to believe.

"You don't want to sit with your boyfriend?" Taura asks, a bit annoyed.

"I've sat with him before," Daisy shrugs.

Christian nods his chin at her. "Missed you too, Daisy."

We sit down and everyone orders.

The food looks nice enough, though I can't honestly say I expect to eat a whole lot of it. I order half a lobster, which is a great meal, because it sounds like a lot of food but it actually yields not all that much in the end.

BJ watches me as the meal is placed in front of me and I take a breath that might sound like I'm steeling myself, but I'm not. Why would I?

"You good?" he whispers.

"Hmm—?" I look over at him, eyebrows up. I nod. "Yeah. Starved."

"Yeah?" He frowns, then shakes his head. "I mean—good."

And then I wonder if he knows—not that there's anything to know, really—nothing's going on, I'm just not dying over food at the minute is all. Appetites fluctuate, that's normal. They taught us that at Bloxham House. So, I don't have one right now sort of, in general? It's fine. Nothing for anyone to worry about, it's just a stress response. Some people eat when they're stressed. I don't.

Beej is still staring at me with not quite a frown, just a weird look on his face that I can't totally place, and then he does a smile that feels forced to me, and grabs my head roughly with his hand and pulls me over to him, kissing me on the forehead.

He says nothing. There's no follow-up. Just a kiss, and I get that feeling again like he's lying to me or hiding something from me—I don't know why?

Daisy elbows me. "Well, aren't you two ever the picture of premarital bliss?"

I flick my eyes at her. "Occasionally."

"Suits you," she tells me. "You two—actually together."

"It's how it's supposed to be." I give her a small shrug.

She nods back, almost coolly, almost as though it's offended her that I've said that.

Her eyes drift somewhere else in the room, but really they drift further away than that, and I know to where.

I lean in towards her and lower my voice to a whisper. "Where is he?"

Her eyes narrow. "Away."

I breathe out a little breath, and flick my eyes.

"What?" she says, frowning a little—defensive. Standard Daisy.

"Nothing." I shake my head.

"No." Her brows go low. "What?"

"He didn't call," I tell her, and I'm very sure that my voice didn't even remotely waver towards the end of that sentence. "When Bridget—"

"He couldn't," she cuts me off.

"Why?" I stare at her, unflinching.

"He just"—she looks away—"couldn't."

I tilt my head and give her a look. "Your brother could do anything if he wanted. Literally, anything at all."

"Magnolia—" She sighs. "Want, for him, seldom takes precedence."

Daisy folds her arms over her chest, and it feels like she's protecting him somehow by doing it.

"He was sad when he heard—" she tells me.

I roll my eyes at her because she's talking about him like she's trying to avoid a political disgrace and I just want to know why someone who I thought maybe, possibly cared a little bit about me hasn't said a single word to me in the worst few months of my life.

"And yet." I give her a little glare.

She rolls her eyes, looks annoyed.

"Is he okay?" I ask quietly.

"Define 'okay'—" she says as she keeps glaring. Which makes me wonder—?

I lean in closer towards her and lower my voice. "Is he sad?"

She curves a brow. "What about?"

I clear my throat delicately as I look over my shoulder to make sure no one can hear us. I'm not trying to be sneaky, I'm just also not trying to start World War III.

I whisper now. "About me."

"You?" she scoffs and gives me a look that makes me feel like an ant. "God, you're so fucking up yourself—"

I pull back. Woah.

"Sorry, I—"

"Un-fucking-believable." She shakes her head, looking away, and I find myself pushing back from the table.

BJ leans over. "You good?"

"Yeah." I nod quickly and I hope my eyes aren't teary because if they are, he'll notice. "Just the loo."

He squeezes my hand and I walk quickly to the bathroom.

I don't care if Julian's not sad about me, I'm not sitting here wanting him to be sad about me. And actually, probably, I'm just being stupid. No one's yelled at me in months, really. The only two people who ever yelled at me anyway were Daisy and Bridget, and they both disappeared around the same time, so—just a recalibration of sorts.

Christian yells sometimes, I suppose. But not much recently.

I stand in the mirror and adjust my necklace. A gold and emerald pendant from 42 Suns.

A girl at the sink recognises me and asks for a photo.

We take one—she's sweet enough—and then she leaves right as Romilly walks in.

She eyes me cautiously. "Are you okay?"

"Yeah." I shrug like I wasn't about to cry had a stranger not just interrupted my downward spiral, bless her.

"She is . . ." She trails. "Feisty."

She is, of course, referring to Daisy.

"Yes." I sniff.

Romilly bites down on her lip, watching me. "Henry said you were with her brother?"

"Oh. Um—" I'm not sure why that's thrown me. "Briefly, I suppose," I say, feeling defensive for some reason. Except that it feels like a lie or maybe something worse. So then I say "Yes" too.

"Did you love him?" she asks gently.

For a few seconds, I stare at the sink that I didn't even realise I was gripping, and then I laugh breezily, shaking my head.

"Daisy can just be so prickly, you know—" I shrug and Romilly nods but her eyes are pinched. She asked me a question, I know she did. I heard her. What's the point in answering? I know the answer.

I clear my throat and look back up in the mirror.

"Terribly rude, raised by a bunch of boys—one extremely lost one in particular." I flip my hair over my shoulders and lean in towards the mirror, pretending my makeup needs fixing but it doesn't.

"Magnolia, come on, are you crying in here—" Daisy says as she bursts through the bathroom door. "Am I not allowed to be mean to you now because your sister died?"

Romilly frowns at her but I don't even look at her when I say, "I mean, that would be my personal preference, yes—"

Daisy groans.

Romilly's frown deepens. "Why would you be mean to her at all?"

Daisy turns to Romilly and scowls.

"Sorry—" She shakes her head. "Who are you?"

Romilly glances at me through the mirror and I turn around now, facing Daisy, arms folded and looking down on her because I'm taller (although arguably she is more deadly). (Though I do postulate that she probably wouldn't kill me.) (Despite her brother's arguably insensitive and mildly hurtful sudden disinterest in me, I do suspect he wouldn't much care for my death.)

"That's Romilly," I tell Daisy and point back towards the restaurant. "She was at the table with us . . . She's Henry's girlfriend."

She blinks. "Henry's got a girlfriend?"

Rom looks offended now. "Christian didn't mention me?"

"I haven't seen Christian in four months. We're not . . . doing a whole lot of talking," Daisy tells her, and I roll my eyes because she talks a big sexual game but I know that's not true.

"Anyway—" Daisy gives her a quick smile. "Pleasure. Can you leave now?"

"No." Romilly shakes her head, looking at her unimpressed.

Daisy cocks her head in Rom's direction. "Is she for real?"

"She doesn't know who you are."

Daisy's face pulls. "Well, maybe you should tell her."

"Tell me what?" Romilly asks, annoyed now and looking between us.

"There you are!" Taura throws the bathroom door open. "Why'd you all just leave me at the table—? It became an instant sausage fest."

"Sorry—" I flash her a smile.

Taura flicks her eyes quickly between all of us and frowns.

"Right. What's happening in here, then?"

Romilly shakes her head. "I've got no idea."

"Nor I." I shrug, flicking Daisy a look. "Daisy disappears for four months and returns home with a hard reset on her bitch factory settings."

Daisy rolls her eyes.

"I just want to talk to Magnolia alone—" she tells Taura, exasperated.

"Why?" I ask, flashing her a bright smile. "So you can body slam what's left of my soul into the wall behind me?"

Daisy growls under her breath and shakes her head. "How someone didn't drop you off at a fire station at birth is beyond—"

"You played right into my hand, Daisy." I cut her off. "Thank you."

Taura nods her head towards the restaurant.

"Come on," she tells Romilly.

"She's mean—" Romilly says to her (not quietly) on their way out.

Taura shrugs. "She's okay once you get to know her . . ."

"*Okay*?" Daisy stares after her, offended, and Taura ignores her.

"I don't know—" I say, staring over at her as the door closes, my arms folded. "I might have picked a less savoury word."

She licks her bottom lip and sighs. "Sorry."

I stare over at her. Glare a little.

"I like that cardigan on you," I tell her, nodding at it as I cross my arms over my chest. Petar Petrov's 'The Kids' oversized bouclé-knit cardigan. "That shade of black really matches with the evil in your soul."

"Magnolia!" she growls as she stomps a foot. "I'm sorry, okay? I mean it. I've been worried about you—"

I frown. "Why?"

Daisy makes a sound in the back of her throat. "Can you not just take the compliment?"

I pull a face. "Was that a compliment?"

She leans up against the sink. "I suppose not."

I back myself up against a stall and keep glaring.

"You didn't call when she died." I try my best not to sound insanely hurt by this. "Neither did he."

"I know." She sighs. She does actually, in all fairness, look sorry. "We were—"

"Friends, Daisy." I shake my head at her. "We were friends."

She tilts her head, a bit sad. "We *are* friends, Magnolia."

"My god." I blink. "How do you speak to your enemies?"

She sniffs, amused, and looks away.

I don't look away though.

"Where is he?"

She looks over at me, eyes weighed down the way their eyes do. "I can't say."

When Julian and I were whatever we were, whenever something happened where I didn't really understand what was going on or he said something that went over my head, sometimes something about it made my tummy fall a foot inside of me; I get that feeling now.

"Is he in trouble?"

"No," she says too quickly. "He's—I don't know." She frowns at the ground in front of her then looks up at me. "He was sad, at first."

"Was he?"

"Yeah." She nods.

"About me?" I ask quietly.

She nods again.

"Okay." I purse my lips, not really knowing what to say.

She looks over at me, instantly defensive. "Do you want him to be sad?"

"No, actually. Not at all—" I give her a look. "I do want him to be okay though."

She licks her bottom lip and sighs. "Yeah, me too."

"Is he?" I ask quietly.

She looks over at me and stands up straighter.

"Are you?"

I cross my arms again, a bit uncomfortably this time.

"How long after your parents died did it take for you to remember it as a normal part of your life?" I ask, and she looks confused. "Like, when you'd wake up in the morning and you knew they were dead without having to remember it."

"Oh," she says; she looks over at me sadly. "Months."

"Really?"

"Yeah." She nods. "Like nine or ten."

"It's every morning." I press my lips together. "And through the day, you know? It'll just dawn on me suddenly—it doesn't feel like the kind of thing you'd forget, but I keep forgetting. Like, I see something on Instagram and I immediately go to send it to her. I have so many screenshots in my phone of things I want to send her—sometimes I send them—"

"Do they still go through?" she asks.

I look over at her and my cheeks go hot. Might as well confess it. She already thinks I'm a terrible idiot.

"I have her phone plugged in in one of our guest rooms. I didn't like it the first time the message went through green, so I plugged it back in."

And I've written an unsent message to myself from her as well so I always have those three dots, as though she's texting me back.

"Magnolia—" she sighs.

"Sometimes I call and leave her a voicemail. Pretend she's just ignoring me because she's angry I bought a mink fur coat from The Row—"

She frowns.

"But I didn't know it was real!" I tell her quickly. "Not until I got home and said to BJ that I thought £17,000 was a bit steep for a faux-fur coat, and he said, 'you're such an idiot—'"

"You are," she interrupts, rolling her eyes. "Such an idiot."

I nod once. "Bridget always thought so."

She sniffs a laugh. "Well, she was the smartest one of all of you."

I give her a look. "Didn't want to include yourself there?"

She shrugs. "I'm pretty smart."

I roll my eyes.

"Magnolia—" She looks over at me. "You're undoing a lifetime of neural pathways. We think of people like habits. That year where I didn't talk to Julian, I still thought of him every day—like a reflex."

"Really?" I ask, except that I know it's true myself.

I thought of BJ every day I was in New York. I'd thought of him every day since I was fifteen, it was impossible to stop cold turkey. I didn't want to stop.

I actually thought of him like it was a workout, the way he smelt, the way his hands felt on my body. I'd study in my mind the way his hair would fall over his face, and it was an absolute torture, and I suppose that tells you everything you need to know.

I think I knew—on some level—if I stopped thinking of him, I was letting him go, and so on that very same level, I still have my sister's contact pinned next to BJ's on the top of my iPhone messages.

I'm not letting her go.

15:41

Dad

I'm sorry about the other night.

What are you sorry about

I upset you.

You're sorry you upset me?

Yes

But not sorry for what you said?

BJ, I didn't say anything bad to you.

I just want you to be happy

Yeah ok

TWENTY-FIVE

Magnolia

From Kensington it's almost a two-hour drive to Varley. Technically, it's in Kent, which is obviously rather large. In the Dover district, if we're being specific.

Hamish went there, which I think is why we all wound up there, really.

Dwerryhouse is the prep school in London where we all went, which is where I met Henry. My parents were—as you can rightfully assume—fairly useless when it came to this sort of thing.

They found out Henry was going to Varley so Harley made a call and then I was going to Varley too.

Lilian was so upset that the boys were going to boarding school, I remember them talking about it at dinner a few weeks before Henry and I started school, and she was tearing up, so sad he was leaving.

I remember watching my parents, my mum nodding along like she understood, as though she had a single maternal bone in her body, like I didn't see the relief on her brow at the thought of being a little less responsible for one of the someones she was barely responsible for at this point anyway.

"She'll love it," Harley told the room, even though he hadn't asked me and I wasn't sure I would. "Love it, won't you, darling?"

I gave him a quick smile and a nod and looked down at my plate. Henry elbowed me.

At least he'd be there, I remember thinking.

My parents arranged for me to drive up with Lil, the boys and Jemima—she was in year eleven at the time. It was strange—it hurt my feelings, actually—that they didn't want to drive me themselves.

It was a big deal, you know? To me, at least. Going to secondary school, a boarding school—water off a duck's back to them though, clearly.

It came up at dinner.

"They have to be there by what time?" my mother gawped.

"Seven a.m." Lil gave her a smile. "Usually a bit later—half eight on a standard Monday—but on the first day of school, seven."

Harley rubbed his head at the thought, nodded his chin at Mum. "We'll get her a car."

BJ stared over at me across the table. He always sat across from me at dinners. He told me later it was for easy watching—cute. Stalkerish, but cute.

He was twelve at the time, and I was just about eleven. He said nothing, just looked sad for me.

I can remember about a thousand times over the course of my life when some member of the Ballentine family was looking sadly at either myself or Bridget.

"I'll take her," Lily said quickly. Flashed me a smile.

"Brilliant!" Harley clapped his hands together, and that was that.

The morning of came and there was absolutely zero fanfare.

Mum was hungover from the night before, face down in their bed. Harley wasn't in it.

I went in to say goodbye to her and she said, "Fantastic, good job—would you be a good girl and bring me a coffee on your way back?"

And I said, "On my way back on Friday?"

And she said, "Friday, Saturday. My favourite days. Love you."

So I went downstairs and Marsaili was up, because of course she was. For one, it was her job at the time, and for two, she wasn't a trollop back then.

She was making me breakfast; she was nervous—she cared I was leaving. I could tell because she was crying over the porridge she was making for me that I wasn't going to eat anyway because it was too early to eat but I definitely wasn't going to eat it after seeing it be made, watching her unknowingly stir in her own tears. Salty. Gross.

I stood in the foyer, waiting for the Ballentines to collect me, when who should stumble through our front door but my father.

Ten to five on a Monday morning, eyes blurry and his shirt undone.

"Hello!" he said, cheery when he saw me.

"Are you home to see me off?" I beamed up at him.

"Um." He frowned. "Yeah. Where are you going again?"

I swallowed. "Secondary school."

"Right." He nodded. "Yeah, came home for that—yep!"

He patted my arm. "Have fun."

I stared up at him.

Kind of a crushing moment, in a lot of ways.

I knew before then, subconsciously probably, that my parents weren't like other parents. I'd see how Hamish and Lily were with the boys, how Barnsey and, at the time, Jud was with Christian. Parents who parented without an absolute and utter indifference towards their offspring. I noted it in the back of my mind how you might notice the colour of a passing car in your peripheral vision, but that morning I noted it how you'd note the colour of a car that was about to run you over.

"Call me when you get up there?" he said, but there was an upward inflection at the end. As though he wasn't quite sure what he was supposed to say. He frowned at himself. "Do you have a phone?"

I nodded. Marsaili got me one. An iPhone 3GS.

Got Bridget one too, and herself, so we could talk to each other. iMessage wasn't out then, it was all green—gross—but we didn't know better at the time.

"Great." Harley nodded. "Talk soon then, darling."

He patted my head and ran up the stairs. I stared up after him and wondered, consciously for the first time after a lifetime of wondering it unconsciously, why they bothered having us.

"Hi," said a little voice from the top of the stairs.

"Oh, hi." I looked up at my baby sister, who was a baby at the time, all of nine years old or something.

She scurried down the stairs and stood a few above me so she was taller.

"Are you nervous?" she asked.

"No." I scowled at her.

"Okay, good." She nodded.

"I'm fine," I told her even though she hadn't asked.

"I know." She nodded calmly. "Henry will be there. And Paili."

"And Christian," I reminded her because I "loved" him at the time.

"And BJ," she added, but I gave her a funny look because that was incredibly irrelevant at that specific moment.

"Will you be okay?" I asked her, looking around our big house.

"Yes." She nodded quickly and sure. "Grand. Excited for the quiet."

I scowled at her again. "That's not nice."

She gave me the same look then as she's given me her whole life when she's unimpressed with me.

"You know there are girls all over the world, Magnolia, who'd die for the chance to learn." Such an annoying nine-year-old.

"Literally—" She gave me an extra-pointed look. "Actually dying to go to school—"

"Yes, but—"

"What are you scared about leaving, anyway?" She looked back up the stairs the way Harley went. "It's not like they're ever here."

I frowned at her. "You."

"I'll be fine." She shrugged.

I frowned more. "I know you'll be fine, you're always fine, but I'm not—"

She rolled her eyes. "I'm not that far away, Magnolia."

"I don't care about you—" I growled, sounding annoyed even though I definitely did care about her. "I'm not—that's not what I'm—" I huffed. "Will you be home when I get back on Friday night?"

She nodded. "Yes."

"Promise?"

She nodded.

"You'll make sure Marsaili cooks a shepherd's pie?"

Bridge rolled her little eyes. "Okay."

"And you, Allie and I will watch the *Big Brother* final together?"

Another eye roll. "Yes."

"Promise you won't watch it before without me—?"

"Promise." She nodded.

And then the doorbell rang. Marsaili let out a cry from the kitchen and Bridget giggled as Mars scuttled across the foyer, swinging open the door.

BJ was standing there.

"Good morning." He smiled up at Marsaili.

She patted his hair—it was a bit more golden back then—and went down the stairs to Lily, who was standing at the boot of the car, crying herself, so they hugged and started talking.

I looked down and Henry waved at me from the car.

"Hello," BJ said to me with a big smile.

"Hi," I said to him with a nervous one.

"Ready?"

I nodded even though I wasn't. "Yes."

"Is this your bag?" He pointed to my suitcase.

I nodded.

"I'll take it," he told me, reaching for it, as he flashed my sister a smile. "Hi, Bridget."

She smiled shyly. "Hi, BJ."

My sister and I locked eyes and I said nothing, then followed BJ down the stairs.

He paused.

"Do you want to say goodbye to her?"

"Not really. No," I said, and he frowned because he thought I was being mean to her but she smiled because she knew I wasn't.

See, I've never wanted to say goodbye to her. I never will.

TWENTY-SIX

BJ

It does happen still, every time I'm out without her—which is wild—I'm not quietly dating her, we're not rumoured-to-be-lovers, we're British bread and butter these days, and I think that makes it worse.

I walk in with Henry over to the table the Hemmes always get in the back corner of Boisdale. Pass some girls on our way who look at both of us like we're the main course they came out to dinner to eat.

Flash them a quick smile because there's a balance to fame that's hard. Can't be rude, can't properly ignore them, because fans—girls like these—we need them, I need them, so you have to acknowledge them, have to be available enough that there's still a buy-in, but not too available that it compromises my actual life.

Been weird vibes with the boys lately, and not because of Henry and Jo.

That's blown over, if you can believe it. We were in a clusterfuck of a wind tunnel for like five years between me and Christian and then Henry and Jo.

Out of it now, clear skies and all that—except something feels different.

Not off, but different. Like, properly changed, maybe? Don't know.

Order a burger tonight almost out of compulsion. Feel like I have to sneak them in whenever I can these days before I go home to a fridge full of green juices and ballerina teas.

Jo orders a cigar, so then we all do. Know I'll cop an earful for it—if she doesn't want me eating burgers, she won't want me smoking cigars, but I'd come home smelling like them either way.

I'll try to get into the shower before she can smell me, tell her it was just the boys if she asks. Don't want her to worry—

I look over at Henry and nod my chin at him.

"Do you like what you do?"

"What?" He frowns.

"Do you like what you do?" I repeat. "With Dad."

He shrugs. "It's a job."

"But do you like it?" I ask, folding my arms over my chest.

Henry's eyes pinch. "Heard you two had a row."

"What?" Jo frowns, chiming in. "Your dad again?"

"What about?" Christian asks, and I flash the peanut gallery an annoyed look before I repeat to them.

"I don't do anything with my life."

Christian shrugs. "You manage to fill the days alright."

"I mean—what's anyone doing with their lives, really?" Jo says, pondering it, and his brother rolls his eyes.

"Here we go."

"I mean it." Jo gives him a look. "What's anyone doing?" He shrugs. "There are too many balls in the air."

I stare over at him, confused. "What are you talking about?"

He takes a puff of his cigar and lifts his shoulders in the air. "Everything anyone does—it's either for love, for power or for money."

"Or sex," Christian adds.

Jo nods and points to him in agreement. "Or sex."

I toss Henry a look, not really tracking.

"Right," I say, eyeing Jo dubiously.

"For me, it's power." Jonah shrugs. Says "power" like how you might say you want another beer. "I want it—it's what I think about when I wake up in the morning. First thing—" Gives me a curt smile and I wonder if that's true. The first thing he thinks about in the morning is power?

"So, for me," he keeps going. "What I'm doing with my life is pointed towards that. But you—" He points at me. "Don't give a shit about that."

"And you—" Henry stares over at our friend. "Are high."

"Yes." Jo nods. "Not my point though."

Henry and I give each other a look. Jo's high just for fucking kicks on a Tuesday night? Historically, not a great sign.

"Man, what are you talking about?" Henry asks him.

Christian snorts a laugh.

"I'm saying it's all for naught." He sinks his drink and his eyes look a bit blurry, now that I'm looking at them properly. Why wasn't I looking at them properly before?

"If you choose the power path, Beej—or the money path. You'll build your dad's company, and he'll be proud of you for a minute then he'll die—" he announces, and Henry's head pulls back.

"Sorry," Jo says, looking between us. "But he will. And then that pride will cease, and you'll have this moment where you're like 'What the fuck did I do that for?'"

Henry shrugs his shoulders, trying his best to keep pace with Jonah's fucking sky-high ramblings. "Well, he's built a company. He'll hand it down to his kids and—"

"So his kids can be tortured as well by the pressure of not wanting to do what he didn't want to do in the first place," Jonah slurs before he shrugs, but it seems like it's mostly to himself. "Not that it's about want, like I don't want to be doing what I'm doing, but I'm doing it," he says to me, but he's looking past me, really.

"I'll probably die doing it," he says to the space behind my shoulder.

"Jo—" Christian frowns, looks a bit genuinely worried.

I grab him by the shoulder. "What's going on?"

Jonah looks at me, blinking. "Hmm?" He shakes his head. "Nothing."

Claps his hand on my shoulder and musters a smile.

"There are a lot of different things you can fall in love with in the world, Beej. I'm fucked." He points to Christian. "He's fucked."

Points to my brother. "Could be fucked, TBC. But you—" He nods his chin at me. "Arguably once upon a time the most fucked of us all, you're probably the only one here getting it right."

TWENTY-SEVEN

Magnolia

For Lily's birthday Hamish booked a super yacht for our combined families to go sailing around Corsica.

BJ and Hamish are still strained. I asked Henry if we should do something and he said something along the lines of, "I know it's insanely hard for you not to meddle, but try"—which I thought was a wee bit rude, but I can't say I have a great grasp on paternal relationships myself, so I don't even know where I'd start.

The room layout proved to be a bit of a catastrophe for the Ballentine girls—all of whom are presently relationally un-attached—because it meant the three sisters had to share a room (Madeline did, of course, have an absolute conniption), whereas the boys, both of whom are relationally attached (or, as their father so demurely put it are 'Going to do it all week'), were given their own respective rooms.

Mum and Bushka each got a room, Harley and Mars and then Lily and Ham.

It's a full house. Boat. Ship? When does a boat become a yacht? And how big is a yacht before it becomes a ship, I wonder?

There's a lot of people here, is what I'm trying to say.

The first two days were dreamy, in a funny way. Almost movie-like in their level of perfection. The perfectionism would, of course, be shattered every now and then when someone would talk about Bridget or say her name in the way that you mindlessly do talk about people you love and who matter to you; she comes up. She comes up and then everyone goes quiet, and no one but

BJ or Henry dares to look at me, like my grief is offensive or too big and bright to stare into the eyes of.

And I'd force a smile and say I'm fine and then I'd get up and go to the bathroom—I think everyone thinks I've got a stomach flu, but I'm just talking to my sister.

She would say I'm being pretentious by referring to the straw Cordobes boater hat from ELIURPI as my 'yacht hat,' and I know she'd be mean about me bringing fifteen swimsuits for a six-day trip, but you need options and have you seen Magda Butrym's latest swimsuit collection? Please, everyone should be grateful I capped it at fifteen.

Earlier today, Allie and I lay on one of the decks by ourselves and we didn't really say much but it was nice to be next to her, to feel the largeness of her grief pressing up against my own, like two giant water balloons that are being filled more and more and more and one day soon, the balloons will be so full of sadness and stretched beyond their capacity that they'll burst and soak everyone in their vicinity, but today is not that day.

Today is water sports.

Hamish Ballentine loves a plan and a scheduled activity.

Parasailing, waterskiing, wakeboarding, Jet Skis—you name it, we're doing it today.

Lily once kneed me in the head when I was in high school during one of Hamish's scheduled activities. We were on a banana boat. I nearly drowned. I went properly under, passed out and everything. Jonah spotted me, dove in and pulled me out.

Sweet boy, he was rather rattled by it in context of his sister. BJ said he thinks it might have repaired something in Jo, as though he'd carried around all these years not being able to save his sister back when it happened, and that after that day, where I almost drowned but he saved me, there was an ease in Jo that hadn't been there for a long time.

All that's to say, neither Lily nor I go near the banana boats.

My family do though because they're about as thoughtful and self-aware as a bag of chips.

"It's kind of incredible, no?" Lily says, her hands on her hips of the navy-trimmed, white cotton and mid-length floral print silk wrap skirt from Gucci, with the navy Belle Vivier embellished suede pumps from Roger Vivier. The latter are arguably not incredibly yacht friendly, but it's fashion over function around these parts. I picked it out for her. She's watching my father as he's sandwiched between Marsaili and my mother on a banana boat.

"I suppose." I stare at them, not particularly liking the feeling of them being praised for anything, but I concede. "A bit."

BJ watches them, shifting on his feet. He looks sort of cross at them, but that's not necessarily new.

BJ and my father have always had somewhat of a funny tension.

When we first started dating, I know BJ was completely petrified of him—but very quickly it became apparent that the person to really fear in my life was Marsaili.

Marsaili ruled with an iron fist. Sometimes.

She was the one who had rules, consistent ones anyway.

Harley would have rules in the hot minutes he felt like acting like a parent.

I could never tell what would propel him into fatherhood; sometimes he'd be the one to pass the Grey Goose, and then occasionally, for no reason I could tell either then nor now, he'd suddenly decide that it wasn't okay for me to sleep over at BJ's house when I was seventeen and would show up at the Ballentine's at three in the morning and demand I go home with him.

BJ always got a kick out of riling him up—and do imagine, BJ dating your teenage daughter—a complete nightmare.

It's possibly my fault, their dynamic.

Something happened when I was younger that no one really knows about except for BJ, which I think put them on a strange foot to begin with. I probably shouldn't have told Beej, I told him before we were even properly together—that holiday in St Barts?—I don't really know why I even told him, I just blurted it out when he asked me something. How was I to know back then that we'd be together forever and it would seed a passive-aggressive undertone to their relationship for decades to come?

We went to a celebrity wedding when I was seventeen for

one of the singers Harley works with often; BJ came as my date. Harley found us at the reception with BJ's hand up my dress and his mouth on my neck, and Harley cleared his throat loudly, waiting for us to stop.

BJ gave him a bleary-eyed grin and said, "Oh, hey, man," and then Harley lost the fucking plot. Threw BJ against a wall, his forearm against his throat. Someone took a photo, sold it—the papers went bonkers for that one.

"Trouble in Gangster's Paradise" was the title I believe *The Sun* went with.

Stupid and a bit racist because there wasn't a gangster in sight, and I don't think he produced that song.

All that's really to say, they've always had a tendency towards being prickly so I'm not alarmed or surprised or even suspicious about BJ's face as he looks down at my father on the water, sandwiched between both his ex and current wives, with a vague expression like he'd maybe rather like to punch him.

"Truly," Lily says, still watching them. "Some couples, once the marriage breaks, they can't even be in the same room—do you know our friends, Vrille and Tommy Thurstan? When she found out Tommy had been cheating on her, my god, inviting them both to your wedding, figuring out the seating chart—it's almost a NATO summit—but then—" She gestures to my parents, zipping around on a banana boat on the Amalfi Coast. "Here these three are, completely functional and—"

I toss her a look. "Well, I wouldn't say completely—"

Lily smacks my arm and gives me a playful look.

"Hey, let's go—" BJ grabs my hand suddenly, pulling me away, and I wonder if I spot a tiny bit of strain on his brow—maybe I do? Perhaps I don't? Maybe he's always a bit strained around me these days?

"Where?" I laugh, giving his mum an apologetic smile.

"Swimming," he says, pulling me towards the other end of the yacht. "With Hen and Rom."

They're at the back of the boat, canoodling like they have been the whole trip.

"All hands where we can see them!" BJ calls as we approach.

Henry pulls away from Rom, whom he's lying on top of on the deck, gives his brother a somewhat despondent look, and sighs, rolling off her.

"You're one to talk," Henry scoffs. "Your index and middle fingers were unaccounted for most of your sixteenth year on this planet, champ."

Romilly smacks him for that, BJ snorts a laugh, and I pull a face.

"How terribly improper to say, Henry." I scowl at him and he grins back, pleased with himself. "Shockingly uncouth."

"No, Magnolia—" Henry shakes his head. "Shockingly uncouth was the play-by-play you tried to give me about the first time it happened."

I gawp at him, furious, but BJ's beaming.

"How'd I fare then?"

Henry rolls his eyes. "She saw colour for the first time."

"That's not what I said!" I yell.

"What did you say?" BJ asks, smiling like that cat who got the cream.

I cross my arms and walk ahead of him. "None of your business—"

"I think you'll find that it is—" he calls after me, except that I ignore him and lay down next to Henry and Rom, where we spend the next hour laughing and talking in the sun in some kind of way that I'm sure looks like a European Summer Instagram montage, and I am happy and relaxed, and my mind is light for a minute, kind of how I think I used to feel. A bit free, unbridled by my new and ever-constant companion, grief, which makes it all the worse when she creeps back up on me as soon as the light starts to fade.

The sun starts to dip behind the horizon and I fall into the ice bath that is remembering my sister.

I excuse myself quickly and BJ gives me a sad smile because he knows me. He's the only one who does, who can spot it a mile off when the clouds come for me.

*

"Why do you only talk to me in toilets?" my sister would ask as I stand in front of the sink in BJ and my en suite.

And I'd say something about her being the human embodiment of a toilet and then I'd feel bad immediately, so I'd take it back.

"Do you even like boats?" she'd ask, peering around.

"They are socially precarious," I concede. "But we're not too far out. If I became terribly overwhelmed, I'd just make one of the boys row me back to shore."

She'd stare at me with a bit of a mean smile. "BJ is so lucky, you're so easygoing—"

I roll my eyes, say nothing, maybe look at my nails, flash her my engagement ring like some reflexive power play she wouldn't even care about because I don't think she's ever cared about being engaged and she certainly didn't want to get married to BJ.

"How's the planning going, anyway?" she'd ask.

I shrug because I don't know what to say to that—it's going. It's being organised, I think I'm the one organising it, I don't really remember. It feels sad and blurry to do it without her.

"Will Dad walk you down the aisle?" she'd ask and I'd look up at her, a bit stumped by the question.

"I suppose." I shrug, not having thought of that til now. The thing at the end of the aisle, that's always been my focus, not how I'd get there.

"It would be rude if he didn't, wouldn't it?" I ask her, and she'd shrug.

"You could walk yourself," she'd tell me. "You're not his property, BJ isn't giving him a dowry for your hand—"

"Is tradition not nice?" I ask.

"Only if it's nice to you." She'd shrug again. "Dad gave us away a long time ago."

"That infers he had us in the first place—" I give her a look.

She'd roll her eyes at me.

"We had some happy memories with them," she'd remind me.

"Oh yeah?" I ask, eyebrows up. "Doesn't ring a bell."

TWENTY-EIGHT

Magnolia

It does ring a bell, actually.

Far and few between were those bells rung, but they'd occasionally dong a couple times a demi-decade.

I don't have a great many happy memories of my parents together or this incredibly happy, picturesque type of family; not the way BJ's was—a life where if you were able to stand on the cusp of time, close your eyes, spin around and point, no matter where you landed, no matter what the year or the circumstance, Lily and Hamish were a united front, consistent and steady parents who loved the company of their children.

A series of incredibly beautiful, classic and traditional squares quilt together BJ's family experience, whereas mine, it's more like the dribs and drabs of memories you have during a night when you're blackout drunk.

Mostly, completely belly up, but occasionally, piercing through the bleakness of it all are these bright, cinematic flashes.

"Your parents are pretty fun," I remember BJ telling me once when I was fifteen and we had gone to Cirque le Soir, only to find my mother and father there, one drunk, one high, respectively.

There was this funny moment where we all saw each other—like we'd all been caught out.

I was fifteen, BJ was sixteen, definitely underage and definitely shouldn't have been there, but then, should my parents have been themselves in the club we were sneaking into? Probably not.

It would never have happened—never in a million years—with BJ's parents. Lily would sooner die than step foot on Ganton

Street after dark on a weekend. So maybe they were in the wrong too. The moment hung there, BJ and I staring at my parents, wide-eyed, their eyes all blurred from the alcohol and the drugs they'd been taking long before we got there.

And then Harley shook his head, cracked a smile and threw an arm around BJ. My mum clapped her hands together and gave Jonah and Henry big cuddles. I think she might have actually kissed Christian on the lips. Like mother, like daughter, I suppose?

BJ had always been a little offish with Harley because of that thing I'd told him before, but he toed the line. He wasn't supposed to know, he couldn't react about it.

That night was the first time I sort of watched him embrace Harley in one way or another, lean into the chaos, try to have fun with it.

It was a good example of how fun it could be when parents don't act like parents. A quick flip through the book of Bridget and my collective lives will give you around forty-five thousand examples of how it can be terrible/scarring/dangerous/illegal and/or traumatic to have parents who don't act like parents, but I think we know that about us already. What you might not know, the stories I keep much closer to my chest, are the few incredible memories I have where it felt like (a) they actually loved each other and (b) I was part of an actual family.

It was late one Saturday night. I was sixteen. Uber Eats hadn't been invented yet. BJ and I had just finished doing what teenagers oft do when left to their own devices in an unchaperoned room with an incredibly plush bed in the centre of it, and we went downstairs to make Marsaili cook something for us, only to discover she'd taken the night off.

"The gall." I blinked at the fridge full of food that I had no idea how to cook. "That's so irresponsible." I stared up at BJ, aghast.

"Not really. Like, your parents are upstairs, Parks—"

I rolled my eyes. "As if they know how to cook!"

He smirked.

"Come on—" I huffed and dragged him to my sister's room.

Allie and she were lying on her bed reading books next to one another in silence, like the adorable little nerds they were.

"Did you know Marsaili isn't here and there's nothing to eat?" I stared over at my sister, incredulous.

"Yeah, she went back to Scotland for the weekend—"

"FOR THE WEEKEND?" I yelled, and Bridget rolled her eyes.

"It's her elderly father's birthday."

I put my hands on my hips. "It's going to be her ward's funeral in a minute if I don't eat something."

Bridget eyed me antagonistically how sisters do. "Do you even like food?"

BJ tossed an arm around me and I gave her a look back. "Sometimes."

"I'm hungry too," he told them with a shrug, which—annoyingly—is what propelled my sister into action.

"We had dinner like three hours ago." Allie frowned at her big brother.

"Well, Al, I burnt all that energy off!" he told her, pleased with himself.

Allie frowned. "Doing what?"

BJ pointed at me with his thumb and both our sisters scrunched up their faces.

"Come on, then." Bridget sighed, leading the charge down the hallway to my parents' room where she just swung open the door without so much as a knock.

And there they were—I shouldn't care to get much into the weeds of it, but do be sure, it appeared a great time was being had by each of them, and were it a movie, I'm sure someone would pay quite a lot for it.

As it were, it wasn't a movie, and still, someone (them) were about to pay quite a lot for it all the same, but rather differently.

"OH MY GOD!" Bridget yelled, smacking her hands over her eyes.

I dove into BJ's chest, covered his face with my hands.

"All the money in the world, and you can't buy a lock?" I screamed at them.

There was the mad scrambling to cover themselves, accompanied by the annoyed grunts of my father and the giggling of my mother as they tried both to cover themselves.

"Disgusting!" Bridget yelled.

"It's nine o' clock at night!" I wailed, and BJ started laughing next to me as Harley wandered over to us, the bottom of him wrapped in a sheet now. He threw BJ's hands off my face and gave me a look.

"When would you have had us do it then?"

"I don't know—" I shrugged. "Once? In 1997?"

He rolled his eyes as my mother came and stood beside him, wrapped in another blanket. She looked very beautiful, I do remember thinking that. She had that sort of curious and special afterglow you get when you have sex with someone you really love, which was a thing I didn't know about until last year when I had sex with some boys who I didn't really love and I didn't get the magical afterglow I've always only gotten with BJ and maybe just one of the others barely ever, but probably not.

She reached over and rubbed my boyfriend's arm affectionately and it made me and Harley both roll our eyes, though admittedly it was difficult to blame her because while every other body on the planet is made up of 60 percent water, Baxter James Ballentine is 60 percent sunshine, and if you could squeeze the arm of Sunshine, of course you would.

"And then one other time in the year 1999." Bridget told them.

"Or!" I folded my arms. "Strictly between the hours of one and three a.m., when you have drugged me out cold—"

"Oh god—" Harley rolled his eyes.

"Cold!" I yelled.

Beej leant up against the frame of their bedroom door and stared over at my dad, that old cocky grin of his I love so much dancing around the edge of his mouth.

"What are you so stressed about, Parksy?" He looked down at me. "Nothing we haven't done before—"

Harley pointed at him, warningly.

"BJ!" Allie cried, covering her ears.

"Well," I tilted my head, conceding. "We haven't done *exactly* that."

Bridget shook her head, unsure. "I don't know if you should, either."

"You can all go." Harley pointed down the hall, but eyed BJ in particular.

"Oh, did you not finish?" Beej asked brightly. "Do you need a minute?"

"I need a minute to bash your fucking head in—"

"Harley—" I rolled my eyes.

"—Dad." Harley eyed me.

"If you say so—" I shrug. "Arguably, I look nothing like you."

I do a little, actually. I don't know why I said that. To get a rise maybe?

Bridget blew some air out of her mouth.

Harley's face pulled, offended maybe. "You look very like me."

"No—" I told him, eyebrows up. "Bridget does. I look like her—"

I pointed to Mum.

He rolled his eyes, exasperated.

"You think you got your skin from your white-as-tits mother?"

"Darling—" Mum sighed, disappointed. "Don't say 'tits,' it's very vulgar."

"Yeah, Harley—" I chimed in. "Don't be so vulgar."

Beej slung an arm around me and said nothing, but lifted an eyebrow and gave him a shit-eating grin.

"Can you, like, hit the fucking pavement, mate?"

"No." I shook my head. "He's going to stay over tonight."

My father's eyes pinched. "In the spare room."

Bridget snorted a laugh and I rolled my eyes.

"Okay," I giggled at his silly suggestion.

Harley looked over at my mother. "He sleeps in the spare room, doesn't he?"

My mother gave him a look and Harley shook his head, pointing at my boyfriend menacingly.

"I'm going to wipe that fucking smug grin off your face—"

"Excuse me—" I positioned myself between my father and my boyfriend. "But you've threatened my boyfriend like four times throughout this conversation when you're the one up here having S-E-X—"

"With my wife!" He yelled.

"Sick." Bridget growled at the same time I threw him a dirty look and muttered "Gross" under my breath.

I looked over at my mother, eyes pinched with a careful caution.

"That looked quite uncomfortable—"

Harley kept shaking that head of his as he breathed out what I think was probably a poor-man's attempt at a measured breath. "I hate this."

My sister cringed. "Yeah, are you okay?"

Allie looked over at her best friend and spoke with much more sexual authority than I'm sure she really has, even to this day. Then again, she is a Ballentine, so who knows?

"Some people like that, you know," she told Bridge.

BJ craned his neck to eyeball his little sister. "But you don't, yeah?"

"Some do." My mother nodded and I frowned at her. "Indeed."

"Indeed?" I scrunched my face up in its entirety. "Indeed you liked it?"

Harley looked offended. "Of course she liked it."

BJ elbowed me playfully and cocked his head back towards my bedroom.

"Should we—"

Harley made a choking gesture at my boyfriend. "I'm going to—"

"Oh—" Beej shook his head. "We're actually not into that sort of thing, man." He flashed Harley a high-beam grin, loving every second of his windup, but not Harley—he took a menacing step towards Beej so I blocked him with my body.

"Move," Harley told me.

I flicked my eyes at him. "No."

Harley nodded his head at my boyfriend behind me. "Break up with him."

"Also no."

Harley growled at the back of his throat then covered his eyes with his hands before he blew out more air.

"What are you all doing in my room?"

"We're all hungry." I pouted.

Another sigh from Harley.

"Yeah," BJ nodded along coolly. "Me and Parks just did a fucking stellar workout and we—"

Couldn't even get the sentence fully out without laughing but that didn't stop Harley from lunging after him. BJ dodged him as he skipped down the hall.

"Actually, darling," my mother called after her husband. "Your wife is hungry also."

BJ flashed my father a quick thumbs-up.

"Nice one." Beej grinned over at him, mid-run, which was followed by growl number three of the evening from Harley Parks, or was it number four? I lost count. So many growls. He loves a bit of exasperation. Marsaili has always said the man would never feel emotion at all if it wasn't for exasperation. I suppose that seems true enough, really.

Harley trudged back towards their bedroom, and he pointed down the stairs.

"Go wait by the door, all of you."

Those two went and got dressed (thank god), then we all piled into the Range and drove to McDonald's.

Context is everything, isn't it? Good memories with the four of us as a family were random islands and atolls that I swam to and nearly drowned trying to stay afloat for, whereas for BJ, happy times with his family were a whole continent. Maybe it's pathetic that that's one of the more tender memories Bridget and I have with our parents, maybe it's not. Maybe subjectively it's fine?

Because when you listen to that story alone, hear it for what it was in the moment, ignore that two weeks before that night I saw Harley kiss that girl from *X Factor* at a club he didn't know I was in, and focus in on the fact that in that moment—that specific moment—he was an attentive husband, a present father and just generally, a funny person to be around—maybe they weren't so bad after all.

TWENTY-NINE

BJ

The next few days on the yacht are good. Easy, you know?

Mostly lying about in the sun, pulling into ports, eating at the best restaurants. Hard to tell how Parks is going with food at the minute because a lot of it's family style or antipasto. What she's eating—or what she's not—bit harder to track.

Less hard to track is her face sometimes when she watches me order.

Ordered shrimp fra diavolo and she blinked about forty times.

Leant in towards her. "You good?"

She nodded quickly.

"You don't look good," I whispered, and the waiter moved on to Hen.

"It's just that shellfish is a very common allergen."

"Right." I nodded, frowning, confused as I gestured to myself. "But I'm not allergic to it. Neither are you."

"But you can develop shellfish allergies randomly, just completely out of the blue."

Squinted over at her. "But I haven't."

"How do you know?"

Pressed the tip of my tongue into my top lip. "Because I'm not allergic to shellfish."

She crossed her arms and looked away.

Rolled my head back and stared up at the ceiling of this old restaurant that's probably been privy to many a relational argument over its one hundred fifty-year history; wondered how many of them were about a hypothetical and completely nonexistent shellfish allergy.

Slipped my arm around her shoulders. "Want me to order something else?"

"No!" She looked at me. "That would be crazy."

She laughed nervously, and I fucking hate her looking nervous so I brushed my mouth over hers and ordered chicken cacciatore.

Little brushes like that aside, it's been good.

Good to be out of London—I always think that, we do so much better when we're out of London. No one gives a fuck about who we are in Italy.

Magnolia out and about with both her parents in London is usually front-page news. Here no one bats an eye.

They've gotten a bit lax though, those two . . . I've seen some wandering hands. Some stolen fucking glances, shit like that.

Told her dad last night to tighten up; he made this noise in the back of his throat like he thought I was being an idiot, overcautious or something, I don't know. Thing is, he's never been cautious. He's not cautious of anything. Never has been. Might go as far to say that he's actually almost willfully reckless—in most areas of his life—but I reckon I'd say here with a regrettable confidence that he's particularly frivolous about anything to do with that girl I've spent my whole life loving.

Always struggle in moments like these not to tell him that I know. Know what he did; what he did to her. Always wanted to throw it in his face, fight him for it, but they have such a complicated relationship as it is.

She hates him . . . almost. Like, has an unreal amount of resentment towards him in general—without knowing any of this new extramarital shit—so I don't want to fucking pile on, make it worse for her, because the thing is, she doesn't actually hate him. Acts like she does, might talk a big fucking game; don't think there's anyone in the world who's hurt her more than him, besides me.

Which makes everything that's about to happen so much fucking worse.

*

It's dusk, we've spent the day off the coast of Fiordo di Furore—taking boats in, laying on the beach. Bit torturous with Parks, who's getting browner and browner every passing minute, eyes are getting brighter and brighter—couple times throughout the day she looked so good I'd look at her, laugh and have to go for a swim.

We all get back on the boat for the sunset, me, her, Hen and Rom on the top balcony. The girls are a few champagnes deep—once upon a time that wouldn't have meant much but then, there's not much to her these days. Nowhere for it to go.

They're trying to do the Dougie. For the daughter of a famous black musician, she has alarmingly little rhythm.

Hen and I are laughing, everything's good and then I make a mistake—though arguably, it's not really on me—I pull her away from the others, drag her to the balcony rail to watch the sunset with me. Never been mad about a sunset, Parks. I like them though, think they're romantic, always have, so she obliges me.

I duck down a bit, rest my chin in the curve of her neck and we fit like we were carved out of the same stone. And we get a good forty-five seconds of that kind of rare peace, blissful, easy feeling of life before I feel her body tense up.

"Oh my god," she says, and I have a feeling before I see it, that it is what it is—that she's seen what she's seen.

Her dad, standing behind her mum, kind of how we are. His body proper pressed up against Arrie's. Couldn't pass it off as mates, no way. Not even as a kind of residual intimacy or the sort of comfortable you might accidentally slip into around an ex, it's proper sexual.

Chin isn't on her shoulder though, why would it be? They weren't fucking carved.

And then she's gone. Parks spins on her heel and runs downstairs.

Cover my eyes, breathe out and say "Fuck" under my breath before I go and run after her.

She's fast, remember?—hated athletics. Probably should have

done it anyway—so I get there right as she's standing a couple of metres away from her parents as she yells loudly, "What the fuck?"

Harley and Arrie turn around quick as anything and her dad's eyes land on me before they go dark.

"You told her?" He glares at me, and his daughter looks back at me, eyes instantly wide with distress.

"You knew?"

I squeeze my eyes shut. Fucking prick.

"No—" I say to her dad, my eyes dark, then I turn to her and nod once.

"Yes," I tell her, then breathe out, already over whatever the fuck is going on, then Hen and Rom jog down the stairs after us. "She saw you—you're not fucking being covert, man—"

"You knew," she says again, but her voice is quiet now.

I tilt my head. "Parksy, listen—"

Her brows dip as she starts filing back through time. "When I walked in on you three in his office on my birthday—"

"They were having sex." I nod. "I walked in on it."

"Oh my god." She frowns, and I can tell her eyes are teary.

"Magnolia—" Her mum steps towards her.

"Fuck yourselves—" She points to her parents and then she turns to me, looks wounded or something.

"You lied to me?"

"I was tr—"

"How long have you known?" She cuts me off.

I look away from her to her parents, her dad drops my gaze—piece of shit. Pretty quiet now for a big man—I look back at Parks.

"Five months," I tell her.

"Phwoar—" Henry breathes out, and I hear Romilly gasp a little. Parks? Doesn't make a peep, just inhales, small sharp breath, it's a pain breath. This is hurting her. Hurting how I knew it would, how I hoped it wouldn't.

"How could you not tell me?" she asks me, sounding small again. Sounds like the girl I fell in love with.

"Tell you what?" Marsaili says from behind us all.

Magnolia freezes, eyes locked on her parents but especially her old man.

He gives her a look, breathes in steeply through his nose.

"Darling—"

Magnolia turns to face Marsaili.

"He's cheating on you," she tells Mars. "With her." She nods her head back towards her mum before she glares over at Harley again.

"It's very Shakespearean, really."

Sounds mean, her saying that. Like she's stabbing for stabbing's sake, but she's stabbing so she doesn't cry, I can tell.

And it all hangs there for a minute, suspended in this weird moment. I've been Harley before, your mind racing as you try to figure out which way the sky's going to fall on you.

Like you're about to read the last sentence of the chapter you're currently living in.

And then . . .

"I knew it," Mars says quietly, shaking her head. "I knew it! You said I was crazy—you said I—" She trails and looks over at Harley. "How could you?"

"Mars," he sighs, rubbing his eyes. "Listen, I never meant to—"

"And you—" Marsaili looks past her husband to his ex-wife behind him. "I trusted you, I let you in our home—"

"I let you in ours first," Arrie says without missing a beat, not a drop of regret in her voice.

"Marsaili," Harley starts. "I'm sor—"

Slap. Clean across his face from Marsaili.

"What's going on?" my mum says, walking out onto the balcony now as well, followed quickly by an "Oh dear" about half a second later once she reads the room.

Mars turns and scurries away quickly and Harley goes after her instinctively then he stops. Pauses. Looks back at Arrie. Gives her a sad almost-smile, then goes after his wife.

And then Parks darts away so I follow.

"Magnolia—" My mum calls for her but she doesn't stop.

My brother runs after us both.

"Parks—" I call to her.

"Don't speak to me!" she spits without turning around, charging towards the back of the yacht.

"Where are you going?" I keep after her.

"I'm getting off this boat," she says, cross, hands on her hips, looking for a way out.

"We're in the middle of the Tyrrhenian Sea."

"Hardly." She rolls her eyes as she heaves a rowboat off its rack. "We're like two miles out from Vettica Maggiore."

I toss her a look, pretend I'm not a bit impressed by that show of strength. "You going to scale those cliffs back up to the mainland?"

"Maybe?" She glares over at me spitefully. She keeps dragging the boat onto the ramp and I get the feeling I'm in for a bit of a night.

"Well, I'll come with you—" I tell her. "Let me just—"

"No!" she growls.

My head pulls back a little. "Why no?"

"Because you're a liar!"

I blink a couple of times. "What?"

She straightens up, stares over at me, eyes all ragged.

"'You might be a fuck-up, but you're not a liar'—that's like, your mantra, isn't it?"

I breathe out.

"Magnolia—"

She folds her arms. Bad sign. "So are you both?"

That hurt, actually. Gutting. Want to say it felt like a low blow but maybe it wasn't?

My jaw juts. "You tell me."

She glares over at me for a couple of seconds and then she gets this look in her eye that I'm well familiar with and then I'm sure, absolutely, I'm in for a fucking night because she turns around without a word, pushes the boat into the water and scrambles in after it.

I growl under my breath. Pull the the Dolce & Gabbana button-up shirt she bought for me off over my head, because like fuck am I getting in trouble for wearing that in salt water—then I dive in after her.

"Parks!" I call to her, paddling after her. "Stop!"

She keeps rowing, but thankfully, not very well.

After about two minutes of rowing away from the yacht, she's lost both oars and is sitting there, arms crossed, not moving in the dimming light.

I swim over to one of the oars—the other one's gone. A gift to the sea gods—grab it, swim it back over to her and toss it into the boat.

I rest my arms up on the side of the boat and stare over at her in the quickly darkening sky.

"You done?"

"No," she pouts.

"Okay." I nod. "You mind if I climb in anyway? There are sharks—"

Her eyes go wide. "Are you joking?"

Shrug my shoulders a bit. "Feeding time's dusk, so—"

She screams and lunges for me, heaving me up into the little boat, and I collapse on her, wet, but again, pretty impressed by those Pilates muscles.

Our eyes catch and I stare down at her, best face in the world, push some hair behind the best ears.

See that soften her a little but she doesn't want to be softened, she wants to be stroppy, so she pushes me off and sits up, arms crossed again. I try not to smile at it, because she's a brat and I don't want her to know that most of the time I think it's funny—feel like if she knew that she'd bloom into this full-blown megalomaniac.

"Well, you've just completely ruined this Des Phemmes embroidered fringe silk Georgette midi skirt!"

I give her a look. "You'll live."

"You lied to me," she fires back.

I nod, sorry. "Yeah."

She glares at me.

"Why?"

I swallow—think about trying to soften the blow—decide not to lie again.

"I didn't think you could handle it . . ."

She looks offended at that. "I'm that much of a mess?"

"Honestly, Parks?" I frown over at her. "Yeah."

She pulls back. "No, I'm not."

"Within reason. I didn't want you to find out about that and not be able to talk to Bridge about it—"

At her sister's name, her face pulls how it always does now, the edges of that mouth I love and have always loved and will always love all weighed down with a sadness I can't free her from.

"But I could have talked to you about it."

"Yeah—" I nod, reaching for her. "I s'pose you could have. Sorry—" Shake my head. "I was trying to protect you. Your dad's never been much good at it," I tell her as I trace the scar on her wrist from the accident.

"No." She stares at it, brows bent in the middle. "He hasn't."

I nod my head back towards the yacht.

"Should we go back?"

"No." Bottom lip out.

I shrug. "Well, we're down an oar and I just dropped my phone on the ocean floor, so—"

"BJ!" She sighs.

I nod my head back towards the yacht.

"Let's go back. Pack up, stay the night, we'll fly home in the morning when we dock at Arienzo."

"Fine." She frowns and hands me the oar, snuggling into me as though she's cold even though I'm all wet. "But I expect you to body block my father if he tries to speak to me."

I kiss the top of her head.

"Nothing I haven't done before."

THIRTY
Magnolia

"Who's your stalker?" Daisy nods at Daniela.

"Oh—" I swat my hand. "Just my very present personal assistant."

"We're at a dinner."

"She drove us here," Taura tells her.

Daisy looks confused. "It's like, nine o'clock."

"I know—" I shrug. "She works incredibly odd hours. Long days. Sometimes she stays over! I kind of forget she's there."

"Yeah," Taura takes a sip of her drink. "She's really stealth."

Daisy stares over at Daniela a few more seconds and then shakes a thought she has away.

"Anyway, how's Marsaili doing?" Taura asks.

It's a fair question. Not that good, is the answer.

She moved into The Savoy, and I feel for her because I've been cheated on before, and yet I suspect she feels maybe as though she's gotten her just deserts.

She hasn't said as much and maybe that's me projecting because it's certainly a bit how I feel—quietly, at a whisper, my mouth pressed up against the ear of my fiancé under the covers so no one can hear me—but I wonder if she feels it too, because she is sad, heartbroken actually. But she's not complaining about him, not dragging Harley's name through the dirt—though he deserves it.

She's rather settled into the situation.

"Sad?" I shrug at the girls. "She's staying at a hotel. I think she feels stupid."

Daisy takes a long sip of her wine. "She should. Once a cheater—"

Taura kicks her under the table and she catches what she said.

"I mean"—she shakes her head quickly—"fuck. Sorry—he's changed, you know like, he's—"

I nod quickly and smile dismissively as though I think it's silly, as though it's not agony for me to think about, as though the thought's not my heart's weak knee every waking day. I flap my hands as though it's nothing, just wanting the conversation to be over now because actually, quietly, between us, in the absolute very dead of night, the bad part of my brain worries that she's right.

Taura grimaces over at me.

"Magnolia, I'll be honest—"

"Okay?" I frown, more scared than I want to be.

"If he wasn't your dad . . ."

"Oh!" I growl and toss the bread roll I've not been eating at her. It bounces off her and onto the floor. Can't eat it now anyway.

Daisy scrunches her nose up.

"Sorry, babe," Taura sighs. "But he is an absolute fucking smoke show."

I roll my eyes. "Shut up."

Daisy pinches her lips as though she's trying not to speak but then she does anyway.

"Okay, but no like, he's proper fit—"

I sigh. "No, he's not."

"Yes," Taura nods. "He is."

"Well," I stare at my nail beds. "He's a shit guy."

"Maybe." Daisy nods. "Wasn't he bachelor of the year right before he got married?"

I roll my eyes. "Yes, but that doesn't mean anything—"

"I think it technically means something—" Daisy considers. "At least, you know, on an aesthetic level . . ."

"He'd be a fucking tomcat in the sack, I can tell—" Taura announces, staring off to a faraway place I never ever want to visit.

Daisy bites down on her bottom lip and nods slowly, deep in thought. "He does give that vibe."

"Daisy!" I stare at her. "I implore you to stop or I will be forced to tell you in graphic detail what it's like to give your brother a blow job."

"Oh—!" Taura's brows shoot up. "I can chime in on this actually."

"I . . ." I grimace, my face pulling. "—sort of hate that."

My stomach does a weird flip and I feel a stab of not quite jealousy but something in the vicinity of it that probably shouldn't be there, and I mentally sidestep whatever that's saying because I don't have the bandwidth.

Taura shrugs as Daisy glares over at us.

"Well, I hate both of you, so—"

It goes on like this for a while. It's weird, I think, that they're my girlfriends.

A girl who, at best, I was wildly indifferent towards all my years at school, and at worst, I out-loud hated for something she never even did; and a girl whose brother and boyfriend I have been involved with. Funny how life works, the people you find who become yours.

"What are we going to do about this one?" Daisy points over at Taura. "Positively miserable."

"Just in matters of the heart," Taura sighs as she throws back her wine.

I feel as though this is the universe offering me a chance to segue the conversation.

"Right." I nod emphatically. "Do we know anyone single?"

Daisy's face pulls. "Your dad—"

And I put a finger on her mouth to silence her.

Taura chokes on her food a little and Daisy blinks over at me.

"You know I've killed people before." She keeps blinking. "In my life."

I roll my eyes. "Okay."

"Really." She moves her head back from my finger. "I have. I've killed people."

I give her a look.

"Okay," I laugh. "Same."

"Right—" Daisy's eyes pinch. "But breaking someone's heart isn't exactly the same as killing a person—"

"And thank God for that. Or we'd have a little Jack the Ripper on our hands, wouldn't we!" Taura beams over at me.

"Shut up." I roll my eyes at her.

"To clarify though, Magnolia—" Daisy stares over at me, eyes wide. "I have actually killed people."

"Daisy," I touch her arm gently. "You might want to tone that joke back. It's a bit weird, niche comedic vein, certainly. Like, you might attract the attention of the police—"

"I have the attention of the police!" she says rather loudly, and my face falters at the depth of her commitment to her weird little joke.

But honestly, I'd never look a universal gift horse in the mouth, so here I dive in again.

"Do you mean Tiller, because actually I—"

"Wait." Daisy shakes her head. "Hold on—are you being serious?" She looks from me to Taura, back to me. "How can you have been with my brother how you were and not know what we do—?"

"Oh my gosh!" I roll my eyes, a bit annoyed at how many times my intentions for this conversation are being sidestepped. "You're both so dramatic. Must run in the family . . ."

"Sure." Daisy nods. "Do you know what else runs in our family? Crime."

Taura's laughing now and I roll my eyes at her.

"Daisy."

"Magnolia!" Daisy stares back at me, incredulous. "Honestly, this is—unbelievable. What is this, like, glued-on rose-coloured glasses?"

Taura nods. "And a true gift to deny the absolute obvious."

"Speaking of gifts and obvious things!" I raise a finger in the air. "Tiller's arse is—OW!" Someone—Taura—kicks me under the table. "—What'd you do that for?" I growl over at her.

"Sorry—" Taura's shaking her head. "Just ignore her. She's like, drinking on an empty stomach."

Daisy glances between us. "What's going on?"

"Well—" I lean forward, chin in my hands. "I was just thinking how, now that you're back, which is so great, by the way. I love having you here—weird death jokes aside—it's brilliant you're back. And that you and Christian just picked up where you left off."

"Okay," she says, suddenly sounding suspicious.

"And you're with Christian, super, super 100 percent committed, and you love him terribly, yes—?"

Daisy glances at Taura and then back at me.

"Yes," she says, eyeing me.

"And you're such a well-adjusted person," I tell her with a smile. "And you're a nice girl who wants nice things for the people you care about, right?"

Daisy's eyes pinch. "Right."

"And you care about Taura?"

"—Yeah?" Daisy says, watching me carefully.

"And she's like, so alone and so sad without—OW!"—Taura kicks me again—"Would you stop that? Your shoes are bejewelled; considering your heritage and mine—this is practically a hate crime!"

"Would you shut up?" Taura says through clenched teeth.

"Oh, don't worry—" I swat my hand. "Everyone's family has a black sheep. And given, sure, yours was perhaps black to the soul, but neverthel—"

"Not about that!" Taura gives me desperate eyes.

"Oh!" I nod, knowingly. "No."

Daisy's looking between Taura and I, confused, waiting.

I clear my throat.

"I think Tiller and Taura would be great together, don't you?" I give Daisy my most brilliant smile.

"Erm—" Daisy's face strains.

Taura reaches for Daisy's hand. "I begged her not to—I'm so sorry—" Tausie shakes her head. "Ignore her. She's insane—unhinged—! She—did you even take your medicine today?" Taura glares over at me.

"I did actually," I give Taura a smug look. "Thank you very much, rude."

Daisy frowns at me, curious. "What medicine?"

"Vyvanse."

"Oh yeah." Daisy nods, thinking it through. "Yeah, totally—I see that."

"Yes, yes—" I roll my eyes. "My ADHD is apparently incredibly obvious to everyone now in retrospect, hindsight is twenty/twenty, blah blah—let's have some foresight. Taura and Tiller, do you see it?"

"No!" Taura growls. "Shut up. Sorry—I'm so sorry, I—"

"Kind of," Daisy squints. "Yeah—?"

Taura stares over at Daisy, blinking. "What?"

"Well, I care about him." Daisy shrugs. "I want him to be with someone amazing, and I don't know a better girl—"

Taura's face softens.

And then I clear my throat. "Um. Wow—"

Daisy rolls her eyes and gives me a disparaging look. "You're exhausting."

"I mean," I gesture to myself. "I'm sitting right here—"

"I know who I'm killing next." Daisy nods to herself.

I shake my head at her, give her a fond look. "The imagination on you . . ."

I give her a chef's kiss and she rolls her eyes.

Daisy looks over at Tausie.

"I'd be happy for you and Tills. Really."

Taura stares over at her, a bit wide-eyed. "Really?"

Daisy gives her a smile that looks to be a little bit strained but she tries for it to look easy, and I think she's incredibly mature for someone as young as her. I was twenty-two when her and Christian began and I was wildly in love with BJ and even still I didn't much care for their union, and she was a near-perfect stranger.

How adult.

"Yeah," Daisy says. "Really."

THIRTY-ONE

BJ

Grabbed a bite this afternoon with Maddie and her friend that she asked me to chat to about modelling. Dylan's her name. Pretty enough, got one of those model faces, you know? Not necessarily like, picture-perfect at all times, bit angular, definitely interesting, high fashion—kind of face girls think is amazing and men are a bit indifferent about.

She's been scouted, wants to get into it.

Maddie called me the other day and asked if I'd meet up with her and I said no, I didn't really want to. And my sister said "Sorry, too bad. I already told her you would so don't be rude," and that's why Allie's my favourite.

So anyway, I'm at an organic café on Westbourne Grove.

The friend's actually not so bad. Most of Maddie's friends are pretty googly-eyed about me and Hen, but this one's pretty normal. When I got there, I gave Mads a hug and a kiss on the cheek, did the same with this girl and she turned her head the wrong way and I got precariously close to her mouth. Whatever, not a big deal—happens to the best of us—same thing happened with another friend of Maddie's and then she wouldn't fucking leave my side for about a year and a half. Parks wasn't thrilled. But this one, Dylan, when it happened she just laughed. I laughed, Maddie laughed, we sat down.

Been there about twenty minutes, chatting away to the girls, when my phone rings.

Look down and my favourite name in the world pops up.

In the scheme of our lifetime there was maybe like, three or four months where she wasn't calling me—the rest of the time she'd phone me up like normal, five or so times a day unless we were fighting, which—maybe you'll remember—sometimes we'd do. Calls from her were and again now are a dime a fucking dozen, so you'd think I'd be over it, that the shine of her would have worn off, but it hasn't. Hope it never does.

Plug my ear and answer the call. "Hey."

"Hi," I hear her smile. "Where are you? I just got home— You aren't here—"

"Oh, you finished early?"

"Yeah," she sighs. "Sort of, I just wanted to work from home the rest of the day."

"Sorry—I'm just with Maddie and her mate, Dylan." I flash the girls a quick smile.

"Oh," she says. "Where?"

"Daylesford. The Notting Hill one."

Wasn't my choice, by the way, but nice to be at a restaurant without Parks that I don't need to lie to her about.

"Oh, will you bring me back a bone broth?"

"Yep."

It's not like I'm lying to her a tonne, by the way. Just like, Mondays, lunchtime, I get a burger at Patty&Bun. Just kind of started doing it a month or so ago. Can't tell Parks, she'd fucking lose her mind—like aneurysms are contagious and I might catch one from a BBQ cheese and bacon burger. Used to lie to her about the girls I hooked up with, so lying about some fries doesn't feel so bad. Doesn't feel great, mind you. Prefer not to be doing it at all, but I kind of need the headspace on a Monday, still feel like I'm my own man, not some fucking muppet eating rabbit food because I'm in love with a vegetable dictator.

"Shall we go out tonight?" she asks me.

"No." I shrug. "Let's stay in."

I'm tired of out, honestly. Tired of navigating how to get places, tired of trying to work out to make sure she's actually eating, tired of figuring out how to protect her from all the shit going on right now about her parents. Out is a lot at the minute.

"Okay," she says, sounds relieved I think.

"See you in a bit." Then I hang up and flash the girls an apologetic smile.

"The ball and chain?" Maddie says with an antagonistic smile.

I roll my eyes.

"How'd you land Magnolia Parks anyway?" Dylan asks, peering over her berry smoothie.

I pull a face. "I didn't land her, we've always been together."

"Not always," my sister corrects me.

I cross my arms and sit back in my chair. "If we average it out."

"Why would you 'average it out'?" the friend asks with a frown.

Fuck, I don't know—because I've framed my life by loving her? Because the most defining things that have happened to me—bar two, maybe—have been to do with her or because of her or with her, and fucking frankly I'm not interested in living or having ever lived any kind of life that was apart from her—won't say all that to this relative stranger though.

"We've been together a long time," I tell the friend. "Even when we weren't together, we were together."

My sister rolls her eyes a bit. "If you average it out?"

"Nope," I shake my head. "Just if you were paying attention."

THIRTY-TWO

BJ

Took some convincing, but I eventually got her around to see her parents.

Wasn't thrilled about it. Cost me a Hermès bag, but eventually I got her to—as she put it—"Schlep it all the way over to Holland Park."

"Hardly a schlep, Parks."

"Emotionally it is," she told me with a straight face, and she's probably right and I don't think she was trying to be funny, but still it made me laugh almost. Covered it though because I didn't want her to have a strop.

Her dad's been on me about getting her to talk to them in general but especially since the red tops broke it. Honestly haven't loved that either, like I'm some coconspirator with them, like we're in fucking cahoots about their affair, like it wasn't an absolute headache for me for months carrying that shit around for them.

Didn't get her to go for her dad in the end, it was for Arrie.

"Please, BJ," Arrie said on the phone to me the other night. "I can't lose her too."

Don't even know if that was genuine when she said it, but I've never lost a child.

Guess I have, actually. Bit different though. They got time with Bridge; we didn't. Don't know which is worse—?

Don't know if there even is such a thing as "worse" when it comes to grief. I've kind of come to think of grief the same way you might think about drowning.

Drowning is drowning, some people might be drowning for longer than others, some drowning might put you on a whole new path once you're through it, sometimes it might change how your brain works if you're cut off from oxygen for long enough, could even cost you your life—the severity of the drowning incident might be scalable but the drowning itself, the grief itself, it's all water you can't breathe in.

It's all been a bit relentless, the coverage, the photographers, the interest in her parents seemingly being back together and as always, Magnolia in context of that.

It's fucking wild to see actually, being on this side of the bullshit people spit about you that's just fucking bold-faced lies. Parks and I have had a tonne in our time, obviously. Sometimes the stories are based on a tiny shred of truth, and then other times, it's like someone just pulls it out of their bollocking arse.

There was one about Parks getting knocked up by Edward from *Twilight* back in the day. Weren't even friends, we all met one night in a club, I was there. She was Team Jacob anyway, never had been a fan of that sickly-white, Victorian man-child. Still, someone got one photo, from one specific angle, made it look like something it wasn't, and it's all fucking smoke and mirrors around here. None of it's real, even if it's real. Even if they're reporting something true, like now, with her parents—there are still lies.

Headlines like "Magnolia Thrilled at Parents' Timely Reunion," and "Magnolia the Matchmaker! How Britain's favourite it-girl used her sister's death to Parent Trap her parents back together."

All lies, all like, proper codswallop. No one cares, they print the headlines anyway.

I don't know how to take this, but I noticed Magnolia put a yellow smiley face on one side of Bridget's urn and a frowning face on the other. She seems to swivel the faces around according to something—her mood? Bridget's? I don't know.

It was frowning when we left.

"Magnolia, darling!" her mother coos to her daughter as we

stand on the front steps of her ex-husband's home that I guess in a way, she never really left. "So wonderful to see you—" Arrie leans in to kiss Parks on the cheek but she dodges it and walks right on in.

Arrie breathes out, sounds a bit disheartened but it's only for a second; she blinks it away, locks eyes with me and lights up, planting one on my cheek instead.

"BJ." She gives me a warm smile and I give her one back. Got a soft spot for her, can't help it. She looks like a messier, white version of the love of my life. Same eyes, that alone is enough to win my allegiance, but throw in the fact that we're all missing the same girl and I'm putty in Arina Parks' hands.

Harley tries to engage Magnolia with a smile but she trots past him, arms crossed, and plops herself in the "boss chair" of the formal living room.

Don't think that's a real thing, by the way. It's just what her and Bridge have always called that seat in their house. The chair itself has changed countless times over the course of our lives but the power that seating position wields remains legend among the Parks. Arrie brokered her big Harrods deal in that chair. Rumour has it Harley bought the catalogue of arguably the biggest male artist in the world while sitting in this chair. The girls swear up and down that Bushka sat here once with someone from MI6 and gave them intel that prevented something happening with the KGB—who knows, but even their parents buy into it because once Harley sees she's sitting in it today, he rolls his eyes and sits down in a less powerful seat.

Parks folds her hands in her lap and looks over at her parents, eyes pinched, poised, waiting—like she's a fucking crime boss, and I wonder for a quick second how much her time with Julian—however brief it was—might have rubbed off on her.

When no one says anything, Magnolia lifts an eyebrow.

"You summoned me, did you not?"

"Summoned?" Harley rolls his eyes. "You're not the bloody Ghost of Christmas Past."

Magnolia purses her lips as she pauses for a few seconds. "I do feel as though a visit from a yuletide ghost might do wonders for your soul."

He rolls his eyes. "My soul's fine."

"No, you're right." Magnolia gives him a sarcastic look. "You're the picture of emotional health."

Her father rubs his face all tired.

"We're so glad you came—" Arrie says, offering both me and Parks a smile, but trying in especially to catch eyes with her daughter.

Magnolia folds her arms in front of herself. "I'm here because I was promised an Osier Wicker Picnic Kelly."

Her parents both glance over at me, probably wondering which of us is footing that £80,000 bill.

"I'm gonna—" I nod my head in the direction of nothing. "Pick it up from Sotheby's later."

Harley flicks his eyebrows at no one in particular, looks relieved. Maybe I'll bill him, the dick.

"I know what you're thinking, darling—" her mother says, sounds more sage and more maternal than I've heard her in years. "Don't worry, they signed a prenup."

"Wasn't what I was thinking," Parks says, shaking her head once, but on the way over here, Magnolia did say "Do you think they signed a prenup?"—but I like being engaged, so I bite my tongue on that one.

Parks looks over at her dad, brows low. "Are you really thinking about getting divorced? Again?"

Harley blinks a few times and leans forward.

"I mean—I'm considering it."

Magnolia scoffs a little laugh, shaking her head. "Your lawyer must have whiplash! Fuck, I have whiplash—"

Harley breathes out his nose, slow and steady. Pretends her disappointment in him doesn't weigh heavy on him, but it does because we're all mere mortals and for some reason, her being pissed off at you kicks your world a little off its axis.

"I don't have to explain myself to you, Magnolia," he tells her, which strikes me as both a brave and stupid thing to say to her.

She leans forward a bit, eyeing him.

"Yes, you do—she raised us."

"Raised you—" He rolls his eyes. Second stupid thing he's done in under ten seconds.

"Yes," Magnolia says clearly. "Raised us. She's not some random up-and-coming singer from America. She raised us. And then you fucked her and married her and made her fully dependent on you and now you're fucking her a different way—"

"I'm not going to leave her with nothing—" Harley cuts in.

"But you are leaving her?" Magnolia asks, eyebrows up.

"I—" Harley shakes his head. "I don't know! This is new—we're"—he catches eyes with Arrie, swallows—"figuring it out."

Magnolia sits back in the chair—throws herself back in it, if I'm honest. Pouty, like a teenager.

They say that people freeze the age they got famous. Means she's stuck at about fifteen, Arrie at nineteen and Harley at twenty-two. What a fucking shit show.

"You're too old for this shit," Magnolia tells them, cross.

"We're not that old," Harley tells her.

"You're pretty old," Magnolia tells him, staring at her nails.

"I'm forty-five," Arrie tells her with a smile.

"I'm forty-eight," Harley adds.

"Positively ancient." Magnolia scowls, staring over at me, like I'm actually going to weigh in and call my future mother-in-law old to her face. "Yuck," Parks adds with a crinkled-up nose, just to annoy them because she's fucking good at it.

Harley gives her a sarcastic smile. "I do so love it when you visit us."

"Is there an us?" Magnolia asks, gesturing between her parents, and even though she wouldn't want it there, and she definitely wouldn't want anyone to hear it, I do because I know her the way I do—I don't even know what I'd call it—? A nervous tenderness, maybe. An undertow of fear to the question she just asked.

And then her dad answers it how I was afraid he might.

"Magnolia!" He growls a bit. "Fuck—can you just give us a fucking minute to work it out ourselves—"

"No!" she yells back, jumping to her feet because they fight like we used to. Ground floor to the ninety-ninth with the push of a single button. "I can't! This all should've been worked out before I was born but you're still acting like children when you have children!"

And then they all go tense, even me, because Bridget's the corpse laying in the middle of every room we all walk into these days, not a one of us ready to bury her.

"A child?" Magnolia says, frowning, thinking about it. She looks over at me for clarification. "Children?"

"Children," Harley tells her firmly, with a frown. He licks his bottom lip and nods a few times, I don't know at what. "Magnolia, I understand that this is hard for you. It's hard for me too—"

"How?" she asks loudly, and I don't think she notices her mum pressing a tear into her own face.

"How is it hard for you?" Magnolia asks again. "How, because you're the one doing it! No one is making you. You did it by yourself!"

Arrie gives her a gentle smile and speaks up. "You know it wasn't just him, darling. I did it too."

Weird time to speak up, if I'm honest. Ballsy, but weird.

Parks glances over at her mother out of the corner of her eye. "I know he didn't." She squares her shoulders. "You don't want to hear what I have to say to you—"

Arrie nods bravely, that crazy woman.

"Yes, I do."

I touch my fiancée on the small of her back. Put my mouth close as I can to her ear. "Parksy, maybe we should go—"

"Don't be silly, BJ." Arrie gives me a smile that I know she means to be brave but really, I can see it, it's all laced with fear. "I'm sure she's said much worse to me before."

I press my hand into my mouth because I fucking doubt it.

I can see it, pooling up behind the tide in her eyes, all the time since Bridget died, this percolating anger, mounting resentment for the way they were (or weren't, depending on her disposition of the day) raised.

"Okay." Magnolia nods once, sounds calm in her voice but I know those eyes. They're steep and she's backed up on the edge of a cliff.

"You're pathetic." Magnolia glares. "He cheated on you and now you're just—back together? How desperate are you?"

And I love her—I know you know I do, but fuck—her self-awareness sometimes . . . ? Doesn't even occur to her that—you know? She can't see it. That she's her mum here and I'm her dad.

Everyone else can but her. Her mum's eyes don't move from the place on the floor they've found, but her dad's, they wander over to me and I give him a little glare. Don't like the insinuation coming from him.

What he did is worse and I only did it once. He's fucked Arrie over more times than I could count on two hands.

It's been a strange watch over the years, actually. Parks thinks her parents were a marriage of convenience because they've lived pretty separate lives for a long time now, but I think that's a coping mechanism for Arrie.

I've said it before, her faces, they're like Parks'. I know them. I see how she lights up when Harley walks into a room, how she sits up straighter when he walks past her, how her stomach tenses when she'd see him touch Marsaili like she was waiting for a physical blow—Harley, I can't read. He's a fucking mystery. He's cheated on Arrie as long as I've been around in some capacity or another and then the person he ultimately leaves her for is the girls' nanny?

Arrie looks up at Harley the same way Parks looks up at me, for some sort of assurance that everything's okay, and he's not consistent with how he treats her in normal life, at least he hasn't been for the last decade, but today he gives her a steadying look, a small nod—doesn't say a word to her but I watch it make her feel better all the same.

Magnolia's too fucked off to see it, not willing to be softened by the reality of the circumstance. She's got an overzealous sense of justice and a flair for the dramatic. I don't know what here she's finding the most unjust—Marsaili being left, her mum taking him back, her dad getting away with all his shit, her parents trying to sort their shit out when she's a grown-up, or maybe just all of it happening without Bridge being here.

Probably all of the above but especially the latter.

I slip my hand into Parks' and tug her towards the door.

"We'll see you soon, yeah?" I tell her parents with an apologetic smile.

Her dad nods, forces a smile he doesn't want to give.

Then Magnolia pauses at the front door and looks over her shoulder at them angrily. "I wouldn't count on it."

THIRTY-THREE
Magnolia

I've avoided her, if I'm honest.

That's bad of me, I know. Selfish. Which I am, by the way. Particularly in an emotional-preservation sense, I'm incredibly selfish. Bridget used to say that to me all the time, and I feel a hot kind of crossness in my chest at my sister for dying and not being here with me dealing with the absolute fiascos we've been forced to call parents.

Initially, she didn't want to see anyone. Just that older sister of hers who flew over from Scotland—the shit one—they were holed up in the hotel room for a few weeks.

I called a couple of times but Marsaili didn't answer, the sister did.

She did text me though, which I suppose is something, though not really at the same time.

About two weeks after the fact, I'm finally asked to come to the hotel she's staying at.

Just me, not BJ. A specific request of which I can't say I was overly fond, but BJ said to take this one on the chin and just go see her, that he'd wait downstairs for me in the lobby, which he does, because he's like that.

Love is so strange, don't you think? The last time I saw Marsaili before all this, she was on a boat off the Amalfi Coast, kissed by both the sun and my father, cheeks that sort of lovely rosy glow you have when you're in love and you think everything is fine, and it's hard to look her square in the eye as she opened the hotel door because the disparity is stark.

Pale skin, dishevelled hair, eyes all sunken and the skin around them worn from wiping away tears I'm increasingly sure my father isn't worth crying over . . .

She opens the door and barely pulls me inside before she's crying again.

"Do you think I'm a fool?" she asks without looking at me, face buried in a tissue.

I sit on the edge of her bed and shake my head at her.

"No, of course not."

"You do." She nods, walking towards me.

"I don't!" I insist before I accidentally pause. "Well—a tiny bit, but—"

"I ruined everything." She sniffs. "And for what? For him to run back to her? For him to ruin me too?"

"Mars," I reach for her hand. "You're not ruined, you're just—"

"A fool?" she says, and I say nothing. Maybe that's bad of me but I don't know what to say. Once upon a time, a couple of years back, I'd have been incredibly staunch that this is exactly what she deserved, but here, now, some time and life and distance between the circumstances then and the circumstances now, I'm not sure anyone should be made to feel like a fool, even if they were one.

Love makes you into one, I think.

It's one of love's lesser qualities.

"He is a fool," I tell her. "And a thousand other worse words. He's always been."

She nods quickly, like the mention of him hurts her. I didn't even say his name, just the air of him, or something—and I feel sad for her because it's a pain I've known well, and I think you can only know that kind of pain in the face of loving someone in that sort of terrible, true way. I haven't ever thought of her loving my father or my father loving her or even possibly my parents loving one another in at all a genuine way. It always felt abstract and distant to me, a two-dimensional, sort of lofty adult love that wasn't visceral, not something you feel in the bones of yourself, nor grounded in the grittiness of the kind of real love BJ and I have or Christian and Daisy have, where we've dug in the earth for it, our hands are dirty but we've cultivated something special; but looking at her face now, I wonder if they had a version themselves of true love.

"And the papers—I know it's shit, but it'll blow over," I tell her. "They're just awful at first—"

Mars nods, wiping her nose with another tissue.

"And I know it can seem impossibly relentless. They're monsters. I didn't really set them up, I prom—"

"I know." She puts her hand on top of mine. "I know you didn't."

"I promise, in a week and a half, the duke will allegedly be having an affair again with the Marchioness of Cholmondeley, or Rush and I will have run off to have a secret wedding or something and they'll move on and they'll stop talking about you and you'll feel like you can go outside again—"

"Magnolia darling—" She takes my hand, shifting in towards me. She opens her mouth to say something and nothing comes out. She frowns briefly, like she's surprised herself by her silence. She presses her lips together and tries again. "I'm going to go back to Scotland for a while."

"Oh." I give her a quick smile. "For the weekend?"

"No." She tilts her head, eyes pinched. "I—don't want to be here right now. Your parents aren't being subtle . . . and I—the media, I—" She gives me a quick smile. "You're much stronger than anyone gives you credit for, Magnolia. I hope you know that."

To be fair to her, it has been a feeding frenzy.

Everything from "Nanny Gets Her Just Deserts" to "Harley's at It Again" to "Arrie Parks vs. Marsaili MacCailin: Everything You Need to Know About Britain's Biggest Scandal."

And it's been interesting—there's been some divide, not everyone feels sorry for Marsaili, and not everyone is pleased for my mother?

I see magazine covers where I'm in the middle, photos of Mum and Marsaili on either side of me, Harley in the corner—"A Family Torn Apart."

That much at least is true. Truer still might be this title: "A Family Tearing at the Seams in Slow Motion."

If Bridget was the thread that held us together, every day without her is a seam popped. I don't know how many are left.

Less than I thought, I suppose, what with all this happening.

"Well," I frown. "Then when will you be back?"

She swallows, uneasy. "I'm not sure."

I purse my mouth.

"You don't have a return date on your flight?"

"I'm going to drive. Take my car," she tells me, followed by a brief pause. "My belongings."

"Wait—" I blink a couple of times.

"Your belongings?" I shake my head. "You're moving to Scotland? You're leaving me?"

"No, darling!" She reaches for my hand and I move it away quickly.

She presses her lips together and breathes out her nose, she gives me a delicate look.

"I'm going home to my family to take a breath—you have to understand how painful this is for me—"

"He has affairs! It's what he does!" I shrug a bit wildly. "It's his quirk!"

She shakes her head. "It's not a quirk I'm interested in."

"You used to be!" I tell her quickly, and she gives me a look as though I've hurt her. "Sorry," I say quickly because I wasn't trying to be mean, it just came out. I stare at my hands.

"So you're leaving," I say, not a question really, just a statement.

"For the time being," she says in a way that makes me think the words are to placate me, not to convey a genuine intent.

"What about me?" I ask, and I feel like I'm seven, trying to get Harley to look up from his newspaper to see the dress I put on to wear to his party.

"Magnolia—" She sighs. "You're twenty-four. You don't live at home, you have BJ—"

"What about Bushka?"

She gives me a sad smile, because she does love Bushka. "I'll miss her, but she'll be okay."

And then I start to feel funny. There's a feeling I get sometimes where it's like there's a raptor scratching away at my stomach from the inside. Or an elephant standing on my throat. Do you know what I mean? But it's only sometimes, and I'm quite sure I'm actually completely fine and I'm just being dramatic. Raptors scratch stomachs and elephants stand on throats and people come and go, that's just life. Parents and guardians come and go, lovers too. Actually, evidentially, sisters as well. People leave, relationships change, one day someone feels like your family and then they have an affair with your father and then they break up and then they leave because they actually aren't your family, and you were a job and that's all and that's fine. It's fine, everything is fine.

"Okay." I swallow quickly and straighten my shoulders. "Sounds like a plan. Have fun."

"Magnolia—" She sighs. "Surely, you of all people can understand needing to get away from London in an instance like this."

"Completely." I nod emphatically as I stand to my feet. "I hope Scotland's a blast."

"Sweetheart—" She sighs, standing and reaching for me, but I take a step away from her.

"I'm fine," I tell her even though she didn't ask. I walk towards the door. "I'm glad for you. You definitely deserve a break after the last couple of years of unemployment, being a kept woman must be so exhausting—"

She frowns. "Magnolia—"

I look over my shoulder. "Goodbye, Marsaili."

THIRTY-FOUR

BJ

Magnolia took Mars dipping out worse than I thought she might. Probably actually worse than Mars thought she might have as well.

Tried to talk to her about it, soften the blow of it all—didn't go over super well when I reminded her that she herself left when she found out about me and Paili.

"You don't get it," she said, arms crossed, annoyed at me. "You have parents who want you."

She says shit like that every now and then, has since we were young. Kind of rough. There's not a lot of room for me to have an issue with my parents, even when I have them, just because in comparison to her mine are fucking saints. But saints are people too, and people fuck up. Not much use talking to her about them though. She sees them in the same golden light she sees me in, which I am by and large very grateful for, but occasionally it serves me as a disadvantage.

Mars leaving or—maybe she'll come back, I'm not sure?—whatever she's doing, it's a type of abandonment. Even if it's not, Parks is taking it as one.

Magnolia likes to leave before she's left. Watched her be pretty one-foot-in-one-foot-out with everyone in the world except for me and the Box Set.

Sort of.

Sometimes if Jonah or Christian don't reply to her fast enough she'll ask me if they're angry at her, and I'll say no, and she'll say, "Are you sure?" And I'll say, "Yep." And even then she'll invent a scenario in her mind where Jo's cross at her for something that didn't happen and she'll make a plan to cut him out of her life forever for the next hour and a half until Jonah texts her back and says, "Hey, sorry, didn't have my phone on me." And she gives me a sheepish smile like she's an idiot (she is) but I reckon it runs in her family because she goes like that for a reason.

Her mum would nip off for a girls' trip for two weeks, wouldn't call, wouldn't leave a note. At best, she'd warn Marsaili; at worst, we'd read about it in the papers when the paparazzi took a few photos.

Magnolia would look over at the photos of her mother pouring champagne into the mouth of a Belgium prince and make a small "hmm" noise and look away.

Shit with her dad was about the same. Away a lot, lied a lot, fucked around a lot, nothing surprised her—I'd see it hurt her though, more than with her mum. This weird sadness that'd barrel over her like a wave—there for a second, then gone.

Girls and their dads, you know? Mayer was right. Mothers, be good to your daughters, 100 percent. But fathers, wind your fucking necks in.

I've never asked her this, don't think I need to. Think I know her well enough to just know without needing the confirmation—modelling for her, it was for her dad. Or because of him, or something—rooted in something to do with him.

It wasn't long after we'd just gotten together that she was scouted.

An agent from NYC that her dad was definitely shagging. He took her and Bridge over for some award show, did this whole bit on the red carpet, photographs everywhere, Britain fucking ate it up. Dad of the year, beaming with his arms around his daughters. "Prettiest dates here," he was quoted saying by *OK!*

She came back from the trip absolutely fucking beaming.

"Beej, guess what!" She threw herself down on my lap in the Carver Hall common room.

She'd been away about a week. Our school wasn't that forgiving when it came to skipping school, unless, of course, your father was a celebrity and made massive donations.

“What?” I pushed some hair behind her ears.

“Ford wants to sign me!” She gave me this big smile.

My face pulled. “Who?”

“The agency!” She rolled her eyes like I was an idiot. “In New York. The modelling agency.”

“No way!” I put one hand on her thigh, the other on her waist. “I mean—yeah. Of course, like—”

Then I kissed her. A lot. Made a show of it. I loved being her boyfriend at school. Loved the fanfare of being that couple at Varley. Makes me laugh now, we must have been so fucking annoying. So in love, so obnoxious about it.

And you know what? I'd be lying if I said I wasn't into it at first, my girlfriend a model.

What sixteen-year-old wouldn't be?

She was always pretty small. Small bones, small frame. Just a little person who happens to have some long legs on her.

Didn't take too long before her eating shifted, but. At first it was just before a shoot or a runway, then it bled into everything else. Mostly, it'd happen when she'd get overwhelmed.

She got a tonne of campaigns. That face, her skin on that teenage body she had? High fashion's dream.

That was sort of when it began, the fascination with her. She went from being a celebrity's kid to being one herself. About a year after she started modelling, I did too and then it all went fucking gangbusters. I was okay with it, kind of did it for a laugh to spend more time with her, we'd get booked for a lot of the same jobs, I liked getting to travel with her, go with her to weird places, just us. But for her, the more jobs she got, the more stressed she'd get, the more she'd naturally fall behind in school but she wouldn't let herself either so she'd just push herself. Felt out of control in every area of her life. Found control in one area in particular: how she looked.

Fifteen was the first time she went to Bloxham House for it. It wasn't her parents that made her go, wasn't even Marsaili—though she'd bring it up with me sometimes, if I was worried, if she should be too—I didn't know what to say, didn't know that I could say anything without betraying Parks, so I didn't for a long time. It was crazy hard to get Magnolia to admit there was even a problem at all, actually. But there was. I knew there was. Her periods would come and go months apart, she'd get dizzy a lot, get drunk crazy easy. She fainted once in the pool at school, nearly drowned. Ms Hurtwood, the girl's housemaster, contacted Bloxham House herself after that. Told me that there were a lot of different ways you can betray someone you love, one of them is letting them hurt themselves.

It was me and my dad who dropped her off. Harley called her into his office before she left, told her he was proud of her. He meant for getting help, but sometimes I think she thought he meant it about her, in general, at that time. Probably put her on a bit of a bad path.

She stopped modelling so much after December third. Just didn't have the capacity for it how she did before. Still did a bit, the odd big campaign here and there, but for the most part, that was her done.

Kind of thought we'd seen the tail end of her shit with food but then every time she was stressed or we'd have a fight or something happened with her parents or her sister, something that she couldn't really control, it'd pop up again. Don't think it was conscious, she'd just lose her appetite. Short spells, usually. For the last few years anyway. But not this time. It's been what—like, five months since Bridge passed? You ever watch the person you love start wasting away right in front of your eyes?

I have. A few too many times now.

8:33

Daisy Haites

It was so good to see you

Thanks

"It was so nice seeing you as well Magnolia."

Ok

Stop!

You love me.

Ok

You do!

Reluctantly.

At best.

Honestly I was just waterboarded with your presence.

Sounds refreshing.

It wasn't

Such an onion you are . . .

So many layers

Please don't quote Shrek

What's 'Shrek'?

I hate you

??

THIRTY-FIVE

BJ

Hen and I go for a bite at Goodman, the Mayfair one. It's not an early dinner, probably got there just before the sun went down, so what, like, eight p.m.? It's late August, it's not getting dark early, and then we don't have a quick dinner either. The Brigham crab on toast is unmissable and so is the Australian Wagyu rib eye. They also have Pappy Van Winkle's 23, which—if you drink whiskey (and you should) it's a must, so we do. Have a couple of glasses of that before we dander back out onto Maddox Street and up towards Grosvenor.

Hen's banging on about how he and Romilly are having their first fight and it's because Henry talked shit about her dad, which honestly, like, fair play. The man's a fucking loon, but girls and their dads, man? Like, don't play with fire—that's what I'm saying to him when Henry whacks me in the chest and nods his chin over at someone on the other side of the street.

My brows go low and my eyes pinch. Can't be—? But it is.

Bushka.

Out, alone. Past ten.

Now look, thank fuck we're not at the dodgy end of town, she's safe as houses up near the embassies on the square, but I don't love seeing it. Can't say that I've ever seen it before actually, Bushka out, wandering alone.

Pretty weird.

"Bushka!" I call to her, darting across the road, Hen in tow. She doesn't hear me so I call her again, and the closer I get the more I can see that I don't think she's okay. She looks rattled.

"Ksenyia—" I touch her arm and she jumps in fright before realising it's me.

"Oh!" she breathes out, relieved. Grips my arm with both her hands. "BJ." She smiles up at me then looks at my brother, reaching for his cheek to kiss him. "Henry."

"What are you doing out here?" Henry asks with a smile but it's hemmed with a frown.

Bushka breathes out her nose and looks around.

"I was out for drink and I got—" She trails, looking around her.

"Lost?" I offer.

She frowns at me, proud.

"Took a wrong turn," Henry offers as an alternative, and that's why everyone fucking loves him.

"Da." She nods.

"Were you by yourself?" I ask her as I shrug off my grey Mastermind World shearling jacket and drape it around her shoulders.

"Нет." She shakes her head. "I was with Arina and Harley." She frowns, mumbles something in Russian under her breath. "Я не знаю, куда они пошли."

Henry and I catch eyes.

"Well, we can't stay out here all night." I give her a smile. "Come back to our place for a drink, yeah?"

She nods, still looking confused. Probably won't give her a drink once we're home because there's a chance she might be already a bit pissed—hard to tell—no two ways about it, Bushka has been for as long as I've known her a semi-functioning alcoholic.

Henry flags a cab and I help her into it.

When we walk through our front door, Parks looks up and then blinks in surprise at the sight of her grandmother.

"Look who we found!" I give Magnolia a big, tight smile all laced with a look.

Her face flickers, confused.

"What a pleasant surprise!" she says, skipping over to us. "Found?" she mouths over Bushka's head, and I give her another look.

"Grosvenor Street," Henry whispers to her. "Wandering, alone."

Magnolia's eyes widen in alarm and she looks over at me before zeroing in on her grandmother, annoyed at her now.

"What were you doing by yourself wandering alone at night?"

"I wasn't!" Bushka shuffles past her, helping herself to the vodka on the bar cart. "I had dinner."

"Alone?" Magnolia lifts an eyebrow.

Bushka squeezes some lemon into her glass. "Нет."

"С кем?" Parks asks, swapping to Russian.

"Parents," Bushka tells her, not looking over as she drops in an ice cube.

Magnolia's eyes go to slits. "Mine?"

Bushka glances over at her, face hard to pick but somewhere between embarrassed and sad, then she nods once.

I hear Magnolia's breathing shift. Quicker and louder, jaw goes tight and she presses her lips together.

"Они оставили тебя?"

"Нет," Bushka says again.

Parks eyes pinch. "Ты лежишь?"

I don't know a lot of Russian, picked up bits and pieces over the years because of the girls. Something about lying.

"Я не вру!" Bushka tells her, eyes a bit wide with an emotion I can't pick. "Пожалуйста, забудь об этом, моя дорогая."

I don't catch a lick of that except for "my darling" at the end.

Magnolia folds her arms over her chest, eyes all cross.

"Fine," she says. "You'll stay here tonight."

"I go home," Bushka tells her.

Magnolia looks over her shoulder sharply and gives her a look. "ы останешься здесь сегодня вечером."

Bushka glances over at me and then follows her granddaughter sheepishly into the guest room.

About ten minutes later I can hear the shower running and then Parks scurries back out to us, brows furrowed. Her hands have already made their way to her hips when she looks between Henry and I, impatient.

"Speak," she says. "Quickly. Tell me everything."

"She was alone, looked lost—" I shrug because I don't know what else to say. I'm as fucking confused as she is.

"This is fucking unbelievable." She's shaking her head, eyes wide, horrified.

I touch her arm, give her a smile. "She's okay, Parksy."

"That's not the point," she tells me sharply, and she's right, actually.

"Yeah," I concede. "I s'pose it's not. What do you want to do?"

She breathes out—huffs, really—thinking face on.

"Who's the scariest person we know?" She looks between me and my brother.

"You," I tell her and she rolls her eyes.

"Julian," my idiot brother says.

Magnolia nods once and pulls out her phone, which I quickly pluck from her hands. She glowers up at me, and I shake my head, staunch.

"Nope." I give her a look. "No, we're not calling our gang lord exes at least until morning."

"But—"

Another look. "No buts, Parksy."

"You don't even have a gang lord ex!" Henry reminds me, merrily.

I breathe out my nose.

"Nor do I, actually." Magnolia concedes, flicking her eyes. "He's just an arts dealer."

Hen tosses me a look before he coughs.

"Course he is," I tell her with a nod, and do my best not to crush her with that truth she ignores.

When she has those fucking blinders on, my god. Can't really complain though, as an absolute beneficiary of those blinders frequently myself.

"Anyway," I put my hands on her shoulders. "Important part is that Bushka's here, and she's safe and—"

"—my parents are beasts?" she jumps in.

Henry nods silently and I press my lips together before I sigh. "Yeah, that too."

THIRTY-SIX
Magnolia

"You look fine," my sister would tell me as I stare at myself in the mirror.

Black cut-out knitted cropped top and the red pleated patent leather miniskirt, both Balmain and the Gucci Black single-breasted 'GG' embroidered wool coat over top.

"Fine?" My eyebrow would lift at the audacity of her. "Marvellous! We all know 'fine' is absolutely my favourite adjective."

Bridget would give me a look. "Does it really matter what you wear when you crucify our parents?"

I'd put my nose in the air, adjust my hair, push some behind my own ears.

"I think it matters what I wear all the time."

"Well." She'd boost herself up on the bathroom counter and look at her nails. I don't know why though, because we all know they'd be unmanicured. It's like looking at a garden that's nothing but grass. "That's because you have a rather skewed perspective on most things and not a very firm grasp on reality." She'd give me a curt smile.

I'd frown over at her. "I have a firm grasp on reality."

She'd fold her arms and give me another look.

"You're talking to a dead girl in a mirror," she'd say, and I'd stare at her, eyes big, feelings hurt because she's a traitor—how could she leave me here like this? And she'd roll her eyes, which is a way that Bridget would say a half-sorry to me without ever having to say it. An eye roll and a quick topical change.

"Do we really feel like this is a good idea?" she'd ask, and I'd nod, sure.

"We do."

"Who is we?" she'd ask.

"Me and you. I'm speaking on your behalf as well—"

Both of her eyebrows up at that, I'm sure. "Over my dead body."

And I'd stare at her because she's an arsehole.

"Get it?" she'd ask, smiling, proud of her joke.

"Bridget."

"Sorry—" Another eye roll. "Look, they deserve it."

"Obviously." I stare into the mirror at myself.

"Just—" Bridget would shrug. "What if it goes poorly and you get sadder and it gets worse?"

I'd look over at her, brows low. "What gets worse?"

And then she'd sort of gesture towards me vaguely with her hands.

And then I'd let out this little scoff, and I want to fight with her now—oh my god, I miss fighting with her so much. About everything—about clothes, about her not answering my calls fast enough, about popcorn (sweet or salty) (me, salty; her, sweet) (me, right; her, clinically insane), about the boys I'd dated, anything—I'd give anything to fight with her again, anything to hear her utter something snarky and annoying under her breath.

Breath is so strangely precious, isn't it—?

There's a knock on the bathroom door before it cracks open.

"Ready?" Beej says with a gentle smile.

"Yeah."

He nods his chin at me. "You look great."

I straighten my shoulders and give him a big smile. "Great is so much better than fine!"

He sniffs a confused smile. "Who said you were fine?"

"Oh, Br—" I catch myself. "No one."

His face pulls, sad, careful maybe.

"Well." He hooks his arm around my neck as he pulls me towards the door. "Next time you talk to No One, tell her I say hi."

Daniela drives us over because it's raining obscenely and I tried to tell BJ that it was statistically more likely for us to have a car crash in the rain and he said it was also statistically more likely for me to start crying mid-walk in the rain when the water ruins my black Joplin 105 suede over-the-knee boots and there are so many things I can argue with but I can't argue with Aquazzura.

We stand under an umbrella at the bottom of the steps that lead up to my childhood home. Phillimore Gardens. BJ and I used to talk about buying it from my parents one day so we could keep it, I don't know why really? It's not where we fell in love, not really, but he holds a funny kind of sentimentality for it, and I suppose once upon a time I did too.

We didn't fall in love here, but much of the love we fell into took place within these walls. And now they feel so cold and empty in Bridget's absence, which is strange, I know. They aren't correlating thoughts, but how much this house makes me think of her snuffs out the good for me. And it's not that thinking of her is bad, I think of her all the time on my own, it's that her bedroom isn't her bedroom anymore. When I made her move out and we moved into our place in Grosvenor Square, they kept my room mostly as it was as a guest room, but Marsaili turned Bridget's room into a sewing room because it was—and I'm quoting her here—"incredibly west-facing."

I asked what west-facing had to do with sewing, but Bridget said what did it matter, she didn't live there anymore ("Thanks to you, Magnolia."), it was their £38,000,000 home, they could turn it into a sewing room if they so wanted, and I begged to differ but it was an argument I lost, though it turns out I was right in the end. It did matter.

Now the only shrine I have for my sister is her bedroom that I haven't stepped foot in since the night she died in it in our old apartment on Upper Grosvenor, that I obviously don't live in anymore but I did buy from the owners because I needed to keep it, and sometimes, on Mondays, usually in the mornings, I lay flowers at the foot of her closed bedroom door because I don't have anywhere to point my grief at except for the vase of her ashes that lives at my Parks House, which, if you'll remember, was an argument I also lost.

BJ nods his head towards the front door before squeezing my hand that he hasn't stopped holding since we left our place.

Daniela stays in the car.

I go to ring the doorbell but then Beej pulls out a key—opening my door, but not before he gives me a tiny wink.

There's magic in those winks of his, I think. I've always suspected that to be true. They make you braver and stupider. I've done a thousand questionable things because BJ Ballentine winked at me and gave me a half-smile and my stomach dropped three storeys inside my chest cavity. I hope he winks at me forever. If there is such a thing as forever because people are so temporal. We're all sort of dying, maybe just in slow motion, do you know what I mean? I bought him vitamins to keep him alive as long as possible, a whole suite of them—LYMA, Elysium, Thorne and Verso—the best vitamins in the world—he scarcely ever takes them, so sometimes I crush them up and sprinkle them on his food when he's not looking, which Henry says is maybe illegal and I say shut up, like hardly.

Buskha's dying too.

Not actually. At least that I know of. But in the way that we're all dying, just probably her faster than the rest of us. That's not to say that one of us couldn't go before her—Bridget did—death doesn't really take any prisoners, does it? Doesn't really discriminate, it takes the chances it gets.

Which is why my parents allowing Bushka to wander alone around London looking like the most robbable woman in the world, what with her Birken, her three-carat diamond earrings, her nine-carat teardrop diamond engagement ring that she's never taken off that indicates to me that her husband, my technical grandfather who I've never met, who died well before I was born, who died actually when my mother was quite young, was probably an oligarch, which feels probably a little uncomfortable for everyone in this day and age, but please remember I am half black too so don't shoot the genetic messenger.

The bag, the earrings, the ring and the £20,000 mink coat (don't talk to me about fur, please. She's like a thousand-year-old Russian, do you think she's not going to wear real fur if she owns it, come off it.)—wandering around after ten at night, an old woman alone—I tell myself that London is safe because we live here and I need it to be, but it can be dangerous. Crime is soaring here, from robberies to assaults to murder and stabbings—yes, thank heavens she was in Mayfair, but there are bad people everywhere.

In fact—I swing the front door open—I suspect I'm about to speak to two of them.

"Oh, darling!" my mother says, standing up from the couch she's laying on when she sees me. "To what do we owe the pleasure?"

I look around the house, confused. "Are you living here?"

She waves her hand through the air. "Staying."

She moves towards BJ, kissing his cheek.

"Are you here to talk about wedding things?" she asks, excitedly.

My face falters. "No—"

Beej frowns a little and steps towards my mum. "Arrie, we're here to talk about what happened with Ksenyia."

"Oh—" My mother swats her hand through the air. "She's fine—"

"Yes." I eye her. "Luckily, but no thanks to you."

"What's this about then?" my father says as he walks out of his office with an apprehensive smile.

My mother gestures to me. "Magnolia and BJ were just checking in that Bushka was okay after the other night."

"Ah." My father nods. "Happy as Larry. Upstairs in her room."

Beej folds his arms, brows low. "You want to just walk us through what happened?"

Harley takes a steady breath, and he's annoyed—I can tell he's annoyed.

"There was just a misunderstanding—" Mum says.

My face pinches. "Was the misunderstanding that you would care for her and you didn't?"

"Easy—" Harley eyes me.

BJ looks over at me and our eyes catch. Me or him, that's what he's asking without asking. I'd rather it be him, but it probably should be me.

I take a breath and straighten up.

"Bushka is at that crazy time in an old person's life where they are practically an infant again. Now listen—" I eye them both. "You dropped the ball with Bridget and I, you cannot do it with her. It was different with us because we had each other and we had Marsaili, but Bushka has no one."

My mother's face pulls, as though something is hurting her.

"So be present for her. Or send her to Alexey—" I tell them with a look. "But you cannot neglect her."

My father scoffs. "I've never neglected a thing a day in my life—"

"A task, you mean—" I frown over at him. "You've never neglected a task."

A scowl appears on my father's face, and I'm not actually trying to actively insult him, I mean that genuinely.

"You're incredibly high-functioning, Harley. You're unbelievably talented, there's no two ways about that—" I give him an earnest look before I say this next part. "But you have neglected much."

That scowl of his deepens. "No, I haven't."

"Every list you've written might be finished, every box might be checked, but I've never made that list and neither did she—" I nod my chin at my mother, now readying to insult him a bit. "At least not until you were married to someone else—"

Harley tucks his chin as his eyes get darker.

"Watch that mouth." He points over at me.

BJ steps in front of me, squaring up.

"You watch those fingers."

"Ah." My father nods, coolly. "I see you're a big man today."

BJ breathes out and shakes his head as he gives my father a little smile. "Oh, we're all big men compared to you these days, champ—"

Harley pulls back. "You're going to talk to me like that in my own fucking house?"

"Yeah." BJ nods, unperturbed. "Or we can go outside if you want—"

Harley nods his head towards the door.

"Yeah, alright, let's go."

"No." I step between them, glancing back at BJ to tell him to stop. I look back at Harley. "If anyone will be bringing you bodily harm it will be me—" Harley rolls his eyes.

"And while we're at it—" I eye him down. "I actually won't be watching my mouth, thank you. Everything I have up my sleeve"—I look between my parents—"you fully deserve to hear. As it stands though, I intend on being somewhat reserved with what I'm going to say to you, so please do hear it with the weight of my restraint."

I take another big breath. "I don't have overly high expectations of either of you, neither individually nor collectively. I did, however, perhaps wrongly assume that you had within you enough decency to look after your own elderly mother." I give my mother a glare.

She opens her mouth to say something and I hold up my hand to silence her.

"I know neither of you had it in you to look after Bridget and I when we were small, but now—" I shake my head at them. "Bushka's a different kind of small. And you have a chance to prove to yourselves—and maybe to me, even—that you aren't entirely despicable people."

My mother stares over at me, mouth agape. "You think we're despicable?"

I blink a few times and then look over at BJ.

"Was I unclear?"

BJ shakes his head coolly. "Pretty clear."

Harley presses his tongue into his bottom lip and shakes his head.

"I know you have an absolute fucking knack for making everything about you, but this isn't—"

"I know." I nod. "It's about my elderly grandmother BJ found wandering the streets alone at ni—"

"Alright—" Harley rolls his eyes, exasperated now. "Let's all calm the fuck down with that, she was walking around Mayfair, not Dorset Street—"

"Right—" Beej gives him a look. "That's the point."

"Magnolia, darling," my mum sighs. "You have to understand—everything that happened with Bridget made us—"

I cut her off.

"Are you really going to blame Bridget dying on you leaving your mother unattended late at night to go off and have sex?"

Harley gives me a look. "And how the fuck do you know that's what we were doing?"

I give him a glare. "An unfortunate but I fear accurate stab in the dark."

My parents trade a look and I know I'm right. I'd probably rather have not been right, but I can tell that I am.

"So how was that Bridget's fault?" I ask, crossing my arms as I frown between them. "I'm actually rather interested to see how you drive this one home—"

My mother sighs. "I didn't say it was her fault, I said that after everything that happened, all our emotions are heightened and we're feeling so much and—"

I cut her off again.

"Yes, the blues are bluer, the food tastes sweeter, the songs sound better—carpe diem, sure, that's fine. не облажайся." I tell her.

"I won't," she says in English.

"You already are," I tell her and then I turn to leave.

BJ jogs after me, tossing his arm around my shoulders again. "Feel better?"

I take a staggered little breath. "No."

Not at all.

THIRTY-SEVEN

Magnolia

Monday morning I decide to work from home. No reason, really. Just felt like it.

It was overcast when I woke, harder to get out of bed.

BJ looks good in all lighting, but there is something about a man in grey, and when I opened my eyes when he opened the curtains to wake me up (because fiancés are the best kind of alarm clock), he was lit up by the grey sky behind him and we had sex because I couldn't help it because I'm only human, and then after that I didn't much want to go into the office anymore.

"I'm off—" BJ poked his head into the shower.

"Where are you going?" I ask him with a smile.

"Gym for a bit, then I want to go in to Hatchards to pick up a book and then I might go for lunch."

"Oh, who with?"

The slightest of pauses that I don't notice at the time because why would I notice at the time?

"Jo," he says.

"Okay—" I brush my wet mouth over his dry one. "I'll see you later."

He nods. "Box Set's coming over for a carry-out."

And then he's gone and my morning carries on much how I imagined it would.

A Zoom with a photographer we're working with next month, a couple of emails, and then mostly just flicking through *Vogue*s and *Harper's Bazaar*s and scrolling Net-A-Porter to spot any pieces I'm wanting to pull.

I skip breakfast, but Daniela brought me a coffee even though I told her not to, she sort of just shoved it in my hand and gave me a disparaging look before she went off to the kitchen to unload some groceries that arrived.

I don't know who they're arriving for, I've never used them.

Just milk, tea and sugar. They're the only groceries I need. And this water I get shipped from New Zealand by the crate, 1907. It's perfect. Try it, I love it. I can't drink any other water now.

And Evian, obviously. But not for drinking—never for drinking!—for face washing.

Oh, and Perrier. Also not for drinking (though in a pinch, I suppose it's fine) but is great for hair washing. And don't give me that silly look—it's hardly my fault, the absolute dire state of London's hard tap water—one could hardly expect me to use non-chelating water on my face. And not a word about the environment or single-use plastics either, because obviously I order them all in the glass bottles.

I head out at about lunchtime to go for a walk. I tell Daniela I want to go for a walk around the park and she gives me a look and says "The park" in air quotes because we both know that just means I want to take the scenic route to Selfridges.

I feel incredibly convinced that if I buy the coral pink small flap bag from Chanel in the patent calfskin with the gold-tone metals then the cloud that's sitting on my brain today will lift and I'll be able to focus again.

I do tell her she doesn't need to come and I can go by myself but she just ignores me and puts her jacket on anyway.

It's funny because it takes a lot of conscious effort to make Daniela walk in step with me, she always tries to walk in front of me even when I'm talking to her.

At first I thought it was maybe that she was just an aggressively fast walker, but then BJ pointed out that I myself am an aggressively fast walker so for someone to be staying consistently in front of me they're probably either doing a light jog or doing it on purpose.

I call BJ on the way—see if he wants to meet up for lunch, but he says he's already on his way to Jo.

We get to Selfridges, I find the bag I want and then I (we?) head up to the men's section to grab a couple of pieces for BJ.

Two monogram scarf-print shirts from Balmain; a black and white one and a brown-toned one, and then the Undercover black patch-lettering cotton sweatshirt because it says 'a wolf will never be a pet,' and maybe that's true but I still love the wolf all the same.

I'm filing through the pieces in the Off-White section when Jonah Hemmes' face pops up right in front of mine, giving me a silly grin.

"Oh, hi!" I smile up at him.

He gives me a big kiss on my cheek.

"Hey, Parksy."

"What are you doing here?" I ask.

He rolls his eyes. "You know, I do dress myself occasionally . . ."

"No—" I give him a look. "You must be running impossibly late—"

His brows bend. "For what?"

"For lunch with Beej."

Jonah's face falters. "I'm not having lunch with Beej."

"Yes, you are, I just spoke to him."

Jonah thinks to himself—trying to work out if he's forgotten something—then he shakes his head, looking over at me, eyes cautious.

"Parks, I was never having lunch with Beej today."

I can hear the blood in my ears all of a sudden, and under my skin around my ribs feels all hot.

I get that stinging sound in my ears though nothing's stinging me and I try to take a deep breath but actually I just end up taking three short ones.

"Hey—" Jo grabs me by the shoulders and pulls me behind a rack so we're less visible to the public.

"Don't do that. We don't know anything." He gives me a

look. "He could be buying you a present. He could be trying on a wedding suit—"

"Then why don't you at least know about it?"

He lifts his eyebrows and gives me a tricky look.

". . . Maybe I do."

"Jonah," I stare over at him. "You lied to me once. For three years. About something I had every right to know—" I swallow and take a shallow breath. "Please don't lie to me again."

He nods quickly. "Okay, well—track him."

"What?"

"You share locations, don't you?"

"Yes, but Bridget said that it's unhealthy to check it and it makes us codependent."

"Well, you are, so—"

"And Henry said when BJ and I got back together that if I checked his location every time we aren't together then it's very indicative of my trust in him." My eyes go a bit blurry. "And I really want to trust him."

"Do you?"

"Well, not right now." I frown. "But now feels like when I should be trying to, doesn't it?"

Jonah nods like he gets it but he doesn't—how could he?

"Give me your phone—" He holds his hand out.

"What?"

He shrugs. "You don't want to break his trust, fuck it, I'll break it—give me your phone."

Something about this feels fractionally better, so I hand it to him and he doesn't even ask for my passcode; he just punches it in.

"How did you—?"

"We all know your passcode," he tells me without looking up. "You're insanely predictable."

I frown.

"He's close," Jonah says, glancing over at me.

"What?" I blink.

"James Street." He nods his head towards the door. "Let's go."

I kind of hoped that Jonah would spend the walk assuring me

that nothing was wrong and everything was okay, but truthfully his face looks sort of pale and stressed. Everyone loves BJ, everyone in the world, he's fundamentally loveable—but no one loves him more than Jonah and I.

Jonah loves BJ unconditionally, would lie for him—obviously—would fight for him, would do anything for him, Jonah has his back 100 percent of the time. He believes the best in BJ blindly, so if Jonah's frowning how Jonah is frowning, I'm fucked.

That's the feeling I've got.

It's just a quick five-minute walk from Selfridges, really.

Jonah's still got my phone, watching it, tracking him.

"We're getting close," Jonah tells me, watching the phone.

Under different circumstances, this could actually be a new hobby of mine. Spying on people is incredibly fun, did you know? Of course, circumstantially speaking, this in particular isn't that much fun but there's a thrill to it that's hard to deny.

However, that thrill is quickly squandered when I find myself standing outside a burger bar—Patty&Bun?—standing at the window looking in.

Jonah's standing next to me, still frowning as he watches on.

BJ's sitting at a table with some random girl. Quite pretty. Looks like a model.

My heart sinks.

"Call him," Jonah says, eyes on his best friend, dark and cloudy. "Now."

He hands me my phone back and it's already calling.

We're watching him through the window.

BJ picks up his phone and holds up a finger to the girl he's with.

"One sec," I see him say to her.

"Hello?" he says as he answers the phone.

"Hey," I say a bit tonelessly.

"Hey!" He smiles a bit.

I clear my throat and try to sound as normal as I can muster. "Where are you?"

"At lunch, remember?"

"Right," I say quickly. "With who again?"

I watch his brow furrow and then he says, "Oh—why? What's going on?"

"With who, BJ?"

And then he looks up and around the restaurant, spotting me on the other side of the window with the person he's meant to be dining with.

"Fuck—" he says. "Parks—"

"Fuck you." And then I hang up the phone.

THIRTY-EIGHT

BJ

She's so fucking fast.

I've never been able to outrun her in my life, do you know how annoying that is? To be with someone like her, a fucking runner, who's not been a runner, ever, hates running, wouldn't ever run for exercise, isn't that kind of runner but is the other kind. The unhealthy kind, like, runs-from-shit kind of runner—always has been. For her to be that kind of runner and to also be the other kind of runner who is unbeatable physically is so fucking annoying, I can't properly wrap the words around it. Give it a go anyway. Leg it after her but I lose her on Oxford Street in a crowd of people.

I did think about it, by the way, telling the truth. This morning when she asked me where I was going I had this feeling like maybe I should—weird, never had a feeling like that about this before, last Monday I didn't think twice, but there was something about today that made me think maybe I should and I ignored it.

The universe does shit like that, doesn't it? Gives you clues, nudges—guides you a bit. And for a minute there, I was going to say to her, "Actually, I'm going to grab a burger today," but then I think about the way her eyebrows bent in the middle when she watched me eat a fried portobello the other day—not judgey, just scared. It's irrational, obviously, I know it is—she's kind of fucking insane. But then, she's always been?

And she's stressed already so I didn't want to make it worse so I caught myself saying that I was having lunch with Jo at Mildred's and she was pleased about it.

Fuck, I hate it when she's scared. She was the other night with the mushroom, because she's an idiot; she was the other night when we were at dinner and I drank wine that wasn't natural; she was the morning after when I was hungover and out of desperation ordered a Sausage McMuffin—which was fucking unreal, by the way—it's a funny kind of scared on her. It's rootless. It's a thing she's decided to point her fear at that's not grounded in anything because really the thing she's afraid of is mortality and she doesn't know how to reconcile that the people you love can just die. Just like that.

Which, actually, that's the kind of thing that's worth being afraid of, but see—she can't be afraid of that because she can't control it. Food, she can control. She's controlled food for a long time. An easy thing for her to both demonise and weaponise against the actual thing she's actually afraid of.

She looked scared when she saw me.

Different kind of scared, rooted in something too. Fuck.

I didn't go to Patty&Bun to meet Dylan, by the way. She just happened to turn up and I was there by myself, she was too, asked if she could sit down, I said yes, because why would I say no? The odds here feel stacked against me. Like, what were the chances of Parks running into Jo and then them finding me and seeing what they think they saw—and I know what she thinks she saw.

Magnolia says she's forgiven me and she's past it, but that forgiveness is wafer-thin ice that's sitting on a deep fucking lake.

I went to our place first. Don't know why. Cause I'm an idiot, all hopeful like that. That she'd actually turn to me instead of running to someone else. Didn't, obviously. Not her vibe.

Call her about forty times but then she switches her phone off.

Call Jo instead but he doesn't answer either, which tells me she's with him at least, so she's safe.

Take a stab in the dark and head to his house.

Jonah and Christian moved in together sometime in the last few months.

Jo finally gave up the Park Lane place, not because he wanted to but because Christian said he didn't want my old room because—and I quote, "fucking yuck"—forced his brother's hand to move it.

Probably good for him.

Houses can carry things, like energies or whatever. That house was good for what it was, for when we had it.

The 'lost years,' as Jo calls them.

We're not in them anymore though, time to move on.

Harcourt House on Cavendish Square, that's where they went. Like proper grown-ups and shit.

I don't flag down a taxi—it can take anywhere between twenty minutes to nearly an hour at this time of day to get from Kensington to the top of Marylebone, but it's pretty much a straight shot on the red line.

Don't get to take the tube much, really. Wish I could, definitely the fastest way around London. But can you imagine? Magnolia Parks on the tube?

I get off at Oxford Circus and then fucking leg it up Regent, take a right on Margaret Street til I hit the square.

Little less than thirty minutes.

I bang on my best friend's door.

She used to fall through the ice all the time before New York, she fell through the ice again that day up at the stones with Taura and Jo and that time we bumped into Paili on the street, but since then, she hasn't, not really. I'll see it on her face every now and then—we'll see a shit article about me in a red top and her face will pull, you can almost hear a cracking but then nothing—she doesn't fall through.

But here, now, she's under, fully submerged and the conditions were—unfortunately—perfect for the hole that she fell through to freeze over immediately and trap her in under.

I'm going to have to punch through to get to her.

There's a scuffle behind it and the muffled voice of my fiancée growling something at Jonah—him saying something back to her and then I hear scurrying footsteps and the slamming of a different door.

This one swings open.

Jo glares at me and I push past him.

"Magnolia?" I call, looking around the apartment. "Parks, please—let me explain—"

Jo sniffs.

I point at him, warning him to shut up.

"Parks?" I call again, heading towards Christian's closed bedroom door.

I turn the handle and swing it open—don't know what I'm expecting to see—her curled up on his bed, him holding her, some old fucking nightmare playing out in front of me, but I don't. She's not in here.

Neither is he.

"He's not home," Jonah tells me gruffly.

I look over my shoulder at him, say nothing. Head to his room instead.

Knock twice before I open the door and there she is.

Glassy eyes, tear tracks down her face, knees hugged up against her chest as she sits against the head of my best friend's bed.

I lick my bottom lip and breathe out my nose.

"Parks—"

"Don't." She cuts me off.

I move towards her shaking my head. "I know what you think happened—"

"Do you, Sherlock?" Jo sneers from behind me. "Fucking clued in, aren't you?"

"Yeah—" I swing around and get right up in his face. "And you aren't at all, so why don't you shut the fuck up and let me talk to my fiancée."

He raises his eyebrows and pulls his head back.

Doesn't like to be yelled at. Don't really give a shit though. Turn back to Parks.

"Listen, right—" I move towards her. "I fucked up."

"Who is she?" Magnolia glares.

"Literally no one—" I shake my head. "Maddie's friend. But we weren't even there together—"

"You're fucking cooked, man—" Jo steps further into the room.

"Would you shut the fuck up!" I yell at him.

"We saw you!" Magnolia jumps to her feet, standing on the bed so she's towering both of us.

"I wasn't with her!" I tell her again, exasperated.

Jo eyes me, shaking his head. "Weird drum to keep banging when we have eyes, man."

I roll my eyes. "She just happened to be there—"

Magnolia gives me a look, all angry and spiteful.

"What a coincidence."

"I told you about her, Parks—" I give her a look. "Maddie's mate. Who wanted to be a model—"

"Mate means 'boy'!" Magnolia yells, fists balled.

I stare up at her and pull a face. "No, it doesn't!"

"Yes, it does! Of course it does! You tricked me!"

I shake my head, staring at her, still confused.

"You fucking gendered a word without telling me—"

"Everyone knows mate means 'boy'!"

Jo makes an unsure noise and shakes his head. "Uh, I don't know—to be fair to him, if someone said 'whatever fuckity blah Magnolia's mate'—"

"Which no one would, as we all know I hate that word—"

"Right—" Jo tosses me a look. "But you could be talking about Taura or you could be talking about Henry or me or—"

She cuts him off, speaking over him.

"You said her name was a boy's name." Magnolia glares.

I roll my eyes. "I said her name was Dylan—" Give her a pointed look. "Because her name is Dylan."

Magnolia stands now, feet together still on the bed. She crosses her arms and looks down her nose at me.

"So why are you lying about going to lunches with her?"

I sigh and stare up at her with heavy eyes.

"I'm not lying about going to lunches with her, I'm lying about eating burgers to you."

Her brows dip. "What?"

I grab her by the waist and lift her down from the bed, put her on the ground.

"I am so fucking hungry—"

She blinks, annoyed. "What?"

"All the time, Parks. I'm starving. I don't want to eat a crunchy artichoke—" I shake my head a bunch. "I want to eat fried chicken, I want those fucking Dutch pancakes at the end of the street, I want to eat every single thing on the Smoky Boys menu and I don't want to feel like me doing it's going to make you cry—"

She lets out this shallow breath and shrugs once. "Okay—"

"Not okay." I shake my head. "Because you aren't okay."

She rolls her eyes and turns from me a bit. "Yes, I am."

I pull her back, angle her face at mine.

"Listen, I know that you're going through the absolute fucking wringer, Parks, and I'm so sorry—" I take a breath. Press my mouth together before I keep going. "I know that eating like this helps you feel in more control of everything happening around you—"

"No—" She lets out a breath that sounds like a laugh. "I'm not—this isn't—"

"I think it is," I tell her.

She shrugs again. "Well, you're wrong—"

"Am I?" I give her a look then nod my chin at her. "What did you eat today?"

"A coffee—"

I nod, waiting for more.

Her lips purse as she thinks.

"Some olives." She shrugs. "Various kinds of grapes . . . Some . . . rather runny potatoes . . ."

I stare at her, unimpressed. "You had a martini—"

"They're very filling," she tells me.

"They aren't."

"Well, I have mine with four olives, so it's practically a salad—"

"This isn't funny." I shake my head and cover my eyes. "I can't do this again, Parks—"

She pulls my hands down away from my face.

"I'm fine," she tells me, but I shake my head.

"You're measuring your food. You're weighing it, counting how many berries you're putting in a smoothie—"

Jo sighs from the other side of the room. "Magnolia—"

And then her shoulders slump a little, face looks sad and I feel like shit for making her feel like shit.

I tilt my head at her.

"We already did this in school, Parks, I'm not doing it again—"

"I'm not trying to lose weight!" She stomps a little foot.

"You've dropped another ten kilograms even though you didn't have five to lose—"

She gestures towards me. "You haven't lost any weight, and you eat what I eat—"

"That's because after I eat your green shit I wait til you're distracted and eat some toast like a fucking normal person—"

She gives me a steep look. "Tell me it's at least Ezekiel bread—"

I shake my head at her, not wanting to lie anymore.

"It's just plain white bread from Waitrose."

Her eyes go wide, panic-struck. "Do you know how bad bleached flour is for you?"

"Parks." I stare over at her. "Bleached flour didn't kill Bridget, an aneurysm did—"

She glares over me.

I press my hands into my eyes for a second, breathe out, then look down at her.

"I'm sorry," I tell her. "I shouldn't have said that."

She stares up at me, eyes teary.

From the other side of the room, Jo catches my eye before he gives me a little nod and quietly leaves, shutting the door behind him.

"I shouldn't have lied to you," I tell her. "I'm sorry."

"Do you promise?" She blinks. "That nothing happened?"

I push my hands through her hair, shake my head as I stare down at her. "Nothing happened." I kiss the top of her head. "Promise."

9:46

Henny Pen 🐓

Heard what happened

You good?

Yeah, I guess so?

A bit scary.

Yeah I bet.

He wouldn't do that to you again

Yeah?

Yeah.

THIRTY-NINE

Magnolia

It's my mother's birthday and she's hired out The Ritz Restaurant. I didn't realise that before we got there—I thought we were actually just dining there, I didn't realise she'd hired out the entire place.

BJ gives me a steadying look as we walk in—he stops in the doorway—doubles down on the look, tilts his head and squints down at me.

All the people in the room that I wish weren't there and even the ones who I don't mind that they are, they fade away how they used to, how I hope they always do.

'You've got this', the edge of his smile tells me.

I nod at him quickly, even though he didn't say anything out loud.

He touches my face with his hand and presses himself against me—subtle but intentional, and I swallow heavy.

"Sunny?" he asks me.

"Increasingly so." I nod again, finding it tricky to look him square in the eye because he's just that beautiful.

A magazine here did a study on our faces once, most of my face exists in the mid-low nineties in the Golden Ratio except for my eyebrows (97.98 percent) and my eyes (98.2 percent), but BJ, high nineties all around. His mouth? 99.87 percent.

His mouth is 99.87 percent perfect—I already knew that myself. But actually, after years of study and research and rigorous data collecting, I can confirm those numbers are, in fact, the slightest bit off. BJ's mouth is empirically proven to actually be 100 percent, entirely perfect.

He runs his tongue over it as he smiles more.

"Good," he says and nods his head out of our moment, and the whole world reappears.

We walk further into this particular hellscape that my mother has constructed.

To be completely honest with you, BJ is massively underdressed for the event now that we're here, primarily because we didn't actually know that we were attending an event. Brunello Cucinelli's black and tan logo-appliqué bomber jacket, a white cotton-cashmere T-shirt from the Zegna and The Elder Statesman collab, with the PA monogram leather track pants from Palm Angels. And Vans, obviously.

That's the good thing about a face like his, it kind of carries whatever he's wearing. He could have worn sweats and still would have been the most handsome man here, I'm glad he didn't though as that would have been mildly awkward.

"Incoming—" BJ whispers, his mouth pressed up against my ear as a society vulture swoops in towards us.

Verity Colson. In the scheme of it all, she's incredibly fringe and incredibly desperate not to be. Overly eager as well. She's not quite as wealthy as everyone else in the room—not that it matters at all, it definitely doesn't matter to me, no one here's as wealthy as me except perhaps maybe Charles Philip Arthur George, but he hardly counts because he's him and I mean that both as a positive and a negative—anyway, I do suspect all that's always quite mattered to Verity. New money is funny like that. So much to prove, mostly to themselves, I think. She likes to be seen strategically with certain people, likes to know as much as she can, tiny details to infer she's closer with you than she really is. She also wears clothes that have maximum brand display just to prove that she's wearing them. She often looks as though Fendi threw up on her. Not tonight though, tonight she's wearing the Jenny Packham Midnight gown, you know the gradient pink one?

Which is fine, it's not a bad dress—bit of an irritating length on Verity, but it could be that Verity is irritating regardless of her dress length, who knows.

"Magnolia, babe!" She kisses my cheek quickly.

"Verity," I muster up a smile. "Hi."

Then she gets on her tiptoes to kiss BJ's, which last for much longer than mine and (oddly) feels significantly more sensual.

BJ gives me a panicked look over her head and I stifle a laugh.

"What a party!" She looks around, pleased to be at it.

And I don't know why she is at it, honestly.

She's not close to my mother. Actually, I think my mother quite detests her. There's a line from *The O.C.* where Anna says to Seth, "Girls want to be chased by guys who aren't into them," and I think that's rather true of my mother. She wants the attention of people who don't give her attention. I told Bridget that once and she looked at me for a long time before she said, "Yeah, I know the type."

I flash Verity a cordial smile. "We actually weren't aware it was a party."

"Oh dear." She cringes, looking from BJ to myself. "How embarrassing."

"Not really—" BJ shrugs, unfazed but now a little off her. I can tell by the bend in his brow.

"And you two!" she coos, touching both our arms, and I stare down at her hand on me. "Finally together!"

That brow of my fiancé's bends more. "Been together about forty years at this point but—"

"Oh, you know what I mean!" She bats a hand and gives him a look like they're the best of friends and he's a silly billy. She looks over at me and beams this smile that's so hemmed with eagerness it nearly makes me sad for her, but only nearly because of what she says next: "Are you so excited to be a wifey?"

My face falters. "Excuse me, what?"

"A wifey!" she repeats.

"Why do you keep saying that hideous word—?" I shake my

head a million times and cross my arms over myself to ward off anymore of her vitriolic hate speech. "Who invited you here?"

"I did," Brooks Calloway says, turning around and giving me a dumb smile.

BJ breathes out. "Oh, fuck."

"Ballentine," Brooks nods his chin at Beej before he leans down to kiss my cheek.

I hold up my hand to stop him. "That's quite alright."

"Magnolia." He nods, pulling a little face. "The picture of warmth, as always."

I give him a tight smile. "What are you doing here?"

"Me?" He gestures to himself, and I nod. "Oh, I was invited."

"By whom?" I ask, eyebrows up.

Brooks' eyes pinch. "Your dad."

I flick BJ a look before I look back at him.

"Wherefore?" I blink twice but flash him another quick smile because manners.

"Uh—" Brooks glances from me to BJ back to me. "Because he hired me."

BJ's head pulls back.

"For what?" I ask.

Brooks shrugs, sniffing a laugh. "I'm like, his guy."

"His guy?" I blink.

"Yep." He nods, pleased with himself.

I look over at BJ, sort of bewildered, and he sort of gives me this shrug.

My face pulls as I think back to our time together, or whatever you want to call it, and stare up at him with squinted eyes. "Sorry, but were you not in finance?"

He nods. "I always had a passion for music though, remember?"

I purse my lips as I shake my head. "I can't say that I do."

"Yeah!" He nods emphatically. "It's actually why I was interested in you in the first place—"

I blink a few times. "Oh—!"

BJ has a warning face on. Chin low, eyes daring.

"Are you trying to be punched?" Beej asks him, and I look over at him, shaking my head.

"Don't—" I tell him as I reach for his hand. "He used me, I used him."

Brooks nods along pleasantly but tilts his head. "How did you use me, out of interest?"

"Well," I shrug. "I was obviously terribly in love with BJ the entire time we were—whatever—"

"Together—?" Brooks offers.

"Sure." I shrug. "I was just using you as sort of—a last line of defence."

"I see." He nods, considering this. "Well, fair play. Worked out for you—" He flashes BJ and I an indifferent smile.

I cross my arms over my chest, feeling a tiny bit awkward.

"Tell me," Brooks says as he swirls his glass of wine. "I always wondered—were you two shagging?"

BJ scoffs. "I wish—"

Brooks glances from Beej over to me. "I just thought because we weren't—"

"You two never slept together?" Verity repeats loudly, and BJ gives her a look and I ignore her.

"No, I just—" Shake my head. "I couldn't stomach the thought of sex with anyone else. Or with him!" I gesture to BJ as an afterthought, as though it might soften a potential blow.

Brooks turns to Verity. "We did other things, don't get me wrong—"

"Okay—that's—shh—" I lift his glass to his mouth and shove it in there. "Enough out of you."

BJ presses his hands into his eye sockets.

"Could you tell me actually—" I stare up at Brooks. "Out of curiosity—does my father know that you cheated on me?"

Brooks tilts his head again. "I mean, did I—"

"I think you'll find literally and technically . . . yes. You did." I give him a pinched smile. "With that other girl that wasn't me."

He breathes out his nose, a bit miffed. "I know you didn't love me—"

"I don't care that you knew I didn't love you—I don't even care that you did it—" I give him a tall look. "Way to read the room, I was in love with BJ—" I give him a sarcastic look.

Brooks rolls his eyes at me and I square my shoulders a little.

"All I care to know is whether Harley knew when he hired you."

Brooks' jaw grinds as he thinks. There are a thousand terrible adjectives I could apply to him but he's never been a liar. Mercilessly truthful sometimes, actually.

He nods a couple of times. "Harley knows, yeah."

"Brilliant." I nod back once and BJ wordlessly takes my hand.

"Thank you," I tell Brooks.

His face falters a little, all confused.

"See you around?"

"Well," I shake my head. "Not if you're dating people that say 'wifey,' no—"

"Okay—" BJ turns a laugh into a cough and starts dragging me away. "Sorry—yep. See you around," he calls back to them before giving me eyes that mean I'm in trouble.

"Magnolia, she used a word you don't like, she wasn't working a corner."

I stare up at him, defiant. "I may have honestly preferred that she were."

He sniffs, amused.

"So I take it you're not going to call me 'hubby' then?"

A shiver rolls through my body and I shake my head.

"I think my clitoris just shrivelled up and died—"

"I can check that out for you, if you like?" He gives me a playful smile.

"I should not like that, to be entirely honest, sweetheart," says the voice of his mother from behind us. "And Magnolia, darling." She touches my shoulder gently. "Don't say 'clitoris.'"

"Well, what would she say instead?" Hamish asks, just to wind her up.

"Oh thank god—" I throw my arms around both BJ's parents.

Hamish glances around. "I thought they said it was an intimate dinner for a few of her closest friends."

"Well," I give them a small shrug. "It is possible my mother doesn't actually know what intimacy means . . ."

Lily says my name under her breath and she smacks me in the arm, trying not to laugh.

I shrug demurely. "It would explain so much."

She gives me a fake-stern look. "Be good."

"You look beautiful, Mum," BJ says, leaning down to kiss her.

Hamish extends his hand to Beej, who watches it for a couple of seconds before he reluctantly shakes it.

I stare over at Lily in the Victoire draped crepe gown in blush-pink she's wearing from Maticevski.

"Did you pick that dress yourself, Lilian?"

She nods, proudly. "I did!"

"Oh!" I look her up and down. "I'm terribly impressed. Splendid job."

From there, we dodged several members of the royal family—both intimate and extended—as well as three celebrities BJ has definitely slept with and one French rugby union player who I nearly slept with once in the olden days when I liked making BJ jealous.

When my mother spots us she does a big song and dance, hugs me, hugs Beej, coos at my dress, goes gaga for my shoes—at least when she focuses her adoration for me on the clothes I'm wearing, I find it believable.

My dress is sublime and my shoes are fantastic, that is fact. It's also a floatation device because it gives me something to talk about to the three people my mother is parading us in front of—and you'd best believe that we are being paraded.

My mother has, for as long as I can remember, been much more concerned with the perceived state of our family rather than the actual state of it.

Nearly every school holiday I ever had in my educational life was filled with at least one random photoshoot for an article someone was writing about my mother and the kind of woman she was. What strikes me as strange is she's crafted her public perception rather meticulously over the course of our lives but then will be photographed topless on a yacht with a bottle of champagne in her hands and maybe a joint in her mouth, and you know what—they loved it.

"Good for her!" the public used to say. "We love a woman who can do both!"—it was a funny sort of experience, watching Britain publicly celebrate our maternal neglect.

The only time they turned on her a little was last year, after the divorce—when she went a bit sideways, so did their perception of her. Her serial dating of men her children's age was less easy to stomach, for whatever reason.

However, since Bridget, she's back in their good graces. Quite adored by them, actually.

Sometimes that makes me jealous, I don't know why with me they can swing between such extremes but with her, she's able to rest fairly easily in the favourable bosom of the red tops.

Why can she be photographed falling drunk out the door of a club when she's thirty-eight and be celebrated for being Britain's Coolest Mum and then when I was photographed falling out of a town car drunk when I was seventeen, I was labelled "The Parks Family Problem Child."

"Do you think it's because she's white and I'm not?" I asked BJ back then, frowning, eyes heavy. The article itself really went on to list several of my indiscretions from that year past, including my grades from school that were still fine but not as good as they previously had been. Of course, no one knows what actually happened that year. And truthfully, even if they did, I don't know what it would have changed. They've always liked to talk about me, how it affects me is irrelevant, it seems.

BJ slipped his arms around my waist in his bedroom at his parent's house. It was December, he was close to nineteen and his forever-beautiful face strained at the thought.

"No—" he brushed his lips over mine. "You're perfect."

And he's right, actually. I myself might truthfully be rather far from perfect, but my skin? My skin is a caramel-chocolatey dream. Bridget later said that actually, they're mean to me just because I'm easy to hate. (Or maybe because I refer to myself as a caramel-chocolatey dream?) (People tend not to like it when you're attractive and you know it, which I am and I do.) (Isn't it weird how if I said to someone, "I have a really good numbers brain, I can do maths crazy fast," they'd be like, "Oh good for you, you delightful, mathy nerd," but were I to say, "I'm quite pretty," they'd be like, "piss off, you big prat"—even though both things are personal advantages.)

Anyway, BJ and her had a bit of a row after she said that, but I think I do see her point actually.

"It's a cheap shot," BJ scowled from the doorway as he watched me laying on my sister's bed, reading another article about how I went to Paris and spent £500,000 in a day on shopping.

"Yes, maybe," Bridget said. "But that was an unlikable thing to do."

"Yes, but I didn't do it!" I insisted. I probably spent a couple hundred thousand, yes, but I was gifted so much as well. Except I couldn't really say that either, normal people don't much like rich people getting free things.

"You're too pretty, you're too skinny and you're too in love." Bridget gave me a shrug. "Of course they're going to try to rip you apart."

They haven't ripped me apart in a while, probably because of Bridge. Small mercies, I suppose.

BJ and I happy together is a fascination to everyone here though—that's not a small mercy. It feels like we're goldfish in a bowl, so we hide in the corner with Bushka and his parents, which usually is my perfect way to spend an evening anyway, but the strain between BJ and Hamish is still overtly present. It's weighing heavy on Beej, I can tell. He's really in his head about it—which I don't mean to be insensitive, but it's really dragging down the vibes with just the five of us in the corner.

Hamish is making more effort to talk to his son than my father has ever made in his whole life combined to talk to me, and BJ's not not talking to him, but they're pretty one-worded answers.

Just when I think Lily is absolutely about to stroke out from the stress of Beej and Ham, someone taps a champagne glass and I look up.

It's my father, standing next to my mother in a dark green wool mohair suit from Gucci, with a cream roll-neck cashmere jumper from Fedeli, with the caramel Cordovan derby shoes from Brunello Cucinelli. He looks handsome, so that's annoying.

He looks down at my mother and gives her a smile.

"Thank you, everyone, for coming here to celebrate Arrie's birthday tonight. It's so wonderful to have you here with us. Arrie, myself, Magnolia and Ksenyia are so grateful for your support these last few months—"

I drop my eyes to the ground, not wanting to catch the eye of anyone here who might think I have ever received or wanted their support—I haven't and I do not. BJ puts his arm around my shoulder and pulls me in towards him.

"I just wanted to take this opportunity to make a small announcement. Obviously, Magnolia and BJ Ballentine are—finally—" Harley looks over at us, gives BJ a wink as though they're friends. "Tying the knot in June next year. You're all invited, of course, and we're incredibly excited."

("All invited?" I stare up at BJ, horrified, and he presses his lips together.)

"Magnolia is going to be the most beautiful bride," he says as he flashes me a smile. "Or the second most," he says, and I definitely feel myself frown, because what the fuck? That's so rude, why would he—and then I realise—I know what's coming. Shit.

I feel BJ stiffen up next to me.

"Arrie and I will be renewing our vows next summer," Harley says to the room, which immediately gasps and "Ooh"s.

My mother holds up her left hand. A new engagement ring on her finger and she lets out a little excited squeal.

I'm very still except for my eyes. My eyes go wide and fall

to my hands in my lap as the whole restaurant breaks out into a round of applause.

I feel dizzy. Suddenly, really lightheaded. The edges of my vision start growing dim and I stand up. I don't even mean to stand up, but I'm on my feet nevertheless—maybe I stumble a bit or something because BJ's next to me now, one arm around my shoulders, the other on my stomach keeping me upright.

Everything is going swirly, or is it rushy? Is everything rushing? I might be fainting. Or am I panicking?

He's saying something that I can't hear, he's shaking his head. He looks annoyed and worried at once. His eyes are heavy, brows low.

He brings me out into the foyer, stands in front of me, close. Puts his hands on my shoulders and looks me in the eyes.

"Deep breath," he tells me, not looking away, eyes locked on me.

I don't realise that I take one, but I must because he nods and says, "Good, again. Another one." I do. This time I feel it, the air cool through my nose and then down into my lungs, my tummy expanding with it.

BJ nods again, licks his top lip. "Good—"

"Darling!" my mother calls from behind us, walking quickly in our direction.

"No—" I shake my head, looking just at BJ.

"Arrie—" BJ gives my mum a look as she fiddles up to us. "Just give her a minute—"

"But—"

"Just a minute," he tells her with a gentle firmness.

"Magnolia!" my father calls, walking over to us, frowning. "Is everything okay? What's going on?"

And it's that last sentence that sort of pushes me over the edge.

I take a big breath that feels like someone's winding a crank that's in my back, and I stare up at my father.

"You're insane," I tell him.

He pulls back. "What?"

"Clinically, perhaps." I nod to myself.

Harley looks confused, glancing from BJ to Mum then back to me. "Come again?"

"Are you joking?" I look from him to my mother. "This is how you tell me?"

"It was a surprise, sweetheart!" My mother smiles, as though I'm silly. "We wanted to surprise you!"

I stare at her for a couple of seconds, incredulous. "You thought I was going to be happy about this?"

She shrugs demurely, nose in the air. "Maybe."

I look at her, exasperated and baffled. "Why would I be happy about this?"

"Oh, I don't know—" Harley scoffs. "Because we're happy?"

"Oh—" I roll my eyes. "Well, if you're happy, then—great!"

Harley shakes his head, jaw jutted. "What are you going on about now?"

"You hired my ex-boyfriend, who cheated on me, to be your—and I quote—'guy'?"

"Well," Harley's face pulls. "Did he cheat on you though?"

My mouth falls open as I stare at him.

"I mean," he keeps going. "Fair play to you because you're marrying him now—" He gestures to Beej. "But BJ was up in your bed every night."

"Did you need to hire him?" I emphasise the "him."

Harley shakes his head as he looks down his nose at me. "Who I hire has nothing to do with you. It's none of your business."

"You couldn't just . . . hire someone else?"

"No." He shrugs, indifferent. "I wanted to hire him."

I nod along like I get it. "And you always do what you want."

"Yes," Harley says loudly. Loud enough that a few people that are nearby glance over at us and loud enough that BJ shifts a little bit in front of me.

"I do, yeah," he says, quieter, but nodding still.

I sniff an empty laugh. "Do you think about anyone but yourself?"

"I don't know—" He shrugs. "Do you?"

"Say that again," BJ tells him, properly stepping in front of me now.

"Ey," my father jeers. "Here he comes." He flicks his eyebrows at Beej a bit menacingly. They've never come to blows, not once in however many years. But it often feels like they might and I've wondered what would happen if it did.

My father's not a small man. Six feet to BJ's six feet two, but he's undeniably jacked. Like, really, really strong. But then, BJ is—regrettably—rather an incredibly good fighter. I've seen him in so many fights so many times since we were young, in real life and on the rugby pitch, and I've probably seen him lose twice. But him against my father, I don't know what happens because I suspect that there's not much my father wouldn't do to win. That said—BJ's been waiting to hit Harley for literal years, so maybe all that pent-up energy might bring him up a weight class.

Not that I think it's actually going to happen—it just feels more and more palpable these days.

Harley nods his chin at Beej. "It's all talk with you."

And then BJ moves towards him, chin low, nostrils flared.

"Nah, man," Beej shakes his head. "I'd hit you in the foyer of the Ritz any day."

I spin on my heel, hand on my fiancé's chest, shaking my head at him. He tears his eyes away from my father's, back down to mine, breathing a bit ragged, jaw all tight.

I turn back to Harley and glare up at him.

"You're unbelievable."

"Unbelievable, am I?" He pulls back, amused. "Thought I was despicable."

"You're both." I stare him down.

He sighs, tired. "Magnolia, I didn't realise you cared about Brooks—"

"I don't care about Brooks!" I huff, annoyed. The nerve! "I've never cared about Brooks—you hiring Brooks is representative of a larger problem within you—"

"Within me?" He scoffs and nods his head at me. "Go on then."

"You never think about how anything you do might affect anyone else around you."

He rolls his eyes.

"Like how hiring an ex-boyfriend of mine might make me feel. Or how sleeping with my agent in the room next door in New York when I was fifteen might have affected me. Or what it might do to Bridget and I if you were to, say, oh, I don't know—fuck our fucking nanny."

My mother shifts on her feet uncomfortably.

"Magnolia, I know that this has all been hard for you—but in the scheme of my life, Marsaili was a blip that I—"

I cut him off.

"So you fucked all our lives for a blip?"

My mother stares at the marble floor, she's sad. I think this might hurt her to talk about. Harley says nothing, he stares at me—"glares" is probably the more accurate term—breathing heavy, eyes me like he hates me.

But do you know what? Same page.

"Fuck you," I tell him and then we leave.

FORTY

BJ

I swear to god, I'm one comment away from beating the shit out of Harley.

It's been a few days since that night—fuck, it was a bit of a disaster, wasn't it?

Magnolia got in the car—bit of a feat in and of itself, that was, but it was raining and her shoes were suede—and then she said she needed to call Marsaili.

And I asked if she really wanted to do that right now and she said she's probably never wanted to do anything less, but that she didn't want Marsaili hearing or reading about it somewhere else.

So she called her as soon as we got home. It was the sort of selfless shit Magnolia does sometimes that she doesn't want people to know she's capable of, but I was proud of her. Stayed on the phone with Mars while she cried and then when Parks finally got off the phone with her, she lay her head down on my chest and cried til she fell asleep.

Do you know how rare it is for her to fall asleep without showering first?

It's happened like, twice. Ever.

When she woke the next morning she was quick to point out we were asleep on the couch and so it wasn't—and I'm quoting here—"heralding the coming of a new showerless regime in our relationship."

That same morning Bushka showed up and said she thought we'd want to take her to breakfast—so we did, and then since, she's actually just not really left.

Which is something I need to talk to Parks about.

So a few days after the fact, I sat Magnolia down and sat across from her, reaching for her hands and holding them.

"Can we have a chat about something?"

"Oh—" She leant in towards me. "Okay. Is everything okay?"

"Yeah, grand—" I nodded. "I love you."

"Okay—" She gave me a confused smile.

"So, like—" I thought to myself for a second. "Your parents fucking suck."

"Yes, thank you." She gave me a look and I stared back at her, breathed out my nose.

"We have to take Bushka."

She looked at me, confused. "Where?"

I lifted my eyebrows. "In."

She copied my eyebrows. "In where?"

"Here—" I rolled my eyes. "With us."

Magnolia stared over at me, blinking a bunch of times.

"You want her to live with us?"

"Yeah," I shrugged.

Magnolia shook her head. "She's not a stray dog, Beej!"

"I know—" I shrugged again. "But, actually—by definition—she is kind of a stray . . ."

Parks flicked me a look before she folded her arms over her chest, looking conflicted.

"Beej—" She took a steep breath through her nose. "You and I, we're only just—" Her eyes welled up a bit and she swallowed heavy, looked at me kind of guilty and weighed down. "I just—got you. I don't want to share you."

I took a deep breath and nodded because I got it—I felt that too a bit.

"I know." I touched her face. "But it's the right thing to do, Parks. Besides," I shrug, "you and me, we've got forever between us." I leant in, pressed my mouth into hers.

"And anyway, with the way she drinks, her liver's going to kick the bucket any day now—"

"BJ!" She laughed, smacking my arm.

"I'm joking—I love her so much. I want her to stay here. She has to."

"Probably shouldn't get that puppy anymore, then." Magnolia sighed and I pulled back, giving her a look.

"Oh no, definitely we should still get a puppy."

"You're ridiculous." She rolled her eyes.

"Only sometimes," I said before I kissed her.

Couple of days pass again and we have one more chat about it to make sure we both feel good—and I'd be lying if I said it didn't feel a bit like a sacrifice, I've waited like, five years to be back with Parks and I've got her now and ever since we've found our way back it's fucking blow after blow, so part of me, part of her—we were ready to just be by ourselves—be chillers in a house we both live in, get married, be married, you know?

But this is the right thing to do, we both know it is.

So I bring in all her favourites, Beluga caviar, these Lavosh biscuits she's mad on and the 1985 R.D. from Bollinger.

Bushka is fucking thrilled by the spread but Magnolia gives me a disparaging look as she sits down next to me.

I nod my chin at her, tell her to talk without saying anything.

"Bushka," Magnolia rests her chin in her hand on the table. "We have something we'd like to talk to you about."

Bushka looks up as she's shovelling as much caviar as physically possible onto her cracker.

"Da?"

Parks clears her throat and tosses me a quick smile.

"We'd like for you to come and live with us."

"Какие?" Bushka looks between us, confused.

"Мы хотим чтобы ты жил с нами," Magnolia tells her again. "Here—" She switched back to English. "We'll turn that guest room into your bedroom and—"

"Нет." Bushka shakes her head.

Magnolia stares at her, annoyed. "What do you mean 'no'?"

"Please—" I reach over and touch Bushka's hand. "We want you here—we'd have so much fun—"

Bushka gives me a tender smile as she pats my hand with her own.

"So sweet and good," she tells me before she looks at Magnolia again.

"Мой ангел"—my angel, I know that one—"this kindness for me is too much—"

"Great!" Magnolia sits up, smiling at her. "Well, I'll arrange the movers—"

"Нет."

"Okay, fine—" Magnolia rolls her eyes. "Daniela will arrange the movers—"

"No," Bushka says, rolling her eyes. "Not moving here."

Magnolia stares over at her, offended. "Почему?"

"Я возвращаюсь в Россию," Bushka says, and I stare between the two of them, waiting for one of them to translate.

"What?" Magnolia frowns, staring over at her.

Bushka breathes out her nose and looks over at me, gives me a tender smile.

"I'm going to live with Alexey."

"No." Magnolia shakes her head.

"Bushka—" I start.

"Why?" Magnolia stands up. "You belong in London!"

Bushka shakes her head. "I belong in Russia."

Magnolia stares down at her grandmother, brows low, sort of glaring. "Why are you doing this?"

Bushka stands, reaching for Parks' hand.

"It make me so happy that you want me here—I will visit," she tells her, gesturing back to the guest room we just offered her. "This will be my room anyway, you can make it like shrine room for me—"

"Well—" Magnolia cuts her off with a frown. "We probably won't if you're not going to live wi—" Then I nip her in the arm as I stand up next to her. "Ow!" She stares up at me, outraged and betrayed.

"I get sign made that says 'Bushka's Room,'" Bushka tells her.

"It should be in neon!" I tell her just to annoy Parks. "Magnolia loves neon!"

"Bushka," Magnolia sighs. "You don't have to go."

"Da." She nods. "Yes, it's time. Alexey has asked for years and I always say нет, but now is right time."

"Why now?" Magnolia pouts.

"Вы знаете почему сейчас."

Magnolia shakes her head and her eyes go teary.

"Пожалуйста не оставляй меня с ними." Magnolia sniffs and Bushka looks sad, she reaches for her granddaughter's hand and squeezes it.

"Я не." Bushka gives her a strained smile and then nods at me. "I leave you with him."

Feels a bit like being knighted, that does, being trusted like that.

I tilt my head, looking down at Bushka.

"At least stay here til you move—"

"Fine, yes." Bushka nods. "They do so much sex."

"No—" Magnolia starts shaking her head.

"They do," Bushka nods. "Like animal. Bang bang bang all day."

Magnolia scrunches her face up.

"But your sex—" Bushka continues. "Is okay!"

"Oh, good—" I stare over at Parks, eyes wide.

"You are young," Bushka tells us. "Have fun, is good to have orgasm, yes?" She pats me on the arm for a job well done. "Good."

"I take it back—" Magnolia shakes her head. "You can leave."

"I go to my room now," Bushka says, ignoring Parks, already walking to it.

"—Not your room!" Magnolia yells down the hall.

"Yes, it is," I call after her.

And then I look at Parks, her eyes all heavy and afraid, and I'm about to wrap myself around her when Bushka comes bustling back out of her room and throws her arms around Magnolia from behind.

"Спасибо," Bushka tells her. Thank you.

Magnolia nods quickly, not wanting to let her grandmother see her cry.

"Of course."

Bushka gives my hand a squeeze and goes to her room.

We sit back down at the table, me and Parks, but she doesn't eat much after that.

Just a mouthful. One. I counted. Shouldn't count, I know, that's fucking helicopter-y of me, but that smacked her around a bit, I can tell. She's cut up about it.

Thinks everyone's leaving her. And to be fair to her, it does seem to be a reoccurring pattern.

I pull her up from her chair and over onto my lap.

Just have her sit there for a few minutes, my chin on her shoulder. Let her stare off into space, think about whatever she's thinking about.

"You okay?" I ask her eventually.

"Hmm?" She looks back at me, so close her mouth brushes up against mine even though we aren't kissing.

"Oh, yeah—grand." She nods. "Great."

I give her a tender smile. "She was so happy we asked—"

"Yeah." Parks nods, not meeting my eyes at first and then she does. Fuck, she's sad. Hate it when she's sad. "She's still going though."

"Yeah," I dig my chin into her shoulder mindlessly. "It's better for her."

Magnolia looks over at me, unsure. "You think?"

"Yeah," I nod. "Alexey's great. He's going to look after her so well."

She nods, staring at the wall. "But she'll be gone."

I watch her carefully. "I know."

She keeps staring at the wall and I can see it, pressing down on her, this fear that they're all leaving her. Abandonment issues, man. I've said it before, I'll say it again. They're fucked up.

I touch her face, turn it towards me. Tell her the only thing that I can think of to say.

"I'm not going anywhere."

FORTY-ONE

BJ

A night out with the boys—Jonah's been a dog with a bone about it—so we head to Tramp.

At first I said that I couldn't, that I think Parks needed me, but he looked sad when I said that, like, out-of-character sad.

He's a pretty difficult bloke to bum out, if I'm honest, and that did it, so I feel like something's amiss, so out we go.

Nights out with the boys hit different now.

It was clubs before, now it's dinners or bars, and when we're there the dynamic's weird, because once upon a time the whole night would have been about tuning random girls and now three fourths of us are locked up so it's just not on the cards—except for tonight.

It became very apparent very quickly that Jonah's sole intent for this evening was to get fucked up and hook up.

Henry's too fresh in his relationship, too absolutely fucking pussy-whipped to be here, so he bails pretty quick once he realises the tone of the evening.

"You coming?" he asks me on his way out.

Shake my head. "Going to stick around, see if Jo's alright."

He glances over at Jo, who's making out with girl number four of the evening at the bar, and tosses me a look. "Good luck."

I look over at Christian and we both snort a laugh.

"Feels weird," he says. "Don't you think? Being out without them."

"Yeah, kind of."

"Are we fucked?" he asks, sort of laughing.

"Hundred percent," I nod. "How's it going with Daisy?"

"Yeah—" he shrugs. "She's the best."

Says it like it's fact. It is. She's fucking sick, like such a cool girl to hang out with. You can tell she has brothers, grew up around boys. No pretences, no bullshit, says it like it is.

Christian looks over at me—stares for a couple of seconds, eyes pinched, thinking before he speaks.

"Julian's back."

I look over at him. "What?"

"Just," he tells me.

"Oh." I nod, make sure it doesn't show on my face that hearing it rattles me a bit.

"Good for him," I shrug.

Christian watches me a few seconds more, says nothing, then looks away.

Julian's back?

Fuck.

Annoys me more than I wish it did, that's my fucking night ruined.

I check in on Jo (on to girl number five) and order us all another round of drinks and we're talking about a documentary we both watched about storms that was just fucking insane. The earth is wild.

Christian's talking about the episode he just watched about volcanoes when I feel a body sidle up close to mine.

I look over my shoulder at the person—it's a girl—her eyes lock on me.

And it's a look, like, I mean, a proper look.

"Hello," she says, batting her cat eyes at me.

I look back at Christian and pull a face. "Hi?"

"Do you remember me?" she asks, tilting her head.

I press my tongue into my top lip as I scrunch my face.

"Uh, no?" I flash her a quick smile. "Should I?"

She presses her lips together and squints at me, playfully. "We had sex."

"Oh, fuck—" I breathe out this sort of laugh. Look at Christian again for help but he just gives me a little shrug.

"Sorry—" Shake my head at her. "I had sex with a lot of people."

She rolls her eyes in pretend offence. "So romantic."

I look at her, my chin pulled back. "I'm not trying to be romantic."

"Are you not?" She smiles up at me, invitingly.

Actually, now that I'm properly looking at her, I remember. Remember the hookup, remember why I did it.

I did it because she looks a bit like Parks.

Can't ever decide if it's better or worse when they're kind of like Parks.

Worse, I guess. I mean, it's all worse.

Skin like my girl, hair kind of the same but not as good, brown eyes instead of green, a less good mouth—enjoyed it enough at the time. Didn't think of her once during or after.

Wonder if she knew that if she'd just fuck off?

I lift my chin, stare down at her a bit. "Do you know who I am?"

She flicks her eyes like I asked her a silly question. "Of course, I know who you are."

"Then you know I'm with someone." I give her a pointed look.

She makes the "Hm" sound as she glances around the room before she gives me a little shrug. "I don't see her here."

I'm frowning now, well off it.

"I'm not going to cheat on her—"

"You have before," this absolute twat of a stranger reminds me.

Both my head and Christian's pull back.

"Fuck off—" Christian scoffs, shaking his head at the fucking audacity of her.

"One time," I tell the girl, even though I don't have to tell her anyway.

And you know what she does? Takes a step closer to me, looks me up square in the eyes and says, "I won't say anything. It can be our secret."

Then she grabs my hand and puts it on her waist.

I stare at it for probably a full second before I snatch it back.

Shake my head at her. "I don't want secrets with you."

"Are you sure?" she asks, voice sultry, and I'm proper fucked off now.

"Yeah, alright," I nod once as I stand and get right up in her face. "Here's one. I fucked you because you look like the girl I've been in love with my whole life."

She goes still and I keep going.

"She didn't want me at the time, but now she does, so why the fuck do you think I'd come back for seconds here with you when I have her waiting for me at home?" I lift my eyebrows, waiting for her to say something, but she doesn't, obviously.

Looks pretty mortified though.

Feel a bit chuffed with myself and she danders off pretty quick.

Christian pulls a face like he's the uncomfortable one but smacks me on the back like he's pleased with me. We try to have another drink after that, but actually I'm done now. I feel sick.

Happens sometimes, still. It's not the first time—girls having a crack even though the papers are talking about our wedding every other fucking day. Most of the time it's one crack, I shoot it down, they walk away.

But that girl tonight, she was persistent and I don't know what made her think she had the right of way?

I don't know how to shake my fucking image that I'm some cheating prick who'll fuck anything for a good time.

It was true once, but it's not true now.

Now, I'm done fucking around.

Now, I feel fucking ill anytime I see someone I was with or Parks sees someone I was with. Now I want to put my fist through a wall every time someone even mentions that I cheated on her.

I check in with Jo one last time then tell Christian I'm heading home.

One positive about not having Parks with me is I can actually take the fucking town car.

Like, yeah, all the walking's fine—her legs have never been better and that's saying something—but how good's driving?

And I'm not even driving myself. Fuck, I miss driving myself.

When I walk through the door, she looks up at me from the couch, a spread of fashion magazines around her, a pad of Post-its and a Sharpie.

"You're home early!" She smiles up at me.

I nod, walking towards her. "Yeah."

She looks at me closer for a few seconds then stands. "Are you okay?"

"Yeah," I nod quickly. "Kind of."

She frowns a little.

"No—" I shake my head once. "Not really."

She walks towards me, touching my waist.

"What happened?"

I press my hands into my eyes and breathe out. "I ran into this girl I fucked about with before—"

"Okay?" Magnolia frowns.

I lick my mouth, feel nervous, kind of sick to tell her, like I did something wrong.

"She made a pass at me," I say quickly.

"Oh," Magnolia barely says.

I swallow. "Grabbed my hand, put it on her."

"On her where?"

"Waist."

Magnolia nods once.

I tilt my head, looking for her eyes.

"I told her to piss off."

"Right." She nods again. "And then what?"

"And then I came home."

"Why?" she asks quietly.

"I don't know." I shrugged. "Felt weird, didn't want to be out anymore."

I grip her waist. "I hate 'out' without you."

"Right." She nods, sort of distracted, not looking at me. Her face has gone weird, pale maybe?

"Are you okay?" I ask, watching her closely.

"Hmm?" She looks up at me, eyes too wide, pretending she's more fine than I know she is. "Completely, yeah."

I breathe out my nose. "Sorry."

She looks at me quickly, nervously. "What for?"

I shake my head and shrug a bit. "Just am."

"Okay," she says, forcing a smile before she swallows, nervous.

"I love you," I tell her.

"I love you too," she tells me back, but the way she says it makes me feel weird.

She moves back to the couch, brows low, breathing shallow, biting down absentmindedly on her bottom lip—

And then I see it—that thing I hate—the part of her mind where the doubt lives, it fires up behind her eyes and then they go rounder.

She swallows heavy. Fiddles with her hands.

Fiddles so much with them that she sits on them only for about twenty seconds before she's back to wringing them.

And I can't watch it—I hate seeing how what I did so many fucking years ago still wrecks her now so I pull off my shirt and get in the shower.

Know she'll follow me. She has to. There's a loose thread in her brain.

I wonder how long there'll be these loose threads, and am I going to spend my whole life cutting them off?

Takes about five minutes for a little voice to sound from the other side of the shower door.

"Beej?" she calls.

"Yeah?"

"Nothing else happened, right?"

I open the shower door and look down at her, frowning.

"Parksy—no." I shake my head. "You know I wouldn't do that to you, right?"

And do you know what—she doesn't say anything. Doesn't even move a muscle.

I stare at her, my chest going tight.

"You do know that?"

She nods this time, but it's unconvincing.

"Parks," I sigh. "I wouldn't."

"Okay." She nods.

I rub my hands over my mouth—think I might be sick.

"Do you believe me?" I ask.

"Yeah, of course," she says automatically.

Then she flashes me a smile as she walks away that's timid and afraid but she doesn't know it is, doesn't mean for it to be either. But I see it, right there, lurking under the waters of us.

There's a monster that thrives on her second-biggest anxiety and her worst fear, used to be number one. Thanks to Bridge, it's been demoted, but only just.

"Parks—" I call to her again.

She looks back. "Yeah?"

"I promise," I sigh. "Nothing happened."

11:17

Julian

Hey tiges

Well well . . .

Look what the cat dragged in

I'm back

Okay?

Can I see you?

I'm engaged.

I know.

Can I see you?

What for?

Just say yes.

No.

I know you want to see me too

No I don't

Yes you do.

Go on . . .

When?

You tell me . . .

Tuesday.

Ok

A week from now. 2pm.

Hah. Ok.

Where?

Daylesford

Marylebone?

Notting Hill.

Bossy . . .

?

Missed it.

Don't.

Haha

Alright.

Julian, is everything okay?

I'll see you Tuesday. x

FORTY-TWO
Magnolia

I didn't mention anything til the night before. Not because I was trying to be a sneak or anything, but because I wasn't sure how he'd take it and I hate fighting with him.

"BJ," I say, rolling in towards him in our bed.

"Mm?" He doesn't look up from his book. *Starry Messenger* by Neil deGrasse Tyson.

"Julian texted me."

"What?" he says, not really registering what I've said.

I see the information processing behind his eyes, then he closes the book and turns to me.

"What about?"

I take a breath and then sort of shrug. "He asked to meet up."

"Okay." Beej nods. "What'd you say?"

I purse my lips. "Yes."

He presses his tongue into his bottom lip, nodding a couple of times. "Okay."

"Okay?" I repeat, eyebrows up.

"Yeah, I guess." He shrugs. "You don't need my permission—"

"I know—" I say quickly, because I don't.

He shrugs again. "Then—"

"I was just trying to be honest," I tell him.

"Right. Thanks." He purses his mouth. "What do you think he wants?"

I shake my head. "I don't know, actually."

BJ's eyes wander over my face, a bit curious. "You haven't heard from him?"

"No—" I shake my head. "Not once since he left."

His head pulls back in surprise. "Even when Bridg—"

"Even when." I cut him off with a nod.

Beej shakes his head, annoyed about that for some reason. Then he tugs me in towards him and brushes his mouth over mine.

"I trust you," he tells me, but I wonder if there's an inch of him that looks a little bit like he doesn't.

FORTY-THREE
Magnolia

Now, do I dress a certain way knowing that I'm seeing Julian Haites and I want him to still think of me sort of how he used to?

Possibly, yes.

Does that make me a bad person? I don't know. Or does it perhaps just make me *a* person? Maybe it makes me both.

It's hard to have someone look at you one way for a length of time and then when you finally see them again, they see you in a different light. I don't much like the light of me changing in anyone's eyes but the idea of Julian's eyes being different towards me makes me feel uneasy in a way that I know it probably shouldn't.

It implies something, I know it does. How deep-rooted that implication is anyone's guess. Bridget's always said that I need a constant top-up of the male gaze due to our father being so negligent, which, to her credit, seems to have proven true enough, and I've always wondered why we're so different in that way. Why she's so fine and I'm so . . . me?

I wear the the cream Leni cotton, cable-knit wool sweater from SEA tucked into Saint Laurent's black horsebit-detail miniskirt and the Loro Piana cognac coloured double-breasted reversible shearling and leather coat over it, with the caramel brown calf suede Piper 90mm suede knee-high boots by Gianvito Rossi and a velvet bow barrette from Jennifer Behr in the same brown as everything else. Because I know he'll like it and I want his eyes to go how they would when they saw me before, which was a way I don't know quite how to wrap words around because sometimes I used to think he liked me—properly liked me—but then, he could so quickly turn on a dime. He could be so cold, so off, completely indifferent. And the way we ended? Well, that just tells you everything, doesn't it?

Daniela and I walk to Daylesford from the apartment, which is barely a twenty-minute walk, and usually I try to make conversation with her but today I don't because I feel nervous to see him. I don't know why?

Silly.

I can't spot him from the street once we arrive, so I go in and in again further when I still can't find him.

I head towards the back. Up the stairs and perch on the top of them, and then there he is.

Back right corner, tucked away, except not at all tucked away.

As big as I remember him—bigger even, perhaps.

You know how with time sometimes in your memories you remember someone bigger than they actually are? I felt like I probably did that with Julian.

That he felt like this huge, big presence, because he—at least at first—sort of felt like a thing that was a bit like a saviour.

In the end, not so much, I suppose.

If I were to think back to that night in the hallway at Jonah's club—which I don't, because why would I?—but were I to recall with vivid memory how it made me feel seeing Julian do that with that girl when he was supposed to be there with me, it felt a bit like watching someone pick up one of your favourite mugs to drink tea from and breaking it on purpose.

He's over there wearing the sherpa-lined black denim jacket from Levi's over a dark grey logo cotton T-shirt from Acne, black straight-leg cargo trousers from Daily Paper and the black Tournament leather sneakers by Common Projects.

He's rather tan, sitting there on his phone, drinking a coffee, and I might have stood there watching him a second too long out of habit, or something—maybe because it feels a bit like seeing a ghost, or maybe because he's lovely to look at, just—he looks up and glances around, the way you do when you can feel eyes on you, and then his eyes find mine.

He gives me a lazy smile and stands as I approach him.

"Oi," he grins.

I give him a quick smile. "Hello."

He pulls a face and rolls his eyes.

"Fuck off—" He reaches for me. "You give me a hug right now."

He folds himself around me and I don't cuddle him back too much because I feel a bit precarious in his arms.

He gives me another smile and then looks past me to Daniela. "Who's this then?"

"Oh—" I shake my head. "I'm sorry! This is Daniela. My assistant."

Julian extends his hand to her, then shakes hers with both of his.

"Julian." He smiles at her. "Good to meet you—"

"Likewise." She nods.

"Daniela, would you mind giving us a minute, actually?"

She nods, "Sure," before going off and finding a table.

Julian looks back at me.

"Sit," he tells me, and I do, across from him.

He watches me for a few seconds and gets this smile on his face that I don't quite understand. Maybe how you might smile at a Rubik's Cube that's beating you.

"What?" I frown at him and he shakes his head, looking away.

"Nothing—" He sniffs a laugh. "Just that stupid face you got."

I frown more, offended now.

He nods his chin at me. "I like this."

He gestures vaguely at my skirt.

"Yeah?" I smile, glancing down at myself.

Knew it.

"Yeah . . ." He nods, still watching me closer than I'd like him to. I forgot how see-through I felt around him. "Alright?" he asks.

"Yes," I nod big with my show smile. "Grand."

He shakes his head a little, face serious. "Don't bullshit me."

"I'm not—" I shrug, airily.

And then Julian stares at me for a few seconds, eyes not quite pinched but serious.

"Liar," he calls me, and the way he looks at me makes me feel small and I hate it.

I breathe in quickly and glare at him, a brief resentment towards him as though he was the one who caused this mess as opposed to just being the person here in front of me now making me look at it square in the eye.

I'd imagine it would be fairly rare for one to abseil down here of one's own volition, and perhaps if it were done by conscious knowledge then it would be a controlled descent and you might know where you even are and how you got there. But for me, death is a valley I've been shoved into . . . without my permission, in the middle of the night, and I don't know how to climb back out of it. That's how I am. How can I say that out loud though? I couldn't possibly. It'd be so un-British. I square my shoulders, put my nose in the air.

"I've known better days," I say to him instead.

He stares over at me for a few seconds, blinking, saying nothing, then he reaches for my chair—"Come here."

He drags me and the chair over to him how he used to and pulls me into his chest.

"Fuck, I'm sorry—" he whispers, shaking his head. "I'm so sorry."

He really does sound it, actually.

I pull back and look up at him and his saviour complex. "It's not your fault."

He lets out this shallow laugh and nods, looking like he might cry. He presses his lips tight together.

He was quite fond of Bridget.

He nods again. "I'm still sorry."

I glare up at him. "So sorry that you ignored me for four months?"

He gives me a look. "I wasn't ignoring you, I was—"

"What?" I ask him, eyebrows up.

He licks his bottom lip and looks away.

I nod, coolly. "Nice."

"What did you want from me?" He shrugs.

"Gosh, I don't know. What about a good, old-fashioned 'I'm sorry your sister died'—"

"I didn't know what to say."

I stare at him, unimpressed. "Literally anything would have been better than nothing at all, Julian."

He nods, resigned. "Sorry," he says, though he doesn't really sound it.

I breathe through my nose, feeling annoyed. "Why did you ask me here?"

He watches over at me for a couple of seconds and his mouth opens to speak but it doesn't immediately.

He swallows once then breathes out. "I just wanted to see if you were okay."

I give him an impatient look and wave my hands in front of me as though I'm presenting myself for his viewing.

I breathe out my nose. "You know it's rather impolite to ask someone that—"

"Only if they're holding on by a thread," he tells me and then watches me closely again. "Are you?"

"Am I what?" I glare at him defensively.

"Okay—?" he asks. "Hanging on by a thread—? Completely fucked—? Pick one." He's impatient and done with my shit now. He's always been done with my shit though.

I look up at him and my eyes go threadbare without my express permission.

"No. Yes. And yes."

His head tilts in that "your sister's dead" sad head-tilt way.

"Can we go for a drive?"

"Ah," I give him an apologetic smile. "I can't say I'm much for driving these days."

He sighs and presses his hand into his mouth all sad and strained about a thousand things I suppose I won't ever understand.

"I won't let anything happen to you," he tells me as he stands up and tosses down a small wad of cash that's without a doubt far too much for the single coffee he's had here.

"Oh, have you taken up traffic marshalling?" I give him a wry smile.

He looks down at me in my seat and takes my hand, pulling me to my feet.

"Parks, nothing's going to happen to you ever again."

I flash him a weak smile. "You can't promise that."

"Yeah, I can," he says, solemn. "I do. On my life." He nods his head towards the exit. "Let's go." He starts moving towards the door.

"Why?" I ask as I follow after him anyway, even though I'm not entirely sure I want to.

He shrugs. "Too many eyes here."

I glance around us. "So?"

"So you're spoken for." He looks over his shoulder at a pair of girls about my age, whispering as they stare at us. "Do you really want to be in the *Daily Mail* tomorrow?"

He nods again at the exits.

"I'm in the *Daily Mail* every day," I call after him.

"Sure," he nods, opening the back door to his black Escalade, which is different to the one he had before. I was rather well acquainted with the one he had before. Then he gives me a playful squint. "But do you really want to feed the beast?"

I sniff, or maybe I huff, I'm not sure—either way, I cross my arms momentarily, then remember Daniela, who's appeared beside me.

"What about—"

"She can sit up front," he tells me, before he opens the front door for Daniela.

She just climbs in, not a second thought. He closes the door behind her and looks back at me, eyebrows up, waiting.

I flick my eyes at him and then he boosts me up into the car, climbing in after me.

I settle in the same corner that I always sat in and he sits opposite, facing me.

That's different. It used to be next to me, but it shouldn't be next to me anymore, so well done him.

He touches a button by his seat and a window partition rises up between us and the front seats. He waits for it to seal shut—and then he looks over at me.

"How's the wedding planning going?"

"Yeah—" I shrug. "Fine."

His face falters. "Are you two not good?"

"No—" I shake my head quickly. "We're good. The wedding is—" I trail. "The wedding's . . . something else." I give him a tight smile.

"Cold feet?" he asks, an eyebrow up, and I scowl at him immediately.

"No!" I adjust my skirt, trying not to look offended. "Brilliant feet! Incredibly toasty feet, in fact, borderline sweaty!—"

He pulls a face. "Yuck."

I roll my eyes at him and he rolls his back.

"What then?"

I purse my lips.

"Well, the wedding's just . . . not really about us."

"What?"

"It rather stopped being about us when they invited Camilla Parker Bowles."

He nods, sympathetic. "You are a bit of a Di-hard."

"As should we all be," I tell him, nose in the air. "Queen of hearts."

He gives me a look.

"I think you might have nicked that title out from under her, Tiges."

I squash a smile and shake my head at him.

"Don't do that."

"What?" he asks, knowing full well what.

I say nothing else but give him a stern look.

He rolls his eyes again and sits back in his chair. He lets out a breath I hadn't realised he was holding.

"Oi, so I have to ask you something," he says, face rather serious.

"Oh." I sit up straighter and suddenly I feel nervous—why do I feel nervous? "Okay."

He rolls his head back and stares up at the roof of the car, blows some air out of his mouth. Wait—is he nervous? What's he nervous for—? He's never nervous.

It hangs there, for many, many seconds. I didn't count them because I didn't know I needed to, but the stretch of time between the announcement of a question coming and the question yet to be asked felt like a decade lived on a knife's edge.

Eventually he looks back over at me, licks his bottom lip and swallows.

"Did you love me?"

My head pulls back and I blink five times quickly.

I swallow, shaking my head as I stare over at him with big, confused eyes.

"Why would you—"

"Call it closure," he tells me with a decided nod.

"From what?" I frown. "You always said we weren't together."

"And you always said we were," he fires back.

I flick my eyes to the roof of the car, press my tongue into the roof of my mouth and breathe out a shallow laugh.

"Why are you asking me this?"

"I don't know—" he says, face strained as it watches me. "I just need to know how to pocket this in my mind."

"This!" I repeat, maybe sort of yelling. "What 'this'!"

"Us."

I purse my lips and glare over at him.

"There is no us," I tell him because that's what he always told me, and then he sniffs, annoyed because he knows I'm quoting him. I do ever so love to use a man's own words against him.

Julian runs his tongue slowly over his bottom lip.

"Yes, there was," he tells the window before he looks back over at me, and his eyes look like a water planet.

I swallow and breathe out, my chin all tucked away now.

"Well, so—" I shake my head. "I don't know then. How do you want to pocket us?"

He presses his hand into his mouth and stares at nothing on the car floor. It's pristine. Freshly vacuumed. Nothing's there.

Julian Haites sits back up and looks me square in the eye, chest not quite heaving but definitely on its way.

"You're the only person I've ever loved, Magnolia."

I hear myself make the faintest gasp and I stare over at him, mouth agape.

"You love Daisy," I tell him quietly, I don't know why—it's all I can think to say.

He shakes his head and his eyebrows look too heavy. "Not how I love you."

I stare over at him, a tiny bit afraid.

"Loved," I say. "Right?

He nods quickly, licking his lips. "Right."

My eyes drift from his and out the window to the pastel colours rushing by us.

I don't even know where we're going. Where are we? Knightsbridge, I think. I look for a street sign, but it's just houses. Ennismore Garden Mews, I can tell now. Such a pretty street, I've always loved this street. I focus on the pink townhouse we pass and tell my stinging eyes to stop it. There's a lump in my throat that I'm wrestling with.

"Did you know?" Julian asks quietly.

I look over at him. He's sitting there, leaning forward in his seat, hands in his lap, eyes bigger than I've ever seen them and then I feel something wet slip from my own eye.

I wipe it away quickly and cross my arms over my chest to put some sort of barrier between us because I feel like I should.

"I didn't know." I shake my head. I take a breath that gets caught halfway in my chest. "You had sex with someone else."

"Yeah," he nods, staring at his hands now.

"You did that even though you loved me?"

"Yeah," he tells his hands.

I press fingers against my lip and take a steep breath.

"Why?" I eventually ask.

He sighs, shaking his head. "It's hard to say."

I give him a slow nod, accepting that strange, twisted fate of mine.

"Bit of a theme there for boys who love me, isn't it . . ."

He loosely points to himself. "Not a boy."

"Could have fooled me." Yes, but you behaved a bit like one.

He shrugs.

And I give him a dark look. "You're not going to hit me with a 'I never meant to hurt you'—?"

"No—" he shakes his head. "I meant to hurt you."

"Oh." I nod emphatically. "Right. Job well done, then. Bravo."

He sighs again. So much sighing.

"You didn't answer my question." He stares over at me.

I put my nose in the air. "I don't know that you deserve my answer."

"I don't." He shakes his head. "One hundred percent, I don't. But I need it anyway."

I stare over at him, frowning as I let out this breath that sounds like a whimper.

How many loves do you get in a lifetime? Fuck. It's undeniable now, isn't it—? I've had too many. None of them are the same, none have felt the same, and all of them I loved incredibly differently.

BJ, I love in an unquestionable way. I love BJ like he's the sun. Blinding, bright, unbridled, unavoidable. He's the thing that sustains the galaxy of me. He drives the currents of me, he dictates the climates and the seasons. I feel his warmth on my face, and when he's gone, it's colder. He is the centre of everything, and the gravity of me is loyal to him above all.

And Christian, I loved, truly I did. I know he mightn't think I did in retrospect but here and now, I can tell that I did. I won't say that it was a pure love; it was painful and convoluted, but I did love him. I loved him like he was the nurse dispensing morphine to me after a surgery. He helped me, he numbed my pain, he saw me through it to the other side of betterness.

And then Tom, who always deserved more than I could ever give him.

I loved him like you'd love the hand of a person who reached down into the water to pull you back up to the surface when you're drowning.

Sort of dazed and dreamy, enamoured in a rootless, drifting out to sea sort of way.

But Julian . . .

I stare over at him in the back of his car as he waits for my answer.

I've never seen him look scared before. It's so unlike him. I quite rather hate it.

I bite down on my bottom lip and nod.

"Yes." I sniff.

I love him like you might love a star.

"Yes, you did?" He stares over at me.

I nod. "Yes."

His eyes go funny, sort of blurry—he blinks twice and then he yells "Fuck!" way too loudly to be anything close to discreet.

My head pulls back and I tense up.

"Shit." He breathes out, shaking his head. "Fuck—"

I watch on in mild horror. "Are you ok—"

"Say it."

"What?" I stare over at him.

"Can you, please? Say it?" he asks. "Now. Out loud—" He shakes his head at himself. "Just so I've heard you say it one time."

I open my mouth to protest for a reason I don't know why and then I stop myself, swallow and look him in the eye.

"I loved you."

He nods a couple of times then closes his eyes for a few seconds, blows some air out of his mouth.

"I have to ask—" He looks back over at me, eyes all heavy now. "Was I ever in with a shot?"

He is a star. Not the shooting kind. Not some flash-in-the-pan meteorite that burns up on entry into the atmosphere. And stars, they're undeniably beautiful, kind of magical. Only come out at the nighttime. Easy enough to ignore. In a sky full of them, a single star can be difficult to tell apart from the others. They don't affect our day-to-day lives, really. You might see it one night and not the next, and it bears no real consequence other than perhaps the sky is a little less wonderful on that particular evening. A star is a star.

"In this world," I give him a delicate look, "with BJ?" I shake my head. "I'm sorry."

"That's—" He trails, letting out this hollow laugh that I kind of hate. It doesn't suit him. His regular laugh is so wonderful. "—fine." He nods. "That's good to know, actually—"

"I'm sorry," I tell him.

He shakes his head again. "No, don't be."

But you see, the thing about stars is that in another galaxy, that star is also a sun.

"If it wasn't him, it would be you," I tell him, for better and for worse.

He blows some more air out of his mouth and catches my eye. "In another life, yeah?"

I nod and offer him a weak smile. "I'll meet you there."

Now you listen and please don't misunderstand me, I don't live in that galaxy and I don't want to—I'm not some intrepid explorer, and this is the galaxy where I live, and I choose to remain here. What we choose matters, I will choose to stay planted on this planet until I die—happily—but it would be remiss not to at least acknowledge in a universe as large and expansive as the one we live in that there are galaxies besides the one I've chosen to dwell in. Canis Major, the closest galaxy next door. That's where Julian is, I think. Twenty-five thousand light-years away and full of a billion stars.

"He's being good to you, though?" Jules asks, watching me, and I realise we're pulling up to our street.

"Very." I nod.

He nods back. "Good."

He flashes me a quick smile before he swallows quickly.

"Are you okay?" I ask him.

"That's terribly inappropriate to ask a person—" he says, quoting me with a look, but I ignore him.

"Answer me."

We've pulled up outside our complex now.

He sniffs. "Listen, I knew I was getting into bed with a tiger the minute I saw you."

I give him a look.

"Just fucking waiting to pounce and eat me alive—"

"I'd never eat you!"

"Just my heart?" he quips.

"Julian—" I frown, a bit hurt, even though I'm worried it's actually me who might always be doing the hurting.

"I'm joking!" he says, but he isn't, I can tell.

I swing open his car door and climb out.

"Wait—" he calls after me then nods towards the entrance back up. "When you walk through that door, from now on, you're no one to me—"

"Oh." I frown.

"My mate's girlfriend, at best."

"I hate the word 'mate,'" I tell him.

He pulls a face. "I don't care."

"And I'm not really his girlfriend anymore—"

"Sure," he concedes.

"And are you two even really friends?" I tilt my head, put my hands on my hips.

"Well, fuck—" He starts shaking his head. "This is going to be easier than I thought."

I purse my lips. "What is?"

"Getting over you."

I look over at him, eyes wide again. "Getting?"

He breathes out and takes a step closer to me. "It's not past tense, Tiges. It's present."

Those midnight eyes of his well up a little but he presses his tongue into his top lip and swallows it down.

"And I'm so sorry for everything that's happened—" He shakes his head. "I did what I thought I needed to do and I don't regret what I did because you are where you should be," he tells me, nodding. "If I'm picking shit for you, I'm picking him. He's a pain in the fucking arse, but he's a good man."

I flash him a tender smile. "I know."

"It's just—" He moves in closer still towards me. Somehow. Had you asked me, I wouldn't have said there was much space between us. Just a galaxy or two, I suppose. He bites down on his bottom lip, his eyes on mine.

"You'll always be present tense for me," he tells me right before he grabs my face and presses his mouth against mine.

It's a strange kind of kiss, it's not big or boastful, but it is rather deep. Some desperation in there too, and a bit of sorrow. It's sweetly familiar and the feeling of his thumb resting under my cheekbone as he holds my face right where he wants it like he used to feels like getting out of the shower and being wrapped up in a warm towel. There's some kind of reckoning in this kiss, a finality to it—as there should be. I don't know how long the kiss lasts, one second—? Five—? I can't tell. But it's Julian who pulls away.

He ducks down so our eyes are level.

"I'm done now, yeah?" he tells me and I nod like a schoolgirl. "And you let me be."

I nod again, eyes a bit wide.

He sort of wrestles with a smile as he stares at me.

"Are you okay?"

"I—" I shrug. "I don't know what I expected today to be, but it wasn't this—"

"Yeah—" He laughs. "Sorry, this was a selfish conversation. Just kind of needed to have it." He offers me a shrug.

"You are a great many things." I stare up at him. "But selfish isn't one of them."

He nods once, barely gives me a very tender smile.

"Go on—off you go." He nods his head towards our building.

Daniela climbs out of the car—I kind of forgot she was there, to be honest—but I follow her into the building.

"And don't you two fuck it up!" Julian calls after me.

I look back and give him an obedient nod and he raises his hand wordlessly to say goodbye.

FORTY-FOUR

BJ

"Hi," Parks says tentatively as she walks back into our place after meeting up with Jules.

"Hey." I nod over at her from the other side of the room. She looks nervous, holding her own finger. "You good?"

"Mm-hm." She presses her lips together, brows low. "Yeah," she says, even though she's clearly not.

"Yeah?" I repeat.

"No—" She shakes her head and rushes over to me quickly, eyes wide and afraid. "Beej, he kissed me."

I stare down at her, run my tongue over my bottom lip, and then I nod.

"I know."

"What?" She blinks.

"I saw you—" I nod my head backwards. "From the window."

"Oh." Her shoulders slump.

It was weird—weird to see.

If you had asked me before it happened to describe to you my worst nightmare, that specific scenario would have been top five easy, and then it happened and I didn't want to kill him, or fight him—didn't even want to fight with her.

Just wanted to see what she said when the shoe was semi-on the other foot.

The truth, so it turns out.

I give her a bit of a smile, touch her face.

"Thanks for telling me though."

She looks at me carefully. "You're not cross?"

I shake my head. "No."

"Upset?"

"Nope."

She starts to look a bit confused. "Jealous?"

I sniff a laugh.

"Sure, but—" Give her a little shrug. "Nothing to write home about."

She looks confused. Hurt, maybe? Fucking girls, man—such absolute twists.

"Really?" she says in this small (hurt) voice.

I grab her wrist, pull her towards me. "Look—he was something to you, I get it—kind of?" I pause, because I do hate this part. "He was something for you when I couldn't be, and I should have been, so I can't even like—be shitty about it, because I'm sort of glad he was there. And then, I know you were important to him—" I shrug. No one told me that, they didn't need to—I could see it for myself with how he looked at her. "Meant something to him or something—"

She shifts on her feet, might see a flash of sadness go over her.

"And yeah, it kind of fucking rips me up inside thinking about you being something to someone else but—" I shrug again. "It was just a kiss."

Parks blinks a few times, confused, then she clears her throat once as she stares up at me.

"I would like to be clear—if you kiss someone else, I will absolutely not be this casual about it."

"Alright," I sniff a laugh, nodding along.

"I won't be in the realm of casual!" she tells me, and I keep nodding.

"That double standard has been duly noted, Parksy."

She crosses her arms and looks up at me, frowning.

"So you're really okay?"

I nod, hand on her waist. "I'm okay."

She purses her lips. "Why?"

I lick away a smile before I deliver my trump card.

"Because you're marrying me."

"Oh," she says, a shy smile finally showing up now. "Yes, I suppose I am."

My head pulls back playfully. "Suppose?"

She reaches for me, laughing.

"Definitely, absolutely, completely irrevocably am."

"That's more like it." I look down at her, squinting. "Do you feel like we should consecrate that?"

She squashes her lips together. "I think we have done so on and off for the last decade—"

"Yeah but—" I shrug. "Maybe once more now for good measure."

She flicks her eyes like she's annoyed and not secretly pleased.

I nod my chin at her. "Shirts off, Parksy."

She does, quiet and obedient. So unlike her. She's barely ever quiet, barely ever does what I ask, kind of gives weight to the moments she's like this.

Taking her clothes off now still hasn't really lost its sheen—I don't know if it ever has. I know you'd think it would have after so long, and maybe our specific journey which got us here has kept touching her up on this pedestal in my mind, which then makes it hard to hate the path we walked to get here, because fuck.

I feel how I did when I was sixteen taking her clothes off for the first time—her looking at me with those eyes of hers, big like pools waiting for you to dive into—dive in, climb in, slip in, fall in, doesn't matter, we're all drowning in them—

Sixteen. We were having sex by then—weird; probably too young. It definitely went to her head . . . Made her think she was way older than we really were. Easy to feel that way at boarding school too, shipped off away from everyone, you feel alone because you kind of are. I mean, it was sort of the thing to do at boarding school, wasn't it? A co-ed school in the country? Girls in uniform? Come off it, what the fuck else were we going to do?

We'd been dating not that long in the scheme of things, felt long at the time, but it was just after Christmas holidays, so can't have been that long.

Four months, at best.

There's something about Parks, like a thing where you're scared to break her? Physically she's pretty small, so there's that, but I've always found—especially when I was younger—that I'd hold her how you'd hold a flower, scared you might crush the petals.

It was a fucking mission getting her into my room that night—not that I hadn't had her in there before but because a week before there was a rumour that a girl from the year above mine got pregnant on school grounds and had to move to Switzerland to have the baby in secret because her father's a baron and peerage is fucking nuts. The entire faculty was on high alert which obviously then made sneaking about that much more fun.

Smuggled her into my room after navigating an army of schoolteachers, she was the prize. She's always been the prize.

She was laying on her back on my bed—I'd kicked Jo out already—me next to her, kissing, just. That's all we'd done til then.

It was her busy hands—she's always been braver than me with shit like this—undoing my school shirt button by button, watching me without wavering with those eyes I'd loved since I was a kid. I was still a kid, I know that. Didn't know that at the time though. She got to my last button and pulled my shirt off, casting it to the floor, and then lay back, hands by her sides, as she stared up at me.

Pinched my eyes as I stared down at her. "What are you doing?"

She shrugged, innocently, knowing exactly what she was doing.

"Parksy—" I gave her a look.

"Beej—" She gave me the same one back and I started laughing. Ran my hand up her leg, up her skirt because—as if I wouldn't.

"I don't know if we're ready," I told her, I don't know why I told her that. I wanted to. I don't think at the time I was even thinking about the shit with Zadie. For ages actually, I think

I blocked it out. Didn't let myself think of it much outside of a handful of times when what memories I do have of it came thundering through on their own without my permission. This wasn't one of those times. I wasn't thinking about it, wasn't scared, didn't feel pressured—I wouldn't say that I'm someone with a spectacular amount of foresight but I will say, Parks has none. She'd never been older than she was in that moment and with her lifetime of parental neglect clutched snug under her arm, she'd felt that strange and terrifying mix of independence and like, a longing to belong—if anything, that's what I saw. Saw how badly she needed me, felt the weight of that at all of fucking sixteen.

"We're ready," she told me, very unready.

"We don't have . . . anything . . ." My voice trailed, and I gave her a look.

"Oh." She pouted.

Even then I hated feeling like I'd disappointed her, don't know how she does it—me and the boys have talked about it so many times now, tried to worm our way out from underneath whatever fucking spell it is, because it's not even that she gets stroppy—which she does—she's been stroppy at me for about six consecutive years now, I don't give a fuck about stroppy. It's something else. It's like tripping over in front of a statue of Jesus, saying "fuck" under your breath and then feeling self-conscious in front of the statue; or feeling a bit like a pervert for making out with someone if there's an animal in the room—can't really explain it. I'll die one day and I'll bet money when I do I'll wander over to those pearly gates and Peter with the book will look down at it, give me a grimace and say, "Ah, you're the sorry bastard who fell in love with the demigoddess. Fuck it, go on in then."

So I found myself kissing her in this big, heavy way, bigger than I planned, heavier than I planned, just wanted her happy. Plus, we had the buffer of not being able to actually have sex because we didn't have protection.

So I undid her buttons with significantly less patience than she undid mine—thought I was going to fucking burst into flames on the spot when her school shirt fell open and I saw her in a bra for the first time.

"Do you like it!" she chirped, never one to shy away from ruining the moment.

"Love it," I said, voice a little huskier than normal.

"Would you like to take it off also, then?" she asked, bright-eyed and bushy-tailed.

I swallowed heavy, nodded a couple of times. "I would."

And now she's here in our apartment that we finally share, and she's looking at me with the same big eyes she did that night in the dorm, the same eyes she'd look at me with most days from there on til it all got cocked up. Every now and then I wonder what my life would be like if she had a normal pair of eyes, but alas, fuck it, here we are . . .

Tug that sweater she's wearing up over her body as I move her backwards against a wall behind her.

Press myself up against her heavy as I can, she tosses her arms around my neck and then with no communication—just a thousand moments like this one under our belt and muscle memory that I hope forever lasts the test of time—she jumps up onto my waist at the same time as I'm about to boost her onto it.

She actually—surprisingly—doesn't fuck around with the buttons on my shirt—rips them open and I look down at them as they bounce all scattered on the floor, give her a puzzled look.

The number of times in my life I've seen her disrespect a piece of clothing—she'd probably sooner disrespect the Pope.

"You right there?" I laugh.

"I'll sew them back on later," she tells me as she tugs the Nahmias shirt off of me.

Give her a look. "No, you won't."

"No, I won't," she concedes, laughing.

I glance down at the ground again.

"Are you trying to prove something to yourself with those buttons?"

She pulls a face. "Like what?"

"Don't know—" I shrug. About Julian maybe? Don't want to say that out loud.

"No—?" She gives me a defensive look. "Are you trying to prove something to yourself?"

"I've been trying to prove something to myself since I was fucking six—"

"Yeah?" She blinks, hands in my hair. "And what's that?"

"That I'm good enough for you," I laugh, but quickly her face goes still and serious.

She climbs down from my waist and then stares at me.

"Are you joking?"

"Yeah—" I shrug, reaching for her. "Mucking about. Climb back up—"

I grab her arse, but she swats my hand away, frowning still.

"Do you really think that?" She blinks.

I sigh a little and roll my eyes. "No—"

She lifts those eyebrows of hers, waiting.

"Sometimes, it's just—" Roll my eyes again, shift on my feet because I feel like a proper git. "I don't know why you picked me."

"Picked you?" she repeats, baffled. "I didn't pick you. I've never had a choice in the matter."

I sniff a laugh, not sure what to say. "Is that a good thing or a bad one?"

"Both, possibly."

I breathe out my nose and tilt my head, she gestures at me.

"You walking into the living room in St Barts, shirt off, broad all of a sudden and you looked so unreasonably handsome—you were so cool and I just—" She trails. Squashes away a smile that makes me feel better. "BJ Ballentine. Like I had a choice."

I swallow as I stare at her.

"In the stars." I nod at her.

She nods back. "Something like that."

Then she slips a finger of hers under the band of my underwear, runs it along my stomach and I give her an eighth of a smile. She takes her own bra off—a black balconette bra from Fleur du Mal. Know that one—I picked it—she slips it off her shoulders like they're made of silk and it lands at my feet softly. I swallow heavy, watch her with big eyes of my own.

She tilts her head, folds her arms over her chest, looking annoyed.

"Are you going to stand there all day or are you going to do something?"

"Oh—" I scoff. "I'm going to do something."

And then I grab her, carry her back to that angular bench she says you can't fuck on, just to prove her wrong.

She is right though, unfortunately. Can't get a grip for the life of me. Every time I push into her she just slides further and further up the bench.

She dissolves into a puddle of laughter at this point, and I don't want to think it's funny, but I do, because everything's fun with her and I guess that's why you marry a person; so then I pick her up, toss her over my shoulder and carry her back to our bed.

Think about tossing her down unceremoniously but can't shake the feeling of her like petals in my hand so I lay her down slow and gentle and then she's back to serious, no more giggles.

I crawl over her, stay, hovered above. She reaches up and traces my jawline with her finger. I don't do anything, just let her, let her grow impatient—doesn't take very long, she's about as patient as a kid in a line at Disneyland—she kicks off my jeans. Light blue ones from Rag & Bone that she got me. Still I do nothing, just hover there.

And then I see her take in this deep breath—I know what it means because it happens all the time—I'm about to be yelled at, so that's when I do it. Drop my weight on her, then kiss her and push into her again all at once because I'm fucking good at this.

In general, but especially with her. We're good at this.

It's not the same as being with anyone else. I'm found when I'm with Parks. Lost all the rest of the time.

You want a metaphor for it? Alright, here goes.

I come from a good family, everyone knows that. My parents

were great, roof over my head. I never wanted for much, really, and still. She's the only home I've ever been interested in having.

Her body is the walls, heart's the ceiling.

I'll live here forever.

"Jo thinks we're Shakespearean," I tell her afterwards, staring up at nothing.

We're lying in our bed still, her on my chest, sheets all bunched up around us.

She glances at me. "We've had our moments."

I lick my lips, try not to sound nervous when I ask it:

"Are all Shakespeare couples fucked?"

"No!" she says quickly, sitting up a little. "Well, some—" she concedes. "But not all. The famous ones are fucked, but the lesser-known ones—Benedick and Beatrice, Orlando and Rosalind, Duke and Viola—"

I look over at her.

"Sometimes I wonder if obscurity helps."

"I'm sure it does." She nods, thinking to herself for a minute before she looks over at me, her chin on my chest. "I'd fade into obscurity with you."

"Yeah?" I smile down at her.

"So happily," she tells me.

I pull her up towards my face so I can kiss her properly again, and after a minute, she pulls away.

"BJ?"

I push some hair from her face. "Yeah?"

"I feel that it's important you know that even if I didn't love you in the sort of stupid, embarrassing way that I do; if I did, hypothetically, have a choice—I would choose you anyway."

FORTY-FIVE

Magnolia

Shoe shopping for the boys' wedding shoes today, so we're back in Selfridges. I actually wanted to come alone, I know all their sizes. Most of the time they just slow me down. Sometimes they're helpful but today is not one of those days.

BJ keeps telling me he's going to wear Vans with his tuxedo ("if I'm even wearing a tuxedo!") and I'm about ready to murder him.

Vans with a tux? Are you joking me?

I don't know who he thinks he is but he's not Seth fucking Cohen, which I told him, and he said, "I mean, yeah. Thank god." Which then that made me cross too (because Seth Cohen was the best boy on that show) (besides Sandy) (see: father issues) so anyway, off I went ahead to have a strop, and ever since, BJ keeps picking completely hideous and random accessories and saying that they'd match his tux perfectly and he's going to get them, and I know he's joking—I know he's not really going to wear the brown Horsebit leather-trimmed shearling slippers from Gucci that—let's be honest—absolutely look like a god-damn Chia Pet.

Oh my god, I just now realised that Chia Pets were grown from chia seeds, like the ones we eat. What an undeniable and absolute glow-up . . . From a frizzy plant to a chic breakfast! That's practically the plot to a Jennifer Garner movie.

"This is nice!" BJ holds up a Kapital Kountry patchwork printed voile, gauze, tweed and felt scarf.

"Put that down!" I snatch it from him, putting it back. "We're in public!"

BJ smirks.

"So mixy—" I look at it again in horror.

"No one's asking you to eat it, Magnolia," Henry tells me.

"You're okay with felt touching gauze?" I stare at my friend, baffled.

"Love it," he says, with an annoying smile.

"Ooh," I coo at a tie from Brunello Cucinelli. The striped knitted cotton and linen-blend in off-white. "This is obviously completely not the vibe but this is sort of incredible."

"Neckties are out," Jonah tells me, and I roll my eyes at him.

"Oh, on the pulse, are we?" Christian rolls his eyes at his brother.

"Actually, neckties were featured in a rather big way on the fall/winter 2022 runway."

"On women," BJ tells Jo with an eyebrow up, and I'm a tiny bit proud of him for retaining that knowledge.

"Fashion is getting more and more fluid—" I tell the boys, and I'm about to launch into my Yves Saint Laurent 1966 pants TED Talk when I spot someone looking lost in the Casablanca section.

"Tiller!" I call to him, pleased.

"Magnolia." He smiles, but does, arguably, sound less pleased.

"How absolutely splendid to see you!" I skip over to him.

He smiles, looking caught off guard. "That's so much enthusiasm, thank you—"

I smile up at him. "How have you been?"

"Great—" He shrugs. "Good, yeah. And—and you?"

He then looks past me to Christian, giving him a ginger nod, who, in return, gives a disastrously unspirited and unwelcoming non-smile smile.

Men.

"Wonderful, yes. Thank you." I pluck the shirt he's holding out of his hand and look up at him, squinting. "A Casablanca man? Really—?"

"Let him be, Parks—" BJ says, and though I'm not looking at him, I can feel there was an eye roll attached to that sentence.

"What's wrong with Casablanca?" Tiller asks.

"Nothing at all!" I say quickly. "It's summery, it's Amalfi, it's fun, it's bright—I love it. It's just, I've never not seen you wear loose-fitted blue jeans, Cons and a grey T-shirt."

He frowns a bit. "Sometimes I wear a black T-shirt."

"Oh." I nod. "I stand corrected."

Tiller gives me a look.

"I could be wrong—" I tell him even though I'm definitely not. "But I feel that perhaps Off-White might be more your speed."

"Or Sandro," Beej offers.

"Sandro!" Henry says, looking over at his brother, confused. "They're so fucking loud!"

Jonah waves a pink, red and white graphic wavy print shirt of theirs in my face. "The subtlety."

I give Jonah a disparaging look before I look past him to Henry.

"I don't know, Hen—" I give Henry a look. "Sure, they don't shy away from a colour pop but they do often stick to classic silhouettes, their summer line has a lot of staple colours, like cream and navy and—God, you'd look wonderful in navy, wouldn't you?" I look back over at Tiller. "Have they made you into that calendar yet?"

"What?" He shakes his head, confused.

I blink away the thoughts of the calendar.

"Are you seeing anyone at the minute?" I ask him instead.

"Uh—" He frowns, looking past me to BJ.

I reach over and snatch his iPhone from his hand.

"I'm going to put Taura's number in your phone—what's your passcode?"

"Uh—what?" He looks at me confused, eyes wide.

"Magnolia—" BJ sighs.

"Quiet," I tell him and look back at Tiller. "Passcode?"

"I—"

"Passcode, Tiller. Quick, come on!" I sigh impatiently as I put a hand on my hip. "I've not got all day. Well, I could have all day, I suppose. I don't have any wildly pressing engagements, and I just had an iced matcha—do you like those? A bit grassy, but sometimes the amount of caffeine in a coffee can make me talk—" I catch his eye. "And talk and talk and talk and t—"

"Five nine five nine," he says in sort of a panic.

"I mean—" BJ rolls his eyes and gives Tiller a look. "Don't tell her—"

Tiller looks between myself and Beej. "I—why—?"

Jonah pokes his head in. "Because then she'll keep doing this shit with other people—"

"Okay." I hand his phone back to Tiller, ignoring the others. "That's her number in there."

"Alright," he nods. "Why?"

I squint up at him and give him a little smile. "Oh, why don't you use those detective deduction skills and puzzle that one out . . ."

He rolls his eyes and then shifts on his feet, a bit uncomfortably.

He clears his throat, glancing from me to Christian, who's a bit away from us, not really paying attention.

Tiller lowers his voice. "Has anyone talked to Dais—?"

"Why?" I ask. "Do you still have feelings for her?"

"No."

I lean in towards him. "Are you sure?"

"Yes."

I lean in a bit further, my arms crossed over my chest. "Do you know, I'm terribly good at getting people to tell me their secrets, people often just tell me things when I want them to, I don't know why—they just—bust, right there on the spot and tell me, I suspect it's because—"

"Because she doesn't fucking shut it otherwise—" Henry tells Tiller, arms folded over his chest.

I glare at him. "Rude."

"Annoying." Henry eyes me back then turns to Tiller. "I'm Henry."

"Tiller." He extends his hand and Henry shakes it. Then Tiller looks back at me. "And I don't—like, I care about her but not in the same way—"

I smile, pleased.

"Well, that's perfect then, isn't it." I tap his phone.

He gives me a look. "You're really pushy."

"I am, yes," I concede. "It'll grow on you."

"No—" BJ shakes his head at the same time Henry scrunches his nose and says, "It won't," which is at the same time Christian—from rather far away—calls, "It never grows on you," at the same time Jonah says, "It actually wears you down a bit over time."

I swivel on my heel and eyeball all of them, unimpressed.

"And yet here you all are, following me around Selfridges like ducklings on a Wednesday, though I asked not a one of you to be here."

Jonah huffs and starts to wander away. "Don't need to get snippy about it—"

I turn back to Tiller.

"Call her!" I tell him.

"Okay," he nods, with a laugh.

"And then call me afterwards to tell me how it went."

"I prob—" He shakes his head and clears his throat. "I won't do that, just being upfront."

"Oh my god!" I turn and look at BJ. "I give and I give and for what—"

"Is it give and give, or is it push and push—?" Henry asks.

"You're on extremely thin ice today—" I tell him, a finger in his face. Henry smacks it away unfazed.

"Oh no." He rolls his eyes.

"Uh—" Tiller points in the direction opposite of us. "I'm gonna—but, uh—thanks for this." He gestures to his phone.

"Oh, absolutely!" I smile at him. "Call her!"

"Okay." He laughs, rolling his eyes.

22:56

Tausie 🩶

What did you do

Today?

Well, first I woke up, a little after 9.

I had a matcha.

I'm really loving them with strawberry at the minute.

Have you tried that?

Did you give my number to Tiller?

Who's to say, really?

He said.

Ah.

Well, then. Yes!

Why?

Did he text you?

He called me.

!!!!!

BRILLIANT!

You're so nosy

I know, don't you love it

Fuck.

Kind of yes.

I wish I didn't but I do because we're going out next week

OHHHHHH MYYYYYYYY GOD

Shut up

Where are you going?

Some bar

Do you actually not know which bar or are you just not saying because you think I will turn up there?

The second one

FORTY-SIX
Magnolia

Terrible days are sneaks, aren't they?

They love to lull you into a false sense of safety. Dress themselves up in the terrible mundane, make you think that everything's okay when actually, nothing is.

Lunch with Henry, Rom, Christian and Daisy. Just me and them, no Beej—he's shooting for Loewe.

We're at The Petersham, in Covent Garden, and the afternoon's been entirely pleasant.

Daisy's finally stopped being a complete brute towards Romilly, and while I wouldn't go as far to venture that she's accepted her entirely into the fold, I would perhaps say that she begrudgingly answers her questions and at least acknowledges her existence.

I've told Rom not to let it get to her, that she'll come around, that she hated me for years and years and now she obviously completely adores me, sort of. Depending on which day of the week it is.

Henry, Romilly and Christian start to talk about a volcano documentary they all watched, Daisy leans over to me and whispers, "My brother said he came to see you?"

"Yes." I nod.

She watches me for a second. "Are you okay?"

I give her a pleasant smile. "Yeah, of course—"

Her eyes pinch. "He didn't do anything—? Nothing happened?"

I purse my lips and think about telling her. I've wanted so badly to tell someone what he said to me for one, because oh my god. And two, imagine being the only girl Julian Haites has ever loved. What an honour, that's how I really feel about it. But even with that honour bestowed upon me—and it surely is one—it doesn't matter. One name, two letters, frequently the bane of my existence and forever, for better and worse, my favourite thought.

Besides, I don't really care for the idea of anyone else knowing how Julian feels for me because I shouldn't like to cause him any kind of discomfort or pain, so even though the urge to tell her bubbles up inside of me like a dam, I just shake my head.

"Nope." I give her a quick smile. "He just checked in."

"Who did?" Romilly asks, pleasantly.

"No one," Daisy snaps. "Mind your own business."

Henry gives Daisy a little glare and tosses an arm around Rom.

"Dais—" Christian gives her a look.

Daisy rolls her eyes. "Fine, sorry."

"You know I've never slept with Christian, right?" Romilly offers her.

Daisy stares over at her from across the table, and Romilly keeps going.

"I'm just getting this really passive-aggressive—"

"It's really more aggressive-aggressive—" I interrupt, and Daisy flicks me a look.

"—territorial, you-want-my-man energy from you, and I don't."

I shake my head. "That's actually just her default energy."

"Fuck off," Daisy growls. "No, it's not."

"Well," I roll my eyes. "It very obviously is, so—"

"It obviously was that towards you because you did want my man. Men, I'd argue. My boyfriend and my brother, you've been with them both so—"

"Okay—" I interrupt her. "There's no need to go around casting aspersions."

Henry and Christian start laughing.

"What aspersions!" She glowers over at me. "What I just said is fact."

I shrug my shoulders demurely. "You say potato, I say po-tah-to."

And then Rom's phone sounds off with a text.

She looks down at it, picks it up and opens it.

Her face falters, confused—that's all I can see—and then, barely moving, she flashes her phone to Henry, whose posture broadens and freezes at once.

His eyes move towards me.

"What?" I say, looking at him confused.

He swallows.

Daisy notices, frowns between us all.

"What's going on?" she asks us all, but neither Hen nor Romilly says anything, so she snatches the phone from Rom and then she freezes too.

I'm racking my brain for what it is—something to do with my parents, probably? Already married? A pregnancy scare? My mum caught Harley cheating on her—? I arm myself with a preemptive eye roll.

Christian's annoyed now, peers over Daisy's shoulder and then quite quickly presses his tongue into his top lip, staring over at me.

"Magnolia—" Christian says carefully and now—it is now exactly—that my stomach knots itself up. Christian never used to call me Parks back when he loved me because it's what BJ called me—I mean everyone does now, but in our youth, Parks, Parksy—they were very Beej-centric names—when he didn't want me to belong to BJ, in the moments where he didn't associate me with Beej, that's when he'd call me my name.

He hasn't called me my name in a very long time.

I stare over at Christian—Christian, not Henry—because for a long time, BJ's infidelity was our bread and butter, it was the soft focus over our entire relationship, the padded wall that hemmed us in.

I can't look at Henry, I can't look at his face as I see what I'm about to see and I know what I'm about to see because I can see it in Christian's brow already.

I hold out my hand. "Give me the phone."

Christian breathes out his nose for a second, face conflicted—then he swallows and hands it over.

I'm not sure what I'm about to see—BJ and someone, to be sure.

I go immediately rapid-fire absolute worst-case scenario:

BJ and Paili again. BJ and Taura. BJ and Bridge. BJ and my mum?

But it's none of those.

None of those and still, my fingers go tingly, the place in my chest where my heart's supposed to be turns hollow and my stomach drops and keeps dropping, probably forever now, always dropping.

It's that girl. From the other day? That one at the burger place, that he "wasn't with." There's four or five photos.

I don't know where they are—Daylesford, it looks like? The one on Westbourne Grove—his hands on her lower back, leaning in, brushing his mouth over hers, laughing, smiling, she's holding on to his arms, looking up at him. He looks happy.

"We don't know anything for sure," Daisy says, the first one to say anything.

"Don't be stupid," Christian tells her gruffly.

"We're jumping to conclusions—" Romilly tells me, and Daisy nods along.

Henry looks between them both. "How?"

"I jumped to a conclusion with your sex tape," Daisy tells Christian.

Christian looks at her a bit exasperated. "Dais, I made a sex tape. There was no conclusion to jump to—"

"Yeah, but—" She rolls her eyes. "It wasn't what I thought."

Christian pulls a confused face. "Did you think it was a sex tape?"

"Yeah, but—"

"Then it's what you thought," Christian tells her with a look, driving his point home.

I'm trying my best to listen to what they're saying because I can feel myself slipping, I'm very, very dangerously close to having a panic attack and there's only one person who knows how to help me stop them and his hands are on the lower back of some other girl.

I need my sister. She'd know what to do.

"Bathroom," I say without meaning to.

"What?" Henry stares over at me.

"I need to go to the bathroom," I tell him. "Now."

"Okay." Daisy nods, pushing back from the table. "I'll take you."

"No!" I say urgently, standing up myself. "No—I need to go alone."

They all stare at me with big, afraid eyes.

"I'm fine," I tell them, even though none of them asked.

"Are you?" Romilly asks carefully.

I don't even look back as I call, "Fine, I said," already on my way to the bathroom.

I lock the door behind me and barely make it to the toilet before I throw up in it.

It's strangely familiar, vomiting because of BJ.

Loving him so much I'm sick to my stomach every time he fucks up, which, let's be frank, he has been known to do.

I make myself throw up the rest of what I had for lunch because no one likes a job half done and then I wipe my mouth, toss the paper in the bowl and flush it.

I stand and face the mirror, waiting for her.

It takes a minute—that scares me—so I close my eyes and wait to feel her.

"Magnolia," she'd say, watching me with sad eyes.

"Oh my god—" I start to panic.

"Magnolia—" she'd say again.

"Bridget—"

She'd tilt her head. "Try and stay calm—"

I shake mine. "Tell me it's not true."

She'd breathe out her nose. "It's not true."

I'd look her square in the eyes, try to find a grip on anything she's saying.

"Are you lying to me?"

"I mean—" She'd glance around this bathroom stall. "This is all lies."

"Stop." I sigh.

But she'd just keep shaking her head. "Why are you in here talking to me?"

"Don't, Bridge—"

She'd gesture back to my friends. "When there are real, actual people outside here to help you—"

"You are real—" I tell her.

"Not anym—"

"Bridget, I said stop!" I yell.

And then it's silent and she's gone.

"Magnolia?" calls Henry's voice tentatively though the door.

"No one!" I say quickly, automatically.

Pause. "What?"

"Nothing." I shake my head at myself. So stupid.

"Parks, there's just a bit of a crowd growing out here—"

I stare at myself in the mirror, try to fix my face. "Why?"

"I don't know—" he says. "I guess they saw you run? Or maybe they saw it, I don't know—"

"Oh." I swallow. "Okay."

"Christian's got the car waiting out front."

I race over to the door and crack it open. "I don't want to drive!"

"Trust me, Parks," Henry tells me with a solemn look. "You don't want to walk either."

"Oh." My eyes fall to the ground.

He takes off his jacket—green and navy panelled leather bomber jacket from Gucci—and drapes it over my head before he fishes out my Sicilian Taste sunglasses from my small black Diana textured-leather tote (both Gucci).

He puts them on for me before he offers me his hand.

I stare at it for a second before I take it.

"Game face," he tells me with a nod. "Give them nothing."

Then he leads me out of the restaurant—a few flashes in there—and out onto the street where there are now a couple of photographers, one of which Daisy shoves out of the way.

Henry pushes me into the car and Christian peels out.

FORTY-SEVEN

BJ

It was my dad who called me. Not Parks, not my brother, not my best friends. My dad.

"What's going on, BJ?" he says, stern.

I've been at a shoot all day. Hadn't yet seen the twenty-five missed calls from him. Hadn't seen the four thousand comments on my last Instagram post where I'm getting fucking barraged for doing something I didn't do. Hadn't see the panicked text messages from Maddie's poor friend asking what to do.

I shake my head even though Dad can't see it.

"I don't know—what are you talking about?"

"The photos!" my dad says, annoyed.

I pause. Fuck.

"What photos?" I ask.

There could be a fucking million photos of me that I wouldn't want out in the wild. The "lost years" that Jo's always joking about, some of them are legitimately lost to me. Days—weeks, even—that I just can't remember. After Parks left for New York? I don't know what happened the first couple of months, I know I was fucked. I've sent photos to girls, not a tonne of them and not usually when I'm in a coherent state of mind, but I have. Sex tape? Could have. I don't know. After she left I was on a sinking ship, I was going down anyway, might as well have gone down swinging.

"You and that blonde girl," Dad says, annoyed.

I shake my head again. "What blonde girl?"

"I don't know!" He's getting impatient. "She looks like Maddie's friend—"

I freeze. "What?"

"She looks like Maddie's friend," he says again. "You know, the one with the weird eyebr—"

"I've gotta go," I interrupt him.

"BJ—"

"Now, Dad."

Then I hang up on him, open my phone and holy fucking shit.

It's from the day I met up with Maddie and Dylan. Remember I said we nearly kissed—came in at each other at a weird angle—it was funny, we laughed. But fuck, it looks bad. It looks intimate. They've cropped Maddie out completely—

These fucking pricks. I stare down at it in disbelief. Why the fuck would someone do this?

I try to call Parks. Straight to voicemail.

Shit.

I tell the photographer I'm shooting with that I've got to go, that I'm sorry—there are still a few pieces left to shoot, he was fucking pissed about it—said I'd call Jonathan myself to apologise.

Practically barrel into my car and pull out my phone.

Try to call her—straight to voicemail.

Fuck.

Try my brother. It rings out.

Try Jo. It rings out.

Try Christian. He declines the call.

My skin starts to feel prickly, hot. Under it, not on top of it.

Ignore how much my stomach feels like it's being actively punched and pull up her location on my phone.

Last seen three hours ago at . . . Henry's.

Put my car in drive and race quick as I can from the location we've been shooting at the White Studio in St Katherine's Dock.

From there to Henry's place on Chelsea Harbour at this time of day? Maybe a thirty-minute drive in today's traffic?

Three hours ago? Her phone must be off.

I feel fucking ill as I make my way over there, for a few reasons.

For one, I know she saw it. Why else would her phone be off? That she saw it at all, looking how they've made it look—all like, happy and fucking tender—I need to get to her, explain it away. That it's everywhere already? A nightmare.

"Bad Boy Ballentine, at It Again." "Magnolia Parks, the Jilted Bride." "Magnolia Parks—Devastated Once More."

At least that last one's likely to be telling the truth.

Every couple of minutes I get this wave of nausea as I think about Magnolia seeing that, how much it would scare her . . .

And then the part that scares me: she believes it.

Believes it enough to just switch off her phone and fuck off to my brother's.

And my brother and my two best friends? Not a fucking call between them?

My mind starts spinning—one thing at a time, I tell myself—get to Parks, explain it, once she sees me she'll listen. I think.

I get to Henry's after about thirty-five minutes. Double park someone in, don't care. Put my hazards on and run up the stairs.

Six flights up, I take the stairs two at a time, practically fucking hurl myself at the door as I bang on it.

And then it opens and Julian motherfucking Haites fills the frame.

I stare over at him in shock at first.

"Oh—" I groan. "What the fuck are you doing here?" I push past him and walk into Henry's apartment. I spin back and look at him, ask a question I don't want to ask but need to. "Did she call you?"

"No," Julian says gruffly.

"So what are you here for?" I stare over at him.

"He was with me," Jo says from behind me and then I look around the room for the first time.

Full of people. Both Haites, both Hemmes, Hen, Rom and Taura. No Parks.

"She should have called me though," Julian says, eyeing me down.

I take a step towards him. "Yeah?"

"Yeah," he nods coolly. "I'll sort you out—"

I give Julian a little shove. "Will you?"

"Oi—" Jo jumps between us and shoves me himself. "Fucking wise up."

I push Jonah's hands off me and glance around the room again, feeling a bit frantic now.

"Where is she?" My eyes land on my brother. "Hen? I didn't do anything—"

"You know what, man?" Henry stares over at me and shakes his head. "I don't believe you."

"There are pictures," Christian tells me.

"They're doctored!" I yell.

"Yeah," Henry rolls his eyes. "Okay. Paili doctored too then?"

I storm over to my brother and push him, hard as I can.

"Fucking shut your mouth." And then I start moving around his apartment, calling her name.

The girls all shift uncomfortably. Romilly whispers something to Henry, who shakes his head as he stares me down.

Wonder how I'm here doing this again—didn't I just do this the other week?—how many times is she going to believe the worst in me? How much of my life am I going to have to spend proving that I'm not who everyone keeps saying I am?

"Magnolia!" I call again and bang on my brother's closed bedroom door. Definitely where she is. Bang on the door.

I can hear her crying now that I'm close.

I bang harder—call her name.

"You need to leave," Julian says from behind me.

Spin around quick and stare at him, stone faced.

"And you need to shut the fuck up."

"She doesn't want you here," he tells me.

"Actually, do you know what else she doesn't want?" I square my shoulders. "You."

I watch that crush him a bit how I meant it to. Don't feel bad either, it's about time he properly fucked off.

He shakes his head a bit, rolls his eyes, tries to palm it off like it's nothing.

I nod my chin at him coolly.

"You think she didn't tell me—?" I stare at him.

"Tell you what?"

"That you kissed her," I announce, and the whole room sucks in air.

Julian's mouth falls open a bit, happy to have the one-up on him for a minute, so I decide to go in for round two.

"You kissed her and then who did she run home to?"

Julian looks away, jaw set and angry so I keep going. Wouldn't mind hitting someone today.

"You kissed her and who did she have sex with that afternoon?" I lift my eyebrows at him. "She doesn't want you, she wants me."

"I know, man." Julian stares over at me, exasperated. "It is you, I know it's not me. So why can't you stop fucking it up?"

"I didn't fucking fuck anything up!" I yell.

"Can you just go?" says this tiny voice from behind me.

"Parks—" I reach for her and she flinches away.

Julian dives between us now, shielding her from me, pushing me away.

"Don't touch her—" he tells me.

"Get off me—" I shove him off and punch him in the jaw in one quick move.

He touches his mouth with his hand, looks down at his fingers—blood—he sniffs a laugh.

"You feel like dying today?" he asks me.

Honestly, a bit.

And then he tackles me to the ground.

There's a loud crash as we knock over a table in the hallway, break a vase—he gets in a few, I get in another one before the boys pull us apart and I see Taura and Romilly clinging to each other's arms and Magnolia crying behind Daisy, who suddenly yells, "Enough!"

Julian and I freeze, both look over at her.

She looks between me and her brother.

"Leave," she tells us. "Both of you. Now. Leave."

"Daisy—" Julian starts, standing up. "I'm—"

"Leaving." She cuts him off and glares at him. "You are leaving." Then she shakes her head and lowers her voice at him. "What are you even doing here?"

"I'm—"

But she cuts him off again.

"Kissing her?" She stares at him, incredulous. "Have you lost your fucking mind? Pull it together."

Julian sighs, shakes his head, silenced by his baby sister who isn't going to let him get a word in edgewise so he just stops talking.

"And you—" She glares at me. "Haven't you done enough?"

"I haven't done anything!" I tell her loudly, loud enough that everyone here can hear me, Parks included, and still she closes herself on the other side of my brother's door anyway.

Daisy gives me a long look. "If that is true, I'd find a way as fast as you can to prove that."

FORTY-EIGHT

BJ

"Oi—" Jo calls after me, jogging down the hall.

"What?" I ask gruffly.

"Are you for real?" he asks, eyebrows up. "They're fake?"

"Yes!" I yell. "Fuck! Yes, Jo—I didn't—"

"Okay." He shrugs. "I believe you."

I look at him, exasperated. "You couldn't believe me inside?"

Jo rolls his eyes.

"Who gives a shit if I believe you, man." Shake his head. "There's only one person in the world who actually counts as far as believing you goes—"

"I know but—"

"It looks bad, Beej," he tells me. "She's already caught you in a lie with this same girl—what do you think she's going to think?"

I sigh, shake my head. "I know, but it's a fucking setup!"

He rolls his eyes, makes me think he mightn't actually believe me. "How?"

"Maddie was there."

He looks confused. "What?"

I shove my hands through my hair, impatient as we make our way back towards my car.

"She's cropped out of the photo."

Get in my car, he climbs in the passenger seat.

"Should I call Maddie?" I look over at him. "Or the girl? Ask her to come here—"

He shake his head, pulls a face. "I wouldn't bring the girl here."

"Maddie?"

He grimaces. "She'd lie for you."

She would too. Parks knows it.

I roll my head back, stare at my car's ceiling.

"So what the fuck can I do?"

Jo breathes out his nose loudly, thinking.

"Well, so—who first ran it?" He looks over at me. "Where's the initial photo from?"

I shrug. "Some article from the *Daily Mail.*"

He lifts his eyebrows, interested. "Does it have an author?"

Jo and I spend the next few minutes figuring out who the author is—loose term—some fucking tosser named Ian Audley. Northcliff House is where all the DMGT offices are. Not too far from here, just a stone's throw in Kensington. Found a picture of him online too so we could spot him and decide to pay him a visit. He looks how you'd imagine, doesn't he?

Stocky, weird hair that's not really like, committing to being any colour in particular—is it brown, is it blonde, is it red?—not overweight. Not well kept. Looks like the kind of person who might get off tearing people like me down.

Jo called the DMGT office on the way over to make sure he was still in—he wasn't—but then, a bit terrifyingly, Jonah fired off a text and within three minutes we had his home address so we head there instead—all the way over in Hackney.

That's a fucking hour-and-a-half drive. What a joke. Still, somehow me and Jo beat him there.

Knocked on his door, no answer. Must have stopped off for a drink or something, celebrate a day's honest work.

Jo peeked through the windows. No one home. No sign he lives with anyone—not surprising, I suppose. Lies for a living, doesn't exactly lend itself to relationship building.

The sun's setting pretty early now we're in late November, and I'm cold without a coat, even with my car's heater on.

Jo glances over at me. "You look like shit."

"Yep," I say, staring ahead.

"Are you okay?" Jo asks, watching me close.

I look over at him, stare for a couple of seconds.

"No, Jo." I shake my head at him. "Everyone I know thinks I'm a massive fuck-up. Including but not limited to—" I list them off my fingers—"my best friend. My other best friend. My brother. My fiancée. My dad. Every girl I know, apparently. And—"

"Beej—" He cuts me off.

"It's fucked," I tell him, shrugging. "I'm fucked. I did one thing, and it was shit, I know it was, but I've spent my whole life since then trying to prove that I'm not who everyone thinks I am. And for what?—" I shrug again. "I didn't even do anything and I'm still whoever the fuck they think I am."

Jo nods slowly, face looks heavy.

"I'm sorry," he tells me.

I say nothing and we both look at the window and say nothing for a bit.

Could be a minute, could be a few—

"Hey, is that him?" Jo says suddenly.

Yep, it is. Bustling down the street, bunched up in a coat and clutching a backpack like a briefcase.

Jo jumps out of my car. I follow.

"Oi," he calls to him.

The man looks down, walks faster.

"Oi!" Jo calls again. "I'm talking to you."

Audley looks back at Jonah.

"I don't want any trouble."

Jo pulls a face.

"Well, you've got a tonne of it coming your way."

"Ian Audley?" I ask, walking towards him.

He frowns. "Who are you?"

He's confused. Squints in the dark.

I shift under a street light and he recognises me, eyes go wide.

"There it is." Jo flashes me a look.

Audley looks between Jo and I. "What do you want?"

"What do I want?" I repeat, staring at him. Make my face look amused and not devastated. Let out a hollow laugh. "What I want is a quiet life in the country with my soon-to-be wife, away from prying eyes and fuckheads like you but I don't think that's on the cards—"

He licks his lips. "I just ran a story."

"No, you're fucking up my life, man." I shake my head at him. "My girl's locked in my brother's room, crying, because she thinks I cheated on her, again. My brother's angry at me, my friends don't believe me, all because I was a fuck-up before but I'm not now! And because you're having a fucking slow news day, you decided to crop my sister out of a photo to make me look like I'm doing something I'm not?"

Audley stares over at me, shakes his head like he can't help it. "It's already gone to print."

"Well, unprint it!" I yell at him. "Take it down!"

"That's not how it works!"

And I'm about to blow my fucking top when I'm pushed out of the way by Jo. He grabs Audley by the collar and slams him up against my car, forearm pressing down on his throat.

"Oi, Beej—how fucked up does a man have to be to get a kick out of spreading shit about perfect strangers? Making girls cry with the shit you talk about them on the internet? Does it make you feel big?" Jo lifts an eyebrow as he presses down harder on his throat.

Audley, he starts choking a little.

"Jo—" I glance at him. Feel nervous, if I'm honest. Never felt nervous about Jonah in my life.

He presses down more still and now the reporter is proper struggling.

"Jo!"

"Listen—" Jonah ignores me. "If he wasn't here—" He nods his head towards me. "It'd be knives out, but here he is. Lucky you, happy days . . ." He releases him and the man stands there gasping, holding his throat.

"Are you going to be a bit more amenable to what we want from you now, Ian?"

Audley nods, clearly afraid.

"Beej." Jo nods his head at me.

"Alright, besides the part where I'm not going to just sue that dumb fucking magazine you work for but I'm going to sue you. You—" I point at him. "I'm going to come for you with everything I've got, and I know just from looking at you, that I've got a lot more than you do already, and I'm going to take it anyway. I'm coming for everyth—"

"I'll print a retraction," he says quickly.

"Yep." I nod. "And?"

"And I'll issue a public apology."

I nod, unimpressed. "What else?"

"What else do you want?"

"Do you have the original photos?"

"On my phone," he nods. "Yeah."

I think for a second, then I tap my car.

"Get in," I tell him.

"No—" Audley shakes his head. "I'm not going anywhere with you—"

"Ian . . ." Jo says, warning voice.

I stare down Audley. "You're going to come with me right now and tell my fiancée that you're a piece of shit who's trying to sell magazines so you made something up and you're sorry that you lied and caused her this pain."

Ian opens his mouth, starts to say something, but Jonah shakes his head, opens the back door of my car and shoves him in.

Quicker drive back now. Maybe thirty minutes, just.

He's quiet for the first little while. Looks annoyed, actually. Like we've inconvenienced him.

"Having a rough day are you, mate?" Jo notices and turns back towards him.

Audley says nothing, gives Jo a little glare.

"People like you think you can do whatever you want," he tells the window, not us.

"People like us?" I spin around. "Funny, I went to lunch last month with my baby sister and her friend, went to work this morning and when I came home, you'd set fire to my relationship. And for what?"

"If your relationship's on fire, that's not my fault," he tells me, quite sure of that.

"Is it not?" Jo stares at him, sniffs a laugh. "What's your problem with him—" Jo nods his head towards me. "He fuck a girl you fancy?"

Audley rolls his eyes and looks back out the window.

"I could have you arrested for assault," he tells Jonah.

"Okay." Jonah sniffs. "Let's see how that goes."

"I could!" he says again.

"Sure." Jo nods coolly. "I mean, I wouldn't. But yeah, give that a try. Let's see what happens . . ."

I toss my friend a look but he doesn't catch it. His eyes are on the road, glaring at it.

"It's just a job."

"No, it's fucking not—" I bang the steering wheel. "We're real people, man. I've got a real girl back home who's crying proper tears because you're a fucking liar."

He's quiet for a second.

"She believes it only because you've done it before."

"Well, thank you very much, Aristotle." Jo rolls his eyes.

I give Jo a look then stare down at Ian.

"Imagine doing something once, one time, when you were twenty and fucked up, and then every time, every chance everyone around you gets, people roll that mistake out in front of you like it's a fucking carpet that you have to walk on. But it's not just me who has to walk it—it's my mum, it's my grandma, it's my fiancée. Do you know what it does to her every time there's a fake story about me and some fucking model I've never even met? When you print a story about how I got some girl pregnant when we were at school? It fucks with her—she's real. I know to you lot, she's this, like, far away abstract idea of a person, but she's a proper person."

He goes quiet after that. Looks at his hand, looks back out the window.

When we pull up to Henry's we take the lift up this time.

Bang on Henry's door and he opens it, begrudgingly.

Everyone's gone now except Henry and Rom.

"She still here?" I push past him, looking around.

Henry nods as Jo shoves Ian into the apartment.

Henry looks at him, confused.

"And who the fuck is this, then?"

"Magnolia?" I call. "Parks!"

"Guest room—" Romilly nods at it and Henry rolls his eyes at his girlfriend.

I swing open the door—don't knock, don't wait for her to let me in—I shouldn't have to.

She's back up against the head of the bed, centred, hugging her legs. Room's pretty dark but still somehow those eyes are fucking bright as the morning star, all rimmed red from crying.

"Hey," I say.

She says nothing.

Then I grab Ian by the back of his collar and shove him into the room.

She stares at him all confused for a couple of seconds, then flicks her eyes back at me, unimpressed.

"Tell her who you are," I say, giving him another shove.

"I'm—" He clears his throat. "Ian Audley. I wrote the article in the *Mail* today."

Magnolia sits up straighter immediately.

Henry snaps his head in Ian's direction and glances back at me.

I lift my eyebrows, impatient. "And?"

Ian sighs. "And I changed the photo?"

Magnolia jumps off the bed, standing now.

"How?" she growls, keeping her distance from us both.

Ian shuffles, uncomfortable. Embarrassed, maybe.

"There was another girl there—" He shrugs like he can't help it. "With her in the shot it was pretty obvious it wasn't a date . . ."

Parks' eyes pinch. "How did you do it?"

He looks guilty now. Hard not to with those green eyes boring into you like that.

"I cropped her out of a few. Photoshopped her out of a couple as well."

She looks at me now—finally—flicks me a look.

"Who was the other girl?"

"Maddie," I tell her.

She looks back at the reporter. "Did you make them kiss?"

He shakes his head. "No."

And then she's back to staring at me, eyes wide and incredulous.

I rush towards her.

"I didn't kiss her, Parks—" I shake my head. "I went to kiss her cheek—we moved at a funny angle, I got the edge of her mouth—"

She stares at me for a few seconds then looks back at Ian.

"Do you have the real photos?"

He nods, hands her his phone.

She scrolls through them at rapid speed and I watch the anger in her face melt all the way down to sadness.

She covers her face with her hand and cries into it.

It might be the first time in our whole lives that she's cried and I've done nothing, just stood there.

Ian looks over at me, uncomfortable—the boys are watching me, waiting for me to move, but I don't because she thinks I'm a fuck-up and that's a hard pill to swallow.

It lasts for a decent length of time, her crying into her hands, face covered. No one moving, saying anything. Nearly a minute, I think.

I feel frozen, like my feet are stuck in dry cement.

I want to hug her, of course I do—don't feel like I can, though. Or maybe that I should? I should be fucking pissed at her. I kind of am, now that she knows I'm not doing what she thought I was.

She gains control of herself, with a steep breath through the nose and some deep breaths.

She wipes her face with her hands and then stares over at the reporter, thrusts him his phone back and smacks him across the face.

I pull back, surprised. Never seen her hit someone that wasn't me. Didn't hate it.

"How dare you?" she says to him, shaking her head.

"I'm sorry, I—"

"Are we a game to you?" She cuts him off. "To talk about and to lie about—?"

Ian says nothing, just stares at her, sort of enraptured and terrified, which are things I frequently feel in her presence, so welcome to the fucking club, mate.

"Get out," she tells him.

Ian turns to leave and Jo grabs his arm on the way out.

"Oi—" He gives him a look. "You know who I am, yeah?"

Ian nods. "Yes."

Jonah gives him a look. "It'd serve you well to remember that they're under my protection."

Ian nods once more and then leaves, slamming Henry's front door behind him.

Magnolia takes a breath and glances between the boys and Rom.

"Can we please have the room?"

They all nod and leave, shutting the door behind them, and once we're alone she rushes me.

I don't want to hold her really, but I do. Out of habit and without thought, my hands go on her waist and her arms slip around me.

"Fuck—" she whispers. "Beej, I'm sorry."

I don't say anything, just nod.

She shakes her head.

"I'm so sorry—" She bats tears away from her face. "I just—I got scared and I panicked and—"

"I know." I nod.

"I'm sorry," she says again.

Never said sorry to me so many times in our lives.

"Yeah," I say, resting my chin on top of her head. I say nothing for a good fifteen seconds and then it sort of just slips out.

"Hey, are you always going to believe the worst of me?"

She pulls back and looks up.

"BJ . . ."

"I'm asking seriously." I stare down at her. "I need to know."

She shakes her head. "I don't believe the worst in you."

"Yes," I nod. "You do."

She goes still and sort of freezes in my arms, eyes locked on me.

"Are you breaking up with me?"

I roll my head back, exasperated.

"No—" I take a step away from her. "I said forever to you when I was sixteen and I meant it, but—" I breathe out a breath I didn't know I was holding. "Fuck, Parks—I can't keep doing this—"

She blinks, looks scared. "Doing what?"

"This—" I wave my hands between us. "This fucking dance where even if I don't fuck up, I'm still a fuck-up and I have to prove to you that I'm good enough—"

"You don't have to prove that," she tells me, looks earnest as she says it. "You don't have to prove anything."

I move back from her.

"You didn't even fucking call me, Parks!" I yell. "You saw it, believed it and switched your phone off."

Feel more betrayed than I realised and shake my head at her, annoyed.

"I watched you kiss your ex-boyfriend on the street the other week and I didn't bat an eye—"

"I didn't kiss him," she clarifies. "He kissed me."

"Not a fucking eye!" I yell, shaking my head. "I asked no questions, I didn't push because I trust you—"

"I trust you." She scowls at me.

"Bullshit you do," I scoff.

She folds her arms, looks scared—fuck, I hate it when she looks scared—"So, well—what are you saying?"

I lick my top lip. "I'm saying we need help."

She frowns, taking a step back from me now.

"What kind of help?"

I stare at her for a second before I say it because I know how she's going to go.

Say it anyway.

"We're seeing a psychologist."

"No—" She shakes her head, backing up against the wall.

"Yeah." I nod, walking towards her.

"No!"

"Yes!" I tell her, toe to toe and staring down at her. "I love you, Parks. I love you and I want to be with you—I would do anything to be with you." Her eyes soften a little.

"Please, do this for me," I beg, really.

She huffs, arms crossed and looks around the room.

Looks put on the spot, flustered almost.

She peers over at me.

"Do you think I'm mad?"

"Yes," I nod, decidedly. "All the time."

She rolls her eyes at me and I flash her a smile.

"Well, what would they make me talk about?"

"Everything," I tell her.

She frowns. "My sister?"

"Everything."

"Billie?" She frowns more.

I give her a look. "Everything, Parks."

She breathes out, hands on her hips, leans back against the wall behind her.

"Are you saying that if I don't go, you'll break up with me?"

I shake my head. "I would never say that to you."

"What are you saying then?"

I take a step towards her, reach for her hand and hold it.

"I'm saying that being with you, as we are, is hurting me."

"Oh." Her whole face falls. Eyes fill up with tears. "All because I believed a fucking *Daily Mail* article—"

"Not all." I touch her face. "We need this."

Try to give her an encouraging smile but she doesn't give me one back, just big eyes and a heavy swallow.

"We've needed this a while, Parksy."

She stares over at me for a few seconds then sits down against the wall in the dark room.

She stares past me for a bit and then glances up at me.

"I feel scared."

I go and sit next to her. "What for?"

"What if they sell all my secrets to a magazine again?"

I sigh. "That feels unlikely."

"It's already happened!"

"That's why I don't think it'll happen again!"

"Well—" She crosses her arms. "What if I'm horribly dysfunctional—?"

"You are," I nod, sure.

"What if they say I'm a mess?"

"Oh, they will." I keep nodding.

"And what if you—"

"Parks—" I cut her off with a look. "Do you think there's anything that I'm going to hear about you in a psychologist's office that I don't already know? I've loved you forever."

I pull her into my lap, press my mouth into the back of her head.

"I need this, Parksy." I hold her a little firmer. "Please?"

She rests her head on my chest and I hear her breathing, feel it fall in time with my own.

And then comes her little voice out from the darkness.

"Okay."

FORTY-NINE
Magnolia

We wake up the next morning when the door to Henry's guest room opens. We slept here all night, evidently—on the floor, against the wall.

BJ presses his free hand—the one that isn't holding me—into his neck, stretching it, and I blink over at his brother, who's staring down at us, eyes pinched.

"Interesting," he says.

I rub my eyes, tired.

BJ cracks his back and sits up a little, pulling me with him.

"What are you two doing down there?" Henry asks, arms folded.

"Fell asleep, I guess."

"On the floor?" Henry frowns. "Next to an empty bed?"

"Yeah." Beej shrugs, tired.

Henry rolls his eyes.

"Well, if that's not a metaphor for the two of you, I don't know what is—"

"Morning!" Rom sings, poking her head around Henry. "On the floor?"

"Mm." Beej yawns.

"Sexy." She nods appreciatively. "Fancy some breakfast?"

I sit up and flash her a smile.

"Yeah, we've just got to make a call first."

BJ looks over at me.

"Who are we calling?—Fuck my neck hurts."

I rub it for him as I tilt my head.

"Do you have a psychologist in mind or—"

His face goes funny, soft focused or something.

He nods. "I do, yeah—"

"Okay," I give him a little smile, nervous. "Book it."

"Alright." He smiles back, not nervous. He brushes his lips over mine.

"Now," I tell him.

"Oh, well, it's like—" He pulls a face as he looks at his watch. The Submariner watch in Bezel steel with the Hulk Green dial from Rolex. "Seven a.m., so—"

I scrunch my nose up. "So?"

BJ glances over at Henry and Rom, then back at me. "Well, she's not open—"

"Oh my god." I cross my arms, liking this less and less already. "What kind of doctor is she?"

"A psychologist," he nods.

I lift my eyebrow, unimpressed. "Who's not open at seven a.m.?"

"Yeah." He sniffs a laugh. "I think that's called boundaries."

I give him a dubious look.

"I think that's called strike one."

21:13

Henny Pen 🐓

So Taus and the policeman . . .

Mmm?

That a thing?

I think so, yes.

They've been texting.

Is that okay?

Yeah.

Of course, yeah.

Weird to watch it play out . . .

But happy for her.

Good!

Is he a good guy?

Very good, I think.

Good

FIFTY

Magnolia

"I don't feel like we owe them this," I tell BJ as I look up at him, holding his one hand with both of my own.

"Oh, we don't—" He shakes his head. "You don't owe them anything, Parks." He purses his lips. "Still think they should know though."

"Why?" I frown, and it's possibly a pointless question because we're already on our way to Holland Park to tell them about December third. Daniela trailing behind us as usual.

The decision to do so wasn't actually incredibly hurried, we've umm-ed and ahh-ed about this for months now, but it was re-brought up over the last week and now we're on our way to tell them, even though I don't necessarily think that they deserve to know, BJ thinks that I should tell them, and I'm trying to be more amenable as a person because I get the feeling that sometimes I have a reputation for being occasionally difficult.

"Because you're their daughter—" He gives me a look. "And this massive thing happened to you and—"

"And they didn't bat an eye." I cut him off.

"They didn't know they had to." He gives me a look. "Plus my parents know. It's going to come up with the psychologist—"

I look back up at him, feel a tight panic I get in my chest sometimes at the thought of the world knowing about her. What they might say, how they might sigh with collective relief that she was spared being the daughter of Problem Parks and Bad Boy Ballentine.

"Really?"

"Yeah." He nods gently. "I mean—she already knows from me, so—"

"Oh," I say and then he stops walking.

"It's up to you, Parksy. We don't have to tell them—" He gives me a look. "We can just go, have lunch with them—"

"For no reason?" I stare over at him, aghast. "Are you crazy!"

He snorts a laugh as he shakes his perfect head and keeps walking.

"Or we can just go home."

I eye him. "Preferable."

"But if it was me—" He gives me a look that's a little bit know-it-all-y but rather sexy and sort of hard to ignore because as I said, sexy, and also I am—I think—a bit adrift within myself, so I rather like being bossed around, except don't tell him that.

"I'd tell them," he tells me rather decidedly.

I slip my hand into the pocket of his caramel brown equestrian-print buttoned bomber jacket by Gucci. "Well, that's because your parents are nice—"

"Why don't we give yours a chance to be?"

I breathe out my nose and look straight ahead. "They'll disappoint me."

"Then we can talk about that in therapy too!" he tells me brightly, but when I don't laugh or even crack a smile he just nods. "They might, yeah."

And then I ask him the question that's worried me since the beginning. My voice comes out funny, quiet, nearly choked.

"What if they ruin her?"

He stares at me for a few seconds and his eyes look a little weary.

"Nothing could."

It's the first time we've been back to Holland Park since Bushka left for Moscow.

She's doing well, by the way. She FaceTimes us most mornings, significantly earlier than either myself or BJ cares for.

I actually think she keeps doing it because BJ sleeps only in his underwear and she's trying to catch a look, and she told me that since being in Russia, Uncle Alexey runs a much tighter ship when it comes to vodka distribution and so I mean, what's she living for if not the occasional glance at my mostly naked fiancé. I can't blame her.

We stand at the front door and knock, and even though I have a key still, it's feeling increasingly less like a home that's mine.

Someone opens the door who I don't recognise—that's hardly new—since my mother's apparently moved back in there's been many a staff change around here.

I told Bridget I think it's a strange attempt at a fresh start; as though they're weeding out as many people who were there for the "blip."

I haven't heard from the blip, really. Just the bare minimum. BJ said he thinks she's just taking time to sort herself out. My feelings are still rather hurt though.

We're escorted to the dining room where there's a full proper spread, a suckling pig, every vegetable under the sun, four types of salad and about nineteen different types of bread rolls.

BJ's eyes go wide at the sight of it and then my mother swans in wearing a kimono, kissing our cheeks and smiling warmly.

"Wow—" I stare at the table full of food. "It's just us, isn't it?"

"Yes—" My mother eyes all the food. "Is there enough?"

BJ sniffs, amused. "To feed Romania, yeah."

"Oh—" My mother swats her hand. "I've never really had to organise catering for anything myself, but with Mars gone—"

BJ glances at me quickly—confused, which frankly, as am I.

"Marsaili hasn't worked for you for some time though, Arrie."

"I know," my mother says, taking her seat with a puzzled look on her face. "She just kept doing it anyway. Guilt, maybe?" She adds as an afterthought.

"Well," I give her a pleasant shrug. "That served her well, didn't it?"

"Have you heard from her?" my mother asks.

"I have, yeah," I lie, trying to make it sound as though we're close like we used to be, that we talk every day when really

I know nothing more than anything you could probably just google if you were so inclined anyway.

She's in Plockton, living with her family. Not working, but she wouldn't have to again in this lifetime should she prefer not to, with the settlement coming her way.

She does think she's going to work again though. She's considering going back to university to get her bachelors in teaching.

She is, of course, not seeing anyone as it's only been about thirty seconds and though I myself would lump her in with the other crazy adults I grew up with, she is the least crazy and arguably the most sound. She's not even thinking about dating, she said.

And I said "same" and she sounded unimpressed by my joke and said "Magnolia."

"She's doing well," BJ tells my mother, and I do just think he's the most brilliant person on the planet, truly, I really do.

The way he said that to my mum shut down the conversation from going any further, it somehow implied this wasn't a topic for my mother and I to be discussing, but somehow it was a warm enough response for my mother not to feel entirely rejected.

He's very good at traversing all the minefields in my family, I think.

I suppose that's why you marry a man. And as well because you love him.

"Ah." My father flashes me a wry smile as he walks into the room. "Here she is! Back to yell some more?"

I flash him a look. "Well, it's not the purpose of our visit but with you here, let's not take it entirely off the table."

BJ nudges me quiet and pulls me down onto the dining chair next to him.

BJ extends his hand to my father, who shakes it.

"Help yourselves," my father says, gesturing to the food, and then a staff member I don't recognise comes around with two bottles of wine and I tell them I'd like both because I feel nervous.

"And to what do we owe the pleasure?" My mother smiles over at us.

I take in a breath and hold it without realising.

Beej reaches under the table, squeezes my knee and then speaks for me.

"There's just something Parks and I wanted to chat to you about." He flashes them a tentative smile.

"Okay." My father frowns, placing his fork down, waiting.

I look over at BJ and swallow.

He points to himself, eyebrows up, asks without asking and I nod.

He gives me a gentle smile, throws an arm around me and then looks back at my parents.

"Right, well—" He mashes his lips together. "Back in school, Parks and I—" He trails and catches eyes with my father. Harley already looks deeply unimpressed by whatever's about to come next.

"She got pregnant," he says—before he shakes his head, correcting himself. "We got pregnant."

Both their faces change immediately.

Harley's completely shocked, and my mother—her face, I actually can't quite pick.

"Did you get an abortion?" Harley asks.

I shake my head.

His face falters as he looks from BJ to me, but I scarcely notice, I'm just watching BJ.

Forever this has been the hardest part for me—what comes next.

Talking about the life we planned so long ago, how difficult everything became for so long after it . . .

Beej gives me a tender smile before he looks back at my father.

"We had a plan, we were going to keep her—"

"Her," my mother says, watching us with the same strange expression. Sadness? Fascination? Both? None? Botox? Your guess is as good as mine.

"Yeah," Beej nods fondly. "Her."

"So what happened?" Harley asks rather unceremoniously.

"We don't know—" I tell him, and Beej glances at me, eyes all big and heavy. "But I miscarried at fifteen weeks."

Mum's mouth falls open and now, finally, I can pick my mother's face. I think she's rather devastated.

"Who knew?" Harley asks, pushing his untouched plate of food out of the way.

"Just us," I say. "And Christian's mother."

Harley pulls a face. "Why Christian's mum?"

BJ licks his lips and gives my father a delicate smile. "She's discreet."

"Right." My father nods once. "Did Mars know?"

I wriggle in towards BJ. "No."

And there's silence for a handful of seconds, all the things they didn't know about us seeping into their minds, changing the chemistry of who we are in context of that new information.

My mother stares over at me, just watching, until she finally speaks.

"Why didn't you come to us?" she asks. She sounds hurt?

I shake my head, not understanding. "Why would I have come to you?"

"Because we're your parents!" she says, rising to her feet.

"So?" I stare at her, like it means something.

So she tries again. "Because I have been pregnant and scared before—"

"When!" I shake my head at her, exasperated.

She takes a ragged breath and barely gestures to me but does enough for her point to land.

I lower my chin to my chest and eye her.

BJ slips his hands into mine.

"I could have helped you—" Then my mother sighs this big, heavy sigh. Not sorry for herself, or maybe it is. Maybe sorry for us both.

"Well," I shrug, "you were going through your baroness phase, so—"

"Don't you punish her for not being there when you didn't let us in—" Harley points over at me. "We could have helped you."

"We thought we could handle it," BJ tells him firmly.

"Yeah?" My father's head pulls back. "How'd that go?"

It's a rather cruel, don't you think? In the scheme of things.

But actually, I wonder if he could perhaps just be a rather cruel man in general.

BJ says nothing, just stares over at Harley, possibly having the same revelation that I am; there are many hats a man can wear, many qualities a person can possess, so many things a person can be, and yet none will destroy you faster than pride.

Harley lifts an impatient eyebrow. "You going to sit there, tell me you knocked up my child and not say a fucking word—"

"What would you like me to say, Harley?" BJ stares at him, unaffected. "It was ten years ago—"

"Cannes," my mother says suddenly.

I blink twice. "Yes."

"You were crying so much—"

The night when BJ and I got back, remember? And we were in so much trouble? I cried for hours—they had to call him.

I nod. "Yes."

She stares over at me and then shakes her head ever so slightly. "Magnolia, I'm so sorry."

BJ clears his throat and gives my mother a smile.

"Every year we go up to the house in Dartmouth—"

"Why?"

"Well—" I frown a little bit. "It's not where she's buried because—we didn't—" I pause. "It happened so quickly—"

"After Parks' surgery—"

"Surgery?" My father frowns.

"Fifteen weeks," BJ says again.

"She'd have needed a D&C," my mother tells him.

"After that—we just left." BJ tells them, and I can see that it's hard for him to say. I've always regretted that part. "We lay a stone at a tree up there."

"Which tree?" Harley asks.

"The one by the lake," my mother tells him, but she's watching us. "I've seen it."

I nod.

"Why?" she asks.

I *'um'* for a good few seconds, and BJ grimaces.

I eye Harley. "I'm not sure you'll love the answer."

His eyes pinch. "Try me."

I purse my lips. "It was her . . . conception . . . point."

BJ squashes away a smile.

Harley nods, unimpressed, but—surprisingly—doesn't make a smarmy remark.

I look for his eyes, try to tell him without telling him that it's an important place to me, sacred even. But he doesn't sense the tone, he doesn't hear me—how could he? We don't know how to talk to each other even if we're using words so I look away from him and turn to my mother instead.

"It's the only kind of burial site we have."

"The third of December is when she died." BJ puts his arm around me. "My parents are coming up this year. We'd love you to join us—"

"Well," I tilt my head. "'Love' might be a touch too eager, but—"

My mother cuts me off.

"We'll be there."

FIFTY-ONE

BJ

Telling her parents went better than it could have gone, but she was sort of jittery for the next few days anyway.

She's never been to see a psychologist—I know, fucking nuts—but I guess, neither had I til I started.

We had a school counsellor at Varley who was actually a really good woman, fairly switched on and observant. She was who Magnolia saw intermittently throughout the years. She had to check in with her as part of her outpatient program at Bloxham House. Parks actually quite liked her, I did as well. Easy to like really. Only that she had a gambling problem.

It was her who leaked to the red tops about Magnolia's grades dropping, her who told them about a bunch of Harley's affairs, her who told the world that we were sexually active.

That kind of fucked with Parks' trust in counsellors. Justifiably so, I guess.

She was actually so in her head about it the night before our first session that I put a melatonin in her mouth and told her to swallow it. Knocked out pretty quickly after that. Slept about eleven hours, which is pretty unlike her these days.

I move the urn to a smiley face today, try to help her feel brave, like Bridge was with us. But when I get out of the shower, she'd made it frown again.

She pinches my finger absentmindedly the whole drive on our way to the office. Not a shockingly long drive, about twenty minutes over to Belgravia. Daniela drives. She's actually a really good driver. Fast, safe, almost strangely efficient, even in shit traffic.

When we get to the doctor's office, Magnolia scurries inside quick as she can, sunglasses on, scarf on her head.

She doesn't speak to the receptionist, just sits in a corner away from the windows.

"Ballentine for Dr Ness," I tell her, even though I know she knows who I am—who we are, I guess.

For one, I've been a thousand times at this point, and two, the receptionist is our demographic. Exactly the age and kind of person who's interested in people like us. Or just us, I guess.

Never made me feel weird for being here, so good for her for that. And to her credit, nothing's been leaked that I come here.

I sit down next to Parks, who's nervously picking her nails as she scrolls on her phone without looking at anything she's looking at.

I kiss her cheek and she looks over at me, flashes a quick smile and then starts tapping her foot like a maniac. Didn't take her Vyvanse this morning, I see. Funny. She gets extra chatty when she's on it.

The doctor's office opens and Claire walks out.

"BJ, Magnolia—" She gives us both a warm smile. "Please, come in."

I stand, offer Parks my hand—she takes it—and I lead her in.

Dr Ness shuts the door behind us, and I take a seat on the sofa.

Parks sits down next to me, ridiculously close.

She stares over at the psychologist how you might at an alien who's about to probe you.

"Magnolia," She smiles. "It's such a pleasure to meet you at long last. I'm Claire Ness."

"Hi," Magnolia says quickly, flashes her a quick smile.

"BJ," Claire looks at me. "Good to see you. Have you been well?"

"Yeah. I mean, crazy lies in the *Daily Mail* aside, yeah."

She nods emphatically. "That was terrible. I'm so sorry that happened. But everything's fine now, yes?" She looks from me to Parks, and Parks looks at me, waiting to answer.

I let out a single laugh and nod. "We're working on it."

"Good." Claire sits back in her chair, pleased. "And how was your morning?"

"Fine, yeah—" I shrug, glancing at Parks, letting her jump in if she wants to.

She doesn't.

I clear my throat. "We had coffee in bed, I read a bit, she worked a bit, then we just headed here."

"Did you walk?" she asks.

"Drove."

Magnolia glances at me out of the corner of her eye.

"You drove." Claire gives Magnolia a warm smile that Parks does not return when she eyeballs her.

"Yes?" Parks shrugs, and I can tell she's on the defensive.

Claire tilts her head delicately. "BJ told me you don't like driving."

Magnolia stares at her for a couple of seconds. "Would you like driving if you'd been T-boned by a car on Vauxhall Bridge?"

"No," Dr Ness concedes. "I suppose I wouldn't."

Parks crosses her arms and shifts away from me a little. She's annoyed.

"Walking's good for you, anyway," Magnolia tells neither of us in particular.

Claire nods in agreement. "Are you very health conscious?"

Parks looks over at me again, nervous. I give her a quick smile, blink out that she's going to be okay and I'm right here.

Magnolia lifts her shoulders carelessly. "I suppose."

"In what ways?" asks Claire.

Parks rolls her eyes like it's a stupid question. "I don't know—I drink a lot of water, I take a lot of vitamins. I exercise most days—"

"You eat well?" Claire says, and it's open-ended, an offer to share.

Parks doesn't like that though because she's not an idiot, so she tosses me a massive glare.

"Do you just sit here and complain about me, then?"

"Talk about you," I say instead, then nod. "Sometimes, yeah. You were my 'reason for being' for a long time."

Her eyes soften at that.

"He's been worried about you," Claire tells her.

Magnolia flicks her a look. "I'm fine."

I shake my head at her carefully. "You aren't."

Magnolia rolls her eyes again and also shifts a bit further away too. I don't know if she knows she does it though.

"Magnolia," Claire leans forward. "You've been through a tremendous amount of trauma for someone so young."

"I'm not so young—" Magnolia glowers over at her, and that's when I become positive that we've a long road ahead. Cross that she's been called young? Fuck me, this is going to be a ride. "I'm the perfect amount of young," Magnolia tells no one in particular, that nose in the air.

Claire keeps cracking on though, the picture of an absolute professional.

"You've had a very complicated life—I'm just here to help you begin the courageous journey of starting to wade through it all."

Magnolia sits back in the sofa, crosses her arms again and glares at Dr Ness.

"Do you find that kind of talk ever works on a person?"

An amused look flickers over Claire's face. "Yes . . ."

Parks rolls her eyes and jumps to her feet. "Well, then godspeed and you're an idiot." She turns to me. "Let's go."

I grab her wrist. "Parks—"

"BJ, I tried!" she whines. "I hate it, she's crazy—"

"How?" I pull a face. "She hasn't really said anything yet—"

"So what are we paying her for?" Magnolia says, exasperated. Just grasping at any straw not to have to unpack a lifetime of shit, I think.

She huffs on the spot. "Such a poor use of money—"

A poor use of money?

I sniff a laugh. "I once watched you mop up some spilt wine on a table with a €500 bill."

She screws up her face and looks at Claire.

"I didn't have a napkin," she tells her.

"Parks—" I give her a look. "You said we could do this."

"Okay, fine—" She shrugs. "Well, we'll find someone else who—"

"He found me because your sister chose me for him," Claire announces.

Magnolia freezes.

"What?"

Dr Ness gives Parks a tender smile.

"Bridget was a student of mine," she starts, and Magnolia just stares at her, blinking. "I oversee the psychology department at Imperial."

"Oh." Magnolia sits back down, hands in her lap.

"Bridget told me she was going to send me her sister's ex-boyfriend because he was—and I quote—'really stupid but pretty great.'"

A smile cracks over my fiancée's face that I haven't seen the likes of since May.

She sits under the shade of her sister's words, rests in them for a second, then looks over at me.

"Did you know?"

"I had guessed." I give her a little smile. "When ten anonymous therapy sessions arrived at my door with a vaguely threatening letter attached—"

She frowns, interested. "What'd it say?"

"Well—that's between me and your vaguely threatening sister."

Magnolia's eyes pinch, but she looks happier.

"I'm here to help," Claire tells her.

Parks eyes her suspiciously. "And sell my secrets to *The Sun* . . ."

Claire nods once, carefully. "BJ mentioned you'd had a bad experience with a teacher—"

Magnolia looks over at me, unimpressed. "BJ seems to mention a lot."

"BJ understands the point of therapy," I tell her, and she pokes her tongue out at me, but it's not playful. Like, she's genuinely annoyed at me but just doesn't know how else to express it in this setting, which makes me laugh, despite my better judgment to not.

"So exactly how well did you know my sister—?" Magnolia says loudly to make me stop.

"Bridget was one of the brightest students I've ever had the pleasure of teaching," Claire tells her.

"Obviously." Parks gives her a look.

"She was an incredibly hard worker."

Magnolia shrugs. "I know."

Claire nods, thinking about Bridge. "Really quite organically wise—"

Parks gives her a demure smile. "It runs in the family."

I shake my head. "It doesn't."

That's glare number twelve thousand from my fiancée today.

Magnolia takes a breath and looks over at Claire.

"Did she talk about me a lot?"

Claire thinks about the question and then smiles.

"She was very protective of you," she said. "There would occasionally be someone in the class who would try to pry into your lives, ask her questions or make comments. She just never took the bait—" She shakes her head. "She guarded you very well."

"I know," Magnolia says, staring at her hands.

"She did, however, speak with great authority about trauma bonds—" Claire says, and that makes me laugh again. Parks too.

It's a strange laugh from both of us, actually. Somewhere between genuinely amused and properly shattered.

Her eyes fill with tears, and she wipes them away quickly, flashing an apologetic smile to Claire for her display of emotion.

I toss my arm around Parks.

"See, Parksy. We're good here." I kiss her cheek. "Handpicked by Bridge herself."

17:54

Tausie

How was therapy?

Fine

Yeah??

Did you like it?

No, of course not.

I'm not crazy.

Well . . .

Quiet.

Date is when?

Tonight.

Call immediately after

What are you wearing?

I don't know yet.

You are, of course, joking . . . yes?

I'm coming to your house now to be dressed.

By me?

No, by BJ

What the fuck

Yes by you, you twat

Oh.

Oh my god, Taura. I wish you'd given me proper time to prepare

What would that have looked like?

I would have pulled pieces.

I'd have made mood boards.

I'd have done you a colour chart.

You did me a colour chart when we were in year 10 and I wore blue eye liner and you said you found it offensive.

We weren't even friends

I don't know, or was I the only true friend you had telling you how much it washed you out?

I'll be there at yours in 15.

Okay, fine.

Is your make up at least done?

You're an absolute animal.

FIFTY-TWO
Magnolia

December third rolls around and for the first time ever, since the first December third, there isn't the same heaviness to the day, which is sort of strange, don't you think?

It's still a hateful day, I'm still quiet when I wake up, BJ still holds my hand more than he would on an average Sunday, we speak less than we normally do during a four-hour drive, but the weight of the day is now spread between us and a handful of people who love us and I think that makes it feel different.

There's not a great use to me looking back on all the December thirds past and wondering how different it all might have gone had we just told our families at the time . . . if we had cracked that day we came back home, the one where I was crying and Bridget had to call BJ, if we'd just told them what we had lost, what had happened to us, what might have happened to us instead of moving forward.

Would they have made us go to therapy? Would BJ have processed what happened with that wretched girl in a way that meant when he saw her that fateful night at that party at the boy's old house that I wasn't at, would none of that have happened? Would we have just lived happily ever after, spared ourselves what I can only imagine is like, several lifetimes' worth of pain, or was all of it necessary for us to arrive here?

Useless to think about, really, but I still wonder it anyway as we're driving along the M5 with BJ playing all his favourite Billie Holiday songs and singing along to them mindlessly with that perfect mouth of his.

It's really not a surprise at all that of all the parental figures who know now what actually happened, Lily is the one who took it the hardest. Lily and Mars, but Mars was different.

She said she felt like she failed me when I told her.

She was upset that I went through it alone, which made me cross because I didn't go through it alone, I went through it with Beej.

She said I should have never have been able to fall pregnant if she'd been paying more attention—if she hadn't been so focused on sneaking around with my father—she'd have been more on top of this, and I said to her that even though it all hurt me impossibly so, I wouldn't change it. Except for the part where we lost her.

I extended Marsaili the option of coming here today as well, but she didn't feel as though she could, not with my parents also attending.

But Bushka flew back in from Moscow. Henry and Romilly are driving her up.

When Beej and I pull into the grounds of the Dartmouth house, Lily practically tackles me to the ground in a hug before I'm even fully out of the car.

She comes up here a lot, enough that we now joke about her having an affair with Mr Gibbs and the only reason that's funny is because he's literally like, a thousand. She's here enough that Hamish is looking for a property down here for them, and I said I think they should move and Lily said, "How could I ever move from London when that's where all my babies are" and Henry said, "Yeah, but none of your babies are babies anymore" and then Lily said, "Your brother is my favourite today."

"Mum—" BJ rolls his eyes, peeling his mother off me, and she sort of hurls herself into his arms instead, briefly, just for a moment, then it's a hand on each of our cheeks, her face all fond and sad.

She's organised a lunch for us all in the greenhouse that's by the tree and I can see from here as we start walking over that it's spectacularly decorated and overly catered for the nine of us. Ten of us, if Mr Gibbs joins, which Lily is insisting he must. I hope he does. He's been very good to us in an unspoken, tender way.

My parents are—of course—the last to arrive.

"Missed the exit," is what my father said as he flashed us all an apologetic smile on approach. Henry leant over and whispered to me, "Is that what they're calling it these days?"

"Magnolia, darling." My mother hugged me. She looked surprisingly emotional. Her eyes skim over what I'm wearing. "I love this. Zimmermann?"

"Saint Laurent." The open-back black and white polka-dot crepe minidress.

"And the 101801 coat."

She nods at the black one I'm wearing before she drapes herself around BJ's neck.

Beej stares over at me, holds my eyes and gives me a small wink before he puts his arm around my mother and starts walking her down towards the tree.

I accidentally fall into step with my father and neither of us says anything for a good almost-minute.

"Are you okay?" he asks in a weird tone and sort of out of the blue.

"What?" I stare at him. "Why?"

His face falters.

"Oh—" I shake my head at myself. "About today?"

He sort of nods and shrugs at once—such a natural father—I give him a quick smile.

"Fine, yeah." I tell him and fight the urge to scurry off to Henry, which I'd much rather do. Henry wouldn't ask me if I was okay, he'd just hold my hand in case I wasn't. But I don't scurry off to Henry, I walk in a curious, sort of pathetic silence with my father instead.

When we get to the tree it looks incredibly sweet.

The garden's the best it's ever been, full of life and buzzing with pastels. Beej asked Mr Gibbs to install a couple of beehives around the tree, and though no bees are out today because it's cold and it's winter, the mere sight of them resting under our tree seems incredibly poetic.

BJ lays down some magnolias that he always has on the new stone with her name on it that's next to the old stone that doesn't and I still like it better anyway, because it was ours and it was all we had for so long.

There is some sort of balmy sweetness to seeing her name written down like that though. I've never seen it written out before. Billie Ballentine.

Romilly lays down some white hydrangeas and pink Mayra's roses because they're my favourite and then Hamish lays down a Ballentine crest ring on top of the stone, which makes Lily cry so BJ goes and hugs her.

I feel like crying at that a bit also but I shouldn't like to in front of so many people, and I realise that even though it's very sweet and very supportive that they're all here, I'm not sure that I actually like it.

I think I have imposter syndrome for my grief with Billie, and I never worried about that before, when no one knew, when I was allowed to carry her loss in my heart just quietly myself, but now that the loss of her lives outside of just my body, I'm conscious of how my sadness might look to other people.

For so long this specific moment in time was the only kind of intimacy BJ and I managed still to foster between us, and it pricks my heart a little, being here now, not just him and I how we're used to, and I wonder if it pricks him too because he stares over at me for a few seconds, his arm still tossed around his mum—our eyes lock and he gives me a tender smile, laced with all our old sadness and all our new hope.

'Are you okay?' he asks without asking.

'I don't know,' I tell him without telling him, and even still he knows.

He gives his mum a kiss on the cheek before he beelines over to me, arms slipping around my waist as he pulls me into him.

He wraps himself around me in this way that I don't think

I'll ever stop loving; just a complete envelopment. It's only achievable—I'm sure—when your bodies have grown up with one another's how ours have. He blocks out everyone around us so I can't see them, tilts his head the slightest bit and doesn't say a word. A tiny moment of privacy between us that makes me feel better about everyone else still being here.

We stay like that—I don't know for how long—no one says anything, no one else even moves a muscle. It's just him and I, saying nothing and sharing everything between us, grieving that tiny life we barely had and the life we planned to give her. His eyes get glassy how they always do on this day and then so do mine, but I think I cry most days these days so maybe that doesn't mean anything.

He gives me a smile that tells me he loves me but that we probably need to get back to the others and I scrunch my face up at him a little bit because what an annoying thing to say and he didn't even say it.

He sniffs, amused, and then shifts my body, turns me around so I'm back to facing the others, then pulls me backwards into him.

He rests his chin on top of my head and Hamish looks over at us.

"Any words?"

Beej shakes his head.

"No," he says, and I think people sometimes forget that 'unspeakable pain' is not just an idiom but also a truth that we have carried around in the depths of ourselves for a very long time.

Hamish nods once at his son and then looks at Lily.

"The garden looks beautiful, sweetheart."

She smiles up at him, and BJ nods his head at her.

"It really does, Lil," I tell her. "Thank you."

She gives me a gentle smile, and BJ starts walking towards the greenhouse, not letting go of me.

"Mum, do you want me to give you a list of all the other places on this property we've had sex so you can get flower arches made for those too?"

"Nope," Harley shakes his head, holding my mother's hand as we walk.

"Quiet, darling," Lily tells him. "You've never had sex ever in your life."

Beej pinches his eyes at her. "Given the current situation, how do you figure?"

"Fine," Lily rolls her eyes, conceding. "Fine, but just the one time."

"Didn't you walk in on them once?" Henry asks, unhelpfully.

"Twice." Hamish nods, then looks at Lily. "The snow, remember?"

"No—" She shakes her head. "That didn't happen."

"And then at the gala—" Henry throws in.

Romilly looks at me, wide-eyed. "You had sex at a gala!"

"Before the gala—" I tell her. "Well, almost—"

Romilly squints, curiously. "Almost having sex or almost walked in on?"

My father rolls his eyes. "Why does that matter?"

"Well, if it's the former—" Romilly starts, and Henry cuts her off.

"It was."

"Then—" She gives me a look, eyebrows up, as we enter the greenhouse. "How were you almost having sex?"

"Well," I take my seat. Place settings and everything, Lilian, that cutie. "I can't quite remember if it was in or not—"

"NOPE!" says my father, very loudly and very clearly, then he pulls out his phone before he answers a call.

"Good job, Beej." Henry drums his hands on his older brother's shoulders. "Way to leave a lasting impression."

Beej shoves him off and then gives me a disparaging look as he sits down opposite to me. "If it was in, you'd remember—"

"But it's never been in, darling," Lily reminds him. "So all's fine."

Lil organised the lunch to be catered by The Hampstead Kitchen and if I'm honest, it does all look quite tasty. This incredible rustic, leafy, overflowing table of too much food, which all looks rather at home in the greenhouse.

I at first only put some dip and vegetables on my plate but then I see Hamish look at it and I don't want him to know so I pile on some chicken and a bit of a fig salad.

After a few minutes, Harley walks back into the greenhouse sort of beaming.

He walks straight over to my mother and I.

"Great news—" He glances between Mum and I. "She's not putting up a fight with anything—"

"Really!" My mother blinks over at him. "All terms?"

"All terms." My father nods, pleased. So pleased, in fact, he tosses me a smile as though we're in cahoots. "Didn't ask for a thing extra—"

My mother's brows furrow. "How curious."

My father shrugs and takes his seat down next to BJ.

"Happy days."

And I don't mean to do it but I do, it slips out of me, the smallest scoff, and for a sliver of a second, I think he doesn't hear it but he does.

My father looks over at me across the table.

"What?"

"Nothing." I shake my head, not wanting to cause a scene in front of Lily and Hamish.

There's something a bit pitiful about my family being how my family are in front of the spectacularly perfect and cohesive family that Lily and Hamish raised. And I know they know how my parents can be, but sometimes, quietly, I do worry that if they were to see how my parents and I can be towards one another, if Hamish saw how my father really must feel about me, that it might make me in their eyes a little less adequate for their son.

"No, what—" Harley stares over at me, eyebrows up, and BJ's looking between us, confused.

I flash him a placating smile. "I said it's nothing—"

BJ's watching me from the other side of the table, brows low.

"And I'm saying that's horse shit—" he says, and the whole table goes quiet—Lily, Bushka, Mr Gibbs, the caterer and even the ducks in the pond. "Tell me what that scoff was."

I give him a tiny glare.

"Oh, I just think it's just so wonderful that you've fucked over another woman—" I give him a curt smile. "Jolly good, happy days."

Harley's head pulls back.

"What the fuck is your problem?"

"Excuse me?" I blink up at him.

"Maybe we should just take a beat!" Lily suggests brightly, but her eyes are round with worry. "It's a big day, lots of emo—"

My father holds a finger up to silence her. "Lil—"

BJ's hands ball into fists, Henry's jaw goes tight and Hamish straightens up a little. They really are such good men, don't you think?

"Every day—" Harley says slowly. "Every day with you it's something. It's just fucking headache after headache, so what is it this time?" he asks, exasperated. "What's your problem now?"

"You are my problem!" I find myself suddenly yelling.

"Parks—" BJ says gently, but the moment for diffusing has come and gone, Harley's on his feet now.

"Me?" he yells down at me. "I have given you everything you ever wanted—"

I jump to mine.

"Except for the only thing I've ever *actually* wanted from you." I glare up at him.

He lifts an eyebrow. "And what's that?"

"YOU!" I yell so loud it echoes around us and through the air and under the ground and in the leaves of all the trees on this whole entire property.

His head pulls back, shocked. Or maybe he recoils?

"I've never wanted anything from you except you—!" I tell him.

My father sniffs a laugh, shaking his head. "Bullshit."

"Not bullshit—" I shake mine back. "My whole life has been

shaped by wanting your approval and needing your attention and I would have done anything for it! Anything—" I stare over at him and bat away the stupid tears that I had been saving up all day to cry later when Beej and I were alone.

"Every weekend, I used to wait for you so I could eat dinner with you and you'd just never come home."

Harley rolls his eyes. "At school, you were with him every fucking weekend—" He gestures to Beej next to him. "And eating dinner—? Catch yourself on—" He sniffs. "You had an eating disorder—"

Everyone at the table sort of lets out a collective exhale of disbelief and perhaps even horror, except maybe my mother, who's sitting there quietly, staring at her hands in her lap.

"Eating food with your old man wasn't high on your priority list, Magnolia."

He sighs a small laugh, trying to break the tension, but it doesn't work, and I just shake my head at him.

"No—" I shake my head. "It was, it just wasn't high on yours."

He rolls his eyes again, dismissive.

I stare over at him, frowning, blinking, and then I breathe out a breath I've maybe been holding my whole entire life, before I say what I say next.

"I think you're really just quite a terrible father."

And that comment sucks the air out of the room—everything goes quiet and heavy, because everyone there knows that I've been lugging that thought around in my back pocket for years and years, never brave enough to say it but never loved enough to let it go.

The way it sounded was strange I thought. It wasn't overly laced in emotion—it mightn't have been laced in emotion at all? Just a statement of fact.

"How am I a bad father?" Harley asks me, tonelessly.

"Harley—" my mother says, looking up at him from her seat.

He doesn't look at her when he (barely) responds—he doesn't look away from me. It might be the most I've ever had his attention in my whole entire life—he just gives my mother the smallest head shake in the history of head shakes.

"Well." I clap my hands together and I can feel everyone watching on with morbid fascination. It's a showdown they've been waiting for—fearing, even—for years. "Here, let's take your question, and we'll flip it, okay?" I give him a polite smile. "Why don't you tell me why you are a good father?"

I lift my eyebrows as I wait for him.

He flicks his eyes, annoyed and offended by the question.

"I've provided you with everything, you've wanted for nothing. I've given you everything you've ever wanted—"

"—Not everything." I cut him off.

"Oh yeah?" He tilts his head. "Go on, what's your lack, then?"

"A dad."

That throws him for a moment, I can tell. He blinks a couple of times and then he sniffs a shallow laugh.

"Magnolia, you're so—"

"And you know what—" I cut him off again. "There was such a painfully easy trump card in there for you just now . . . So obvious to anyone, if only it were even partially true . . ."

Harley lifts his eyebrows, waiting, impatient.

"You could have said that you love me."

BJ shifts in his chair. I'm not looking at him, but I can feel his eyes on me, sad for me. Worried for me.

Harley rolls his eyes again. "Magnolia—"

I shake my head at him. "How at the back of your mind must loving me be that right then, in that specific moment just now, it didn't even occur to you to say it."

He presses the tip of his tongue into his top lip and looks annoyed.

"Of course I—" He sniffs, like he thinks this is all ridiculous. "—love you." He shrugs and I can't help but roll my eyes and that makes him angry.

"There are more ways to love someone than by fucking saying it all the time." He points over at me. "I have given you a very good life—"

"You can have it back," I tell him with a quick shrug. "I don't want it anymore."

"Oh, okay. I guess I'll just take away all my money, then?" He cocks a brow and I give him a dirty look—the whole table is so unbelievably tense—Lily is gripping a wine glass so tightly I think she's running the risk of it breaking in her hands.

"I don't need your money," I tell him, shoulders back. "I have my own money."

"Yeah," Harley quips. "And where'd you get that?"

"From my grandparents," I tell him with an eye roll. "The same place you got yours—"

"I'm self-made," he tells me, he says it like it's a warning.

"No, you aren't—" I tell him with a dismissive head shake. "You just didn't take a free ride—"

His jaw juts out and he glares over at me. "You've always been an ungrateful little shit—"

BJ stands up now, faces my father and touches him gently on the shoulder.

"That's a warning."

"Always—" Harley keeps going, doesn't even break eye contact with me to acknowledge what BJ said. "Bridge was grateful at least, had her feet on the ground, her head screwed on."

Now Henry next to me stands up as well. Says nothing, just stands.

Do you know, I could sort of feel this moment brewing for some time now. I could feel the atmosphere around us shifting, how you can smell the rain in the air before you can see it or feel it.

I knew I was about to be delivered some sort of catastrophic blow, and you'd think I'd shy away from that but I can't because it feels like poking a wound—sure, it's sore, but there's something honest about it. There's something true to it and it's too intriguing to stop. Like knowing when you open a door you're going to unleash a hideous life-sucking monster, but you sort of need to know what the monster looks like or else you'll just wonder about it forever so you open it anyway.

"You know, when he called me—" Harley nods his head at

Beej. "There was this second before he said it, where I knew what he was about to say—knew it, like, could feel one of you—that something had happened." He's thinking out loud, eyes pinched, lost in a memory. "And there was the moment before he said it where I didn't know who it was going to be about and when he said Bridget, there was no part of me that was relieved that it wasn't you."

My eyes go a little bit wide and my mouth falls open.

He gives a half-hearted shrug. "Kind of wished it was."

And then BJ tackles him clean off his feet.

It surprises Harley, I think—it takes him off guard, the ferocity with which he's knocked over—Lily screams as her hand flies over her mouth, and Bushka's swearing in Russian. Henry pulls me behind him—BJ gets in a good three or four punches before Harley throws him off of him and stands to his feet, chest heaving, both his mouth and nose bleeding.

Harley looks over at Hamish all ragged.

"Nothing to say, Ham?"

Hamish looks from Harley to BJ, eyes all dark.

"Henry," Hamish looks at his other son. "Go give your brother a hand."

Harley sniffs. He shakes his head, spits out some blood, then gruffly wipes his mouth before he eyes BJ.

"I've wanted to hit your fucking face for a long time—"

Beej nods coolly, "Same, old man."

Harley beckons BJ over to him. "Let's go then—"

BJ shrugs, unbothered. "I've already hit you three times."

"Four," Henry tells him, standing close behind.

"Four—" BJ nods, cocky. "Come on, I'll give you a swing."

Harley snorts before he takes one and BJ dodges it with ease. Flicks him a little look that would have driven my father mad before ducking another swing but the third one—an uppercut—Harley doesn't miss and it hits BJ, knocking him backwards, and Henry sort of catches him, keeps him on his feet—and Harley looks pleased, truthfully. To have hurt him or gotten a swing in, maybe he's wanted to punch BJ as long as BJ's wanted to punch him, I don't know—but what then happens next happens all so very quickly and rather intuitively.

See, Harley would never have known because he never came to any kind of anything to do with our school, but BJ and Henry were an absolute force on the rugby pitch, and everyone knew from every school that they played against that if you fucked with one brother, both of them would fuck with you.

BJ's dazed for maybe about four seconds before without a word between them, Henry and BJ both charge at my father.

"Oh my god—" My mother stares on in horror.

"Hamish!" Lily cries, hands on her face. "Do something—!"

I stand there sort of frozen, eyes wide as I huddle with Romilly and Bushka, both watching on, mouths open.

"Hamish!" Lily yells again. "Make them stop!"

And now they're beating the absolute shit out of my father. BJ and my father were a fairly evenly paired fight but BJ and Henry versus him, he can't win, he can't get a swing in edgewise.

"Stop!" my mother cries, running towards the boys. "Please, stop!"

She grabs BJ's arm and he looks at her for a second—it sort of snaps him out of it—with his hand he blocks a punch from Henry that would have absolutely, without a shadow of a doubt, broken my father's nose.

Harley stands up, worse for wear, incredibly ragged, and glares over at me, as though it were me he was fighting.

My proxy, I suppose.

"I meant every word I said," he tells me and then my mother lets out a tiny cry that I don't know what to do with.

"Say one more word to her and I swear to god, I'll put you in the ground," BJ tells him.

"Get the fuck off my property—" he says in a low growl.

BJ rolls his eyes, completely dismissive. "Fucking piss off—"

Harley grabs my mother's hand and pulls her towards the door, shaking his head at kind of everyone collectively, but really it's just for me.

He points to where the stone lies for our girl.

"I'm lopping down that tree," he tells me, unflinching, and then he drags my mother away.

Bushka chases after him, yelling Russian obscenities, crying so much that I can't really hear her properly but I do catch a "Отвали" and a "Ты сын шлюхи"—Hamish goes after her, maybe because we're all worried Harley's so unhinged he might say something terrible to an old woman as well.

I wait as long as I can for him to be as far away from me as possible before I let out a cry that doesn't even sound like my own.

I think I sort of collapse a little, BJ catches me on the way down, sits on the floor of the greenhouse, cradling me.

His mother, his brother, Romilly, poor, sweet Mr Gibbs and even the caterer all crater around us, looking down at me with these big, awful, miserable eyes.

And I'm crying too much to say it out loud but I hear Lily whisper it quietly to her son herself.

"BJ, what if he comes for the tree?"

BJ's face pulls in a sort of fearful strain and he says nothing, because what can he say? I wouldn't put it past Harley at this point.

Mr Gibbs puts a hand on her shoulder.

"I won't let him through the gate."

FIFTY-THREE

BJ

Parks and I stay up in Dartmouth that night, Hen and Rom too. Mum and Dad drove Bushka home once the chaos of everything died down—but what the fuck?

I don't know what to say to her—it's just the culmination of that thing that I was saying where like, our base level of parental experiences are so fundamentally different, I don't know what to do.

I mean—what do you say after that?

That he didn't mean it? That's probably true, I don't think he did. I think he's just a fucking arsing prick who can't lose and felt like he was, so he brought a gun to a knife fight.

I've seen them fight before, seen things escalate between them in these sort of catastrophic, snowballing kind of altercations but today was proper fucked.

A K.O. hit.

I carried her into the house after that, she was frantic—it's why we're staying up here, it wasn't the plan—she's worried he'll come back and fuck with the tree.

I don't think he would—I don't—I think it was an empty threat—cruel and callous and like, fucking impossibly insensitive and unkind—but hollow.

But then there's a part of me that wonders, what if—? Maybe? He looked wild enough, got that unhinged look in his eye—I know it, had it myself. Magnolia, man—she'll fucking drive you to madness, evidently even if you're not in love with her. There's something about her that can get under your skin and it fucks you up. Makes you look stupid, sound stupid, act stupid—coming back here with a chainsaw sounds stupid, but I'm not willing to risk it so we stay.

I take her upstairs to the room with the lock that we love—bypass the bed, I know she needs a shower—I sit her on the edge of the bath, kneel in front of her, and I'm sick. Like, sick to my fucking stomach at what he said to her.

I don't know what to do, how to undo what Harley said, make sure she knows that it's fucking bullshit, that he's a liar—that she's none of the things that he said she is and that actually, she's still the best person I know.

She sits there, shoulders sunk, head low, hands in her lap.

The last time I saw her this slouched, she was fucking unconscious. Do you know how much you have to hurt someone like her for her to slouch like that?

I slip my hands into hers and look for her eyes.

"I can't believe he said that to you."

She blinks twice, dazed. "Really?"

"Really." I nod. "It's so—" Shake my head, breathe out my nose. "Fucked, Parks. I mean it. It's—"

"Will you tell me about the day you knew you loved me?" she interrupts suddenly, and I pull back.

"What?"

"The day that you knew you loved me," she says again. "Can you tell me about it?"

"Why?" I frown over at her, confused. "You know—"

She swallows and glances away, thinking. Pinches her hand absentmindedly but I squeeze her fingers gently to tell her to stop.

She looks back at me, a weird look on her face. Not sad, definitely not happy, just like, kind of resigned, maybe?

"Whenever we're with your parents, every time, there are things they do—these small—" She breathes in what she's saying, shaking her head as she goes. "—Almost invisible to the eye, little ways that say they love you without saying that they love you."

I stare over at her, I'd be lying if I said I knew what she was talking about.

She purses her lips while she thinks of an example.

"How your mum's head tilts when she looks at you; or how your dad always shows you something from the internet that he thinks you'll like; or how your mum force-feeds you and how your dad always tries to kick the ball with you—I know they love you without them saying a word, but if I asked Lily to tell me about the moment she knew she loved you, it would without a doubt be the second she lay eyes on you, if not possibly sooner." She straightens up, raises her chin a little before she flashes the quickest smile. She swallows again. "That moment doesn't exist for me."

"Parks—" I barely say, and she shakes her head quickly.

"I don't actually know that they love me—"

"Yes, you do—" I nod quickly. Can't stomach the thought. "You know they have to—"

"Why do they have to?" She shrugs.

"Because—" I shrug back.

"Because why?" she asks me calmly.

I stare over at her, the person I've loved most in my life, find it fundamentally incomprehensible to think about someone not actually loving her if they were allowed to, and I can see the sting of what he said to her slowly starting to creep on to her like a shadow that falls on you when the sun's gone.

I look up at her on the edge of the bath and shift off my knees so I'm sitting on the floor facing her. I lean back against the vanity and take a big breath.

"Well, I've loved you in many iterations over the course of our short but fucking drawn-out lives—"

She smiles a little.

"You, to me, at all of six years old, were the hottest four-year-old—"

She shakes her head. "Terrible sentence, absolutely not."

"Yep." I laugh. "Instantly regretted it—"

She stifles a laugh and I look over at her, don't try for a second to disguise the softness in my eyes that always lives there but I usually throw a blanket over because I don't want to look like a wanker all the time.

"You were fucking shit at kicking the ball around, Parks—but you said you liked my face and that blew my mind because the second I saw it, I was already obsessed with yours—"

She gives me a quarter of a smile.

"I kind of suffered in silence for a good few years there—I remember you gave me a soccer ball signed by Beckham for Christmas that year and I was so excited I went upstairs to find you something else besides whatever Mum bought you, and I gave you a necklace of my mum's that I took from her drawer, and you were so happy but it was from Cartier and she wanted it back—"

She starts laughing. "I remember that."

"Marsaili made you give it back and you cried."

Parks keeps laughing.

"I made a promise to myself that day, I'd never do anything to make you cry again—which admittedly, I fucked that up a bit—"

She gives me a look.

"But I remember that feeling, I got it then, still have it now. You happy at all costs—that's the goal." I nod.

She slides down from the bath onto the space of floor in front of me, watches me, eyes big, waiting.

"Your first day at school, you were so nervous. I told my dad the night before we picked you up that I loved you, and I was—what, thirteen?—asked him what I should do, and he gave me this fucking annoying smile, now that I'm thinking of it—" I laugh, shaking my head. "Fuck, it's such an annoying smile! He still gives it to me now—"

"What did he say?" she asks quietly, tucks her feet under herself, hugs her knees.

"He said 'I think we should play the long game.' And I was like, 'What does that mean?' And he said, 'Walk her to the car in the morning.' So I did."

I give her a small smile, can't really smile big at that memory, she looked too sad at the time, too scared.

And then I pull a face, eyebrows up.

"I did hate being at school with you back then because you were so fucking into Christian—" I laugh and so does she. "It made me sick."

I laugh again.

"St Barts," I tell her, "besides here, will always be my favourite place in the world. I don't know what light that place cast me in so that you finally looked my way, but thank fuck for it—" I chuckle, and she's watching me with big eyes.

"Could have died happy after that trip, the feeling of you like, wanting me back? Was some kind of fucking high that like—I mean, shit—I've done it all, every drug I could do, I've done—"

She frowns at that, never liked drugs.

"None of them have come close to feeling how I felt when I grabbed your hand when we were running from Mum with the champagne, and I pulled you behind a wall and I let go and then you stared down at my hand—like you were annoyed about it, that I wasn't holding it anymore. And then you took a step towards me anyway."

Her mouth twitches, eyes all round how they were that night too.

"And then you kissed me," I tell her like she doesn't already know and I smile at her now how I did back then, like so fucking pleased with myself.

Parks laughs on the floor of the bathroom.

"I loved you then," I tell her with a nod. "Different than before though, because then you felt like you were actually mine."

"I was," she tells me.

I reach over, touch her face. "Still are."

"Then coming back to school, figuring our shit out and properly being together—first time in my life I felt like a man, like I was responsible for something, finally. That first day back at school, Jo was so in my ear about playing it cool with you, and I was fucking stupid because I listened—" I give her a look, like she doesn't know it already, like she hasn't crucified me for it for the last decade, how after St Barts once we were back at school I didn't talk to her for a week. Depending on who you ask, that's an exaggeration. Jonah was well adamant not to look too eager.

"You can't be too keen with girls like her, Beej," he told me, knowing full well I'd been keen on her all my fucking life.

Parks rolls her eyes at me on the Dartmouth bathroom floor, waiting for me to keep going.

"But I remember watching you get out of that town car in your uniform and thinking—" I stare over at her, lick my lip, nod. "*—Fuck, it's going to be a really good year.*"

She laughs again, cheeks pink.

I look over at her. "Been a really good life, actually."

She wriggles in closer towards me. Wants to be close to me, doesn't want me to stop though.

"Billie made me love you in a new way," I tell her. "That was the biggest shift, you know? If you'd asked me before that I would have said I always loved you in this like absolute, sort of—I don't know—I guess, like, star-crossed kind of way, but then after that—" I smile at her, weary from the thought of that day—this day, I s'pose—nine years ago. "I was unreasonably in. Hopelessly in." I nod over at her and she nods back.

"We were different after that," I tell her. "We didn't love not being together before but after that, it hurt. Like you'd go home on a Saturday night—"

"When?" she interrupts, outraged at the thought of it.

"Oh—" I shrug. "Like, sometimes."

She rolls her eyes. "Barely."

"Barely, yeah." I nod. "But when you did go home, it was like—hot aches in my arms and my body, you know? Like, when you have a chill—"

"Oh," she says. Swallows heavy.

I stare over at her, think twice about what I'm thinking about saying—say it anyway.

"Breaking up was big for me," I tell her, and she looks nervous, instantly. "Just this like, fucking sobering revelation of not just how much I loved you, and how I'm better when I'm with you, and that I'm fucking nothing without you, but that like, I'd never get past you, ever—" I shrug, kind of surrender to the idea of it. "And that was—" I trail, thinking back to it. Fucking scary, is what it was. There was a time there where I wasn't sure, legitimately, that we'd actually work out, and I knew I'd have to just live with loving her.

"I tried—like, proper tried—to get over you and I—" Shrug my shoulders. "Couldn't. Here I am." I give her a look. "Still here."

She watches over at me, nodding quickly like she's telling herself, saying it so she believes it. "Still here."

I reach over, hold her hands.

"I wish I could tell you all the ways that I tell you I love you without telling you that I love you, but I don't know what they are—"

She kind of sighs and I look for her eyes.

"Because I think at this point all of me is a big fucking ode to just loving you—"

She crawls towards me, settles in, head on my chest.

"But in case that's not good enough, can I maybe just tell you to your face forever that I love you, and that your dad is a piece of shit."

7:24

Lilian 💕

Darling, I am so sorry he said those things to you

It's okay! I'm fine.

That was beastly of him.

He was just being silly, Lil. I'm fine.

I love you 💖💖💖💖💖

I love you too ❤️

You're brilliant

I know

And very funny!

I know

And so much stronger than you realise.

Thank you ❤️❤️

And arguably you're the most beautiful girl in the world.

You have three daughters . . .

Actually darling, I think you'll find I have four.

FIFTY-FOUR

BJ

Jo sits across from me, brows low—pissed.

Shakes his head. "Has that ever happened before?"

"No—" I rub the back of my neck. "Not really. Like—the thing with Tom, I guess?" I shrug. The lamp, by accident, remember? "And one other time besides that."

Jo squints. "What time?"

She was seventeen, probably? We were out one night at a club—can't remember which one. Cirque Le Soir, maybe? Anyway, Parksy was well tipsy before we even arrived, but once we got there, we found her dad. With someone else.

"Like, proper with someone?" Jo crosses his arms, staring over at me.

"Yeah." I shrug. "So she started yelling, got her phone out, started taking photos, filming it, saying she's going to show her mum, send it to the red tops—classic Parks shit—"

Jo sniffs, amused.

"But then Harley jumped up, grabbed her phone and threw her phone in the ice bucket—"

"Funny." Jonah chuckles then shakes his head at himself. "But not."

"I don't know why that was the part of it that sort of pushed her over the edge but it did—she started yelling at him, but bad. Like, 'You're fucking shit!' 'You're a piece of shit!' and 'You're the worst dad in the world!' and then he got up close in her face and said real calm and low, 'That's fine, I never wanted to be a dad anyway.'"

"Fuck." Jo blinks at the story.

It was bad. Hearing someone say out loud something you've always worried about yourself? Fucked up.

She didn't say anything, just sort of stared at him and then bolted, as she does.

Fucking loves a run, doesn't she? At least it's not me-specific, I suppose?

I stare over at Jo, nodding slowly. "Bit of a circus after that—she drank more, got like, blackout drunk—blacked out, woke up the next morning—" I take a big breath, sort of relieved to get this off my chest. I give him a look. "Didn't remember a thing."

His face falters. "What?"

I shrug. "Completely wiped."

"You didn't tell her?"

I toss him a look.

"How the fuck am I going to tell her her dad said that to her face?"

He frowns. "Shouldn't she know?"

"No—" I shake my head. "Why? What's her knowing that going to do? Me knowing it makes me fucking sick and it's not even about me. I don't want her to know."

He frowns more, thinking it through.

Jo has a weird relationship with his dad too. Jud sort of just fucked off after Remy died. Didn't technically leave, didn't stay in any way that counts either. He's been around more lately, before Barnsey's coma but especially since. Hard for the boys though. Both of them shrug it off, act like it's nothing to them but I've seen up close what it does to a person, shit parents. Barnsey would have softened the blow. It's still a blow though.

Jo's face pulls. "The other day and this—you think he meant it?"

"No." I shake my head, sure. "What happened at the club, it's how I know he doesn't. He was with that fucking leggy model from the 2010s—you know who I mean? The American. Huge boobs—"

"Oh yeah," he nods. "Her."

"It was her at the club, and I could see it on him—embarrassed. Like, he was losing face in front of her, that's why he cracked it."

He is proud like that, always has been. Bridge was right—pride is dangerous—of all the things in the world that sound a bit benign but could take you out in the end? It's pride. Maybe she knew that because of Harley. I never thought to ask.

He came up to Parks' room the morning after, stood in her doorway all sheepish, and she looked at him how daughters do—eyebrows up, she goes, "What?" Like he was annoying her, like she'd say to him any old time—Harley looked at me, confused—I looked at her—

"What?" She frowned over at me, confused now too.

"Nothing." I shook my head, looked back at Harley.

He frowned over at his daughter. "You have a big night last night, then?"

"No." She shrugged, batting her eyes like an innocent. She straightened up. "We went to a club and then came home."

How many kids could tell their parents they went to a club and they don't fucking bat an eye?

"What club?" His eyes pinched, trying to bait her.

"I don't know—" She shrugged, annoyed. Flicked me an impatient look. "Why?"

His mouth pulled, baffled—did she really forget? Could he be so lucky?—he watched her a couple seconds more, waiting for a crack in the veneer that she'd never let him see, even if it was there. It wasn't. There are no cracks in her, she's flawless.

Her face didn't move the way faces sometimes do when they're lying, so her dad's whole face relaxed, relieved.

"No reason," he said, then he turned and walked back down the hall.

I glanced over at her. "I'm going to grab a juice from downstairs—do you want anything?"

"A smoothie, please," she told me, and I gave her a quick nod.

"A green one—!" she called after me.

Gave her another nod.

"Green but if you can ask her to make it taste more like

strawberries and bananas, but with the nutritional value of like celery and spinach and spirulina—"

I paused to give her a look because you have to give her looks or else she'll drive you mad, and then I ran after her dad.

"Oi—" I called to him, all of nineteen at the time.

He spun around, brow cocked. "You talking to me?"

"What the fuck was last night?"

Rolled his eyes like I'm an idiot. "We both had a bit much—"

Lowered my chin to my chest, eyed him for that.

"What you said to her—"

"Come on, I didn't mean it—" He rolled his eyes. "She doesn't even remember."

"Yeah, but I remember."

He gave me an indifferent shrug.

"Seems like your burden to bear," Harley said to me.

"And really you never told her?" Jo asks again.

"I'm not trying to fucking unravel her completely—" I give him a good scowl. "Anyway, what he said the other day was worse than the first time."

That makes him sad.

"Is she okay?"

"Yeah. Like, no—" I shrug. "But yeah. I don't know—" Shake my head because that's about as coherent as I can be about this shit.

Nod my chin over at him.

"What about you? What's going on?"

"Nothing—" Jo takes a sip of his drink. "I had Banksy's birthday the other night."

"Yeah?"

Jo nods.

"She happy with it?" I ask.

"Yep." Nods again.

"She still with the teacher prick?"

He shakes his head. Looks annoyed.

Interesting.

I mean—not actually interesting, pretty fucking predictable. But physical discomfort present on Jo's face is a development.

"Remember the ex?"

I squint, thinking. "The ex? Like, the one we—"

Beat up. Is the end of that sentence that I don't say.

He was a prick too.

With the exception of Jo, Bianca Harrington has rubbish taste in men.

"Yeah—" He flicks me a look. "They're back on."

I pull face. "Shut it."

Jonah breathes out his nose, looks stressed about it. Like, proper stressed. Heart's in it, stressed—I don't know that he knows that though.

"On on?" I say even though, obviously—I'm not a fucking idiot—I just want to see where this goes, need a bit more to prod him with.

Jo gives me a dirty look. "I don't know."

Tilt my head a bit. "But you care . . . ?"

"What?" He scowls. "No—" Shakes his head a lot.

Sniffs a laugh, rolls his eyes, does about forty things at once with his stupid body to prove he doesn't love this girl that he definitely does.

"I care how I care when you were fucking about with twats, I don't care like care—"

My eyes pinch. "Right."

"Shut up."

I lift my shoulders. "I didn't say anything."

Jo swats his hand through the air and breathes out, looks a different kind of stressed.

"I don't have time for that shit anyway—" he says, but I don't know that he's saying it to me? Slips out of him, bit unconscious. Not a real thought. At least not one he meant to share.

"What's going on?" I ask him, watching a bit closer now.

"What—?" He blinks, like he's out of a trance. "Nothing."

But he's lying now, I can tell. Whatever it is, it's something.

"Jo—" I press my tongue into my top lip, shake my head. "What's going on?"

He stares over at me, big long look—bit weird—he's about to

spill his fucking guts though, I can see it, bubbling to the surface. He opens his mouth to say something and then he frowns, shakes his head at himself—but, like—barely?

My best friend breathes out his nose.

"Nothing."

18:31

Gus W 🤍

Hey. Heard what your dad said to you . . .

How?

Doesn't matter.

So Taura

Yeah.

lol

Are you ok?

Why does everyone keep asking me that?

I don't know.

Because it was fucked?

I'm fine.

Like, actually?

Yes.

Doesn't sound like you . . .

🙄

Talked to him since?

No

But that's hardly indicative of anything.

He's never been my first port of call for a chat.

Has he talked to you?

Nope

You know how he goes . . .

Loves escalating things more than they need to be.

Flare for the dramatics.

Sure

Runs in the family, I think.

FIFTY-FIVE
Magnolia

"So," Claire gives me a psychologist-y smile. You know the kind. Warm-ish, reserved, profiteering off of my perpetual traumas, etcetera etcetera. "How have the last few weeks been?"

"Excellent." I give her a quick grin back. "Great. Really wonderful."

BJ shifts in his seat next to me but says nothing.

"It was December third," she tells me, and I don't, for even a second, allow my face to reflect the pain that day conjures in me. I give her another controlled smile.

"Yes, it was."

"Would you like to share a little bit about that day?"

I straighten up a tiny bit. "No."

She nods once, then writes something down.

It feels so judgey when they write something down, don't you think?

"BJ said you and your father got into a bit of a tiff?"

"Hmm—" I pretend to think back to the day, as though it were something I have to try to remember, pretend that what he said hasn't played on a loop in my stupid little mind since then. "Oh, that—?" I shrug airily. "Just a small one."

She tilts her head. So patronising.

"I understand he said some quite unkind things to you?"

I shrug my shoulders again, easy breezy. As though my father's words were nothing more than some kicked-up sand that brushed across my face in amongst an ocean breeze.

I mentioned it before, unspeakable pain. I can't actually speak about what happened out loud—I don't know why?—as though speaking it out again might make it possibly truer than it already is.

There are so many aspects of what happened that I hate and that terrify me . . . that he said what he said at all—that he said what he said in front of BJ—in front of BJ's family? So now all these people, who I suspect probably already knew that he wasn't all that mad on me to begin with, have now a glaringly hideous, undeniable confirmation that that is, in fact, the truth.

I flip my hair over my shoulders. "Sticks and stones, Claire."

Her face looks sad for me, possibly in a genuine way. But I don't want her genuine sadness, I don't want her pity. I don't need anything from her or from anyone else over the age of forty.

"Words can really very much so hurt you," she tells me with some kindness in her voice that I'm not interested in hearing so I give her a look like she's a little bit hopeless, mostly because I think—I wonder if—?—am I the hopeless one?

"Claire, I've had people lie and speak shit about me for years. People have pulled me apart from the seams of myself since I was fifteen—" I give her my most brilliant smile. "I'm fine."

BJ rubs his hand over his mouth absentmindedly.

"Okay." She nods, giving me a curt smile. Then writes something else down again. Typical. She takes a big breath while looking at her notebook and breathes it out her nose. "And how are you going with Bridget?"

I glance at BJ before I look back at her. "What do you mean 'with Bridget'?"

"You've been having some trouble letting her go, I've heard?"

I look back at Beej—glare, actually. "Heard, have you?"

"Sending her texts, leaving her voicemails—that her ashes sit at the end of your bed—?"

"Just sometimes." I roll my eyes at that last one.

She gives me an encouraging smile. "Where else do they sit?"

And the answer is sometimes on the couch with me or on my desk while I work but I get the feeling those answers might incriminate me in some way so I cross my arms over my chest instead and try a different tactic.

"If not the end of the bed, where else would I put them?"

"On a shelf?" she suggests. "In a closet, in—"

"In a closet!" I interrupt her. "Bridget hates closets, obviously, did you not see what she wears if she's left to dress herself? My god, it's like a Macklemore video—"

"It was," Claire says a tiny bit firmly, before she watches me and then BJ reaches over and rests his hand on my knee.

I blink. "What?"

"Past tense," she tells me. "It was like a Macklemore video."

"Alright." I shrug. "Whatever—"

Claire stares over at me for a few seconds before she puts her pen down and rests both her hands in her lap.

"Do you talk to your sister still, Magnolia?"

I turn sharply towards my fiancé and knock his traitor hand off of me.

"You're unbelievable—"

"Parks—"

I shake my head at him. "You're telling on me?"

"No, I'm not t—" He rolls his eyes. "She was my psychologist first."

"Who you made me go to!"

"I know!" He nods. "But before you started, I'd already told her that my fiancée talks to her dead sister in the bathroom—"

"Why?" I demand.

"Don't know—" His head pulls back and he shrugs sarcastically. "It felt relevant."

"How?" I ask him, jaw set.

"Is your head cut?" he asks loudly before he blinks twice, looking all annoyed now. "Fuck, Parks—"

He pushes his hands through his hair, which I wish he hadn't done because I do love his hair so much, and I get jealous when anyone touches it that isn't me, even him. There's just so much of it, it's so thick and always tousled in a way that feels styled, but it's just like that! I've checked! When we were together at school I was positively convinced that BJ had to be waking up early to do his hair, so one night I did a camera in his dorm room and filmed us sleeping without telling him to catch him. Imagine my dismay when I then discovered that actually, he's just horrifically, naturally flawless. Imagine my other dismay when watching that video back I accidentally caught Jonah and—never mind—we don't talk about that.

"It's always been you and me, Parks," Beej says, staring over at me in Dr Ness's office. "If you're happy, I'm happy; if you're fucked, I'm fucked; if you're grieving, I'm grieving—"

"That's actually—" Claire clears her throat. "We call that codependency."

"Um—" I toss her a disparaging look. "So not the time for one of your outbursts, Claire—"

"We don't often consider it to be a good thing." She keeps going.

I glower over at her. "Claire, for the love of god, would you please read the room."

I gesture my thumb towards her and give BJ a look and he immediately looks at Claire apologetically because he's annoying like that.

"Go on," I wave my hand impatiently at him.

"If you don't move on from Bridge, I don't," he tells me. "If you're living with your dead sister, so am I, Parksy. I'm allowed to talk about it—"

"Must it be to her though?" My voice lowered now, as I nod as discreetly as I'm able to towards Claire. "What with her social skills of a simpleton raised in the wilderness—"

"I actually went to Bassett House," she announces, and I look at her suspiciously.

"If you say so . . ."

"I did," she tells me.

I purse my lips. "Okay."

"Magnolia—" She blows air out of her mouth as though I'm annoying her and I just wonder if this woman has even an ounce of professionalism in her at all.

"I understand that every authority figure you've had in

your life has either disappointed you, betrayed you or abandoned you—"

I look over at BJ, completely appalled by this awful woman.

"That's so rude—" I whisper to him.

"I'm not an authority figure," she says over me, voice stern. "I'm not trying to be your mother. I'm trying to help you navigate the insanity that is so clearly your life—"

I put my nose in the air. "Whatever do you mean by 'so clearly'?"

Beej sniffs a laugh and gives me a hapless look.

"I mean—" She clears her throat. "Your grandmother left, your childhood guardian left, your father rejected you, your mother sounds incredibly passive—"

I shift uncomfortably, and whisper to no one in particular, "It's dreadfully improper to just assume that about a person—"

And she keeps going on with her horrible tirade anyway.

"You're planning a wedding while harbouring a decades-old eating disorder and talking to your dead sister in the toilet."

I glance between the two of them.

"You both have been saying 'dead' a lot today—"

BJ breathes out his nose quietly, eyes heavy and sad. "Because she is, Parksy."

I look over at him, eyes raw like he's just slapped me. I blink twice, reject the sentence, and think about those incredible majolica printed polished calfskin clogs I saw during my morning scroll. Exquisite work, Dolce & Gabbana . . . Truly, something else.

"Have you ever said it, Magnolia?" Claire asks, back with the head tilts now. "Out loud?"

I cross my arms over my chest. "Said what?"

"That she's dead," Claire says, unflinchingly.

I press my lips together and swallow.

"No."

She picks up her pen again, poised to write another thing, and I shake my head quickly.

"But not for any reason that you need to write down on your secret notepad!"

Claire glances at BJ quickly before she looks back at me.

"It's not a secret notepad—" she says. "It's just—"

"Then show me what it says!" I tell her, peering over as best I can from my chair. "Flip it around."

"No." She rolls her eyes a bit but puts her pen down again. She takes a breath, and relaxes her face. "Magnolia, why haven't you said it yet?"

I shrug. "Just for normal reasons—"

"Like what?" she asks.

"Like . . ." I flick my eyes upwards, racking my mind for those normal reasons. "I don't want to make anyone uncomfortable—"

"Uncomfortable with what?" she asks.

". . . With what happened to my sister."

She nods once.

"And what happened to your sister?"

I lick my lips and shrug. "We were in a car accident."

"Yes . . . ?" she says, upward inflection at the end.

I purse them. "And then she had a headache."

"Okay . . ." She nods, eyebrows up, still waiting for the terrible more.

I cross my arms again.

"And then she had an aneurysm," I tell her and then I lift my shoulders like it's water off a duck's back.

"And then what happened, Magnolia?" she asks quietly.

I take a breath.

"She—" My voice stops short and I frown at myself because they're just words. I swallow, take another breath. "She—um—"

I clench my fists, as I glare over at Claire, digging my nails into my hands. I breathe out all the air that's in my lungs, breathe myself flat until my ribs fall heavy against my diaphragm and a pain starts spreading out from the centre of my chest and it's a different kind of pain to the one I feel without my sister, and I think to myself how fascinating a reprieve that is: pain for pain.

And give that to me, please—fuck—I'm begging you. Empty lungs, burning chest cavity, a shallow but distracting agony from the kind I feel always now anyway.

I press my hand into my mouth to cover my lips, which are trembling, and then BJ shakes his head and grabs my hand, squeezing it tightly.

"Died," he says for me.

Claire's face falters a bit, her eyes wander from myself to BJ and when her eyes leave me, I bat away a tear I shouldn't like for her to see.

"Yes," Claire says, carefully. "And I'm so sorry that she did."

I'm not so sure that she is though, she might just be a sadist who loves to prod at painful things to watch you squirm. If I was a sadist and I was clever (which I suppose you'd have to be in order to be a certified psychologist and the head of the department at Imperial) I'd pick a job that would let me poke at things that hurt people, like she's doing now to me, so I just stare over at her and say nothing.

She leans forward a bit, watching me with her eyebrows bent in the middle.

"Your sister was an exquisitely bright young woman," she tells me with a smiley nod. "Completely up to her ears with so much promise and so much sarcasm—"

I don't mean to smile at that but I do.

"And though I know you feel the incredibly personal weight of her absence in your life, I must assure you, Magnolia—" She tilts her head again, though admittedly it's mildly less annoying this time. "That her loss also belongs to humanity. The entire world is undoubtedly worse without her."

I nod once because that is fact, and then BJ lifts my hand to his mouth wordlessly and kisses it.

She puts her notebook down on the side table next to her before she looks back at me.

"Would you do something for me?"

I eye her, suspicious. "I'm inclined to say no . . ."

She smiles, a bit amused.

"Would you, in the next week or two, go to Bridget's room at your old apartment and just look through her things?"

I scrunch my face up. "Why?"

"Because no one has touched her belongings in nearly seven months—"

"So?"

"So Bridget is dead, Magnolia," she says with a completely straight face. "Something you've avoided, fairly successfully these last few months, but she is dead. And we need you to start accepting that."

I fold my arms over myself, defiantly.

"Well, what if I'm not ready to do that?"

"You aren't." She simply shrugs. "This is just the beginning."

23:42

Bridge 💩✨

She kept saying you're dead.

Can you believe that?

So rude.

And like, very morbid.

...

FIFTY-SIX

BJ

Today in my own session with Claire, I got in trouble for finishing Parks' sentence the other day.

Not trouble, because Claire's not my mother, but she did say I have to "allow Parks to arrive at her own conclusions about grief," or something. That buffering it for her only prolongs the process. Pretty hard to watch though. Made me feel sick, a bit. Not like Magnolia's ever really been an absolute top gun in the area of emotionally processing information, she's avoided most painful things with sheer willpower and a dash of neglect for most of her life—and yeah, unhealthy and whatever, I know we need a change, I know she needs a hand wading through all the shit that's been hurled at her til now, but fuck—that was rough.

Had dinner with Hen after my session, he said the boys were acting weird. Which they are—I haven't seen them like this before?

We've been friends for forever, right—? Basically, anyway. Jo and me, we've always been pretty honest. I'm sure there's some shit he wouldn't tell me, and same, but for the most part, I trust that what I see with him is what I get.

What the boys do, it's never really bothered me. I've never felt a squeeze from it, never felt like we were all that different—I didn't have a negative association with it, I guess. But these days, I don't know—? Something feels off. Different, maybe?

Could be in my head.

I head home after dinner, Daniela assured me that before she left, she'd make sure Parks ate something so I don't rush.

Walk home instead of drive out of habit, kind of like walking now—don't tell Parks, her head's big enough as is—takes me about fifty minutes, it's a nice dander.

Hit the button up to our place in the lift—opens right into our apartment—and do you know, I hear her before I see her.

This like, completely undone sobbing.

My heart drops in my chest.

"Magnolia!" I yell for her, but I don't know if she can hear me from here. The crying doesn't stop, doesn't even pause enough to take a breath. I barrel out of the lift the second the doors open. I call her name a bunch of times—I don't know why? For me or for her? I need her to know that I'm coming for her and I need me to know that she's okay—which I don't—for about ten seconds anyway.

I follow the sound to the living room where I find her, sitting on the floor, a box full of shit in front of her and she looks up at me, eyes all big and terrified—says nothing, keeps crying.

"Hey, hey, hey—" I get down onto the ground next to her. "What's wrong, Parks?" I pull her into my lap. "What's going on?"

She buries her face into my neck and keeps crying.

I start looking around for clues. The box—what's in it? I squint over at it. Some books, a journal, maybe? Some clothes—

Fuck, it's a box of Bridget's stuff.

"Parks?" I pull back to see her face and she looks at me, her eyes all red from crying for however long she has. Use my thumbs to wipe some of the wet away. "Talk to me."

She takes a couple of massive breaths—staggered, choking breaths—like she's fighting for her life for a drop of air and then she looks at up me and says with a quivering bottom lip, "I'm just a watch blown together in the desert by a blind man!"

My brows furrow and I pull back from her, confused. And then I see the book cast off to the side.

"Oh shit," I sigh, roll my head back a bit, then stare over at her. "Who the fuck gave you Richard Dawkins?"

Hands fly to her face and she's back to crying. I peel her hands from her face and make her look at me.

"I found it—in—Bridget's—stupid room!" she tells me between sobs.

I didn't realise she was going there today. I told her to tell me when she was planning to go back to their place so I could be there, and I should have picked it, how she brushed it off, how agreeable she was about me going with her, I should have known she wouldn't—I don't know why? Something to prove, maybe? To me? To herself? That she's fine even though she clearly isn't?

"No wonder she was so grumpy all the time," Parks tells me, wiping her nose with her sleeve. "It's incredibly hopeless out here."

"Out here?" I repeat, carefully. ". . . In life?"

She nods, bottom lip about to go again. "And after it."

I breathe out this laugh, not because I think it's funny—I'm relieved, maybe? Glad she's okay, or whatever the fuck she is right now. Not okay, probably technically, but okay enough—I shift her in my lap, hold her against me.

"It's not so bad here," I tell her.

"Yes, it is," she says, but it comes out all muffled because she's talking directly into my neck. "It's awful."

"Parksy—" I shift her back, touch her face. "It's okay—it's technically just a theory—"

She gives me a look. "It's rather compelling though."

"Evolution?" I blink. "Yeah, I'd say so—"

"So he's right?" She shrugs, eyes welling up again. But to be fair I wouldn't say that they ever really un-welled these days. Constantly welled or on the cusp of.

"It is all pointless," she manages to say before another little cry cracks out of her and she covers her face again.

"Hey—" I shake my head and pull her hands away again. "I didn't say that."

Push my hand through her hair, watch her carefully—if I'm calm, she's maybe not calm but she's at least calmer.

She sniffs, grabs the neck of my T-shirt and wipes her nose with it before she peers up at me.

"Is this what you were crying about with your dad?"

I pull a face.

"I wasn't crying—" I roll my eyes. "And no."

"Yes, you were," she tells me. "About the meaning of life, remember?"

"No, I remember—" I flick her a look. "I was angry at him because he said I have nothing to show for my life—"

"Oh—" she squeaks. "That's so sad!"

And then she starts crying again, balled up in my lap.

I pause for a second, think through what I'm about to ask her, whether it's wise or not—not, probably. Do it anyway.

"Parks," I clear my throat, eye her carefully. "Are you on your period?"

She pulls back. "I beg your pardon!"

My mouth opens to say something but nothing comes out. I force a smile instead.

"Bit erratic, is all." I grimace. "A lot of feelings."

"Well—" She gives me an exasperated look as she crawls off my lap, putting some distance between us. "Excuse me for just now realising that everything's pointless and hopeless and meaningless and—"

"I know the meaning of life," I tell her with a little shrug.

She rolls her eyes.

"No, you don't."

"Yeah," I nod. "I do."

"Well, go on then—" She folds her arms, an eyebrow up. "What is it?"

"I'm not going to tell you," I gesture towards her. "That's cheating."

"No, it's not—" She pouts, squaring up all proud. "Are we not one, BJ? What's the point of marriage if—"

I roll my eyes at her.

"We're not married yet," I remind her, and she pokes me.

"Give me a clue—" she whines.

I squash a smile.

"The answer's like, right in front of your face—"

"Just tell me!" she sighs, despondent.

I clear my throat.

"'There is something infantile in the presumption that somebody else has a responsibility to give your life meaning and point . . . The truly adult view, by contrast, is that our life is as meaningful and full and as wonderful as we choose to make it.'"

She frowns again.

"What?"

I nod my chin at the copy of *The Blind Watchmaker* she's clinging on to for dear life.

"Finish that book, Parksy. We'll figure it out—"

She gives me a petulant look.

"I thought you already had it figured out—"

I pull her back into my lap.

"Well, I'll help you figure it out too then." Press my mouth into hers, smile against it. "Because you're a bit slow to start, apparently."

She nods quickly, swallows, flashes me a smile but her mind's far away racing somewhere, I can tell.

Gets lost in these spiral thoughts of hers sometimes. Always has.

"Hey—" I touch her cheek again because, like, I can't help it. "Parks, everything's going to be fine."

She looks at me, brows low, that perfect face all heavy.

"But how do you know, Beej?" She gives me a hopeless shrug. "There are just so many shitty, terrible things happening all the time—People die. Babies die. Blind men don't get to have watches—"

I purse my mouth and squint over at her.

"Sure, yeah—" I nod, clear my throat. "Did you actually read the book—or like, open it and point to a page?"

But she doesn't even hear me, I can tell because if she had, she'd have smacked me in the arm or something, but she's just staring up at me all fawning, eyes unfocused with her blurry thoughts.

"BJ—" She looks up at me, face completely serious. "What if we die and it's just . . ." She shakes her head, blinks a thousand times, mouth opens but she says nothing, like she's too scared to speak the words she's thinking.

She swallows, takes a staggered breath.

"Just . . . black, empty nothingness?"

I give her a gentle smile and nod a couple of times.

"Then I will find you, Parksy." I stare down at her, hold her a bit tighter. "And we'll be in the black empty nothingness together."

00:41

Bridge 💩✨

You honestly read the worst books.

“At least I read”

that’s what you’ll say I know,
so don’t even bother.

Wouldn’t hurt you to pick up something nice
and easy every once in a while,
like The Princess Diaries or something.

Give it a try.

•••

FIFTY-SEVEN

BJ

I have lunch with my parents today. Don't know why.

Because it's been a bit and Mum asked and I find it hard to say no to her because she's the best?

Shit's still pretty weird with me and Dad, felt kind of naked when I walked in without Parks. Don't use her like a shield or anything but I guess my parents—Dad especially, he's not going to pull at strings if she's there. Especially not at the minute.

Starts out fine. Chit-chat a bit about life and the girls—Jemima's got a new boyfriend, Madeline's wanting to swap her university major again, and Al is doing better—thinking about going away on that trip her and Bridge had planned—but still not great, but to be expected, right? Best friend dies all of a sudden, what do you do with that? The world doesn't stop for grief, that's a fucking shit thing to discover at all of—what? Twenty-three?—and it feels like such a massive injustice—it is, isn't it?

Parks and I learnt that one pretty young. Grief stops you in your tracks but doesn't even throw a pebble onto the footpath of the world. They just step right over it.

But my mum hasn't been at me for weeks about lunch because of Allie. They're not worried about Allie; Allie has parents who give a shit about her.

They're worried about Parks.

My parents took it on about twenty years ago, worrying about those girls. Parks and Bridge were extensions of our family before me and Parks were what we are. Mum's been stressed out of her mind wondering how Magnolia is—not just about Harley (a lot about Harley) but all of it.

"How is she?" Mum asks once our mains are served.

"In pain, actually." I nod, tack on a quick smile on the end. "Sad. Figuring it out though."

"Life?" Dad asks.

"Yeah." I give him a shrug.

"Well," Mum smiles. "Who isn't?"

"This guy, apparently." Nod my head in Dad's direction. "Got it all sorted."

"Haven't figured it all out," he tells me, taking a sip of his coffee. "Got a few loose ends—"

I flick him a dismissive look. "If you say so."

"I had an affair," he says suddenly, and I stare over at him, eyes wide, blinking a fucking million times.

What the fuck?

"Hamish—" Mum says, and I look over at her. Can't fucking believe it. Who the fuck's doing that to her—? Hurting her like that.

I don't say anything, just stare over at him. The fabric my mind's made of unravelling at lightning speed.

He what?

My dad looks over at my mum, then gestures towards me. "He needs to hear this."

Mum looks over at me, her face pulls all strained. Can't read it either, is she sad for her? Sad for me? Sad in general?

She looks back at Dad, nods.

"A while ago now—" he says.

"When?" I ask, sharp. I'm angry.

"You were at school," he tells me.

"What the fuck—?" I stare at him, shaking my head. Look over at my mum. "Did you know about this?"

"Of course she knows—" Dad says, rolling his eyes at the same time Mum throws me an exasperated look.

"Of course I know."

I sigh, watch over at her. Reconcile quickly in my head why

she took it so hard when she found out the reason Parks and I first split was because of cheating.

"Mum—"

"I'm okay, darling." She gives me a smile that's dignified and proud and she's such a fucking legend. "Really."

"How?" I stare over at her. Doesn't make sense. I never saw it? How didn't I see it?

"I was sad for some time, but things happen—" she says, and all she does is offer me a small shrug. "You stay, you get better."

I stare over at her for a minute, gain a new layer of respect for her, which I didn't think I could because she's fucking tops already.

Look back at Dad, jaw set.

"With who?"

"My assistant," he says, without missing a beat. "Bit of a cliché, really—" Tosses me a half-baked smile that I don't return. "Embarrassing."

My eyes pinch.

"Why'd you do it—?" Look at my dad like he's a stranger. "It doesn't make sense—" Shake my head again. "You were so in love."

"I am so in love," he says matter-of-factly. "Still."

"But—"

"So were you when you cheated on Magnolia, weren't you?" He asks that like he's asking if I want one sugar or two.

"Yeah, but—"

"I made a mistake, BJ," he tells me. "That's it, really. Became closer with her than I should have—"

Cut him off as I stare over at my mum.

"And you were what—? Fine with it?"

"No, I wasn't fine with it." She rolls her eyes like I'm ridiculous. "But I forgave him."

I say nothing for a minute, try to hold together the parts of my life up til now that feel a bit like lies. Or maybe they aren't? Maybe it's all the same still—? Is it possible this changes nothing? Feels a bit like it should change everything but the older I get, the more I love the person I'm in love with, the more sure I am that—I don't know—I'm not leaving her for anything. Don't care what she does.

Shake my head as I stare over at him.

"Why are you telling me this?"

"Because I want off the pedestal that you've put me on," he tells me, unflinching.

"Yeah—?" I roll my eyes at him. "Where the fuck was this confession five years back, then?"

Lift my eyebrows, stare at him, unimpressed. "When I was a fucking mess because of what I did—?"

"BJ." He gives me a look. "We didn't know that's why you and Magnolia broke up until a few years ago—"

"And still, nothing?" I jump in. "Happy to let me feel like a piece of shit—"

My dad breathes out his nose, calm and steady. "You feeling like a piece of shit has nothing to do with me."

Mum frowns. "Hamish—"

"It doesn't, Lil," he says with a shrug. "It's because he's not doing anything with his life—"

"Oh fuck—" I breathe out. "Not this again."

"Yes, this again," he says louder than Mum would want him to. Not a yell, not a normal pitch either though. "Because what do you have to show for your life—"

Mum sighs and gives him a look that looks like a warning. "Hamish—"

"Her!" I yell, and it's a proper yell. There's a clatter of a fork dropping from some other table and everyone around us goes quiet and I proper don't give a shit so I keep going. "I have her to show for my life." I give him a look and a shrug like I'm sorry except that I'm not.

"She's the only thing I've ever properly wanted in my adult life and I've got her. She is the home I've spent years building. And I don't have any regrets—" I tell him and then stop myself, reconsider. Reword it. "Well, I have some, but—" Roll my eyes at myself. Definitely have some.

Give my dad another shrug and ignore the face my mum's got on where her eyes are this sort of heavy kind of worried, the unease she gets on her face whenever any of us are a bit off with each other—I don't care. That's a lie. I do care, actually. Makes me feel like shit seeing her upset in any capacity, but in the scheme of this all, I don't care.

"What am I meant to be showing?" I ask Dad. "Who am I showing it to? What's it supposed to look like—this thing I'm meant to have to show? Who's it supposed to be acceptable to?"

Lift my eyebrows, wait for him to unravel this great mystery for me.

"Is it a lack of a degree? A lack of a doctorate? Do you wish I was a lawyer—?"

Dad breathes out his mouth, loud. "No—"

"Then what is it?" I ask, but I guess it's maybe more of a demand. "What's this thing you're so fixed on that I'm obviously not doing? Is it a nine-to-five?"

"No," he says, eyebrows up.

I stare over at him, nod a couple of times.

"I'm good, Dad." Give him a little shrug. "I'm not fucking about. I'm off drugs. I'm with the girl I love, we're getting married—and the second she lets me, I'm taking her the fuck out of London and we're going to go someplace where they don't give a shit about us and we're going to grow old together and—"

"I love that plan, darling," Mum tells me quickly. It is sincere, but really she's trying to diffuse the situation.

I take a breath and throw her a quick smile.

"Thanks, Mum." Sound more tired than I mean to. More tired than I realised I was.

"Hamish—" Mum eyes him. "You don't have anything to say—?"

My dad opens his mouth but I'm spooked now, whatever it is, I think I'd rather not hear it. I don't want him to tell me it's a shit idea or that she'd never go for it and that it's still a lifetime amounting to nothing that he can quantify.

"Actually," I push back from the table. "I've got to head."

"BJ—" My dad sighs.

"I've got to pick up Parks from the office."

"We'll come with you—" he tells me, voice up, sounds—not nervous, not sad either. Something though. I shake my head.

"No, better not—" Flash him a smile. "She's not up to much at the minute."

My dad nods once, like he gets it. Or maybe like I'm a fucking prick. Could be either.

I lean down, give my mum a kiss.

"We'll see you at dinner this week, darling, yes?" She gives me a hopeful glance.

I nod. "Yep."

And then I leave.

23:19

Tausie ❤

Do you believe in God?

What?

God.

Do you believe in him?

Um.

Shit.

Maybe?

Why?

Just wondering.

Okay.

You okay?

Yeah.

And do you think he wears a Patek Philippe or is more of a Swatch Watch salt-of-the-earth kind of guy?

Who?

God.

Obviously.

I'm not even convinced he's a guy

Oh okay.

Fair

So perhaps more of a Cartier?

What?????

Never mind

FIFTY-EIGHT
Magnolia

We have therapy today—our last one before Christmas and the new year—and for the most part we've talked about Billie and BJ and I, except for these fifteen minutes where this lady keeps trying to pry again about what happened with Harley and I've said I don't care and she's been trying to prove to me that I do and to what end? What end? I don't know, honestly—don't make me say it—don't make me but I will.

Smells like a sadist, that's all I'll say.

"You're angry," Claire tells me, and I hope to god she didn't spend all those years in university only to arrive at that conclusion because fucking duh.

But I shan't admit that to her. I give her a polite smile that I hope enrages her a little.

"I'm not angry."

"You've internalised it," she tells me.

I give her a bit of a patronising look. "I've internalised nothing."

Actually, I've internalised plenty, I know that, but people like us aren't often afforded much time to decompress.

"Magnolia—" She gives me a stern look. "Your father told you he wished you'd died—"

BJ shifts next to me, picks up my hand with his and mindlessly holds it.

"Mhm." I give her a quick smile.

"And you feel nothing?" she asks.

I shrug my shoulders demurely. "I didn't say that."

"Well." She sits back in her chair. "What do you feel?"

I say nothing and so she presses more.

"Surely you must feel something, Magnolia," she tells me. "Something. Anything—!"

"Do you want me to be sad?" I snap. "Would it make you feel better if I was sad? Because, truly, I don't give a shit. He's never been a good father, so when he said that I wasn't losing something or discovering something, it wasn't this live-time rancid revelation of what kind of man he is, he's always been shit," I tell her very clearly and maybe a fraction louder than my finishing school teacher would have preferred.

I clear my throat and tuck some hair that isn't out of place behind my ears anyway.

"He's always been shit," I tell her again, calmly this time. "He just was shit in public this time."

She nods a few times, thinking, considering.

"That's sort of catastrophically shit—" she tells me. "Has he always been that shit?"

"Yes," BJ says too quickly. Without a thought.

I look over at him, give him a look.

"Don't—" I shake my head at him.

"Magnolia," he says—my name. He's saying my name. That's how I know he means business.

I keep shaking my head, because I know what he's about to say, what he's about to talk about, but I don't want him to say it and I don't want to talk about it. It's always there with him, thinly veiled, his finger on the trigger, waiting for the right moment to pull it.

There is no right moment to pull it, all it would do is get everyone in trouble, so what's the point?

I give BJ a dark look.

"Don't."

He sighs. "Parks—"

"BJ!" I scowl at him but really my eyes are begging. "Please don't—"

He breathes out his nose, barely raises his hands in a tacit surrender as Claire looks between us, curious and perhaps a little concerned.

Nothing to be concerned about though.

It's all in the past.

"You didn't answer my question . . ." Claire says gently after a moment.

It's entirely expected that over the course of our lives as humans with humans, those humans will—inevitably—disappoint us or betray or hurt us or be less than we hoped them to be. But how much, I suppose is the question.

When does a normal amount of to-be-expected human error cross over the line and become an unacceptable amount?

How many affairs? How many models in clubs? How many missed birthdays and ballet concerts and family dinners constitute as too much?

At which point does the understandability of why one is absent give way and shittiness enter the building?

I stare over at Claire and frown, thinking about what she's asking me.

Has he always been this shit?

I open my mouth to say something but nothing comes out so I shrug instead.

"Yes," BJ says quietly from next to me, nodding his head, face set. "He has."

We're walking home from Claire's office, BJ's holding both my hands with one of his, and he's quiet.

Upset I think because I didn't let him talk about the thing he wants to talk about, but it's not his to say.

I don't say anything even though I wonder if I should because I think it's quite draining, therapy—don't you think? Drives you to drink, almost.

And then my brain swan dives through about fifteen thoughts in a few seconds.

Have I drunk any water today—? Not really. Just a bit. My mouth feels dry—but that could be from my medicine—did I take my medicine? I think I did. I need to get one of those pill reminders. Or I could just set a reminder in my phone. Maybe I should do that for water—?—and get a water bottle. Givenchy have a really cute one I like, actually. I should order that when I get home—I wonder if Daniela ordered my crate of 1907? Why is the water in London so bad, do you think? It's so hard and bad for your skin and your hair. Which reminds me, I need to book in with George Northwood about bridal hairstyles. Oh, fuck—I really do need to pick my reception dress. I don't know which one between the Galia Lahav and Giambattista Valli.

"My dad cheated on my mum," BJ says to me completely out of the blue, and I stop in my tracks.

Blink a million times trying to absorb what he just said but it slides right off my brain. Absolutely in no fucking world. No.

I turn back and stare at him, shaking my head,

He says nothing, just nods a couple of times.

I reach for his hands.

"When?"

He sighs. "Years ago."

I tuck my chin a little. "Does your mum know?"

"Yeah." He nods again. "She was there when he told me."

"When did he tell you?"

He shrugs, shoving his hands into the pockets of his textured-finish cream shearling hooded bomber jacket (Saint Laurent) as he keeps walking. "The other day at lunch."

"I'm so sorry I wasn't there—" I tell him, my skin prickling with guilt. How completely and terribly self-absorbed must I be right now to not even notice this in him.

"No—" He shakes his head, looking down at me. He throws me a quick smile. "It's fine—I think it's fine."

My face falls a little, confused, and he gives me a look.

"I don't mean fine like that." He takes my hand mindlessly. "I mean like, they're fine—"

My eyes search over his face, looking for clues. "Are you?"

His brow bends, all weighed down in the middle, and I hate it when it does that, even though actually, honestly, I sort of love it because god—he's so beautiful, at all times, in all stages of life and emotion, even the ones that weigh heavy on him.

"I thought he was like—" Beej sighs, lifting his shoulders as though he feels stupid. "—Perfect."

I give him a little shrug and smile. "Like father, like son."

His mouth pulls almost apologetically. "Runs in the family . . ."

"Yes," I tell him, quite sure. "It does."

He flashes me this small half smile and does one single nod, but there's something to his face? Like he's sad or resigned, or something.

"I meant perfection." I stop walking to clarify, not letting go of his hand. "Not cheating. Perfection runs in your family."

BJ flicks his eyes, jaw going a little tight. "He's not perfect."

I raise my eyebrows up. "Because he made a mistake?"

He grimaces a little, all uneasy, and seeing him like that makes everything in the universe of me feel entirely off-kilter.

"It wasn't just once, Parks," he tells me and I won't lie. That specific morsel of truth hurts me and feels like it squashes me on the inside a little bit. My mouth tugs.

Poor Lily, wonderful Lily. Good and kind and deserves the world, Lily. No wonder she was so upset when she found out why Beej and I really broke up.

BJ swallows.

"I don't know why she stayed with him," he tells the ground with a frown.

"Oh, I do," I tell him, very quite sure, and something about my tone lightens his face up a bit. He licks away a smile.

"Yeah?" He sniffs. "Spit it out, then."

"Well, perfection isn't exempt from humanness," I tell him, straightening up. "You've done so many stupid things, and made so many completely insane mistakes and you've—"

He squints at me. "Is there a point in here, or—?"

I give him a look and roll my eyes a little at his impatience.

"You're still perfect." I shrug matter-of-factly. "To me."

His eyes pinch.

"Not because you didn't do those things, but because you do other things that maybe, in the scheme of it all—all being life—" I clarify for him and he rolls his eyes.

"I'm tracking, thanks."

"The way you love me and the other things that you've spent our whole lives doing weigh more in the equilibrium of my heart than any mistake ever could. You might have torn us in two once upon a time, but we're not stuck back together with sparkly washi tape and all the shiny things about us that everyone can see. We're held together by clear fishing wire and white thread that no one but us can really see."

He takes a step towards me, smiling a bit now. "Like what?"

"Like when you ordered my engagement ring the week I told you I was staying in London. And that night last year when you came home with me because I was sad and drunk and I needed you, even though you had a fake girlfriend—"

He gives a little shrug and presses his lips together.

"She was a real girlfriend."

I roll my eyes. "If you say so—"

He breathes out a laugh, shaking his head.

"Like every time you've shielded me from my parents, and defended me, and fought for me. Like how you let me take your pulse even though you think it's weird—"

"—It is weird," he cuts in.

"How we're walkers now," I go on, ignoring him. "How you bring me cups of tea in bed every day with the right amount of sugars according to the day. How you look at me when you think I'm not looking. How you were on the worst day—"

And at that, he gives me a tender smile.

"And on the other worst day," I add, giving him a little nod. I swallow. "If that doesn't make you perfect then"—I shrug—"perfect doesn't exist. And if it does, and it's not that, then it's stupid anyway, and I don't want it. Whatever you are classifiable as—" I nod my head at him. "It's the only thing I'm interested in committing to."

His mouth twists playfully as he moves in towards me. He slips both hands on my waist.

"I should like to think—" I start to say and then leave it for a beat because I might be a little power drunk from being so listened to and so watched by those golden (but technically not golden) eyes. "Or at least, I would hope very much, in some sort of bright, shimmery, glittery way, that Lily is still with your dad because he loves her how you love me."

BJ's eyes go soft. "Not possible."

I hold his face with both my hands and smile at him gently before I say what I'm about to.

"They nearly had a child die once, remember," I say, and he falters, struck by the thought.

"Perhaps," I say to him, and my hands don't move from his face. "They're somewhat versed in trauma bonds as well."

FIFTY-NINE

BJ

Christmas Day came and went, and it was a weird one for a couple of reasons.

Firstly, we didn't see the Parkses at all, we stuck to my side. Usually a Ballentine Christmas has a lot of fanfare. Something with everyone we're vaguely related to up at my grandparents' in Much Hadham, but not this year.

Henry, Mum and I decided it was probably too much for Parks. Between Bridge and the wedding and her parents—even in our family where they've known her for decades, there's an air of fascination we were all keen to keep her from, so it was a tiny Christmas at Mum's. And Dad's.

That was the other weird part. I still haven't really felt like speaking to him, neither's Henry, who knows because I told him—but the girls don't know, and Mum doesn't want them to, so we can't even really not talk to Dad, so it was just weird.

Mum cried. She said it was nothing, that she was just tired and cooking a ham is hard, but nothing's hard for her, she's a fucking wizard. I know it's because we're all out of sorts.

Me and Dad aside, it was all our first Christmas without Bridge and it was fucked, that's all there was to say about it. Felt her absence in all of it. At the dinner table, opening the presents, watching Christmas movies—

Parks barely said a word the entire day, just followed me around room to room like my little shadow. Even followed me to the bathroom once.

"I just need a wee—" I told her, pointing to the toilet.

"Oh." She frowned a bit, like my basic bodily functions were inconveniencing her ability to stay by my side.

I sniffed a laugh and pulled her into the bathroom.

Pressed my mouth against hers, and then gave her an apologetic look because I had a quick slash.

Can't be alone today, not even for a second.

Washed my hands, dried them, picked her up and sat her on the counter—a hand either side of her.

"How's the weather, Parksy?"

She put her hand on my face and smiled a bit sadly, didn't say anything. I kissed the inside of her hand and then we stayed in there until Madeline banged on the door and started yelling about us getting a room.

For New Year's we went to the Madeira Islands with Henry, Rom and Bushka, which was—I'm being completely serious—the best New Year's Eve of my fucking life.

Easy time, no drama, just laughs and champagne and my girl(s) and my brother.

Mum was dropping hints like mad leading up to it for an invite, and I've never not invited my mum to something I could tell she wanted to come to before, but I couldn't stomach Dad at the time, so I had to sidestep it. Felt like shit for that.

It was around then that the amount of calls and texts I received from her daily went from a (somewhat) healthy one or two up to about fourteen.

That's a lot of calls. Well too many. I don't want to talk to anyone fourteen times a day. Fuck, I think if Magnolia called me fourteen times in a day, I'd block her number, but I can't block my mum because she's my mum.

Henry called a few days ago and said I had to go and see Dad, not even for Dad's sake, but because Mum was calling Henry now too and he's had it and please, for fuck's sake, fix it or he's going to change his mobile number and then all her maternal worry will be funnelled at me and me alone and I think I'd rather die than risk Mum calling me thirty times a day, so now I'm on my way to meet my dad for lunch.

Sat down across from him at Colbert on Sloane Square, don't say much to him before I order a glass of the 2017 Château de Pibarnon. He orders the same, which is how I know he's trying to make amends. Not a fan of that sort of leathery, earthy, mineral-y type of wine. Got it anyway.

He watches me for a couple of seconds, face still, a bit stoic.

"Are you okay?" he asks eventually.

"Yeah," I shrug. "Why?"

"About me—" He blinks. "What you learnt the other day."

I purse my mouth. "Yeah—" Shrug again. "I—I don't know? I guess." Scratch the back of my neck. "I didn't love it."

It's weird, I won't lie. Thinking your dad's one thing all your life, only to find out he's just another fuck-up same as you—

He sniffs a laugh. "No, that's fair."

He flags down the waitress, gestures for me to order. I get the chicken because the French do it fucking well and he orders a croque monsieur because he's never gone past one on offer a day in his life.

He sits back in his chair.

"Do you have any questions?"

Yep, actually. Like a fucking million of them.

I nod over at him.

"How long did it last?"

"About four months," he says, completely calm.

I pull back. "Oh, shit."

Dad nods, weird face—wouldn't say he's completely unfazed, he's not uncomfortable though.

"How was Mum when you told her?"

"Shattered," he tells me, and my heart fucking plummets. "Worst day of my life. Other than—" He gestures to me and I wonder if maybe Parks was right.

"I hated seeing her like that." He's not looking at me now, eyes on the memory, frowning at it for a few seconds and then he looks over at me. "Broke myself doing that to her."

I scratch my neck. "Why'd you do it?"

He blows the air out of his mouth, thinking. Shakes his head a bit.

"I . . . honestly don't know." He stares over at me, squints like he's trying to understand it himself. "I think back on it now and there's not any kind of banner excuse that makes what I did okay. I just did it—" He shrugs with his mouth, not his shoulders. "She was attractive, she was good to me, made herself available to me—and it wasn't that Mum wasn't any of those things." He pauses, looks away again. "I loved your mum actively as I was doing it, I don't think back on that phase of my life and feel like I wasn't in love with her at the time, I was. I think I just got complacent in it."

He takes a breath, breathes it out. "And then along came this exciting sort of firework in the banality of my day-to-day life, and I acted on an impulse." He takes a sip of water and for the first time in the conversation, I think I see the sort of shame you'd expect to see on him.

"And then I kept acting on an impulse for a while."

Throw back some wine. "Why?"

He stifles a smile as he nods his chin at me.

"Would you believe me if I said being the CEO of a supermarket chain isn't as thrilling as it sounds—?"

Makes me laugh, only give him a chuckle though before I lick it away and then he shakes his head at me.

"I don't know—what you said the other day, Beej—it actually gave me a lot of pause." Purses his mouth. "Made me think."

I sort of lift an eyebrow, waiting.

"I'm an arsehole" is what he says next.

I say nothing because it catches me off guard, so he keeps going.

"I'm honestly quite floored by you, BJ. I've spent so much time worrying about you, worrying that you'd make mistakes, go too far again, lose Magnolia—lose your life—" He pauses as this flash of pain cracks over his face and I feel guilty and shit and like I'm a bad son.

Dad keeps going.

"I hadn't realised, I guess—I was too distracted by the

worrying and the projecting of what I thought your life should look like if it were healthy and if you were okay, so much so that I just . . . fucked it." He gives me a helpless shrug. "And missed that you are, actually, okay."

I stare over at him, not really sure what to say. My parents are encouraging, always believed in us, always told us as much as well, but somewhere around my early twenties my plan for my life and my dad's plan for my life diverged and it's obviously been an area of contention for us since.

"I think it's actually incredibly admirable, your philosophy." He nods, approvingly. "You're more right than I am. And I can't say I won't worry. I hate crypto. What the fuck is an NFT—"

"Dad—" I roll my eyes because I've explained it so many times.

"It's stupid, Beej."

I shrug. "Parks sold the NFT of our first kiss to a Chinese businessman for like, £500,000—"

His face scrunches up in pure confusion. "I don't—what?"

I groan a little. "Jonah took a video of it at the time. And she wanted to prove to Henry that NFTs are stupid so—anyway, it's a long story with very little point other than I guess Parks proved herself wrong and she has a weird, big fan in Beijing."

Dad doesn't love that, pulls another face, but this time I think it's out of concern for her.

Licks his lip and then sighs.

"I'm your dad, Beej—"

My phone starts ringing, but I silence it because this feels important.

"I'm always going to worry about you—" he tells me as I get a text message. "That you're going to be okay, that you've got enough, that you're going to be covered when I'm gone, but—"

And then I get another text message. And another. And another.

So I pick up my phone to check quickly that everything's okay and that's when my face falters.

"Oh, fuck," I whisper under my breath. "I've got to go."

Punch in a text, flick it back to Tausie.

Dad frowns.

"Is everything okay?"

"Um—" I keep staring at my phone. Shake my head. "I need to get back to Parks—"

My phone rings again. It's Taura.

"Yep," I say, standing to my feet. "I'm already on my way—no, you go too—I'll meet you there—"

I hang up, look at my dad.

His face pulls, suspicious.

"Was that a fake call so you have an excuse to leave?"

"What—?" I pull back. "No, Dad—Fuck. Do you really think I'm so—"

"No—" He shakes his head quickly. "I just—"

I roll my eyes. "Unbelievable."

He sits back a little, face serious now.

"Then what's going on, BJ?"

I press my tongue into my bottom lip, and breathe out, annoyed. "Someone leaked it." Push my hands through my hair and watch my dad's face try to work out what exactly's been leaked. "Magnolia's eating—it's everywhere."

His eyebrow bends in the middle—looks crushed for her, actually. He properly loves her. Always has.

He nods his head towards the exit. Tells me to go without actually saying anything and then I run to the tube.

Quicker than an Uber at this time of day and I'm home in less than thirty.

Fight my way through a sea of photographers that are outside our complex—catch eyes with the doorman, who looks sorry for me and tired for me and probably fucking pissed off for himself too. Put my glasses on so they can't see my face, because it's what they want. A certain photo at a particular angle so they can twist the story to say whatever they need to say for it to sell.

Get out to our place and I can see they're in our room—Tausie's burning a hole in the floor with her pacing and Parks is sitting on the edge of the bed, eyes wide and nervous.

"Oi—" I say as soon as I walk in.

She springs to her feet as soon as she sees me and bolts into my arms.

"You okay?" I ask the top of her head.

She pulls back and looks up at me.

"How did they know?"

"I don't know—" I shake my head. "We'll figure it out."

"It's too late," she says, eyes teary. "It's already out there—"

"Where, exactly?" I look from her to Taura. "Who ran it?"

Taura gives me an exasperated look. "Everyone's running it."

Magnolia covers her hands with her face, a bit devastated, and then sits back down on the bed.

"Parksy—" I kneel down in front of her. "Listen, it's not fair—that they do this to you—it's complete shit, but you have nothing to be ashamed about—"

"Yes, I do—!" She scowls. "Of course I do. I'm twenty-five. I have an eating disorder I've had since I was fifteen. The articles say it, plain as day—" She flashes me her phone to show me.

One of the usual shit-slinging rags has consulted an alleged expert, insinuating how truly curious it is that she's still struggling with bulimia after all these years.

"That begs the question—why does she still have it?" they're quoted as saying.

Doesn't have bulimia, by the way. Hates throwing up more than anything, almost. Avoids it at all costs, if she can. Would never do it voluntarily. Disordered eating, not eating at all—now that, she's a pro at . . .

Just goes to show you how shit these people are. Don't care what they're saying, doesn't even have to be factual, just has to be salacious.

I shake my head—and this, it fucks me off because whatever she has, they gave it to her. At least in part.

She didn't have an eating disorder before they put her up on their pedestal, on their covers, calling her the "Best Body Since Elle"—before that, there wasn't an overt interest in her beauty, she knew she was attractive, I guess. Boys at school always made a bit of a deal about her, but I don't think she was paying that much attention. She hadn't really worked out its function, how to use it as a commodity. Didn't realise it was one.

And then she got her deal with Ford, and then Storm, and it was a combination of the fact that Arrie was in a real comeback in her career at the time, and Harley was fucking killing it, and then sort of randomly one night, she and I were out with the Box Set—she was fifteen, I was sixteen and someone, some photographer, took these really fucking cute photos of us. Really basic shit—me on the street, her on the sidewalk, her arms hooked around my neck, my hands on her waist, and we were laughing and kissing and talking, and it was completely regular. It was like normal kid shit, except we look how we look and were wearing cool shit. Someone printed the photos, then everyone printed the photos and then the fascination was born.

She didn't lie down willingly under their microscope, they clubbed her over the head and dragged her there.

They did this to her. Built her up and then would tear her down, splash photos everywhere of her drunk and eating fries so she wouldn't eat for a week; taking purposely shit photos of her—do you know how fucking hard it is to take a shit photo of her? You've got to try. It doesn't come easy—they'd photograph her eating at restaurants—mid-bite, because they're fucking monsters—say shit like, "See, she's just like us!"

And she isn't. She's better. She's better and they all fucking know it, it's why they're like—obsessed with her or whatever they are—and I know it sounds like I'm biased, but I'm not. I hate it, I don't want it for her, I see how it makes her go. I wish so badly it would stop.

They—whoever they are. The media, the public. Call them whatever the fuck you want—they adore her and they tear her limb from limb in the same breath, and when your base-level, born experience of love ranges somewhere between for-show and indifference, what do you do with that? How do you fucking process that?

"Parksy—" I hold her face in my hands. "Oi, it is on you

to get better, that much is true—but you've got nothing to be embarrassed of. I'm not embarrassed—"

"That doesn't count." She rolls her eyes. "You're never embarrassed of me—"

I pull a face at her. "I'm always embarrassed of you. The other week with Tiller—?" I shake my head. "Fuck me, that was stressful—"

"What was?" Tausie asks with a frown.

"Nothing!" Parks says quickly at the same time I tell her, "She made him give her his phone passcode—"

Taura groans. "Magnolia—"

Magnolia glances from her to me with the absolute utter indifference you'd expect from her when she's getting in trouble. Blinks twice. Shrugs.

There's a pause, Taura's eyes pinch.

"What was it though? Can you write it down?" Taura asks, and I point at her as a warning because these fucking girls, man.

I shake my head, try not to look amused but I am. Refocus on the little puddle in front of me.

"Parks, you do embarrassing shit all the time and I love you anyway, but this—" I gesture to the invisible darkness that's nipped at her heels for the worst part of a decade. "This isn't it. And they're fucked in the head for running it. Proves they don't know how bad this can be, how much this can frame a life—"

Change a life; fuck a life; take a life.

"Whoever did this—" I nod at the article on her phone. "They're not even a real person."

She breathes out, shakes her head. "It doesn't matter, Beej, because now everyone already knows and they're going to talk about it for months, and they're going to take photos of me eating, and then they'll analyse what I'm eating, and they'll watch my body to see if it changes and—"

"Yep." I nod. "That's true."

No point in lying about it. They will.

Take her hand, squeeze it. "They are going to do that because they're fucking sons of bitches and it says everything about them and nothing about you, Parks—"

I watch her for a sec, this girl I love more than anything being fucking trashed again by the same fucking fuckwits who talk about her and us out of habit and without cause, reason or merit—she takes this big breath, sad, lip trembling, gives me a smile, trying to be brave. Taura reaches over, takes her phone from her, logs her out of all social media accounts and deletes the Safari app before she hands it back to her.

Parks says nothing but gives her friend a grateful look, and I wish Tausie didn't know to do that but she's had to before and she'll fucking have to again and that gets me. Feels like a fire lights under me, actually. Rage-fuelled, fucking over-their-shit, out-for-blood kind of fire.

I pull out my phone.

"Oi," Jo says on the second ring. "Fuck—I just saw it, man. I was about to call you—is she okay?"

I take a step away from her, look over my shoulder at her, feel crushed as I watch her fidget nervously—lower my voice.

"Not really," I tell him and walk into our en suite.

"Was it him?" I ask Jo as I look around the room.

Still a work in progress in here, but less obviously. The tarp's gone off the bath now. Our cleaner said she couldn't stand to see it anymore and the contractor was taking too long. Cleaned it all up like it's usable, even though it isn't. Like either of us ever have a bath anyway.

"I don't know. I'll figure it out though—" Jo talks quieter. "Want me to pay him a visit?"

"Yeah," I say on a reflex, then I pause. Never paused to think when it comes to Jo before but I do now. "Don't do anything like, too stupid—"

"But a bit stupid?" He clarifies.

"Yeah," I nod. "A bit stupid. Warrants a bit of stupid."

"Yep," he says before he hangs up. "On it."

17:28

Mars ♡

I'm so sorry, Magnolia.

I can't believe it.

Are you ok?

I don't know.

Not really.

Is it quite as everywhere as it seems?

Yes

Is BJ with you?

Yes.

Good.

I'm sick over it, truly.

Who would release that?

I'm so sorry.

xx

SIXTY

Magnolia

"Why do you always wear the same outfit?" I ask my sister's reflection in the mirror.

"Um," she'd breathe out a bored breath. "Because you're fixated on me in my final moments and this is what I was wearing—"

"Fixated." I sidestep the part about final moments. "My, my, we're fond of ourselves today, aren't we?"

She'd roll her eyes. "I don't daily summon an apparition of you to bathrooms, do I?"

I frown. "Would you like more to be in other clothes, then?"

"I'm dead, Magnolia," she'd tell me. "I don't care what I wear."

I stomp my foot, then wash my hands for no reason.

"Why does everyone keep saying that?"

"Saying what?" Bridge would ask. "That I'm dead?"

I pout at the mirror and she'd shrug indifferently.

"Because I am . . ."

I lick my lips and stare at my incredibly fine French manicure before I shake my head and look back at the ghost of my sister.

"What's it like?" I ask her.

"What's what like?" she'd ask.

I'd give her an impatient look for not tracking me because she should, because isn't she like, magically divine or something now? "Heaven."

She'd shrug. "Don't know."

"How don't you know!"

She'd give me a look. "Because you don't know—"

I ignore her. "Is it very white and bright, then?"

She'd sigh. "Do you want it to be bright and white?"

"No—" I flip my hair over my shoulders. "Not necessarily."

"How do you want it to be, then?" she'd ask all begrudgingly, and I do everything in my power to not cry—I don't. I don't cry. I don't even well up.

I straighten myself up in the mirror.

"Real." That's what I want it to be.

Her eyebrows would bend in the middle at that, sad for me a bit, and worried.

But everyone is a bit sad and worried for me these days.

"Anyway," I shake my head. And clear my throat. "We haven't really talked about it—Harley, I mean. Can you believe that he said that?"

"Well," she'd shrug. "Sort of."

"Bridget!" I scowl.

"You did never call him Dad," she might tell me.

I'd glare at her. "I can't believe you're saying that—"

"I'm not saying that, Magnolia." She'd give me an exasperated look. "I'm not real. I'm you—" Another pointed look. "So you obviously think that this is probably your fault—"

I swallow. "Is it?"

She'd shrug. "Is it?"

I open my mouth to say something back to her—when BJ calls for me.

"Parks!" He yells from our room and then the bathroom door opens. "Your mum's here."

I sniff a laugh. "Good one."

"No—" He rolls his eyes. "She's actually here."

"Oh." I scrunch my face up.

How curious?

BJ stares at me, head tilted in a way that makes his jawline just . . . immaculate. His brows are a little heavy with concern for me—he forces a smile, and I know he knows I was talking to my sister.

"What's she here for?" I ask.

He pulls a puzzled face and shrugs, giving me a tight smile, then offers me his hand—do you know about his hands? Have you seen them? Besides all the tattoos about me and us that are perfect that you know about—and those two dead bees on the back of his right hand he's getting lasered off because sometimes I just start crying if I stare at them for too long. He's had "MKJP" tattooed on his left ring finger, which I opposed at the time because I said we weren't married yet and he said I wear a ring, so he should too, so I said well then just wear my family crest ring and he said it needed to be more permanent and that he hasn't taken me off for twenty years, so he won't start now. He got my sister's name tattooed on the back of his left hand as well, bottom, near his thumb. I've always loved that his hands are covered in me—that all of him is, I suppose—but the hands especially, because for all those years where he was touching other people, he was doing it with hands that were riddled with me, and I hope that it made whoever he touched that wasn't me feel like they were doing with him the sexual equivalent of the anti-legitimists plundering Notre Dame in 1831. A complete desecration of something that they had no business being near in the first place.

Besides all the obvious and obnoxious reasons I might love his hands (of which there are currently thirteen and counting) I've always loved them just for their shape. There's something incredibly sexy about good hands, don't you think? I'm not sure why. BJ's are big but not cartoonish. Strong fingers but not stumpy or too thick. His nails are short, he bites them—not nervously—he says that teeth are our god-given nail clippers. Bridget once said, "What about your toes, then?" and he told her she was "fucking sick."

I couldn't tell you if I love them as much as I do because of how they feel when he puts them on my face or if it's because of how they feel when he holds my waist, how it feels like I've slipped back through time and forward into more time and I could be fifteen or I could be eighty-five and his hands will still feel the same on my waist because there's just something about them, even though they're just hands. Arguably, a fairly mundane part of one's body, but the argument falls flat on its face once you've been touched by Baxter James Ballentine's.

I take that hand of his that I love and follow him out to my mother.

She gives me this overly bright, almost anxious smile as I stand in front of BJ.

"Hello, darling." She smiles as she moves in to kiss my cheek. I don't recoil, I don't respond at all.

"I've been meaning to come by since everything happened—"

"Have you?" I ask, backing myself into Beej to make myself feel braver. He slips an arm around my waist.

"Been a few weeks, Arrie," Beej tells her over my head, and his tone—it's bizarrely neutral. He's barely ever given my mum shit, he has a little soft spot for her which I used to be jealous of, but Taura says it's because our eyes are the same and so he can't help it.

"Christmas has come and gone." He nods at her, unimpressed. "We didn't hear a thing."

"Well." She tilts her head as she glances between the both of us. "In our defence, neither did we—"

I say nothing and BJ nods coolly. "What would you have had her say?"

My mother breathes out and somehow the very air of her sounds diplomatic. She gives him an apologetic look before she casts the dregs of it over to me. "It's been a big few weeks . . ."

"Are you alright, darling?" she asks me, eyebrows up.

I lick my lips. "About what, Mum?"

She gives me a demure shrug. "Your father, darling."

BJ's grip around me tightens some—I don't know whether it's conscious or not—and I lift my eyebrows, pursing my lips. Don't count backwards to work out how long it took her to think to have this talk.

"Last week it was publicly announced that I've struggled with an eating disorder for the last decade and I didn't hear a thing from you—"

"Well." She gives me a look. "That wasn't really news to me, sweetheart—"

I nod as though I understand.

"I've lost my sister, I've lost a baby, my grandmother's moved back to Russia, my lifelong carer has moved to Scotland because—" I gesture to her. "Well, you know. Multiple affairs. I've watched you and Harley each have multiple affairs, break up and get back together. I've been publicly cheated on, I've had my heart torn entirely from its chest and hung up in the streets for people to point at. I've lost my best friends, I've fled the country, I've had the media pull me apart completely and yet you have never once before asked me whether I'm okay."

She clears her throat quietly, almost nervously, then she swallows.

"Are you?"

I stare over at her and blink a few times before I shake my head quickly.

"I am so sorry for the vulgarity—this isn't something I would usually say but I've just no idea how I might otherwise put it—"

She frowns a little, waiting. "Okay?"

"Um—" My eyes pinch as I think it through. "Please, I am begging you, please—piss off."

She breathes out and looks past me to BJ.

"BJ, darling, can we have a minute?"

I shake my head. "No."

She rolls her eyes a little, but it's an odd roll. She's not annoyed but more, insecure?

"Magnolia, I—"

"Whatever you tell me, I'll tell him anyway. Whatever it is—" All I can offer her is a shrug. "So save me the back and forth."

Her eyes tighten, annoyed she's not getting her way but I lift my eyebrows up in defiance and wait.

"Fine—" She flicks her eyes before moving backwards and sitting down in the armchair behind her.

I don't sit, there's no part of me that feels overly moved to make whatever's about to come from her mouth more comfortable for her to say.

She breathes out a sigh and places her hands, folded—just how we were taught at finishing school—in her lap. She gives me a delicate look.

"I was very young when I had you," she tells me. "I'd only been in London a few years but my career had taken off—"

I give her one bored nod. "I know."

"And I met your father, and I just thought he was the most exquisite man—"

I cut her off with a scowl. "Why?"

BJ subtly pokes me in the back at the same time my mother gives me a look—almost defensive. How I might look at someone if they spoke badly about BJ.

"He was so handsome and talented and rich and—"

I glance at her dubiously. "Mother, your family was worth nearly a billion pounds."

She shrugs. "I didn't have access to my accounts until I was twenty-one—"

"And you were . . . ?" BJ prompts.

"Nineteen," she tells him with a nod. "When I met Harley." Then she looks at me, eyes earnest. "Darling, you have to understand that I've loved your father very much—since the moment I met him—"

I scrunch my face up.

"Didn't you have a years-long affair with Hugh Grant after I was born?"

"Yes, but—"

"And why do people sometimes suggest Taye Diggs is my paternal father?"

She shakes her head, frowning. "Because we were in a shoot once together, and he's beautiful and you're beauti—"

"And wasn't there another rumour going around in the nineties that my real father was Tupac?"

"Yes." She rolls her eyes. "There was, but he had died by the time you were born—it was one of those silly ones that didn't even make sense to run, but they ran it anyway—"

"Sure, yes, but—" I nod. "I mean—it doesn't speak exquisitely to the argument that you've loved Harley since you met him, but go on—"

She clears her throat again.

"See, the thing is, darling, I wouldn't say in the strictest sense of the term that you were a 'planned pregnancy' . . . "

"Oh." I flick my eyes, unimpressed and unsurprised. "You don't say."

She swallows and then licks her lips before glancing over at me with big eyes.

"At least not by your father."

Do you know, for the longest time in my relationship with Harley, there has been this puzzle I've been trying to solve. Just, trying to figure out why we are the way we are, why he is the way he is—the best way I could describe it is my brain's felt like the three reels in a Vegas slot machine that won't land or can't land and they've just been spinning around forever and ever, diamonds and crowns and sevens whizzing by at the speed of light—

My eyes widen and I feel BJ's grip round my waist very briefly go slack before it tightens again, extra.

My mouth falls open.

"Mum!"

Beej shakes his head at her. "What the fuck, Arrie?"

"I know—" She shakes her head, sorry. "I said I was young! And I loved him, and I wanted to be with him!" she says like it's an excuse. "Just him—!" she says, eyes wide. "And he was seeing so many other people at the time, and I wanted him to stop—"

"So you forced him?" I stare over at her.

She shakes her head quickly.

"I didn't see it like that at the time but—" She trails and presses her lips together.

I press the tip of my tongue into my top lip, thinking.

I stare over at her. "Did you make him stay with you?"

"He offered," she tells me. "He was being honourable—"

"So you forced his hand into becoming a father—" I nod slowly and then—ching, ching, ching—three cherries in a row.

"'Forced' is a bad word," she says, somewhat like a politician, before she squares up, an almost-proud look on her face. "I feel he rose to the occasion."

"I mean—" I glance back at BJ briefly, blink at him in genuine surprise. "Do you really?"

My mother breathes out her nose.

"Magnolia, darling—" She gives me a look. "I understand that we have disappointed you many times throughout your life but really, you live a very nice existence—"

"Right, okay. Yeah, absolutely—there are aspects of my life that are incredibly charmed," I concede. "But do you really look back over our lives, him as a husband to you and a father to Bridget and I, and think, 'Wow, a job well done'?"

Her mouth tugs in a way that might have made me feel sad if I wasn't too busy feeling all betrayed by her right now. Which is weird. I didn't know I held her in high enough regard to allow her to betray me.

"No." She swallows as she holds her own hand in her lap. "I suppose not."

And then it goes quiet.

The slots have landed, sure—but now it's spilling out a lifetime of coins everywhere, out the mouth, slipping through my fingers, all over the floor—

"Does he know?" BJ asks her over my head and it snaps me out of it.

My mother nods and BJ blows some air out of his mouth.

He kisses the top of my head absentmindedly. Or maybe it's intentionally—I don't know, I'm not looking at him. I could tell if I were looking at him.

"That's why you let him have all the affairs," BJ says, staring over at her.

My mother squares her shoulders a little, lifts her chin.

"I had some too."

I can't tell if she's saying that defensively or out of some strange sort of pride and I watch her, quietly, processing the implications of what she's saying.

An 'oopsie baby,' that's what I'd assumed I was until now.

Just the product of them being reckless and young and famous and having too much sex with too much alcohol, and one night they got drunk and forgot a condom and voilà—me.

That was the story I invented around my birth, which—truthfully, looking at it with subjective eyes, it's not actually a fantastic story—but I suppose there's some appeal to it . . . Sure, it lacks the conscientiousness of two people who are already committed to one another and who've decided they're going to make a baby together and raise it together and love it together; which is how BJ was conceived, by the way. Obviously. With great intentions and high hopes. Sure, maybe mine lacked those things, but in the very least there's something a tiny bit rock and roll about being a love child or an act of passion.

Alas, it turns out my story of how I came to be is neither.

"So, he's never wanted me—" I sort of ask, sort of state. And then I find myself nodding as I quickly add, "I presumed as much—"

I flash her a quick smile and I hear BJ breathe out in this heavy, sorry way. I added the "I presumed as much" to dull the patheticness of the situation, but obviously it wasn't enough because I can feel it radiating off my well-loved, well-adjusted fiancé, this anxious pity. It feels how I used to feel for him when I'd watch them pop his shoulder back in during a rugby game without medicine so he could keep playing.

I don't know how we can pop this shoulder back in though.

My mother thinks for a moment, choosing how she responds to that carefully. I don't ask why. We all know the answer at this point in the conversation. Though it does strike me as a tiny bit odd that it doesn't seem to cross her mind to just lie to me, spare my feelings. I think the fact that it's not even a consideration implies where we, as a family, are at. The cat's out of the bag. No going back. Why lie?

"Sometimes," she says delicately. "I think you perhaps felt difficult for him because—through no fault of yours, darling"—I'm flashed a quick, apologetic smile from her—"you sort of were the physical embodiment of my entrapment."

I've wondered before how it might feel to be shot.

Not somewhere stupid like your arm or your leg, that would just hurt—obviously—but a kill shot—well, that sounds interesting.

A head, you're dead, obviously. Quick, painless—unless they miss. You hear about that, don't you? People surviving a bullet to the head—they can survive for a lifetime as long as it doesn't move.

A shot through the centre of you—that's got to be something else, doesn't it?

How do you think it feels?

Like nothing, maybe? Because it's too much, too bad, too final and so your brain knows not to let you feel it.

I don't feel anything at that. Isn't that funny? At least at first.

ADHD is crazy, actually. My brain, how fast it moves at any given moment—that the hyperactivity, it's not me bouncing off walls, it's a thousand thoughts each minute bouncing off the walls in my head.

And there are parts of it that are wonderful, I notice things other people don't, I'm detail-oriented, I pick up patterns well, I think I'm quite clever, truthfully. I like how I think. I wasn't sad when they diagnosed me with it, it made a lot of things about me make sense, and about us and how I am and how I can be and why—it answered a lot.

It can be bad though. It can be a waterboarding of thoughts. Just—cloth over my brain's face, and all the thoughts in the world being poured over my mouth and nose and you can't breathe because if you do you'll choke on them—

I have a lot of thoughts about this. I'm the biggest Powerball jackpot in the world and the thoughts are the balls blowing around inside that glass thing and then the mechanical arm rises up with a random ball and drops it down the slide into the forefront of my mind.

I suppose, all things considered, it's somewhat understandable my father is how he is with me, but if my mother became purposely pregnant, and she decided that she would have me to keep him, where was she? If she wanted me, where was she? Reason would then conclude that she didn't actually, and my existence is nothing more than the signature on a binding contract she made him sign.

There's something about not being wanted by parents that stings in a way that's rather difficult to wrap words around and to convey to anyone else if they've not experienced it.

An entry-level bleakness to the whole world, I think. Because it's—anti-Darwinian. People are programmed to love their young. It ensures the continuity of our species. And if the people who are hardwired to love you can't or don't or refuse to—what does that say about me?

And now I feel it. From my trachea to my tertiary bronchi right down to my bronchioles—all the air that's in me evaporates on the spot. As though someone put cling film over my face and I'm gasping for air but there is none—all the air in all the world is gone. Evaporated.

BJ feels it—somehow, I don't know how—he turns me around to face him, ducks down so we're eye level.

He touches my face, holds it in his hands and gives me the most serious look he's ever given me in our lifetime.

'I love you,' he blinks in our language.

I hold his hand to my face with my own and press into myself the only love I've never really questioned and feel my lungs expand again with the air they've found.

It all makes sense now really, doesn't it? Why Bridget was his favourite, why they got along so much easier? She was planned. Wanted. Not a bear trap on the ankle of his life.

Arrie sighs.

"This is all my fault," she says as she moves towards me but BJ raises his hand to stop her and she does, in her tracks.

She lets out this sharp, little breath.

"BJ—"

"No, Arrie." He shakes his head at her before he looks at me again, holding my eyes up with his.

She edges closer to me still, taking her chances.

"What happened at Dartmouth, sweetheart—" she starts, and I turn to look at her, eyes all heavy with rocks in their pockets. "He was speaking from years of pent-up frustrations—most of which should have been directed at me but—"

"Weren't," BJ says, eyeing her darkly.

She nods once.

"Weren't," she concedes. "He's always spoken too quickly. He loves to win an argument, darling, you know that—" She licks her lips, shaking her head. "I know he would be terribly sorry for how this all has hurt you—"

"Yeah?" BJ tilts his head at her. "That why he's here and not you?"

My mother gives him a look.

"He's not good at apologising."

BJ shrugs. "Then there's not much merit to her forgiving him—"

"I'm fine," I tell BJ quite suddenly, and my voice does—I personally think—sound rather convincingly fine. I can breathe again, there's air back in my lungs, my thoughts are flying around at the speed of light—but what else is new? When you have parents like mine, rejections happen and you hold them in your hand for a minute and that minute is horrible and terrible and painful and then you fold it up, file it away into a cabinet that's the size of the O2 and maybe it might be the thing that sinks you one day but today is not that day.

BJ tilts his head. "Parks—"

"I'm fine, BJ." I give him a shrug, imagining all the ways I was feeling a moment ago falling off my shoulders as I do. "He said nothing we didn't already suspect he felt—"

"Alright." He nods at me, jaw set. "Then I'm not fine. It's bullshit how he spoke to you—I won't let him talk to you like that." He glares over at Arrie. "Neither should you—"

I touch his arm gently. "I do think your reaction at the time may have already expressed to him that, in your eyes, he had crossed a line . . ."

I offer him a small smile, and his face softens for a fraction of a second before it goes dark again as he looks at my mum.

"And in your eyes?"

"BJ, darling," she sighs. "Please be patient with him—he just lost his daughter—"

"The one he wanted," I clarify for BJ with a smile that's made up of bravado and trauma.

My mother's face pulls. "Sweetheart—"

"It's fine, I said." Shaking my head, giving her a dismissive smile. "All of it. It's fine." A little shrug. "Revelatory if anything."

She frowns a little, unsure.

"Are you sure?"

I nod. "Mm-hm."

She lifts an eyebrow in cautious hope. "Really?"

I shrug, not sure what else I can offer her.

She presses her lips together for a second, thinking.

"You see, I just don't want it to—you know—" She gives me an apologetic smile. "—during the wedding, to look uncomfortable or feel uncomfortable for either you or him—"

BJ's eyes go to slits but my mother keeps going.

"Or for anyone to have anything to talk about that might—"

"Oh—" I cut her off with a nod. "You're here for appearances."

"No!" She shakes her head quickly. "No, darling. No, no. I'm here to help you understand him—"

"Do you understand him well, then?" I roll my eyes. "Is that why you have such a stellar marriage?"

She puts her nose in the air.

"You're more alike than you think you are—"

My head pulls back a little. "That . . . might be the cruellest thing anyone's ever said to me."

"You both lash out when provoked," she tells me. "When you feel cornered, you—"

"So does a brown bear," I interrupt. "And yet, I wouldn't say we were brothers—"

BJ squashes a smile.

She shrugs helplessly.

"I just wanted to give you some context—"

I nod once. "I appreciate that."

She swallows, eyes suddenly looking a bit hopeful.

"Really?"

"Um—?" I frown a little bit at her eagerness for my appreciation. "Yes. I guess? I mean—" I swallow. "Contextually, you did a terrible thing that, contextually, set my father and I up for a lifetime of contextual losses but—" I glance at BJ quickly then back to my mother. "Sure, I suppose there's some . . . level of appreciation in there—?"

She lets out a breath as though she's relieved.

"Well . . . Good." She nearly smiles but not quite. "Good. I'm—well, to be honest with you, I'm quite relieved." She breathes out a single laugh. "To get that off my chest, you know? That was a lot to carry for twenty-four years—"

"I'm twenty-five," I tell her, and BJ puts his hands on her shoulders, guiding her towards the elevator.

"Alright, Arrie, well—that was—" He gives her a tight smile. "Yeah" is all he says, and then he presses the button down.

The door opens and before she gets in, she leans in towards my fiancé and says something quietly.

He stares at her, face serious, and then he nods once.

The elevator doors close and he looks over at me, face all crushed for me.

"Are you okay?" he asks, arms open, and I walk into them how I always have, the same way you walk into a church. A bit broken and looking for salvation.

I don't say anything, just nod.

"Look at me—" he says as he tugs my head back by the hair and finds my eyes. "Don't bullshit me. Are you actually?"

"Yeah—" I shake my head. "I don't know."

His face pulls. "That was a lot—"

I nod again. "I guess."

"You guess?" He blinks. "Fuck, Parks—I get that she was aiming for context but that was—"

"It's okay, I think—" I cut him off. "I think something about this makes it better."

He looks completely confused now. "How?"

"I don't know—?" I shrug, trying to think through it myself. "Maybe because he didn't meet me and get to know me and then not want me—he's just not wanted me all along."

BJ frowns more, unsure. "—Is that better?"

"I don't know—?" I shrug. "But I don't suppose that it's worse."

SIXTY-ONE

BJ

"You'll look after her, won't you?" That's what her mum whispered to me the other night on her way out.

"Always," I nodded back.

A lot to unpack there, if I'm honest. Was that a handover? Some sort of official transference of her daughter's duty of care? Or was it some sort of acknowledgment that she knows even if she tried, I don't think Magnolia would let her be a mother to her anyway?

Parks is sitting cross-legged on our couch when I walk in tonight, bridal magazines spread around her, tabs all sticking out of them, a notepad by her side.

She jots something down before she looks up at me, gives me a smile that's such a nothing smile, like—mindless, like it's no big deal me wandering into the home we share together, just happy to see me—stops me in my tracks for a second. Sounds mundane, I know. It is.

I've been chasing the mundane with her since I was fucking seventeen, and here, now, finally almost ten years later, we've got it.

Mundane is relative, I suppose. Had to battle my way through about ten paparazzi to get into the building and she's still on a bit of a social media lockout because people can be fucking soulless shits—but here she sits on a couch we picked, in the home I bought us, with both our names on the title.

Walk over, kiss her on top of her head, then sit down in the armchair across from her.

"Good day?"

"Yeah—?" She shrugs. "I worked from home. Had some meetings—and just now, I'm looking at some things for the wedding—which do you prefer?"

She flashes me two photos of the same place settings.

I squint at her.

"Is this a trick?"

She frowns. "No?"

I nod over at them. "They're the same—"

Her head pulls back. "You are of course joking, yes?"

"Uh—" I squash my mouth together, decide to tread carefully. "Yeah—yes!"

"BJ—" She rolls her eyes. "The plates are entirely different colours."

I roll my eyes at her, snatch the photos from her hands to inspect them myself.

Both very gold. That's all I can see, really. One's got flowers on it, I guess.

"Eden Turquoise and Aux Rois Or," she says, even though I didn't ask. I never ask and it never deters her from telling me anyway. "Bernardaud."

I look over at her. "This the vibe you want to go with?"

She shrugs. "It seems fitting to the Mandarin, no?"

I nod, looking at the photos again.

Hear us both sigh at the same time and I look up at her, give her a weak smile.

She blinks. "You don't like them?"

I tilt my head at her. "They're beautiful—of course they are—"

She nods, face unsure. "The day isn't about us, though, so—just pick one. I can't decide."

"This one." I wave the one that's a bit blue, I guess. "I've got a thing for flowers."

That makes her smile.

"Do you?" she asks, abandoning her magazines and finding her way to my lap.

"Yep." I nod. "Love them."

She cuddles into me. "What did you do today?"

"Had another tattoo removal session."

She perks up and peers down my shirt before she looks back up at me, chuffed.

"She's nearly gone!"

I nod. "On our way."

"Do you feel silly for that now?"

Flick my eyes at her, because if you give this one a fucking inch . . . "Sometimes."

She shifts on my lap, settling in. "Well, you should."

I dig my chin into her shoulder.

"Want to grab some dinner?" I ask, casual. Ask it how I'd ask anyone, like I'm not nervous about her answer, like it's not weighted at all, even though it is.

About ten fucking photographers downstairs, is what it weighs.

"Mmm—" She hums, pretending to think about it. "No."

I nod, try not to look disappointed or worried. That never helps.

Push the hair from her face.

"You eaten yet today?"

Her eyes flick up to the left—thinking—her mouth pouts and she shrugs.

"No."

I nod again, swallow, tilt my head. "Maybe you should?"

"I don't know—" she says, climbing off my lap and tidying up the magazines over on the couch. "What even is the point of eating?"

She says that like someone would say "What's the weather like today?" And she says it to the couch, not to me.

"What?" I ask, watching her carefully.

She turns around, hugging the magazines to her chest and her sister's copy of *The Blind Watchmaker* to her chest.

"It's like watering a house plant that lives on a rocket ship, that's running out of fuel, that—for whatever reason—is nevertheless hurtling towards nothing but infinite blackness," she says, eyes big, scared puddles, and I'll fucking fight Dawkins in the street if I see him, I swear to god.

"Would you water it?" she asks me, brows up. Question's genuine.

I breathe out.

"Yeah, probably—" I nod and shrug at the same time.

"Why?"

I walk towards her, take the magazines from her hands and the fucking book as well, set it all down on the coffee table and then I slip my hands around her waist.

"Because you don't know what's on the other side of the blackness, Parksy," I tell her.

She looks up at me, face all worried.

"Maybe nothing."

"Or maybe everything—" I give her a look. "Parks, there's no point not looking after yourself while you have the chance, what if the whole point is to nurture the life you have—"

"But for what?" She frowns, looking a bit distraught. "What's the point if we're all just going to live til we die and then what—"

"Alright," I nod to her point. "Say this is it, Parks—say all it'll ever be is what we have right now in these moments on this planet as we spin wildly through space—" I give her a look. "Even if that's true, then it's the only true thing we've got, so it's your duty, Parks, to the universe, to look after this—"

I tap her chest, wait for her to say something, but she says nothing.

I breathe in through my nose and out again, sounds like a sigh. Suppose it is, really.

"And if that's not reason enough to look after yourself, Parksy"—tilt my head at her—"do you love me?"

Her face falters. "Of course."

I nod once. "How much?"

She pouts a little. "The most."

"It hurts me," I tell her. "You're hurting me, Parks—when you do this—when you don't look after yourself—"

"Beej—" she interrupts, frowning, and I shake my head at her.

"No, listen—" I adjust my grip on her, hold her firmer against me. "One day, I want you to care about eating because you care about you—because you care about your wellness because it's yours, and because it's yours, it's inherently valuable, but until that day—" I give her a tall look. "If you love me how I know you do—care about it for me."

She sighs, glancing away, and I nudge her face back towards mine, hold it there so she's looking into my eyes.

"Parks, your wellness is intricately linked with mine," I tell her. "I'm working fucking hard to be well. And I really—" Shake my head, shake off the feeling in my throat that feels a bit like I could cry. "I need you to be okay, yeah?" I tell her with a nod.

She gives me a tiny, weak one back. "Okay."

I give it space for a couple of seconds before I try again.

"Can we order something in, please?" I ask carefully. "Anything you want."

She nods and I pull out my phone and start scrolling through Uber over her shoulder, til I find Kensu Kitchen and wait for her to say it. Her lips are pursed, all heavy in thought.

"Sushi," she says eventually, and I kiss her on the head, smile like I didn't already have it pulled up and ordering our favourites.

SIXTY-TWO

BJ

After that talk we had, I feel like Parks made some solid steps.

We left the house for coffee the next morning, and she went into the office for a meeting.

Stayed around Hanover Square so I could pick her up after it and then we walked over to Liberty, did some shopping.

The paps followed us but we knew they would. Planned for it even. Brought my AirPods, gave us each one, played her a bunch of songs that were themed around "fuck this" and/or "fuck you."

Didn't completely drown them out but it made her laugh at least.

Therapy today, about a week after the fact, and I know Claire is going to bring up the eating because we haven't really ever talked about it properly.

She asks for the background, when it first started, when first I noticed something, how she's been feeling—all the shit you'd expect her to ask.

When it started, any triggers, how many times she's been in treatment for it—

Magnolia "ums" on the answer to that one so I jump in.

"Twice," I say on her behalf, and her face falters, mouth falls into a purse.

I look at her, confused.

"Three times," she says, looking at Claire, not at me.

I pull back. "When three?"

Her eyebrows bend in the middle and she looks uncomfortable.

Does this weird breath, like she's nervous or something.

She swallows. Definitely nervous.

"When I was with Christian."

"What?" I stare over at her.

She takes a big breath, licks her lips. "Well, after we broke up, I had quite a bad spell—"

"How bad a spell?" I cut her off.

She crosses her arms over her chest and barely meets my eyes. "I was involuntarily committed to Weymouth Street for a couple of days—"

"Parks—"

"And then Christian drove me up to Bloxham House and I had to stay there for a month."

"Fuck—" I sigh into my hands, cover my whole face with them. An old, familiar wave of nausea rolls through me, and I don't know why—I shake my head. "Why didn't you tell me?"

She stares over at me, looking small. Holds her own hands. "I thought you'd be cross."

I lift an eyebrow. "At which part?"

She swallows. "All of it."

Flick her a look, unimpressed. "Well picked."

"Well—" She crosses her arms, annoyed. "I don't feel like you should be."

"Why's that?" I cross mine back.

"Because it's not at all about you—" She lifts those shoulders of hers. "You're making something not about you at all, about you—"

And I cut her off.

"You in danger is about me, Parks!"

She rolls her eyes. "I wasn't in danger!"

Give her a look. "You were in a hospital on your own because you can't look after yourself—"

She gives me a little glare. "I wasn't on my own."

My jaw sets. Take a breath.

"He went with you?"

She swallows. "Yes."

Breathe slowly out my nose.

Of course he fucking did.

I know when too. I know exactly when—

I wasn't seeing Parks much then because we hadn't patched shit up yet, so I didn't know she wasn't around, didn't expect anything.

During that initial breakup phase of ours, she'd go into hiding sometimes anyway, just because if she ever left the house it was too much.

Anytime she was seen with anyone—Henry, Christian, Jonah, singers her dad worked with, literally fucking anyone—they'd run it that she was with them—like, "with them" with them—so she wasn't about that much. But I never put it together that neither was he.

There was this month that year when Christian was away all the time. And we all just assumed that he was seeing someone he didn't want to tell us about or someone who lived far away—did Henry know, I wonder? Of course, Henry fucking knew—knew and he didn't tell me? Even now? Yeah, I'm pissed.

Blink twice at her. "Did you not think you could come to me?"

Parks pulls a face. "Why would I 'come to you'?"

"Because I'm me!" I tell her loudly—maybe louder than I should, because Claire shifts in her seat.

Magnolia clocks her—briefly—goes back to pretending like she's not there.

"So?"

"So I would do anything for you!" I tell her, shake my head at her and mutter under my breath, "But I guess you're you, so—"

Magnolia's head pulls back. "What's that supposed to mean?"

I stare over at her, wonder if now's the time to say it—? I know I have to eventually, but she's sitting there looking defensive and her eyes are glassy.

"Nothing," I say, looking away. Disengaging.

"No—" She shakes her head, overtly not disengaging. "You obviously meant something by that, what did you mean?"

Breathe out my nose. "Nothing, Parks."

Claire leans forward with a gentle smile. "BJ, perhaps now's a good time to—"

"No," I say quickly and firmly.

Magnolia looks between us. "No what?"

"Nothing." I shake my head. "Leave it."

"Tell me," she says, watching me, brows low.

I keep shaking my head, unmoved. "Nope."

The session sort of tanks after that, all goes a bit fucky and shit. She powers down and I'm too annoyed to keep chatting about anything so it kind of just peters out and we leave, head home, not really talking.

I say I have to meet up with Jo, which I don't have to but I want the excuse to be away from her for a minute.

Her eyes don't go hurt when I say that either, she's pissed too. Wants space.

Gives me a tight smile and walks home being trailed by Daniela.

By the time I get home later it's past dinnertime and she's already in bed—hair pushed up, all of this month's *Vogue*s from around the world and she's circling and tabbing them, marking pieces of interest. Take a peek at Bridget's urn for any clues—frowning face. To be expected, I suppose.

I stand in the doorway and she glances up at me without moving her head.

Still pissed then, I guess.

"Hey," I say.

"Hey," she says back before looking back down at the magazine.

I sigh, pull off my T-shirt as I walk into the bathroom.

Shower even though I don't feel like it because I'm marrying a fucking psycho, brush my teeth, pull on some sweatpants and get into bed with her.

I'm in there only for a second before it happens, and I knew it would.

She's predictable—doesn't want to be, tries not to be—but even her trying her hardest to be unpredictable is predictable as fuck, so I know what's happening before it happens.

She goes still, I'm not even looking at her and I know how her face is, probably—brows low, nose pinched, mouth pouting.

"What was she talking about?" she asks after about a minute of silence.

I breathe out, say nothing, let it hang there.

She glances over at me, but not really. Turns her head a bit towards me but doesn't give me her eyes.

"I asked you something," she tells me.

"And I told you to leave it."

"No!" she snaps, looking at me now. "The last time you wouldn't tell me something that I wanted to know, you'd fucked my best friend, so tell me now—"

Jut my jaw out at that—fucking low blow. "Nope."

"BJ—"

I give her a warning look. "Don't, Parks—"

She rolls her eyes and throws back the duvet from her body, springing to her feet.

"Whatever—" she says, already halfway out the door and darting down our hallway.

I breathe out, annoyed. Fucking typical.

"Where the fuck are you going—" I call to her and she doesn't answer so I'm on my feet now too, walking after her. "I'm talking to you—!"

She spins on her heel, eyebrows tall.

"Oh, now you're talking to me?" She blinks twice. "That's funny because now I'm not talking to you—"

"Alright—" I nod coolly. "Yeah, fuck it, why not?"

She shrugs passive-aggressively.

I give her a look. "Are you ready?"

She gives me a bratty, impatient smile that's almost all eyebrows.

"I'm angry at you."

She sniffs, amused. "You're angry at me?"

I nod once. "Yep."

"Okay." She frowns dubiously. "Might I ask what for?"

"For leaving me," I tell her without missing a beat.

Her face falters.

"For leaving you when?"

"Fuck—" I scoff, sort of shake my head and nod my head at once. "Exactly, yeah! Thank you. Pick a time—"

Her eyebrows go low as she thinks about it, confused.

"I've never left you."

I stare over at her, incredulous.

"You've never left me?" I repeat. Let out this breath that sounds a bit like a laugh except it's all dripping in how much it's all killing me. I gesture to her here in the hallway. "You just did it—"

She rolls her eyes and takes an exasperated breath.

"I'm angry at you! I didn't want to sleep next to you—"

"We don't do that!" I cut her off, yelling. Probably shouldn't yell. Don't really want to be the kind of man who yells at his wife, but I do it anyway. "We don't just leave each other, Parks—or at least I don't—"

"What the fuck are you talking about?" She scowls at me, hands on her hips. "When have I ever left you?"

"Paili," I tell her, and her head pulls back a bit.

"What?" she says, voice a bit softer now.

"Paili." I say it again, glare over at her a bit, even though I don't mean to. "You left me when you found out about Paili—"

Her chin drops, eyes go tight.

"You're joking," she says to me, watching me with these eyes like she thinks I've lost my mind. Lifts an eyebrow. "You're angry that I left you when I found out you slept with Paili?"

I nod once. "Yes."

She rolls her eyes, scoffs.

"You've lost the plot—" She almost laughs, but I shake my head and cut her off.

"If we flipped it, Parks—" I gesture between us. "I would have stayed."

She folds her arms over her chest defensively.

"Bullshit."

"Nope—not bullshit." I run my tongue over my bottom lip. "If you came to me, told me you fucked Christian, which—"

Her fists go to balls and she yells, "I've never fucked Christian!"

And I give her a look like I don't believe her but I think I do. Give her that look mostly because she's pissing me off and I want to piss her off too.

"But say you had—" I shrug. "Say you did it drunk one night at a party, and you came and told me—yeah, it would have fucking crushed me. Yeah, probably I would have proper murdered him, but then—I'm not leaving you for anything—"

Her eyes are flicked up, not rolling them but like, permanently up at this point.

"You're talking in hypotheticals," she tells me. "You don't know what you would have done if that happened to you—"

"No, I do—" I shrug, jaw set. "Because leaving is what you do, not me—"

She does this thing sometimes—like, this hurt blink as she straightens herself up, chin down—affronted, or something.

I'm aware of my breathing now. It's fast, but I'm angry. And scared, if I'm honest.

"Parks, do you know what it's like to love someone how I love you and always wonder if they're actually going to stay with you?" I stare over at her, hope I don't sound as fucking pathetic as I'm pretty sure I do. "Do you know how that feels?"

Stands there for a second, watching me with a frown as she breathes out her nose and then she swallows and walks over to me, stands toe to toe with me, reaches for me.

"I'm going to stay, Beej," she says, super quiet.

I glance down at her, chest still breathing all heavy. "Yeah?"

She nods quickly, eyes big, voice little. "Yes."

Jut my chin over at her. "Prove it."

She frowns again, and swallows. "How?"

I shrug once.

"Just stay."

14:12

Christian

Oi, we need to have a chat

Ah fuck

What have I done this time?

Bloxham House

Oh.

Yeah shit.

Fair enough

Meet for a beer?

Lamb and Flag?

I'll be there in an hour.

SIXTY-THREE

Magnolia

We're at dinner tonight with Taura and Tiller. Our first official double date—so cute. They're so cute, actually. It's the first time I've seen them together in like, a together capacity, and it's just—they do things for each other quite mindlessly. He pulls out her chair for her, pours her water, she spits out her gum and offers him the wrapper to spit his out—very in sync about regular things, but the older I get the more I understand that it's the regular things that make a relationship.

I think my great pursuit in life is going to be regular.

BJ orders for the table, a bit because he's sexy like that, but mostly I think so I myself don't have to, in front of a room full of people watching with prying eyes and camera phones not-so-discreetly at the ready to see what I eat.

I stare over at Tausie and Tiller, sort of drink them in, if you will.

She's completely gorgeous, we know that. In general, her hair is somewhere around the dirty blonde mark, and she can go either way. Though at the minute she is very and undeniably blonde, over the course of our little best friendship, she has had both properly brown and truly blonde hair, and I'm somewhat annoyed to report she looked completely spectacular with both. Because of her skin, I think. Quite olive, with the dream-dusting of freckles. And then those big hazel eyes—the colour of which she acquired from her German father—but that wonderful, cat-ish, almond shape is thanks to that mother of hers. Half Singaporean and half Malay. She's a rather successful singer over in Singapore, did you know? A knock-out voice. Wildly beautiful—obviously, she made Taura.

And then Tiller—fuck. I think we can all breathe a collective sigh of relief that he wasn't much on my radar during the "lost years" because I would have absolutely thrown myself at this man.

Biggest, whitest smile that touches all the way to his jarringly blue eyes. Then that wavy blonde hair and skin that isn't too white for a white man.

They're just . . .

"You're a very attractive couple," I tell them, crossing my arms over my chest. "Were I not so secure I'd almost be threatened by you."

"You're not that secure," BJ says with a pleasant smile as he takes a sip of his water.

I give him a look as though he's ridiculous. "I'm very secure!"

Taura and Beej exchange looks, as though they're unsure, and I stare between them, aghast.

I gesture to myself. "I'm beautiful."

"Yes." BJ nods once emphatically. "Insanely so, but—"

"But what!" I interrupt him very crossly, and Tiller pulls an uncomfortable face on the other side of the table.

"But—!" Taura says loudly, taking over. She clears her throat and speaks more delicately now. "There are some—abandonment issues, at play . . . Sometimes."

I roll my eyes and make a 'pfft' sound. "We all have those."

"I don't—" Tiller says at the same time BJ says, "Maybe just with you but—" while Taura says, "No, I'm fine."

I stare at them collectively, all-around displeased.

"Really, Taura?" I glare at her. "No abandonment issues when your mother's off swanning around Singapore, living her dream life as a singer without you by her side?"

Tiller leans across the table and nods slowly.

"That did feel secure," he whispers but I'm not sure he's being sincere.

Taura laughs, then shrugs lightheartedly. "No—she's really good at calling me."

I roll my eyes again and look away, muttering under my breath something about her being emotionally dead inside.

Tiller glances between us all, as though he's trying to track our dynamic and playing catch-up. I suppose he is.

"So, how do you all know each other?"

"Well," I clear my throat, gesturing between BJ and I. "We're engaged."

Tiller rolls his eyes. "Yes, I know."

"We all went to school together," Taura tells him. "Magnolia and I were in the same year—"

"—But we weren't really friends," I add.

"Oh." Tiller says.

"Well, we weren't not-friends, I suppose," I say, thinking further on it. I didn't dislike her during our school years, I was just wildly indifferent towards everyone who wasn't in our immediate friendship group. "I wasn't overly friendly during school if you can believe it—"

"I can believe it." He nods, rather sure of himself, and Taura and Beej both stifle a laugh. I frown at them all.

"I've been extremely friendly to you—" I tell him, a bit miffed.

"If not too friendly—" BJ says under his breath to Taura, but I catch it too, so shoot him a look.

"You have," Tiller nods, appreciatively. "But when we came in and sat down, that girl came over and started talking to Taura, you didn't say anything and just, like, glowered at her the whole time."

I look at BJ. "I thought I was smiling?"

His face pulls as though he's thinking about it and he nods. "May have missed the mark on that one by an inch or two."

"Or ten," Tiller says, and the others smirk.

"Okay, well—" I give him a little glare. "You're new, so—quiet."

"And we're back to friendly!" Tiller gives me a playful smile and I roll my eyes, a tiny bit off of him but not too off him because, fuck—he's very handsome, and I'm only human and while I've got you here, what do you think it's saying about me that I find it a little bit sexy when a man is mean to me? Actually, never mind. And don't tell Claire.

Tiller turns and looks at Taura. "So when did you become close?"

"About a year and a half ago?" Taura guesses with a shrug.

"Well," I wave my hands between Taura and BJ. "These two were obviously close for a good deal longer before that—"

Tiller's face falters.

"Oh—" He blinks. "Did you two—"

"Magnolia—" Taura sighs at the same time as BJ says, "Fuck, Parks—"

I grimace. "Uh oh—"

I stare over at Taura, giving her a million sorrys with my eyeballs, but the glare she's giving me is thwarting them off.

Taura takes a breath as though she's winding up to say something, and then Tiller cuts her off.

"No, it's fine—" He shakes his head, looking from her to me and back to her. "It's just, we haven't—" He trails, glances over at BJ and I sitting across from them, albeit one of us a bit more awkwardly than the other now.

Tiller swallows and clears his throat.

"We haven't done the, like—" He shrugs. "Who . . . chat."

"Well," I give him an apologetic smile. "If it helps open up the conversation, we all know you've had sex with Daisy—"

"Magnolia—!" BJ growls and I look over at him. He gives me a singular shake of the head and a firm look.

"And!" I glance back at Tiller, grinning bigger (and sorrier) now (and Taura says "oh god—"). "If it makes things less awkward here—specifically, with these two—" I gesture at my fiancé and my best friend. "I too have seen Taura naked."

"Okay—" Tiller laughs once and throws Taura a look.

"She looks great," I tell him with a nod. "Great body. Surprisingly big boobs—"

Tiller smiles somewhere between appreciatively and knowingly. "I'm familiar with them." He glances at Taura, squashing a smile. "Big fan."

Taura covers her mouth with both her hands and wipes away a smile that's both amused and mortified.

And then no one says anything for about twelve seconds, which is such a long time, so then I say, "I don't have very big boobs."

"Oh, fuck—" Taura drops her head in her hands and Tiller starts laughing.

BJ tosses an arm around me and peers down my black and gold sequin-embellishment bustier minidress from Balmain.

"No, they go alright."

I turn and look at him, mildly offended. "Alright?"

"Nope—" He shakes his head quickly.

"No, they're not alright?" I blink.

"Yes!" BJ says loudly, trying to overcorrect now.

I purse my lips. "Yes, they are just alright—"

"Fuck," he laughs, scratching the back of his neck. "Perfect! They go—perfect, is—what I meant."

Taura pulls a face, and says under her breath, "Took a while to land that plane."

"Yes, Taura, it did, didn't it?" I glance at her before looking back at BJ. "Would you prefer they were bigger?" I ask, arms crossed over my chest, pretending to be madder than I am.

He thinks for a couple of seconds.

("Answer faster." Taura whisper-growls, and I squash down a smile.)

BJ exhales. "I'd . . . prefer . . . this conversation to be . . . over." He shoots me a quick smile at the end.

"Me too." Taura nods once.

"I don't know, I kind of like it—" Tiller says, appreciatively.

"What—Magnolia's small boobs?" Taura asks, pointing across the table at them.

"No—" Tiller shakes his head quickly.

"Well, that's a bit rude—" Taura says, pretending to be offended on my behalf, but she's smirking, all pleased with herself to have dragged him under the bus with the rest of us.

Tiller looks over at BJ, keeps on shaking his head. "I wasn't—"

"Oh, I know, man—" Beej shakes his head. "They're fucking incorrigible."

"We are," I concede. "And apparently rather flat-chested."

Taura flicks me a smile over the table. "Speak for yourself—"

Tiller rubs the side of his head. "I think I'm getting a headache."

"Oh no—" I reach over the table and touch his arm. "I do just think we'd all—collectively—feel so much better if you would just . . . put on your fireman uniform and—"

"Parks—" BJ laugh-growls.

"He's a policeman," Taura tells me.

"Detective," Tiller corrects her.

"Wait but—" I pout. "But their uniform's terrible—"

He looks over at me for a couple seconds before shaking his head. "We don't have a uniform?"

"Yes," I nod. "I know. Hence the terrible."

Tiller holds my eye, smirks. I suspect he'll fit in just fine, don't you?

Then he leans back and crosses his arms over his chest and looks between BJ and Taura.

"So, when did you two—" He trails.

"Years ago—" Tausie shakes her head, and she looks the smallest bit nervous. "It was stupid—he was still really in love with Magnolia, and they were this big, crazy mess and—"

"See," I rest my chin in my hand. "I thought, once upon a time, BJ had cheated on me with Taura, but he hadn't." Dramatic pause. "He had sex with my old best friend, Paili, who—"

"—Sucks." Taura injects.

"Very much." I nod once. "She told me BJ slept with Taura, and so I hated her for a very long time."

Tiller's face sort of bends heavy under the weight of all the information, thinking through it, looking for the answer to the only question he asked, which evidently, neither Taura nor I supplied.

"About four years ago, man," BJ offers with a curt nod that looks like it might be bro-code for 'Sorry I used to fuck your girl.' Tiller holds his eye for a few seconds then nods. He glances between us.

"You're all very—" He waves his hands about, nondescriptly.

"I mean—" I scoff. "They are." I gesture over to my fiancé and my best friend. "I've only had sex with BJ in our friendship group."

"Right," BJ nods, less sure. "And Julian."

I scrunch my nose, unsure. "I don't know if I'd classify him as in our fr—"

"And Christian," Taura adds, merrily.

"Well—" I start. "I'd hardly—"

"Wait—" Tiller cuts in, staring over at me wide-eyed. "You and Christian?"

I hold my hand up, shaking my head. "No, no—"

"Yes, yes," BJ says, mimicking me.

I look at the man who's dangerously close to sleeping on that terrible, angular bench he loves so much, and point at him a warning finger and I wait for him to be quiet before I turn back to Tiller.

I give him a smile as though I think everyone else is being silly.

"I actually would really love it if we as a group, moving forward, agreed to pass a motion to classify Christian and my collaborative sexual experience as a failure to launch—"

BJ bangs his fist on the table like a gavel at the same time as Taura declares, "Motion denied!"

"Why?" I pout. "I mean, honestly—how does one truly, ever properly, conclusively define sex—?"

And in unison, Taura says, "P in V" and BJ says, "Penetration." And I roll my eyes at them, growling under my breath.

"Well, of course you two absolute hoe bags would know how to define it—"

Taura shoots me a look over the table and I look at Tiller and give him a big grin.

"I mean—" I clear my throat. "She's a *lovely* hoe bag."

". . . And we're done with the champagne," BJ says with a nod, moving my glass away from me.

Tiller laughs and pushes back from the table.

"I'm going to use the restroom," he tells us all, but he touches Taura's arm, smiling at her in a way I love.

Once he's out of earshot I lean over the table and grab her hand.

"Quick, quick!" I whisper urgently. "Have you had sex?"

"Magnolia—" Taura rolls her eyes. "You're such a nosy parker."

I stare at her, unimpressed but also unfazed. "So, yes," I deduce.

"Parks—" BJ lifts his eyebrows and I can tell by the look he's giving me that I'm about to receive some dull soliloquy about being impolite and minding my own business and respecting people's boundaries. "You can't just—"

But then Taura interrupts like a burst conversational fire hydrant.

"Yes!" she squeals, thrilled. "It was so incredible!"

"Nice—" Beej nods, appreciatively, and I scowl at him.

"A touch pervy."

He rolls his eyes. "I said 'nice,' I didn't ask her to send me a photo of her feet."

Taura frowns over at him. "Are you into feet now?"

He sighs, exasperated. "No."

"How incredible are we talking, Taus?" I ask, eyebrows up and scanning the room to be sure he's not on his way back yet.

"Like—" She shakes her head, cheeks all pinky and full of swoons. "Very ten out of ten out of ten—"

I press my lips together excitedly.

"Is he as incredible without clothes on as I imagine him to be?"

"Yeah," BJ gives me the look. "I'm the perv—"

Taura nods at me, ignoring Beej. "Statuesque."

BJ frowns between us.

"Do you know, I have a pretty good body—" he says, but we're not listening.

"Incredible." I nod to my friend, appreciatively. "So what's his vibe?"

Taura's face falters. "Towards what?"

"Indian food," I tell her, deadpan, before I toss her a look. "Sex, Taura, my god. Keep up."

BJ looks over at me, eyes wide. Gives me that warning finger of his.

"You need to put a fucking lid on it, Parks. You can't just ask—"

"Oh—" Taura says over him, and he just sighs, head rolling back up at the ceiling. "Um. Sweet at first, but pretty in control of the situation the whole time—"

I purse my lips, thinking. "Vanilla?"

"Yeah." Taura nods.

"Oh—" BJ frowns on her behalf, but Taus shakes her head quickly.

"No, I think I like it—"

"Oh!" I stare over at her in surprise. "Oh my god—"

"Stop—" She rolls her eyes.

But I shake my head, not stopping.

"You liking vanilla sex is massive."

"Well." She flicks her eyes between BJ and I. "It is massive, so that helps."

I squint over at her, suspiciously. "How massive?"

"No—" Taura shakes her head as though this here now is me crossing a line.

"Come on!" I pout. "I'd tell you how big BJ is—"

She flicks her eyes uncomfortably between us. "I know how big BJ is."

Beej and I give each other a no-look high-five and Taura rolls her eyes.

"But do tell me," I say to her again.

She gives me a look. "No!"

"Come on," I frown.

And then BJ sighs, pressing his hands into his eyes. "Oh, no."

"What?" Taura and I say in unison, looking over at him.

He's shaking his head, looking somewhere far away.

"I'm just thinking about how—" He glances over at me.

"I'm going to have to do parent-teacher conferences with you one day."

"Well," I tuck my chin and scowl up at him. "That was very uncalled for."

He gives me a playful look. "We'll see."

Then he flags down the sommelier to talk about wine.

"Oh!" I clap my hands together, and kick Taura under the table, leaning over to her again. "Pick an oblong vegetable—"

"No!" Taura growls.

"A carrot!" I say, watching her face for clues—nothing. "A zucchini!" I say a few seconds later. "Corn on the cob?"

"Oh, god—" She sighs.

"An eggplant?" I keep guessing, unperturbed.

She gives me a look. "Magnolia—"

"Oh no, Tausie—it's not like a rutabaga?"

"What's not like a rutabaga?" Tiller says with a pleasant smile, sitting back down at the table.

"Nothing!" Taura yelps at the same time I sort of scream, "Hi—!" admittedly with an overly enthused smile.

"Hello!" I keep going. "Back, so soon! Such an efficient bowel you must h—"

Then Taura kicks me under the table and I yelp and smile less. Tiller looks between us, confused but perhaps already a bit amused.

"What are you talking about?"

"Um—" I purse my lips. "Vegetables?"

"What?" Beej says, tapping back into the conversation.

"Tiller—" I give him a pleasant smile.

"No—" Taura says, shooting daggers at me across the table and I ignore her.

"If you had to identify as one of the following vegetables, which would you say you feel the strongest affinity towards—?"

("I'll kill you," she whispers under her breath.)

Tiller tosses me a baffled look.

"A kinship, if you will—"

(*'Dead to me,'* she mouths across the table.)

"Um—" I clear my throat. "Carrots . . . zucchini . . . corn on the cob . . . eggplant . . . a cucumber . . ."

"Cucumber," BJ says, nodding to himself. "If I was a vegetable I'd be a cucumber."

He thinks about it a little more. "But like, a big one. Not the ones that come in the small packs. And not room temperature either. Super cold and fresh. And not weedy, like—the thick ones, you know? Not bendy."

Taura snorts a laugh and BJ flicks his eyes from her to me suspiciously before he puts it together, rolling his eyes and shaking his head, barely concealing how much he loves us on that immaculate face of his.

I reach over the table and poke Tiller.

"Pick," I tell him.

"I am sorry about her—" BJ says to him over the table.

"Zucchinis are nice—" I tell both Tiller and Taura.

"Bit watery—" Taura says, and I pull a face.

"What does that mean?"

Tiller's eyes dart between all of us, confused.

"Um—" He shakes his head and clears his throat. "Does it have to be one of those?"

Taura tilts her head, considering. "Er—"

Tiller's brows go low as he thinks about it. "My favourite vegetable is a butternut pumpkin."

"Ouch!" I barely say before BJ throws his arm around me and covers my mouth, laughing with his eyes all wide.

"What?" Tiller asks Taura, confused.

She glances at me over the table, BJ's hand still covering my mouth, and she licks away a smile.

"Nothing."

SIXTY-FOUR
Magnolia

It's Jemima's thirtieth birthday at Coworth Park, which is about forty-five minutes outside of the city.

BJ and I drive up ourselves. I had to have a mini-intervention with Daniela actually, I think she might be a bit of a workaholic. When she heard that we were driving up here, she insisted she come, and I said, "It's a Saturday," and she said she didn't mind, and I said that it was quite alright, and she said it'd be her pleasure, and I said perhaps we needed to look at expanding her understanding of "pleasures then," and then BJ nipped me in the back and took over the conversation.

He insisted that we wouldn't need her and if we did, he promised to phone, but that really, he was fairly sure that we could survive a weekend without her.

It was a nice drive up, you know—other than the driving part. But it sort of felt a little bit like the olden days.

BJ's hand on my knee, me swatting his hands away when he'd venture them higher and higher, both of us laughing, both of us pretending that every time we drive towards another car my whole body doesn't go into an intense panic where for a split second I can't really see or hear.

He doesn't say anything about it, he doesn't make me feel silly for it—just every time we start driving towards another car, he'd turn the music up, try to drown out my mind and screeching tyres and scraping metals I'd otherwise hear.

The party's both inside and outside, which is ambitious of Jemima, but you're only thirty once, I suppose, so good for her. It's mid-January now, so the outside part is under cover with too many outdoor heaters to count and barely any guests because they're all inside.

We say hello to Lily and Hamish, and they're doing so much better, by the way. BJ and Ham.

BJ kisses his mum on the cheek and sort of folds himself around her the way sons do on their good mothers, and then he turns to his dad and hugs him too. For less time, but I haven't seen them hug in a while.

That lights both Lily and Ham up like a bloody Christmas tree.

And then I spot Allie in the corner next to Madeline and a friend of theirs, but she looks bored.

I pull Beej away from one of those old-woman friends you know because of your mother who insists you call her "Aunty," even though she's not one, and her interest in BJ is absolutely non-familial in nature, let me tell you. I know hungry eyes when I see them, especially when they're pointed at my fiancé.

"Thank you," he whispers into my ear, kissing it as we walk over to the girls.

Madeline gives her brother a big hug and barely acknowledges me, and the friend can't seem to look either BJ or myself in the eyes, but never mind.

Allie stands to her feet quite quickly with a funny look on her face.

"Is Jonah okay?" she asks us.

I look from her to BJ, unsure what she means.

BJ's face pulls. "What?"

Allie's face goes still but her eyes dart between us nervously. "You didn't hear?"

His brows drop low. "Hear what?"

And then Allie looks over at me for a moment, she looks a bit distressed, actually, but I don't know from what. She swallows.

"There was a shooting at one of his clubs last night—I saw it on the news."

"Oh my god." I blink, and BJ's eyes go wide, his face paling instantly.

He reaches for his phone in his pocket and I reach for his hand.

Allie takes an anxious breath—she wouldn't have wanted to be the one to tell someone something like this. She's not like that.

I look at Beej. "Did you know? Did he say anything?"

I don't know why I ask that because I know the answer from his face.

Beej shakes his head anyway as he raises his phone to his ear, his perfect face caving under the weight of the worry he has instantly for his best friend, and I stand there waiting to see if our friend's alright, my heart pounding away in my throat for the full nine seconds it takes for Jonah to answer.

"Fuck—" BJ sighs, relieved, into the phone, as he shakes his head. "What the fuck, Jo?" He sounds angry now—catches my eye and nods his head away from us.

I nod, and he kisses me mindlessly on the cheek.

"Tell me what happened—" I hear BJ say as he plugs his ear, walking away.

I sigh.

I sigh in disbelief and stare over at Allie. "London's really gone mad, hasn't it?"

She nods with big eyes. "I think I'm going to go away soon."

"What do you mean?" My head pulls back. "Where are you going?"

"Well, do you remember Bridge and I had that trip planned?"

"Oh." I frown, thinking about it. "Right. The Asia one. You're going to go anyway?"

"Yeah, I—maybe." She shrugs and I wonder if guilt flashes over her face, which isn't what I wanted to make her feel. "I think so. Mum says it'll be good for me—?"

"I do too," I nod quickly, because I want her to feel like she can, not that she shouldn't.

"Really?" She looks over, eyes nearly something like hopeful.

"Yeah." I smile as encouragingly as I can, which is hard because something about Allie leaving feels like more of Bridget being taken away, but that's my problem, not hers. "That's special, Al—will you go alone?"

She tucks some brown hair behind her ears.

"I guess so? Unless—" She trails. "Do you want to come?"

"Me?" I blink, surprised.

"—And Beej!" she adds.

"Oh—" I shake my head. "I don't think we could—with the wedding, and—"

"No, totally!" She nods. "I completely understand."

"But by yourself, Al—" I give her an impressed look. "That's very brave."

"I just sort of feel like if I had di—" She cuts herself off and swallows. "Bridget still would have gone, don't you think?"

I nod. She would have.

"So where to exactly?"

"Oh," she shrugs, "I don't know yet—Bridget had a plan somewhere, but I don't know where it is—" She rolls her eyes. "It was in a diary or something—"

We stare over at each other for a few seconds.

"She's such an analog loser," I say, much without thinking, and we both laugh and tear up at once. I brush away the one that escapes my eye quickly and flash her an apologetic smile—I'm not sure why—I know of all people, she gets it.

"BJ's stupid therapist is making me go through Bridget's things if you want to come over this week?" I offer. "Have a riffle through—? See if we can find you that plan."

She nods and forces a smile. "Please, yeah." And then she watches me for a couple of seconds, a bit of a frown there. "Are you packing her room up?"

"No," I say quickly. "I'm just—she has me looking at her things and I put some of them in boxes to bring them to my house because I don't like to be in that apartment now."

"Oh." She nods and flashes me a smile.

"It's all really boring—" I sort of laugh but it's being choked by another emotion I don't want to feel in front of all these people. "It's just mostly like, books and journals and—" I shake my head. "Psychology papers she seems to have been reading for the thrill of it."

Allie smiles.

"Some photos of us—" I gesture between us. "A lot of pens. God, she loved a shoe with a buckle, didn't she?"

Allie cracks a laugh and a couple tears roll down her face, and she doesn't wipe them away with any great urgency. They sit on her face, catching in the light of the sun, plain as day for everyone to see that she's feeling anything other than wonderful, that her life experience is something other than idyllic, and I wonder what that must be like?

Beej walks back over to us, pocketing his phone. He flashes me an exasperated smile, before he clocks his teary sister.

"You good?"

She sniffs once, nods and then smiles. She excuses herself but not before she kisses his cheek.

He waits for it to be just us before he nods his chin at my lifted eyebrows, waiting to hear about our friends.

"The boys are fine," he says.

"But they were there?" I ask.

He nods.

"Oh my god! That's mental—" I shake my head in disbelief. "Was anyone hurt?"

"Yeah." He sighs, face looking a bit strained. "A couple of people, actually—"

And then I have a scary thought and my heart's arms lift up, frozen, like they're being arrested.

"Was Julian—"

"No—" Beej shakes his head and gives me a strained smile. "I mean, he didn't say—" He shakes his head. "If something happened to him or to Daisy, we'd have heard—"

"Right." I nod, telling myself that's true. "No, you're right. Sorry—"

He cocks his head to the side. "What are you sorry for?"

"For—" I trail and then flash him an apologetic smile. "I shouldn't care—never mind."

His eyes pinch dubiously. "You shouldn't care if someone you were in a relationship with was hypothetically shot?"

"I—but he wasn't, so—" I stare up at him. "Right?"

"Right." He nods, frowning and smiling at once. "But text him."

He nods at my phone that's tucked away in the Venus La Petite crystal-embellished satin clutch by Benedetta Bruzziches.

"Really?"

He shrugs, permissively, so I do. I pull out my phone, type his name.

13:51

Julian

Are you okay?

Is Daisy?

Yeah, we're good.

Okay, good.

I look back up at BJ and feel my body relax.

"They're fine." I flash him a grateful smile as I put my phone away.

BJ looks at me with this sort of pinched smile for a couple of seconds before he hooks his arm around my neck, drags me in towards him and kisses me.

A not quick peck or brushing of mouths, not even a snog, but like a proper, big kiss. Like a tipsy-kissing your crush with reckless abandon at a club in Ibiza kind of kiss. I peel myself away from him (barely) and look up, surprised.

"Okay," I laugh, breathless and self-conscious, glancing around at some of the nearby eyes that are definitely on us.

He nods his chin at me, smirking, pleased with himself.

"What?" he asks coolly, unwrapping himself from around me.

I straighten out my floral embroidered Swiss Dot strapless

gown from Elie Saab, and barely look at him as I say, "That was quite a kiss."

He shrugs, but I know he knows.

I put my nose in the air. "Very typical male of you."

"Oh," he laughs, head pulling back. "Was it now?"

"Mm-hm." I nod once. "All cute and territorial—"

He squashes a smile and shakes his head. "I fucking hate it when you call me cute—"

I nod a couple of times.

"Julian hated it when I called him cute too." I give him a look to make sure he knows exactly what I'm playing at, and then he drops his chin to his chest and glares over at me a little, but he's smirking. He presses his tongue into the side of his mouth to cover up a smile he'd never give me the satisfaction of seeing in its fullness. He is annoyed, but he likes it.

He grabs me by the waist and pulls me over close to his face.

"You're a fucking shit-stirrer," he says, licking away a smile.

I smile up at him, pleased to have found a new little trick.

"Will speaking about Julian always elicit such a fun, sexy reaction from you?"

He presses his lips together and stares down at me. "Why don't you give it a try?"

I purse my lips, flick my eyes up and try to think of something to say that's quite sexy but that's also un-diabolical for us in a long-lasting way.

"He really didn't like it when I called him cute, but he did like it when I—" And that was it—that was all I had to say, before his hands were on my face—and I've talked about his hands before. They're perfect and they're so big that his thumb sits just to the side of my mouth and the rest of his hand wraps all the way around to the centre back of my neck.

It's a rough kiss, not a gentle one. I can feel the jealousy in how his fingers press against me and I don't mean to but I smile against his mouth because to be completely honest, I've been an object of desire for lots of people—I've been wanted by many men—and all of it feels good, I would be lying if I said it didn't—being wanted is my weakness, I think.

But being wanted by BJ? There's nothing like it. I've had cocaine before, at school, and it was an odd experience. I would say publicly that I didn't like it, but—don't tell anyone—actually, part of me did quite like it. And it makes sense now, but at the time I didn't know I had ADHD, and everyone else around me was happy and euphoric and having fun, and I was super focused and aware and my brain went very, very still, which it never did—and if we knew to look for it that would have been a big clue but we didn't—and so because my experience was so terribly different to everyone else's, it made me feel stupid and so I said I didn't like it.

I didn't get the high that most other people seem to get, so can't confirm this with any undeniable, factual accuracy, but I imagine being wanted by Beej feels like the high people want from narcotics. Best feeling in the world. Sometimes I can't see straight in the pursuit of it. Look at my track record, it's right there. I'll do anything to make him want me. He is the master and I'm just a dog doing tricks to please him.

I take this little staggered breath as he shifts back from me, and he looks pleased.

"Sexy enough for you?" he asks, eyebrow up.

I straighten up and try to regain my composure, because yes, he is my weakness, and yes, I would blindly do anything to be wanted by him, but best not let him know that, don't you think?

I clear my throat.

"I'm not sure—" I give him a demure shrug. "Julian would often—"

And then he goes "Hah!" and pulls me to the far side of the party with eyes that don't just look like trouble but are actually, historically speaking, very, very trouble-y, but that's okay because he wants me too now. He usually does, but every now and then—something happens and he gets this look, and it's . . . do or die trying.

As though someone's turned up the magnetic field between us

and there's no such thing as too close—you'll see in a minute, I know how this goes. This was how we spent our school years. Stolen moments around too many people in the weirdest, most cramped spaces. His head pressed against mine, heavy breathing, chests heaving. Nothing, not even air, between us.

And I'll put up a bit of a fight because I'm me, and because if I do, making him work for it, that's the slow-release version of the only drug I'm interested in: him.

He's got this squashed smile as he's staring down at me, tongue pressed into his bottom lip—he shakes his head.

Says "Fuck" under his breath and kisses me again.

Our bodies are like warm wax melting into each other and I need to fucking pull it together because that kiss wasn't conducive to a slow release.

I pull back, flick my eyes up at him, bite down on my lip and smile at him.

He breathes out a breath to steady himself, and then his wandering hands slip down my body, stopping just ever so south of the small of my back. There's something so lovely about a man touching you on the small of your back, but there's something unspeakably sexy about being gripped just beneath it.

BJ tugs me against him and holds me there, tilting his head, biting down on his bottom lip, biting away a smile.

I give him my most convincing look of reluctance.

"We can't—"

He gives me a dubious look. "They've got rooms here!"

"We don't have a room here!"

"But we could . . ." he says, eyebrows up. "We could find the coat room—? Or a quick shag in the back of the car—"

I let out an incredulous laugh. "The car is right there, in plain sight—!"

He shrugs, completely indifferent.

"Nothing we haven't done before—"

I point at him. "That was never exhaustively proven."

"We have had sex in cars a thousand times," he tells me. "The Maserati might be up for debate, but we've fucked in my car, we've fucked in your car, in Jonah's car, we've fucked in Henry's car, we've—"

"Cheers, man—" Henry grimaces in passing as he flashes Beej a quick thumbs-up as he walks past us on his way to a waiter with hors d'oeuvres.

Beej sniffs a laugh, pulls a face and waits til Hen's out of earshot again.

"We've done it in a lot of cars, Parks. In more precarious locations than under a tree at my sister's thirtieth—might as well have a quick fuck in the back of this one." He nods over at his black Wraith we drove up here.

"A quick fuck?" I blink up at him. "I beg your pardon!"

"Oi." He tilts his head, baiting me. "Don't be such a toff."

I flick him a look as though I'm annoyed and not ever so detrimentally more attracted to him for it.

"I am a toff," I remind him. "As are you—"

"Come on." He bites down on my shoulder playfully and my resolve is weakening.

"Not a lot of room in the back of that Wraith," he says, eyes wandering all over my body how his hands would like to. "It'll be fun."

I breathe out my nose, and hope that my face hasn't given me away yet, that the answer is obviously yes. If the equation is his hands on my body, the answer is always yes.

Sometimes I don't much care for either public or daytime sex, it just seems sort of improper and I can get a bit in my head about it, but then—that top lip is calling my name, all extra pink, begging for me to kiss it and to bite it, and he gives me a quarter of a smile and I know he knows he's won.

"Fine," I huff, squaring my shoulders, before I glance down at myself. "Wait, but what if my dress gets crushed and overtly needs an ironing and your mother sees—"

"Then my mum finally will have to come to terms with the fact that sometimes when a man and a woman love each other very much, they take their clothes off and—"

I roll my eyes and smack him quiet and he laughs, slips his

hand into mine, and we move towards the car and everything is normal, everything is fine—and then suddenly, it's not.

Not in a way that anyone else would notice, just me. It's one of the sweeter things decades of life with a person can offer you, the ability to notice the smallest nuances in the posture of a person. He doesn't freeze, he doesn't even go stiff. His fingers tense in the most unnoticeable way, but I notice it. His stomach tenses and he swallows quickly, before he removes his hand from mine and places it on my waist instead—it feels different to how it did a moment ago, and then in a voice that sounds completely, totally normal, he says—"Hey, should we go?"

It's that hand of his on my waist—I've felt his hands on me like this before. When we've been out and something's amiss, or when someone he doesn't know gets a bit too close to me. It's the same hand he put on my waist when I was seventeen and we were in Prague and we were mugged at knifepoint.

Something, or someone, somewhere behind me has flagged to him as a threat.

I look over my shoulder, trying to see what he sees, but I don't.

Beej nods his head in the direction of the car.

"Come on, let's go," he says again.

I nod and take his hand that's stretched out now and waiting for me, but as I do, I take one more look over my shoulder—

And then I see this woman. About thirty. Dark hair, a tiny bit too much lip filler and eyes like a fox.

She glances our way and her eyes snag on BJ—not weird, really. Everyone stares at BJ, he's BJ. I stare at him all the time and I live with him; it sometimes simply cannot be helped, I get it.

And obviously, over the course of the last few years I've encountered many a woman that BJ has had sex with. I wouldn't say it's exactly an uncommon occurrence—and it usually goes the same way.

They're awkward, he's somewhere between awkward and apologetic, and I'm quite rude, because—please, for the love of god, fuck off—and I can tell most of the time, there's some discomfort there or maybe even remorse, once they've seen us together with their own eyes. Every now and then there's a girl who's really sexually aggressive, really proud to have fucked about with BJ Ballentine, wears his past-hands on her body like a pageant crown. They'll have a bit of a faff around him, cause a scene, make sure everyone in the vicinity knows what they did and how many times they did it. They'll flirt with him, sometimes flirt with me, bat their eyes for an invitation they're never, ever going to get—but this woman, standing over there with the fox eyes . . . it's different. How she's looking at him—I've never seen it before. It makes my stomach feel like jelly, actually, because she's looking at him with some air of ownership, as though he is a thing she has possessed.

And then BJ's hand is back on my waist again and immediately, I know who it is and who he's trying to protect me from.

It's a misplaced kind of protectiveness. He's protecting me how he wishes he was, removing me from the situation that he couldn't remove himself from.

I turn to face him, look him in the eyes and touch his face.

"Go to the car," I tell him calmly.

He frowns, scowls, almost. "What?"

"Get in the car," I tell him again, firmer now.

"It's fine—let's just get out of here," he says, eyes on the ground now, shaking his head, so I duck down and grab his eyes again.

"I love you," I tell him first. "It's not fine."

"Parks—" he starts, but I cut him off.

"If it were the other way around, Beej—in no world would you walk away from a person who hurt me how she hurt you, so do not ask me to—" I point over to his car again. "Now, please. Go to the car."

He licks his bottom lip, and I can't read his face. It's a terrible face, and BJ doesn't have terrible faces. Scared, angry, hurt, afraid, lost, ashamed—all of the above?

But then he turns, walking straight to the car without saying a word to anyone.

It is hard to love someone so much, I should like to say that.

When you think about love, there's an innate softness attached to it, do you know what I mean? Maybe it's that whole "love is gentle, love is kind" thing, and it is true. There's a tenderness to loving someone. It's Vaseline on the screen of how you see them, rose-coloured everything, picking wildflowers, gentle fingers dragging over cheeks and butterfly kisses.

But there is another kind of love.

A love like ours—you drown in it, fill up your lungs with it, choke on it and cough it up as you lay there dying.

There's a violence to loving someone sometimes.

BJ has fought for my honour a hundred times and he will a hundred more, I'm sure, because he loves me and that's what you do when you love someone.

That is what you do when you love someone.

And I'm not Daisy—I don't take Boxercise, I'm strictly a Barre and Reformer girl—I don't know how to fight, at least not with my hands.

I don't have a thought in my mind about what exactly it is I'm going to say to her—I'm marching on over there before anything's formulated in my mind.

She's standing with Jemima and Stephen, and when I approach, Jemima beams at me how all Ballentines (bar Madeline) do when they see me.

"Magnolia," she smiles. "Where's Beej?"

"Oh." I tilt my head. "The strangest thing happened, something suddenly came over him and he's feeling so unwell, I'm sorry—"

"Oh, no!" Jemima's face falls, sad for her brother. "So you're heading off."

"In just a minute," I nod and give her the sincerest smile I can muster in this given moment. "We'll do dinner," I tell her. "The four of us, to make up for it."

Jemima nods and then I turn to Zadie, who's not angled her body in my direction how a normal person probably would, but is instead peering over at me out of the corner of her eye. Down at me, actually. She's quite tall, because I'm not . . . not tall. I'm five feet eight, but she's taller than my mother, who's five feet ten. She's thin but tall.

"Excuse me," I give her a frosty, controlled smile. "Can I borrow you for a second?"

Zadie arches those already-arched eyebrows and points to herself.

I nod again, coolly.

Jemima looks a bit confused but Stephen pulls her away nevertheless.

I stare up at her, she—who's caused the person I love more than everyone and everything on the planet more anguish than I'd ever wish upon my worst enemy. I suppose (though in a way that's substantially less significant) she's caused me much grief as well.

I watch her face, waiting to see some hint of regret whisper over it, some sort of clue that she's sorry, or that she wishes she'd behaved differently, or even that in her mind, there's been a misunderstanding, but—nothing. She just stares back at me, a vague, vacant smile sort of present on her terrible, puffy lips.

"Where's BJ?" She glances around capriciously for him and there's a kind of fury in my body now that makes me feel shaky, but I hope that it's just on my insides and not showing on my outsides, because someone like her would see it as weakness but it's not. It's an anger that will seed in me and spread across the universes, traversing through time and space, and it will reverberate forever and ever until she's on her knees begging for forgiveness.

But here, in this horribly unjust universe where she bears no real consequence for anything she's done, she just stands in front of me blinking, as though what she just asked wasn't laced with a lethal dose of cyanide but is instead just a normal, everyday run-of-the-mill question.

How someone could be so flagrantly apathetic about hurting anyone the way she is about how she hurt BJ—and it's BJ! When you hurt BJ you're not just hurting a person, you're hurting light and wonder and summertime itself, you're hurting the air around us and the galaxy incarnate, and she's blinking in my face with the nonchalance you might expect someone to sport if you've just informed them they're sitting on an ant.

It's such an outlandish indifference, actually, that I wonder if maybe she doesn't know I know?

Nevertheless, I clear my throat and stare up at her anyway.

"We've never met, so I want to preface what I'm about to say by saying this: I don't make threats very often—"

Her eyebrows lift taller and she sniffs but I ignore her and keep talking.

"And I certainly don't make ones that I can't make good on, so when I say what I'm about to say, I want you to hear it and heed it . . ." I blink a few times. Wet my lips, square my shoulders. "I know what you did."

And for the briefest of seconds, her face falters.

I keep going.

"If you ever speak to BJ again, look at him—even utter his name, I will know and you will die."

She scoffs, it's dismissive. She rolls her eyes and glances away like she thinks I'm being stupid or dramatic, so I move my body into her line of sight and take her eyes again.

"Do you know who I am?" I ask with a tilt of my head.

Her jaw goes tight. She looks annoyed.

"Everyone knows who you are."

"Okay," I nod, appreciating the honesty. It'll play rather well into my next hand.

"Do you then know who I was with last year?" I ask, an eyebrow up.

And then there's a sharp inhale from the demon girl. She blinks several times in quick succession. I mightn't strictly like to know or acknowledge what exactly it is that Julian does, but I do know it's enough to scare people.

"Oh, so you do." I keep nodding. "Good."

I clear my throat.

"Julian would do anything I ask. If I ever see you again, I will ask him to do this." I lean in closer towards her. "And I wouldn't lose a second of sleep over it."

She breathes out a sort of scoff as she rolls her eyes, trying her best to look unbothered, but I can tell the tables have turned and she can feel it.

"So what, you just want me to never come back to London?"

I laugh at her question like it's silly and give her a smile that matches. "Only if you like living."

She glares over at me a bit. "I think you're all talk."

"Oh!" I lift my shoulders up as though I'm excited. "Why don't you take that chance, then—" I lift an eyebrow. "I've always wondered how far Julian would go for me and this feels like a happy way to test it."

SIXTY-FIVE

BJ

I don't remember the drive. From the party back to our place—? Don't remember it. The best I can remember are trees. Wooshing past the windows. The party was a bit of a drive, I remember thinking that on our way there. More than forty minutes outside of the city. So, lots of trees.

When Parks told me to go to the car—that was . . . weird—because I wanted to get the fuck out of there, needed to. But she wasn't coming with me, took me a couple of seconds to realise that. She was sending me to the car.

I've never left her before in any kind of place or situation that could hurt her, so her telling me to go and then her staying felt fucked. Unnatural, against all my most basic instincts.

I've protected her my whole life, but I think that was her point? I think she was protecting me.

I don't know what happened. I didn't speak when she got into the car. I didn't ask, she didn't offer. I don't think I had words in me anyway, I don't know why.

Bit stupid, really.

Hasn't sat behind the wheel of a car in five months, Parks, and it won't cross my mind til a week from now what it actually implies that she did. That she just climbed into the driver's seat, pulled out of the car park and drove all white-knuckled the whole way home.

I don't know when we got back to our place. When did we park the car—? She hates parking.

And then—did we take the lift or the stairs? It's all a blur.

I go to our bathroom, splash some water on my face. Sit down.

On what? I blink a couple of times.

The edge of the bath.

I look around and that's when I spot her.

Standing at the doorway, watching me. Eyes all big and heavy.

She frowns, a bit like she doesn't know how to help me.

I don't know how she can help me either.

Nothing's wrong, I guess. I just—feel like shit.

Nothing happened, seeing Zadie after however long, it's like, fucking all rushing back to me, it's just—shit.

Parks steps out of her shoes—the little gold ones with the butterflies—leaves them by the door. Walks over wordlessly and she kneels in front of me, between my legs. She stares up at me, looks—I don't know—sick? Nervous?

I give her the weakest smile of my life, don't know why.

She shifts her legs under herself, sits on them, shoulders square.

"Is that the first time you've seen her since—" she asks gently, trails at the end.

I swallow.

"Well, since Paili—"

"Oh—" She shakes her head, like she forgot. Maybe she did. "Of course."

She puts her hand on my knee.

"Are you okay?"

I look down at her, breathe out my nose—I don't really know what to say?

I drop my chin into my hand, rub my mouth, thinking back.

"You know I—don't even really remember it? I remember before and I remember after, but—"

She nods, sad. "That's a bad feeling."

My face falters, my stomach drops and I stare over at her intently.

"How do you know about this feeling?"

"I don't—" She shakes her head quickly, other hand on my other knee to placate me. "Not how you do," she clarifies. "But it's a bad feeling to not remember things in general. I've drunk too much with you and not remembered the night and you're you—" She shrugs. "You'd never do anything to hurt me, and even then it's still a rather uncomfortable feeling—so for you, Beej, I—"

"I told Henry a couple of months ago," I tell her suddenly.

"Did you!" She blinks, surprised. "How come?"

"I don't know—" I shake my head. "I just, had a thought one day, like maybe she tried it with him—"

And then Parks' face goes still for a second before it's just fucking rife with panic.

"Did she—"

I run my tongue over my bottom lip.

"Yeah—"

"No!" She gasps. "Oh my god, no—I can't—"

"No, Parks—" I tell her quickly, give her a bit of a smile.

"She tried," I tell her.

He said Zadie came up one night—sounded about the same, actually—he was about thirteen, asked if he wanted to play *GTA*. He said yes, because why wouldn't he? She gave him a Smirnoff Black and he thought it was weird but like, kind of cool because she was attractive. And then when they drank them, she told him she'd go get another—

"And then you walked in—" I tell Parks.

"I did?" She blinks, surprised.

I nod.

She frowns, thinking. "I don't remember."

"Hen said you walked into his room, looked at her, scrunched up your whole face—" Squash a smile at the thought of that specific detail. "And said 'Who are you?' And she said 'Just a friend' and you said 'Henry doesn't need another friend' and stared at her until she left—"

Magnolia flicks her eyes up to the left, trying her best to remember but her face just settles on a confused frown.

"And then you told her to tell Mum to order in Chinese," I tell her, nodding, smiling a bit still because of course she fucking did.

Magnolia stares over at me, brows bent, not blinking.

"You saved him, Parks," I tell her.

Her face pulls and shoulders droop. She swallows. "But not you."

Give her a strained smile. "Not me, no."

Her eyes go teary and heavy. "I'm sorry."

"No—" I shake my head. "Fuck," I sigh, relieved. Push some hair behind her ears. "Better me than him."

Her head tilts and she reaches up, touching my face.

"You're a very good man, BJ," she tells me, but my eyebrows dip because I'm not so sure.

"What?" She frowns.

I shake my head, pretend like it's nothing, not just my worst, absolute fucking deepest worry.

She takes her hand back and sits up straighter, looking more poised again.

"Tell me," she says.

I breathe out my nose and mash my lips together, thinking how to word it.

"It scares me," is what I go with.

She tilts her head the other way now, confused.

"What does?"

I swallow, like I'm scared saying it out loud means it true.

"That someone hurt me and the way I made myself feel better was by hurting you." I tell her that staring her straight in the eyes. Feels like the least I can do.

She reaches for my hand.

"You weren't hurting me on purpose."

I give her a weak nod because what else can I give her?

"Still hurt you though," I tell her, like she didn't already know.

She nods.

Breathe out my nose, try not to cry. Press my tongue into my top lip.

"I'm so sorry—" I tell her.

"No—" She shakes her head a million times, quick as she can. "I know—"

And then she pulls herself up from the floor into my lap, perching on my leg.

"Will you do something for me?" she asks, gently.

I glance around—we're on the edge of the tub. She's sitting on my lap on a bath—I stare at her for a couple seconds, waiting for her to realise, but she doesn't seem to so I just nod.

"Close your eyes," she tells me.

I close them.

"And think about that night—"

I open them again and look over at her, brows low.

"The Paili night," she clarifies, and my face pulls uncomfortably.

"What is this?"

"I read a paper by a German psychologist on something called Imagery Rescripting—"

My face falters. "You what—?" I shake my head. "Why?"

She sighs, impatient.

"It was in a box of Bridget's things—" She shrugs. "I actually thought it was about Walt Disney's Imagineers, but it absolutely really, really wasn't, but then I wondered whether maybe it would be good for you and kept reading it anyway."

I love her.

"Okay," I nod, not a puddle of a man.

She gives me a pleasant smile. "Do you know what it is?"

I nod. "I do."

"Shall we try it, then?" She gives me a gentle smile, tall eyebrows.

Another nod from me, then a shrug—like there's anything I wouldn't try with her, anyway.

Parks nudges my face with hers, telling me without telling me to shut my eyes, and I do as I'm not-told.

"You're at the party," she says. "And I'm not there because I'm sick. But Henry's there, and Jo's there, and Bridge and Al—"

"—Christian," I add.

"And Christian," she repeats. "And everything's fine, and then that beast of a girl walks in—and then what?" she asks, shifting on my lap. "We'll pick a new past."

I open one eye and peer over at her—she gives me a gentle smile—I swallow, close them again.

"She walks in," I start. "I see her. I—" Pause. Imagine for the millionth time what I would do if I could do it differently. "I walk out," I tell her. "Immediately. Don't even think about it, don't get my keys, don't find my phone, just leave."

She's doing this thing—and I don't even know if she knows she's doing it—holding my hand in her lap, rubbing her thumb back and forth over mine. Such an understated way of touching another person, it's so unobtrusive, and still, it does what she means for it to.

"I head to you—run, probably. Because I've been drinking, and I feel like shit and running helps a bit—" I shake my head at own babbling, but she squeezes my thumb.

"Okay," she says and waits.

"Let myself into your parents' house, go upstairs—you're in bed." My brows dip at the memory. "So many tissues scattered around your bed, and I'm pretty sure they'd been placed there for dramatic effect—"

"They had not," she says, and even though my eyes are closed I fucking know her nose is in the air. "I was very snotty."

"You'd never be 'very snotty,'" I tell her, still not opening my eyes. "You're too prim."

And then I'm smacked in the arm. "I'm not prim—"

I open my eyes and give her a look.

"Okay," I say in a dumb voice. "Are you also not beautiful? Are you also not fashion's Rain Man? Are you—"

She rolls her eyes, and gives me an unimpressed look for a half a second before she straightens herself out again. Pokes me with one of those fingers of hers I love.

"Keep going."

I stare at her for a couple more seconds before I do. Take a breath. Close my eyes again.

"You've come to my house. I'm in bed. I'm unwell. I'm extremely snotty and there are thusly the appropriate amount of tissues—"

I sniff a laugh, squash down a smile. Re-centre myself in the moment.

I remember how I felt that night, on my way to tell her after I'd done it.

So fucking sick, like sick to my stomach. Chugged a litre of milk and rode a roller coaster fifteen times sick. And full of dread—I've never been full of dread before but I was then. Like, properly saturated to my bones in it. Felt it in all of me, in my fingers, behind my eyeballs, in my pockets—and I remember thinking that night, maybe I could tell her. Maybe I should—maybe she'd understand?

And I stood outside her bedroom door for a minute or two before I opened the door that would break us up—tried to work out which was worse to say.

Decided that me being a fucking arsehole and cheating on her was better than me being something weak that someone fucked once a bunch of years ago. I remember deciding I'd rather her look at me like I betrayed her rather than risk her knowing that about me and not wanting me for that reason.

It was a properly visceral fear I had back then, what would change if she knew. That day on the boat when she asked me why, wondered about telling her then too—couldn't bear it—couldn't tell her about Paili without explaining the rest of it, because Paili's less than half the truth.

So even in this, this retelling of events, sitting here in the bathroom we share, in our flat we own, with her on my lap, my heart is pounding when I think about how I would have felt telling her that.

"I go to the bathroom—" I start. Swallow. "Throw up, probably, because I feel sick and I'm fucking scared to tell you—"

"Why?" she asks quietly, and I breathe in her question through my nose, feel it move through my chest.

"Because I . . ." I trail, pause, breathe out. "I don't want you to go off me." I shrug like it's stupid and not my worst, darkest fear. "Or think I'm weak or some shit like that—"

And she doesn't say anything, just presses her mouth into my shoulder and kisses it.

"You come after me," I tell her. "You're worried. Touch my

cheek, read my face like a book. You ask me what happened—" Take a breath. "And then I tell you."

"Do you look at me when you tell me?" she asks, but it's all muffled by my shoulder.

Shake my head. "No—"

"Why?"

"Because I'm chicken shit—" I shrug and I feel her shake her head, so I open my eyes to find hers glaring back at me.

"You are nothing of the sort, so try again," she tells me very firmly.

I breathe out, stare at her.

"I tell you, but our eyes don't meet because I'm ashamed."

She nods once, accepting that, closes her eyes and bows her head against my shoulder so I shut mine again too.

"And then you start crying"—I shrug—"because you're you, and you love me how you love me, and—probably, I cry now too, because you love me how you love me, and nothing shifted," I tell her. Tell myself. Breathe in the truth of that.

"Nothing on your face shifts in how you're looking at me—you're looking at me how you always have, and I realise," I shake my head a bit. "That I was worried about fucking nothing for so long—" I swallow, take a breath.

"And then you hug me," I tell her. "But you know me and you know what I need, so you let me hold you like you're the one who needs it and not me." Fuck, I love her. "You probably cry a bit more."

"Probably," she says softly.

"And then I kiss you."

"Okay," she says as she kisses my cheek. "And then do we have sex?"

"Yeah," I nod. "Because it's you, and I'm okay. And I'm in control—" I shrug and open my eyes, staring over at her. "And it's you."

She nods a couple of times, staring at me with these round eyes, and then she climbs off my lap and into the empty bath, blinking up at me.

She swallows once.

"Would you like to rewrite some history?" she asks in a small voice.

I look down at her a bit surprised. Tilt my head.

"You don't have to do that—"

"Oh," she sits up a little. "I would like to, if you'll let me." Another swallow. "If you want to."

I press my tongue into my bottom lip, stare so serious at the girl of my dreams it's almost a frown as I nod.

"I want to."

I pull off my shirt and toss it aside as I climb in, hover over her.

She's watching me with big eyes, kind of nervous.

It's funny. Something about it feels like the first time. Like there's a newness or—I don't know.

She holds my face with both her hands, searching my face for I don't know what—all the time we lost maybe?

I brush my mouth over hers gently and then pull back from her a bit, start unfastening her dress slowly and she doesn't take her eyes off me.

I tug the dress down her body—smile at her little, chest moving up and down quickly with her nervous breathing, and she swallows heavy.

I drag my finger down the side of the only body I've ever wanted to do this with, and I know she's wearing matching underwear because she's her, but I don't look. Don't need to look. I'll see them again eventually. Maybe not, I'm not sure if she wears underwear twice.

I lower myself down on top of her and she slips her arms around my waist as I do, trailing her fingers over my lower back, just above the band of my Calvins.

Not like her—pull back—give her a suspicious look.

"Where's the handsiest girl in England today, then?"

She gives me a flick of a glare. "She's quite sober, so she's not here—"

Sniff a laugh.

"This is all you, Beej," she tells me. "You're the boss."

"I'm the boss!" I beam down at her.

She gives me a look, pretends to be annoyed. "For now."

I concede with a shrug. "I love being bossed around by you."

She lifts her chin, face all proud.

"Yes, well, I am a very benevolent queen—"

"Yeah?" I tilt my head as I stare down at her. "And what am I?"

"The king, I suppose," she says with a shrug, before quickly adding a caveat. "Who's the boss and in control right now, of this specific situation, but in general, the queen is his boss—"

"Alright—" I laugh as I brush my mouth over hers. "The queen can shut up now."

She zips her lips with her fingers and then sets her hands down at her sides, staring up at me, eyes big and waiting for me.

And then I kiss her in a big way. Crashy. Waves on a cliff.

Slip one hand behind her head and use the other to unbuckle my belt.

She helps. Undoes the buttons to my shirt—silk, Gucci, has a horse on the back of it—then kicks the pants picked to match it off my body like she's treading water, smiles up at me, pleased with herself.

I brush the strap of her bra off her shoulder then kiss it.

Kiss lower and lower and her breathing gets faster and faster.

People prattle on about twin flames a bit these days, all these fucky twats on TikTok weakening the stock of it—pisses me off because they don't have it, we have it.

What Aristophanes was going on about in *The Symposium*, it's me and Parks.

In Greek mythology, when they were first created, the humans had four arms and four legs and a head with two faces. And then when the humans tried to climb Mount Olympus Zeus considered them a proper threat, so he split them in half and they were condemned to spend forever looking for their other half to make them whole again.

Lucky for me, I found her when I was six. Been a bit of a

fucking journey but here we are—pretty Greek, this journey of ours, all things considered. An odyssey of our own.

And I don't let myself mourn it—what was. It's done. Already happened. But maybe also properly done now in the other way too.

It's the best thing anyone's done for me, her doing this. This conscious amendment to the worst thing I've ever done, that I did to her, and that she's down here with me, in here—fuck, I love her—I push into her and her breath catches a little, how it's always done, even when we were too little to be doing shit like this.

She's not closing her eyes as much as she usually does, she's watching me, making sure I'm good.

I tell her I am in blinks and she swallows, runs her hand over my cheek. Getting sweaty now. She keeps it there, hand on my face—makes it impossible to look away. Like I'm looking anywhere else anyway, what with the self-professed benevolent queen staring at me with the only eyes I see when I have mine closed.

We've had some great fucks, me and Parks. Proper spectacular, earth-shattering shit. Sex with her is like sex with no one else. Don't hate me, but it's that twin flame shit again—speaking without speaking, a whole fucking language in our blinks and bodies that move like magnets, I'm south, she's north. My truth north, isn't she?

Fuck, I love her.

And this. Especially this, because this is different.

She's nearly there, and same, because—just because.

It's not rough or crazy fun, her nails aren't in my back how they usually are, fingers aren't in her hair, knotted and pulling, her neck's not thrust back and she's not panting how I always want her to be—but her hand's still on my face and her eyes are locked on mine, teary and big and—fuck, now mine are too—

That makes her nearly smile but not all the way because whatever this is here is too serious for smiles.

And then it's happening and of course, it's fucking incredible because it's us and I feel it through all of me; fingers, toes, down my legs, through my arms, up my neck, in my stomach, in my pockets, and even though neither of us make a sound that isn't our breathing, it's magic. Like, the best kind of magic. Phosphorus in the water kind of magic. Northern lights kind of magic. You know, like, blue lava, frost flowers, shooting stars. That kind of magic—proper, real magic.

And it's no big deal, just the thing that made us hold each other a bit differently because it was right there in the fucking middle of us, made us fold our bodies around the angles of it to get close to each other, the worst thing I've ever done—her and her quiet breaths in our broken bathtub with her hand on my face blew it away.

00:22

Bridge 💩✨

There are so many things I want to tell you.

•••

SIXTY-SIX
Magnolia

We sit across from Henry and Romilly at breakfast. Chiltern Firehouse.

Rom's eyes pinch as she watches over at us.

"There's something different—"

BJ tosses his arm around me and pinches his eyes back at her before he takes a drink of his Fireman's Drill. Which is a cocktail, yes, but don't be judgey, as a matter of urgency, next time you're there, order it and get back to me.

"Yeah?" Beej says with an evasive smile, eyebrows up, inviting her to guess why, but she won't.

Couldn't, I don't think. But she's right, there is.

The other day in our bathroom, it did something to us. Or undid something in us, maybe?

It's just been a bit different. Familiar and new at once.

Uninhibited in how we love each other, no elephants in the room, no terrible monster to skirt nervously around anymore—it just feels a bit how it used to before it happened, except also with the retrospect of the years we've lived since then as well.

"Yeah," Romilly's eyes search over both our faces for clues and I wriggle in towards BJ a little more, because—not even air.

He breathes out his nose and it feels calm and easy and he glances down at me, gives me the smallest of smiles that even if Henry and Romilly catch, they'll never understand the depth of it.

Henry's eyes pinch. "Did you get married secretly?"

"No!" I laugh, but my eyes light up at the thought. "Imagine, though!"

"Have you picked a dress yet?" Romilly asks as she takes a bite of Henry's bacon.

"We've narrowed it down to five," Henry says, tossing me a pleased smile.

"Five?" BJ scoffs. "How many do you need?"

"For the day—?" I list them off my fingers. "Ceremony, reception, leaving."

"Okay," he says, unsure. "How many suits do I need?"

"Just one." I shrug and flash him a smile. "The day's not really about you. Or me, anymore, either—" I frown to myself briefly before I plaster back on my happiest smile.

"Magnolia—" Romilly tilts her head, sorry for me. "I'm sure if they—"

"It's flown the coop." BJ shakes his head. "It is what it is."

A means to the only ends I've ever been interested in.

After that, BJ and I head to our appointment with Claire. We walk, take the long way through the park. A little more than an hour from Marylebone to Belgravia at the pace we're moving today, which is rather leisurely, but we both have long legs so it might take you longer.

As we're about to walk up the stairs to the office two girls stop us on the street, teenagers, about fifteen or sixteen—they ask us for a photo.

We stop and take one with them and Beej asks them questions about themselves because he's always been better at this than I am, but as we're standing in front of our psychologist's office I think to myself that a few months ago, I would have fretted myself to death thinking of people knowing we go here, and now, I sort of just hope that they don't post it and if they do, that no one figures it out. It's just a thought though, it's not a fret.

A great deal of today's session is BJ and Claire talking about him seeing that terrible girl again, and he's brave and articulate when he talks about how it made him feel. He tells Claire about how I had him go to the car, that it sort of annoyed him and it was something he was grateful for all at once. That it made him feel a bit stupid (which I interject to say that wasn't even sort of my intent) but that a part of him could appreciate someone defending him.

Claire turns and gives me a curious look. "What did you say to her?"

"Oh, yeah—" Beej sits back on the couch a little and looks over. "I didn't ask."

"Oh—" I shrug. "You know. Just some stuff—"

Claire rests her chin in her hand, waiting for me to expound.

BJ's eyebrows dip. "What kind of stuff?"

I shrug again. "Just stuff."

He gives me a sort of 'What the fuck' look, and I subtly nod my head back towards Claire because we're still not friends and I don't know if I trust her.

He rolls his eyes and leans over towards me and I cover my mouth and whisper a paraphrased version of what I said to the terrible woman.

He pulls back and looks at me with a bewildered face before he lets out a little laugh, shaking his head.

"I mean it!" I frown, not liking him not taking it seriously.

"No—" He shakes his head and reaches for my hand. "I believe you. I know that's true, it's just—" He sniffs again and smiles the tiniest bit. "I love you."

"So what happened after you saw Zadie?" Claire asks us, and I purse my lips, pressing my fingers into my mouth. I glance over at BJ, waiting for him to answer.

"Um." He flashes her a controlled smile. "We went home. Kind of—worked through some stuff—?"

He glances over at me to gauge whether that was an acceptable answer.

"Okay." She nods with a smile. "What kind of stuff?"

"I forgave him for sleeping with Paili in the bath," I tell her matter-of-factly.

"Okay." She blinks a couple of times. "Wow—that's—wow."

BJ's eyes shift over to me, top lip not quite smiling but resting in its happy place.

"How did you do that?" Claire asks.

("She's so nosy," I whisper under my breath to him, and he covertly nips me in my side.)

She does hear me though, I can tell, because she gives BJ a look before she rewords her question.

"Why did you do that, Magnolia? What made you decide to?"

It could be a million things.

Maybe it's because I'm stupidly in love with him, or maybe it's that I don't want to be with anyone else so it has to stop mattering to me. It could have been because I saw her, and I saw how it made him go—all in a way I'd never seen him go in any other instance—and I hated it. I hated how he looked afraid and ashamed and exposed, and it made me feel so sick and so guilty that when he saw her that one time, however many years ago, and he would have felt just as scared and just as shit—if not perhaps more so?—and then because of what happened after he saw her that night, he had to process that and everything else on his own without me. Or it could just be that these days I care less about how once upon a time he hurt me and more about wanting nothing to ever hurt him.

"I want to be with BJ, regardless," I tell her. "No matter what, I suppose. I've been without him before, it's not a life I'm interested in having—"

He glances over at me, eyes a little soft at the edges.

"The why I forgive him is because it's him and I don't want to be without him, and it wasn't that I decided I wasn't going to—I knew three years ago that I needed to if we were going to work, it wasn't a decision, it's that I was ready to."

She sits back in her chair and looks a bit impressed with my answer, and I'd be lying if I didn't say having the approval of a woman the generation above me thrills me a little.

And then she goes and ruins it by asking another fucking question.

"What made you be ready, do you think?"

I tell her, squaring my shoulders proudly, "Why isn't 'because I love him' a good enough answer?"

She gives me a patient smile.

"It's not that it's not good enough; it is good enough. It does need to be anchored to something though." She glances from BJ to me. "Because you've always loved him but you've not always forgiven him—"

I look over at my fiancé, and he puts his hand on my knee, that face I love waiting for the answer too. He's nervous, I think. That maybe I'll take it back. Which, I suppose, is fair enough, I have been known to be occasionally inconsistent and sometimes (but barely ever) erratic—

I shrug, glancing at BJ briefly before I turn to Claire, somehow it feels easier to say to her than to him.

"I just sort of realised—what he did had become the centrepiece of our relationship. Like it was a giant candelabra that sat in the middle of us, and it was covered in all sorts of wax from all the candles we'd put on top of it to try to make our dinner not be ruined by this stupid fucking candelabra that was just right there, all the time—and we'd have to crane our necks around it to talk to one another, and I'd have to duck and weave to see him through it, and then when we saw that awful girl—"

"—Zadie," Claire says.

"Yes, her." I give Claire a dark look. "I don't know, seeing her was like—" I shake my head, looking for the words. "An earthquake that knocked the candelabra off of the table, and then I could see him all unencumbered again."

I look over at Beej and he gives me an eighth of a smile.

"And the candelabra's still there—" I tell Claire. "She didn't obliterate it. But I just have no urge to pick it up and place it back in between us."

She nods, and I think she approves. Of course she does, that metaphor was completely brilliant.

"So, where have you placed it then?" she asks, because she's tedious like that.

"I don't know." I roll my eyes, a bit grumpy now and feeling shortchanged that no one mentioned the metaphor. "In a storage unit somewhere outside of the city."

BJ squashes a laugh and Claire nods, jotting something down before she looks back up at me again.

"Magnolia, do you understand that some days, you will wake up and forgiving BJ will have to be a choice—a decision you choose. It's not a feeling you always get to live with."

"Yes, obviously." I roll my eyes at the ridiculousness of her. As though I'm going to drive to a storage unit outside of the city? Please. "My sister told me that a long time ago."

BJ smiles over at me with this fond look he reserves just for her. "Did she?"

I nod at him.

"To forgive," Claire says. "That's a verb. That's doing—"

"I know what a verb is," I growl, crossing my arms.

"Well, can you do it?" she asks, eyebrows up, and BJ's watching me closely now. He's not frowning, his eyes aren't pinched, but his jaw's tight and his breaths are short.

"Can you forgive him even when you don't feel like it?" Claire keeps going. "Can you love him anyway?"

I give her a polite smile.

"I know that you're fairly new here, and I understand that you know him. Sort of—" I add as a caveat, because I shouldn't like her to get too comfortable. "And me, barely—" Which is true, so I don't know why BJ and Claire both look as though they smother a laugh when I say it. "If there's one thing that you should know about me, Claire, it's that I've always loved him anyway," I tell her firmly.

"Always," I say again, for good measure.

Beej reaches over and slips his hand into mine, squeezing it, and then he looks over at Claire, eyebrows up as though he's waiting for something, but I'm not sure what.

And then she does one, single decisive nod.

"Well then, as Esther Perel would say . . . your relationship is over."

My face falters with a thousand blinks and BJ's falls to a genuine scowl, and he opens his mouth to say something and then she beats him to it with her eyebrows all up in this sage, annoying way.

"Would you like to begin building a new one together?"

ASIA TRIP

MUST DO:

- SPRING EQUINOX AT ANGKOR WAT

- HOT AIR BALLOONS OVER TEMPLES OF ~~BAN~~ BAGAN!

- VISIT THE IFUGAO RICE TERRACES OF THE PHILIPPINES.

- SWIM IN THE KHAO YAI NATIONAL PARK WATERFALLS

- DIVE THE WRECKS AT CORON, PHILIPPINES

- MOTORBIKE THE MAE HONG SON LOOP IN THAILAND

- TREK HANG SON DOONG CAVES OF VIETNAM

- CLIMBING KAWAH IJEN ~~VOLCANO~~ VOLCANO, INDONESIA

- CAMPING ON PALAU KAPAS, MALAYSIA

- VISIT GUNUNG PADANG, WEST JAVA

- PLAIN OF JARS, LAOS

20:39

Allie Ballentine

Look what I found

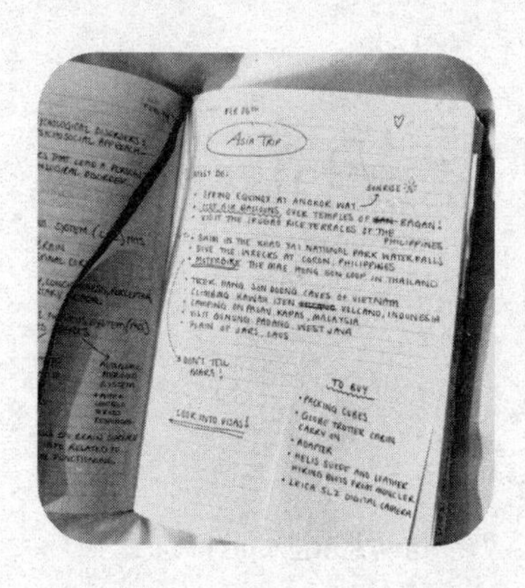

!!!!!!

Oh my god

You found it

There's a must do list

There's hotels nearby the sites that she researched for you to stay at

Ways to travel around

Thank you.

For finding this.

This is incredible.

It's a very outdoorsy trip, Al

A lot of climbing and trekking.

Did Bridget like outside this much?

I didn't know

The outside's just so cold here

That is true

And rainy.

What are the Plain of Jars

I have literally no idea

Well, good luck then

SIXTY-SEVEN
Magnolia

For BJ's birthday this year, he and I go to Heckfield Place. It's an hour away in Hampshire and we did talk about taking the plane for me but it would have been about a thirteen-minute flight and that made me feel silly. Plus everyone was so mean to Kylie Jenner when she took her jet out for a couple of minutes, and I can't be having people be mean to me right now, I'm just not in the mood.

So we drove—or, Daniela drove. Beej sat in the back with me, it was a little less scary than usually, I'm not sure why.

It wasn't my favourite thing, and I'm not rushing to drive unnecessarily again, but it was okay.

I do love Heckfield Place.

We've been before, not since we've been back together properly though.

It was one of those places we'd come to sometimes "for work," those trips we'd take to be alone without saying we wanted to be alone. We'd share a room and a bed and play make-believe for a day or two, pretend we were some strange version of the thing we actually are now, so I love it. I love being back here with him like this.

And we could have gone to an island, of course, or the Six Senses in Douro Valley—I thought about Rosewood Castiglion del Bosco or maybe even Villa Treville—but there is just something about him and I in the countryside.

The greenery, maybe. It used to feel as though it was mocking us but now it feels like a promise.

We didn't ask anyone to come with us, but no one was cross about it except Jonah, and even still, it was only barely.

Four nights in The Long Room, which is the best room in the property, and all we did was take walks and do spa treatments and more walks and some more adult activities on said walks, and it was the quietest birthday either of us have had in years and it was kind of perfect.

"We should never invite our friends anywhere again," he said as he kissed my cheek, an arm around me in the back of his car as Daniela drove us home.

Which, of course, did not happen. Jonah and I already planned him a dinner at Socca, and I'd been feeling rather tense about it because Taura wasn't going to bring Tiller, but then I realised Jo's bringing Bianca (though they are still playing the "just friends" card) and Henry will obviously have Romilly, so I told Tausie and now she's bringing Killian and it all seemed fine in the abstract but the closer we draw to the dinner, I wonder if Jonah might behave like a right brute towards Tiller or if by way of miracle, he will behave. And then of course there's the Tiller-Taura-Daisy thing we'll be navigating. Taura and Daisy have talked, I know they have—but Taura says less than normal. She said she asked Daisy if they could talk about it and that Dais said yes, but then just didn't follow up, which is a bit weird.

"She probably just feels weirder than she thought she would," BJ said on our way to dinner. "It's weird to see someone you were with be with someone else."

"Oh really," I blinked up at him, sarcastically. "Dated a lot of people, have you?"

"No—" He sniffs, looking down at me with a quarter of a smile. "You have."

"Oh!" Jo crows when we walk in forty-five minutes past our reservation time. He stands, opens his arms and hugs Beej before turning to me. "How are you this late—we planned this?"

"We got distracted." I shrug helplessly.

"With a fashion thing or a sex thing?" Jonah asks, sitting back down.

"Uh—both." BJ scratches the back of his neck then flashes him an apologetic smile. "But I haven't had birthday sex in like, seven years."

Nearly the entire table grimaces silently so I say what we're all undoubtedly thinking.

"Well—at least not with me." I flash him a quick smile and he rolls his eyes.

Hellos to everyone and all the birthday faffing for BJ—and then I notice two spare seats still at the table and no Daisy and Christian. I suppose they got distracted themselves.

"Did you have fun on your trip?" Banksy asks across the table as I sit down.

And I nod, smiling at her pleasantly. "Oh, it was perfectly idyllic. You and Jonah should go—" I say that last part at the end just to gauge her response and she lets out this flustered laugh and her cheeks go pink and her eyes dart around a bit, which is all a bit interesting, isn't it?

"Jonah—" I say to him across the table, wanting to see how he might react. "Hampshire was lovely, thanks for asking."

"You called me twice on your drive back," he says, flicking a look from Beej to Bianca. "It's an hour's drive."

"I think Bianca would like it up there," I say to him with a closed-mouth smile, watching for clues.

"I'm sure she would," he says, fairly unperturbed, and even sort of scrunching his face up at my smile, which is rude, and then BJ pinches me under the table so I pinch him back because I think he's nipping me a bit much lately, but then he nips me again so I do it back and then we're under the table nipping and pinching, trying not for anyone to see, but the detective, of course, notices.

"What are you doing?" he asks, watching us, and we freeze.

"Nothing sexual," I say with a wide, plastered-on smile, before I unclamp my forefinger and thumb from my fiancé's body, that will most definitely be covered in tiny bruises tomorrow, because nails.

"I wouldn't be so sure, knowing them—" Henry says, eyeing us.

"Are you American?" Bianca asks Tiller curiously.

"Yeah," he nods, smiling at his fellow countryman. "Whereabouts are you from?"

And then they start a conversation in American and I plant some common-ground seeds for Taura and Romilly; shared interests (Henry excluded), similarities and topics they both really organically latch onto such as the terror of AI as well as the wonder of Gwyneth Paltrow, and with that, I excuse myself to the bathroom.

I do actually need to go, but while I'm there, I have a quick chat with my sister because it's been a few days, maybe even longer than that.

"It's all coming up roses," she'd tell me with a smile.

And I smile back for a second because I've felt a tiny bit of lightness in my step lately but then I shake my head because I shouldn't.

"Not all," I tell her solemnly.

When I get back to the table, Christian's finally arrived. And I don't notice it immediately, that the table's a tiny bit tense when I get back, I don't sense that everyone's a skosh uncomfortable—well, I do, but I just thought it was probably one of those conversationally awkward silences where someone bossy finally puts their foot down and makes everyone pick from the menu once and for all.

So I drape myself over Christian's shoulders, hugging him from behind, and then go to kiss Daisy's cheek next to him when I stop short—holy shit.

Not Daisy.

That's not Daisy at all.

My eyes go wide and I clock the faces of everyone else at the table, all of whom look as bewildered and perturbed as I do, perhaps with the exceptions of Jonah and Tiller.

I press my lips together and sit back down in my seat, which as the fates would have it, is between BJ and Christian, the latter of whom I turn to.

I take a big breath and then breathe it out my nose before I calmly ask, "And who's this?" I point to her.

"Hi!" says the girl, upbeat, blonde, really bouncy, wavy hair. Pretty. Looks American but that 'hi' sounded English. "I'm Sasha."

"Hi, Sasha—" I nod at her, trying to but barely smiling. And then I turn my head to look at my old friend. "Christian, who's Sasha?"

Christian glances over at me, and because of who he is and what we were and what he was to me, I know him well. I know his face. Something is tragically amiss.

"Sasha"—he flashes me a quick smile—"is my girlfriend."

That smile though, it's dim. Everything about him is dim.

"I'm so sorry—" I stare at him, incredulous. "What?"

"Yeah—what?" BJ says, looking over at him. The whole table, all of them, pure shock, and all our eyes on Christian, except mine because mine are on Jonah. His hands are laced together and he's looking at nothing at the table, tongue pressed into his top lip.

"It's quite fresh," Sasha smiles.

"Is it?" I blink twice quickly. "How fresh, Sasha? Out of curiosity."

"Um—" She looks over at Christian, eyes bright as she thinks. "Gosh, probably like a week or two?"

"Huh." I pull a face as though I'm tracking it all. "Amazing. Christian—" I look at him. "Shall we have a quick chat?"

"No—" he shakes his head. "I'm good."

"Wasn't a question," I tell him.

He flicks me a look. "You *asked* a question."

"Okay," I nod curtly. "Let me rephrase—I'm going to talk to you now." I rise to my feet and pull him to his. BJ and Henry exchange looks and Taura and Tiller are whispering, but Jo, he's oddly quiet, and I hope he doesn't think for a minute that I've not noticed.

I look back down at this alleged girlfriend of Christian's.

"Nothing to do with you of course, Sasha—! Not at all!" I give her a strained smile. "In the wake of my highly publicised eating disorder—it's so comfortable, isn't it—? That you're here—?" I flick my eyes between Taura and Romilly before I look back at the new girl. "Don't get me wrong—please!— I'm absolutely thrilled to be dining tonight in the presence of a complete and total stranger. How exhilarating!" I keep that forced smile of mine firmly in place. "Are you a ballerina? Are you a murderer? Who knows—? I guess we'll find out soon—Christian—!" I glower up at him and grab his wrist before I drag him away. "A word."

I pull him around the corner away from all the eyes and out of earshot and he shakes me off his wrist.

"Get off—"

I stare at him for a couple of seconds before I overenunciate the following words:

"What—*the*—fuck?"

He rolls his eyes, looking down his nose at me a bit.

"You know, some people are scared of me—"

"Wow!" I roll mine back, unimpressed. "What a brilliant lot to have in life—! Regrettably, however, mine appears to be that I'm the only person alive willing to call you out on your shit—"

He lifts a brow. "And what shit might that be?"

I point back in the direction of the table.

"Who the fuck is that, and why am I being forced to eat dinner with a stranger?"

"She's not a stranger—" He crosses his arms. "She's my girlfriend."

I cross mine. "What's her name?"

"Sasha."

I give him a look.

"Full name."

He pauses for a second. "—Sloan."

I pull a face.

"That's a singer," I say at the same time a flash of annoyance flashes over his face and he says, "Fuck, that's a singer."

His face tugs in thought, trying to remember. "Uh—"

"Christian—" I look up at him, my tone different with him now. It's quieter, more serious. "Where's Daisy?"

"We're done—" he says with a shrug.

"What do you mean you're"—I imitate his shrug—"done?"

"I mean we're done, Parks," he says again, and I can see it right under the surface of his eyes. The truth he isn't telling me.

Then he shrugs again. "She's back with Rome and I'm with what's-her-name—"

"Sasha," I say for him, unimpressed.

He nods. "Yeah."

I lift a dubious eyebrow. "Sloan."

He shrugs. "Could be."

I shake my head and look up at him. "What happened?"

"Nothing—" He groans, rolling his head back. "Just, wasn't working—"

"It just wasn't working?" I repeat back to him, incredulous. "No!" I stomp my foot and give him a little shove. "Bullshit!"

His jaw goes tight. "Not bullshit."

I shove him again. "Yes, bullshit!"

He gives me eyes that are a warning.

"Stop it—" he tells me, and I give him a look.

"Or what?" I ask, my eyebrows up, daring him. Then I shake my head, annoyed and disappointed in him. "You were so happy! And you were good! It was g—"

"She fucked Rome," he says loudly, cutting me off.

I blink a million times and I don't believe it.

"No—" I shake my head. "When? She wouldn't—"

Christian swallows and then gives me a firm look. "Whatever you think you know, you don't, okay?" He nods. "You misread it. We were a fucking mess, we've always been a fucking mess—"

"Christian—" I touch his arm. "I don't believe Daisy would do that to you. Are you sure you—"

"Oi, Parks—" he sighs, in this way that strikes me as strange. Not broken how I'd imagine him to be broken by this, but defeated and tired. "I don't give a fucking shit what you believe. It's done either way."

SIXTY-EIGHT
Magnolia

I haven't been here in quite some time now. What—going on nine months, I suppose? I've always been quite fond of it here, it's big and regal and quite like a museum. Somewhere between neoclassical and Georgian revival.

The men at the gate don't immediately let me in, and I get cross and stroppy and then Kekoa sees me arguing with them and comes out.

"Magnolia," he says with a bit of a frown. Weird. People barely ever frown and say my name. "We weren't expecting you."

"Must I be expected to drop in on my friends?" I ask him with a polite but sort of impatient smile.

His mouth twitches and he doesn't smile, though I suspect were he not on the clock, he may have.

He leads me into the house and up to Daisy's room.

He gives me a closed-mouth smile that seems entirely too indifferent towards me, and I wonder if he's cross at me on Julian's behalf?

Maybe. He'd be a good friend if he were.

I knock on Daisy's door.

"What?" she calls through it—ever the picture of manners.

I poke my head in.

"Always with the charm."

Her face falters from her bed, where she's sitting cross-legged.

"What the fuck are you doing here?" she asks, surprised.

I pull a face and walk all the way in. "Hello to you too—"

"What are you doing here?" she says again, staring at me.

"What am I doing here?" I repeat back, blinking a few times. "What the hell is going on?"

She rolls her eyes, climbs out of bed and then picks up her duvet, tugging it up to the top of the bed to sort of lazily make it.

"Christian and I broke up—" She shrugs to the pillows she's propping up against her bedhead.

"You and Christian broke up, shrug?" I copy her, eyes pinched.

"Yeah," she says again with an indifference that just doesn't compute in my brain.

I stare over at her, shaking my head.

"You and Christian broke up, and now I have to have dinner with strangers—?"

"Um—" She tosses me a very unsympathetic look. "I guess."

"No." I shake my head firmly. "I refuse, no."

She rolls her eyes. "Then don't go to dinner—"

"Or—!" I give her a curt smile. "Why don't you stop being a fucking twat and go and work it out—"

"No—" She scowls.

I think for a second. "Is this about Tiller?"

She rolls her eyes. "No, it's not about Tiller."

"Then what's it about?" I ask again. "Did you have a fight?"

Her mouth pulls and she swallows.

"I don't care about Taura and Tiller, I'm happy for them—whatever—" She shrugs. "Christian and I didn't have a fight. I slept with Rome." She gives me a curt smile.

I stare over at her and get this odd feeling buzzing around in the back of my head that I'm talking to a stranger. Some other Daisy that isn't the one who's my friend.

"When?" I ask quietly, I'd wonder whether she'd mention it.

She shrugs like she doesn't care. "On and off since Dubai."

"When were you in Dub—"

And then she says '*fuck*' under her breath as she shakes her head, fixing up the things on her nightstand, which is an absolute fright.

Wine glasses, tumblers, books, used tissues—positively revolting!

"Doesn't matter," she says. "Christian found out, and we're done."

I take a step towards her, lift my eyebrows gently.

"He loves you," I remind her. "I know he does, and I know it feels impossible now, but I promise, it'll—"

"No!" she says, a bit savagely now, and something about her eyes makes me remember that once upon a time, a very long while ago, I may have been cautious of this girl. "I don't want your promises. It's done."

I frown over at her. "I feel like there's something you're not telling me—"

"Magnolia—" She says my name as though the very sound of it annoys her. "There are about a thousand things I'm not telling you, and haven't told you and won't ever fucking tell you because we're not friends."

My head pulls back and I feel as though I've been slapped, but she keeps going anyway.

"We've never been friends!" Her eyes pinch. "You fucked my brother, so I had to learn to tolerate you. And then I dated your friend, so I had to learn to be around you—but we"—she points her finger between us—"have never been friends."

And even though she's hurt my feelings, and even though I can feel my eyes stinging, I try my best to give her a look that implies we both know better. "That's a lie."

She tucks her chin a small bit. "Are you calling me a liar?"

"Yes!" I tell her as I roll my eyes. "Obviously. I literally just made that inference, right now."

She sniffs a laugh. "Brave."

"And you're stupid!" I tell her and she looks taken aback briefly before her en suite door opens and Romeo Bambrilla walks out in nothing but a towel.

I stare at him for a few seconds—because, oh my god. Oh my god! The depth of his hotness is truly . . . wow. The brown skin, the light eyes, the dark hair all wet from his shower. From one mixed-race person to another, like, truly, job well done, Bambrilla parents—but then I look away because—Christian, you know—? And fuck him.

Romeo wanders over to Daisy, pulling her into him, and kisses her in a way that strikes me as both unnecessary and frankly a bit crass.

He pulls away eventually and looks over at me, with a painfully cool smile.

"Magnolia," he says with a flick of his eyebrow.

Daisy crosses her arms over her chest.

"What are you doing here?" he asks as he tosses an arm around Dais.

"She's leaving," Daisy says, leaning into him, and she glares over at me.

I stare over at my friend, or—whatever she is. "What's the matter with you?"

She breathes in through her nose.

"Goodbye, Magnolia," she says as she turns on her heel and climbs back onto her bed, Romeo crawling onto it after her, and she almost had me—almost, but I hear a waver in her voice, the softest cracking in the history of cracking, but of course that's quiet—Daisy's already all cracks—she's one of the most broken people I know.

My eyes pinch. "Right."

And then I march downstairs to the one I'm sure has the answers.

I don't knock on his office door before I open it—though I do briefly hesitate as I reach for the handle to open it, brace myself that, knowing him, I might see something that I'd rather not, if I were given the choice.

I turn the door handle. Julian looks up from his desk—thank god—and looks confused.

He stands. "Are you okay?"

"What?" I blink, confused. "I'm fine—"

He walks around his desk and over to me, frowning.

"Nothing's wrong?"

I shake my head, looking up at him, a tiny bit disconcerted.

And then Julian gives me an exasperated look. "Then what the fuck are you doing here?"

My chin tucks to my chest and I stare up at him with hurt eyes. "Why do you both keep talking to me like that—? What's the matter with you—?"

He ducks down a little and sort of yells in this overenunciating way, "What do you want?"

That throws me briefly. I count my blinks—four—why is he being like this?

"I want to know what's going on with Daisy and Chris—"

He cuts me off, nodding his chin to the door behind me.

"You need to leave."

I stare up at him, incredulous. "I beg your pardon?"

"Did I stutter?" He stares back, unfazed.

I let out a frustrated growl and stomp my foot.

"Why are you all talking to me like this?"

"Why did you come here?" he asks in this loud, sort of mean voice. "You can't just show up like this—"

"Why?" I shrug. "You did! You came to my house when you thought BJ and I were over and—"

"And are you?" He jumps in.

"No, but—"

"So what the fuck are you doing here?" he asks through gritted teeth, and I take a breath—my head is reeling. He came to me, I thought it was fine. I thought we were okay?

And then he lifts his chin, stares down his nose at me for a second.

"You heard about Scotland," he says.

"No?" I look up at him, completely lost. "What happened in Scotland?"

"Barnes," he says, and it takes me a good few seconds of blinks and blank stares before it lands.

"Scotland Barnes—?" I stare up at him, and he says nothing. "You're dating Scotty?" I ask, and I can't tell whether

I ask it quietly or if it just sounds quiet because everything else has been so loud until now.

He looks annoyed I asked.

"No—" He gives me a bit of a dirty look.

"She's great—" I shrug. "I like her, she's funny, she's really cool, she's—"

"I don't give a fuck if you like her," he tells me, still cross.

"You brought her up, not me! I'm just saying that—"

"Stop saying things!" he yells loudly, and my mouth snaps shut.

Julian shakes his head, annoyed.

"Is this what you came here for?" he asks, glaring over at me; he was quiet as he said that but then he starts to get louder again. "To check in—? Fuck me up?"

"Fuck you up?" I shake my head, baffled. "And how, exactly, might I do that?"

And then he looks at the ceiling and yells, "With ease and with your eyes fucking closed!"

"What?" I say, back to quiet.

But he's not.

"Why are you here, Magnolia?" he yells loudly, and angrily, and—there's something else—? Something I can't quite pick . . . Stressed, maybe? Or worried? But why would he be worried?

I cross my arms and glare at him a little.

"I feel like you're up to something—"

He stares at me for a split second longer than he should, and it makes me nervous I'm right.

"Up to something?" Julian sniffs and rolls his eyes, moving past me to one of his shelves. He shifts something on it before he turns back around, looking at me as though he thinks I'm stupid. "Yes." I nod curtly. "Up to something."

"Go on then—" Another eye roll. "Enlighten me. What am I up to?"

"I don't know yet—" I huff as I cross my arms. "But I can tell something's wrong."

He gives me a sarcastic look. "Can you?"

"People who love each other don't just suddenly stop being together!"

"Yes, they do!" he roars, a bit ragged. "It happens all the time!"

"Not without a reason—" I shake my head as I move towards him.

He lets out this sort of tired, bewildered laugh. "You think I made Daisy fuck Rome?"

"No!" I stomp my foot. "I don't think she did it at all!"

He stares over at me a couple of times, blinking as though that's thrown him.

"Something's happened—" I eye him. "Tell me what happened."

"I don't know!" he says, shifting back from me.

I take another step closer to him. "Yes, you do."

His jaw goes tight. "No, I don't—"

"Don't lie to me!" I yell now properly for the first time.

And then he gets right up in my face, jaw clenched, eyes dark. "What happens with me and my sister, what goes on in this house, has nothing to do with you, yeah?"

I shake my head at him. "You can't just cut me out."

"I have cut you out!" he growls, and he's talking with his hands now. "You're with someone else—"

"What's that got to do with anything!" I stare over at him, confused."

"Why are you here, Magnolia?" he says again, shaking his head. "What are you doing here? I didn't ask you to come—I don't want you here—"

"Daisy and Christian belong together, and if you've—"

"If you're here about Daisy, why the fuck aren't you talking to Daisy?" He cuts me off. "What are you in here fucking barking at me for?"

I give him a long, stern glare.

"Because Daisy has never been the primary problem in her own relationships, you have."

Julian's jaw goes tight as he looks away from me, and he

shakes his head as though I don't know what I'm talking about but I do.

"And there are perhaps two people in the whole world who will call you out on your bullshit, and one of them can't come to the phone at the moment because Romeo Bambrilla has his tongue down her goddamn throat, so whatever's going on, whatever you're doing—"

"—Shut up," he says, interrupting me.

"No—" I scowl at the ridiculousness of him. "You shut up. Whatever you're doing, stop."

He runs his tongue over the bottom of his lip. "You're so fucking out of line—"

"I don't care—" I shrug. "Leave them alone. Let them be—!"

He tilts his head and his eyes fire a warning shot.

"Fucking stop telling me what to do."

I stare over at him, defiant. "Then stop acting like an arsing lunatic!"

And what happens next, if I'm honest, it did give me the tiniest bit of a fright.

He gets completely right up in my face, nose to nose, but not how he used to—and it rattles around my mind how strange life can be, that once upon a time in these very same walls, that he'd pressed his nose against mine, and his mouth against mine and even his heart (so it would turn out)—and that now his nose hovers not a centimetre from my own, and yet there isn't so much as inch of tenderness to be seen for miles.

"I swear to god, Parks—" he growls through clenched teeth. "Tell me what to do one more time."

"Are you really in my face like that?" I whisper to him, my voice probably a little more threadbare than I'd like it to be. "What are you going to do, Julian? Are you going to hit me—?"

His eyes flick down my face and I wonder if—for a second—he thinks about it as he stares over at me all threatening.

And something about how he's looking at me and speaking to me snaps on my pride like an elastic band, and it's as though I jerk awake. I square up, chin and nose in the air, and take a step towards him even though there's already nothing between us. It forces him backwards, he takes a step. It destabilises him for a moment.

He licks his lips and crosses his arms over his chest.

"Do you think I'm scared of you?" I glare at him.

He sighs, tired. "You should be."

"Well, I'm not." I flick him a look. "Because I know you, and you're all fucking talk—"

He's shaking his head again, runs his tongue over his teeth. He glances over at me, still annoyed.

"How did you get here?"

I shrug. "I walked."

"You w—" He stops short and makes this sort of laugh, sort of scoff, and presses his hand into his mouth.

"Did you bring Daniela with you?"

"What—?" I frown, shaking my head. "No? How do you—" He's always been good with names, I guess. "I ducked out while she was—"

He growls and covers his eyes with his hands, and he says something under his breath that I can't completely make out but there was definitely a "Fuck," and poor old Jesus may have gotten a mention.

"What?" I say to him, a bit put off by that last part of the performance.

"You need to go," he tells me.

"What?" I sort of laugh at the ridiculousness now.

He nods. "You should go."

"You should go!" I yell.

"We're at my house!" he yells back.

"I don't care!" I say. "You're acting so weird! You need to wind your neck in—"

"For what, Parks," he asks, chin jutted. "What did I do?"

"I don't know—" I glare, fists balled. "But I know you did something!"

"Yeah?" He crosses his arms over his chest that I used to rest on, and I feel like he's daring me to figure it out. It's there, something's there, he's done something, I know it. "How do you figure?"

"Because I know you," I tell him. "And I know your faces. You look guilty and you look like shit—"

The edge of his mouth kicks up, the faintest hint of a cocky smile.

"I've never looked shit a day in my life."

"Very few days, Julian, absolutely." I nod. "And only when you're lying."

He looks away from me and swallows. "Are you done?"

I nod quickly. "Very much so."

I step around him and start towards the door.

"Delete my number—" that terrible boy calls to me, and I nod once, happy to oblige. "I want you to fuck off." He points over at me, staring me dead in the eye, and then lifts a brow. "Am I lying now?"

I stare back at him for three, four, five seconds, and wonder whether it hurt him as much to say that to me as it did for me to hear.

"Don't come back here," he says, a look on his face that I hate.

"Why would I?" I shrug. "It turns out I don't know a single person who lives in this stupid house—"

Julian points to the door and I walk to it, not looking back at him once.

In the foyer, Daisy and Romeo are standing on the stairs and Daisy's face, it's still hard to read—has she been crying? Is she afraid? I pause a few metres away from her.

"If you need anything—" I say to her.

"I don't," Daisy cuts me off.

"If you do—" I talk over her, but she interrupts me again—

"Didn't my brother tell you to leave?"

I stare over at her for a few more seconds. "Listen to me, Daisy. If you need help—"

She swallows and blinks and then rolls her eyes, and now they won't meet mine anymore.

"I will come for you," I tell her.

SIXTY-NINE

BJ

I sit across from Jo at Apollo's Muse and take a drink of my negroni.

"Oi, what the fuck is up with Julian?"

Jonah rolls his eyes dismissively, has a long sip of his tequila. Straight, no ice.

"Fucked, if I know—"

I frown a bit. "What do you mean, fucked if you know—? You're his best friend."

His jaw juts a bit. "We're not as close as you think we are."

I pull a proper face now. "Since when?"

"Since—" Then he shakes his head, lets out this frustrated puff of air. "Fuck. Never mind. Why, anyway?"

"I don't know—" I shrug. "He was just a prick to Magnolia when she saw him the other day."

Jo looks over at me. "When did she see him the other day?"

"I don't know?" I say again. "The other day, a few days ago—"

He leans forward. "What did she see him for?"

"She went to see Daisy about Christian, and then got into it with Julian because she—"

"What do you mean?" Jonah asks, brows low now.

"You know her, man—" I sniff a laugh, shaking my head. "Like, nosy and shit. Just trying to work out what happened with Christian and Dai—"

"What the fuck?" Jonah says loudly.

Loud enough that I pull back in my chair, eyeing my best friend. Loud enough that it drew a few looks.

I lick my bottom lip and stare over at him a few seconds, let it hang there, make sure he knows no one raises their voice when it comes to her. Except maybe me when she's doing my head in.

"She was just trying to help," I tell him, and he shakes his head.

"She can't go there—"

I give him a dumb look. "Why?"

"Because," is all he says.

Annoys me a bit. "Because why?"

"BJ—" he says, proper frustrated now. "Fuck, I swear to god—"

I nod my chin over at him. "Since when?"

"Since—always?" He shakes his head. "She should have never gone there in the first place!"

"Hold on—what?" I frown, brows low now. "Are you fucking joking me—? You let her date him—"

Jonah looks away quickly, sort of says under his breath, "I didn't let her do shit—"

"Jonah—" I say loudly, staring over at him. "What the fuck is going on?"

"Nothing," he says quickly, and I don't buy it for a fucking second.

I press my hand into my mouth and lean in towards him over the table—look at my old friend—properly look—sixteen years of friendship under our belts. A tonne of shit between us, fuck-ups and piss-ups and knockouts, the best nights, the worst nights—first person I call if I'm in shit. I know him—I don't think anyone knows him better than me, or at least—used to be that way.

"Would you stop fucking lying to me?" I tell him.

Jonah shakes his head dismissively.

"I'm not lying, man—"

"Yes, you are!" I say louder than I mean to—a few eyes turn our way so I lower my voice. "So tell me, what the fuck is going on?"

Jonah leans back in his chair and folds his arms.

"They're dangerous," he says with a shrug.

I roll my eyes. "No shit—"

"No—" He gives me a look. "I mean *dangerous*."

"Alright, sure," I say, a bit lost. "Same as you, right?"

He turns, glances over his shoulder—for what?—tucks his chin to his chest, looks over at me, eyes low as his voice is.

"No."

"Come on, man—" I roll my eyes now. "Don't be stupid—"

"BJ." Jonah says my name and his voice sounds different. Serious, like. "I need you to promise me—you don't let her near them again."

"Jo—" I sigh and shake my head. "No—like what's—"

"Beej—" He looks me in the eye. "Swear it."

I lick my lips and roll my head back.

"Jonah—"

"How many fucking times, Beej—? Have you said a single word and I've just said, yeah okay, fuck it—" He shrugs. "Just followed you blindly. Trusted you enough to listen when you ask me to?"

I stare over at him and feel a bit queasy out of nowhere. He's glaring at me now.

"Would you please, for fuck's sake—for once in your life—extend me that same courtesy?"

"Alright—?" I shrug, what else can I do? "Whatever, yeah."

Rub my jaw as I try to think through what the fuck is going on here. Has something happened? If something had happened, surely they'd—

Shake my head, shake that fucked-up thought away.

"I don't think she's heading their way anytime soon anyway. She said Julian was a prick—"

Jo scratches his neck. "How?"

"Just an arsehole—" I shrug. "Told her to piss off, or something—"

"Right." He nods a few times to himself. "You make sure she does."

SEVENTY
Magnolia

Taura sits back in her Powis Mews flat, with a cross look on her face.

"Did you ask her if she's cross about me and Killian?"

"Yes," I nod. "She said she doesn't care—"

"Well, was she lying?" Taura asks, and I can tell she's worried.

She's worried because she'd never have ever gone there if Daisy cared still, but now I can tell Taura really likes Killian.

"No," I shake my head. "I really don't think so. But the whole thing was strange—her and Romeo immediately back to a thousand completely out of the blue."

Or maybe not out of the blue?

"Yeah—" Tausie squints. "That is weird."

I tuck my chin to my chest and purse my lips before I say it.

"Christian told me Daisy slept with Rome. Like—" I leave it hanging with a look. "*Slept* with him."

Taura shakes her head, not believing it either. "No."

"Well, no, that's what I thought too, but then she said it!"

Taura stares over at me. "To you?"

"Yes." I nod.

Taura's shoulders slump. "That's kind of fucked, I don't believe it."

I don't say anything, just mull on it all, all the things that felt like loose ends that now are severed instead.

"Did you see Julian?" she asks, watching me.

I nod.

"And?"

"And he was a fucking prick."

"He was?" Her head pulls back. "To you?"

I nod.

"I thought you said everything was fine with him—?"

I shrug, as lost as she is. "I thought it was."

She flicks her eyes up and pulls a face as she thinks to herself.

"Do you think Julian still has feelings for you?" she asks as she flicks her hair over her shoulders and I once again have the urge to tell someone what happened, what he said to me—but still don't. Less this time to protect him and more this time because I don't think it reflects on me well that someone can say they love me one day and a few months later tell me to fuck off out of their lives. I don't want her getting ideas.

"Well—" I clear my throat. "Before, I'd have thought possibly, maybe, he had some very residual feelings, left over for me—but now, no." I shake my head. "You wouldn't talk to someone how he spoke to me if you did."

I give her a quick smile.

"Do you care?" she asks, head tilted.

I put my nose in the air.

"Well, only in the way where I find it horribly inorganic and completely uncomfortable for anyone at all to dislike me even remotely."

She rolls her eyes at that before she asks somewhat carefully, "Did you tell BJ you were there?"

"Yes." I frown at her. "Of course."

And I don't like the implication.

She shrugs a little apologetically, but mostly like it wasn't a terrible thing to ask or infer.

"What did he say?"

Not a great deal, if I'm honest. He put his hand on my face and listened, brows low, nodding along. His face went a bit dark around the part where I regaled that Julian had told me to fuck off and not come back. And he wasn't cross that I went there, but I could see him thinking about something or processing something and then he sort of came to and kissed me.

'I'm sorry he spoke to you like that,' BJ said, and then he went on to say— "Beej thinks I shouldn't see them anymore—" I tell Taura.

She frowns a little at that and then goes to say something, but then someone clears their throat behind us and Taura's face lights up.

"Hey!" She smiles at Killian, standing to her feet and draping her arms around his neck in a way that makes me feel happy for them. "You're back."

"I'm back." He smiles down at her coolly.

"And I'm off." I jump to my feet.

"Oh—" Tausie shakes her head. "You don't have to."

"No, I do—" I glance at the skirt I'm wearing—the Blanca embroidered velvet miniskirt from Isabel Marant. "We're meeting BJ's older sister, her new boyfriend and his parents for dinner later and I need to have a steam first."

Taura flicks me a look. "You need a steam?"

"Look at me like that all you want—" I shrug, unfazed. "I'm the only one in our group who has a steam regimen and washes their face with Evian—"

"—Sorry, you what?" Killian cuts in, but I ignore him.

"And I'm the only one who consistently has absolutely fucking radiant skin so, you do the math."

"You're also the only one who's the daughter of a literal nineties supermodel," Taura says, but it feels diminishing of all my work with water so I pretend I don't hear her and keep putting on my dark brown faux-shearling coat from LVIR.

"Is Daniela downstairs?" Taura asks.

"No." I flash her a smile. "I'm just going to walk."

Tiller looks over at me.

"I'll walk you."

"Oh—" I shake my head, not liking the feeling of being a pain. "I'm fine, I walk everywhere. It's only four o'clock—"

"Yeah—" He shrugs. "But it's still pretty dark."

He turns to Taura and kisses the corner of her mouth.

"Be back soon."

We get into the lift and he pushes down.

I glance over at him.

"It's really just—a thirty-minute walk."

He breathes in through his nose. "Would BJ let Taura walk home in the dark?"

I look at him again out of the corner of my eye and then the lift dings and the door slides open.

"No, but most people are happy to be driven."

"Most people aren't T-boned by a rogue car on Vauxhall Bridge."

I say nothing but don't protest any further. It is a tiny bit darker than I anticipated anyway, so I appreciate it.

"My mom would have killed me if I let a girl walk home alone," he says, shoving his hands into the pockets of his 4 X 4 Biggie grey hoodie from Ksubi. Taura picked it.

That's a lie, I picked it and told her to buy it for him. I'd have bought it for him myself but I suspect we're not in a place yet where he'd willingly let me dress him, but hopefully soon because those eyes of his are just begging to be accentuated.

I smile up at him. "That's very lovely."

He shrugs as he glances down at me. "It's the American way."

I nod twice. "Is the American way also a terrible health-care system and a loose grasp on the historical context of the Second Amendment?"

He doesn't quite smile at that but he barely conceals it either.

"No ADHD medication today?"

"No, I took it—" I shake my head. "That's just what I think."

He nods once. "Fair enough."

He presses his lips together and something about his face, I can just tell he has something to say. I peer over at him, waiting for him to say whatever it is, but it takes all the way to Lonsdale Road for him to actually say it.

"You can't just—go wandering into a gang lord's house."

I cross my arms over my chest.

"I don't think"—I clear my throat—"that that's actually his job."

Tiller gives me a look. "It really is."

I roll my eyes. "Okay."

"No, Magnolia—" Killian says, stopping walking briefly. "Actually."

I square my shoulders.

"So you, as a detective at the NCA—"

"—you remembered my job!" He smiles at me, pleased.

"Knowingly dated the sister of a—" I use quotation marks. "'*Gang lord.*'"

"Yes," he says, unashamedly, and something about the straightness of his face makes me feel a bit nervous and pay closer attention.

And then right when we're at the corner of Pembridge and Bayswater Road, there's the obnoxious sound of an engine revving and tyres screeching and these bright headlights, and I jump in response (because—cars) and before I even have a chance to react beyond that, Tiller grabs me by the shoulders and pushes me back into a wall behind us, sort of bending his body around me like a shield.

The car revs again how those men with the tiny penises love to do with an engine; you know who I mean. The sad ones who hire a Maserati for a day and drive it altogether too loudly around Regent Street on a Saturday, and you wonder to yourself how small one must feel in one's self to be convinced it's a good idea to do something like that.

And all of that happens so quickly—the lights, the engine, the tyres, the me-being-thrown-against-a-wall-but-not-in-the-sexy-way—and I'm not sure what Tiller's waiting for to happen, but a few seconds pass and the only sounds I hear are those of the people on the street around us whispering or laughing, and then I see the flash of a few camera phones, and I stare over at Killian all wide-eyed, our faces oddly close for two people not romantically interested in one another.

"Sorry." He straightens up. "I just—" His voice trails as he reads my face, which says in big, bold letters *'what the fuck?'* He shakes his head. "By-product of my job. Assume the worst."

"Sure." I nod, watching him carefully. "Bit of an overreaction to . . . tyres."

He flicks his eyes at me and then laughs, licking his lips as he nods.

We cross the road and keep walking, in silence now.

A minute or so passes.

"Make sure you—" I nod my head back behind us. "Tell Taura. That'll be in the papers."

He glances at me, uneasy.

"The Wedding's Off! Magnolia and Her Mystery Man," I say, guessing the title.

He breathes out his nose, sort of a laugh, sort of not.

"Do you hate it?"

I nod. "So much."

"People know it's shit though, right?"

I shake my head. "No, I think—most people think we are the things they say we are." I shake my head more. "I don't even think people think we're people."

He lifts his eyebrows, makes a face I don't quite understand and puts his hands back into his pockets.

We're mostly quiet until we pass Clarke's, which I love and feel as though it's a bit underrated. BJ and I go there quite often. The menu changes all the time (which I hate but BJ likes) but all the food is incredibly seasonal. I think I like it there extra, because not once when I've been there has anyone come up to us, there's a nice quietness to it.

I tell Killian to take Taura there and he says he will, and then he bites down on his bottom lip, thinking on something.

"What did you think Julian did?" he asks eventually. "When you were together?"

I shrug. "He's an arts dealer."

"He's an art thief!" he says loud enough that it takes me off guard a little and I don't think I believe him and then my mind snags on Kirchner's *Street, Berlin* hanging in his bedroom, and I wonder—?

"Is he in trouble?" I ask quietly, staring over at Tiller. "—Is Daisy?"

He rubs his hand over his mouth and looks stressed when I say her name—our eyes catch and I feel a kinship towards him, because I think he understands. He's with Taura now and I wouldn't be with anyone other than BJ, but still I wonder if we both harbour an unshakable tenderness for those siblings we used to love.

He frowns rather seriously. "I think they've always been in trouble."

"Is it Julian's fault?"

Killian sniffs a laugh. "Almost always, yeah."

I lift my shoulders trying to figure out what to do.

"Well, do I need to go back there and sort him out?"

"No, Magnolia." He gives me a stern look. "You need to go home and stay away from them."

I frown defensively. "They're my friends."

Tiller frowns down at me for a few seconds.

"Then get new friends," he says before he starts walking again. "That goes for the Hemmes too—" He calls back over his shoulder.

I stare after him momentarily.

"Are you crazy?" I chase after him.

He spins around, brows back to low again. "Are you?"

"No!"

He shakes his head. "I don't think you understand how dicey this situation is with them—"

"What situation?" I shake my head back.

"Just—" He pauses. "—Them!"

"I've been friends with Christian since I was six," I tell him defiantly.

And then he retorts with equal defiance, "Then you have been friends with one of the most dangerous families in England since you were six."

"You're being dramatic." I roll my eyes, walking ahead of him now because I don't want him to see on my face that he's scared me.

"No, I'm not. You're being naive."

SEVENTY-ONE

BJ

"He was being silly, right?" she asked once Tiller left.

Appreciate him walking her home—good man.

"About the boys—?" she asked in a small voice, like she was nervous to hear my answer.

She said something about a car revving and him reacting fucking weird, and I had this thought for a second—wonder if—? But no. No, because I know that if anything, like—Jo would have done something.

He would have intervened.

Tiller's a cop, he hears about the worst shit all the time—his hippocampus is probably just fucking always on high alert.

"It's not really that bad, is it?" she said to me, upward inflexion, brows low. "Are they, I mean—?" She swallowed. "—Bad?"

I watched her face pull, sort of afraid of the answer that was hanging on the tip of my tongue. I don't know anymore, that's the truth.

"Of course, they're not bad," I said to her, thinking of the lifetime between us all that tells me so. I've seen both of them fight for the honour of girls neither of them know. I've seen them take money out for homeless people, thousands of dollars on the spot. They're good sons, they're good brothers. They've looked after me, and Parks and Hen when we've had alcohol poisoning, they've defended our names when we weren't there to do it ourselves. Jonah's covered my arse a thousand times in a thousand ways, more loyal than a naval officer is to his country—but are they good?

Define 'good.' Are they in line with the law one hundred percent of the time? No.

Does questionable shit happen in their name? Yes.

Would they do something ethically or morally wrong purely for personal gain? Listen—is that the measure of bad—? If it is, fuck.

I held her face with my hand and gave her a look that I hoped would wipe all those thoughts that were scaring her away.

Couple days later, Jo and I go for lunch. Annabel's, just. Nice and easy.

After, we walk down towards Piccadilly to kill time while I wait for Parks to finish work.

We pass the little Sainsbury's on Stratton Street because the other day I saw Magnolia eating some Galaxy Counters (not Minstrels? Weird, I know) but I was just fucking happy she was eating anything at all, so I nip in to grab a few.

While I'm standing in the checkout line, I spot a couple of girls hunched over a magazine looking down at it then over at me, whispering, and I throw Jo a despondent look.

"Oh, fuck—" I sigh. "What now?"

Jo glances over at them and nods at the magazine.

"May I?" He holds his hand out to them, waiting, and they sheepishly pass it over. He flicks through it before he shakes his head. "Same old."

"Who this time, though?" I ask with a grimace.

"Oh, that blonde fucking—the model one, you know—?" He shrugs unhelpfully. "American. Walks with the wings and the knickers."

"Oh." I nod, knowingly. Breathe out my nose.

Jo looks over at me, eyes pinched. "You did shag though, didn't you?"

"Not recently—" I shrug in defence.

His jaw juts a little. "How 'not recently'?"

I give him a dirty look for that. "Piss off."

He closes the magazine, putting it down where it doesn't belong.

"Don't worry about it—"

"I am worried about it though, man," I tell him as I tap my card on the terminal. Give the checkout woman a quick smile—"Thanks"—I look back at Jo. "It's too much for her." Parks, I mean. Not the checkout woman. "I fucking hate London—"

"So leave," Jonah says with a shrug.

I look over at him. "What?"

He shrugs again. "Didn't you say Allie asked you to go on her trip?"

I tilt my head. "Yeah, but—"

"Go," Jo says like he's telling me to stop by the ATM.

But then I think about it for a few seconds, kind of get this electricity skittering through me at the thought of being away from here with her.

I look over at him cautiously.

"Do you think?"

"Yeah—" Jo nods, thinking more on it himself. Like before he just said it to say it but now he's saying it because he's thought of it.

"For sure, yeah—for Parks to get out of here—" He gives me a look. "For both of you—it might be exactly what you need."

It might be. Feels like there could be some truth in there, plus, it's kind of our roots. Everyone thinks it's me and her and London, but actually—it's me and her and anywhere.

"Away from all the shit with her parents—" Jo keeps going. "Away from this shit—" He nods his head back towards the magazines. "Away from like—" He shakes his head like it's aimless, but I know him so I know it's not. "—Julian, even."

But that's enough to me; I stop walking, turn around and stare at him.

"What the fuck's going on, man?"

Jonah gives me a look like I'm an idiot.

"Wouldn't you rather she be away from Julian?"

My face pulls—because, maybe, sure, at one point I might have? But now—

"I don't—" Give him a little shrug. "Can't say I'm that worried about it."

"Float it to her, just," Jo says again. "I think she might go for it."

I look over at him, nod a few times. "Yeah, okay."

We turn onto Sackville Street, heading to Sotheran's without talking about it.

Don't say much for a bit. Find a *Midsummer Night's Dream* from 1908, clothbound and illustrated by Arthur Rackham, so I buy that for Parks, and the first edition of *We're Going on a Bear Hunt* from 1989 because one day, me and Parks will have a kid and who wants the regret of not buying this when I had the chance hanging over my head?

I hand the shopkeeper my card, flash them a quick smile.

I look over at Jo.

"You'd tell me, yeah?" I stare over at him. "If something was—like—" I pause, don't even really know how to say what I'm trying to say. Mash my lips together. "If she was—in . . . danger—? You'd tell me, yeah?"

Jonah frowns and blinks twice.

"Yeah. Of course—yeah." He shakes his head, and then he gives me a long look.

9:30

Daisy Haites

I shouldn't have talked to you like that

No, you shouldn't have.

I'm sorry

That's okay.

Are you okay?

Yeah.

Do you promise?

I promise.

I love Rome.

Okay.

And we are friends.

Yes we are friends.

I never want to hear you say I'm dramatic ever again.

You deserve a BAFTA for your performance the other day, my god.

SEVENTY-TWO

BJ

I sat on it for a few days. Didn't go straight to her about it, wanted to mull it over, make sure it really was what I actually thought was best for us, it is.

Feel like being here is a fog pressing down on us.

Last night when we were going to sleep she asked if I wanted to go away on the weekend, and I said "Sure, yeah. Why?" And she said, "Just because"—so I feel like she has the urge to get away too, just doesn't totally know how to do it.

I get home that afternoon after having checked back in with Al that she's still open to us coming and she was like, very, very ecstatic about the idea.

On the way out my dad stopped me and said he thought it was a good idea, felt like it was what all the girls needed, Bridge included.

When I get home, Parks is on the couch, legs tucked under herself, frowning like someone was being mean right to her face, looking between two books that she's holding both at the same time.

Left, *The Blind Watchmaker*; right, *Existential Physics*.

I nod at them.

"Just some light reading, then?"

She looks up at me and says, "Mmm," before she looks back down and keeps frowning between the books.

I sit down on the coffee table so I'm directly across from her.

"I wanted to talk to you about something . . ."

She looks up at me, eyebrows up.

"London's pretty fucked at the minute," I tell her.

"Totally." She nods.

"And I feel like maybe it'd be good for us to get away for a while—?" I say, eyebrows up and watching her closely.

"Absolutely," she says, nodding with a sort of glazed-over smile. "One hundred percent."

I squint at her, trying to gauge what's happening.

". . . Is there anywhere in particular you'd be keen on going, or—?"

She blinks a couple of times and smiles, more focused now. "For dinner, you mean—?"

I squash my lips together.

"You listen to anything I just said?"

"Mm-hm." She nods and gives me a quick smile.

I nod at her, not buying it.

"Repeat it back to me."

Her mouth falls open.

"Umm. Well—" She gives me a curt smile. "I would, except that I don't like your tone—" She purses her lips and she's full of shit and I still want to kiss her anyway. "And I think you're being patronising . . . and an . . . ableist—"

I lift an eyebrow, nodding, intrigued. "An ableist?"

"Yes," she says decidedly.

I squint over at her. "Sticking with that?"

"Mmm—" She flicks her eyes around, considering. "I think so."

"Magnolia—?"

She smiles at me pleasantly. "Yes, BJ?"

"Would you like me to repeat what I said?"

"Oh—" She shrugs, breezily. "Only if you feel you weren't clear the first time."

I give her a look and her shoulders drop a bit.

"I wasn't listening the first time," she says, and I laugh, pulling her over onto my lap.

I like this—the ADHD thing—I mean, she's always had it. I like knowing about it. Feel like we could have navigated things a bit differently if we knew about it before. Maybe wouldn't have had our primary means of contraception at school hinged on her remembering to take a pill, maybe would have entered into all our heated conversations knowing that she'd feel one thing all at once in a way that can take over her mind, and then later reason would come, would have tried to learn telling the difference between when she's actually listening to me and when she's just responding.

"Magnolia," I say again as I kiss her shoulder.

"Yes, BJ."

"I had a thought—"

"And I am listening!" she declares with a big smile that shifts quickly into an apologetic one. "—Now."

I flick her a look, squashing a smile. "You know how we always said it was London, not us, that was the problem—"

"Yes." She nods. "Although, sort of in retrospect, it was probably a little bit us—?"

"Yeah—" I sniff. "A little bit." I dig my chin mindlessly into her shoulder. "I feel like we need to get out of here for a bit—"

Her eyebrows dip. "What do you mean?"

"Let's go somewhere," I say with a shrug.

"Well, I said about Devon on the weekend, didn't I?" She looks at me. "We haven't been to Hotel Endsleigh in a while—"

I give her a small smile, push some hair behind her ears. "I meant a bit further away."

"Like, France—?" she asks.

"Sure," I nod. "France, America, Tahiti, Australia—I don't care—just, I want us to be away for a while."

"BJ—" She sighs, rolling her eyes. "We're planning a wedding."

I give her a look. "We're planning a circus."

"And who will herd the monkeys if I don't?" she asks.

My eyes pinch. "I don't think you herd monkeys?"

She gives me a look. Right, let's try another route.

"The wedding planner," I tell her, and she gives me another reluctant look but I can see her resolve already weakening, so I put my hand on her waist and squeeze. "Come on, we don't even like it—we're doing it for them, not for us." I shrug. "What does it matter whether the china's perfect and how the aisle looks?"

She frowns a bit at that. "It's still our wedding."

I nod. "The part about the wedding you care about is the dress, yeah?"

She straightens up, proud. "And the vows."

I shrug. "I don't care about any of it."

And that—I realise quick—wasn't the right thing to say. She's completely off me for that. Whole face scrunches up in offence. "Not even the vows?"

Touch her chin with my finger, lift it so she gives me her eyes again, and then I look at her all solemn. "I avowed myself to you a long time ago, Parksy."

She blinks twice, face shy.

"I don't need new ones. I'm in." I give her a shrug. "Always have been."

She swallows heavy, eyes go to mush. Feel it in the air that we're probably going to have sex in a minute, and then she conjures a frown again, still wanting to have a strop because she's like that.

Arms cross, little glare in her eyes that's at least 50 percent manufactured.

"You don't care about any single part of our wedding?"

"Nope—" I shake my head. "I care about the day after," I offer with a shrug.

That doesn't appease her much, though. Eyebrows shoot up and she stares at me like I'm ridiculous.

"The day after?" She blinks.

"Yeah," I nod, coolly, ready to deliver my trump card. "The life with you."

I flick my eyebrows at her, knowing before I even look at her how her face looks.

Eyes like rock pools at sunset. Soft and calm and a few different colours at once.

"Oh," she says, swallows again.

"The fanfare of the day, that's for everyone else—" I say to her, and she pushes her hand through my hair.

"I'll take the tomorrow," I tell her.

She jumps to her feet, spinning around to face me again, mouth pursed, hands on her hips.

"Okay, well—so how long for?"

"A while." I shrug.

Eyebrows go up. "For any reason in particular?"

I blow some air out of my mouth.

"How about because our private lives are fucking fodder for the red tops?" I say, and her face pulls. I squint at her, apologetic. "You saw the magazine?"

Parks nods, quiet.

"You didn't say anything?" I ask, feel a bit worried that she didn't.

She shakes her head.

"Why not?" I ask.

"Because I trust you," she says, nose in the air.

Kind of smile at that, stop it short before it gets too big though because I don't want to look like a fucking idiot. And then I see her face flicker with more there, so I lift up an eyebrow and wait for her.

"And because I know you've hooked her before a while ago, but since then she's had a lot of work done—which, fair play to her, I don't judge, if she feels good, that's great, it's just—" She gives a demure, little shrug. "Not really your speed anymore."

"No," I stand up, sniffing a laugh as I put my hands on her waist. "I've only really ever had one speed." Press my mouth against hers for a couple of seconds before I pull back.

"What do you think? Want to run away for a bit?"

Parks purses her lips, thinking. "Just you and I?"

I give her a squint. "And Allie?"

"Oh." She pulls back, less hesitant now.

"Bit of a last hoorah for Bridge," I offer. "Take the trip she couldn't—?"

Her lips twist in thought. "Just us and Allie?"

I nod a couple of times.

"And the girl in the mirror," I say as I look down at her, my head tilted to the side.

Our eyes hold and she gives me a shy, almost nervous look.

And then she nods.

"Okay."

22:17

Henny Pen 🐓

I'm coming!

Vulgar.

Funny

That was a good one

Don't act surprised, I'm hilarious

Soon I will be the funniest Ballentine

Do you mean the funniest looking Ballentine?

Went and took yourself out of the running there with that one . . .

I know that was so shit.

I meant on the trip

Really!

Yeah

Why?

Rom's got to go back to America for a few weeks anyway. Don't know what I'd do in London otherwise

Cute

And clingy

That's how I've described you for years

How the tables have turned

SEVENTY-THREE

Magnolia

I stare at my closet with pinched eyes, hands on my hips.

"Do you think I'll need the Loro Piana sherpa jacket?"

Gus clicks his tongue. "In southeast Asia?"

"Yes." I nod.

"In March?"

"Mm-hm." I nod, glancing over my shoulder at him.

Gus blows some air out of his mouth, thinking about it. "I think you'll probably be okay without it."

"Hmm." I move my head side to side. "Why risk it though?"

And then I toss it into my open suitcase from the Casablanca x Globe-Trotter collaboration.

I hold up the extremely pink floral-embroidered gown from Carolina Herrera against myself and tilt my head in the mirror as I hum again.

"Attending a gala while you're there?" Gus asks, and I give him a sharp look.

"I could."

"It would be very like Bridge to go halfway across the world to attend a gala," he says to me, and I pinch my eyes at him and he pinches his back, so I put the gown in the maybe pile.

"Spoken to your dad lately?" he asks after about thirty seconds of silence.

"Who?" I ask, because I'm funny like that, and then I shoot him a look and he rolls his eyes.

"Of course not," I say. "I don't speak to him at the best of times, let alone when he makes a public spectacle wishing I were dead."

Gus purses his lips. "That's a bit of a paraphrase."

I hand him the soft beige reversible belted shearling coat from Brunello Cucinelli to fold and he gives me a look.

"And yet much of its intent all the same."

His eyes drop from mine and he looks sad for me or sorry for me, or caught a bit because my father is his boss, or whatever.

There's something quite enigmatic about my father, I know that much.

BJ and usually Henry are the only two males I know who don't fall for his shit.

He's a bit of a black hole, there's something rather magnetic about him. Men lose time in his presence, at writing retreats with him, people won't speak to their significant other for days. It's as though there's a gravity you slip into in my father's presence that's stronger than any reality might offer you.

Julian is quite fond of my father, and Julian would consider himself a great reader of people. Let that be a measuring stick for how enrapturing a man he can be.

Gus, even after working with Harley now for nearly five years, still isn't quite immune to his charms.

He's aware he can be a bit shit, but I think he thinks it's all fair play. The way we all know that celebrities are usually absolute whackadoos and you make excuses because they grew up in a boy band or she was on Nickelodeon and kissing a Jonas brother when she was fourteen or something.

Comes with the territory, is what I mean. Which is true, much of who Harley is comes with the territory.

Every now and then I can tell that Gus thinks Harley's being silly or tempestuous. I know that when Harley hired Brooks that Gus thought he was a few sandwiches short of a picnic, but to be completely honest, I've enjoyed the stories I've had regaled to me since then.

I—and I cannot stress this enough—for the life of me, cannot understand why Harley hired Brooks.

He'd drive him mental, I know it. Gus says they actually fight all the time, which I love. I have a working theory that he subconsciously hired him so he'd fight with Brooks instead of my mother, which is weird, but sweet?

Can narcissistic arseholes be sweet?

"Where are we with Jack these days?" I look over at Gus so I can properly see his face, lest he try to lie to me about it.

I fetch my little Schuyler Maltese compact mirror from Jay Strongwater and slip it into my little Tangerine crystal-embellished gold-tone clutch from Judith Leiber Couture, so I can talk to my sister whenever I need to.

That's going to be my primary handbag for the trip. I've never had a primary handbag before, it's quite restrictive, stylistically speaking. I suppose that's why so many people have black bags? Completely boring but rather versatile?

"Good—" he says, squinting, as though he's not so sure. "I think good."

I stop what I'm doing and look over at him, waiting for more.

"Okay."

"He's really one-eightied with that Taj Owen."

I nod once, proud on his behalf. "So he should."

Gus's face pinches, looking much less sage than it often does. "I'm not entirely sure I trust him anymore?"

I nod, rather familiar with the perils of not trusting the person you love.

"In my limited experience," I give him a small smile. "It's rather difficult for someone to earn your trust unless you open yourself up to being completely tortured and hurt by them again."

"Oh, good." He gives me an unceremonious look that turns a bit suspicious. "I don't like you having sage relationship advice that makes sense—"

"What can I say, Gus?" I shrug, flipping my hair over my shoulders and continuing to pack. "It was bound to happen eventually."

He rolls his eyes and at the same time, removes both the green Ribbon Candy stilettos from Gianvito Rossi as well as Prada's black gabardine après-ski boots from my suitcase.

"Unnecessary, Magnolia—" He eyes me. "You don't need these."

"I might."

"You aren't going to the snow!"

I glare over at him. "Life is a journey, Gus—and you, just—don't know where it'll take you."

"Totally." He nods emphatically. "But I do know it's not taking you to any snow fields, so—no."

We have a little standoff with our eyes and then he rolls his first, which I think we all know means I won.

"So Hen's going too?" Gus asks, refolding some things I already folded.

"He is." I nod.

"Why?" Gus asks.

"Oh," I shrug. "Romilly has some things she has to finish up in America so she's going back there for a little while, and I don't know—he said Christian said it in passing and then he thought, 'why not—?'"

Gus nods, accepting it.

And same, I accept that too. That's completely perfectly, totally acceptable. Nothing at all to get caught up on mentally. Except that—there is this one thought, somewhere deep in my mind. It feels like a scratching at a window, when it's dark at night and you're home alone, and it's probably just a tree—but it mightn't be just a tree?— It could be something a bit more nefarious, it could be something that was there all along . . . A threat that you knew about, in an abstract kind of way, but it always felt so far away and so unreal—even if it was a bit, technically, real—it never actually posed any genuine threat . . . except sometimes, at nighttime when you're alone in your house and there's a scratching at the window that— But as I said, it almost definitely probably is very likely to be merely a tree branch.

But what if it wasn't a tree branch?

So I told Henry to come with enthusiasm. And when BJ grumbled about his brother tagging along I was quick to make sure he knew I wanted him there, because even if it is just a tree branch which I'm sure it is because there's literally nothing else, no other possible thing on the planet it could be (except one other thing that it definitely, absolutely couldn't be because none of them would allow it). And besides, it definitely is just a tree branch and anyway, those are actually very dangerous and can take out your eye.

I'm not worried about Taura at all because I don't have a reason to be, because nothing at all is wrong other than there are branches in the world, which isn't technically a threat, and also, she's with Tiller now.

"Woah," BJ says when he walks into the room, interrupting my little mental slip and slide, which I'm grateful for, but also barely. Because everything's fine.

He eyes my two large suitcases, one medium suitcase and the Centenary 125 carry-on from Globe-Trotter, which doesn't match the other two, but I don't know what I'm wearing on the plane yet and brown matches a lot of my wardrobe and a small silver briefcase sort of gives *Deal or No Deal*, no?

Can I just say—I know it might be beneath my tax bracket to admit it but one time BJ and I found an arcade version of *Deal or No Deal* and I think we spent about £2,000 playing it. It's a cracker of a game. I don't blame Meghan Markle for partaking in it one bit, it's highly addictive.

"Parksy—" Beej clears his throat, eyeing my suitcases. "Do you remember when I said this was going to be like, a singular-suitcase trip?"

"Yes!" I wander over to him, slipping my arms around his waist and grinning up at him. "That was a funny one. You don't get enough credit for your wit."

I boop him on the nose and he blinks a lot.

"Did you just boop me?" he asks, staring at me.

"I—" Boop him again. "—Did."

"I'm leaving you," he tells me with a straight face, and I roll my eyes.

"Really, man?" Gus says, walking over to him to hug him hello. "Booping's the line—?" Gus shakes his head curiously. "Not Tommy, or Julian or Christian—a little—" he reaches over and boops BJ too.

BJ gives him a tight smile that is 80 percent amused and 20 percent actually annoyed.

"I'm not helping you carry these around Asia." He points nondescriptly to my suitcases.

I pout. "Yes, you are!"

"I'm not." He shakes his head.

"But what about in sickness and in health?" I frown. "This is my sickness."

"We haven't said the vows yet." He gives me a look.

"So it was all for show—?" I stare at him. "Your cute, sexy spiel about already being avowed to me—? What was that?"

Gus looks between us, eyebrows up, waiting.

"—Heard about that speech, man." He gives Beej a wink. "Very sexy stuff."

BJ rolls his eyes.

"I have promised to love you forever a thousand times, Parks." He lifts an eyebrow. "I have, however, never promised to herniate discs for you. One bag."

Then he boops me on the nose and walks out my room.

"I'm going to unpack all my lingerie!" I call after him.

He pokes his head back through the door very immediately, eyebrows up. Gus chuckles as BJ blows some air out of his mouth.

"On second thought—" He squints back over at me. "What's a couple of extra suitcases between lovers?"

22:41

Tausie ❤

What will I do without you??

Have very incredible sex with the fireman.

*detective

But he does dress up as a fireman for you, yes?

Magnolia.

Taura, if the answer to that question isn't 'yes', I'm sorry to say but that man is cheating you out of what is rightfully yours

You're an idiot.

I'm going to miss you

Me too.

I won't be long.

A mere blip on your radar, if your radar is filled with emergency responder role-play

At least I know what we're doing for your bachelorette night?

TILLER?

☹

Jokes.

SEVENTY-FOUR

BJ

Even though I tell her she should, Magnolia doesn't tell her parents we're going away for a while, not even her mum.

She does tell my mum that she can tell her mum "if she sees fit" but also clarified she wasn't sure why or how it would affect them, considering she doesn't live there and they've not been parentally responsible for her since she "left uteri" (her words, not mine).

We fly out in a few days, we're all pretty relaxed about when, exactly. But Taura and Tiller are taking a trip to Hvar tomorrow, so Parksy's having a goodbye dinner with Taus and Gus.

Goodbye seems a little dramatic. There's not really a time limit on the length of our trip, that's all. Could be going two weeks, could be gone six.

Hen and I have a night with the boys, not as a goodbye—because what are we saying goodbye for?—and it's weird, because it's not a *good*bye, right? But then, it's something.

As soon as we walk in to Boodle's and spot the boys, there's a weight to it.

Jo jeers when he sees us, same how he always does, and I wonder if it's in my mind—tell myself that it is—but I feel like the edge of his smile sags a bit. Like, there's an innate heaviness to him that wasn't there before and now it's there all the time.

Henry's asking the boys about Scotty, their cousin who's in town. Always wanted a crack at her but she was strictly off limits to us all according to Jo, and even that conversation—benign as they come—bears this strange conversational weight I don't understand.

"She been here a while then?" Hen asks.

Jo shrugs. "A bit, yeah."

"Holiday?" I ask.

Christian has a drink of his Sazerac. "Scotty loves a holiday."

"Needed a break from Australia," Jo says.

I smack Christian in the arm. "And that girlfriend of yours, what's her name—?"

"Sasha," Christian and Jonah say in unison.

Henry and I exchange amused looks.

I nod my chin at Christian. "How's that going?"

"Yeah." He shrugs. "Fine."

"You like her then?" I ask, curiously.

"Sure, yeah." He blinks, takes another drink. Fuck that, he fucking sinks that drink, actually. Calls over the waiter, orders another round without asking if anyone else wants more, more is coming.

I've watched Christian properly love two girls now, one of them was mine. I know what he looks like when he loves a girl and he's not even in the fucking ballpark.

I sit back in my chair, cross my arms and shake my head at him. "What are you doing, man?"

"What?" he asks with a frown.

"I don't want to cross a line, but actually—what are you doing?"

He shrugs, gets a look on his face.

"I don't know what you're talking about," he says, even though he does.

"Oh, come off it—" Henry jumps in. "I get that Daisy cocked up, but what's the point of dating some girl you're not into?"

Jonah looks over at Christian, gives him this long, weighted look that I don't understand but I also don't like. Does this thing with his eyebrows, this flick up. Says something to his brother that I don't know about, that I'm not meant to know about, that I get the feeling we've been kept in the dark about.

"She's hot, she's good in the bedroom and she doesn't talk a lot." Christian shrugs. "Checks my boxes."

"Since fucking when?" Henry gives him a look. "You've been into two girls, ever, and they're the mouthiest girls in the world."

Don't even give my brother a side-eye for that, I'm too interested to see how Christian responds.

But it's not Christian's response that flags to me, it's Jo again. Angles his jaw towards Christian, flicks his eyes, watches.

Christian rubs his mouth, tired.

"Can we change the subject?" he asks.

I nearly say "To what?" but I don't because something about it all feels too fucking sad.

Henry brings up The Ashes, which we're going to this year with Dad, asks the boys if they want to come. We bang on about cricket for a bit, Hen asks how their uncle is, the Australian one, Scotty's dad—the conversation fucking nosedives again.

I don't make much of an excuse for it when I go to the bar to order, just for a fucking reprieve.

Jo follows me up there and I wish he hadn't, because it forces my hand and he knows it.

He leans against the counter, looks straight ahead.

"If you've got something to ask, just ask," he says to the top shelf.

I look over at him. Squint. "You're in some shit."

He juts his jaw. "Didn't hear a question in there."

"I didn't ask one," I tell him.

He says nothing. I order us a couple of negronis. Turn around. Face the other way.

"How bad is it?" I ask.

He presses his lips together, squints at the top-shelf whiskeys.

"Fuck," I sigh under my breath.

He looks over at me, annoyed. "I didn't say anything."

"You didn't fucking have to," I whisper back, voice sharp now. I lean towards him, quietly ask, "Do you need money?"

He gives me a dirty look. "Fuck off."

I turn to him, eyes dark. "Then what the fuck is going on?"

He shakes his head a bit. "Don't talk to me like that—"

"Or what?" I ask, standing up straighter.

Jonah rolls his eyes. "I'm not going to fucking fight you, man—"

"Not going to talk to me, not going to tell me the truth—just going to fucking fade away, act like a prick so I don't even bother to try—?"

Jo's jaw goes tight and he looks away, and I go to say something and then my phone rings.

Glance down at it.

Parks.

Answer it.

"Hey."

"Beej?" She sounds panicked.

"Parks—?" I plug my ear. "What's wrong?"

"It's terrible!" she says, distressed. "Completely terrible."

I take a step away from Jonah. "What is, Parksy?"

"Today's March sixteenth!" she says.

I frown. "Okay?"

"The number one thing on Bridget's list is the spring equinox at Angkor Wat. That happens once a year and it's in three days!"

"Okay," I nod, glancing at Jo, and honestly, fucking keen for a reason to leave Boodle's and London in general.

"I'll be home soon, we'll figure it out."

I hang up, look over at my best friend.

"Everything good?"

"Yeah—" I shake my head. "Just Parks shit. I've gotta—" I point my thumb towards the door and Jo nods once.

"Hen—!"

My brother looks over from across the club and I motion my head towards the exit. He gives me a confused look.

"999," I call to him, and he stands up quickly, so I clarify.

"But like, not really—" I say, and he rolls his eyes.

Him and Christian hug and then they both walk over. Christian throws his arms around me, gives me a hug as well—Jo and Henry skip it, but not surprising considering the last few months, but me and Jo—

We stand like, a metre apart, I give him a fucking weird shrug.

"I'll see you when I see you?" I say.

Jo nods. I nod back.

And then I'm about to walk away when he just tosses his arms around me in this bear hug—hardly hug him back—try to.

"Look after yourself, yeah?" he says to me. "And Parks."

I nod, feel a bit worried, if I'm honest.

I look at him again, properly. "Are you sure you're good?"

And he gives me a smile that I know is forced.

"Everything's going to be good."

SEVENTY-FIVE

BJ

So, it turns out, the spring equinox does only happen once a year, and it happens this year, in now—two days.

Magnolia is fucking freaking out, and we're up shit creek.

Dad said we can take our plane, but he's got it with him in Canada til tomorrow, and if we wait til tomorrow, we won't make it to Angkor Wat in time.

Magnolia is refusing to ask her dad for his, so no dice there.

Felt weird asking Jo, like we'd be tossing ourselves into the middle of something.

So here we are—the four of us—me, Parks, Henry and Allie at the Thai Airways counter at Heathrow, too many bags in tow thanks to my fiancée, trying to get on the next flight to Cambodia—and are you ready for this? There are no direct flights.

"What's a 'layover'?" Magnolia asks no one specifically, and yeah, she does use air quotes.

Henry cringes and says, "Not it," under his breath and ducks away.

Magnolia follows after him, leaving me and Al to sort the seats, and thank fuck.

Heathrow to Bangkok, three-hour layover and then Bangkok to Siem Reap.

Here's the catch. That first flight—eleven hours? Economy.

Allie gives me a look, eyes wide both with amusement and maybe some light terror.

Once everything's checked in, I walk over to Magnolia and my brother, who are waiting there with my mum.

"All good?" Lil asks with a smile.

Allie grimaces and Magnolia looks at me with a sort of expectant frown.

"Good news—" I flash her a smile. "We're on the flight, we will one hundred percent make it in time for the spring equinox, assuming there are no delays and we, like, run off the plane into the car we've hired . . ."

Parks' eyes pinch. "Okay?"

"In other news," I press my tongue into my top lip and say the first part real quick. "We're flying economy. Who wants to get drunk!"

Magnolia draws in a breath and her eyes look off to the side and then she—nothing. She says nothing.

My mum pulls a face and Henry waves a hand in front of the perfectly still Parks, and for a full five more seconds she doesn't even blink and then she looks at me, blinking.

"I'm so sorry—what?"

"Economy."

Her head drops and she looks to the side, eyes wide, processing.

"Is the part of the plane where people who aren't heiresses sit," my brother says unhelpfully.

"An heiress?" She blinks. "First economy and now I'm reduced to an heiress?"

I lean in close to her and whisper very quietly, "I think you'll find by definition you are technically a Russian heire—"

—don't get to finish that sentence though, because my fiancée's spindly little finger smooshes into my mouth to quiet me.

"Lilian—" She points at my mother, who has given her a maternal look. "Don't look at me like that, okay?" She glances between all of us. "I know what you're all thinking—*Oh Magnolia, she's so ridiculous, she can't fly commercial*—be quiet!"

("None of us said anything," Allie whispers to Henry.)

"We're all like this," Magnolia says, waving a finger in all our faces. "No one wants to fly commercial when you can fly private. And certainly, no one wants to fly economy when you can fly first—" She looks at me, eyes wild, a tiny bit frantic. "Why can't we fly first?"

I move her to the side, away from my family—because, yes, she can be a bit of a brat, and yes, she is ridiculous—but she is who she is and I can see she's about to spiral.

I hold both her arms, duck a bit so we're eye to eye.

"It was a really full flight, Parksy. We were lucky to get on."

"Is this a weird joke, where we'll get on the other side of security and then you'll say 'Gotcha!' and I'll say 'What the fuck?' and then we sit in first?"

I shake my head. "Unfortunately, no. And actually—" I look at my watch. "Because we aren't flying first we have to go through normal security, so we should get a move on."

She stares at me blankly, pressing her lips together as she thinks on something.

"This does feel like Bridget's fault somehow, don't you think?" she eventually says, and it makes me laugh.

"Yeah," I nod. "It's got her name all over it."

"What's in the jar?" an airport security guard asks Parks as she's squinting at the X-ray machine.

"My sister," she says, not really looking at the man. And then she glances up and flashes him a smile.

The security guard looks taken aback, and Magnolia looks over her shoulder at me for help.

I point to the jar. "Ashes."

That doesn't seem to settle the security guard's worries.

"She obviously died before we turned her into ashes," Magnolia adds unhelpfully.

The supervisor waddles over to us. "Do you have the death certificate?" he asks.

"Excuse me, no—" Magnolia frowns. "What a funny thing to carry around—? Who'd ever think to—"

"I have it—" I say, pulling it from my bag.

Pretty on-brand for Parks to just try and bring a dead person on a flight without looking up what you need to allow it.

Hand it over and Magnolia's looking at me with big, grateful eyes.

The supervisor recognises the name on the certificate and ushers us through pretty quickly after that, handing Bridge back to Parks on the other side.

I walk over to her, touch her face.

"You said she died." I give her a sorry smile. "I've never heard you say that out loud before."

She flashes me a quick smile and her eyes fill up a bit, but I brush the one that spills over with my thumb before anyone can see, because she's like that.

For what it's worth, Parksy only cried once between security and boarding the plane when the, and I quote, "horrible woman in the Kathmandu microfleece jumper and the non-branded espadrilles hit her with her stupid nylon backpack."

"What even is JanSport?" she asked me through tears, and Henry disguised his laugh as a cough.

But honestly, that was about it for the theatrics, except for when we boarded the plane and Magnolia closed her eyes and insisted I lead her through the cabins like a blind person so she's not "forced to live the next eleven hours with the knowledge of what could have been."

Unsurprisingly, Henry and Allie elected to sit apart from us.

"56A," she says, giving me a strained smile as she sits down. And then she sort of wriggles in the chairs. "You know, this isn't so bad—"

I sit down next to her. And honestly, it fucking sucks. I squint over at her.

She shifts around in the seat, glancing side to side. "So spacious!"

I give her an unsure look. "Is it?"

"Mmm!" she hums. "So roomy!"

She buckles in Bridget's urn like it's a minor on her lap.

I frown. "My shoulders don't fit."

"Well, that feels like a humble brag—" she tells me.

I nod my head covertly towards the very tall, very white man that's now sitting in 56C.

"Parks," I whisper at her. "There's a stranger next to me—"

"Oh!" She leans too forward and smiles over at the stranger too much. "How nice! A friend!"

At which point I stand up and scour the plane for my brother.

"Did you give her something?" I call to him.

"Just a benzo!" He shrugs innocently and I give him a fucking unimpressed look before I sit back down next to her, grimacing a bit.

"You alright?"

"Oh, yes!" She nods. "I was quite nervous before about sitting in the tiny chairs with the large people, but Henry gave me a great thing and now I'm great." She wriggles in her chair more. "I think it's rather commodious!"

I let out a laugh. "What the fuck are you on about?"

She flicks me a smug look. "I bet we all wish we had an eating disorder now—!"

"Magnolia."

She flashes me a smile. "Sorry."

I lift an eyebrow. "How sorry?"

She laughs, looking out the window. "Not that sorry."

SEVENTY-SIX

Magnolia

We did, of course, have sex on the plane, because what else do you do for eleven hours in economy otherwise?

Sleep poorly and develop a neck injury—? We did that as well.

I waited for Beej to fall asleep before I went back to the bathroom by myself, stood in the mirror and waited for her.

She'd burst out laughing at the sight of me.

"Four hours in economy and you look like you work at the town mill in 1876."

I'd flick her a look and she'd give me a smug one back.

"Where are we off to?" she'd ask because we haven't spoken in a few days now. That's bad, don't you think? Bad of me. It's been a busy few weeks, is all.

"We're taking your trip with Allie," I'd tell her, pleased with myself a bit.

"The one around Southeast Asia?" she'd beam, and I'd nod.

"How many suitcases did you bring?" she'd ask, and I'd wash my hands for no reason, just good hygiene is all.

"I don't want to talk about it," I'd say, my nose in the air.

"So too many, then?" she'd say, and I'd roll my eyes.

"BJ cross about it?"

I shrug demurely. "Who's to say, really?"

She'd give me a look and I'd close my eyes and study it, the angle her eyebrows would make on her face when she was unimpressed, the crinkle in her nose, the creases around her eyes when she'd squint at me, all the directions her mouth could pull—no one gave a look like Bridget, I love it when she glowers at me and it knocks around my brain like a glass bottle being kicked through an underpass that she won't ever give me that look again in real life with her actual face and her actual eyes.

It was a three-hour layover in Bangkok, which went by fairly quickly, what with all the space and open air at my disposal outside of the airplane.

We paid our way into a lounge, showered, and got dressed for the spring equinox, because BJ said there's zero turnaround.

What does one wear to the spring equinox, did I hear you ask? Great question, I wasn't completely sure—it's the sort of thing I wished I could ask my sister, a bit because she'd know the answer but also because I know the question would annoy her so much, but she's not here to answer it, so I took a stab in the dark and decided on the sky blue button-embellished broderie anglaise-trimmed polka-dot silk minidress from Alessandra Rich and the cognac Titya studded leather clogs by Isabel Marant with the ivory ribbed cashmere socks from The Row.

Not long after I'm dressed, it's time to get on another plane for the second flight, in which we did fly business, but it was only an hour's flight or thereabouts.

Annoyingly, Henry and Allie both said they slept the entire flight, which seems rude because I think I went to actual sleep for about an hour and then after that, kept trying to tell myself that I was asleep when I was in fact awake and resenting BJ for sleeping for the remaining nine hours of the flight.

When we arrive in Siem Reap, there are two cars waiting for us, one for the luggage and one for us.

It's not very far from the airport to Angkor Wat, just six kilometres or something like that—but it's already light out and my stomach is in knots.

"You know, they say that technically either side of today it's still pretty centred—?" Henry offers, turning around from the front seat.

"But it's not the spring equinox." Allie frowns next to me.

"And—" I give Henry a look. "'Go to Angkor Wat on some random day in March' wasn't what was on Bridget's list."

I drum my fingers on BJ's bare knee—he's in the navy and tan GG Supreme intarsia-knit shorts from Gucci.

He throws an arm around me, plays with my bra strap absent-mindedly as he looks out the window.

Everything around us looks a bit hazy, and only just starting to get a hint of light. A lot of trees. More than you'd think.

"Woah—" BJ says as we approach the site.

"Four hundred two acres," Allie says. "It's huge—" Then she kicks the back of Henry's chair to get his attention, nodding to the driver. "He knows we're in a rush, right?"

"Yes, Al," Henry sighs, impatient.

The sky's getting brighter, and the traffic is slowing—it would appear there are quite a few people here to see the spring equinox—we're about to pass under this giant carved stone gate when BJ whacks the back of Henry's chair.

"Let's just stop here and run—"

I blink at him. "Run?"

"Yep," he says, then nods his chin at the urn. "Give me Bridge."

I give him an uneasy look and he gives me an offended one.

"You watched me play rugby all of school, how many times did you see me fumble that ball?"

I breathe in through my nose, still not handing Bridget over.

"Conversely—" Henry pipes in. "I've seen you just drop things for no reason at all. You'll be standing there, completely normal, sometimes not even moving and then—bam!—butterfingers out of nowhere."

I roll my eyes and stare Henry down long enough to know I am not well pleased, but then I hand Bridget over anyway.

BJ nods his head towards the temple.

"Let's go."

And then we are running for our lives, ducking and weaving through probably literally thousands of people—the clogs were, in retrospect, a bad idea, but in my defence I didn't know we'd be going for a run when we got to Cambodia.

"It's also called the vernal!" Allie says as we're running.

Henry glances back over his shoulder at her. "What is?"

"The spring—" She takes a breath. "Equinox."

"Oh," Henry says as he darts around a fairly large tourist.

"People observe it all over the world—" Allie keeps going even though we're still running and she's fairly out of breath. "In Japan it's called Shunbun no Hi"—breathing break—"and the Mayans celebrated it"—gasping breath for air—"the Persians too!"

BJ throws me a quick look over his shoulders and I think we both collectively wonder if we've made a mistake holidaying with the *Encyclopaedia Britannica*.

"The Shang dynasty was allegedly born from the vernal equinox—" she says.

(Henry stares over at me. "Make it stop.")

"—The Celts and the Druids"—gasps for air—"and it was celebrated by the Cybele cult in ancient Rome! You'd have liked it, Beej"—stops running for a second, bends over to catch her breath, but doesn't miss a chance to slight her brother—"tonnes of drinking and sex."

BJ throws her a look and I frown.

"Allie."

She flashes me a smile. "Sorry."

Henry laughs, catching his breath as well, and then BJ stares up into the ever-brightening sky.

"Come on—" he nudges me and eyes everyone else, then off he goes.

I am faster than him but he's very fit. He's much fitter than I am, and stronger. He never, ever asks me to open jars for him.

And I know, you're thinking—what does *she* eat out of a *jar*?

Caviar, mostly. For Bushka. But while we're on the topic, sometimes we have fig paste—that can be hard to open. And honeys, we always have varying types of that. At the minute we have Manukora, which BJ said was overpriced, but how would he know, and besides, inflation, or something? And then from Flamingo Estate we have a bunch of the Will Ferrell honeys, but that was for charity so it doesn't count. We do have a jar of peanut butter that Henry and I bought out of curiosity once, it was like, £700 for three six-ounce jars. Standard Reference Material 2387. It has a really boring label too. Fascinating. What were we talking about?

"Are you going to talk the whole time, then?" Henry says, equal parts breathless and exasperated, to his sister.

"Well," I consider. "It is very Bridget-esque."

"That's what I'm going for—!" Allie nods emphatically. "All the things she'd care about"—breath!—"I'll care about."

"And I'll be unenthused as you tell me them," I say back to her. "—Just to keep everything in a realm of realism."

"Okay—" Allie nods, flashing me a tired smile. "Hey, Beej—how much furth—"

And then BJ stops running, still in his tracks. I actually bump into him, because I wasn't paying too much attention where I was going, but you'll be pleased to know he doesn't fumble my sister and he manages to also steady me.

"Oh, shit," Henry says, staring up at the sky, jaw ajar.

And then it happens.

It's an odd moment actually, where it feels like somehow the whole earth takes a collective gasp and holds its breath as this little orb of light floats up, perfectly centred above the centre temple tower, and as the sun rises, BJ lifts my sister's smiley face side towards the sun, high as he can in the air, giving her the view she deserves, even if she can't see it how she'd have imagined she would have.

It's more golden than I could explain to you, even if I were to try really, really hard. A bit as though all the sky and the land has been dipped in honey and sprinkled in topaz and amber and citrines—

BJ hands Bridge over to Henry and then pulls me in front of him, his chin resting on top of my head, arms wrapped around me.

Do you know what the spring equinox is, actually?

It's an ancient celebration, obviously, as Allie said . . . several times, in several different ways.

It means the winter is over, spring is coming. And as I lean back in my fiancé's arms, I wonder if that's perhaps a promise?

Something my sister is saying to me through a light in the sky that's a hundred fifty million kilometres away, because life doesn't end at death, I don't care what you say, it can't—it mustn't. It mightn't look how it did before when they were here, and maybe Bridget isn't as close as that nice veil theory people have where they're just a whisper beside you through a curtain we can't see, but maybe she's somewhere—? Pulling strings, rising suns and promising that there's hope on its coattails.

"Wow," I say, staring at it.

Beej kisses the back of my head. "Yeah. Wow."

"It's so beautiful," Allie says, eyes wide and enamoured.

"Never seen anything like it—" Henry shakes his head. "You can like, feel it in the air."

Allie sniffs, smiling up at it. "It's really incredible—"

Henry smiles down at her, throws an arm around her shoulder.

And everything is quiet and everything is still, everybody on the grounds at this time is tranquil and zen, even birds—it's so peaceful.

I breathe it in—hold my breath—release.

Open my eyes, look around—feel at one with the world, feel at one with BJ, but we've been one a while so that's not that exciting.

I elbow him covertly.

He leans forward around me to catch my eyes.

"Now what?" I whisper very, very quietly.

He pulls a face. "It's been about eight seconds—"

"No, totally!" I shake my head, letting out a little laugh. "My mistake. Silly—"

I purse my lips and take another deep breath as I glance around at our fellow spring equinoxians—spot a few odd ones.

I look back at BJ, nodding my head towards the woman who hasn't washed her hair in a good few years and is giving herself a sound bath.

"They love a sun around here, don't they?"

BJ starts laughing.

Henry moves in towards us. "What's wrong?" he asks.

BJ nods his head towards me.

"Old John the Hesychast is bored."

"Who's that?" asks Allie with a frown, and I shrug because I don't get it but Henry chuckles, so I guess he does.

Henry gives me a look. "We just got here?"

"I know, but—it's already moved?" I shrug.

"Yeah, Magnolia—" He gives me an annoying look. "It's the sun."

"Right." I nod. "Now we've collectively established that it has in fact moved—that brings me to the question of the hour—" I give both boys a dumb smile. "Now what?"

"Well, wait—" Henry sighs. "Should we say something?"

"What do you mean?" Allie asks, glancing at me.

Henry shrugs. "Like, should we say something." Shrugs again. "About Bridge—? It's what we're here for."

"Oh." I purse my lips, frowning a bit. "Yes, sure. I suppose."

I gesture towards him, giving him the floor.

BJ takes Bridget off of him, swivels the urn so the smiley face is facing him. Henry rolls his eyes.

"Bridget Dorothy Parks was one of the coolest girls I've ever met," Henry says, firmly. "Funny, clever, like brilliant"—he nods emphatically—"wasn't she, really? So smart. And witty and dry. Sarcastic. Beautiful. And I have to say"—he gives me a long look, eyebrows up—"honestly, I'll literally regret it forever, I think, that I didn't have a crack."

Allie's mouth falls open and BJ starts belly-laughing.

I stare at him, not blinking. "Henry!"

"What?" He shrugs. "She was hot, Parks—" He gives me an apologetic look, then the same look to his sister. "Sorry, Al."

Allie shrugs.

"And don't get me wrong—" Henry raises his hands as though he's an innocent. "I love Romilly, I do. But I reckon I would have loved a snog from the little Parks—" he announces further, and I scrunch up my face. "She looked like she would have been a good pash—"

"Ew!" I stomp my foot.

"Oh, Beej has kissed her!" Allie points to their older brother as though she's helping.

"Fuck off." Henry stares at his brother, wide eyes, flicking his eyes from BJ to me to BJ, then he shakes his head. "No, but actually, piss off and tell me everything."

Beej rolls his eyes. "She was, like, fourteen. She hadn't kissed anyone before—"

I cut in.

"Remember that party when we were at school and she wouldn't kiss Dean Vinograd and people were calling her weird and someone started a rumour that she was leaving Varley to join an alpine convent—"

"—You started that rumour," Henry tells me, and I roll my eyes.

"Well, I'll have you know that she told me she got a tonne of action because of that rumour because men love to have a crack at sexually unavailable women, so—"

"Yep, fair play." Henry nods at the same time BJ says, "Yeah, that is true."

"Anyway." BJ gives Henry and I shut-up looks. "She was scared because she hadn't done it before, got all in her head about it—" BJ shrugs. "So I kissed her. In front of Parks."

"Nice." Henry nods, appreciatively.

"Harley saw," I add.

Henry grimaces. "Fuck." He pauses, thinking. Nods his chin over at Beej. "Good kiss?"

BJ glances over at me and starts laughing before he does a bit of a "fuck it" shrug.

"Yeah, actually." He laughs. "She was a good kiss."

"Fuck," Henry says, under his breath. "Shoulda coulda woulda."

"Is that it?" I blink at Henry, trying to look unimpressed. "That's your big send-off?"

Hen shrugs. "If I can't say I wanted to give her a snog now, then when can I?"

Allie considers this and gestures to herself. “I could have lived with never.”

I point over at her in solidarity.

Hen rolls his eyes. “Smartest person in every room, at every table she sat at. She was brilliant. I loved listening to her fucking school you two idiots with her psychobabble—” He smiles, thinking about it. “I will miss that. I loved not knowing who she was going to open fire on with a random diagnosis—”

“That she was always painfully right about—” Allie adds.

“Yeah,” Hen nods. “Like, unbelievably astute.”

The mood goes sombre and everyone feels her absence pressing up against us like water behind a dam wall. A building pressure of missing her and wishing she were here and mentally adjusting to how life has to look now that she’s gone from it and acknowledging how uncomfortable it is that death came for her, all of twenty-two years old, and all the things she didn’t get to do in that tiny, short life—

I press my hands into my eyes and try not to cry, unsuccessfully. I do cry. Louder than I would in England but hopefully still not so loud that a tourist sees and takes a photo. BJ wraps me up in himself, holds me against him.

And then I hear Allie crying too. Henry hugs his sister again.

“It’s okay, Parksy,” BJ tells me because what else can he say. “She’s okay. Wherever she is—” He gives me a little shrug. “Standing at the pearly white gates reading Immanuel Kant while she waits for the rest of us, or backstroking around in the infinite nothingness where she will—for eternity—chew our ears off about fucking trauma bonds and about geometric infinities.”

I sniff a laugh, and he holds my face in his hand.

“Wherever she is, it’s good. I know it is.”

“How?” I ask.

He shrugs like it’s easy. “Because she’s there.”

SEVENTY-SEVEN

BJ

We step into the very bare, white-tiled, black-bunk-bedded room where our luggage is waiting for us.

Parks lets out this dry laugh.

"No, no, no, no, no, no, no—" She shakes her head.

"Allie," Henry frowns, looking over at her. "Are you sure?"

"Yes!" Allie nods, sure. "This is it! She wrote it down—!" She flashes us Bridget's plan.

Magnolia looks around the room, completely scowling.

She pokes one of the beds with a single, stretched-out index finger, then she looks at me, unsure.

"This tiny bed has a ladder that leads up to another tiny bed—?"

I squash a laugh down, but Henry doesn't, she hears and glares at him.

"Wait, how on—" She counts us in her head, pointing—one, two, three, four—she squints, thinking it through. "There are four of us and there are six beds—you don't think—"

And then the door swings open and some guy walks in.

"Oh my god!" Magnolia yells proper top of her lungs. "GET OUT!"

And then launches into Russian—

"Тебе лучше уйти! Я видел общежитие! Мы этого не делаем, понятно? Не сегодня! Не сегодня, сатана—"

I don't catch a lot of it at the top, I think she might have said *'not today, Satan.'* Allie clamps a hand over her mouth in a sort of amused horror, which, welcome to my life, Al.

Parksy keeps going at Russian warp speed.

"Ты очень высокий, но мой парень очень сильный, и он убьет тебя. Он сумасшедший! Он убьет тебя до смерти. Тебе нужны деньги? Это ограбление?"

Something about *'my boyfriend is crazy and he'll kill you'*?

And this poor fucking guy—standing there, eyes wide, like, actually petrified—the most beautiful girl in the world bloody screaming at him in Russian.

"Uh—" He looks over at me and Henry, nervous. "This is my room—I'm staying here too—" He nods, not sure to who. Himself, maybe? He points to a T-shirt and jumper on one of the bottom bunks. "That's my stuff."

Magnolia's eyes go wide in disbelief.

"You're—you're staying in here too?" She points to the floor. "In this room?" She blinks. "Voluntarily?"

Henry covers his face with his hands.

The guy glances over at me, unsure. "Yes."

Magnolia squints at him. "You a stranger, in here with us—" She points to herself. "With me."

The poor guy flicks his eyes between the rest of us, almost like he's asking '*is* she *okay*?' but I don't want to push the boat out with Parks right now by giving this guy a leg to stand on. It's a dog-eat-dog world, man.

"With you, yeah." He nods then forces a smile. "I'm—"

"Oh—" She shakes her head quickly. "We need not exchange names—BJ, this gentlem—" Press my lips together because she can't even bring herself to call him a gentleman, and I wonder how many times in my life I'm gonna get hit in the face because I fell in love with a bleeding idiot.

Magnolia clears her throat demurely. "This"—uncomfortable pause—"man, has predator glasses on—"

"They're clear aviators," he tells Henry and Allie. "They're just clear—"

And then Parks squints at him, pointing to his shirt.

"What's that in your pocket, is that a—"

"Kazoo!" He smiles, pleased. "Yeah."

He blows on it and Parks looks over at me, eyes wild, before she looks back at him.

"You, sir, are a menace."

He looks a bit disheartened at that. "Do you not like the kazoo?"

Henry gives him grimace that's laced with a smile. "You're travelling alone, aren't you?"

The Kazoo Predator frowns. "How did you—?"

"Parksy—" I grab her attention with a look. "If Bridge picked this, don't you want to at least give it a—"

"Because, no—" she says, already shaking her head. "Right, I know she's weird, but she's not this weird."

Al looks around. "I feel like this looks different to the photos . . . ?"

"Maybe it's gotten worse over time?" Henry offers.

"No listen, I know this isn't what she picked because one time at a sleepover Jonah made us all watch *Hostel*, remember?" Magnolia looks between us all. "And Bridget was so scared afterwards that she insisted she sleep in my bed for a month."

Henry gives Magnolia an unsure look.

"Bridget insisted?"

"Fine!" she growls. "I was scared and I insisted, but Bridget was too. She was very put off by the Dutch for a good few years after that—"

I roll my eyes at her as I lay down on one of the bunks.

"She'd never stay in a hostel, I know that for certain," she says.

I look around the bunk beds, feel myself less inclined to stay here than I'd like.

I grimace. "There's more room in a can of tuna."

Magnolia huffs impatiently. "Tuna doesn't come in cans."

"Yes, it does," I, my siblings and the stranger all say at the same time.

Magnolia looks between all of us. "Ahi tuna?"

Hen rolls his eyes. "You can can anything."

Magnolia turns away from Henry, nose in the air. "Well, I've only ever seen it fresh or in a jar—"

"That's because you're you," Henry says to her with a look.

And then Allie goes, "Oh, shit."

I sit up because I'm the oldest and I'm with a bunch of fucking idiots.

"What?"

Allie glances around all of us with an apologetic smile.

"I got a letter wrong."

Henry's eyes go to slits. "What?"

"Whoops!" Big, awkward smile from Al. "It's actually A-M-A-N-S-A-R-A. No 'T' in there—"

"Allie!" Magnolia growls from the back of her throat.

"Sorry!" My little sister shrugs helplessly. "I'm sorry, it was an innocent mistake—"

Magnolia starts grabbing her bags and wheeling them towards the door.

"You nearly just got us murdered by a kazoo-playing maniac—"

Kazoo raises his hand. "I'm—I'm not a murderer."

"Uh—" Hen grimaces. "To be fair though, lad, that is straight-up something a murderer would say, so—"

Kazoo considers this. "Does the kazoo make me . . . murder-y?"

"Oh, look—" Henry pats his arm. "It doesn't help."

My brother wheels his and Allie's bag towards the door and gives the guy a merry shrug. "Anyway, we're going to get out of your hair—"

Magnolia pauses awkwardly at the door, looking back at the man.

Her face pulls as she stares over at him gingerly.

"May I—?" She points to his kazoo.

He nods, surprised but a bit pleased.

She reaches carefully into his pocket and then delicately puts the kazoo in the bin.

"You'll thank me one day," she tells him with a sorry smile. "As will your breast pocket—" She gestures to the shirt pocket he was keeping the kazoo in. "You know you aren't supposed to use those. Just for a pen, perhaps. Or a handkerchief—" Quick pause. "Which is like a tissue for rich pe—"

"Alright!" I cut her off there and pull her out of the room.

SEVENTY-EIGHT
Magnolia

The very last trip we went on as a family of four, I was almost seventeen and Bridget was just fifteen, which is a commentary on a lot of things, I'm sure. We've been away since with each other of course, but not just the four of us. We were staying at Il San Pietro di Positano, and it was how you would imagine it to be.

My parents took The Virginia suite and Bridget and I each stayed in a couple of the prestige rooms. We could have shared, I don't know why they didn't book us into one. We fell asleep in the same bed every night anyway.

It was during one of their parenting highs that they'd each go through, but I don't know whose it was. Some teen psychologist probably released a book around then that really grabbed their attention—*How to Have Daughters and Influence Them* or something. I should look into that and see if this trip correlates to any parenting trend around at the time.

All I know is we were taken to Italy and my boyfriend wasn't allowed to come. Which was weird, because if we ever went on a Parks family vacation, which—obviously, we went on many a vacation, yes, but almost always with other people like the Ballentines or the Beckhams or the Richies, who acted as relational diffusers, if you will—but every now and then we'd go away with only my parents and they'd almost always let me bring BJ and Bridget bring Allie because we were then very distracted and they didn't have to pay any kind of attention to us, but this trip it was no bueno.

"You can live without him for a week, Magnolia," Harley said, rolling his eyes.

"No, I can't!" I cried, very dramatically. "You can't keep us apart! We're not Romeo and Juliet."

"No, exactly. You aren't Romeo and Juliet," Harley said with a pointed look.

My eyes pinched at him. "What was that tone? I didn't care for that."

"Darling," my mother said, touching his arm to quieten him. "He simply means that you and BJ will be completely fine apart for the duration of our six-day trip apart."

"But where's she going to get that D?" Bridget said, big grin on her face, and I jammed my finger so hard into her side and that's one of the ways I know how tough she is because she didn't even squirm.

"Vitamin D, I meant, obviously." She flashed a quick smile.

Harley gave both of us a long-suffering look.

"Magnolia doesn't have sex!" Bridget kept going. "She's never even heard of it. She's a precious, virginal flower"—I roll my eyes—"and when I hear noises coming from their bedroom, I know they're just exercis—"

Another finger in the rib for her at that point.

Bridget gave them a decisive nod. "They exercise a lot."

"BRIDGET!" I yelled, and Harley put both his hands on his head.

"He's never coming over again," he breathed out.

(BJ did, in fact, come over later that night.)

"Well," I stomped my foot, crossing my arms. "If BJ can't come, then Allie can't come!"

"Hey!" Bridge pouted, and I gave her a brat smile.

Harley's face pinched. "Bit different."

"How?" I frowned.

"Allie's my best friend!" Bridge said, eyebrows up.

I shrugged my shoulders. "BJ's mine."

"Allie is a girl!" Harley clarified needlessly.

I pointed to myself. "You're discriminating against me because my best friend is a boy."

"No, I'm discriminating against you because you have sex with him all the time," Harley said, eyebrows up and daring.

"Well." My mother wobbled her head side to side. "To be fair—"

Harley raised a finger without looking at her—"Not the time, Arina"—and then gave me a helpless shrug as though she tried her best.

"Bridget could be into girls," I said with an innocent shrug, just to be annoying.

"Yeah, but I'm not." Bridget rolled her eyes. "So it doesn't count."

"So, let me get this straight." I squared my shoulders, eyeing them all. "I'm being punished because I have a loving, healthy relationship with my—"

(Harley blew some air out of his mouth and said under his breath, "Healthy is like, a touch subjective.")

"—boyfriend," I talked loudly over him. "Whom I love and whom loves me, and we express our relationship how everyone in the world expresses love and attraction, and were we living in biblical times—"

("—Which we aren't," Bridget interjected, and I gave her a short look to silence her.)

"—we'd have been married like, three years ago—"

(Harley breathed in sharply through his nose. "I wish you were married three years ago.")

"—so because I'm normal and good at sex—"

("Fucking hell." Harley covered his eyes again.)

"—and I'm lucky enough that the person I'm sleeping with also happens to be my best friend, I'm being punished?"

Harley groaned and stared over at Bridget, grimacing.

"Sorry, Bridge."

"What!" She stared at him, eyes wide.

"She—regrettably—has a point." He shrugged. "Kind of."

("Kind of?" I frowned, and they all ignored me.)

"No Ballentines," Harley said, walking away.

A week or so later, Bridget and I were laying out on the beach club level on those orange sunbeds they have. I don't know where our parents were. I think I remember seeing my mother get on a yacht earlier that day, without Harley, and I think I remember seeing Harley by the pool with someone who wasn't my mother.

Bridge was buried in *A Little Life* by Hanya Yanagihara and I was on FaceTime with Beej, complaining about everything and showing him my very bright and very pink Triangl bikini and how brown I was.

He kept saying he was just going to fly there, that Harley couldn't stop him, he doesn't own all of Italy. BJ at nineteen was so much fun, so unstoppable, so brazenly sure of everything and nothing all at once.

In retrospect now, I can see he was very much so living in the wake of his injury, quite adrift with not knowing what to do. He went to university for a hot minute, but the minute was so hot it's scarcely worth talking about.

I can't completely remember whether by then he had quit or he was about to—but it was in that phase where he was—retrospectively—very listless and very distressed that his life wasn't going to look how we thought it might, and that manifested in a spicy combination of being the most attentive, protective boyfriend on the planet, partying like his life depended on it and really cementing himself as one of the most in-demand male models at the time.

I did sort of like the abstract concept of the potential drama of BJ arriving in Italy to spite my father but he'd have to have missed a Vetements shoot to do it so I convinced him not to.

When we hung up, I turned to my sister next to me and gave her a glare because I felt like fighting. But she was reading and definitely wasn't like, reading how I sometimes read when I am consciously trying to ignore someone but am really just waiting for them to notice me so I can keep ignoring them, she was properly reading, so she didn't notice the death stare I was giving her.

I cleared my throat—re-glared at her—she didn't even glance up.

I cleared it again, staring at her intently, and without looking up she said, "Do you need a drink or something?"

"Bridget!" I growled.

"What?" She finally looked over at me.

"I'm cross at you!" I told her.

"Oh no," she said, unbothered, immediately looking back down.

"It's all your fault that they're not here, you know."

"It's literally your fault," she said, nose still in that book. "Because you're selfish so you made sure Allie couldn't come, and BJ only couldn't come because you're a big dumb crumpet."

I sat up immediately.

"I'm not a crumpet!" My mouth fell open, offended. I crossed my arms over my chest. "You're a crumpet."

She rolled her eyes. "I'm a virgin."

"Yes, I know." I gave her a look. "It's painfully obvious."

She sat up, frowning and a bit proud.

"People want to have sex with me," she said, nose in the air.

"Who—?" I look over at her, interested. "Are you making things up, or do you have actual names?"

"Rowan MacCauley asked me on a date last week, and Raphael Aldebrandi is Snapchatting me a lot—and they're like—" She gave me a look.

"Is he being rude?" I frown, defensively.

She shook her head. "They're just, very like . . . topless, downward angle, hint of a dick root—"

I poked my tongue out in disgust, before I sat up a little straighter, interested now.

"Who else then?"

"Timothy Cadwallader. And Dean."

"Oh my god—" I blinked at her. "Have sex with Dean."

"No—" She rolled her eyes. "He's—"

"—super hot." I cut her off.

"Yes." She rolled her eyes. "But stupid."

"How?" I frowned, not believing her that someone who looked like nineties Ryan Philippe could possibly be stupid.

She lifted her eyebrows. "Do you not follow him on Snapchat?"

I rolled my eyes at her ridiculousness. "I don't follow fifteen-year-olds, I'm not a predator—"

"You're sixteen," she reminded me.

I shrugged demurely. "Practically seventeen."

"But literally sixteen."

I breathed out my nose and then we had an argument about whether I was more sixteen or more seventeen, and I said because I turn seventeen next month I was definitely more seventeen, and she just kept on saying "Yes, except you are literally sixteen, so—" which was so annoying because she was technically right?

Anyway, then we had a big fight after that. She said she spent the last three days doing nothing with the most boring person on the planet who does nothing but talk about fashion and society shit that no one cares about. ("If no one cares, why does *Tatler* exist?" I asked her, spitefully, and she said, "Only people who are in *Tatler* read *Tatler*," and I said "Well, I'm in *Tatler*.") And then she said I was self-absorbed, and actually the worst person to go on holidays with, and I asked how and she said because every day we just do what I want to do, "which is nothing" and she's over it and she's going to take a cooking class in town tomorrow and I'm not invited, even if I want to come.

"Why would I ever want to learn to cook!" I yelled after her.

"You wouldn't!" she said, on her feet by then and backing away from me. "You're too basic."

We did not sleep in the same room that night, and I was briefly grateful that my parents had been stupidly excessive and each given us our own.

I called BJ and cried for a little while, but that was annoying because he's always loved my sister and he'd never trash her, even when I want him to. So I was saying all the mean things she said and did, and he sort of just gave me an apologetic smile and said "Yeah" a lot.

So then I got cross at him, so I called Paili and Perry to complain about Bridget and they were much more compliant, and agreed with me on all my points about how rude she was, and insolent and sullen, and then still, I didn't feel better at all, and I had a terrible sleep because the only person I hate fighting with more than Bridget is BJ, and it seemed I was fighting with both.

The next morning at breakfast with our parents—the only time of day we were guaranteed to see them—Bridget asked me if I wanted to go to the cooking class with her, but I was still feeling stroppy about the day before, so I just rolled my eyes and said "As if."

So that day I went back down to the beach club again except by myself this time, and did the same thing I'd done all the other days before this one, except this time, I sort of hated it.

For one, these slimy men (ranging in age from probably about twenty all the way up to fifty) kept coming up to me, enough times that I eventually asked a waiter for a marker and wrote on a napkin "I am 16" and left it on the side table by my head. That would never have happened if Bridget was there, not because she's not beautiful—she completely was—but she had a real "don't fuck with me" kind of energy to her, which I suppose I must have somewhat lacked, because I have been fucked with many a time.

But beyond that, I just didn't much care for the being alone.

I didn't like not having anyone to say my passing thoughts to, and I didn't like having no one to be annoyed with, and I didn't like having to remember to drink water in between Limoncello spritzes, and I didn't like sitting there all the livelong day in that terrible internal silence that happens when you have space to think and no one to fill it with, and then I began to wonder why on a family holiday I was with no family?

I eventually went back to my room and sat on my balcony and read.

The balconies in the prestige suites really do have this sickening view of the Mediterranean and the Amalfi Coast, like wild—I sat out there for a few hours towards the end of the day, ignoring the insane bubbling in my mind about why our family is the way our family is by reading *Extremely Loud and Incredibly Close*.

"Are you reading?" said the fractionally smarmy voice of my sister from behind me.

"Oh my god!" I jumped to my feet, throwing my arms around her neck. "You're back, thank god—!"

She pulled a face, confused, and I shook my head to explain myself.

"I've had such a dumb, terrible day!" I told her, pulling her over to where I was sitting a moment ago. "I realised that doing nothing is only really fun if you have someone to do it with, and also that men are opportunistic when you're by yourself—" She made a concerned face at that. "—and actually, I think I mightn't like being alone that much?"

Bridget rolled her eyes. "No, really?"

"—so tomorrow whatever you want to do, I'm in!"

She looked at me suspiciously.

"You'll hike Path of the Gods with me?"

"Oh, ew!" I said without thinking, and then paused, trying to be more democratic with my answer. "Uh—that's just so . . . laborious"—I flashed her a quick smile—"would you consider picking something else?"

She gave me a pinched look, annoyed.

"Pompeii," she said, folding her arms over her. "I'm going to Pompeii tomorrow."

"Great!" I nodded. "Sounds great, and super relaxing. Nothing says 'holiday' like vaporised organs and blood from a pyroclastic surge!"

I gave her a big grin and she looked at me suspiciously.

"How'd you know that?"

I shrugged. "*National Geographic.*"

"Oh." She pursed her lips and drummed her hands on the table, probably a little less excited about the trip at that point upon realising she wasn't going to be able to lecture me the whole day about stratigraphic observations.

"Do you think it'll always be like this?" I asked her eventually. "Us and them?"

"What do you mean?" She frowned a bit.

"I mean," I lifted my shoulders, trying to communicate what had been tumbling around my head all day. "When we go away with BJ and his family, Lily and Hamish never go off by themselves—or maybe they do once! Like, one time per holiday they'll go and do something just the two of them that's adulty, but the rest of the time they're just always there, doing things with us or taking us places, or at the very least, like, having dinner and stuff with us."

"They have breakfast with us," she says, eyebrows up like it's a terrible, pathetic offering.

"Yeah, and it's like, half a grapefruit and bye—!"

Bridge gave me a look.

"They're not even spending the days with each other, you know?"

"I know," she said.

"So why bring us?"

"Because it's what they're supposed to do—" She sighed. "They're trying."

I rolled my eyes. "They are not."

"I think they are—in their own way," she said, chin in hand. "But yes, I think it'll always be like this. In some way or another, probably."

"Do you wish they loved us more?" I asked rather quietly and quickly. I think that was the first time I'd ever acknowledged that out loud, at least to her. "—Or that we were less alone?"—I added quickly to soften the blow of the sentence before—"Or that like, it was different?"

"Sort of." She pressed her lips together, thinking. "Sometimes—I mean, yes, of course—" She looked over at me. "But Magnolia, you don't even want it—"

I scowled at her for telling me what I do and don't want. "Of course, I do!"

My fifteen-year-old sister gave me a very pointed look on that Positano balcony. "You have led a very sexually active life for a seventeen-year-old—" ("I thought I was sixteen!" I interrupted because we're sisters.) "—if you had normal parents who cared—" her face pulled in discomfort, because it's a hard thing to admit to. It's a hard thing to feel. So she added as a caveat, "—in the obvious ways—you'd never have the same kind of relationship with Beej that you do."

I looked at her defiantly, not wanting to be grateful for them for anything, least of all one of the best parts of my teenage life. "BJ has a great mother who's normal and he—"

Bridget rolled her eyes. "Lily lives in denial. She thinks BJ's a virgin."

"That's actually a very incredible skill set," I remember musing to myself. "Maybe I should try that."

Bridget gave me an exasperated look.

"My point is, there are good things about how our parents are—"

"Besides getting to have sex, which we just established is possible with a good parent as well—" I give her a look. "What else?"

"Well—" She gestured towards me. "Romilly, as an example—" Who, for context, was very soon about to be ripped away from all of us at Varley. "Her dad is an absolute nutter. And he's so loud, and she's opinionated, and he's so involved in her day-to-day life, she thinks what he thinks—"

"That's not true—!" I rolled my eyes.

"Yes, it is!" Bridge nods. "Cassius Followill is an extension of his father's mouth, he picked a fight with Mr Driessen in science because he didn't refer to evolution as a 'theory' . . ."

I gave her a dubious look.

"And Romilly always talks about God but I can tell she doesn't really believe any of it, she just thinks she does because her dad's always banging on about Him."

I flicked my eyes. "He's a minister."

My sister shook her head. "The gift our parents never meant to give us was not caring enough about our foundational formation to ever want to toss their hat in the ring."

My head pulled back in quiet horror at the terribleness of that sentence. "That we get to decide who we are ourselves, Magnolia—" She shook her head, smiling a bit. "That's really brilliant."

I felt my shoulders slump a little. "I don't know who I am—?"

She looked over at me, very sure. "I know who you are."

"Who?" I asked, eyebrows up.

Her whole face pinched in this new way, that it would again a million times from that moment until she gave up on moments recently; she was—at all of fifteen—about to deliver her first impossibly astute, always honest and often brutal diagnosis.

"You're quite complicated, I think." Her brows lowered ever so slightly in thought. "You're clever, more than anyone would realise"—she gave me a pointed look—"more than you'd want anyone to know. You hide behind your beauty, I think you think if people think that's all you are then when people disappoint you it'll hurt less than if they really knew you—"

I remember frowning at that, not knowing whether it was true or not at the time, but not liking it either way.

I gave her a defiant look. "None of those things are who I am, just possibly things I may or may not do."

She gave me an impatient look and breathed out her nose. "You are Magnolia Katherine Juliet Parks. Yes, you are the product of two creatively brilliant but emotionally reckless idiots. Yes, you're obsessive, and you're detail-oriented, and you're pedantic, and you're warm, and you're generous, and you're silly, and you're kind, and yes, you are many of those things because our parents are who our parents are. And you might hate that, you might hate it forever, and that would be okay!" She gave me a look that was too all-knowing for a fifteen-year-old, but that was her. She was always like that. "I don't see them ever just like, suddenly turning into Lily and Hamish or Rebecca—"

She shrugged to make her point. "—this is probably what it will always be, and you might feel like you're on the back foot because they haven't given you a road map and they don't seem at all interested in drawing you up one either, and I know that knowing you, you will find it incredibly hard to then accept them in any way as actual parents, and so you'll probably feel lost for most of your life"—definitely scowled at that and she definitely didn't care—"so if you feel lost some days and you don't know who you are and you don't feel like you're theirs, like 'Parks' is just a name you happen to share with them, just remember that I know who you are, and you're my sister, and that's my name too."

My crowning achievement, probably. One of two.

Being her sister, being loved by him.

It is funny though, how one's crowning achievements do nothing to dull the throbbing pain of your deepest, oldest hurt. Because your brain might trick you into thinking that it might.

It's been a good few weeks of doing Bridget's list.

After Cambodia we went to Myanmar, and after that, we went to Thailand, where we went to those waterfalls and then that bloody Mae Hong Son Loop (shut up, I don't want to talk about it. I nearly died fifty times and BJ is an impossible arsehole who kept swerving on purpose so I'd get scared and hold tighter which—I know!—sounds both sexy and cute, but I assure you it was neither). Not on Bridget's list was the Amanpuri, which we also stayed at because to be quite frank, I needed a week to recoup—if you knew the kinds of hotels those absolute jokers had me staying in, you'd question who I am.

I mean, hotel rooms that cost double digits—not even triple—double! Madness.

Anyway, then we visited those plain jars in Laos. Taura would have liked them, actually.

And now we're in the Philippines, on Banwa Island, which was a deal I struck with everyone else when they broached the topic of the Mae Hong Son Loop with me.

We were on the mainland before for the rice terraces she had on her list in Ifugao, and then we spent a week in Coron. Bridget had wanted to dive the wrecks there—which we did—kind of terrifying and a little bit amazing?

And Allie wanted to visit the Twin Lagoon and Barracuda Lake.

"Oi," Henry says, sitting down on a sun lounge next to me. Beej is teaching Allie how to play golf, Henry was supposed to be teaching her that, but I knew that wasn't going to last. Henry's too pragmatic and logical—funny and kind, of course—but if he and Romilly have babies one day, I hope they call BJ to teach their children to ride a bike, because as the only person Henry ever has semi-taught to ride a bike, I can confidently say he doesn't have the patience for it.

He just kept letting me fall? I was six—I think? I don't know, I bumped my head a lot—and I remember I'd never had so many bloody knees in my life. We were up at Hamish's parents' estate in Much Hadham, and I remember Ham coming out totally livid and Henry was well in it, and then BJ took over because he's cute like that and I learnt in an hour.

"What are you doing?" he asks, moving in closer to me.

"Just thinking." I shrug.

He lifts his eyebrows. "About . . . ?"

"A holiday." I smile. "With Bridge and my parents. The last one we took together just the four of us."

"When was it?"

"Oh—" I shake my head. "Like, nine years ago or something."

A frown whispers over his face at that.

"What?" I ask, and he shakes his head quickly, face all apologetic.

"Sorry—" He flashes me a smile. "I didn't mean for that to—just a bit shit, is all."

"Yeah." I nod.

And I think that's the way best to describe it, actually.

A bit shit.

It's rather difficult to reconcile, don't you think? All of it, but especially the part where people won't necessarily ever be who we want them to be or need them to be.

That can be quite scary to reckon with.

I think sometimes there can be screaming revelations in your life and then other times, there are the kind that dawn on you like a sun that creeps up slowly over the horizon, and it happens with a subtlety and a grace where you don't even completely recognise that you're realising something until it's high noon and the sun is blaring in your face and you've gone a little bit blind from it—

My father, my mother as well—neither will ever be the parents I want them to be when I needed them to be them.

Even if Harley became the absolute and irrefutable best father in the world in the next day and a half, I'm twenty-five. I don't need a father now, I needed him when I was seven and twelve and fifteen and seventeen, and now I'm grown and I don't need him at all, except in all the ways that are too late.

And that's not to say there isn't still some sort of mournful anguish in me, because there is—I don't know what for though?—for a want I've had forever that will lie dormant and unmet from now on until I die?

That's a rather tragic thing to come to terms with too. No matter how much better my parents become, regardless of whether the cheating and the affairs stop, even if my mother stops dating boys my age, even if Harley became a fucking eunuch, no matter how much they may evolve and develop as people, I will never have—when I needed them, at least—a mum and a dad. I may have had some variant of a mother and a father, but having borne close witness to what it looks like to have a mum and a dad via the Ballentines, I know that having a mother and a father isn't the same thing as having a mum and a dad.

"Hey," Henry elbows me. "I'm not your dad."

"Are you not—?" I give him a silly look, which he ignores.

"But I am your brother."

My face goes soft.

He nods his head towards me, chin lifted, a bit proud. "I feel like I had a hand in the raising process—"

I nod in emphatic agreement. "If not arguably more than either of my so-called parents."

He rolls his eyes.

"I know you have this long-standing fear of being alone, and that Bridget's death like—ostracises you in your family unit. Probably in a way that I reckon you'll find particularly confronting—"

I frown up at him.

"Did Bridget just take over your body?"

He breathes out a laugh. "Right?"

He shifts his body a little so he's looking at me properly.

"There's a bit of it where I can't—you know—like, make the shit with Harley better, I can't make him act how he should. I can't make him say sorry or make him turn up when he should, but I can turn up." He tells me very solemnly. "I know you know this, but you don't need them, Parks"—he shrugs—"you don't need parents anymore, you grew up without them anyway, and what you have now is us."

He gives me a steadying look.

"Me and Beej and Tausie and Rom and the boys. My parents. Gus. A hand-picked family."

I don't know what to say because I'm not usually this sentimental in an out loud way, so I put my head on his shoulder.

"Will you walk me down the aisle?" I ask him. "At the wedding?"

He looks down at me and smiles a bit.

"Honour of a lifetime."

SEVENTY-NINE
Magnolia

There's a volcano on the east coast of Java called Kawah Ijen that, as soon as we started looking into, we understood fairly quickly why Bridget would want to go there.

A few of these other ones I've been so-so about. Obviously the motorcycling across Thailand one went down like a lead balloon with me, and I definitely thought I was going to die in the Hang Son Doong caves.

But this one, with all its electric blue fire—I'll go ahead and say it—colour me intrigued.

We went to this ancient megalithic site called Gunung Padang in West Java, which was equal parts boring and a bit incredible in this mind-boggling way.

BJ really enjoyed both that site and the Plain of Jars in Laos solely for the reason that he was able to keep bringing up that time at Taura's birthday where I became a rock wizard to impress the guide and to annoy him.

Every time anyone would even muse a question to themselves, he'd say, "Better ask the expert—Parks?" or "Oh, Magnolia knows all about rocks, don't you, Parksy?"

The entire thing turned out to be a bit of a kerfuffle—Banyuwangi is where you're meant to stay before you do the hike, which was an inward hike of the soul in and of itself.

Beej spent a half a day researching places "Magnolia would stay" in Banyuwangi, but there weren't a great many options. I really pushed for us to stay somewhere else with a proper resort and just helicopter in and I think BJ was so tired of me peeking over his shoulders and saying things like, "Eleven pounds! For a hotel room? That's not even the price of a decent green juice," and then Henry would say mean things like, "You know, it's not too late to back out."

Eventually I got cross and left and Henry followed after me and said, "Parks, do you think Bridge would helicopter up?" And I was forced to say no because it's the truth, and he shrugged and said, "So we can't either."

Which is how we wound up at the £180 per night Dialoog Banyuwangi. And listen, it's not exactly la Hôtel Ritz, but nor is it an underpass in Hackney.

We walked into our suite, and BJ peered over at me, a little grimace on his face, waiting for my verdict.

"The decor is a bit festive," I told him, and he rolled his eyes and slipped his arms around my waist.

"You ready for tomorrow?" he asked me.

The last thing on our list for Bridge is the volcano.

I shrugged and flashed him a small smile. "How would I feel if I were ready?"

"I don't know." He smiled back. "I don't know if you'll ever feel properly ready, Parksy." Then he kissed the top of my head. "But you're going to be okay either way."

Beej and Allie have gone to great efforts planning this, we've got a guide and someone's organised lunch, because apparently there's no restaurants at the top of the mountain or something—

For the first time in the history of ever, BJ picked my outfit. He said I'm not reasonably equipped to pick my clothes for the day and that I can't "hike in a ball gown or whatever," and I said, "Do you think I'm some kind of idiot?" And he said, "Okay, show me what you think you're going to wear." I flashed him the white Love Parade embroidered terry polo set from Gucci and he rolled his eyes, but when I reached for my black Fendi Rockoko boots, he immediately said 'no' and moved me away from my suitcase(s).

Thus, as per his choosing, I'm wearing the Barocco print leggings and matching sports bra (both from Versace, obviously) with the terribly clunky black Peka Trek hiking boots from Moncler, and BJ's Intern slogan-print black cotton hoodie from Off-White. Our hike looks like it's sponsored by Condé Nast Traveller—not literally, of course, because none of us are so lowbrow that we need to accept any kind of sponsorship.

He packed a backpack for us with water bottles and Bridget and some snacks and I see him pop in my compact mirror, and I love him.

I did say, "I'm not sure Bridget would appreciate spending the night in your bag, actually," and then he said, "Should I crack a zip and give her some air?" and I frowned at him for that, but thought it was secretly rather funny, and then I wondered what that meant? That I could find humour in anything to do with my sister? Is that a good thing or a bad thing, I can't tell?

After that we have an early dinner with Hen and Allie, where at the end of the meal, at 5:30 p.m., they made all of us take a Nytol at the table so we all would go to sleep early because this fucking ordeal of a hike starts at midnight.

Which, first of all—absurd! What is this? A fucking college hazing? Nope, it's just my sister being an arsehole from beyond the grave again!

It's about an hour and a half drive from the hotel to the base of the mountain, so I slept during the drive too.

I've always liked sleeping in cars with BJ. There's something about falling asleep on him and waking up where I'm supposed to be that feels like I've found a shortcut through life that I wish I could replicate in every single sphere of it.

When we arrived at the car park at the bottom of the Ijen volcano BJ wakes me up by pushing his hands through my hair and kissing the top of my head.

But apparently that didn't work so I was actually awoken by Henry clapping loudly in my face and then he and BJ had a fight because BJ called him a "fucking prick" and then because Ballentines do surprisingly poorly without a full nine hours of sleep, it escalated a bit from there.

Allie and I leant against the van, tired, and our tour guide watched on in amusement, whipping his phone out to film them, not because he knew who they are, I don't think—just because it was a pretty good fight, like all of theirs are.

It really wasn't so bad except for when Hen shoved BJ and he nearly dropped Bridget, which was how they pulled it the fuck together—Allie and I gasped so loudly and both lunged towards the ashes of my sister and the boys were so rattled that they just stopped and both looked at us sheepishly and laughed nervously.

I rolled my eyes and walked over to the tour guide where he fitted us for gas masks.

"Very sexy." BJ grins at me as I put mine on and give him an unimpressed look for his behaviour a moment ago.

"You're nearly thirty," I tell him.

"Fuck off!" He gawps at me, offended. "I'm twenty-fucking-seven."

"That's late twenties."

"That's mid," he says sternly, and I roll my eyes.

"Are you going to fight your little brother when we're grown-ups and have babies of our own?" I ask him, eyebrows up.

"If he claps in the face of my sleeping wife," he nods his head, tightening the strap on the headlight I've got on as well. "Yep."

I roll my eyes again but secretly like him for being like this.

It's dark, the walk. And steep. Both things that I think I'm grateful for because my mind is intensely busy today. I have so many racing thoughts, and I'm grateful that no one can see my face as I'm processing them, and no one has spare breath in their lungs to speak and interrupt my train of thought.

I do feel as though I'm walking towards something, or climbing up to it.

We stop a little bit of the way up at the first base camp, where our guide gives us our gas masks again and says it's time to put them on, which I was glad for because it smelt like nothing my nose had ever smelt before, ever, and I hope it never has to smell again, and then we're back to walking.

All in all, it takes about an hour to reach the blue flames.

And it is—actually—breathtaking.

Like a river, almost. On fire, though. Dripping down a mountain, this insane, neon-electric-blue flame that moves and drips like water.

"This can't be real—" Henry says, voice muffled by our masks but eyes all wide.

"It's because of the sulphuric gases," Allie tells us, even though none of us asked, but it makes me happy. I knew she would because Bridget would. "The lava comes out from the crack in the earth super hot, and if we were here in the daytime, it'd look like any other lava or volcano, but because there's so much gas here, when it's combined with the lava, it sort of—ignites it? It's the burning of the sulphur that's blue, not the lava."

I don't say anything but try to observe it as much as I can, to the best of my abilities; as though me seeing it is the way Bridget gets to.

We stay there for about a half an hour before our guide tells us we're going to have to keep climbing if we want to make it to the peak for sunrise.

So back into the darkness we go, just, the tiny dots of light up the side of the mountain like moving stars, each of them a headlight.

And it's funny how much this trek feels like the physical embodiment of my last year in a single moment. This confusing, horrible walk in the dark; I'm falling all the time, tripping over everything—BJ's trying to help me but he's in the dark too.

A sort of floundering that I mostly hate, but that feels distinctively like living, so it's impossible to hate it all the way through.

That's been this year for me. I've hated it, fiercely for the most part—but then, is this not just the human experience?

Shoved into this impossibly deep lake of loss and losing, barely keeping your head above it, then drowning in it, choking on it, somehow surviving against all odds and then reemerging a little bit reborn.

We reach the peak and it's dark still.

That feels right. That's sort of how I feel in general, actually. A bit as though I've climbed this absolute fucker of a mountain, and that maybe I'm nearing the part of it where I might be okay, which doesn't even really make sense because ten minutes ago I was gasping for air in the same way a month ago I was crying because I saw a waterfall my sister would have liked.

Grief is funny like that, how it ebbs and flows from you, it's not corked like champagne, a bottle that bursts open, fizzes all out until it's empty. It's more like a kind of weather. A kind of wind. Sometimes it's these horrible gusts that you feel undeniably, hurts your ears, makes you close your eyes, chills you right down to your bones, some days it's a pleasant breeze that blows across your face and it's neither sad or bad, it's just some kind of unspeakable tenderness. Some days you feel no breeze, that's started happening to me—I don't know how I feel about it yet—not that I don't think of her, I sort of think I'll think of her every day for forever, but more that, when I do, it doesn't necessarily feel like someone's dropping a crystal vase inside my chest. That's not to say I don't still have days where I'm a glassware shop situated somewhere along the San Andreas Fault and there's an earthquake and things are falling and breaking everywhere, but there was a time where every day felt like the big one California's waiting for—just total demolition. I suppose it doesn't feel like total destruction anymore.

And I can feel it coming, like the sun I'm waiting to rise—it's finally getting lighter—another dawning revelation and I know what I have to do—I wonder if a part of me always knew this was what I'd have to do but just shielded that knowledge from the rest of me knowing that I'd reject it if I knew it consciously at the start.

BJ comes and stands behind me, chin on top of my head, pulls my body back against his. He doesn't say a thing because he doesn't have to, I think because he probably knows too. Bridget didn't write a will, why would she have? She was tiny, too young to think of such terrible things, she wouldn't have cared about assets and where they went, to charities or something I presume. That's what I did with them, divvied them up between various organisations I know she's always been fond of.

There's only one thing that was hers that, in the absence of a will, was left largely unaccounted for, and that was her sister.

And while there's no way to empirically prove that this is true, much of the data we have would suggest that Bridget left me to a one Baxter James Ballentine.

So it's with his chin on top of my head and his body pressed against mine that makes me brave enough to allow my brain to think of the scariest thought it's ever had in my whole life, and actually, I resent that I even have to have it at all—I don't want to have it, I've never wanted to have something less—but then everything that's happened has happened now and I can't undo it, I can't change it. This is it, this is what I've got—and maybe all it is, maybe all everything is, is just that houseplant on a spaceship that's on fire flying into the darkest black of the infinite nothingness, and maybe still my best chance for surviving is letting go of everything that is or has been hurting me.

Bridget, my parents, how terrifyingly out of control the whole world is and how that makes me feel—

The sun rises, finally rises, and I get this rush of feelings—elation, relief, sadness, fear, gratefulness, mourning—and somehow the view feels supernatural and otherworldly and I feel as though I'm floating out of my body a bit, except I'm not. My feet are planted firmly on the ground next to my fiancé's, right where Bridget left them.

BJ adjusts his grip on me, wraps himself around me more, which is a clever thing he's always managed to do, right when I think we've reached our most peak level of closeness, he finds a way to be closer still, and I do believe with my whole heart that Bridget would never have left if she didn't know I had BJ. I know that might sound crazy, I know she didn't commit suicide, I know it wasn't her choice—but your body knows. It knows more than we ever want to think it knows, it stores thoughts and feelings and traumas in different regions of it, whether or not Bridget herself consciously knew that she had an aneurysm is irrelevant, because her body knew, and I don't think the part of her that knew that would have allowed the rest of her to leave until she knew I was going to be okay.

Which is in one breath, terribly hard to think about, and in the other, I'm so glad that I am where she wants me to be and that she got to leave knowing I'd be okay(ish) without her, and it's as I'm thinking that, that the sun casts this peculiar light on my sister's urn—it's a beautiful light, but it is odd. Extra golden, extra bright, the kind of colours that nature makes on purpose so they get stuck in your mind.

I look over at the others and pick up her ashes.

"We're going to have a talk," I tell them, and both Henry and Allie look a bit confused but BJ doesn't. He hands me the Jay Strongwater compact without saying a word and I give him a grateful smile, then I carry her away to a spot up here that's a bit more isolated.

I put her down and then sit down next to her.

I flip open the mirror and I don't even have to wait to see her, I just see her.

I swallow nervously.

"I'm going to leave you up here," I say.

"Sorry, what?" She'd blink.

"Well, I was actually going to throw you into the volcano but it smelt so bad down—"

She'd cut me off. "—You were going to what!"

I give her a look.

"Just kidding—" She'd shake her head. "I'm kidding. Good girl"—she'd give me a small smile—"You should."

I nod, not entirely sure because I always want all her approval on everything. "Should I?"

"Yes." She'd nod. "Definitely."

I nod back, eyes filling with tears. "I'm scared to do this without you."

"Magnolia," she'd sigh and give me a look. Somewhere between exasperated and sorry for me and maybe, if I was lucky, a hint of tenderness in there herself. "You're already doing it without me."

"This is different—" I take a sharp breath in through my nose. "I don't know how to"—sharp breath—"I don't know how to be"—swallow—"me . . . without you."

She'd tilt her head. "Yes, you do."

And I'd roll my eyes at her for making it sound easy when nothing about this is.

"You can't be who you were before anymore, that's true—" She'd nod. "That Magnolia died with me, but this one's fine—" She'd nod her chin at me, looking for a rise, and I'd give her one because I'm easy to bait. I open my mouth to say something in protest but she'd beat me to it.

"This one's great," she'd say, rather firmly.

I look over at her, unsure. "Really?"

"Yeah," she'd nod, and maybe her eyes would well up a little bit too. "I'm proud of this one."

I swallow and nod a lot. I breathe out my nose because I don't want to cry on top of this mountain in front of a bunch of people I don't know, but I do anyway.

A few baby tears slip out and roll down my cheeks, and for the first time in my life, I don't smack them away. I let them sit there, I try not to worry about who could see them or use them against me, and instead wear them like these tiny badges of honour, little proofs that I knew the best girl in the world and that she died and that I'm still here without her.

"Have you found heaven yet?" I ask her because I need closure.

"Have you?" she'd counter.

"No."

She'd roll her eyes. "Then no."

"Bridget—" I give her a look.

She'd give me the same one back. "Magnolia."

"Wait—" I sit up straighter. "Do you know the meaning of life up there?"

She'd shrug. "Yeah, probably."

"Can you tell me?"

"Magnolia—" Bridget's eyes would pinch. "For the billionth time, if you don't know, then I don't kn—"

"Okay, okay—" I shake my head, annoyed because she's annoying. "Don't fracture the moment."

She'd give me a long look with a careful gentleness to it, and I know what's coming.

"I'd like you to let me go now, Magnolia."

"Why?" I ask, even though I think I know why.

"Because it's what needs to happen for you to be okay," she'd say. "And you will be okay."

I nod a lot. "How do you know?"

She'd look at me, the slightest bit offended and indignant. "Because I'm leaving you in the most capable hands."

She'd nod her head in the direction of those capable hands over there with his brother and his sister, a light shining on his face that makes all of him golden like he really is on the inside anyway, and I can't help but feel as though my sister made that shade of gold this morning, wherever she is, especially for him, so that he could be cast in it, frozen forever like an eternal sunshine-y promise.

"I love you," I tell her, sniffling.

"I know," she'd shrug.

I lift my eyebrows. "Any parting words?"

She'd scrunch her face. "Uh—"

"Like . . . you'll always be with me?" I offer.

She'd shake her head. "That's not how death works though, is it?"

"Or that you'll live inside of me?" I suggest as an alternative.

"I will do no such thing!" She'd scrunch her face up again. "The mess in there—so chaotic!"

I roll my eyes and feel a kind of relief to feel how annoying she can be sometimes.

"That I'll feel you in the wind, or something—? I don't know!"

"The wind—!" She'd stare at me. "Fuck."

And I'd breathe out my nose, properly annoyed at her now because she's difficult sometimes, and she'd roll her eyes all annoyed at me being annoyed at her.

"Enough with the eating shit," she'd say, voice stern. "You're done with that, yeah?"

I say nothing, and she'd give me a look.

"Magnolia, you're smart enough to develop a coping mechanism for your lack of control in the world that doesn't involve you emaciating yourself."

That feels, somehow, like a fair enough point, so I nod once. "Fine."

"And don't stop going to therapy," she'd say, and I frown immediately.

"Why!"

"Because you're mental," she'd say without missing a beat, and I frown defensively.

"Hey—"

"And—" She'd give me a tall look before delivering this next one. "You should try and forgive Harley—"

"Are you crazy—!" I stare at our reflection, eyes wide. "No!"

Her head would tilt to the side and she'd breathe out her nose. "You'll be better for it."

"I don't care—" I shake my head. "Why are you so annoying?"

She'd roll her eyes.

"He hasn't even said sorry," I tell her, and she'd nod and shrug.

"And he mightn't ever, Magnolia, and then what—?" She'd lift an eyebrow. "You're going to be the sad, fatherless girl all your life because your dad's a stubborn prick?"

"Maybe," I'd tell her, nose in the air, and she'd roll her eyes.

"On behalf of everyone, I'd beseech you to not."

I'd cross my arms over my chest, square off with her how I used to in the olden days when she lived here.

"Hey, Bridge," I'd tell her, looking her straight into our eyes. "I have loved, more than I can say, being your sister."

She'd nod. "I know."

I'd wait a long few seconds where she'd say absolutely nothing because she's an absolute punish of a girl and then I'd lift my brows and eye her down.

". . . And you've loved being mine too."

She'd roll her eyes. "Okay."

"Bridget!"

"Okay, fine—" She'd flick her eyes. "I have."

I can feel my throat getting tight again so I nod quickly, tell myself how my sister would if she were really here that it's going to be okay.

"Thank you for being the brave one and the clever one and the wise one and the safe one and the dependable one and the thoughtful one and—"

"Believe it or not," she'd lift her chin, proudly. "I learnt most of those things from my older sister."

I'd shake my head. "I don't believe it."

"Okay, well—" She'd roll her eyes. "I mean, no one thinks you're wise so—"

"Bridget!" I'd growl.

She'd nod her chin again back towards the others.

"You should go," she'd tell me, and I'd shake my head.

"I don't know if I'm ready."

She'd nod sure, because she knew everything. "You're ready."

"Only barely," I'd tell her.

And she'd nod again. "More than you think."

I stand up and both my legs and my heart feel like jelly.

"See you soon?" I say to our reflection.

She'd give me a small smile, and I think she'd be a bit sad because I know how much she loves me.

"Not too soon, please," she'd say, because that's not what she'd want for me.

"Not too soon," I say, nodding. "But one day again."

And then I close my little mirror, lay it down next to her ashes and let her go.

EIGHTY

BJ

I stare over at Parks laying face down on the sun bed. So brown at the minute, which is both unreal and annoying.

Unreal because she's so fucking hot and it's the best, and annoying, because she's so fucking hot, it's the worst.

Proud of her though. Really proud of how she handled it with her sister up the mountain last week, she cried a bit afterwards.

Cried more when we got back to the hotel, but that was in part because "she couldn't stay at these 'double-digit' hotels anymore," so now we're here. The Four Seasons Resort Bali at Sayan, which is way more her speed.

We finished the list, we could have gone home—weren't ready though. None of us said that, we just felt it for no real reason.

Came over to Bali pretty mindlessly, or so I thought. I thought we just needed to be here longer, needed more time out of London, it wasn't conscious why we came here but I think I know now, just took a minute.

Henry and Allie are on some Ubud bird-watching walk, which Henry really wanted to do because of course he fucking does. Out of all of us, who was the most likely to become a bird-watcher in his old age—? That fucking idiot, 100 percent.

But I'm happy they're gone. I plan on using their absence well.

I dive in the pool to cool down and clear my head, but thing is, my head is clear.

I kind of just wanted to splash her, get her attention.

She glances over at me, fake-glare in her eye.

Push myself up out of the pool, walk to her, stand over her, blocking the sun she's laying in with my shadow on purpose and she smacks me away like she's annoyed, but it's all any old reason shit, and I just want to be close to her.

I grab her wrists and pin her down on the sun bed, wrestling her for a few seconds before I wrap my cold, wet self around her warm, dry little body and she screams and laughs and tries to wriggle away but I don't let her, she smacks me again, once for good measure, and then rolls in towards me, glancing up.

I push some hair behind her ears.

"Did you finish *The Blind Watchmaker*?"

She nods. "Yes."

"And?" I lift my brows. "What'd you think?"

She shrugs, a bit annoyed. "I don't know—"

I sniff a laugh, kiss her nose because it's the best one on the planet.

"No massive revelations?" I ask her.

"No," she frowns, crosser now. "It's a bit depressing."

I press my tongue into my top lip and look over her face.

What a fucking face.

I've loved this face all my life. It's the sun I pray to, and if what we have is a temple, I built it with my bare hands—I nearly died trying to build this fucking thing. Built it til my hands were raw and bloodied. And I'll die on the altar of loving her, happily too. That's not a waste to me.

I push some more hair behind her ears.

"My dad, right—" I nod over at her. "All these years, he's been banging on about what I'm doing with my life, that I have nothing to show for it and—"

"I know." She frowns in defence of me. "I hate that."

"But he's wrong," I tell her with a shrug. "He admitted that too, did I tell you—?"

"—Did he!" she interrupts, smiling over all delighted, but I ignore her.

"And then you, with the meaning of it—fuck, you're both so unbelievably literal—"

"Oh, okay—" She rolls her eyes. "Is this where you tell me the meaning of life, then?"

I nod, pleased with myself. "It is."

She props herself up a little and arches an eyebrow. "Go on then, pray tell."

I gesture towards her casually and she scoffs a small laugh before she lifts an amused eyebrow.

"Me?" She points to herself. "I'm the meaning of life."

"Yeah." I nod, coolly. "I don't know, Parks"—little shrug—"I don't see much beyond like, just a life together."

"Beej—" She rolls her eyes. "That's very sweet but—"

"No, I mean it." I prop myself up on my elbows. "Like, money we have. And stocks are easy and flipping property's pretty brainless for me. We'll always have money, but none of those things seem like what I want to spend my life doing."

She gives me a curious look.

"What do you want to spend your life doing?"

Bite down on my bottom lip, give her a quarter of a smile. "You."

Rolls her eyes straightaway at that.

"BJ—"

"I'm serious," I tell her, putting my hand on her waist, pulling her in closer towards me. "I want to like, build us a home—"

"You?" She blinks. "From scratch?"

She tilts her head in doubt.

"Do you want it to be liveable?"

"Shut up." I flick her in the arm. "I'm going to grow us a garden, with zucchinis and strawberries and turnips—"

"You don't eat turnips," she jumps in to tell me.

"Of course I fucking don't!" I look at her, exasperated. "They're rubbish, but they're easy to grow—"

She starts laughing and it's my favourite sound.

I keep going. "We're going to have animals—"

"—What kind of animals?" she asks, eyes pinched.

"Some dogs, a cat, some chickens—"

Her head pulls back, blinking in surprise. "Plural?"

I ignore her, carry on. "Maybe some sheep. A horse. A cow. A llama—"

"—Absolutely no." She shakes her head firmly and I tilt my head and shrug my shoulders.

"We'll circle back to the llama, then—"

She flicks me a look I know well, where she's trying to look like she's over my shit but she loves my shit, and I love her shit, I want it all. I touch her face, give her a look so she knows I'm serious.

"I want to raise our kids—"

She lets out a surprised laugh. "Our kids?"

"Yeah," I nod, grinning down at her. "A boy and a girl."

"Oh, okay!" She pulls a face. "Sorry, I must have missed their birth—"

I shrug.

"—When you're ready," I tell her.

She nods back. "When I'm ready."

"I just don't see much beyond that—" I tell her pretty breezily, but then I look at her all serious. "You are the thing I have to show for in my life, and that won't ever not be enough to me."

Her eyes go soft so I hold her face because I can't help it.

"It's like, wild that we're here, Parks—" I tell her, my eyebrows up. "There are so many fucking times it went pear-shaped, but there's just no life I can think of where if you're here, that I'm not like, finding my way back to you . . ."

I shrug and she swallows heavy.

"Because it's you—" I say, nodding over at her. "At Mum and Dad's place, over by the mantelpiece, do you know where I mean—?"

She nods back. "The awards wall."

"Right—" I flick her a smile. "They have Henry's masters up there next to Jemima's doctorate and Allie's degree and Maddie's like—what, I don't know—fucking participation ribbon—?"

She squints at me. "Be nice."

"Why?" I pull a face. "She hates you."

"Be quiet!" she growls. "No one hates me."

"I'm going to make them hang up our wedding certificate," I tell her with a nod.

"Well," she considers. "Perhaps not the original."

"Yeah," I nod. "Fair."

"And is it not a touch dismissive of your siblings' hard work all these years—?"

I look at her like she's mad.

"You don't think us having our names on a fucking wedding certificate was hard work—?" My eyebrows are sky high. "No one's worked harder, Parks, fuck—"

I breathe out, exasperated, and she gives me an unimpressed look.

"Listen," I tell her. "They're going to hang it up because in a hundred years no one's going to give a shit that Henry graduated with honours, or that Mimes is a"—I pause—"fuck"—I pull a face because I'm a shit brother—"what does she do? Foot doctor?"

"Otolaryngologist," she tells me, and I nod in appreciation.

"No one's going to give a fuck that Jemima is the youngest ear doctor in a decade—" ("Well, they might." Magnolia interrupts but I ignore her.) "—but they'll talk about us."

She looks at me, eyes actually soft but trying to look suspicious. "Will they?"

I look at her like she's stupid for questioning it.

"A love like ours—? Are you joking?" I give her the magic smile. "We're what the poems are about"—give her a little poke in the ribs—"they'll write TV shows about how much I love you."

She tucks her chin but keeps those heavy eyes of hers on me.

"This life we've like, fought proper battles for—what?—half our lives, almost—?" I sniff, amused. "Yeah, of course, they're hanging that up. It's like, the only thing worth hanging up—"

She looks unsure about that.

"—I think there are some other things worth hanging up too, like—"

"Sure, yeah—" I shrug. "Like birth certificates and shit."

She flicks me a look.

"Parksy—" I say her name to bring us both back.

"Yes," she says, staving off a smile.

I tug on her hair. "I know you're scared about what everything means—"

"Perhaps a bit less so now," she tells me, proud of herself how she should be.

I smile at her because I'm proud too.

"I know losing Bridge opened this can of worms in your mind about the meaning of it all; like, if we're all just going to die anyway, what's the point—?" She doesn't nod but I know she's tracking me, waiting and listening.

"You are," I tell her. "You're the point. Or—" I shrug. "We are, I guess—" Her eyes go soft. "—love is. And it doesn't make sense and I can't hang my hat on it—neither can my dad—and it's unquantifiable, but I don't care what anyone says, because it'll surpass all space and all time and maybe when we're dead there won't be a framed degree to prove we lived on the planet—"

"Um—" She clears her throat to interrupt because she's fucking impossible. "I actually do have a degree."

I roll my eyes. "I know."

"From Imperial College," she reminds me.

I roll my eyes again. "I know."

"Okay," she shrugs. "So that could go on a wall too, is just all I was saying—" and then she shakes her head. "Sorry. Go on."

I give her a long look.

"Okay, so maybe when we're dead there's one degree on a wall somewhere that proves you lived on the planet and barely graduated—" ("BJ!" she pouts.) "But maybe better still, someone sits under that tree of ours and feels how much I loved you."

And now she's all mush.

"Like,"—I shrug—"maybe that's what the northern lights are—once upon a time, a thousand years ago, a Viking really loved the fucking shit out of this one girl and that's what it is—proof that he loved her all over the sky." I shrug again like it's not insanely mind-blowing. "Proof that love is this sort of inimitable, like metaphysical, transcendent thing. Proof that love actually is the only thing worth spending your life trying to do, you know?"

I give her a little smile and she stares back at me for a couple of seconds before she wriggles in towards me, presses her lips heavy into mine.

"I love you," she tells me.

"Marry me," I tell her back and then her eyes pinch, all confused.

"I . . . am . . . ?"

"Now," I say with a nod. "This week."

Her head pulls back but I know all her faces and there's intrigue there.

"What?" she says, quietly.

"Here." I keep going, shaking my head. "Let's do it here—I don't want to wait—"

"But—"

"And we hate our wedding—!" I frown a bit. "Hate it so much—I don't want to wear real shoes!"

She huffs. "BJ!"

"I'm joking—!" I roll my eyes. "About the shoes. Kind of"—I pause, pull a face to wind her up—"I am serious about the wedding, though."

She swallows, eyeing me. "Really?"

"Yeah," I shrug, all breezy. "I'll promise to love you forever anywhere."

Parks presses her lips together, thinking for a bit, before she breathes out.

"Bridget wanted to get married in Bali, do you remember?"

I nod once, smiling a bit.

"I do remember, yeah."

I lift up my eyebrows, hopeful and pretty fucking excited already.

"One more thing for Bridge?"

She nods, smiling now too in a way I know means she's proper happy.

"One last thing for Bridge."

EIGHTY-ONE

BJ

Alright, if you've ever planned a wedding then you know that planning one can be fucking hard.

Planning one in a week—?

Well, shit.

I told Parks I'd do it all.

Said to her to arrange for Taura to bring the dress and I'd organise everything else.

Getting everyone over here was the easiest part.

It's the best outcome for us because it's the tiny wedding we wanted away from all the London fuckery.

The boys are flying out, so is Tausie and Rom.

My parents are flying in with Mars and Bushka.

I think Parksy said Daisy's coming too even though shit's still weird with Dais and Christian.

She said she invited her mum and that she's going to come even though her dad isn't coming.

She got a bit weird around the topic of paying for it all, which she's never done in her life.

Like I give a fuck who's paying for it—it doesn't matter. Said I'd pay for all of it, I'd fucking love to, but Parksy said that she'd pay for it herself, said she had to because the girl's family are the ones who are supposed to do it, but then Henry overheard it and said she couldn't pay for it herself, that it was "too sad"—shot him a fucking sharp look for that one—and then my parents were on the horn saying they were paying for all of it, and that they are her family so they're allowed to, but she refused that option.

So then Henry said he'd pay for it, but that was annoying, and I said why would he pay for it instead of me paying for it when I'm the one marrying her?

And then I reckon my mum probably called Mars or Bushka, because then Bushka called Parks and they had a conversation in Russian, and now she's paying for it.

Now, I can't say I've been able to give myself years of time to research this, but as far as I can tell, there's really one place to get married in Bali.

The Bulgari Resort in Uluwatu.

It was an absolute fucking nightmare getting it on a week's notice, I can't lie. We're getting married on a fucking Wednesday but I'll take it—leave it to Parks to redeem Wednesdays for the world.

There's not a lot of problems that don't go away if you just throw money at them, that's an ugly thing people don't really want to hear but there it is, it's true.

We got the venue, they're doing the food.

I know who Parks' favourite florist is, so I'm flying her in and a bunch of hydrangeas, forget-me-nots, Juliet roses, lilies of the valley and magnolias, obviously.

Mum's bringing my suit over.

We're flying over Emilie White, who was always going to be our photographer, Parks was well decided on that even before we were doing a small wedding. "Why not Annie?" Arrie would say every few weeks. "You've known her all your life, Magnolia. It feels like a slap—"

"She's of course invited to the wedding, Mother—" Parks would roll her eyes. "It's just too obvious. Everyone would guess I'd have Annie shoot—"

"And why wouldn't you! She's Annie Leibovitz!"

Magnolia would give her a firm look. "We're having Emilie."

The cake's being flown in the day before from Lily Vanilli

because, who else—? She's always been Parks' go-to. I order like, ten of them though because fuck it, I don't know how to pick what our wedding cake should look like, so I pick all the ones I think she might like.

The wine selection here in Bali is pretty shit, so I'm flying in a bunch of that too.

It's a lot, I know. We sound mad, but I've waited all my life to marry her, and it's going to be the fucking best day of our lives, but even if it wasn't—even if it was just me and her alone on a cliff, promising all official the same shit we've promised a thousand times before, I'd be happy as Larry.

Actually, as long as I'm next to her, fuck Larry, Larry's got nothing on me.

EIGHTY-TWO
Magnolia

The day rolls around rather quickly.

Taura and the boys all arrived three days ago, Romilly the day after with Lily and Hamish and the girls, then Daisy and Marsaili flew yesterday too, same as my mother, though I've not seen her yet, which I'm not precious about.

Bushka flew out the moment she heard of the wedding, which was equal parts sweet and chaotic, possibly with a fraction of an edge towards the chaotic.

Planning a wedding in general is actually quite horrible, but planning it in a week with a language barrier—oh my god, I'm marrying a saint. BJ really ran with all of it, he didn't ask me anything, didn't tell me anything unless I asked—and I did ask, because all our lives, I've been the one who picks the restaurants and plans the parties and the trips, and I can't say that I'd necessarily look at BJ and think to myself, *There he is, the most organised man in the world!* But to his credit, everything I asked him about he had covered. Once we locked in the venue, then it was just catering, flowers, photographer, we don't need a seating chart because it's so small, he's sorted the cake, Lily's bringing his and Henry's suits, as well as our rings—the only sticking point was who's going to marry us. That was a bit of a conversation, because for one, for a Balinese wedding to be deemed legal in the UK, there are some hoops we'd need to jump through, so we're actually going to have to get legally married again quietly back home anyway, which then opened up the floor of who would marry us here.

We met with several ministers back in London and none of

them felt super right—not that they felt wrong, but we aren't overtly religious. I did have the idea of seeing whether we could get the editor-in-chief of *National Geographic* to marry us but I think he thought we were joking when we asked him and it was a bit weird. BJ suggested Anna because *Vogue* is really the book that I live my life by, but we felt it would create a knock-on effect. If Anna was there, why aren't the Arnaults? Why isn't Annie there? Or Tom Ford, or the Beckhams and the Richies and the Paltrow/Martins, or Donatella or Marc or Alessandro? Our world is too small and too large at once, and you can't invite some people without offending all of the others so it's full Box Set only and our families, not even extended, really. Grandparents, yes. Aunts and uncles, no—with the exception of Uncle Alexey and his wife Mika, a little because I want to stay in his good graces, but mostly because he's looked after Bushka and I'm thankful for that.

While I am inviting my paternal grandparents (even though we aren't that close, it felt decidedly cruel to exclude them), I'm not inviting my Aunty Araminta and her husband Tim, because she's incredibly close with two of BJ's aunts, and we can't invite them because they'd insist on bringing their children who are teenagers and knee-deep in TikTok, and it doesn't matter if we put a social media embargo on the event, those tiny trollops will find a way to post about it anyway. We're all a bit worried about Maddie, honestly. Henry said he's going to steal her phone as soon as she arrives and hide it til after the wedding.

Anyway, all that's to say, after much consideration and some protest from me, Jonah is who will be officiating the ceremony. The antithesis of a priest, I know, but he has been a big champion of our love.

I was worried he'd be a bit of a clown about it but Christian told me he's been practicing in the mirror every spare second he has, so I feel a bit better about it.

If anything in all the planning has gone awry or if anything's amiss, I don't know about it. The only thing I was really charged with was making sure my dress arrived, except that was a tiny bit difficult as I hadn't fully landed on which I was wearing.

I'd narrowed it down to a few, and that was okay because before, I needed a few. Rehearsal dinner, ceremony, reception, leaving dress, a handful of dresses for the shoot we're meant to do for *Vogue*—but now I think I just need one, maybe two.

Getting married in London at the Mandarin with all the fanfare that would have surrounded us would have required a certain kind of dress that getting married on a quiet cliff in Bali with twenty people does not. You can't just deposit one into the other, it's not a neat and easy copy and paste.

Some time ago, Elie and I drew up a dress together and I had it made. A full, fairly constructed crinoline skirt all supported underneath by organza, with teeny-tiny angel-hair straps on a very fitted bodice made of the same smoked-white crushed silk dupioni. There was a schlubbed and crunched effect to the fabric that made me think of a freshly washed linen duvet, and probably the first time I remember consciously and viscerally feeling safe in my life was wrapped up in a duvet with him in St Barts.

The dress was completely gorgeous, and I loved it and I was sure BJ would love it, but I ruled it out quite quickly because it wouldn't have looked right against the setting of our planned London wedding, but here—

Well, here, it's probably rather perfect.

I'd always sort of fancied a mantilla veil, so I had one of them made up with a mostly raw edge but with a light sprinkling of little white lace forget-me-nots around my face.

For shoes, I went with the white Averly 100 bow-detailed faille pumps from Jimmy Choo, even though you can't really see them under my dress, it's sort of nice to know they're there still.

BJ and I slept apart last night, because tradition or something—I don't know—Lily made us do it. All it really meant is I had a fairly bad sleep the night before my wedding.

Henry and Taura have been with me all morning—they tried to make me eat breakfast, but I barely did. Not in the way that

Bridget would be cross about but in the way where I'm nervous and the weight of the day sits heavy on my mind and stomach.

It's a sunset wedding because sunsets in Uluwatu are mad. I don't remember where it was in Bali that Bridget said she'd have liked to have been married, but if I were a betting woman, I think it would have been around here. Maybe not at The Bulgari, knowing her, but somewhere here.

My makeup's done now and I'm about to get into my dress so Henry ducks out for a minute so I can change.

With Tausie's help, it takes about five minutes for me to be all fastened into the dress when there's a knock at the door.

"—Come in," I say because I presume it's Henry but it's not.

The door swings open and Harley Parks fills the frame.

I can't even imagine what my face looks like, and I don't say a thing.

My father looks over at my friend. "Can you give us a minute, Taura?"

She looks over at me, almost asking permission to leave.

I don't really want her to leave, actually, but for some reason I don't say no.

I feel a creeping panic starting to rise in my chest.

Try to tell Taura with my eyes to go get BJ, but I don't know if she speaks our silent language.

She closes the door behind her and Harley stands here, shoves his hands into his pockets awkwardly.

I stare over at him.

"What are you doing here?"

"It's your wedding day," he tells me.

"Yes," I nod carefully. "But see, I didn't invite you, so—"

He nods his chin over at me. "You invited your mother."

"Right." I nod once. "Although I didn't give her a plus-one"—I give him a pointed look—"historically, she hasn't always had the most wonderful taste in men."

His eyes drop from mine for a second before he takes a breath and looks back over at me.

"A father's supposed to give his daughter away," he tells me like I don't know, like it hasn't been a little worried thought in the back of my mind since BJ first asked me.

"They are." I give him a curt smile. "Do you happen to know any?"

He flicks me a bit of a despondent look.

"Harley"—I cross my arms over my chest—"you gave me away a long time ago."

His brows go low and he looks confused.

"I was eleven, leaving for boarding school. You stayed out all night, patted my head on the stairs. You didn't even drive me yourself—actually, you didn't even walk me to the car—"

"Yeah." He presses his mouth together in a bit of a grimace. "I dropped the ball on that one."

My head pulls back, incredulous.

"That one?"

His head tilts as though he's saying '*come on*,' but I won't come on.

He breathes out his nose.

"Who's walking you down the aisle?"

"Henry," I tell him, my chin in the air.

Harley nods a lot while he does a frown that looks a bit like thinking. "That's a good choice."

I look at him out of the corner of my eyes. "I know."

And then he takes a big breath, squares his feet—his face looks oddly strained as he rubs his hand over his mouth.

"I fucked up," he says.

"Yes. Plenty." I nod, unfazed by his candour, before I tilt my head. "But to which time specifically are you referring?"

He rolls his eyes and takes a step further into the room.

"You're hard to parent," he tells me.

"How would you know?" I fire back.

"Listen—" he sighs. "If you want me to go, I'll—"

"I want you to go." I cut him off with a nod.

He shrugs, jaw a bit jutted, and I wonder if he looks a bit hurt.

"If I do, you'll regret it."

"Oh, why?" I blink a few times and smile at him pleasantly.

"Are you going to threaten to take away my money again, or destroy the one vestige of my baby that I have on this earth?"

"No—" He frowns a bit at that, kicks nothing on the floor uncomfortably. "I meant more like, one day when I die, or something—"

He and I stare over at one another, eyes locked in this strange way, a bit stuck, a bit baffled, a bit proud, a bit surprised and I maybe even find myself just the slightest bit amused at that last comment.

I shake my head a little and give him a look.

"Well, that feels in very poor taste—"

"It does," he grimaces. "I'm sorry."

I move past him towards the vanity mirror where I've all my jewellery options set out in from of me. I pluck the handmade and painted Anise Magnolia earrings by Danielle Frankel from the table and put them on because I still have a wedding to get to.

"Also, it sounds incredibly unlikely," I catch his eye in the reflection of the mirror. "What—with all that dancing on your grave I'll be doing."

He doesn't even roll his eyes when I say that; instead he moves closer to me and reaches inside his jacket pocket, pulling something out.

A folded piece of paper. He offers it to me.

"This is for you," he says.

I frown at it before I turn on my heel and pluck it from his hand.

"What is it?"

Harley nods at it for me to open it and I sigh as though I'm not the least bit curious, even though I absolutely am.

I look down at it and it takes me a few seconds to work out what I'm holding, and then I look back up at him, eyes wider with a surprise and a tenderness I'd prefer not to be there.

"It's the deed to the Dartmouth house—" he tells me.

I shake my head. "But—"

He cuts me off.

"I shouldn't have threatened that. That was fucked." He nods to himself. "It's yours. It's done, it's already in your name."

He gives me a little shrug.

I look back down at it and swallow away the little lump in my throat. I fold the piece of paper back up and hold it, feeling awkward now.

"Thank you?" I say, but it sounds like a question.

He just nods back and then he swallows and takes another step towards me.

"I didn't mean what I said," he says, head tilted to the side a bit.

"That's funny." I file the deed away in the jewellery box for safe-keeping before I flick him an unimpressed look. "—because after you said it, you backed it up by saying you meant everything you said."

He blows some air out of his mouth and shrugs, like he can't help it.

"I was in the moment."

"You're a piece of shit," I tell him without a thought, and he just nods, doesn't look angry or defensive when I say it either.

"Yeah," he concedes.

I shake my head at him, my chest starting to feel hot and tight. "You wished I was dead?"

"No—" His face pinches in something that looks like a wince as he shakes his head quickly and then it hangs there.

Nothing. Just nothing hangs there, the same thing that's always been between us. Nothing.

I glance around the room, uncomfortable, and still he doesn't speak.

"Oh," I flash him a stiff smile. "That's so sweet, say less—"

He gives me a bit of an exasperated look and presses his tongue onto his bottom lip.

"I get along with Bridget." He closes his eyes for a second, and I watch the train of grief hit him square on. He swallows. Fixes his tense. "Got along."

I stand tall and look him square in the eye.

"And me?"

"You're a fucking pain in the arse—" He waves his hand towards me. "You make me so angry." He shakes his head. "You're impossible to please, nothing I ever do is good enough for you, and—"

"And you never wanted me in the first place," I tell him in a voice that's surprisingly upbeat.

He breathes in sharp, holds it for a few seconds and presses his lips together.

"She told you," he says with a nod.

I say nothing, just stare over at him, blinking all calm and unimpressed.

"Fuck," he sighs and shakes his head.

He stares at the ground for an undisclosed period of time. Is it ten seconds? Is it sixty? I don't know.

He takes a big breath and looks down at me.

"Shit. Alright—" He presses his hand into his mouth again. "No, I didn't." He nods in this conceding kind of way. "Arrie got pregnant, told me she didn't want to get rid of it—"

"'It' being me," I clarify for no reason.

He nods. "'It' being you, yeah." Then he sighs again. "And you were mine, so—"

"I know," I tell him, looking at my cuticles (which rather desperately need the attention of Ama Quashie)—I can't believe I'm getting married with these barely manicured hands.

I flick my eyes back up at my father. "I checked."

He pulls back, surprised. "You checked?"

"Yes," I nod.

He nods back. "When?"

"In school—" I shrug and I see some surprise flicker over his face, and decide it's worth clarifying.

"When there was a rumour circulating I was"—I purse my lips—"Usher's child and not yours."

He nods a couple of times slowly.

"How'd you do it."

"I told Arrie I needed some hair of yours for a contest." I

shake my head and roll my eyes. "She's not so clued in on what might constitute as a contest—"

He nods again and sniffs a laugh.

"I checked too," he tells me.

"You checked!" I growl, instantly offended. "That's so rude—!"

His head pulls back. "How?"

"It just is!" I stomp my foot and glare at him. "Everything you do is rude and repugnant, and how did you anyway—?" I shake my head at him. "BJ would never steal my hair . . ."

He gives me a look.

"BJ's probably got a fucking blanket made out of your hair—"

I fold my arms over my chest and glare at him, and Harley rolls his eyes.

"I nicked some from your hairbrush."

I put my nose in the air. "How do you know it was my hair-brush, it could have been anyone's—"

"Could have been anyone's, yeah," he nods. "But it was in your old bathroom, and it was one of those fucking stupid boar brushes that you love that cost a fucking arm and a leg—"

"Mason Pearson?"

"That's the one," he nods.

I lift my shoulders, acquiescing a tiny bit. "It really is a top-tier brush though, to be completely frank—"

He smirks a bit. "I'll have to give it a try sometime—"

"To what end—?" I flick him a look. "You're practically bald."

"Oi—" He points at me. "This is a buzz cut with a medium fade!"

I shrug just to annoy him. "If you say so."

"It fucking is!" he says loudly and then the door opens.

Henry pokes his head in, frowning.

"Everything alright in here?" he asks me.

I flick my eyes from Henry to my father. Harley's eyebrows go up, waiting to see if I'm going to have him kicked out.

I swallow once, and look back at Henry, nodding quickly.

"I'm okay." I flash him a little smile. "Thank you though."

He watches us a few moments longer to be sure, and then ducks back out, closing the door behind him.

Harley clears his throat.

"I haven't stepped out on your mother this time around."

I scrunch my nose up. "Okay?"

He shrugs. "Just thought you'd like to know—"

"Do you want some sort of prize—?"

He rolls his eyes. "No—"

"Also," I give him a look. "It's been like five months so why don't we just hit pause for a moment, before we crown you husband of the year—"

He gives me a bit of a long-suffering look, takes another big breath and swallows.

"I'm sorry for what I said to you," he tells me.

"Okay." I nod once.

"And I'm sorry that you found out about—" His voice trails and he pulls an awkward face.

"—About how you didn't want me?" I say for him.

"Yeah." He nods uncomfortably.

And then we stare at each other. I don't know why, I don't know what he's waiting for, what I'm waiting for—? I don't know how to do this.

I glance around the room awkwardly before my eyes land back on him.

"Do . . . you want me to say I forgive you—?"

"No." He shakes his head. "You shouldn't."

"Good, because I don't," I tell him with my nose in the air, even though I'm not sure that it's true.

He sniffs a laugh and then sort of nods but I think it's to himself. His eyes move from mine and look past me, as though he's remembering something.

"I felt tricked when your mum did that. And I didn't blame you, like"—he flicks his eyes at me—"consciously, I mean. But sometimes I guess I did. It'd crop up a bit, like the part where I never wanted to be a dad, never wanted to be tied down." He shrugged. "Sometimes I'd see you and Bridge, and you'd have these looks on your faces, and I knew what you wanted and I just"—his face falls a bit, actually—"didn't have it in me."

He swallows, face a bit pained.

"And then, by the time I probably did have it in me, like I'd figured out a bit how to be a—I don't know, whatever—" Dad is the word neither of us can respectively be or say to one another. "—you already had him." He nods his head behind him in the vicinity of wherever BJ might be. "Didn't need me."

I lift an unimpressed eyebrow. "So you just decided to remain shit?"

He juts his jaw and nods slowly. "It was easier than having to square up with how bad I fucked up with you two."

My face squishes into a little ball of disbelief. "And so to remedy that fuckery, you kept doing it?"

He sighs. "I'm seeing a psychologist—"

"I should hope so!" I stare down my nose at him.

Harley rolls his eyes at me and then lifts his brows up.

"Lily said you've been seeing one too."

I cross my arms again. "Mm-hm."

"Like it?" he asks.

I give him a look. "No."

"Neither—" He sort of laughs. "It fucking sucks—"

And I nearly laugh but I catch myself on the tail end of a smile. Harley's eyes hold mine and he nods his chin at me.

"We're quite similar, you and me."

"Okay," I roll my eyes. "Well, there's no need to lash out—"

That makes him laugh properly this time and then his face softens a little.

"I'm really happy for you, Magnolia." He flashes me what I think might be a small, sincere smile. "Relieved that you're okay"—he nods a few times, as though he's almost telling himself—"that you're going to keep being okay with him. He's a good man—"

"I know," I tell him proudly.

He motions his head towards the door.

"I'm going to head off."

I nod a couple of times, and point awkwardly in the direction of the deed.

"Thank you for that."

Harley nods back, and then his face pulls and he looks sad, or something—?

"You look really beautiful," he says with a tender smile.

"Yes." I roll my eyes. "Obviously."

He sniffs a laugh again and then swallows.

"I love you, Magnolia."

"Ugh!" I yelp sort of in surprise and not horror, exactly, but I don't think I'm pleased about it, I think my face is a bit scrunched up. Harley blinks twice, all startled.

"Yuck—!" I pout. "Fine, whatever"—I shake my head—"you can come to the wedding. Just stop being weird!"

He gives me a look. "I said I love you—?"

"Well—" I hold my hands up to stop him. "Let's hit the brakes on surprise expressions of affection, shall we—?" I glare over at him a little. "God—it's my wedding day, I don't need this kind of stress—"

He gives me an exasperated look again, and he turns to walk away and then I remember what Bridget said. Or would have said.

"Wait—" I say to him, and he turns around. "I have something to say to you."

He looks ever so fractionally nervous. "What?"

I take a big breath, deep, let it lengthen me.

"I've been very angry at you for a very long time," I tell him and he nods a bit. "—Like all the time, for as long as I can remember, and until like, right then—" I point back to where we were a moment ago. "—when you just said that, I've been angry at you."

He gives me a sarcastic look. "I mean, you hide it really well—"

I take a step towards him and touch his arm, which I don't think I've ever done and I mightn't do again, but here I am now.

"I relieve you and I release you from my hurt so that I may be set free."

He stands there, blinking, and says nothing for a full seven seconds.

"What about me?" he asks eventually. "Do I get set free?"

"From what—?" I roll my eyes. "All your responsibilities and your bachelor-style life? Please—"

His head pulls back, but his eyes are amused and I shake my head a lot really quickly.

"Sorry, shit—!" I flash him an apologetic smile. "I take it back."

He tilts his head, trying to follow along. "You take my releasing back?"

"No, the part after it," I tell him. "It's a habit, you know—?"

He nods once. "Got it." His eyes pinch. "Think it'll stick?"

"No—" I shake my head, quite sure of this part. "I think you'll annoy me in fifteen minutes, and I'll have to go meditate for a week to find the zen to say it all over again with gusto, and that will be the cycle I live in forever—" I shrug as though I'm already beaten by the system. "But I will just keep choosing to release you, because I can't wait for you to care anymore."

Harley gives me a long look.

"I do care," he tells me.

I give him a tight smile. "We shall see."

He nods once, opens the door and walks out.

I perch on the vanity for a second, grip it, take a breath.

And then Henry pokes his head in back into the room, he sees me sitting there and darts over.

His head tilts.

"Are you okay?"

"Yeah," I nod. "I think so."

"Was he—a dick?" he asks, confused. "Or did he—"

I crinkle my nose, confused. "He said 'sorry'—?"

Henry blinks a few times, and his mouth tugs in surprise.

"Wow."

I purse my lips. "Yeah."

He ducks down a little so we're more eye to eye. "Are you ready to become a Ballentine?"

I smile up at him.

"Very."

EIGHTY-THREE

BJ

Standing at the top of the aisle, I swear to god, I nearly flipped my fucking lid when I saw Harley sitting next to Arrie, and I was about to toss him out when Taura saw me and intercepted. Said that he came and said sorry to Parks and that she said he could be there—I mean, what the fuck—we don't spend one night together and this is what I miss—?

Feels pretty sacred standing up here by myself.

By myself, with Jo.

In the London wedding plan, everyone was up here with us, but now if they're standing with us, that's like half our guest list.

Mum's already crying and actually, so is Dad.

Marsaili's sitting a few rows behind Magnolia's parents with Bushka and Alexey.

My dad jumps up and darts over to me a couple of minutes before the ceremony's due to start. Fixes my bow tie that doesn't need fixing.

"I'm really proud of you, Beej," he tells me with his weighty smile, and I have to swallow heavy to keep myself in check.

He tugs on the lapels of my custom tux from Tom Ford. Shoes from him as well. No Vans, because I like to live a day into my marriage.

"Did she pick this?"

Give him a little cocky look. "Nope."

"Wow." He nods, impressed, before his face softens. "You told me you loved her a really long time ago, do you remember?"

I nod. "I never stopped."

He gives me a proud smile. "You never stopped."

He pats me on the arm affectionately and then takes a seat back down next to my mum.

And then I hear it. The start of the song she's walking down to. In London it was going to be Pachelbel's *Canon in D Major* because what else would she walk down to in London, but here it's all us, so it's a bit different.

Everyone stands and you'd think I'd be nervous, but like fuck I am—waited all my life for this. No part of me is unsure, I'm not worried, I'm not stressed, I'm just ready—fucking chomping at the bit for it.

My heart is beating fast, I'll admit that—but don't read into it—it always goes fast when I'm about to see her, and I've always loved her in white.

And all I can think is that we made it, we're here. And it was hard and fucking brutal, but it was worth all the things that it took for us to get here, I'd do it all again. Twice, and over broken glass.

And then Jo puts both his hands on my shoulders and squeezes them and I look over right as "Marching Bands of Manhattan" by Death Cab for Cutie hits the twenty-five-second mark in song and the whole fucking world goes dim. There's a new sun in the universe, and it's hanging off my brother's arm, walking down an aisle to me. It's stolen all the light and all the good and all the beauty from everything else around it—if there are even things around it, I don't know—? I can't see them. I'm blinded.

Her face is shy—best face in the fucking world—and her eyes on me, all weighed down all heavy and serious with the weight of this moment.

She gives me the smallest fraction of a smile and I give her a full one back because I can't help it.

She looks so beautiful—which, she always does, but this is some kind of joke. This is a joke, she can't be real—

But there she is, halfway down the aisle to me to promise a bunch of shit to each other that we've always promised anyway, but I'm just happy to be here.

She's almost at the top now—and I know how this is meant to go—seen it before, I mean, fuck—we've even practiced it, but then it happens anyway.

A couple of metres between us and I cross them in a second, shift that veil from her face and her off the ground and kiss her because I can't help it.

She laughs, her mouth against mine, and any tenseness in her body unfurls in my arms. There's some ruckus and noise from our family.

Primarily from Jo, who's yelling that I'm stealing his thunder, but I'm not. I'm just stealing kisses.

I plant her back down on the ground, give her a tiny nod and a little wink and dart back up to the top of the aisle where I'm supposed to be.

Magnolia turns to Henry and wordlessly, he fixes her veil and unsmudges a bit of pink from the edge of her mouth, then he offers her his arm again to finish the best walk she's ever been on—in my opinion, anyway.

When she reaches me—she's blushing now—she laughs but I reckon I can see some tears under there too.

Henry smacks me on the back a couple of times before he gives me a massive hug, then turns to her, kisses her cheek and takes a seat next to Rom.

I glance at Parks, give her the magic smile and offer her my hand.

"Dearly beloved—" Jonah starts, and I roll my eyes.

"Shut up!" I tell him, and Magnolia and everyone laughs.

"Welcome, everyone," Jo says instead. "To the long-awaited wedding of Baxter James Ballentine and Magnolia Parks." He pauses, smiles at me and Parks, can tell how happy he is for it.

He looks back out to our family.

"It's a massive honour for me to be up here, but it is one I feel like I deserve—" He gives me and Parks pointed looks. "Because the last couple of years with these two idiots has been an absolute punish."

Everyone laughs and Magnolia gives me a look.

Jo holds his hands out towards us like he's a priest.

"—But here we are. Now—" He claps his hands together. "When they first asked me if I'd officiate their wedding, my very first thought was, *I'm going to get smited up there*—"

Parksy shoots him a look and Jo pulls a face, straightening up quickly.

"Ohp!" He makes an uncomfortable noise and adjusts the neck on his shirt. "Getting the bad eyes from the boss—I'll save all this for my speech later, will I?" He gives me a nod. "So, uh—" He glances between us as though he's asking the question. "Vows then, yeah?"

Magnolia frowns a little and glances at me, unsure, and I know I'm going to be in trouble for repping Jo as hard as I did to marry us, and know I probably shouldn't think it's funny but I do. I squash a laugh as I look at my babbling best friend.

"Vows would be great," I tell him with a wink.

"Parksy," Jo nods his head at her. "You're up."

Magnolia nods once, obedient—obedient! Hah—first time for everything.

She turns and looks up at me—best dress I've ever seen in my life, but I can't describe it because if I do, it'll come out sounding rubbish. Just trust me on this. Your eyes have never seen anything as beautiful as the girl standing in front of me. She swallows, nervous again now. Her eyes are wide—Bambi-like, you know?

She takes a big breath.

"How many loves do you get in a lifetime—" She gives me a quick smile. "That is a question I've pondered on for a lot of years now . . . And I've come up with varying degrees of the same answer. That there are lots of different kinds of love that life may afford you the chance to experience over the course of one's life—some terrible, some misguided, some well-meaning, some dangerous, some wonderful but benign, some painful, some—when you lose them—are agony." She sniffs and swallows. "If you're lucky, you might get a great one, and I know I'm the luckiest, because I got two."

I give her a gentle smile, hope it makes her feel braver, I

wouldn't want her to cry in front of all these people, unless she wanted to, in which case, fucking cry away—but it's not like her to want people to see her vulnerable.

"There's been so much history and space and time that has run through us over the course of our relationship, and I know there's an air of mystery to us; to how we love each other. I know people often don't understand it, and I'm sorry for them—" She says with a tiny shrug. "Because getting to love you has been the most wonderfully human thing I've ever had the privilege of doing in my life"—that makes me smile and she keeps going—"and I know that people look at us, look at what's happened between us and with us, and wonder how we are the way we are, and sure—trauma bonds"—she flicks me a look—"but also, mostly, primarily you. We are the way we are because of you. Because you didn't give up. Because you loved me first and you loved me better and you loved me braver, and"—fuck, she's going to make me cry—"so I guess what I'm trying to say is, thank you?"

She says that with an upward inflection and it makes me laugh, keeps those tears at bay a bit longer.

"And also, that if space and time and history has taught me anything, it's you are the love of a lifetime." She says that very decidedly.

"You are the thing that the poets wrote about, you are what the choir of angels is singing about, you are the thing that clouds part above and the sun beams down upon. You're every butterfly, in every stomach. You're my every tender thought.

"You're a warm towel when you get out of the shower on a cold night. You're the tea you hold to your chest when you need a minute to yourself. You're the feeling you get when you're inside and safe and dry and it's dark grey outside and it's teeming down."

I swallow heavy, press my mouth together. *Don't cry.*

"You are what He saw in the garden when He said it is good," she says, and with that, she wipes a rogue tear from her cheek, and I rub my nose to keep it together.

"Loving you is the thing I grab first when the house is on

fire, and the house has been on fire before"—she gives me a look—"and it might even catch on fire again. I really hope not, but if it does—how much I love you will forever and ever be the first thing I reach for."

Jonah stares at her a bit in awe—so do I, but I always do.

He nods once. "Alright then"—he glances at me—"Beej?"

I look over at her, lift my eyebrows playfully as though this isn't the most holy, solemn moment I'll ever experience on this planet.

She gives me another tiny smile, mostly with her eyes this time, and I give her a small wink before I start.

"Right," I tilt my head as I stare over at her. "This actually came at a really bad time for me because I gave you such a hell of a speech the other day—" I nod back in time at everything I said so she'd marry me now.

She smirks.

"Like, really top-notch shit. So easily could have been my vows, but I didn't think that'd go down exceptionally well if I just said now what I said to you then, even though it was fantastic and even though it's still all true—" I pause dramatically before I start again. "I have loved you in many iterations over the course of our—"

Magnolia starts laughing and no one else gets it but they weren't supposed to, it was just for her.

Her face is proper lit up now, how it should be. I smile over at her, pleased.

"I was six when I fell in love with you, everyone knows that, I bang on about it all the time"—I shrug—"but no one bangs on about the math of it," I tell her, and her face falters a bit.

"That's twenty-one years of loving you." I nod. "252 months, 1,095 weeks, 7,665 days, 183,960 hours and 11,037,600 minutes where I have loved you and if that can translate into anything, please let it speak to the depth of my commitment to you, Parks, because it's yours."

She watches over at me, chin a little tucked. She swallows heavy.

"I think of you when I wake up, like a habit. I open my eyes and then I think of you"—I tell her with a shrug because it's just fact—"not necessarily in some great, profound, Shakespearean way but in the way where you are my very first thought and have been for"—I gesture with my hands—"evidently, for a long time now."

"And I know when I say it like that it can sound a bit like an enslavement or an obligatory responsibility, but it's not, even if it is." I shrug haphazardly. "No one feels sorry for monks—well, I do a bit because sex is awesome, but we're all fine with it because it's a noble, worthy cause," I say before I nod my chin over at her. "You are my noble, worthy cause."

She wipes her eyes and—fuck, I don't want to cry.

"Parksy, you're not just my first thought, you're willfully my second one and my third one and every one thereafter, because when I am dead"—grimace over at her for saying the D-word—"Sorry. But when I am, that's what they'll say about me. That I loved you. That I still love you. That even if I die, when I die, and I'm old and I'm ready and god willing you've died first because otherwise—up front," I turn to our friends and family. "—sorry to everyone." I turn back to her. "If I die, when I die—it will echo through space and through time, and it'll brush up against the edge of this universe and press into the next one that I loved you more than anything."

She brushes away another tear and I give her a smile that I hope steadies her and then I clear my throat.

"I have, in our time, been a bit partial to a maritime metaphor. Don't know why—" I shrug as I think about it. "There is some gravitas to boats, I think. And there's some truth in the simile of tides and shores, and you and me and how we always come back, washing up on the shores of one another. Probably fairly apt as well because you have undoubtedly"—give her a bit of a look—"been the face of nearly every storm I've weathered in my life. Not saying it's your fault, just saying that—" I shrug. "You are the force that I have reckoned with and will continue to reckon with every day of my life."

I hear my mum let out a little sob and I look over at her, amused, before I look back at Parks and she laughs and her eyes are fucking magic right now. The diamonds are out. Take a breath. Swallow.

"Sailors and wayfinders, yeah—? Since the beginning of time, have used the stars to guide them. As you well know, Parks"—I give her a look and a nod—"we're in them, we've always been in them. So you can forget Altair and Vega." I swat my hand through the air. "If we were born when people were assigning stories to the stars, they would have given us a galaxy. A bit because it took us a while to figure our shit out," I concede with a shrug and she lets out a quiet laugh. "But mostly because I'd have insisted that I needed a star for each reason that I love you—which is what—?" I pull a face as I try to remember. "—roughly, one hundred billion stars and still, not enough—"

And I take a big breath, try to stave it off but I can't, my eyes fill. I sniff, swallow heavy.

"See—shit—" I laugh at myself, embarrassed, wipe my face with the back of my hand. "Here's the thing." I clear my throat again. "You turned me into a mess of a man." I shrug, defeated, because I am for her. "The kind of man who sees stars and us in them, and who buys bee baths and sets them up around Kensington Gardens Square and checks they're full every day because the bees aren't fucking dead"—clock my mum, flash her a quick smile—"Sorry, Mum"—look back at Parks—"They've never been. You turned me into the kind of man who could see a flower cast in a certain light and cry over it, because if you love a flower how I love a flower, how I've always loved a flower—" I say that part slowly, hope that she lets it saturate all of her. "Loving something how I love you . . ." I blow some air out of my mouth. "Fucks you up"—look at Mum again and grimace. "Sorry again!" Look back at Parks. "Willfully fucked, Parksy," I say with a nod.

"I am the fox and you are the flower, and you have tamed me."

She smiles shyly at that.

"'People have forgotten this truth, but you mustn't forget

it'"—I give her a pointed look—"'that you become responsible forever for what you've tamed.'" I take a step towards her, give her a half a smile.

"So that is my vow to you. I will stay tamed by you, forever." I nod once. And then add as an afterthought, "And then all the other stuff too. I'll protect you, I'll provide for you, I'll listen, I'll respect you, adore you, trust you, laugh with you, grow old with you, have babies with you—all of it, I'm in." I shrug. "Whatever the fuck you need, Parks."

"Well, shit," Jo says after a few seconds of silence.

Parks lets out this laugh-cry and it's more emotion from her than I was expecting. Makes me pull a face, which makes her sort of laugh and sort of cry more.

"We're going to do the exchanging of the—"

"Just—" I hold up a finger at Jo to silence him for a second. Wipe that almost-wife of mine's face with my thumbs. Kiss her on the top of her head.

"Almost there," I tell her, and she nods quickly.

I look back at Jonah, brows up. "Go on, then."

Jo gives Parks a look, waiting for her go-ahead and she nods once.

"Do you, Magnolia, take BJ to be your lawfully wedded husband? Do you promise to love him and cherish him, in good times and in bad, in sickness and in health, for richer and for poorer, for better and for worse, and forsaking all others, keeping yourself only unto him, for so long as you both shall live?"

She looks over at me and says more calm and more sure than I think I've ever heard her:

"I do."

Jo smiles and then looks over at me.

"And do you, BJ, take Magnolia to be your lawfully wedded wife? Do you promise to love her and cherish her, in good times and in bad, in sickness and in health, for richer and for poorer, for better and for worse, and forsaking all others, keeping yourself only unto her, for so long as you both shall live?"

I grin down at her. "Yeah, I do."

"Alright then," Jo nods, absolutely fucking beaming as he looks between us.

He reaches into his pocket and fishes out our rings. Custom Polly Wales. He flicks me a little look.

"Home stretch, baby," he whispers, excited.

He hands Magnolia my wedding ring—and now my heart's fucking thudding, I don't know why? Only thing I've ever really wanted finally in front of me, or something?

"Repeat after me, yeah?" Jo says to her, eyebrows up.

"With this ring," he says, and she says it after him.

"With this ring—" She places it on the top of my ring finger.

"I thee wed," she repeats after Jo. "And all my worldly goods," she eyes me a bit suspiciously on that one. "And everything I am," she says, nose in the air, fighting off a smile. "Body, mind, soul and spirit," she swallows heavy. "I endow to thee, til death do us part."

Then she slides the ring on my finger and I'm smiling so fucking big, I can't help it.

And then it's my turn.

Jo drops her ring into my hands, then smacks me on the arm.

"With this ring," Jo starts.

"Parksy, with this ring," I start, squashing away a smile.

"I thee wed," I say with a nod. "And all my worldly goods, and everything I am," I say, watching her, eyes sincere. "My body, my mind, my soul and my spirit, to thee I do endow." Fuck, I'm crying again. I sniff, laugh, try not to feel like an idiot. "Til death parts us."

I slide that ring on her finger, tilt my head and give her a look I've waited a lifetime to.

Jonah's talking again now, and I know I should be listening but I'm not, I'm watching her watching me.

I press my mouth together, not even kind of holding back the smile that's there, and why the fuck would I?

I just married her.

It's not until Magnolia lifts her eyebrows, and I know those eyebrows, they're waiting eyebrows—like, impatient eyebrows—that I realise I've tuned out so much to whatever the fuck Jonah's been saying that I missed him say arguably the best bit.

"Fuck, man—sorry—" I grimace. "Can you say it again?"

"What?" Jo snorts. "That I now pronounce you—"

"Yeah," I cut him off. "Pronounce us."

Jonah rolls his eyes and Magnolia's laughing properly now.

"I now pronounce you husband and wife," he says proudly. (And then tacks on "You idiot," under his breath so my mum can't hear him.)

I smile over at Parks, take a step closer to her and put my hand on her cheek—why do veils make girls look extra fit?—

"I know you're not big on public displays of affection," I say quietly to her.

She whispers back, "I'll make an exception."

"Good." I nod once, and then I kiss the fucking shit out of her.

One hand in her hair, the other on her waist, slightly dipped but all of her pulled tightly against me. I think I can hear the clapping and cheering of the people around us who love us but I don't care—I'm not kissing her like this for show, I'm kissing her like this because we made it. Took us a minute, took the long way home to get there but we're here now and I wouldn't change a fucking thing.

EIGHTY-FOUR
Magnolia

BJ hired out every possible part of this hotel that there was to be hired. There were five different locations for a wedding on the resort and he hired all of them, had each of them set up so we could choose the one that felt best on the day.

Most of the reception's been taking place in the part of the resort called The Mansion, it's a bit more secluded and offers a bit more privacy compared to the other areas.

The day has been perfect, and I'm now in dress number two—an Eisen Stein gown from their Rose Blanche Fall 2023 collection. The gown—if you can believe it—is called Bridgit. I loved it before I knew that, but once I found that out—anything to feel closer to her, you know? BJ is having so much fun. I love watching him have fun.

That's how I've always known we're it. I love watching him do everything. Laughing, driving, showering, brushing his teeth, breathing—all of it, I love it all.

And he's having the best day. Dancing with his grandma and his mum, sitting in the corner with the boys and his dad having whiskey—making eyes at me across the room in a way that makes me feel fifteen again, except I'm not fifteen. I'm twenty-five, and I'm married.

And my heart feels so full it could burst, but also there's an ache in me that I sort of wondered whether it might show up, or if it would be a gentleman and stay away for the day, but it doesn't—how could it?—I never wanted to do this day without her. I've never wanted to do any of them, but especially not this one.

I just need a minute, so I slip out while no one's looking and make my way up to La Terrazza.

It's so pretty up there, a garden all tucked away and overlooking the Indian Ocean. It's just oceans for days.

I take a minute, do some breathing. Try to feel my sister even though I let her go and I'm trying to be a grown-up and live without her, but there are days you need your sister and today is one of them.

"Hey, Ballentine," says my favourite voice in the world from behind me.

I turn around and look at him, immediately feeling a bit shy because he's all undone in the sexiest way.

Tux jacket off and buttons well undone, hair all messy because he's been shoving his hands through it as he's been dancing.

His cheeks are a bit sun-kissed, so his eyes are brighter than normal and his mouth is pinker and I swallow because, I mean—wow.

I tuck my chin and glance over at him. "Hi."

"Waited a long time to call you that," he tells me.

"I've waited a long time to be one."

He scrunches his nose as though he's unsure. "You've always been one."

I smile again, and I suppose the edges of it might give me away.

He walks over to me, slipping his hands around my waist as he tilts his head.

"Are you okay?"

"Yeah," I nod.

He watches me closely. "Happy?"

"Yes." I smile up at him.

He touches my face. "You can say no?"

"No—!" I grab his hand. "No, it's just—"

"Bridge," he says for me.

I nod a few times. "Yeah."

"Do you know," he smiles at me, a bit proud of himself. "I've actually prepared for this."

I look up at him curiously. "What do you mean?"

"Couple of things," he tells me. "One—" He reaches into his pocket and pulls out a black diamond necklace, emerald cut, a little more than a carat.

"What's this?" I stare at it.

He grimaces. "I might have stolen some of Bridget's ashes a while ago—?"

"Oh my god!" I snatch it from his hand to look at it in morbid fascination. "You turned her into a diamond?"

He nods as I find a light to look at it under.

"Did you decide for it to be black or did it just come out that way, because that would be very telling—"

"No," he laughs. "I picked it."

"Oh." I frown.

"Felt like her."

I nod. It does, I suppose.

He watches me carefully. "Do you like it? I wasn't sure if you would—"

"No, I love it," I tell him. "And I think because you turned her into it, not me, that it means you'll be haunted instead."

"I mean, I'd prefer to not be haunted—?" he says with a shrug.

"How did you know to do it?" I ask him, and he shrugs again.

"I don't know." He looks a bit baffled himself. "Just felt like I should?"

Then he nods at it in my hands.

"Can I?"

"Please—" I say, lifting my hair up from my neck so he can put it on me.

I press it against my chest and know it's probably in my head but I do feel a tiny bit closer to her still.

I turn around and look at Beej, smiling up at him.

"Thank you."

"Yeah." He pulls a face like his thoughtfulness is nothing. "Of course."

Then he reaches into the pockets of his trousers and pulls out something else.

I look at it, confused.

Index cards—?

"I've got another thing here too," he says.

I purse my lips, waiting. "Okay?"

"I wrote her wedding speech," he says, then pauses—"Or what I think her speech would be."

My eyes go wide. "Have you?"

He nods once. "Yep."

I straighten up a little.

"Alright," I nod. "Let's hear it."

The boy that I just married clears his throat for dramatic effect.

"Trauma bonds—!" he says loudly, and I start laughing, shaking my head.

He grins down at me. "Joking"—he pauses—"but I'm not joking because she probably would."

"Yes," I concede, because she probably would.

"I know some people mightn't know this," BJ says in his best Bridget voice. "—but Magnolia's actually really smart."

I pinch my eyes at him. "I don't love that 'actually.'"

He pulls his head to the side.

"She wouldn't have cared," he whispers.

"No," I pout. "I don't suppose she would have."

He gives me a tiny wink and then keeps going.

"She hides it a lot of the time, I think. Like she's scared of people judging her as an intellectual being instead of a sexual one, like it might hurt her more, and maybe she's right—?" He shrugs on behalf of my sister.

"People are not kind about her a lot of the time, and it's made her hold herself differently in context of the way she allows the world to see her."

He gives me a proud look for that very Bridget-esque sentence.

"She's on show at all times, for everyone, in one way or any other. Except for me and except for him."

Beej points to himself.

"And that's kind of all you want for someone when you love them, you know?" he shrugs. "For them to be able to be fully themselves with the person they're with, and she is. She's annoying with him, she's whiny with him, she's entitled"—I frown up at him, and he whispers—"this is her talking, not me."

I roll my eyes.

"She's a bit mindless," he keeps going. "But I mean that mostly in a good way. There's a thoughtlessness to how she is around him that's kind of important, I think. She's really free when she's with him, like she relaxes when he's near her"—my face softens a bit at that—"and she looks sixteen still, how she looks at him. Eyes all big and doe-like"—he leans down towards me, eyes locked on mine—

"Bridget?" I say, eyebrows up, and he snaps his head back, laughing.

"Now," he claps his hands. "I don't know whether they would admit this themselves so I'm going to on their behalf, because honour where honour is due—none of us would be here if it weren't for me."

I roll my eyes, because she would say that.

"BJ's in therapy because I made him be," he says and then tilts his head the way my sister used to. "You're welcome."

I smile a bit.

"And Magnolia . . ." His voice trails and he pulls a face. "We're working on it."

I roll my eyes again.

"But," he says, and honestly, he really is good at sounding like her. He has her mannerisms down to a T. "It's important to celebrate the milestones, because he really fucking needed a therapist"—I start laughing—"and I don't know if they would have worked their shit out without a therapist, so if everyone wouldn't mind raising their glass to me—"

He gives me a playful look.

"I'm joking," he says, glancing down at his index cards and reading them for a second, then he looks back at me.

"A lot of you probably wonder what it was like to grow up with Magnolia as a sister." He pauses.

"Annoying obviously, look at her—"

I roll my eyes.

"Plus," he adds, "she's ridiculous, and she's a handful. And kind of a brat—"

"BJ." I frown.

"I know," he whispers as himself. "She's so mean sometimes, but she did call you that a lot and I'm just trying to be authentic."

I blink twice and wave for him to carry on.

"She's impulsive, and she can be tempestuous, and she's really fucking spoilt—"

"Alright, wrap it up," I tell him, and he squashes a smile.

"It's hardly her fault though, what with a name like 'Magnolia,' they brought this on her—on us all!" He says as Bridge before he ducks down and whispers to me as himself, "Which"—wide eyes—"we need to talk about. What the fuck?" He frowns, tilting my chin up to his eyes with his finger. "Are you okay?"

I nod. "Yeah."

"You promise?"

"Yes." I smile now.

"Because I'll fight him."

"I know." I touch his arm, gently. "Keep going."

He looks down at his cards again. "She cares too much about clothes—"

"Take that back!" I yell, cutting him off.

"But, oh my god!" he says loudly over me. "She is loyal."

That placates me a little and I look at him, waiting for more.

"There were so many things that were annoying about growing up with these two." He gestures to both himself and then me. "The papers, for one, that was always a bit of a pain." He checks his cards and I see a little smile breeze over his face, the kind he makes when he's amused himself. "But worse still was the fact that they just had sex everywhere"—dramatic pause—"Everywhere! I mean it." He nods like she would.

"Everywhere—Harley, Dad, I mean"—shakes his head—"if you knew . . . it wasn't just your Maserati, and"—BJ gives me a stern look—"I do maintain that on a technicality, she lost her virginity in the back of that vehicle—"

I give him a look.

"BJ."

He shrugs. "You did."

"BJ!" I stomp my foot.

He points to himself. "I'm Bridget, and I'm just saying," he shrugs, and then leans down to whisper in my ear, "though as BJ, I will say that as more time passes the more sure I become that she might be right."

I stare at him in disbelief.

"I think about it sometimes," he whispers, still himself. "And you did make your sex face." My jaw falls to the floor and he grimaces. "I'm sorry, but you did."

I shake my head at him, aghast. "You get a hint of penetration and suddenly your whole world flips on its head."

He laughs and touches my face because he loves me like that.

He clears his throat, back to Bridge.

"It wasn't just the Maserati, Harley, it was your McLaren and your Bentley and the Hennessey."

I flick him a look, I don't know the names of the cars we've had sex in but we've had sex in a lot of cars.

Cars were easy to sneak away in, stolen moments that could have been innocent moments, we might have just been out for dinner or a drive, but no, we were driving to Hampstead Heath and finding a low-hanging tree to park the car and have sex. I don't know which cars, but there were cars and sex was had.

"It was the jet," he keeps rattling off places as my sister. "It was your office," he says as though Harley's here. "It was your office too, Hamish, don't look so pleased—in your bed, Lily, in the chalet in Switzerland, in the master bedroom of the St Tropez house, Harley—and it was strategic because you were only gone for two hours—"

I smack him in the arm.

"Stop!" I laugh.

But he doesn't.

"In the villa at Valldemossa—"

"BJ!" I stomp my foot, but I'm still laughing.

"I mean," he shakes his head as my sister, "they were unstoppable.

And not covert! The amount of times I walked in on them"—he blows some air from his mouth—"I should be in therapy."

I give him an unimpressed look.

"And it sounds gross, and you know what"—he considers—"let's calling a fucking spade a spade, it was a bit gross but then"—he shrugs for her—"I guess I have to admit that it was a bit romantic too . . . That it was a bit special to see people love each other how they love each other—"

I stare over at him, and my eyes go softer.

"And it took an absolute age for us to get here, but I always knew you would," he says, sounding like a know-it-all the way she always did. "Always had a feeling it was going to work out—"

He clears his throat and keeps going.

"My sister's dated a few people, in case you didn't know—"

I give him another look.

He shrugs haphazardly like Bridget used to when she would casually toss conversational grenades.

"And some of them were honestly great, top-notch guys"—a pause and I literally already know what's coming—"and Julian."

I bite away a smile and give him a look and he gives me his cheekiest grin as he laughs.

"I said that," he whispers. "Not Bridge."

"I know," I whisper back.

"But I could tell—" he says, because that's what she'd say. "Even when they couldn't tell, I could. That they were it." He lifts his shoulders, conceding to our love. "In the stars, or whatever they prattle on about."

"And I was right," he says, nose in the air how hers goes. "That's the most important part, that is the takeaway."

"I was right," he says with her signature smugness. "And they are together, finally. Properly." His face softens too. "So then actually, not just I am right, but all is right."

A tear slips out of my eye and BJ smiles at it, lets it sit there for few seconds before he wipes it away with his thumb.

"So," he says in his Bridget voice. "If you all wouldn't mind raising your glasses—" I raise my invisible glass into the air. "—to my sister and my first kiss."

I laugh and a few more tears slip out.

"To my sister," I say, reaching for BJ's hand.

He lifts my hand to his mouth and kisses it as he smiles all tender and lovely.

"To my sister too. And—" He pulls an uncomfortable face. "To definitely not my first kiss."

23:19

+44 7700 900 274

Congratulations.

Genuinely, properly happy for you.

Both.

Who is this?

I don't have this number in my phone?

Hah.

Good girl.

Do you really not have my number anymore or are you just being a brat?

Julian?

Tiger?

I have been tamed.

Did you delete me?

Yes.

Good. I deserved it.

Yes you did.

Do still, for all I know.

Do still, definitely.

Noted.

Anyway, I'm happy for you.

That's all I wanted to say. Keep me deleted.

Tell BJ I said hi and to watch his back.

Julian.

No but send him my love.

Why?

There's no winning with you . . .

Goodbye Julian.

Bye Ballentine xx

EIGHTY-FIVE

BJ

We honeymooned for a bit more than a month after the wedding.

First down to Qualia in the Whitsundays, then up to the St Regis in Bora Bora. After that, we flew over to the Montage in Kapalua Bay, and finally, back to our roots over in St Barts, where we stayed at the Rosewood.

Some of the happiest, easiest weeks of my life so far.

Coming back to London was a bit of a mind fuck. Interest in us was at an all-time high.

We managed to avoid the paparazzi at the airport by giving someone we know who's a bit shit a bad tip, but they were waiting for us when we got home anyway.

Swarms of them, more than when Bridge died.

We were on the cover of every magazine, and you know what? Someone leaked shit from our wedding too.

If it was anyone we know I'll fucking kill them, or if it was a bougie-arse hotel guest, fuck them—but if it was some little Balinese kid who makes Rp5,000 a day, fair play to him. That'd make me sort of happy. I hope he just got the check of a lifetime.

Happy enough to be back home though, I'm happy to be doing normal life shit with her.

Funny how marriage changes everything and nothing all at once.

We sleep together how we always have, she's the first and the last thing I think of every day, I walk her to work, I kiss her up against all the walls we have—the same old shit and yet somehow, it is still different.

A new weight, or a new layer to us or something?

Whatever it is, I love it.

I love being a husband, even though it doesn't feel different to being a fiancé.

I love being responsible for a person, fucking love being tamed. Tame me forever.

Besides us, shit here's good.

Henry and Rom are going well still, super in love and annoying. Jo's doing better, seems more like his old self? Not completely, but it wasn't like before we left.

Christian and Daisy are—fuck it, never mind—talk to one of them.

Tausie and Tiller are inseparable these days, and life, all in all, feels pretty fucking sweet.

I go to my dad's meetings now sometimes. Not because I'm going to be whatever he does—I don't even know what he does—but because we play golf after and he's a pretty good hang.

Parks is good—still going to therapy, still being a fucking brat about it most of the time, but she's going, so I guess that's the bit that counts?

She and Harley are possibly doing better—? Not ready to put any real stock in that just yet but since we've been back he's asked her to lunch twice.

The first time she made me come and the second time she said she could go by herself, but later said she regretted that because she still doesn't really know how to talk to him or what even about.

It just feels like coasting, all of it.

And I know it won't always be like this, I know we're in the honeymoon phase or whatever, but—fuck, it feels good.

After the fucking iron-man marathon of a journey we took to get here, I'm happy to coast, feel the breeze that is loving her around me as we do all the mundane shit that's a part of normal life, the kind of shit I've waited a lifetime to do with her.

Shit like this—fix a bathroom in the first home we own together.

Our contractor grimaces at me, apologetic for yet another delay on this fucking bathtub, and I shake my head, swatting my hands at him.

"Do you know what, honestly, man—" I give him a sincere look. "We never use a bath, just forget about it—make it look good, but we don't need it to work."

"Wait, no—" Magnolia says from the doorway. I didn't know she was there. "Don't do that."

I look over at her and frown, confused.

"What?"

And she shrugs innocently.

"Well, it wouldn't be the end of the world if one of us decided to take a bath one day—"

I press my lips together, a bit puzzled.

"Do you want to take a bath one day, Parksy?"

"No, actually—" She crosses her arms, walking towards me. "I don't. Because it's like the bath is a teacup and I am the teabag and I'm not interested in brewing a giant cup of human tea, so—"

I screw up my face. "Sick."

"I know!" She nods emphatically. "I don't know why people like baths so much—?"

"That's not a"—shake my head at her—"them problem; that's a you problem, for sure."

She bobbles her head around in disagreement.

"Sorry—" The contractor glances between us. "Am I fixing the bath, or—?"

I stare over at her, wait for her to make the call.

She gives me a carefree, absentminded smile and then looks over at him.

"Yes please, if you don't mind."

EIGHTY-SIX

Magnolia

I've been a bit nervous to tell him, see—? So I avoided it for the first few days, and then those few days turned into weeks—I didn't mean to keep it from him, it just, happened to turn into something I was keeping from him.

Plus I've been so busy at work—terrible excuse, not an excuse at all—but now I've left it so long, weeks and weeks, I'm worried that when I do tell him, he'll be a bit cross?

And what if he's cross anyway?

It could happen, it's happened before.

I'm sitting on our couch drinking a cup of tea and watching *Vicar of Dibley* reruns on television, when I hear the front door close.

Beej has been out for the day. Golf with Henry and his dad, and then they went to Sushi Samba afterwards with Lily.

They asked if I wanted to come, obviously—but I didn't feel much up to going. I'm a bit off food.

"Oi," he yells. "I brought you back the yellowtail, the toro ceviche, and the rockfish tempura," he calls from another room in the house and I hear him wander through our home. Such boring little sounds, things like his shoes on the wood in the hallway, the taking off a coat and hanging it up, dropping his keys in the bowl—I love his boring little sounds.

He stands in the doorway of our living area and leans against the frame.

"Hey—" he says, watching me.

"Hi." I give him a quick smile and then keep watching the

TV, because it's the one where their stained-glass window breaks and they're trying to raise the money for it.

He flashes me the carry-out bag.

"Thanks," I say. "I'm not so hungry—can you pop it in the fridge for me?"

His eyes pinch with that old suspicion.

"I just don't want raw fish today," I tell him with a breezy shrug. "My stomach's been funny."

"Oh." He frowns for me. "Sorry—"

I give him another quick smile and go back to watching the television. He scratches the back of his neck, eyes still on me.

"Hey, Parksy—"

"Mm?" I say, not looking at him.

He clears his throat.

"Beautiful darling, love of my life—" he says, and that gets my attention.

I pause the show and look over at him suspiciously.

"What?"

He walks over to me, arms crossed over his chest.

"Did you buy a house without telling me?"

"Yeah," I shrug. "Tonnes."

He blinks. "What—?"

And I grimace, stutter and say, "Uh—no, I mean—"

He gives me a strained smile. "It's just . . . the sort of thing couples usually run by each other before doing—"

"Right." I nod, trying to follow along. "But I mean—I've bought real estate without telling you before—?"

"Well, that was different." He rolls his eyes before he thinks about it and pulls back, face confused. "And, when—?"

I pout a little and decide that now is probably not the time to bring up that little six-bedroom cliffside villa that I also bought in Sorrento the other day, so I roll my eyes at him instead.

"It's okay." He kneels down in front of me and pushes some hair behind my ears—"I mean, I'm not cross. But it's just"—he shrugs—"married people normally chat before they buy a house, is all—"

That doesn't sound right, I think to myself, and I squint over at him.

"You mean *poor* married people."

He rolls his eyes.

"No, I mean married people."

"Okay, sorry, I know." I shake my head and breathe out my nose, frustrated at myself. "I just was trying to figure out what the best way was to tell you—"

His face pulls a bit confused. "Tell me what?"

I swallow nervously, my eyes go wide and I tuck my chin.

"I don't want you to be cross," I say.

He lifts his eyebrows. "About what?"

"Well, about any of it!" I shrug.

"Any of what!" he says, getting frustrated now.

"Well, I bought the house because it was always the plan and I thought then maybe if you weren't organically super happy because we've just gotten married really, that maybe it would help sweeten the pot or something, but maybe that was a bad idea, now that I know you think real estate is a"—I use quotation marks—"*'mutual decision.'*"

BJ presses his lips together, biting back a smile, and then something clicks behind his eyes and he locks them on me.

"Parksy, where's this house you bought?"

"On the Isle of Mull."

"The Isle of Mull—?" he repeats, head tilted. "As in . . . Tobermory?"

I swallow nervously once more before I nod.

His eyes go wide and he grabs me by the shoulders.

"Shut up—" He stares at me, shocked. "Fucking shut up, are you serious—?"

I can't tell if he's happy or sad or angry or annoyed or weird or—

"Yes?" I say quietly, because I'm not sure where this is going.

And then he pulls me off the couch and down onto the floor with him, mouth fallen open.

"Actually?" he asks.

I nod again.

He lets out this incredulous laugh and he throws his arms around me, toppling us both over and onto the floor.

He doesn't let me go, kisses my face a thousand times—he goes from laughing to looking confused, back to laughing.

"Fuck." He bangs his fist on the rug and looks over at me. "You were right."

I told him in Bora Bora that I had a feeling that the condom broke, but he said he was positive it didn't.

"I hate it when you're right," he says, smiling a lot though. "And you'll have a fucking monument of your rightness that'll follow us around forever in the shape of our child."

I nod, a bit pleased. "I will."

He touches my face. "When did you find out?"

"A couple of weeks ago."

"Weeks—!" He stares at me how I knew he would.

He props himself up on his elbows and frowns at me. "You've kept this to yourself for weeks?"

"Just two or three."

"Who knows?"

"No one." I shrug. "Just you."

His face gets a bit serious. "Why didn't you tell me."

"Because so many bad things can happen in the first twelve weeks, I just—didn't want to tell you only for something bad to happen. It felt safer, I suppose."

He waves his finger between us.

"We got married, remember?"

I flash him a sarcastic look. "I recall it vaguely, yes."

"Whatever happens, Parks"—he shrugs—"we're in it together."

"Very lame," I tell him solemnly, and he nods at the criticism.

"Yep," he concedes. "But with this—with everything—please, just—tell me everything, forever."

He reaches over, interlocks our hands.

"And you're alright?" he asks, eyebrows up. "You feel okay? Everything's alright? Are they all good?"

I give him a proud little smile. "I am thirteen weeks and all is well."

His face lights up and then he leans in, brushing his mouth over mine.

He pulls back after a few seconds, laughing.

"Thirteen weeks!" He grins. "That's like, halfway there!"

"It's not." I shake my head.

"Almost!"

I keep shaking my head. "Not at all."

He laughs and I press my nose against his.

"Beej—" I say, and he lifts his eyebrows, waiting.

"It's a girl," I tell him quietly.

He stares over at me for a few seconds, long ones too—he says nothing. Then he rolls on his back and stares at the ceiling, truly I mean it, probably for about a minute.

"Ah, fuck!" He laughs again. "I'm fucked!"

"Why!" I pout at him.

He looks back at me like I'm an idiot.

"I'm a sucker for a Parks girl." He shrugs. "Never met one I haven't loved."

That makes my eyes go as big as my heart feels.

He pulls me over towards him and on top of him. "Are you happy, Parksy?"

I stare down at him, my chin in his chest and his arms wrapped around me.

Long, deep breaths that hit the back of your chest, easy eyebrows and blinks that bounce with ease because there's nothing heavy left between us. Open windows, light pouring through, birds chirping on fingers, old-fashioned movie twirls in the arms of the boy of my dreams—am I happy?

I give him a small smile. "Yes."

He gives me a calm one back.

"Scared?" he asks gently, eyebrows up.

I nod quickly. "A bit."

He presses those bee-stung lips of his together—that clever little mouth that's gotten me in all kinds of trouble all my life—and then his eyes do that twinkly thing they've always done where it's kind of sexy and kind of exciting but it's also this tacit, wonderful invitation that I'll always, always accept.

"Yeah, same, Parksy." BJ Ballentine nods his chin over at me coolly. "I'll make it pretty fun, but."

Acknowledgments

Benja, I just love you, and I love our life together. It's absolute bedlam 80 percent of the time, but I wouldn't want any of it with anyone else. Full farm forever. For all the parts of this book that are tender to me, you have changed my life by loving me how well and as consistently as you have.

Junes and Bels, if we were to be using my books as little markers for our life as a family, this is the first one where I feel like you two will be really feeling the pinch of my busy-ness and sometimes-absence. You are the most wonderful, gracious children in the world. Thank you for your flagrant indifference towards my career, it makes me happy.

Emmy for being my bff but also for giving Magnolia a face every bit as beautiful as BJ has banged on about it being for all these years. This is my favourite cover we've ever had. She's divine.

Maddi, for being the glue and our whole family's knight in shining everything. You are sunshine in our lives.

Amanda, for everything you do and have done, I know I am chaos, thank you for bearing with me.

To Luke and Jay (and the rest of Avenir)—it's been one of the most fun parts of all this, doing it with my brothers. Thank you for always saying yes and rolling with it.

My brilliant team—everyone from WME, but Hellie in particular—for being as long-suffering with me as BJ is with Magnolia—I am sorry for this, but forever grateful. Caitlin and Alyssa, thank you for being in my corner and forever at the ready. Hilary, Nicole and Sylvie, thank you for adopting me. And my publishers, both Orion and Dutton, Celia, Cassidy, Emad, John, Sarah and everyone else—I am forever and ever grateful for your incredibly hard work and patience with me. I know I can be an absolute wing nut and disastrously particular, thank you for bearing with and trusting me.

And lastly, Magnolia and BJ. Thank you for letting me tell your story. Thank you for consuming my mind and my life how you did. Thank you for getting stuck in my mind and keeping me up at night. It has been one of the greatest joys of my life so far getting to share you with the world, and I am so delighted with where you've found yourselves. You two changed my life. I will love you so fondly forever.